THE PHOENIX FEATHER IV:
DRAGON AND PHOENIX

ALSO BY SHERWOOD SMITH

The Phoenix Feather I: Fledglings

The Phoenix Feather II: Redbark

The Phoenix Feather III: Firebolt

THE PHOENIX FEATHER

4

DRAGON AND PHOENIX

SHERWOOD SMITH

BOOK VIEW CAFE

THE PHOENIX FEATHER IV: DRAGON AND PHOENIX
Copyright © 2022 by Sherwood Smith

Published by Book View Café Publishing Cooperative
304 S. Jones Blvd., Suite 2906
Las Vegas, NV 89107
www.bookviewcafe.org

ISBN: 978-1-63632-051-9

Cover Design by Augusta Scarlett
Interior Design by Marissa Doyle

ONE

TO CONTINUE THE STORY of the Phoenix Feather, we shall visit each of the children whose parents still treasured that gift all these years later, though neither had ever been sure what it really meant.

We begin with the youngest of the three: after seven years away, Afan Arikanda was going home.

The knot in her heart ached as if seventy years had passed since the day she walked so easily behind her First Brother Muinkanda onto the army ship and sailed north to army training. The harbor at Imai looked so much smaller than it had when she was ten years old!

She stood at the rail of the trader on which she'd bought passage as it drifted in on the tide. She scanned the harbor slowly, hungrily, noting every detail both familiar and unfamiliar — including two places where she might rent a one-person sailboat.

She had thought hard about whom to visit first. Filial piety dictated that she ought to go to her parents, and yet she knew they would both want to know the latest news from Ari's Second Brother Yskanda, serving an apprenticeship at a scribe house not far from the governor's mansion.

Ari smoothed her sleeves and robe, then checked that the front part of her hair was neatly bound up in its ribbon and hanging more or less orderly down her back in the style typical for young maidens. The only part of her appearance that might be amiss would be her battered martial artist's boots, but the hem of her outer robe came down to the toes of those boots, and if she remembered to walk in small steps, surely no one would notice them.

It was habit to stride along, shoulders shifting from side to side, a walk she'd consciously mimicked at Loyalty Fortress while she lived in the guise of a boy, until it had become her normal gait. As a small child she had run everywhere, a shadow at her older brothers' heels. She hadn't learned to dress and walk like a girl until this year, and she still thought of the clothes and the walk as a disguise.

She hitched her pack higher on her shoulder and looked around. Ayah! She spotted a girl her own age carrying a basket, head bent against the sea breeze coming off the ocean, and imitated her walk. Smaller steps, balance point in the hips, all as Madam Nightingale had taught her. Ari minced her way past the central square, the Justice House, and up the grand street with the fine stores. Master Bankan's scribe house was here, that much she remembered.

The street didn't look so grand now. Though this was harvest time, and she had expected it to be much hotter so far south, the ship had finally landed after a series of violent thunderstorms. Puddles lay everywhere. The crimson of the year's luck and fortune couplets still affixed to doorways looked tattered in many places. She skirted around a couple teens her own age wearing the aprons of apprentices, as they took down banners of Hungry Ghost Month.

She sketched hungry ghost wards as she passed, then forgot them all when she saw BANKAN HOUSE.

Would Yskanda be very tall? Might he even be starting a beard? No, he wouldn't, if he was living among people of rank, she reminded herself as she mounted the stairs to the front entrance. Young men stayed clean-shaven till they married, or were appointed to their life's work, whichever came first in their family tradition. She could not imagine Yskanda with a large, drooping mustache, and snickered nervously.

"Greetings of the day," a girl her own age said from behind the counter, her gaze raking down Ari from braids to her wet hem and back up again. The blob of light around her shimmered and fluoresced until Ari impatiently blinked it away—at least she had learned to suppress seeing those distracting lights around people.

With the aura gone, Ari mentally followed the counter tender's gaze, assessing her own appearance: dark brown hair, blob face dominated by a pair of fuzzy caterpillar eyebrows, plain-woven rose-colored robe edged with magnolia blossoms. Hopefully she did not notice the travel pack Ari carried over one shoulder, with wrapped implements sticking up that could be anything — but were, in fact, a very old sword and the two halves of a fine fighting staff made by Ghost Moon monks. Ari had sketched deflection wards on that pack and on the weapons as well.

The counter girl's expression reflected her assessment of Ari: not noble, which would require service obsequiousness, but not a beggar to be booted back out, either. "What service do you seek?"

"Greetings," Ari said, consciously going back to the local dialect. For all these years she had been speaking the common version of Imperial, first the military dialect, and then that of the gallant wanderers. "I'm looking for my brother. He should be in his last year or so of apprenticeship. Or maybe you could tell me where he is, if not."

"His name?"

"Afan Yskanda."

The counter girl's eyebrows shot upward. "Afan Yskanda?" she repeated, and her complexion changed as she said, "Please honor us by waiting a moment while I fetch the master."

Ari's happy anticipation cooled to curiosity, even a little worry. That girl hadn't said Yskanda's name so much as exclaimed it. Of the three of them, eldest brother Muinkanda was expected by the entire family to achieve greatness — a phoenix feather drifting down from the sky on her parents' wedding day had augured that — but Ari had never expected anything more challenging than spilled ink to happen to quiet, dreamy, gentle Yskanda.

A very short time later a man came out. He was dressed in four layers of silk, the sleeves not only knee length but tasseled. This could only be Master Bankan himself.

"My brother?" Ari asked, too worried to remember her manners. "Did something happen to him?"

"No, esteemed Miss Afan," the master scribe said very quickly as his jade-ringed hands patted the air between them. "That is, yes, he has, ah, accomplished much. Ayah! Every year's end we receive a letter from him, brought by the imperial courier ship. Very proud of him, we are—the youngest to pass the Imperial Examination in—"

"Imperial Examination?" Ari repeated, interrupting. "Don't you have to go to the imperial city to take it?"

Master Bankan did not like being interrupted any more than anyone else does, and he was used to the utmost respect—however, he was also aware that he was babbling in his shock. One of Afan Yskanda's mysterious family, after all these years?

His lips pressed into a line of displeasure, but then he forced a smile, and said soothingly, "If our honored visitor would care to see the letters, I believe we might have saved them. I will be delighted to personally look in our archive. If you would deign to wait in our rudimentary visitor's parlor through here. Apprentice, what are you standing around for? Fetch tea—the best service—and a plate of our finest delicacies."

"At once, Master Bankan." The round-eyed girl sketched a bow, then flitted away.

Reminded of her manners, Ari also bowed, but her habit was the gallant wanderer bow. "Please forgive me. I haven't seen Yskanda since Year of the Eagle," she said earnestly.

"Quite understandable," the master scribe said, again with that broad smile that didn't reach his eyes. "Please, Miss Afan—"

He gestured to a side room. Ari went in, but she didn't sit. She stood where she was, listening to the master's steps hurry away. She did not trust this situation. Yskanda on the imperial island?—how was that even possible?

She looked around the room, which had two doors, one opening into an inner court. She hesitated, wondering how long it would take to fetch those letters. If they even existed? She shook her head. She had no reason to mistrust the master, except for that false smile. And that odd business about the letters. Surely they would know if letters were saved or not?

He'd been talking so quickly, almost at random. It was too easy to imagine him leaving her to wait while he fetched . . . whom?

Always, always, there was The Story at the back of her mind, resulting in her parents becoming fugitives from a vengeful prince who now was emperor. Emperors, she had learned to her horror, had a *very* long reach.

Moving quickly and quietly, she hitched her pack over her

shoulder with one hand, slid open the door to the courtyard with the other, and stepped noiselessly outside. She dodged around ornamental trees, then paused and shut her eyes, concentrating. She still had not mastered the sensing of others around her, save in the form of blobby lights. There was a cluster nearby. She slipped that way, and heard voices through the oiled paper window.

"... Yskanda? Really? I thought he was a story the seniors made up!"

"Go look in the guest chamber if you don't believe me."

"Unless she's already been rounded up by the governor's guards."

"Why the guards? What did Apprentice Afan do?"

"Nobody knows, but all the seniors said the imperial ferrets snatched him right off the street. It was Year of the Rooster, my first year—"

"And there's a standing order for those with front desk duty, if anyone asks for Afan Yskanda, they are to be detained while the governor's guard is summoned—"

"Miss Afan?" That came from the direction of room Ari had just left.

Ari glanced around, then with a practiced leap used a branch of the pine to vault to the roof. A few running steps, and she dropped into an alley. *Detained while the governor's guard is summoned.* A description of her would be going out right now: girl of sixteen, wearing a rose robe, dark brown hair worn down in the style of unmarried girls.

Another leap, a dash down a narrow alley between buildings, and she found herself in a tiny court between the back of a shop and its supply shed. The door to the shed was not locked. She dashed inside, then crouched down, knees tight under her chin, as a sob ripped its way up from her heels.

Yskanda? Grabbed by the evil emperor? If he was gone, what about her family? Were they all—

She could hear the calm, kindly voice of Ul Keg, the monk who had tutored Ari and her brothers while her father was away with the fishers and Mother was dispensing medicines and healing charms to villagers. "Don't imagine a dragon when you see a dragonfly," he'd say when Ari began to wail, "But what if?"

She fought the sobs back, wiped her stinging eyes on her robe, and forced her shuddering breath to calm a little. What did she know for certain? Yskanda was no longer at Bankan House. Taken not recently — Year of the Rooster, the same year that she left Loyalty Fortress and became a gallant wanderer. He was not dead, because he had written letters. *If* that was really true, and . . .

She was doing it again, imagining the worst. She needed to concentrate on the few real facts she'd heard. Then act.

She snapped a bit of Essence light, which was about as bright as a dozen fireflies. That was good enough. She shucked her outer and inner robes, which she wore over the shirt and the loose riding trousers common to most laborers and gallant wanderers. She pulled out her roomy, road-worn tunic of dull brown from her days as Brother Ryu of Redbark. She put that on, sashed it, then undid the ribbon in her hair and in a practiced movement, wound the heavy mass into a boy's topknot and skewered it with the wooden hair pin that Shigan had given her.

She stuffed the robes into her pack with her sword and staff. She refreshed the eye-deflecting wards over her pack, then added one over herself. There was no possibility of making herself invisible. But the ward would blur her unless someone stared straight at her. And they would only do that if looking for a girl in a rose-colored robe.

There. No more Miss Afan. She was Ryu again, a teenage wanderer who appeared more boy than girl.

Time to leave before searchers came poking around. Now that her appearance had changed, her best hiding place would be in the crowd until she figured out what to do next.

She peered out, gained the alleyway, then slipped into the flow of traffic along the boardwalk paralleling the shoreline. She stopped to buy herself a steamed yam, and then, eating it, she sauntered toward that street again for a quick scan. Yes, there were governor's guards in their fancy blue tunics, broad-brimmed feathered hats, and with tasseled swords, darting here and there on what Ari saw in an instant was a badly organized search.

A pair of guards turned this way, both scrutinizing the faces of all the young females on the street. Ari spotted a bookseller's stall and strolled over to examine the wares. Among the usual stacks of *The Twenty-Five Virtues, Conversations with Kanda, The Five Elements* and *the Dialects of Enlightenment* were histories, and behind those, storybooks. These were far more popular than the proper literature. Ari joined the small crowd examining the stacks.

Her eyes lit on a title: *Firebolt and the Mine of Shame.*

Firebolt—that was the nickname Ari had had stuck on her after one of her first adventures as a gallant wanderer. She fought the burning tide of a blush. No one knew who she was. No one glanced her way. She took in a pair of boys with the gangling limbs of fifteen or so, standing together as they read the book, and picked up a copy herself. She stood behind the boys, trying to look like she was part of their group. She was peripherally aware of the two searchers glancing among the customers around the bookseller's tables.

They moved on, and Ari let out a breath.

"See? He commands demons!" one of the boys said, his voice cracking.

"It's all just a story," the other scoffed. "Like this governor with the pig's head. No emperor is going to put a pig-man in as a governor. This was a real governor, but the storyteller made him a pig-man, and the daughter a snake-woman, to make it more interesting—"

"Shut up, ancestor, and read to yourself."

Was this Rosefinch's book? Ari looked down at the drawing on the cover. It had the rough-hewn look of art made by carving the drawing into a piece of wood and then stamping the page. She remembered when Second Brother Yskanda had cut up his hands experimenting with such art, including making his own ink. The problem had been the paper—he could never quite make it smooth enough to properly take the ink, and so he'd gone back to brushes.

Ari blinked away memory, though it hurt a little. She missed her family so very much, and here was gentle, dreamy Yskanda—a prisoner?

She turned back to the book, hoping that Rosefinch had not written that Firebolt was a teenage girl. The Firebolt in the drawing was shaped like a man, with broad shoulders. The only recognizable features were the eyebrows, here depicted at a fierce slant that reminded Ari of Shigan's winged brows.

Shigan—an imperial prince.

She still found that difficult to reconcile with the Shigan she had trained with, sparred with, slept and ate beside.

At least the story-Firebolt was a man. Good. She put the book down without reading a word and looked about her more slowly. All these books — and she had not read a one. No, that wasn't true. There, near the front, were Kanda's *Conversations*, and Mana Ta's history — books she had read as a small child while the rest of the village children ran about, or worked alongside their parents. As she looked down at an illustrated report of the latest doings of the imperial court — something about trade treaties — she had an uncomfortable sense of . . . ignorance?

She walked out, the knot in her heart tight again. In the village of Sweetwater, even at Loyalty Fortress, she had been better educated than most of the others. But that was when she was ten.

Now? After years of hard work on martial arts, she still had only that education of a ten-year-old. How her mother would mourn her ignorance! It was time to read again — when she could afford books. Not just those tales, which were full of entertaining images instead of truth.

A temple bell gonged in the distance, followed by the brassy bong of the big bell behind the Justice Building, changing the hour from second to third Horse; Ari made herself a promise that as soon as she found her mother, she would beg for forgiveness for all her resistance to learning what made the world what it was. She would study with good will.

But first she had to find Mother.

She wandered toward the temple, working on her Essence breathing. She had survived many terrible situations since she left this island, more than half of which she had shared with Shigan, without knowing his secret. She had kept her own secret, without ever sharing her family's origin, secure in the belief that as long as she never revealed anything, her family would remain secure and safe on Imai Island.

What to do next? Her parents would not be in Sweetwater, not with Yskanda taken. What if . . . No.

Start with what you know, she told herself. Yskanda, imperial island. Maybe writing to his old master each New Year's. Yes, go ahead and assume the letters were truly from him — it was just the sort of thing he would do. He would not write home, because there was no post taken to the farther reaches of the island, ever. Few villagers knew how to read and write. Her parents, living under new names, would never write a letter that might be discovered by some spy of the emperor.

Therefore, the most likely result was that her parents had

either gone to rescue Yskanda once they found out he had been taken—and they would have found out, surely, when the village tax goods were taken to the governor, because of course Ul Keg would check on him—or else they had gone to Burning Rock Island. Her brothers and she had been taught that if any of them were discovered by the emperor's people, the rest were to go to a shrine or temple, and make their way to Burning Rock Island, home to the shamans and monks dedicated to the Snow Crane, God of the Abandoned.

A small measure of calm poured through the fire inside her: there was the island's main temple to the Snow Crane just ahead. She could see the top of the pagoda.

That was the place to start.

A month and a half later, she stood on the spectacular volcanic wreckage of Burning Rock, near the outermost reach of the empire. The great golden disc of the full Phoenix Moon sailed high in the sky. From the valley below, as singing larked upward through the somnolent air, she followed behind a row of departing pilgrims.

She had missed her parents by a week.

A *week*.

They had been living under assumed names, but it was easy to put together the clues.

At any other time, Ari would have found it kind of funny that her mother had been living as a man, just as Ari herself had begun her travels as a boy. The clues were too specific.

Brother Yan might have been born something else, but on this island, we ask no questions. Such matters are between pilgrims and the Snow Crane, God of the Abandoned . . . his face scarred so badly, though the healers did a lot . . .

Brother Brick, yes, he will be missed—until the accident, he was so strong, one of the strongest, though he must be nearer to fifty then forty. Eyebrows kind of like yours . . .

"Accident?"

"He said he fell on his knees. Shattered them, absolutely shattered them. Such a shame—no one could imagine how hard he must have fallen, so agile and strong a man, too! The healers at least were able to knit the pieces together. He could not stand, yet he and Brother Yan insisted they sail. We believe they received word about elders, and of

course family matters must come first . . .

Thwack! The now-familiar clatter of sail battens rattling down presaged the lifting of the prow as the ship came to life. Ari moved to the rail, an island of grief in a sea of harvest hilarity. There was what-iffing, scaring herself with the worst possible possibilities, and there was adding up the scraps of truth, and putting them together into a grim whole.

Yskanda snatched off the streets of Imai Harbor and taken to the imperial city.

Her father, who moved like a trained warrior, suddenly suffering an "accident" that no one had seen: it was clear that the emperor was collecting the entire family, probably to execute them together. The next target would be First Brother Muin, living under an assumed name in the army. Which would be easy enough to figure out—if they hadn't already.

However, all three of her elders would know how to take care of themselves, unlike Yskanda.

Therefore, she would go to the imperial island and get Second Brother out.

Two

FAR BACK WHEN WRITING was confined to divination symbols carved on shells, years of famine and war caused a desperate set of refugees from the empire to set sail to the east, in hopes that the goddess who had gone beyond the rising sun would take mercy on them and guide them to a new land.

Whether or not the goddess was responsible, the refugees, who were nearly starving by then, came at last to two great islands surrounded by hundreds of tiny islands. The refugees brought with them the ancient form of the empire's language and its customs, which included the planting and harvesting of tea, and the knowledge of, and value for, silk.

The desire for silk never diminished, though the Easterners' islands are ill-suited for the growth of mulberry trees, but they discovered that the soil in the temperate zones produced a remarkably flavorful red tea, very different from the infinite variety of greens and silvers of their former homeland.

The Easterners call their land an empire, though the Empire of a Thousand Islands deems them a kingdom, having only the two great islands—one of these being mostly desert from which comes the coal and copper with which they pay tribute along with the very popular red tea.

As for the swam of tiny islands, their denizens, shipbuilders all, have an unfortunate tradition of turning pirate the instant an undefended trade ship appears on the horizon.

Especially if it might be carrying silk.

The craving for silk (and the piratical method of acquiring it) has been a constant in dealings between the Easterners and the Dragon Empire (the sometimes-epithet the Easterners have traditionally bestowed on their former homeland). Meanwhile, the exceedingly high price charged for red tea had inspired shady practice from enterprising Thousand Island smugglers, creating tension between empire and kingdom over the centuries.

The Easterners' desire to be acknowledged as an empire—equal among equals—formed the basis for this new treaty now that there was a new young king on their throne. The treaty, which would enable that king to assume the trappings of empire, would be sealed with the marriage between the Easterners' Second Prince Er Haz and the Emperor of the Thousand Islands' adopted daughter, Imperial Princess Lily. That treaty would grant a special price in the tea trade not given to the rest of the world.

All emperors love tribute. Why was Emperor Guiyan of the Empire of a Thousand Suns considering this paradigm-shift? That will require looking westward, which will come. For now, the empire's court smiled eastward amid much mutual flattery and gift-giving.

One of the seemingly trivial but crucial points to be settled was where the marriage was to take place. Behind the humble disclaimers, each side demanded the respect their rulers thought due, but there were many other considerations, such as the Easterners' discovery of an empty treasury following the sudden death of their king.

When the Easterners were given to understand that if they refused to permit their prince to marry the princess in her native land, she would be required to travel to the east with her own entourage, suitable for an imperial princess. There was much behind-closed-doors discussion. Prince Er Haz had come west with a single ship and six fast warships. On a high-ranking graywing letting it slip to one of the honored guests that Princess Lily would require an armada of at least nine war ships, plus suitable escort, the Easterners had retired dismayed—where were they going to come up with an equal number? Because of course Prince Er Haz could not be overshadowed by his prospective bride.

More to the point, who was going to pay for it?

Another soft murmur in the right place at the right time brought up the idea of two weddings. After all, if the prince and princess married in the imperial capital, then the imperials would host it. And *that* meant that the newlyweds could share the same accommodations going east, and once everyone was on home ground, they could have another wedding, as large or as small as they desired.

Therefore, when New Year's Two Moons ended the Year of the Ox and inaugurated the Year of the Tiger, instead of the customary celebration of the emperor's birthday and the imperial family observing the ritual at the ancestral shrine, there would be a Heaven's Blessing ritual, open to all the court, below the steps to the Hall of Supreme Harmony. After which there would be an imperial wedding.

The next day, the newlyweds would sail eastward, treaty in hand.

And the honor of escorting her from the empire side (after much debate among the Minister of War and the high commanders of both navy and army) was to go to Celestial Waters Admiral Lin Hu, accompanied by the new General of the Magnolia Army Han Menek.

The new General Han would be leaving Green Jade Island for escort duty before New Year's — and, everyone agreed, most of all Duke Yulin of Green Jade, the son of Cavalry General Falik, Panther Captain Falik Tan, would become the new garrison commander, young as he was.

He would also celebrate the New Year by marrying the duke's second daughter.

With all that understood, we now return to First Brother Afan Muinkanda, still living under the name Ryu Muin. He, like his Loyalty Fortress cadet companion Dun Duan, was a silver seahorse lieutenant, at the very bottom of officer rank — but they were shortly to be promoted when Falik Tan took command of the garrison. Muin and Dun would get their kingfisher feathers in their hats as captains, Dun's brother Trickle would rise to quartermaster, and Muin's orderly Fenig In would become weapons master.

Falik Tan still led an undermanned company, but filling out its numbers was a very low priority, well behind the urgency of

Commander Han's huge force getting ready to travel to the east, and preparations for garrison handover, and also preparations for Falik's wedding. Falik was just as happy over the lag in replacements; though he had only two captains under him at present, he had known Dun and Ryu since their Loyalty fortress days, and trusted them to carry on without him having to supervise.

All of them had slowly become adjusted to Green Jade Island's seasons of sericulture, which were very different from the rice farming seasons the Dun brothers and Muin had grown up with as small boys on tiny Imai Island in the southwest. At their arrival in mid-spring, it had even seemed the island of low hills and pleasant streams was utterly uninhabited, except for the city denizens, and the garrison. All the silk farmers were busy with their worms, and tending the mulberry trees that fed them.

Muin and the rest of Falik's small company watched from a distance during summer, as the green hills full of mulberry trees were stripped to brown twigs and branches. They'd become accustomed to that when summer slid into the Three Sleeps, during which the silkworms begin to spin their cocoons.

The rest of the empire might celebrate Harvest Festival, but the silk makers scarcely looked up to see what the moons were doing — or even if they still circled in the sky — until the advent of White Snow: racks and racks and racks of cocoons. Followed by the steam of boiling cocoons, and the sough of unreeling threads.

It wasn't until the advent of winter at Sky Wishes Day that Muin and his fellow garrison newcomers discovered that the island was not uninhabited after all. The harbor city had been always mildly busy when Trickle went on errands there, but now, it seemed, everyone was out, preparing for New Year's Two Moon celebration — and in the Silk Islands, the weddings that people were too busy for in spring and summer.

As for garrison life, despite his pending promotion, no one took Dun Trickle seriously, least of all himself.

Trickle knew very well what people thought of him, which meant when he'd stumbled on what might, *might* be a serious matter, he didn't tell anyone. No one would believe him. He doubted himself, which meant gathering proof.

The two Dun brothers and Muin had dressed in plain clothes and left their swords behind, Muin feeling bare without his blade carried in his left hand. Muin had not seen the harbor city since their arrival on the eve of the Kraken Boat Festival. The elder brother Dun (who hereinafter will be referred to as Dun, differentiated from his brother Trickle) had twice been in the city, but as Dun the Pangolin, quartermaster for Falik's Company.

Today, however, they were not on any military errand.

They had to shop for a wedding present.

And Trickle, who knew the city well—he and his brother Dun the Pangolin were famous for their skills at scrounging — was their guide.

Muin shook his head as he walked a trail running along the ridge behind the harbor town. "Falik! Getting *married!*" He shook his head again.

Dun chuckled under his breath. "Seems like yesterday we were crowded in our hut trying to figure out what to say to a girl if we ever met one."

"Not just a girl, a *wife.*"

Trickle looked askance. "You talk as if Falik were still beardless. He's *twenty-three.*" To nineteen, twenty-three is old, if not quite doddering.

Muin said mildly, "He told me he was expected to marry her when he turned twenty-five. I guess the governor changed his mind. Though I can't think why."

"Oh, I think it was his consort," Dun said. "Wants Second Miss married so she can get Third Miss matched before she runs off with someone unsuitable."

"Like us," Trickle put in.

Muin laughed—though knowing it was true. Falik's prediction that they would like the affable, kindly Duke Yulin had proved to be correct. It was his consort, Oru Nayi, who regarded them as trespassers when they had to go to the mansion for any reason. Her first daughter had been successfully married to the heir to a marquis, the head of an old family. She had not liked her second daughter being betrothed to the mere son of a general, though that had been somewhat mitigated when General of Cavalry Falik had been awarded the title of count, and made governor as well as commander over one of the northern islands with a crucial naval base. But she was determined to find a very fine match for her third daughter, to make up for this lapse.

Her grace Oru Nayi was unaware that her ostensibly

modest, obedient daughters made excuses to come to the garrison as often as they could, where they were very popular.

"Third Sister is too smart to run off for the sake of love," Muin said. That came out a little more heated than he'd intended.

Dun cast a mildly inquiring look Muin's way. "Not a romantic, eh, Ten-Blade?"

Muin waved off the subject. The brothers did not know The Story, of course, so they wouldn't know why Muin did not find tales and ballads of runaway romances with rich and powerful nobles or royalty in hot pursuit the least bit romantic.

He glanced down at the rooftops, many with gargoyles set along the ridge before the upturned ends, and pointed at the main road snaking in the usual curves. The tops of banners could be made out, bobbing along the main street, as distant echoes of drums and trumpets beat the air. "Here's what I don't understand," he said. "Palanquins. It takes how many strong men to lift one of those things, just to carry one person? Why is that practical? I get that nobles don't want to get their silken slippers dirty in the road, but why don't they ride in carts?"

"They do ride in carts," Trickle said. "But only the really rich and powerful get to have palanquins. I think there might even be a law about it. There is about everything else."

"Nobles do everything differently," Dun commented. "Commoners think about practicality. Nobles don't have to. I can see the shops. Shouldn't we be heading down that way?"

"Not yet," Trickle said.

Dun shrugged; Trickle knew the pathways. "Consider the duke. Married at, what, near fifty? He couldn't have been younger. Who does that, besides nobles?"

"What I don't understand," Muin said, "is all this giving of presents. Did they do that at your end of Imai?"

Both brothers shook their heads. "What would we give each other? Mud?"

Muin snorted. "Presents when they first meet someone. Presents back again when they return the visit. Presents for all these occasions—Falik says the house the duke has set aside for them is already stuffed to the beams with fine things. Which he'll scarcely get to see if we get transferred again. And yet everybody coming to the wedding has to come bearing more fine things."

Dun sighed. "Trickle, are you sure you aren't lost? We're

still above the rooftops. We aren't likely to see many shops from here."

"Just a bit farther," Trickle said, scanning rapidly, then once again peering at the horizon.

Muin noticed he'd been doing that a lot. After a meandering exchange during which they debated what sort of present would be least objectionable, as none of them had the any notion of what constituted taste for nobles, beyond costly, Muin finally said, "Trickle, is there a problem?"

"No, really, no."

Dun knew his brother better. He held out a palm, eyes toward the sky. "And I'm testing for rain while hearing the wind."

Trickle flushed, but gave his head a determined shake, his gaze still on the horizon.

Muin sighed. "How can you know which road we're even on if you . . . Trickle, you're watching for someone." He stopped. "Who?"

Dun also stopped. "The navy! Coming for soon-to-be General Han—of course! You think they'll get here today? Were there pigeons?"

"Yes. And yes."

Muin shot an accusing glance at Trickle. "You knew that? But you hurried us out as soon as we swallowed our breakfast, insisting *today* we had to look for gifts? We ought to be back at the garrison! There's sure to be an inspection—"

Dun waved that off. "The commander's people have all that in hand." He eyed his brother, who suddenly pointed at the horizon.

"There."

The three stopped, and from their vantage halfway up the palisade, peered into the hazy sunshine. Sure enough, a notch on the horizon slowly resolved into a sail.

Muin's distance vision was the best. "That's navy ship rigging," he said presently.

Then Trickle took them by surprise. "Run."

His elders looked at him, but he was already speeding along the pathway. They followed. Trickle did not run long. He had planned this expedition very carefully.

When Dun caught up with his brother, he dealt him a cuff across the back of his head. "Trickle, have your wits flown?"

Trickle had stopped behind a cluster of thick, thorny shrubs.

Concealed behind them, he peered down the cliff, toward a rooftop and what appeared to be a large bamboo cage, then out to sea. "Now to see if I'm right."

"About what?" Dun's customary good humor had begun to fade, irritation taking its place. "Trickle, Han will forgive us a lot, but Falik won't like our fooling about when the commander is preparing to leave . . ."

Muin caught his arm. He saw, as Dun did not yet, that all vestiges of humor had vanished from Trickle's cheerful face. When Dun glanced his way in question, Muin said, "Trickle. What's this about?"

Trickle compressed his lips, his gaze still on those distant vessels. Dun braced for confession of some prank gone wrong (for his younger brother was, after all, still only nineteen); Muin didn't expect much more of import. Still, both were startled when Trickle said, "Do you remember Pink Plum? At the Dancing Fan, when we were garrisoned at Milky Springs with Old Turtle?"

The grimness of that posting seemed a hundred years ago, instead of just last winter. "One of the upstairs girls," Dun said. "I didn't like her. She was too . . ." He shrugged.

"Too nosy?" Trickle asked with an odd expression.

"Yes."

Trickle sighed. "I thought she was just curious, and she talked a lot, so I learned things about the town. Who was the best at — oh, never mind that. Here's why we came to this spot. I saw her here, on the Street of Sweet Breezes, one day last summer, when I was arranging fodder."

"So?" Dun said impatiently. "She probably came from here."

Trickle ignored that and went on stolidly. "She had a parrot on her shoulder, and she dressed differently — like the merchant girls, not in those flimsy things the entertainment girls wear, with all the bangles. But I knew her. I called a greeting. At first she ignored me and kept walking. I thought she didn't hear me, so I yelled out, teasing, the way we had at the Dancing Fan. As soon as I said, joking around, you know, that I remembered kissing those two little star moles behind her ear, she stopped and gave me a big smile."

"She knew you. If this is going to be about your prowess — "

"She asked," Trickle cut across grittily, "how I was, then before I could say much of anything she told me she changed her life. Inherited a shop selling birds from her grandmother. She was trying to live a respectable life. I could see all that at a glance. Certainly nothing wrong with any of that. I had the fodder to get, and I could see that though she was smiling she really didn't want to be there with me, so I wished her a blessing from the God of Wealth, and we went our separate ways."

Dun scowled at his brother. "How long is this going to take?"

Trickle said doggedly, "We're up high. They won't have seen the ships from the wharf yet. Anyway, I didn't think anything of it, though I saw her from time to time, always along the wharf or the lower street, always chatting with people. Then, it was right before the silkworms' Third Sleep —"

"Three Sleeps," Muin said.

Trickle snapped his fingers. "Three Sleeps, yes. I saw her again. You can see over there, where the boot-maker has his workshop." He pointed beyond the bamboo cage, to a house on the other side of the stream. "I was there when you sent me to fetch those new boots, and I saw her in the house below. She'd come out to the cage, where there was a pigeon walking around on top. The bootmaker was talking, so I waited, but glanced at her — and saw her taking something off the bird's leg. Then she chucked the bird inside the cage. She looked around — and she saw me. The bootmaker paid her no heed. I think he's short-sighted, for he bent close to his ledger when we totted up what the garrison owed."

"Are we going to find out why that's important?" Dun asked. "We have a present to buy."

Trickle crossed his arms. "She gave me that same big smile, the Dancing Fan smile. How could I not have seen how false it is? Anyway, she called over for me to join her in a cup of tea soon as I finished. I did, only polite, and she served me a decent tea while chattering on about how much she missed her sister back on another island, and she had these birds, so why not train one to fly letters back and forth? She pushed a tiny piece of paper into my hand. I didn't want to read it, but she seemed to want me to, so I looked at it, and saw a lot about baking osmanthus cakes, and fried breads, and some man who might propose — nothing that was my business. I said that was great, it must save her a load of tinnies, having her own messenger bird, and I thanked her for the tea and said I had to go. Which I did. Do you think the ships can be seen from the wharf yet?"

Muin had been shifting his gaze downward as well. "Not quite yet—you'll see the barrel boys bringing the ropes and getting ready."

"Oh, right," Trickle said.

"Go on," Dun commanded. "Though I still don't see how that brings us here behind this thorn bush when we ought to be back readying for the farewell inspection, present or not."

"Because two days later I had to run a message to the Registry for Captain, that is, Commander Falik. While I was there, I was chatting with the clerk, a boy probably no older than sixteen, obviously new and proud of his promotion from apprentice to clerk. He was telling me all about how people think Registry is boring, but the files tell stories, and I don't know why I did it, but I asked, can you find out the story behind the bird shop? He said they weren't supposed to share those files with just anyone, but seeing as how I was part of the army . . . I gave him a string of cash, but I probably could have offered a single tinnie, it was so clear he wanted to show off how important he was. He went and got the ledger, and showed me that it had sold recently to one Pa Jan. Sold, not inherited. There was no grandmother there. It had belonged to someone who owned four stores."

Dun stared in silence, a slight frown between his brows. Muin crossed his arms.

Trickle, seeing their attention was not thoroughly on him, said, "The first of this month, as you know, the courier ship is expected. I was down at the naval house to run messages, but they were all running around, so I was sitting under the eaves of a tea house when I saw her again. I thought about that lie about her grandmother, and was wondering if I should ask her or not."

"Grandmothers being a hot-water topic," Dun muttered.

"But the courier came in. I waited to finish my tea—I knew that they take their time before going to the harbor master for messages—I saw her join those talking to the navy boys who came off the courier. She had that big grin, and the parrot on her shoulder danced around, making the navy boys laugh. Then she peeled off and went the other way, and I headed to the navy house, dropped off the messages and picked up the pouch the navy messenger had just put down. Then, I don't know why, I went up this way to get to the path back to the garrison."

Trickle pointed below. "I reached that point there, beyond that clump of willow, when I saw her there, reaching into the cage. She put something on the leg of a pigeon and tossed it into the air, then went inside the house."

"So?" Dun said.

Muin got it. "You think she might be some kind of spy?"

Dun's eyes narrowed. "Spy," he repeated. "Why didn't you say something before?"

"Because I'm not sure," Trickle said. "What would a spy look like?"

"Exactly like that," Muin muttered.

Trickle rubbed his jaw. "She could be writing to her sister, but it all seems so odd. I always see her when the navy ships come in. She lied to me about the grandmother—and I didn't even ask. It was the same when she pushed that letter at me. I certainly didn't want to see someone's private letter. I thought, the navy ships coming in to fetch Commander, that is, General Han and his captains away was due soon, I'd bring you, if I could. When you said the other day that we have to have presents for Falik and Second Miss, I thought I'd try to get you down here when the navy ships are expected."

Dun gave a short, quick nod, then lowered his voice, as if they could be overheard from that house in the hollow below. "I think the ships can be seen from the wharf now."

Indeed, the busy wharf had become a frenzy of activity, as if a seed had been dropped among ants. The three waited in silence, Trickle muttering under his breath, "She'd be making the parrot dance . . . chattering . . . they're moving toward the harbormaster now, is my guess . . . she'd be turning toward the hill. Climbing the hill . . . maybe stopping to blab to someone a lot of stuff they don't want to hear . . . She should be here now . . ."

All three gazed at the path below the house. Birds squawked in the wicker cage. A crow cawed high behind the three.

Trickle was just giving a sigh, and muttering, "I was wrong, it's been—" *Too long* got cut off when Muin grabbed his arm and hissed for silence.

Below, a woman appeared in the tiny court between the huge cage and the back of the house.

"That's her," Trickle breathed.

Pa Jan carried something in one hand. The three young men

watched as she took a pigeon from the cage of colorful birds, clipped something to its leg, then tossed the bird upward. A pigeon fluttered up into the air, circled around, and then began flying toward the ocean.

"I wish we could catch that," Trickle whispered as the woman went back inside the house.

"We can catch her, and wring the message out of her," Dun said with uncharacteristic grimness.

Muin had been thinking fast. "No," he said. "That was my first thought, but you remember what Old Shaz told us at Loyalty, the best spy is a known spy."

Trickle looked from one to the other. "You believe me, then?"

"I believe she's sending messages to someone. It could be to her family. After all, why would a spy be here? I could see one at Gold Jade, and there is probably a dozen of them at Blue Jade, which seems to get attacked by pirates or Easterners every few years, but *here?*"

They glanced up at the snow-topped mountains behind them, only a part of the formidable natural defenses on this the smallest of the Silk Islands. Muin went on, "There's always a chance it isn't a letter to a sister—and I don't like it that notes have gone more than once on the days when the navy comes in."

"Should we go tell Han? Falik?" Dun asked.

Muin slowly shook his head. "Han's about to leave, and Falik's got enough to think about—and we've got no proof. It'll be one more worry when he's already got plenty. I think we ought to take care of this ourselves."

Trickle nodded. "What I wanted to do is set up a watch, and I even have the right person. But I'd have to pay her, and I don't have anything to pay her with. She's a bird caller. I found out by accident last summer—but there isn't much to be made doing that, so she works for a tea master. She has two children. She can't go without pay."

Muin grunted assent. "I can arrange pay through Falik. If she can intercept those birds before Pa Jan gets them, I'll pay double. Let's see what's in those notes."

Dun clapped Trickle on the shoulder. "Take us to the main street. Let's stay low until we're out of sight of that cottage. We have a present to buy."

THREE

THE ADVENT OF AN imperial wedding involved the entire capital city.

Preparing for New Year's Two Moons always meant scrubbing the front door and changing out the couplets on either side of the door frame, but this year no one was satisfied—least of all the inspectors from the Imperial Household Department—until every door was painted, the calligraphy on banners perfect, and each street and alley was swept into tidiness. There were those whose entire job was to walk the streets to ensure that no horse or dog droppings stayed long enough to gather flies. But as each dung cart earned the bearer some tinnies, that job was enthusiastically carried out by many enterprising youths from the poorer sections of the city where the river sometimes flooded in spring.

Not everyone was in a festive mood. First Imperial Princess Manon was utterly disgusted by the expense and effort the imperial palace put into this wedding between the emperor's adopted daughter, Imperial Princess Lily, and the Easterners' second prince. To see that mutt Lily, whose father was a commoner, the center of court entertainments, dinners, poems, and plays was enough to almost make the first imperial princess regret having turned down the marriage first.

Almost. The repellent idea of being wife to a second prince in a foreign court steadied her, especially when she considered a lifetime of seeing those horse teeth, that chinless face, and the mouse-colored hair about which could only be said that at least it wasn't the ugly rust color so common in the east.

She did give in to the impulse once or twice to dress especially well in order to demonstrate to the foreign prince what he had missed, and the most magnificent of the entertainments was a night of opera hosted by her and her mother, the second imperial consort. But her true intent, as was her mother's, aimed at pleasing the emperor. Manon's goal was to become crown princess; her mother's, empress.

And that, she decided, as the last days of the Year of the Ox brought ever more elaborate festivities, meant she must find a project that would impress the emperor as well as benefit the empire. He still had yet to assign any tasks worthy of an heir to her, but as far as she could discover, nor had he given any such task to First Imperial Brother Jion. Therefore she must come up with something appropriate, something an heir would accomplish.

The idea came the during the last court event of the year, which was the signing of the trade treaty with the Easterners.

In the capital the ordinary people entertained neighbors, co-workers, and extended family. If you wanted the spirit tigers who roamed abroad every Year of the Tiger to keep demons, ghosts, and bad luck from the family home, now was the time for all feuds to be ended, quarrels mended, and debts paid.

In the imperial court that meant peace treaties — and to celebrate the signing and the double seals on the treaty, the emperor had decided to bestow the newest art from the court artist on the Easterners.

Now we come to the third of the Afan children, Yskanda, who had been snatched off the streets of Imai during the Year of the Rooster, and had lived in the palace as a hostage ever since.

Before the painting, which had taken the two court artists full six months to accomplish, was removed by palace graywings to the Hall of Glorious Justice, it was stretched out along the wall in the largest gathering hall of the scribe building for the scribes and artists to see.

Court Artist Yoli stood before it, everyone else respectfully back lest they impede his view. He rocked back and forth from heel to toe in his silken slippers, his wild white brows lifting as he hummed to himself.

At last he turned to Yskanda, tall and extraordinarily beautiful, modestly standing to his right and a bit behind. "I have to admit, my young assistant, I was not certain that your idea would work. But it is magnificent."

Yskanda bowed to the court artist, of whom he had come to be genuinely fond. "It is entirely your work that shames my poor efforts." His sincerity rang in his voice.

"Nonsense," the old man said crisply, but he was secretly pleased.

They both turned to look once more. The banner scroll, painted on silk, depicted the imperial sampans — each painted with fine detail from life — traveling through the watery passage called the Journey to the Cloud Empire. The great cascades were there, and the wild variety of orchids. The whole was mostly done in shades of silver, gray, white, and blue, except for the orchids, which framed the whole at either end, and for the central image, the imperial sampan. At the center of that the emperor dominated the whole, and to either side Imperial Princess Lily and the Eastern second prince, three fifths the size of the emperor. The rest of the imperial family surrounded the two, and then, smaller again by a fifth, the remainder of the imperial court.

The court artist had painted this crucially important central section. Yskanda had done the rest.

"There is not a weak spot in it," Yoli said at last. "I regret that we will never see it again. But that is to be expected." Many of his own favorite pieces had vanished within the imperial family's private residences, never to be seen by him again — or they had been given as gifts to courtiers, and likewise were inaccessible.

The emperor said much the same later that night, when the august company gathered in the great hall stood much as the apprentices had, staring and staring. Many of the ministers and the imperial relations who had been on the Journey found a way to get close enough to look for their painted selves, and then stepped back, smiling. Others who were not depicted, or who had not even gone, found the eye ever led back to the mysterious crags with beautiful pagodas glimpsed among the rocks, then to the ethereal fogs and the mighty cascades that shot rainbows shimmering in the air.

"This," said Second Prince Er Haz in his heavy accent, "is truly magnificent. His majesty my imperial brother will shed tears over such a priceless gift." He said *imperial,* not *royal*: the true purpose of this treaty was to accomplish the paradigm-shift from kingdom to empire. Tribute now became trade. He consciously adapted his language to reflected that.

There were many who were surprised that Emperor Guiyan had conceded this entirely paradigmatic change. Emperors like to be on top, and they love their tribute. But he was not going into the true reasons why — those who knew numbered fewer than ten, and half of those were elsewhere.

As for the emperor, at that moment he was not haunted by the strategic concerns that we will get to in due course. He looked at that painting from one end to the other, hating to let it go.

Then he got a happy idea. "Send for the artists," he said to his chief graywing, Bitternail. "I wish to reward them — and to make a request."

An emperor's request, everyone knew, meant dropping everything to execute the imperial whim, however long it would take.

Court Artist Yoli Jiwa and Assistant Court Artist Afan Yskanda came as soon as they could be hustled into their formal court robes, and Court Artist Yoli's eyebrows, mustache, beard, and wild white hair could be more or less tamed by his graywing Chrysanthemum's patient hands.

On their entry from the back, First Imperial Princess Manon's gaze arrowed to Yskanda, and stayed there. She fought to control the thrum of her heart whenever she saw Afan Yskanda. The attraction she loathed as a weakness (for a common-born man deserved no better) had died down — or so she had believed for the half-year since she'd seen him last. But his sudden appearance, more beautiful now that the last of boyhood softness was planed from his face, hit her just as hard.

She gazed unblinking, her turmoil not quite hatred, but he never looked up, his hands hidden in his modestly sized, plain sleeves, his head bowed.

If there had been the least hint of awareness, that hatred would have ignited. But there was no report (and she had put herself to the trouble of finding out) of him having any lovers. Any visitors, even. He appeared to be entirely cloud-minded, devoted to his brushes and inks the way a monk is to his wooden fish and sutras. If he had preferred another, especially someone low-born, she would have found a way to destroy both. Sometimes she lay awake imagining it.

The emperor had been speaking; Manon consciously looked away from Yskanda as Melonseed brought forward a carved chest on a tray, whose contents clinked promisingly. The two court artists knelt to receive it.

"Divide that up between you as you see fit, Court Artist Yoli. Assistant Court Artist Afan. And turn your talented minds to finding a way to present the royal wedding in paint form. They Journey to the Clouds must remain a memory for us, as this splendid painting goes with Imperial Daughter to her new home. But I would like her wedding memorialized for *us*."

The two bowed and retreated. Manon once again forced her gaze away from Yskanda — and that was when she got her idea.

How could she have not seen it? Imperial Father was proudest of his lineage. What if she wrote a history of the Jehan family? No, not the family. A history of the rulers, and what each had accomplished. Their thoughts on matters — there was a daunting number of dusty scrolls and books and papers to go through, but she prided herself on her scholarship.

There were also the rulers' personal papers, kept in a vault somewhere in the emperor's own pavilion. If she could get permission from Imperial Father to read those, or some of those, would that not suggest to him that she was worthy to become their successor?

Oh, yes. A fair and objective investigation that culminated in Imperial Father's glorious reign, which would crown the Jehan Dynasty for centuries to come — it would be the first of her great writings as the second Sage Empress.

While she smiled unhearing at the courtiers' tedious speeches of good will, the court artist and Yskanda were bent over against a scouring wind as they hurried back to their workroom. Late as it was, there was no retiring for the night.

As soon as the graywing had lit the lamps again, and they were alone, they faced each other in dismay. "We have *one day* to plan it," Yoli said hoarsely. "Even if I was your age, I couldn't do it. Not in a day."

Barely a day at that. The following night — the last of the year — the emperor would retire to the imperial tombs for his customary vigil. He would return at dawn, at which time all the white decorations now going up all over the city would be ripped away, revealing the tiger banners and couplets in doorways. The imperial family would gather along with court and the visitors, as well as Yoli and Yskanda, for the Heaven's Blessing ritual.

After that, there would be the wedding procession.

Yoli sighed, his shoulders slumping. "We only managed the Journey to the Clouds because I made so many sketches of the court during the entire Journey. You made those sketches of the young imperials and ministers' children. We also had a full archive of past artists' drawings of the Journey, every angle possible, to draw on. But how are the two of us to scurry alongside the wedding parade sketching madly, probably in sleet, judging by those clouds?"

Yskanda was thinking fast. The court artist was correct. They'd had a wealth of material to use, except the hardest part had been to design the whole. That had also been true the year before, when Yskanda had done a smaller banner hanging of the imperial garden. But now he understood how to compose such long works. The question was, how could they get that necessary wealth of material to draw on?

"Actually," he began.

Yoli, who only thought in hanging scrolls, blinked at him in hope. "Go on, youngster."

Yskanda said slowly, "In a way, I believe I can use the form of the Journey banner scroll, in that we were always on water, in the passage."

Yoli looked puzzled, but still hopeful.

"In the same way, the wedding parade will wind its way in a gradual circle through the city, which we can open into a line for our painting. So . . . what the emperor . . ." A pause to bow in the direction of the throne. ". . . might enjoy is a view of his capital as seen along that great and ancient street, with the wedding party at the center, just as court was at the center of the Journey painting. All the shops and the ordinary folk, including the imperial court and all the banners."

"I can see that," Yoli said slowly. "But even if we get the senior scholars to run along beside us, sketching as best they can, how will we make certain they are all not drawn to the same picturesque horse, or to the first imperial princess?"

Yskanda was already thinking ahead. "By keeping our sketchers in one place?"

"But . . ." The court artist frowned. Then looked up. "I think I see what you mean. Then we will be using all the senior students, and probably half the staff. Oh, they will not like having their holiday snatched away — they will curse us to a hundred generations."

"Maybe not," Yskanda said — and it was his turn to be hopeful. "If we made it clear they will be a part of a great work? We might even have them add to the whole."

"Supervised," the court artist said. "Supervised, yes, it might do. In that sense it is no different than the senior assignments, each to a specific part of the garden. And if it doesn't, at least we will have an immense number of sketches to work from. Yes, let's try that."

"I'll go along tomorrow morning and break up the street into parts."

"Yes. Do that. We can assign one or two senior apprentices to each part — they are used to that. For details you and I can always go back to the street . . ."

Yskanda paused, wondering if he'd even be permitted to go into the city. He suspected he would — his rank in any other circumstance would assure that — but with guards. It would be said that they were there to keep him safe. If it was the emperor's order, no reason need be given at all.

". . . very much easier than going back to the Journey passage," the court artist was saying, his mind entirely on the project. "And we'll assign our best portraitists to just sketch the wedding party — yes. That's the approach. Another to sketch only the palanquins. We can get Nan Hereg to get the ministers. No, two, we'll put at least two on that."

"Instructor Nan might be best to capture their faces, and her senior apprentice the details of their clothing, perhaps?" Yskanda suggested diffidently.

"Yes, yes, yes. You and I will sketch the imperial family." Court Artist Yoli eyed Yskanda. "You will still have to envision the whole."

"I think I have the trick of it now," Yskanda said modestly. He was smiling — with confidence, Yoli was relieved to see.

However it was not true.

Yskanda did not have confidence in himself the way it was generally understood. He fretted about details, and of course about being good enough. That was until he sank into a project and forgot himself entirely, which opened the floodgates for art to flow unhindered. He never thought about himself as creator of a picture once it was done; his hand was merely the instrument of . . . inspiration. (He still struggled with the idea that he was in any sense an Essence-wielder.) He only had eyes for the picture itself—after which his uncertainties rose again around him like ghosts in anticipation of the next challenge.

But this time, for once, he did not think about failure. He was actually relieved, something he would never say aloud. For one thing, he did not have the time for the usual worries. And secondly, the entire court had heard the emperor make the request.

That gave him the perfect excuse to avoid First Imperial Prince Jion.

FOUR

THE YEAR OF THE Tiger dawned.

The augurs were off by a day in predicting good weather, in spite of all the prayers.

Both weddings—the great imperial wedding, whose magnificence would fill the booksellers with drawings and written accounts over the next month, and the wedding on Green Jade Island, which had importance to no one but the island's inhabitants—were both attended by wild winds and spates of snow and sleet. At least the sky over the capital cleared long enough for the Heaven's Blessing ritual—though many shivering there in the open silently wished it had been rained out.

But inside the beautiful, vast ancestral manor of the Yulins, the gathering of relatives, friends, and the garrison officers enjoyed the warmth and light as Duke Yulin's and Ducal Consort Oru Nayi's Second Miss and new Garrison Commander Falik Tan bowed to Heaven and Earth, to present and absent parents, and finally to each other.

Cheering crowds surrounded the happy couple. Falik Tan looked absurdly pleased as he held tightly to his consort's hand, his face nearly as red as his handsome crimson and gold robe.

Out came the hot wine, and the first toast was offered by the smiling duke, as his consort looked on with a complacent smirk, and a sharp eye on her third daughter lest she show any interest in those admittedly handsome, but definitely no-family young captains placed as far down the row of small tables as she could put them.

Not far enough. Mama did not see Third Daughter's surreptitious hand signs, in approved army fashion, signaling that there would be a gathering of young people as soon as the elders toddled off to their rest.

Then a trumpet announced the feast, and a train of servants brought in trays of steaming dishes. Muin's stomach was a gaping cavern by now; he had been up before dawn, helping Falik with a hundred different garrison tasks. The duke had decreed a honeymoon for the newlyweds until Fire Wishes Festival, which would leave the duke's private guard and the garrison sharing custody of the island's security. How that translated out, Falik, Muin, and Dun knew very well, was that Lord Oru would do his best to order them around, and they would have to carry on with their regular tasks around his interference.

Muin sniffed his favorite chili and garlic mussels, and held his breath, waiting until the elders and those of higher rank got plates set on their tables. The captains were next. He fingered his chopsticks in readiness to pounce —

"Captain Ryu." A whisper at his shoulder.

Muin turned, to see the young recruit who had messenger duty this evening. "What is it?"

"Quartermaster Dun, sir."

Dun Duan had been promoted to take charge of the infantry, and Trickle was now quartermaster. He would not dare some kind of joke now. What else would he be doing? Then Muin remembered the spy and the pigeon-watch duty, half-forgotten in the wake of the unending tasks of the past few days.

He stood, smiled, and when Falik glanced his way, Muin made a surreptitious sign that he needed the privy, and followed the messenger out.

They found Trickle in a side hall, with a wet, shivering conscript. Trickle said, "The bird watcher got it. Sent it with Vo here." He pointed to the wicker cage next to the young conscript, who was dripping on the floor. Inside the cage a pigeon murmled.

"Message?" Muin asked.

"Right here." Trickle held out a tiny strip of paper.

Muin took it, and squinted down at the tiny characters. He was never a good reader at the best of times. Holding it next to a lantern, he made out words: cakes . . . decorations . . . Tiger. As in Year of the Tiger.

"We were wrong," he said, aware of a mix of emotions. Relief, yes, but hard on that disappointment. Ashamed of such an unworthy reaction, he said, "It's from her sister. Wrap it up again and release the bird."

At this, Conscript Vo said, "Excuse me, Captain. This ignorant one hesitates to speak, but the woman, the bird caller, she said to sniff it."

"Sniff it?" Muin repeated.

"That's what she said, Captain."

Muin held the strip of paper to his nose, but smelled nothing. He lowered it. "What am I supposed to smell?"

"She said she opened the capsule, and smelled lemon, Captain."

"Lemon?" Trickle repeated. "This time of year?"

Muin drew in a slow breath, his mind arrowing back to his cadet days. Fifth year, when for a month or two their fellow cadets delighted in elaborate codes and methods of getting secret messages back and forth. Lemon juice used as ink was one of the simplest — milk, also.

In silence he held the paper carefully over the top of the lantern. The others took a step nearer, and before their astonished eyes, marks in light brown appeared between the characters describing decorations for a New Year's Two Moons celebration, one between each of the four lines.

New moons. Get out.

And below that, a tiny panther mask.

Footsteps approached. All turned — it was Dun. Muin held out the strip silently, and in equal silence Dun took it. "What's this — a code?" He scowled. "New moons — the darkest night of the year. The panther — who else would draw a mask like that but the Shadow Panthers?"

"Took a navy ship last year, made it look like pirates," Muin said. "Burned a harbor. But what would they want *here?*"

Dun's usually easy face hardened. "Let's get that spy and find out."

Muin held up a hand. "No."

"No?" the others all spoke.

"I know what Falik will say," Muin stated. "The best spy is a known spy. We should put that paper back on that bird, and let it fly. No. Copy it out first, including the code, writ in lemon. Nothing to raise her suspicions."

Trickle's scowl was a thunder of dragons. "But the spy!"

Muin said, "Trickle, you were an orderly, so you didn't hear Old Shaz on the history of spies, who often are no more than scouts. All they know is their orders. They don't get to hear why, or how their information will be used — no one wants that information being pried out if the spy is caught. She likely doesn't know anything. Further, if she goes away, we can detail someone to follow her."

"Shadow Panthers." Dun spat to the side. "I remember that lesson about the spies. You're right. So what do we do? If we pull Falik out of his wedding, especially on his wedding night, the whole family will curse us to ten generations. Worse, everyone will be blabbing — we may as well hand off the note to the spy and give her our thanks."

"We don't tell the family anything," Muin said with the ease of one who had never had grandparents, much less uncles or cousins.

His mind was on Falik, who had not even told Muin and the Dun brothers he was engaged until they were about to dock at Green Jade Island. After all those years together. And all the last week, any time someone made a bawdy joke, he'd blush. Even so, Muin could tell he was looking forward to his wedding night — as was Second Miss. "We'll give Falik tonight. And tomorrow. We can't send anyone out in this weather, at risk of capsizing, so the call for reinforcements can go out tomorrow night just as well."

Dun shook his head. "Even if it went out yesterday, there are bound to be questions, beginning with, who says the attack is here, just because the spy is here?"

Muin frowned. "That's true — this is the smallest of the Silk Islands, with the best natural defense of any of them. It's never been attacked, unlike Blue Jade, and even Gold Jade. Only White Jade is as peaceful."

Dun said, "Also, it'll take how long to get a message to Blue Jade? We've only got a matter of days, if our guess is right. The closest is Old Turtle. What if he doesn't believe us?"

Muin waved off the what-ifs. "We've still got to send him a pigeon as soon as the weather clears. Also, we'll send someone to report to Blue Jade, and beg for reinforcements. That's what Falik would want."

Dun and Trickle nodded, the latter with rare sobriety. They all had seen how Muin often knew Falik's orders before he spoke them. Not surprising, after following him since they were all boys.

"Should we tell the duke? Or Lord Commander Oru?" Dun's voice flattened at the mention of Lord Oru, who ran the duke's well-dressed guard as if they would never face any worse challenge than muddy boots.

"No," Muin said. "No one but us is to know." He spoke slowly as he worked things out in his mind. "If we're right, then the element of surprise is ours, not the Shadow Panthers'. We need to keep it that way if we can. If they think they have us cold, they might come in lazy. That's a guess, of course."

Dun said, "Right. What we know is, we are severely undermanned."

They all looked at each other. "The timing," Muin said, "is suspicious." He shook himself. "But again, we're guessing. Let's work with what we've got. No one to know. Including the spy. Trickle, you're good with a pen. Use some lemon. Copy the message and the secret message. Get it on the bird, get the bird in the air, and go back to barracks. Vo, we'll give you the reward to carry back to the bird caller, with the caution that no one is to say anything."

Dun stroked his jaw. "How will we defend this place, if no one is to know, or to do anything?"

"Who said we won't do anything? Falik will want silence, I'm sure of it," Muin said slowly. "He was always that way, wasn't he? As for getting ready . . . I'll wager he'll want a ruse. Perhaps — yes, he'll surely want us prepared to defend, which of course we'll do right at the coast where the enemy would have to land. But he'll want to call it just another exercise, now that he's commander. A war game. 'Let your plans be dark and impenetrable as night, and when you move, fall like a thunderbolt.'"

"Number seventeen, Lao Sha's Strategies," Dun said, nodding. "One of Falik's favorite quotes."

They did their best to give Falik time, but no one was surprised when Falik turned up at the garrison the next day, no sign of wedding clothes. He looked a little sheepish as men grinned, or clasped their hands and called out "Congratulations!" — some in a meaning tone that caused him to blush anew.

But he was very much the new commander when he walked into the garrison command office, saw Dun, and said, "Where's Ryu?"

"He's out doing an inspection, Commander," Dun said.

"Of what? Everyone seems to be busy cleaning up after the storm."

"If you would like some tea, Commander," Dun invited, sending Trickle a look as he held out his hand toward the empty inner office.

Falik understood at once, and as soon as the door was shut, said, "I saw Ryu walk out yesterday. He was gone a long time for a man who hadn't eaten all day. Don't tell me he was in the privy. What's going on?"

Dun told him, and laid the crumpled paper before him, with the code words burned in between the cheery blather about New Year's preparations.

Falik looked up. "I wish Trickle had brought it up long ago — I would have sent a courier straight to Blue Jade insisting we get our reinforcements right away."

They all knew that they ought to have had a full company by now. There had been no real need until recently — Han's company had been larger than most, with two extra captains and their twenty-five plus support, and Green Jade's biggest problem for generations had been squabbles between fisher fleets. Of course the commander at Blue Jade would consider them a last priority when shifting people around, especially with news of raids, wild searches, and chases going on up north.

"Trickle wasn't sure it was really anything," Dun protested, and in the way of people facing the unknown he reassured himself, and his listeners, with what they already knew as fact. "We don't really even know if we are the target. Who will believe us? This island has the best natural defense of any of them, and the fewest people. Why would anyone want to attack it?"

Falik waved a hand. "I have no argument with your reasoning. I still would have liked to be told. But done is done. Ryu is, what, out inspecting the coast where they'll surely land?"

"Yes, Commander," Dun said.

Falik grunted. "Good. That would have been my first order. My second will be send a pigeon to Commander Wei at Milky Springs Garrison, and a courier to Blue Jade to beg for one of the fleets to back us up."

"Ryu did that this morning."

"Excellent." He frowned at the paper. "I hate to let a spy go unmolested, but I think you're right about how little she probably knows. From everything I heard, the man who calls himself Master Night doesn't share power, which means he won't share any information his tools don't need to do their part. Let's put someone very good at shadowing on her, and see where she goes, if she does leave. And keep that bird caller on the job intercepting pigeons!"

He looked around. "I rode over as soon as we made our bows to my parents-in-law. Noyu is far more reasonable than her mother. She doesn't expect me to spend two weeks sitting around throwing arrows in a pitch pot while we make eyes at each other as newlyweds. She's busy with her own concerns. That's the nice thing about having known each other since we were small."

"Third Miss rode down the hill earlier this morning, I think to see if Ryu was here," Dun said, fighting a grin. "She said to expect to see you both."

Falik blushed again. "Noyu is over at the infirmary, delivering a lot of the precious herbs we were given as wedding gifts. We scarcely need that much medicine at our age! We'd better start planning . . ."

He frowned into the distance, the others waiting in silence. Then he looked up. "I must report to Duke Yulin. And he will want Lord Oru there . . ."

He got up abruptly, as if having said this much had crossed some invisible boundary. "Whatever happens is fate." He left soon after, adding words of praise for their prudent silence so far.

He was back that night, and curtly gestured Muin and Dun into his office, his expression as hard as they had ever seen it.

"Didn't Duke Yulin believe us?" Muin asked — from long habit dropping honorifics with each other as soon as they were alone.

"Oh, he did. They did," Falik added bitterly. "Lord Oru wants to command any defense."

"Lord Oru?" Muin said, appalled. "He's never worked with us—he doesn't even know how to . . ." He stopped there at the mute misery in Falik's face. "Politics," he muttered, trying to get hold of himself.

Falik looked grim. "This is what you get, the higher your rank. Civilian nobles who have only trained with a fawning swordmaster in their family courtyard telling us what to do. Unless you have a tally or edict from higher above, they have the rank."

Muin grunted. "I was afraid that might happen," he said, unrolling a map. "This is what we have. They can't attack anywhere on this island but here." He tapped the harbor, one of the few north-facing ones in the empire; the entire southern portion of the island was nothing but broken rock below a snow-topped, sky-scraping ridge, riven by deep chasms.

They stood in silence, contemplating the map that they had already learned in a general sense, but now that they might very well be facing attack, improbable as it seemed, they bent to study it with all the concentration of the old days at Loyalty, when the stakes were honor merits—and the cheers, or sneers, of fellow cadets.

Now the stakes were their lives, and those of the people they were there to protect.

Muin had been studying the map so much he had it memorized. It was comforting in a sense to look at that impossible-to-attack south side. Their problems were confined to the north side, which sloped gradually down from the mountains. These slopes were terraced ages ago by the ancestors of the present inhabitants, who had discovered that there was not nearly enough rain and heat for rice, but mulberry trees flourished better here than anywhere else. And so sericulture was established.

Below the terraces, now all winter-bare, stretched a deep chasm cracked millennia ago by some unimaginable cataclysm, with thundering cascades that had deposited the silt that created the arms of the bay. That chasm lay east-west, separating off the shore from the mountains behind, almost like the first axe blow of a god clear-cutting the northern portion of the island. The chasm ended at either end with crashing rivers feeding the great flow.

The bulk of the island was connected to the long line of the shore by the remains of a mighty landslide that formed a slope, with a bridge over the last gap. That bridge was a miracle of building; it had been fashioned over the chasm, above a drop so deep that one sometimes could look down onto eagles drifting lazily on the air.

The civilian's idea of defense would be to abandon the harbor city and the duke's manor, withdraw across the bridge, and destroy the bridge after them. No enemy could get at them then — but that would leave them in a siege situation, with the enemy occupying the harbor, and all possible trade. And rescue. The garrison had been built deliberately on this side of the bridge, squarely athwart the road to the bridge. The standing orders, handed down for generations, had been to defend the harbor city — and the duke's ancient holdings

The garrison was solid stone, made from island rock. There was abundant water from the nearer, narrower cascade. A little higher up, on its own promontory, sat the ducal manor, as large as a small city, its backdrop the larger and more magnificent cascade.

Falik stared at the map. "We can see that defending the garrison and the manor on its hill would divide us into two forces. If we defend right at the shore where the enemy has to land, there we're strongest, and the enemy is weakest. But Lord Oru," his voice husked, "disagrees. Perhaps it is my fault. I know him — I've known him since I was a boy. We should have told the duke, and him, at the outset about the spy . . ."

He shut his eyes against the vivid memory of Lord Oru taking offense as soon as Falik told them about the supposed bird seller. "*We* ought to have known *first*," he'd said. "I am nothing, I realize, and expect little. But not to inform the duke is an insult to his rank and his venerable standing . . ."

Lord Oru had gone on in that vein for some time, but we need not record it all.

"Ayah! Let us be calm," the duke had said at last, when his brother-in-law showed no signs of letting up; indeed, Lord Oru had begun to insinuate that nothing better could be expected from those of humble beginnings who jumped in rank. Meaning Falik. Once launched onto this topic, he got a second wind until the duke interposed, adding mildly, "Everyone knows that I have never seen so much as a sword raised in anger. And besides, we are all family now." He smiled at Falik, who rose and bowed back.

Lord Oru was silenced, but Falik knew then that he had

made a very great error; Lord Oru was not going to forget what he regarded as a deliberate face slap.

Muin's thoughts ran parallel. He shook his head. "If you'd told him, he would not have kept quiet. He'd tell his precious guards, and what was to stop any of them talking to a wife, or a brother, or one of the women at the *Loving Ducks*? Any or all of these people would then chatter about it over tea to cousins, friends, in-laws, the salt seller, and a day later everyone knows. Including that spy."

Dun murmured, "Is he really that stupid?"

"He is not stupid," Falik said with painstaking honesty. "I expect it's unfilial to be enumerating the things I don't like about him, so I'll confine myself to observing that I do not believe he would, or could, keep silence."

The implication that Lord Oru could not keep a secret was a misjudgment. Where a matter touched on his own pride, he was as silent as the stones around him; the duke's guard was at the moment three times the size of Falik's force. They had their own weapons yard and corrals for the riding skills so important to nobles. Lord Oru prided himself on his skill with a sword — everyone had praised him as he was growing up. He also thought of himself as a leaderly figure on the back of a horse.

He had found Commander Han intimidating, but Han, now a general, was gone. After Han and his company departed for imperial escort duty, Lord Oru had ridden down the slope to the garrison to see how these low-born captains of young Falik conducted weapons training. They were young, and he was ready to instruct them — his duty as an elder — inwardly anticipating the notion of thus commanding the garrison as well as the guard.

Muin was in charge of training.

What Lord Oru saw was Muin's revised version of Heaven and Earth. Muin had changed the training to benefit the army's tactical strength in line maneuver.

Lord Oru stared down from the gallery at those whirling blades, the lines moving together to back each other up, and knew he could never match that. He rode away again, reflecting that they were front line grunts, expected to bear the brunt of any fight in order to protect their betters. He, as a nobleman, would command from the rear, where he could see everything.

He never went back again, but kept his dismay a profound secret.

Lord Oru meant to prove to himself, and to the world, that he was a better commander than a parcel of common-born barefooters. Spurred by that image of himself on horseback, banners waving behind him, Lord Oru objected to every part of Falik's defense plan, until he got what he wanted: full control, his much larger force the leaders, and Falik's small company as reinforcement.

"But the manor outgrew its walls generations ago! The new wall is barely the height of a man—the place is indefensible," Dun burst out.

"You know that," Falik stated. "I know that. Luckily, Second and Third Miss understand that, so they'll be laying retreat plans if the attackers make it that far up the hill."

The Dun brothers nodded vigorously—they knew the sisters could, and would, take over commanding the huge manor staff.

Falik said, "At least we know we cannot count on Lord Oru. We've a few days to plan around him. We, as Lord Oru's reinforcements, can be stationed anywhere," he said grimly. "It won't be our fault if we are in the way of the attack when it lands."

Muin stared down at the floor, loathing nobles worse than he ever had. He shook off the useless anger, looking southward toward Te Gar as he thought, "Mouse, I really wish you and your Essence were here with us now."

FIVE

PRINCE ER HAZ'S FIRST thought as he and Imperial Princess Lily made their three bows was that marriage custom had not changed in essentials since his people left the empire in search of a better life.

"The ritual is complete!"

Prince Er Haz met his bride's gaze through the sheer veil. He could tell by how unnaturally straight she held her head that the magnificent headdress of mostly gold, covered with rubies, was much too heavy. He himself was sweating profusely in his gold-encrusted crimson robe, dragging a train fully as long as a man — it felt as if he dragged a man behind him. But five layers there must be, his and his bride's human essential nature deeply hidden, though everyone was aware it was there. It was the same in their manors on both sides of the sea: royals and nobles had bedrooms separated by gardens and courts and gates from the vulgar gaze of the world. But after all, a bedroom was still a bedroom whether you were a king or a street sweeper, and every man or woman was naked beneath five layers or one.

The thought sparked an inadvertent smile, and as Lily carefully stepped up beside him, without moving her unnaturally posed head, she whispered in his language. "Mirth?"

"Tell you soon. Only the tea ceremony left, and we'll be able to get out of these clothes."

She could not nod without setting her headdress a-jangle, so she whispered, "Yes."

Ayah, yes. She had only to get through the tea ceremony without her head being pressed down between her shoulders turtle-fashion, and then the horrible headdress could go back into its vault. If she kept her mind on these practical matters, she could forget the heartache that never seemed to lessen.

At least her mother had prevailed with respect to the all-important tea ceremony, pointing out that to include all the consorts would only go to emphasize the fact that they were honoring the bride's parents first. It was permitted at all because an emperor was an emperor, but the groom's parents were unfortunately with the ancestors. There could be no parity even when they got to the east.

The emperor had agreed.

Lily and her groom offered tea to the emperor and to her mother the first imperial consort, who looked on with misty eyes, as the second imperial consort sat like a block of beautifully carved ice. She was furious at this defeat — to her, it looked very like the first consort was above her, a step closer to empress. Especially now that her mutt of a daughter was marrying an imperial prince, and there was her annoying son Jion sneaking his way back into his father's grace.

But, she reflected with satisfaction, when Manon married, she would make certain that *she* would be the only consort offered wedding tea before the eyes of all the guests. A *true* step closer to empress — especially if Manon was made heir.

Her goal now was to see that it happened.

The tea ceremony finished, and Lily was permitted to leave through a side door while the young men kept the bridegroom back for toasts. The wedding guests were conducted to the tables for the banquet, everyone in strict rank order. Though winter hit hard beyond the walls, inside it was warm, even sweltering, with so many people so close together and hundreds of candles burning.

Lily paused in the quiet hallway, gladly accepting the cool cloth brought by her maid. She threw back the veil and closed her eyes, daubing her face and neck.

She had intended to consciously note every detail of the throne room, the guests, the feel of the air, the smells of candles and incense. She knew she would miss home, even with its tribulations, when she was gone forever. According to all the poems, the bad memories would fade to poignance, and the good ones would become treasures. She was so grateful that she and Prince Er Haz had managed to find friendship as they fumbled their slow, painstaking way into the other's language while the elders decided their future.

But as she stood there, clutching her elbows through the heavy, gold-embroidered cloth, she realized that she had meant to remember everything, but all she recollected was the sheen of tears in her mother's eyes.

The wedding was over. The treaty was signed. Now she was expected to go to the bridal chamber, and tomorrow, to leave her home and family forever. She walked resolutely toward the door, then paused when she heard a step.

She turned slowly so that the headdress would not tinkle, and here was Jion, her only true sibling by the mother they shared. His black eyes searched hers, a new expression since his return from wherever he had been. "I arranged a little surprise, a gift. I hope. But you can look, and choose to do what you like," he said quickly—awkwardly. Why this awkward-ness? He was never awkward.

He led her not down the hall to the guest chambers decorated in red and gold brocade for the newlyweds, but through a side door in this august building into which she had never before set foot. The second imperial consort, and her daughter when they were all small, had seen to that.

At the end of a tiny hall was a door that had a peephole. He stood aside. Wondering, she rose on tiptoes to peer inside, reflecting that it had been made for a man. Then any questions about the need for such a room fled when she recognized the high forehead and the broad shoulders of Ze Kai, whom she had hoped to marry. Whom she still loved.

She turned to Jion, who murmured, "I—you never said, but I saw. I thought . . . you ought to have a chance to say goodbye. If you want."

Lily had made it through the entire day dry of eye, but she was undone at this kind gesture. Her eyes blurred as she whispered, "Thank you, but . . ."

"I'll stand guard. Anyone comes, I'll insist on taking them for toasts. But it probably ought not to be long."

Lily's maid, standing at the side with head bent and hands in her sleeves, looked terrified. Lily was going to say something when Jion went to the maid, and murmured low as he pressed something into her hand. Lily saw the wink of gold. The old Jion at fifteen never would have remembered the servants, though he had often made impetuous, generous gestures to his fellow imperial children, Manon most of all. The maid nodded, and Jion stationed himself at the door.

Reassured, Lily unlatched the peephole door and slipped inside.

Ze Kai rose to his feet, and started to come toward her, but checked at the sight of her in her wedding clothes.

She had not spoken a word to him since the day her mother had summoned her, and, weeping silent tears, had informed her that it was she, and not Manon, who was to be the treaty bride. They both knew that Manon would have been the cause — and Lily didn't blame her. Who wanted to go all the way to the East if she didn't have to?

The inward struggle Lily fought, without telling a soul, was at the thought of Manon marrying Ze Kai. Her heart found that unbearable — but reason said she had to bear it.

Ze Kai looked devastated. He had a powerful family, but powerful families had been destroyed at a stroke. For his, and their, sakes, she forced herself to say, "We ought not to be here like this. If anything ruins the treaty, it will be terrible."

"I know," he said huskily. "Though Jion promised to keep watch. Surprisingly, I believe him." Ze Kai's smile was crook-ed, and Lily laughed, remembering how impetuous Jion had been before he left. "Whatever he did while he was missing, it seems to have . . ." He made a gesture — even now he was too much a courtier to imply criticism of an imperial prince.

So Lily said it for him. "Improved. It's true. Perhaps we've all grown up."

Ze Kai took another step toward her. "Lily, I can't stand to think of you with someone else. And alone out there with those eastern barbarians."

He held out his hands, and she took them. His trembled as she said gently, "But I won't be alone. The emperor gave my father permission to go with me, as my secretary. Also, my loyal maid Ri-Ri will be with me."

He blinked a couple times, then said, "But a maid cannot protect you. At least your father can write — if a letter can be smuggled out unread. I will have to take comfort in that."

"I truly do not believe I am in any more danger than I would be here. I have spent a lot of time with the prince. He is a good man."

Ze Kai looked down at their clasped hands. "I *hate* the thought of you with anyone."

"Then don't think of that. Think of his kindness. Passions are ephemeral—everyone says so—but kindness can last a lifetime."

Ze Kai's fingers clung to hers, hard. "I'm glad your father will be with you. I've always respected Scholar Shan." He took a step closer; his breath stirred the hairs that had come loose from under the headdress. She lifted her face to his steady gaze.

She knew he was going to kiss her, and she wanted it so very much . . . but one would never be enough. She said, "I wanted to beg you. If you marry Manon. Be patient with her."

Ze Kai recoiled, his mouth that had softened flattening to a thin line. "What?"

Lily forced herself to go on. "She's smart, and beautiful, but I don't believe she has ever known kindness in that manor."

Za Kai gripped her hands so hard her knuckles crepitated and she winced. His eyes widened and his grip instantly loosened. "I'm sorry, I'm sorry," he murmured, and bent to kiss her fingers.

"It's all right," she said. "Really."

He shook his head. "It's not—that's not the way I want you to remember me. Lily, I will never marry Manon."

"If your family—"

A swift tap at the door, which then opened. The pair pulled their hands apart as not one but two figures entered—Lily's maid, and Assistant Court Artist Afan Yskanda, he of the beautiful face and the benign spirit.

Lily gazed in astonishment as the assistant court artist sat down at the one table in the room, and with a few swift movements unrolled some very fine paper, on which she was surprised to see a half-finished sketch of herself. He had brush and ink ready, and bent over it as the maid bowed to Lily and Ze Kai before saying, "His imperial highness says to go out the back way—they're coming." Her eyes were huge. "It's the *princess!*"

There could only be one princess who would rush to investigate after having seen that not only was Lily gone, but also Ze Kai was missing from where his family was seated for the banquet.

Ze Kai glanced from the maid to the drawing and back to Lily. "I'm impressed," he murmured, coming forward to kiss Lily once, hard. She kissed him back, with equal passion, then stepped back, trembling from head to foot, and he understood as she did that that would have to suffice for them both.

Lily's maid bowed her head; Afan Yskanda did not even look up.

Fighting against rage and grief, Ze Kai stepped past Lily to Jion in the doorway. Their eyes met. Ze Kai said, "I will not forget this." Then he wheeled about and vanished through the servants' door in a ripple of silk.

Bewildered, almost dazed, Lily had a heartbeat to assume the pose she saw on Yskanda's drawing before the rustle of fabric announced a newcomer. Here was Manon herself, pushing past Jion. She scanned the room in one fast glance, betraying the tight mouth of disappointment, then it was gone, and she said smoothly, "Prince Er Haz is on his way to the bridal chamber. They are looking for you."

Jion leaned his shoulders against the door. "I dragged the assistant court artist in here to make a sketch of Lily for me before she disappears. Did you get enough, Assistant Court Artist?"

Yskanda rose and bowed to them all in rank order before saying, "This incompetent of no talent has the essential lines, and will attempt to finish the details elsewhere, your imperial highnesses."

"Then let's get Lily out of that headdress before she faints from the weight," Jion said to the maid. "Manon, I'll walk her over. I claim brother's privilege."

Manon's lips parted. Everyone in that room knew that First Imperial Princess Manon had insisted, ever since they were little girls, that Lily was not a *real* sister. Besides, Lily thought narrowly, that flash of disappointment had been revealing however quickly it had been smoothed away. Manon had indeed come to make trouble. And having not found the scandal she hoped to find, Manon had no reason to stay.

"I will go back and tell our honored mothers that there will be no further delay." A whish of fine silken skirts, and Manon was gone, leaving only the scent of her apricot blossom perfume.

Jion held out his hand, smiling. Lily realized the assistant court artist had slipped out the side door as quietly as he had appeared.

Seeing the direction of her gaze, Jion said under his breath, barely loud enough for her to hear him, "Yskanda won't say a word. Really."

"I believe you. He has a gentle face," Lily murmured as they started down the hall. "Thank you for everything," she added, not daring to speak Ze Kai's name in those silent halls — who knew where eyes and ears could be located behind all the potted plants, statues, and spirit screens.

"I'm going to miss you," Jion went on. "I'm sorry we did not have more time. It's worse because I know that's my own fault."

Not wholly his fault; the second imperial consort and her daughter had worked hard to separate them and keep them that way. She had never wanted to make trouble between Manon and Jion. Though Manon's successful campaign to build a wall between Lily and Jion had hurt her, she had also hoped that Jion might bring the best out of Manon one day.

But this last bit of malice on Manon's part — it really was just that, malice, coming directly before Lily would be out of her life forever — and Ze Kai's fervent *I will never marry Manon* and above all the fact that she would never see Jion again past this very day, broke past the barrier she had set around herself.

She waited until they reached a clear area with no listeners in view, and murmured, "Jion, there is something I must share. I hope it is nothing. But Manon has been seeing a man at the bookstore."

Jion's first reaction was a hoot of laughter, which he managed to smother. But he found that hilarious, his studious elder sister tumbling into mad passion after all?

"Should be good for her," he said. "All that studying can't be."

Lily's head turned sharply, though he saw nothing in the dim passage but themselves and the maid trailing discreetly. "Perhaps. Except that this man is much older, and her manner is that of youth to an elder."

"Oh? I understand some women like much older men."

Lily felt the press of time, and though she had struggled a long time over whether she ought to speak or not, now that she had begun, she had to get it all out — she had to make him understand, if she could. "I make no claim to identity, but when I saw him, there was a stray beam of sun on him, and I could see that he had those same pendulous earlobes that are common in the Su family."

"He's a Su relative?" Jion asked. "Why wouldn't she see him at Su Manor? Or for that manner, summon him to the palace?"

"He might not be a Su. I made it my business to identify the uncles and cousins," Lily admitted. "He is not any of them. So it could be a shared characteristic."

Jion accepted that. "It's common enough."

They only had one hallway to go, then would separate forever. "Jion, *listen*." Lily halted, the decorations on her heavy headdress swaying. She gripped his wrist. "I saw her with the same man before we left for the Journey to the Clouds last spring. The restrictions had been lifted—you remember—and so I was able to visit the temple again. Probably ought to have told you long ago, but I was so frightened—the first time I saw her with that man it was around the time that her mother had one of her maids killed, along with her family, it was rumored. And you were so young at the time."

Jion looked into her earnest face. "Now that I think of it, the imperial guards would have chased everyone out before letting her inside. What exactly happened?"

"The *very* first time was . . . I think you were twelve or thirteen. And it wasn't me, it was Ri-Ri who saw them first. We'd gone to the temple, which has a side entrance under a grove of redbark trees. I always left that way, because it's so peaceful, and the fragrance—ayah, never mind that. The point is, that way passes down the alley behind the bookshop, divided off by a low wall of trumpet vines. These are full in spring, sparse in winter."

"All right—I think I remember the temple there."

"Ri-Ri was going ahead, because we'd thought about visiting the bookshop. It was a warm day in winter, the back doors open, and Ri-Ri looked through the trumpet vines, and glimpsed Manon. So she warned me with a finger to lips when I caught up. I looked, too, and saw her in earnest conversation with this man. They had gone to that back doorway, perhaps to speak alone? The sun was on him, as I said."

"And you didn't know him?"

"No."

"Could you describe him other than the earlobes?"

"With difficulty—remember, I was looking between vines.

Sometimes you recognize people, but how to describe their features . . . ayah, it's beyond me. I thought nothing of it, except wondering that she would be permitted to talk to strangers, only maybe she wasn't? The guards were out front, so he would have had to pass them . . ."

"Unless he had been waiting inside? But that suggests a planned meeting," Jion said. "And he would have been cleared out by the guard. That *is* strange, now that I think on it."

"I didn't think much of it at the time, either. Except to be relieved that I had avoided an encounter. We saw them again a year later—we were watching out—and that's around the time the second imperial consort had her maid killed. So I kept silent, afraid on Ri-Ri's behalf."

Jion was very aware that he was about to lose her forever, and wished very strongly she had told him before. "What should I do?"

Lily was silent for a stretch, then said, "You must do what you think right." She looked into his face, then in a pent-up rush unburdened her heart further. "There is little time. *No* time. You may go ahead and believe what I say comes out of spite, or dislike, but I wish you would consider why Manon was only permitted an hour of dance a day, but you were encouraged to spend entire days with dance tutors, while she studied? I know, I know, you love to dance and do not wish to inherit the throne—you think she's worthy—but also consider how very dangerous some of that training was that you got in that manor, with the both of them looking on and encouraging you to do more."

Jion wanted to dismiss her words as spite, except he'd never known Lily to be spiteful. But it would be so much easier to do that than to face the fact that his beloved sister . . . No. It was too simple. She *did* love him. She could have told imperial father any number of wild things he'd said in the past, but she hadn't, or he would have heard about it. "It's her mother's influence," he said. "According to Grandmother Empress, Honored Second Mother has been having maids strangled since she was a teenager. Manon might be passionate about rank, but she's not like that. I know all her maids by sight, and they've been with her since we were small, except for two, and she let both those go to get married—no, one died of sickness that year." *Poisoning.* They still did not know who lay behind that.

Lily pressed her lips against exclaiming *How do you know*

that is true? Because she did not know, either, and in any case her time had run out.

The chains and gems on her headdress tinkled softly, betraying how she trembled. "One more thing and then we're done, because it's only observation, and not proof: Manon frightens me more than her mother does. Because the second imperial consort is clever, but not smart. Manon is very smart."

Voices echoed down the passage, and now it was really too late. A heartbeat later they were seen, promptly surrounded and swept off to the bridal chamber. Lily's girl cousins among the Ran family led the singing as she and the Easterner prince linked arms and shared wine. Then, amid last blasts of hilarity from the boy cousins, the bridal pair were left sitting side by side on the bed.

The prince's well-born companions and the empire's princes led the way out. Jion's head was swimming with emotions. He—badly—wanted to reject everything Lily had said. But he knew that that would be foolish.

He caught sight of Ze Kai with some of the other ministers' sons. There seemed to be no uproar; Ze Kai avoided Jion's gaze. So at least he'd gotten away safe.

Vaion, completely heedless, began chattering at Jion's side. "Next will be us, you know. Ah, probably Manon first, and may she be sent to a far island. You'll be next, Cousin Siar most likely. I'm safe for a few years—thank all the gods in Heaven! Married! I don't even want to think about it. . ."

There was one last matter. Jion looked around, wanting reassurance, but Afan Yskanda had vanished along with the court artist and the scribes.

But Yskanda would never say a word about what he'd seen. Ironic, Jion thought, how much he trusted someone he had not spoken ten words to since summer. All Jion had seen of Yskanda was the evidence of his work. Yet when Jion had pulled the elusive assistant court artist aside before the ritual to ask for this favor, Yskanda had assented instantly, as if they had been chatting and playing Circle yesterday instead of half a year ago.

Strange, how you could completely trust someone who just as completely did not trust you. And likewise—his mind drawn back to Lily's words about Manon in spite of his wish to forget the entire thing—how someone you had trusted could prove to be . . . what?

SIX

WHEN ARI LEFT MADAM Nightingale on her quest to see her parents again, she had taken a modest amount of money, figuring that once she reached Sweetwater village on Imai, there would be no more need for money.

As a result, she left Burning Rock, at the extreme southern reach of the empire, with scant coinage, which only brought her back as far as Imai again. She walked the wharf from ship to ship offering to work for passage.

Do you navigate? No.

Can you repair sail? No.

Do you cook? I can prepare congee over a campfire.

She was chased off impatiently, and after all that rejection she was tempted to find gallant wanderers and reveal her identity as Firebolt. Except that there were few gallant wanderers to be found at this extremity, it seemed. That and her close call with Master Bankan on her previous visit made her worry that in her Firebolt guise, or even as Ryu, she might turn up on some list to be arrested. She had never forgotten the sight of that imperial ferret arriving at Benevolent Winds' harbor in a fast navy courier just as she was leaving — that had been a very close escape.

She earned what she could and walked the wharf every day, until she was finally hired on as a drudge aboard a trader full of merchants.

Within a day she understood why they needed fresh hires at every stop. She did not mind doing the grunt word the crew did not want to sully their hands with. It was no worse than being an orderly back at Loyalty Fortress. The problem was not only the surly captain, but two of the merchants had taken an instant dislike to one another, which divided everyone else into armed camps. Twice she forgot to blink away the auras, and found herself with such a collection of sour, dreary colors shot through with the irritated orange of smoldering resent-ment, and found her inward parts unsettled in an unpleasant way until she remembered to shut those colors out of her perception.

At least Ari had the run of the ship. In the moments she wasn't working, she was able to find odd corners to practice her various drills as well as she could under far from ideal circumstances. Otherwise she avoided the sullen crew and the crabby passengers as much as she could, especially during the most dismal New Year's Two Moons celebration she could remember.

Everything changed when the ship approached a narrow passage between treacherous, rocky juts. The passage was filled with anchored ships, packed tight from bow to stern. Ari's trader shed its wind, the crew sheeting up the sails tight and dropping anchor.

Though they could plainly see faces on the ship directly before them, the wash and hiss of rollers smashing the rocks not fifty paces away at either side, the moan of the wind tearing down the rocky canyons, and the squawk and call of hundreds of seabirds wheeling about overhead prevented them from shouting from ship to ship.

The captain scowled, assessing those restless green waves, and turned to the crew. She was not bringing her trader any closer to that ship ahead. She snarled, "Lower the rowboat. You." Pointing to Ari. "Row ahead. Find out what's going on."

Ari was stuck rowing to the ship in front of them, as breakers higher than a rooftop surged and splashed, tossing her boat about. She had to ply the oars — wishing the entire ship's complement wasn't watching from the rail, for she could have hopped to the next ship with her lightness skill, or ridden on her sword to the front of passage, instead of arduously working through icy gray-green waves with a shivering wind tearing at her.

At least the ship ahead of them had been watching. As soon

as she got near enough to hear and be heard, a sailor called down, "There's a wreck on the rocks ahead, at the narrowest passage. No one can get by until it's cleared."

"When will it clear?"

"No word from ahead. We've been here four days!"

Ari rowed back, and after she and the boat were hauled up again, she reported this to the captain.

One of the merchants shouldered up and harrumphed. "Would the great and honored captain please inform these insignificant passengers why we cannot turn the ship about and sail another way?"

The gray-haired captain's eyes narrowed at this thin, icy veneer of politeness over a tidal wave of sarcasm, and retorted with her own brand of sardonic politeness. "If the honored passenger will deign to explain to this inexperienced and ignorant captain how we are to turn about in this fast current, with the wind entirely against us, without being dashed on these fine rocks almost within spitting distance, this humble beginner will be most happy to comply."

Everyone looked at the barnacle-dotted, guano-decorated rocks not far away, where breakers crashed, sending spray the height of a three-tiered pagoda, and fell silent.

The captain said, "We've ten days of stores, and once we're through this passage, it's only four days to Pearl Bay, which is the nearest harbor. I know it's two islands west of where we ought to be, but we can resupply, and then be on our way."

With a lot of grumbling, the passengers went back below, out of the freezing wind.

Everyone turned in early that night, with only two look-outs on deck, both sleepy; the ship wasn't going anywhere.

Ari was mildly tired from an arduous day, but her mind was restless. Why not go see for herself? It would be an excuse to practice her flying, which she had not been able to do since she first figured out how last summer. She unwrapped Sagacious Blade from her bundle of belongings. The pearl in the pommel gleamed with gathered light, looking like a star; Master Ki had told her that a rock had been cast down from Heaven, its essence worked into the blade. She bundled up as warmly as she could, carried the sword to the deck, then sketched Essence charms over it and her body

She knelt on the blade. After months of not daring to risk flying, she was half-afraid she would have lost the knack. But as Essence surged up in her, she fixed her gaze firmly on the highest mast, and the sword rose swiftly into the air.

The icy wind battered her. She concentrated on the Essence deep inside, igniting it into a ball of warmth inside her. She had gone so long without practice, a pulse of worry tightened her neck. She tried to breathe it away. She might tire faster than she could pull Essence from this icy, howling wilderness, but at least her fingers, nose, and toes would not go painfully numb as quickly.

No one in the ragged row of ships looked up. Two didn't even have lookouts. Confident she remained unseen, she let the wind ferry her down the row until she reached the narrowest part of the passage, exactly like a bottleneck, as beyond it the ocean was clear to the east and west.

She looked around in the light of the fading moons, both as close to each other as they got all year, but waning.

There was no wreckage, just two ships jammed rail to rail. Puzzled, she hovered between them at mast level, shut her eyes and concentrated on seeing life forms with her weak, unskilled inner sense.

Tiny lights darted about—sea birds. Undersea life was vaguer, blurrier. And scattered in clumps, with a few stationary singles—probably sleeping—were human light blobs. A tight cluster of them sat near one side of the hull. She turned her gaze to that side, sinking the sword through the icy wind until she could see a row of scuttles.

She hovered close to the hull until she could smell the brine-soaked wood. Voices rumbled from the other side of one scuttle. She fixed her gaze on the ship's hull beside that scuttle, which was open the merest crack to let in a bit of air.

". . . drink any more. The brothers will surely arrive by tomorrow and every one of you needs to be looking sharp as a sword."

"We heard that this morning," someone muttered.

"Pan Paleg, what is that you're bleating over there like a demon's goat? You think whining is going to get you your mask?"

Ari had been losing interest by the breath, but at the word "mask" she stilled. There were a number of sects that wore masks, for varying reasons. But the situation, even the snarling, made her want to find out if these were Shadow Panthers.

The first voice went on, "They'll be here. And I can promise, whoever looks hung over come morning is staying here with the wreck. The rest of us sail to join the attack force."

Attack force?

But the voice was done — all that Ari heard was low-voiced muttering, and the clink of ceramic bottles put back on a shelf that must have been directly on the other side of the hull from where she hovered.

Follow Big Voice, she thought — and concentrated again, though dizziness clawed at the edge of her vision, balanced on the sword as she was, in a buffeting wind, while trying to keep her inner focus on a blob of light. She clamped onto the sword, breathing in, breathing out, tongue curled as deeply as she could with the tip behind her front teeth as she fought against the incipient vertigo.

The Big Voice blob stopped . . . over there. She opened her eyes, then realized that meant the other side of the ship. She set her gaze on a mast above, rose, and then made her way to the ship's lee, where the wind wasn't quite as harsh.

This scuttle was open wider, letting out warm, stale, sweat-tinged air. ". . . pack of stupid brutes." That was Big Voice.

"They've been holed up here three days longer than we expected," another voice soothed.

"They shouldn't be complaining at all. If we had Scream-ing Hawk back, they would be far better trained."

The name shocked Ari. These definitely were Shadow Panthers. Attack force? Where, and when?

And what could she do about it?

Big Voice went on to complain bitterly about the stupidity of the new brothers, none of whom would ever get a mask.

"They don't have to," said the second, reasonable voice, laughing easily. "All they have to do is fight where we tell them. If they aren't any good, they die."

Big Voice, who didn't like complainers, went right on complaining. "I don't see why we have to bother with the small island after all. Isn't all the wealth on the big one?"

"Gold Jade Island also has the largest garrison," Second Voice pointed out. "But most important, Master Night wants Green Jade. Ayah! I'm content with Green Jade — it'll be easy. Easy is good. If I wanted to be a hero I'd be over there *on* Green Jade, sweating under Young Falik, ha, ha, ha."

Young Falik? How many Faliks were there in the army or navy?

The conversation rambled on, all brag and threats. She scarcely listened, thinking furiously. There was one Falik she knew, and she remembered First Brother mentioning once that he hadn't brothers or cousins. That didn't mean there were not other Faliks in the world, but she shook that off. Green Jade Island — Shadow Panthers — brothers coming, and this ship was to join their attack force.

She'd heard enough.

Fury burned through her; she soared up and into the fierce wind, back to the trader. There, she tucked Sagacious Blade under her bedding and slipped down to the carpenter's area where the trunk of tools sat, the carpenter and mates snoring in hammocks nearby. Moving with meticulous care, she took the chisel, the hand drill, and the mace, then sped back up to retrieve her sword.

She flew down the wind to the two ships, then took the time to sail all around them. One, nearest the rocks, had only a couple of people aboard. It looked old. Badly kept. There was no sign of anything stored on deck. Remembering what she'd heard earlier that day, she suspected that this ship was going to be sacrificed as the "wreck" that would clog the narrowest part of the passage — it seemed from what she could see, the Shadow Panthers wanted the ocean between wherever their fleet was coming from and where it was going free of other traffic.

That was a guess. She had facts before her: this ship was full of Shadow Panthers expecting to join an attack.

"Let's see about that," she said to herself.

The wind snatched her words away as she maneuvered to the stern. After all the travel she had done lately, especially these past days as general grunt, she had learned a great deal about how ships were constructed.

This ship would not be going anywhere without its rudder, which was attached by sockets. She had had to help repair and replace one of those sockets her third day out to sea. Working from kneeling on a sword, in an icy wind, was not easy — but she had the tools, and she had fire. At first she feared that the fire she called up would smell on board, but the wind took care of that.

One by one she loosened the sockets so that the first time the rudder was thrown over to guide the ship out to sea, the sockets would give way and the rudder would fall off.

In pieces.

Then she went to work with the drill and the chisel, making a hole in every compartment on the attack ship. Nice slow leaks.

The wreck was even easier to damage, so that the Shadow Panthers could not move to it. Her last act was to detach the rudder entirely. The splash was indistinguishable from the roar of the breakers on the rocks.

By now her head was buzzing. But she was far from finished.

She brought up more inner fire, knowing she would have to get some rest, and soon. But first she had to get a look at the chart.

She returned to the trader, and ghosted to the captain's outer cabin where the charts were kept. The lookout was snoring steadily. Moving with care, she fetched out the chart, shut her eyes, and called up a tiny firelight.

She unrolled the chart, and scanned rapidly. She put her finger on the passage they were in, and scanned the surrounding islands—

What did he say? Green Jade Island?

There, the western end of the Silk Island cluster. Chill shivered through her when she saw how close it was to where she was now. That is, closer than Te Gar, and much closer than the imperial island. But how far was "close" on a map? How long before the Shadow Panthers got there? She knew so little about how to calculate war ship travel times—serious map work would have happened the next year if she had stayed at Loyalty Fortress.

Also, she had never flown such distances before—she was going to have to find another ship, but how was that going to work? And yet she just had to try to get there first, and warn Falik. Maybe he might even know where Muin was . . .

No, address the immediate danger first. She could indulge the what-ifs later.

She retreated to her bunk, packed everything up, ready for a fast departure. She had to get a little sleep—but she set her mind to waken before Phoenix watch, just as she had done in her orderly days.

She looked around, then decided to lower the rowboat again. Captain Surly and the rest were going to have to think she rowed away to escape them. Who would blame her?

SEVEN

FIRST BROTHER MUIN HAD not thought about the phoenix feather since he left Loyalty Fortress. He'd decided his senior year that if there was "greatness" in his future, it would come in Falik's shadow. Falik was admirable in all ways, and his greatness would be honorable as well as glorious. All Muin wanted was to gain enough merit so that if he met the emperor again, he would not have to bash his face into unrecognizability. Instead, if offered a reward, he could reveal his true name — and ask for forgiveness on his parents' part, so they could live without worry.

This goal reached far deeper in him than the "path to greatness" ever had. It was so deep that he could not bear to talk about it even at the best of times — and now, as danger threatened them all, such goals seemed about as graspable as the stars overhead.

And yet he still believed in Falik's greatness. As the tension rose around him in Green Jade's garrison, Muin watched Falik as each new bit of bad news arrived, wanting to see that greatness manifest.

Muin ran into commander's office to meet Dun, who had come from the other direction, looking angry. Dun waved a pigeon paper.

"Old Turtle refuses to release our former company," Dun exclaimed as Muin stepped to the window to observe cross-bow drill in the slushy yard. He'd just finished working the conscripts through his version of Heaven and Earth, which the men privately called The Sweat. "Says they're on maneuvers with the training base on the other side of Table Hills Island—"

"Which could even be true—"

"—and that he cannot release the emperor's ships or men on a guess by a sloppy bunch of fresh-out-of-training cadets."

"The coward," Muin snapped.

"We don't know that," Falik said, his voice tired. "He might believe we're completely wrong. And we might *be* completely wrong. But the important fact is, he is within his rights. He has no orders. Our evidence is a tiny slip of paper whose provenance we cannot prove. He has no ships for transport, and without orders from above, he can't commandeer a fleet of fishing boats."

"He won't," Muin stated, arms crossed. "He could commandeer all those local fishers. And I wager my head the Minister of War would agree, once the report goes in."

"If," Falik reminded them, "we're right."

That was the problem. They did not know for certain.

"Has the spy made any movement?" Falik asked.

"Not that our people can see," Dun reported. "Trickle has them well out of sight of the bird house, which means we don't know what she might be doing inside. She doesn't go to the wharf anymore to flirt with the sailors, but that could just be winter."

Falik gave his single nod. "We have to wait to hear from command at Blue Jade. Our courier should have reached them by today, or tomorrow at latest." If the weather had not been too stormy and the wind contrary: they all knew it, but no one said it.

Muin's mind had gone on to a more disturbing idea: wondering if this Master Night had known that Green Jade Island Garrison was undermanned.

He kept that to himself, and Falik dismissed them to their duties.

The next day, Pa Jan left the wicker cage door open, hefted a pack over her shoulder, and headed down to the wharf, where she hired a sailboat for one. Trickle's watchers reported that she told the hires she was going out for a day on the water now that the weather was fine, and she left her parrot as insurance.

"That's our sign," Falik said, his expression tight. "If she comes back, I'll offer my neck to the executioner myself. Let's evacuate the harbor. Keep announcing that they are to bring all winter stores, and leave extraneous things. Quartermaster Trickle, I hope your follower was dispatched to trail her?"

"Yes sir," Trickle said, then paused. "Should we send another pigeon to Old Turtle?"

Muin sighed. "We know what he'll say — that we're young and stupid, getting excited because an entertainment girl turned bird seller decided to take a sail. He hates us — whatever we do he'll see as wrong."

Falik did not disagree. "Nevertheless, we'll report it to him anyway. And also send a messenger to apprise the duke and Lord Oru."

The next day the snow was back, but the garrison turned out in force, and chivvied the angry, reluctant, bewildered harbor inhabitants into packing a few clothes and as many of their food stores as they could into carts and bags and barrels. They had never been forced out of their homes before! They were going to complain to the duke!

They were offered the empty space in the garrison where a full company should be, or opportunity to go over the bridge and up into the mulberry terraces to friends and relatives.

It was a nightmare. In spite of Falik's repeated orders to take just what they needed, most were pulling carts full of bedding, cages of chickens, and all kinds of oddments, with the family savings buried somewhere in the clutter that seemed necessary to people who had never had to pack up before in their entire lives.

At least, from the looks of it, they had heeded orders insofar as bringing their kitchen stores, judging by the baskets, sacks, and barrels of rice, vegetables, and dried meats. Possibly half crossed the bridge, complaining as the bitter wind whistled down the stone chasm under them, and vanished up the many ancient paths in various directions. The rest decided to squat right there in the garrison, some from a sense of safety, but there were those who felt that if the garrison was going to turn them out of homes their families had lived in for generations, it could take care of them.

Those people were housed in the empty barracks where General Han's three companies had been.

Now the wait.

By nightfall, as a snowstorm moved in, the atmosphere tensed. That many civilians shoved into military quarters meant for a tenth of their number brought its own stresses, especially as most of the complainers began sending handy sons or daughters up the hill to protest to the duke and ask for justice from him. Which brought Lord Oru down to the garrison to make things worse by summary judgments and unwanted advice to Commander Falik. Who had to listen because the man was his elder, and a noble, despite being in a parallel position command-wise.

The fourth time he came down, he said, "The duke's orders, and I am to command the defense."

Falik said, "We'll be happy to follow you, but I feel it is my duty to offer to take the brunt of the beach defense."

Muin held his breath; this was their last chance to try to get Lord Oru to listen to reason.

Lord Oru threw back his head, his golden hair clasp gleaming in the wintry light, the golden eagle worked into his beautiful armor glinting. "I know the territory before the manor, which is my honor and my duty to defend. You will do well to defend your gate."

"Lord Oru, forgive this foolish beginner, but I ask for instruction: it is my understanding that if we fight on two fronts, we weaken both," Falik said as humbly as he could.

Muin's hands tightened into fists behind his back. "Whereas," he couldn't resist saying, "if we combine together and attack them while they try to land, we can do the most damage."

Lord Oru turned angry eyes his way. "No one," he stated, "invited you to speak. Commander Falik, I expect you to discipline your unruly subordinates." He wheeled about, his crimson cloak flaring, and marched out, his silent honor guard at his heels.

Falik shook his head as he raised a hand to silence protest. "Never mind him . . . I might as well send up a lantern to the wish stars." As if regretting having said that much, he walked out.

A tense day followed, bleak and cold, the light watery and

dim as snow flurries blew sideways, mixed with ice. Then came the darkest night of the year. No one slept that night, which remained quiet except for the wind whipping down the mountains and moaning below the chasm, nearly drowning out the thundering hiss of the cascade.

Morning brought gray sea, gray sky, gray light.

Everyone went about their duties, ignoring the increasingly loud mutters from some of the displaced harbor people. The sun crawled across the sky behind the clouds, and darkness closed in once more.

Morning brought a lookout racing in, "Ships on the horizon!"

Falik knew the answer, but he followed procedure — emphasizing control and calm. "Did we receive a pigeon?"

The young orderly on duty squeaked, "No, Commander!"

"Then we shall prepare for hostile intent. Send a messenger to summon Commander Oru," Falik said curtly.

The man bowed and ran out.

For the past days — ever since Falik returned from his visit to Duke Yulin — Muin's and Dun's "duties" had included running drills on what they called their "reinforcement."

Presently the word came that the ships were offloading rowboats in numbers. That, the imperial navy would not do without first executing the proper flag signals and receiving acknowledgment from the naval tower in harbor: this was indeed an invasion.

Falik said, "Those warships out there can carry two hundred, maybe fifty more if there are no horses or any big war weapons."

"Which they will have to land," Muin said. The garrison possessed two medium-sized catapults, which his cavalry had been practicing with every day. "That gives them near to two thousand. We're seriously outnumbered — all we'll be able to do is harry their flanks."

Falik said, "That's what we'll do. They'll want to take the town first. Remember the mercenaries? I expect these will follow the same plan, capture commoners and threaten to execute them unless we surrender. So we'll have them under our aim until they figure out the town is empty. Us behind cover, them in the open, let's call that the same effect as doubling our numbers, especially if you make every shot count."

Dun's crossbowmen had been drilling every day: one

shoots and drops to reload as the second shoots, turn and swap places.

"Make every shot count," Falik repeated, almost gently. A vein beat in his temple. Muin was aware of his own heart racing as Falik said, "To your positions."

They dispersed to get into place, and we shall leave them there for a moment.

Out on the water, Master Night was angry that his sixth ship had not shown up, which would bring him his treasured Gate Breaker. But he had twice the number of defenders, and there was little likelihood of all elements falling to his favor again; Pa Jan, his spy, had assured him that the garrison was crucially undermanned — and that commanded by mere boys fresh out of military school, who would be completely taken by surprise — so he'd given the go-ahead, making a rousing speech that promised loot and prisoners to play with and whatever else his men desired, after a little hot work.

His flagship sailed into the bay with rowboats full of armed Shadow Panthers stretched like wings to either side, each twenty-five warriors led by a mask. Master Night stood at the prow of his ship, pointed his sword, and watched in satisfaction as his Shadow Panthers rowed toward shore in a formidable line.

He knew that there was no actual directing the battle from there — his masks all had their orders. He let the men think he was going to lead, but his ship slowed as the rowboats shot past on the breakers toward the beach, the men roaring and brandishing their weapons.

And then things changed.

At first he thought he was seeing spots in his eyes, until he noted that they all followed the same arc. First bombs, then rocks hurtled from either side, behind wharf walls: catapults.

"They know we're coming," Master Night said to no one in particular. Furious, he wondered who had talked — he'd find out and kill them.

Rocks arced into the tightly packed boats, shattering attackers and boats alike. Someone knew how to aim — more shots reached home than splashed harmlessly into the sea. But then he realized there were only the two catapults. Seeing boats smashed to splinters angered the rest. Master Night swept his gaze over his force, satisfied that the paltry attack had not even slowed his men down.

As soon as they beached, the Shadow Panthers charged into the harbor town, two masks on either side directing fifty men to find and kill the catapultiers. But they had slipped away, the catapults doused with oil and set on fire.

The Shadow Panthers, balked of their prey, ran shrieking and smashing whatever was in reach. When they kicked down doors to start grabbing children to force the surrender of the town, they found empty rooms.

House to house, empty.

Teams met at an intersection. "No one on this road, Brother Mask."

"Nor this alley!"

"Ayah! These shops are empty!"

"Set fire to anything you can—"

That's when a gunpowder bomb, lobbed by one of Dun's men, landed in the midst of the knot and exploded. Then on the rooftops, his defenders rose with their crossbows, and began shooting in twos, as fast as they had drilled all week.

"It's an ambush!" one of the masks roared. "Withdraw! Withdraw!"

A segment of the attackers roared their way back to the beach, where they discovered two of Muin's men having come in behind to stove in the bottoms of the boats. A fierce battle broke out among the splinters until a firework shot into the air. Smoke bombs exploded among the Shadow Panthers, behind which Muin's men, who were now familiar with the warren of tiny alleys and houses jumbled together, melted away as the enemy dashed fruitlessly about, getting rapidly lost.

They gave up the chase and streamed up to the wharf, where the most experienced of the masks rallied the attackers, shouting and roaring for silence. "Look, there's scarce a handful! Yes, we got ourselves ambushed—they knew we were coming—but—"

Someone in the back muttered, "So we retreat?"

"Who said that?" the mask shouted. "Come here so I can gut you, rabbit! What do you think will happen if Master Night sees us crawling back to the ship like whipped dogs? This is where the real fun begins! We outnumber them! The town rats have to be hiding in either the garrison or the duke's palace. We're taking both! So let's get out of reach of these rooftop heroes and head up the mountain!"

The Shadow Panthers ran back to the beach, and moved

parallel until they were well out of reach of rooftop attackers, then started in a mass up the road toward the garrison.

Two teams of Dun's crossbowmen harried them from the rocks, but there were too many. Those Shadow Panthers who had brought shields — most hadn't, expecting an easy win — were pressed to that side, as the others thundered up the road toward the garrison, blood lust lending them speed.

The race was on — unseen by the attackers. Muin's and Dun's men had slipped up the narrow goat-path to the palisade below the garrison, which Trickle had brought his brother and Muin down what now felt like a hundred years ago, when they first discovered the spy. It was a dangerous path, but they knew it; they got to the garrison ahead of the attackers, and then, with sinking heart, they dropped bombs onto the path, destroying it. It was inevitable that the attackers would find it, but a force could not come up the east side now.

The day ended with the garrison besieged.

The Shadow Panthers twice charged the garrison gates and walls, to meet a lethal rain of crossbow quarrels. "One shot to a man," Muin reminded them as he strode back and forth along the sentry walk.

Before too long the blue-white expanse of snow was dotted with dark lumps of fallen Shadow Panthers. The sun went down early, but the enemy did not retreat. During the night, the masks tried three more times to breach the gate, both by charging and by stealth, but the garrison was ready for them, popping up before they reached the top to pour flaming oil down on the ladders.

The masks called them off to regroup just as the drum tower rapped out the change to Turtle Watch.

The leading masks met. "We were supposed to get our supplies from the town, but it's emptied. Nothing left even for the rats," one reported, scowling in the uneven torchlight.

"There isn't much left on the ships," another observed. "And I feel weather coming on."

No one wanted to row back to the ships and risk the wrath of their commander.

The oldest of them grinned. "So we reverse the orders, while we wait for Gate Breaker to catch up."

"How do you know they will?"

"They know what the boss will do to them if they don't," was the answer. "Let's take the manor tonight. They should have plenty to eat."

A roar of anticipation rose.

And in the garrison, a roaring cheer rose from the defenders, joined by the two captains and their commander, but when Falik, Muin, and Dun were alone, there was no celebrating. During their last two years at Loyalty Fortress, any war game army that got itself locked into a siege situation lost, with no merit points. The instructors had warned them repeatedly that sieges were a last-ditch defense, usually won by those with the most supplies, and that was very seldom the defenders.

"They've retreated," reported a sentry.

"Thank you," Falik said. "Serve out a meal, and rest in rotation, watch on watch, as ordered."

The sentry saluted and ran to carry the orders to the rest.

"That means they've moved on to the manor," Falik murmured to Dun and Muin.

No one spoke. Muin drew in a shaky breath. They were all exhausted. They had been on their feet since dawn, after two nights of scant sleep. But no one could sleep.

Presently an orderly brought in a meal, and they forced themselves to eat, remembering lectures on the importance of keeping up one's strength by grabbing food and rest when the opportunity came. Falik forced down half his fish cakes, then stood by the window staring out, but not at the courtyard — his profile had lifted.

The other two reached his sides in two heartbeats. There, on the high ridge high above, beat the flames of fire: the ducal manor was in flames.

"It's got to be merely the front buildings," Muin said. "Lord Oru probably fell back to the gardens. That's an absolute labyrinth in there, with plenty of water. I'm sure that fire looks worse than it is."

"That's right," Dun said, and then turned away. Leaving the last of his dinner untouched, he sat down and began fletching arrows, as if he could will his words into truth.

"My wife is there," Falik said bleakly — which they both knew. She had gone to her maiden home at his insistence, as their small manor house had no defense whatsoever, beyond a low wall that mostly kept animals from leaping over to raid the fruit trees and harry the chickens in the kitchen yard. Even the animals had been evacuated to the garrison.

Muin said, "Second and Third Misses know that warren of

a manor better than anyone. They'll have found find a good spot to hide, probably in that honeycomb of caverns under the ancestral shrine."

"I hope I . . ." Falik stopped there.

They divided up the watches, and all three endured a largely sleepless night.

EIGHT

THE NEXT DAY, THE Shadow Panthers tried again to storm the garrison. Tiny ruddy-gold glints of fiery death began to arch over the walls.

"Fire arrows!"

Falik's garrison summarily bundled the townspeople back inside, though there was scarcely room to sit. The defenders went about with shield in one hand and bucket in the other; tubs of water had been set out in readiness at the outset. It was a day of putting out fires, and returning fire for fire for each ladder the enemy tried to bring up.

The Shadow Panthers retreated when a sleet storm came on with sunset. At midnight, one of Trickle's spies who had crept down to watch the lower part of the city, reached a section of wall along the palisade, and was hauled up, shivering, by the sentries.

He reported that the attackers had moved into the houses along Peaceful Ocean Way. "They didn't bring siege-breaking equipment off the ships," he said as he trembled, clutching hot tea in a fragile porcelain cup painted with dancing water dragons, given to Falik by his wife. "They keep talking about Gate Breaker, which is supposed to be here. And they're smashing into shops and houses and carrying off wood. Which they'll turn into ladders and rams."

"We'll burn them as long as the oil holds out," Falik said.

Nobody talked about what would happen when the defenders ran out of arrows and quarrels for the crossbows.

The next day dawned clear, mercilessly clear, revealing great clumps of Shadow Panthers coming back down the mountain from the manor after a two-day orgy among the duke's wines and winter supplies. They deliberately sauntered just out of arrow-shot in order to brandish the loot taken from the ducal manor. One of them, wearing a mask, sported Lord Oru's famous gilt-eagle armor and his crimson cloak.

Another proudly bore a spear on which had been stuck a large, round object with hair dangling down. Falik looked away, once he recognized that hair as his uncle-in-law's. His burning gaze tracked the rest, but the duke's nearly white head was not there.

All of the Shadow Panthers save a small occupation force at the manor attacked that night. The savage response that threw them back demonstrated better than words how the defenders felt about the looting of the ducal manor: every body that fell had at least four or five arrows in it, some a dozen.

Falik said nothing after the enemy horns blatted the retreat, but next day he went around from man to man, quietly reminding them that every arrow must count. A number of enterprising craftspeople from town had begun dismantling furniture (including their own) to fashion new arrows. Pillows and quilts were ripped open for their feathers.

Falik, Muin, and Dun praised them, but it was not going to be enough.

That night brought a sneak attack.

The Shadow Panthers had hammered together a moveable roof, and under cover of that brought ladders.

The two middle-aged owners of the Loving Ducks and the Three Sailors, who, under ordinary circumstances ran rival inns, had together concocted a wickedly lethal plan; all the chamber pots had been emptied into cauldrons, which they had built fires beneath. Warriors and townsfolk alike gave those cauldrons a very wide berth.

But when the ladders were set against the walls and attackers began to climb, buckets of burning, oily offal were poured down, setting off howls of outrage as well as fires.

Falik went over to commend the women.

The eldest bowed, and everyone cracked jokes about stink bombs and demon tea, but under cover of the mirth, she said in an undervoice, "We are running low on cooking oil."

Falik murmured, "I know."

A fourth, a fifth, a sixth attempt, always at night.

All were thrown back—meanwhile, Muin had raised a group of volunteers to sneak out under cover of darkness.

He had been promoted to a cavalry captain, an honor for one so young. And he'd become a good rider. But he was at his best with his boots on firm ground. Instructor Fumig had once said that one could learn a great deal about ground by paying attention to vibrations under one's feet. Muin had always remembered that, and he attributed his uncanny ability to always know where he was, even in the inkiest night, to this sense. What's more, he could unerringly tell where the enemy was. It had won him war game after war game during their fifth year, including the one that netted him the nickname Ten-Blade.

It aided him now as he led his little force under cover of darkness to harry Shadow Panther stragglers, and attack the edges of their camps then vanish into the night. Shadow Panther parties gave chase—and didn't return. Three times that happened, until the masks decided to endure it.

"Once we win, and we will," the masks promised, "we'll hunt them down, and every one of them will pay, and pay, and pay, until they beg for death."

Another day passed, and another, a slow and torturous drip of time. The garrison and the townspeople still had to eat. The garrison had to fight. The inevitable occurred: the daily count of ammunition dwindled rapidly. As did the food.

"Two days more," Falik said softly, when he, the Dun brothers, and Muin met one cold, wintry morning. "If they keep making forays like those. Maybe three."

The sentries on the tower watched the sea at least as often as they watched the enemy. But the horizon remained clear: no reinforcements. On the tenth day, fights broke out among the harbor inhabitants when people were accused of hoarding. Falik walked among them, unarmed, and tempers cooled—but sideways glances once he passed threatened trouble to come.

Falik's answer was to send Trickle's staff around to collect everything, to be pooled and guarded by the army. At the accusation that the army would steal food, five elders were invited to help guard, and at mealtimes, to insure that everyone got a fair amount.

After that, they went on half rations, once a day. They resisted killing the goats and the three cows, for once they were consumed, that would also take the milk away.

Arguments broke out over the chickens, some wanting to preserve them as layers of eggs, others wanting one last, good chicken dinner.

The chickens lost.

At the end of Turtle watch that night, Falik called everyone together. "We are out of arrows," he said. "Command is bare— we're sitting on the floor. Those who can spare trunks, boxes, and barrels, we will keep an exact accounting."

No one asked who that accounting would be given to.

The next day was filled with sawing, sanding, fletching. When fishhooks bent into arrowheads gave out, wooden arrowheads were made, sharpened to lethal points.

They ran out of wood by nightfall.

That night a blizzard howled, so thick that no one on either side could see much beyond their hands.

Many families gathered to pray, to hold one another, to sing, to sleep.

Some began arguing fiercely with one another about what the garrison should do—hold out to the end—charge right now—can't they find any other weapons—

Falik sat in his command center with his head in his hands.

Muin and Dun kept everyone away. The final decision on what to do had to be Falik's. Couldn't they see how terrible it was? But as it happened, the decision was made for him. Light had begun to blue the east when a lookout raced upstairs.

"Ships," he cried. "Two ships, on the horizon, coming out of the west."

Falik's head jerked up. Muin had been dozing while leaning on a desk. He thought he'd been dreaming. "What?"

By the time they all had left the building, crossed the main courtyard, dodged the water tubs, and climbed to the north wall, the light had begun to lift a little more, and there were two smudges on the horizon.

"Looks like traders. Really battered," a cobbler, who had once been in the navy, commented.

That did not sound like the imperial navy. Hapless traders arriving at the wrong time?

Or more raiders?

Falik's mouth tightened. "Let's go to the wall."

Muin's heart crowded his throat as they climbed the north wall and peered out. He tried not to hope . . . and it was soon heartbreakingly clear when the traders turned toward shore that these were Master Night's ships.

The garrison watched as huge pieces of metal-reinforced wood were landed, put together by many willing hands, and then, as the Shadow Panthers shouted insults and threats or just roared out their frustration and anger, Gate Breaker, a massive battering ram, was trundled by hundreds of pushers up toward the garrison. It had a metal roof, protecting the ram in its swing of chains.

The defenders began using the last of their arrows, but these clattered harmlessly on that roof as the ram nosed right up to the great gate. "Swing!" a voice howled under that roof.

"Ho!" the team shouted in unison.

"Swing!"

"Ho!"

"SWING!"

"HO!"

And, BOOM.

The gate reverberated under the blow.

Falik called everyone together, defenders and defended alike. "My company, I am proud of you. Under Muin you have become as excellent as ten-year veterans. Subjects of the empire, any who wish to fight, I will personally lift the edict against the holding of arms. We will share out the swords, spears, and even the practice weapons as long as they last. Everyone has a right to defend themselves."

The company sent up as hearty a "Yes!" as they could.

"We may win, we may not. But it is our duty to defend to the last. Once they breach, I will have the honor of leading the charge, once more at the head of my cavalry," he said when he saw Muin's mouth open. His gaze was cold as the snow out there, but steady, his stance firm.

All right, Muin thought, you lead. That's only right. But I will shield you until the last.

He resettled his hat with its captain's kingfisher feather and tassel. He saw Dun and Falik twitching at sashes and checking that their swords were loose in the scabbard.

They shared out a meal as the steady BOOM . . . "Ho!" . . . BOOM . . . "Ho!" reverberated through the garrison. It went on all night. The Shadow Panthers traded off in teams, men replacing others without ever losing the momentum or rhythm.

The first crack was a sound rather than a sight, midway through Tiger Watch.

The gates shattered just after the first bleak, blue light of dawn lifted in the east.

Falik mounted his horse and led the charge as Shadow Panthers tried to shove their way past each other around the Gate Breaker to be first inside to the kill.

Furious at how utterly they had been betrayed by the gods, and by that damned phoenix feather, Muin used his spear to cut a swathe through the attackers pouring in. He rode hard until the horse slowed, nickering and leaping over fallen foes. The charge was so furious that Falik and Muin together actually drove the enemy back outside the gates. But then the horses sidled, for horses will not willingly tread on human bodies if they can help it, especially when they are still moving. First Falik then Muin leaped down and began fighting hand to hand, as the horses ran off.

As soon as Muin's boots hit the ground he became a fury of steel, his sword whirling. But there seemed an endless number of snarling faces coming at him; he fought to get to Falik's broad-shouldered figure ahead, intending to defend him to the last, until he saw Falik go down.

With a roar of despair, Muin scythed his sword like a demon from the depths of Hell to get to the commander, but the numbers surrounding him grew and grew . . .

. . . until an eerie rushing noise surmounted the bloodlust.

Defender and attacker looked up, startled, as a comet flashed down from the heavens, fire streaming.

But unlike a comet it leveled into a gout of fire that smote the air.

Then a voice, amplified by Essence, shivered through the defenders' bones, "Down!"

The defenders as one threw themselves flat.

A gout of fire shot over their heads to hit the Gate Breaker, which resisted the fire until its metal glowed hot as a sun, then —

VOOM! It exploded.

Muin tried to get to his feet, but his body had become heavy as stone, his right leg not working at all. He peered down, blinking sweat and blood out of his face. The world spun.

"Muin? Don't move."

Did he know that voice? He knew that voice!

He threw back his head. The comet had vanished. A round-faced boy dashed in a circle around him, wielding a staff so fast it hummed in the air. From attacker to attacker the boy whirled, whacking right arms and ankles and knees.

The mask Muin had been fighting lunged up, but before Muin could grope for his sword, crack! The staff hit both elbows. "Choose a different life," the boy muttered to the mask, who roared curses back and tried to kick Muin's head.

The staff hit the man's knee, and the mask fell. The boy leaped over him and fought in a circle around Falik and Muin, once, twice. Two, three, ten more Shadow Panthers fell before that staff — then the boy paused and slung the staff out in a level strike. Another gout of flame shot over the heads of the Shadow Panthers, followed by a blast of hot air that knocked them spinning.

"Retreat!" a mask howled.

Another echoed, "Retreat!"

"That's right," the boy shrilled. "Run! Here's some fire to get you going!"

And as Muin watched, nearly witless with astonishment, the boy swung the staff in a perfect horizontal strike and for the third time, flames shot low over their heads.

The attackers fled, some screaming.

Muin struggled to rise. He knew that voice. That straight-armed strike, The Farmer Mows the Grass — how often had Father exhorted them to plant the feet just so, and swing from the hip?

"Mouse?" His voice came out a whisper.

The round face turned. "You're wounded." She ran to him, her eyes worried. She was indeed Mouse, though no longer a small girl. But her honest gaze under those straight brows so like his, her unremarkable nose, were his sister's features.

He made a tremendous effort to gather his wits and ignore

the pain igniting in his body. "Falik," he croaked.

"He—" Ari saw the still figure, surrounded by more still figures, and turned helplessly back to Muin.

"He can't be." Muin forced himself to his feet, ignoring the white agony, and dropped down to his knees beside Falik. Sluggish blood ran from Falik's mouth, and from countless wounds. "Thank the gods. Still alive . . ."

Barely. Muin shook his head, anguish nearly destroying him.

But then his sister hunkered down and pulled a small pouch from inside her clothes. ". . . Restoration Pill," she was saying. "This one is yours. Take it! You're very badly wounded."

The pain made every word a torment to concentrate on. "What?"

Ari saw at once that Muin was fighting for comprehension. "Essence. In this pill. Restoration. Take it, First Brother, please—your wounds are terrible."

"No." Muin's bloody hand shook as he pointed at Falik lying there so still. "Give it to *him*. Now."

Ari hesitated, eyeing her brother, who seemed to be bleeding from every limb, The gash in his leg was especially horrible. She wanted him to swallow the medicine, but she could see decision in the set of his shoulders.

Gulping down her protests, her grief and shock and worry, she took the last pill out of the pouch she had carried all this time, and gently but firmly worked it past Falik's cracked, bleeding lips. She massaged his throat, then sat back on her heels. "I don't know if it was in time . . ."

A greenish glow, like the first light of spring, flashed over Falik. The wounds still bled, but his breathing was no longer shallow.

The brother and sister stared at one another—then the sound of footsteps brought back the rest of the world and its demands. "I'll find you. Don't say anything about me," she said in an urgent undervoice. And to Muin's surprise, she put her finger to her lips.

She turned her face away from Trickle leading an armed party and disappeared in the crowd.

Muin's limbs did not want to work. He tried to look for his sister, but darkness was coming on fast, though the sun had risen . . .

He toppled over in a faint.

NINE

OUT IN THE BAY, Master Night had been caught midway between annoyance and exultation when the two traders coming out of the west put up the panther banner among the streamers warding weather and wind demons.

When the front one neared, he scowled across the water at one of his masked leaders, who he instantly recognized by his size and by the red armor he favored. "Where *were* you? And where is my war ship?" he shouted. "We saw you in the Snake Passage — but you were too drunk to join us? Where is my Gate Breaker?"

This was terrible!

"Master Night, we were sabotaged! Our rudder, *and* the rudder on the old tub we brought along to block the passage, on your orders. We knew you needed us, so we didn't have time to build a new rudder. We took over two of the traders penned behind us in the passage, and transferred Gate Breaker over, piece by piece." He pointed violently at the deck under his feet, in case Master Night had not noticed that he was standing in the prow of a trader.

"You were supposed to *block* the passage and follow this fleet, with no one knowing who you are — no one to see us passing by," Master Night roared. "What do you think the purpose of protecting our passages was?"

"But we *did* protect your fleet from being seen! We did block the passage! There were five ships penned up behind us — they saw nothing!"

"They saw you take two traders, you four-eyed rat. Unless you killed everyone on those five ships, now they're spreading word about that!"

"No, Master Night! When we took these two traders here, we hid our tattoos, and wore green headbands."

A second man shouted, "When we forced the merchants overboard, we told them we were Redbark sect!"

The first mask added, "As revenge for Screaming Hawk. So if they went straight to the imperials, it'll be Redbark they go after!"

Master Night threw back his head and laughed. The masks exchanged covert looks of relief. The first mask added obsequiously, "Then there was a vicious storm with winds that drove the current back so that we were stuck for days in one place, which is why we're so late. If you don't believe me, look at our sails! Our masts!"

As the two offered their explanations, Master Night had indeed been scrutinizing the sorry excuses for traders. They did look like they had been through a war with demon winds.

When he spoke again, it was in a far less surly tone. "Save it. Get Gate Breaker in there and bring down that garrison!"

"As you order!" the mask then howled, "Haul wind for shore!"

Master Night watched with satisfaction as the battering ram was landed, put together with commendable speed, and rushed up the hill. At that point he could not see much, but he was satisfied; when he retired to a hot meal, he could hear the boom of the ram echoing around the bay.

That continued all night. When it stopped, he had just begun breakfast. Gloating, he told his orderly to bring his tea out on deck, in hopes he'd see something of the conquering of his new realm — but then, unaccountably, he saw huge sheets of fire. Once. Twice — amid a deep boom that echoed all around the bay. Then a third stream of fire.

After that last one, the churned-up snow on the garrison road vanished in a long swathe as though burned away. Then a mass of figures swarmed down, resolving into his Shadow Panthers. On the run?

They began to swerve toward the harbor, probably to hide like rats. He flung his tea crashing to the deck and began to howl threats that no one could actually hear—then halted when an enormous sheet of fire gouted up from the wall of the harbor town. Master Night forgot his curses and blinked rap-idly, trying desperately to see from his safe position on the bay.

The swarm of Shadow Panthers veered away from the harbor town, and headed toward the beached boats still sitting on the shoreline, half filled with snow.

Master Night began stamping about his deck in impotent rage, shouting a mixture of threats, curses, and orders that could not be heard from the shore, when someone gave a shout: "Fire! Fire! Fire!"

Wham! That was when a gust of hot wind slammed into Master Night's ships. His flagship shuddered. The masts creaked. On the beach, figures struggled to get to the boats. Then a thin, bright length of light flashed and arced at the back of the swarm—a staff glowing with fire?

"That's Firebolt!" That was one of the tattooed brothers, standing near the rail. He pointed shoreward. "I swear it is!"

Master Night bellowed, "A thousand golden dragon-boaters to whoever kills Firebolt!"

The rest of Master Night's fleet in the bay strained to see the battle on the beach—then a horn blatted from the wharf, the wail echoing back from the low hills: *Enemy ship in sight.*

From the east emerged five war ships, in the lead one of the long, narrow fast ones called spear ships, built to ram.

Master Night stared. Naval reinforcements? But he'd sealed off communication . . .

Then he remembered the beginning of the defense—and the lack of surprise. Someone among those supposedly fresh cadets had had the wit to send for help at the outset.

Pa Jan was going to pay for that. But first, Master Night had to get away.

He turned his back on the boats desperately rowing toward him. If they were fast enough to get on board, fine, if not, they deserved whatever they got for running.

"Set sail, straight west," he shouted.

Ari hovered in the air, crouched on Sagacious Blade, having obscured herself with deflection charms. She was still shocked by the sight of Muin bleeding from too many wounds to count, surrounded by enemies. Half a breath more and they would have slain him.

She peered down at the ships in the bay. Which man was Master Night? He had to be the one standing so arrogantly on the prow of the lead ship, feet spread, hands clasped behind him, in a position of command. He wore an elaborate mask that winked with gold in panther stripes decorating the black. His clothes were very fine. Above the mask she made out abundant gray hair threaded with silver.

Master Night's war ships, now on the run, had a more favorable angle of wind as they began to pick up speed. The distance between them and the incoming naval ships widened slowly as she hovered above, utterly sick at heart.

What to do? What to do? She was so tired. She had thought herself so clever, ruining those rudders and causing the leaks — and had managed to miss what now was so obvious, that those Shadow Panthers in that passage days ago would abandon their ruined ships and take someone else's.

She was stupid, stupid! She wept out of hot rage, beyond exhaustion after days of sky chases into icy winds and snow, between sneaked passage on ships going eastward, or naps snatched when she had to land. She was pretty sure she'd slept on the roof of one of those traders below — it was very familiar.

She had *tried* to get ahead, but ships sail night and day, whereas she had to rest, especially when flying over water with no fire below; it had gotten increasingly harder to draw enough Essence to keep in the air, so fatigue and hunger had made her trips shorter and shorter, with the need for rest more frequent.

She was almost too late.

Once again it was fury — and the discovery of fire deep below the surface of this island — that had given her enough Essence when she saw that familiar ship, and that battering ram, and realized what had happened.

Stupid!

What to do now? The Shadow Panthers were scrambling into the boats that hadn't been smashed and rowing desperately toward Master Night's fleet as navy ships inexorably approached from the east. She could set them on fire from the air . . . beginning her on the path of death. The fire was ready, it simmered in her in spite of the tiredness, but . . .

She squeezed her eyes shut. All right, she had not thought out her steps in that passage days ago. She should think now.

What would Instructor Shaz say?

He'd say to look at the Circle board . . . Those rowboats below were not going to outrun the coming navy ships. So she'd leave them alone. The traders were caught in the bay, with the outer flank of the navy ships cutting off their retreat westward. The Shadow Panthers who had stolen the traders had taken the time to boom their pairs of cannon over from their sinking ships, along with the battering ram she hadn't known about. She could see them loading the cannon now.

How to stop that? Fire—but then she would forever give away the element of surprise to both sides. If she wanted to use fire to keep those ships from battering each other into bloody splinters, she had to wait and mix her fire in with their shots . . .

She blinked the tiredness back; naval warfare is excruciatingly slow to begin. The traders, far less disciplined, fired first on the naval ships. Four splashes fell short of the spear ship, which came steadily on, its two cannon at the prow with crew standing at the ready.

The traders were reloading . . . All three ships shot at the same time.

Now, Ari thought. The boom from four cannon firing at once echoed around the bay; in the noise and smoke, Ari threw down two bolts of fire. They weren't very large anymore—she was too tired—but each hit the foresail on a stolen trader.

Splinters exploded from the front trader's prow, and flames licked up the sails.

"We're on fire! We're on fire!"

The little boats from the shore, crammed with men on retreat from the garrison siege, plied oars desperately to get to their retreating fleet. Some of the boats caught up with the slower ships in Master Night's fleet, and men swarmed up the tumblehome of the ships, abandoning their boats. But the remainder, though they plied the oars desperately, could not prevail against the power of the wind. Master Night's ships were in full sail now, leaving behind the desperately rowing warriors. The traders with the burning sails, as well as those in slower rowboats, were left to their fate.

As the naval ships closed in on the former attackers and began rounding them up, Ari wearily turned her gaze back toward the garrison. She had to find Muin, to make sure he was still alive.

Muin was unconscious only a few breaths. He came to, finding conscripts on both sides, their hands supporting him. He tried to take his own weight, but agony shot from his leg through his eyeballs and he nearly collapsed. Wounds he did not remember getting clamored with excruciating pain, but the worst was the thirst.

Trickle seemed to appear out of nowhere, with a cut on one side of his head, blood dribbling into his ear. "Navy arrived! They're going after the ships in the harbor. Brother took your company in pursuit of the enemy," Trickle said into Muin's face, the way people do when they have been repeating words several times. "Orders?"

Muin's wits wanted to wander after his departed strength. He forced his mind to immediacy. "Falik?"

"Breathing," Trickle said. And then in an undertone, "Bad."

That meant Muin had to think of what Falik would want. What would he do? Dun in pursuit of the enemy over land, navy over water . . . Whatever Mouse had done, appearing out of nowhere like that, the Shadow Panthers still outnumbered the defenders. "Everyone inside. Tend the wounded. Lock gates."

Trickle nodded on each command. "Wounded being brought in. Our dead as well. I'll give the order to lock the gates after the last is in."

"Food . . ." Muin grunted as his helpers eased him down onto a table. "No . . . sit up . . ."

"This regretful physician begs the captain's pardon, but these wounds need to be tended at once," came an authoritative voice.

The duke's physician! Where had he come from?

Muin gave up trying to think as his trouser leg was mostly cut away, and then fresh agony made him wonder with a sort of bitter humor if being questioned by enemies or imperial experts hurt any worse than being patched up after battle.

He got one brief break when Trickle showed up with what tasted like a honeyed ginseng decoction. Muin drank it down, then said, "Falik?"

"No change." Trickle glanced over his shoulder; someone had wound a bandage around his head. "Physician says that is a good sign." Trickle then reached over, and carefully picked up something . . . Muin's hat! "I found this on the field. I wiped it down as well as I could."

Muin kept his gaze firmly on his hat as the assistant to the physician finished cleaning and bandaging his cuts. The phoenix feather might have been a mirage, but the kingfisher feather on that hat, he had *earned*.

He must keep earning it. He had to get back on his feet. What would Falik want?

Time somehow passed in a haze of pain, then Trickle reappeared with more nasty-tasting brew. He said, "If you get it all down you get to rest."

Muin drank half of the medicinal tea, choked, coughed, then Trickle helped him to his bed. Torpor made him woozy, but pain would not let him sleep.

After an eternity of trying unsuccessfully to find a position to lie in that hurt less, a flicker on his eyelids caused him to look up into to a candlelit face.

A familiar face. "Mouse!" He started up, then pain slammed him back.

"Ari," she said, low-voiced. "No more Mouse. Hearing that is like trying to put on shoes you wore at ten."

"You're a girl again." He pointed a finger at the waving lock that had slipped over her shoulder. The front part of her hair was pulled back and braided the way girls in the countryside do, tied by a ribbon. What's more, she was wearing a rose-colored robe with magnolias stitched on it. But he could have sworn he'd seen her in topknot and fighting clothes.

"No, don't try to move. The only one worse wounded than you is Falik."

"Alive?" Muin asked.

"Barely."

Muin blinked again, trying to recovery memory. "You said . . . you gave him . . ."

"A Restoration pill. It was given to me. By Yaso. You re-member?"

"Your orderly," Muin said. "At Loyalty. And at Te Gar? What happened? You didn't want me to say anything. Recognize you. I remember that much." It hurt to speak, but everything hurt anyway, and he had to know.

"About that. I'll tell you, but first you need to get this watery congee down. I promised the physician."

Muin struggled to sit, but fell back. Ari lifted his head and slid a pillow behind him. "While you get the congee into you, I'll give you a report. I know everything. Ayah, most everything," she amended, thinking of the mistakes she'd made. But that was knowledge, too. "I know a little news about your army. And I know more about your attackers than anyone here."

Muin said, "How are Duke Yulin and his family?"

"Duke *Yulin*?" Ari repeated, appalled. "They just said 'the duke.'"

A brief smile twitched Muin's lips. "Yes. I felt the same. Till I found out there's a warren of Yulins. All over the empire." And at Ari's doubtful expression, "Think about all three Sweetwater villages. Is everyone alike?"

"No, of course not."

"We're a family of five. Not used to clans. They can be big. With three times the entire north end of our island. He's alive?" It was tiring to talk so much. He swallowed more warm congee.

Ari gave a quick nod. "I was told that the duke is alive, though he suffered some obstruction of the meridians around his heart when the attackers broke through your defenders at the manor looking for people to slaughter."

"Not mine. It would have been . . . ayah! Go on."

"His family is fine—I'm told the daughters had an old tomb hiding place under their shrine. There is to be a funeral for a lord related to the duke's wife when the mourning observance days are done."

"I should be on my feet by then," Muin murmured. He had never liked Lord Oru, but he would pay the proper respect. Especially if he had to do it for Falik, too.

He flinched internally from that thought.

Ari wedged another pillow behind him so that he could sit up better, and as she spooned congee into him, she said, "Yaso made the pills, but there wasn't time to learn how they work, or what they do. I had three. They are all gone now." She grimaced. "I don't know if it was good or bad to save a guard with one, and not keep it for Yskanda."

"Would he need one . . . in Imai?"

"About that," she said again. "There's so much you don't know, I'm not sure where to start. But I'll try. Second Brother is a prisoner."

Muin jolted, trying to rise again, but Ari pushed him back. "He's at the imperial palace. The emperor's ferrets got him,

Year of the Rooster—"

"Rooster? I was there *after* that," Muin whispered, appalled. "I went there, me and Dun, too, accompanying Falik when he took the Imperial Examination. That was spring of the Rat Year. I didn't know he was in the prison."

"Imprisoned, but I don't think he's *in* prison. Though he could be. Do they let prisoners take the Imperial Examination? Master Bankan claimed Second Brother passed it, though I don't know how much to believe of what he said."

Ari then went on to tell him about her unsuccessful quest, including what she'd overheard from the apprentices' gossip at the scribe house.

"So it's only my guess that the ferrets, or someone, chased Mother and Father to Burning Rock," she finished. "I say ferrets instead of imperial guards because no one at Burning Rock talked about guards in armor and weapons. There was only this story about Father suddenly turning up with his knees ruined from a fall, pushed in a cart by Mother, both coming from the beach, where a sailboat had been seen anchored not far off. To a lot of shamans and monks, it looked like father had an extremely violent fall, but to me, that sounds more like a fight, doesn't it? Kneecapped with a club or staff. Father would never let himself fall on his knees hard enough to smash them."

"Yes," Muin said, jaw clenched. "Sounds to me like a snatch gone bad for Father. I hope it went worse for the snatcher. Must have, if Mother and Father survived."

"Then, in spite of his knees being so bad he couldn't walk, he and Mother sailed away alone, or nearly alone. The monks thought it had to be family need, but the only family is us."

Muin nodded, swallowing the last of the congee. The warmth gave him a little strength; he hadn't realized until then that he had been shivering.

"But we don't *know*," Ari said. "Father never liked what-ifs, so I'll stop there. I'm on my way to the imperial city to find Yskanda and free him. That is, I was, until I stumbled on those Shadow Panthers. They blocked up a passage in a rocky cluster to the west. I discovered they were to join Master Night's fleet. And leave a wreck there to keep the ships behind them from getting into the larger passage till they were gone. I don't really understand why they had to keep other ships blocked like that."

Muin said, "Subjects are forbidden to have war ships, much less a fleet—learned that fifth year, when we did games with navy cadets. Unless it's a licensed trade convoy. My guess is, Master Night pulled stolen ships from several rat holes. Blocked the ways first. No one saw where they came from. Or saw his fleet."

"Now it all makes sense! Here's the rest of the story. When I heard they were Shadow Panthers, I did what I *thought* was smart, I detached their rudders, but they took two of the merchant ships stuck behind them in the passage. What's more, they had that battering ram. Which I hadn't even known about. I handled that badly," Ari added, still full of remorse. "I don't know what happened to the traders and their passengers —"

Muin said, "Not your fault. *You* didn't attack the merchants. The guilt is solely on the Shadow Panthers. They'll pay for it. But Second Ry — ah, Mou — that is, Ari. Who helped you destroy the rudders on war ships?"

"I did it by myself," she said.

"How? What have you been learning at Te Gar Garrison?" When he saw her gaze slide away, he said, "Is this one of your *about thats*?"

Ari's shoulders hunched up, making her look like she had when they were little, and she'd gotten caught pelting Second Brother and Muin with rinds from a rooftop. But she had never done that unless she'd been left out, or told she was too small.

"Little Third," he said. "What happened?"

"I left the army," she said quickly, gaze shifting around the room.

"When?"

"Directly after I left Loyalty. The supply ship took us to Te Gar, but I didn't go to the garrison."

"Why not?"

"Because I didn't want to be in the army," she said, chin up. "The army was your path, not mine. I learned a lot at Loyalty, but I also learned my path is Essence, and even if the army did train for Essence, I still had to hide myself. Or get sent to guard princesses, and where are princesses but under the evil emperor's nose?"

Muin eyed her. "All that is true. Why do you still look like you grabbed a boiling kettle?"

"Because I joined the gallant wanderers. But I only fight for justice."

Muin scowled. "The *Shadow Panthers* are gallant wanderers!" His voice cracked. "*Whose* justice?"

"Ordinary people," Ari shot back, arms folded. "And there are plenty of good gallant wanderers. Like you said about clans, they're all different. And yes, I do make mistakes," she admitted. "Like ruining those rudders, and not finding out about the battering ram. But I *try* to think ahead. And not to hurt anyone, even nobles who set up rotten mines that kill people. Every time I break an arm or a leg I tell them to choose better lives."

"Rotten mines?" Muin tried to remember the details of gossip that he'd heard the summer before, something about mines, and gunpowder — a commodity the army and navy were very protective of — and a mysterious sect that has resulted in a massive shift of army companies to search — which, in turn, had contributed to Falik's new command being severely undermanned.

"You weren't part of the outlaws who attacked the Su mine at Benevolent Winds, were you?" He watched her eyes widen with surprise, then slide away. "You were there?"

"That was me," Ari said with honest indignation. "There was no outlaw sect. The only outlaws are ones like these Shadow Panthers. It was another sect who helped me burn down one of the Shadow Panther recruiting manors!"

Despite the agony in his ribs, Muin sat up, and grasped her wrist. "Sister, *that* was you?"

"Yes. I'm trying to tell you! It was for justice, and what's more, I'd do it again."

"Arikanda, if you're in any way related to the one they call Firebolt —"

"That . . . might be what some call me," Ari said in a tiny voice, glaring down at the calluses on her palm as though they'd grown legs and had begun to crawl away. "I hate it."

Muin fell back, groaning. No wonder she'd run off the battlefield! She had to know she was on the Capital List . . . What was his duty now? "Sister . . . Arikanda . . ."

"Just Ari, for now. I don't dare use my full name, especially Afan."

"At least you've got that much sense." Muin's voice was hoarse. "Ari. You are on the Capital List. Dead or alive. A huge reward offered."

"But I didn't do anything bad! It was all good." She hunched up exactly the way she had when small.

The door opened then, and Trickle walked in, bearing a steaming pot of tea with healthful herbs brewed in. "Here's your next dose," he began, then stopped when two startled, pale faces turned toward him.

He looked from to another of the twin expressions then back again. Alarm shot through Ari, who had shared a hut with Trickle while she was at Loyalty. Though she'd been ten years old. She saw his gaze stop on her hair ribbon, and she saw his thoughts shift toward "girl" and stop there.

To help that impression, she raised a hand and began to twirl the ribbon in her hair the way Lie Tenek had taught her. It felt very awkward.

"Have I met you, miss?" Trickle asked. "You look familiar." He then made a discovery. "You look like *him*." He set the tray down and gazed from Ari to Muin again.

Muin said quickly, "This is my sister. Who . . ." Invention failed him.

Even when he wasn't wounded and exhausted, he'd never been able to lie. She jumped up and minced toward the door in her best Madam Nightingale girlish steps. "Ari is my name," she said in a wispy voice. Too wispy? Muin looked like he was going to be sick.

She executed a maidenly bow in the style Madam Nightingale had taught her, and said in a more normal voice, "Came to find my brother, and they put me to work."

"And welcome you are," Trickle said, rolling an inquiring eye Muin's way. He was always ready to flirt with a promising girl, but not an officer's sister. Even if that officer was someone he'd known since they were all boys. "Where did you come from? You never said you had a sister, Captain Ryu."

Muin looked blank again, so Ari spoke up. "I was supposed to become a temple scholar, but I wasn't good enough."

"And so you came to find your brother? Are you with those ships that followed the navy in? You're from Imai, too, aren't you? Any news from the old island?"

"Not when I left last summer." Ari simpered, and twirled her ribbon again.

"Probably not ever. It's too small — interesting events fly right overhead," Trickle said, laughing at his own wit.

Both side-eyed Muin, whose expression had taken on a stuffed look.

Ari picked up the empty congee bowl. "I'll carry this back to the physician," she said sweetly, bowing to both, and rejoicing to make her escape. That had . . . not quite gone as planned.

"Stay close by," Muin said in a somewhat strained voice.

TEN

ARI BOWED AT THE door and whisked herself out, wincing inside at how badly she'd messed that up — and to think she'd gone in thinking that Muin would hail her wearing girl robes as a brilliant idea! She knew that most of Muin's ire was worry about her, and that he was scolding the mouse because he couldn't get at the tiger — which, if she was the mouse, the tiger would be . . . pretty much everybody who was chasing after Firebolt.

On both sides.

She took the bowl down to the garrison kitchen, and wondered what to do with herself. The place was swarming with people. She discovered by listening to bits of conversation that the harbor town folk were apprehensive about returning home — everyone expected another attack, and rumors were flying everywhere. Including about Firebolt. But all the descriptions of Firebolt were of a huge man slinging fire from both hands.

The "huge" was probably due to her pack. She had been carrying it over her shoulder all this time, with wards on it to deflect attention, but when others squinted to see her, they surely saw a blurry dark thing.

She found a dank, ice-cold storeroom that had once contained barrels and boxes of arrows, judging by bits of feathers and splinters of wood here and there. She swiftly changed back to her Ryu clothes, which were so much easier to fly in. She also bound up her hair in a topknot, then renewed the deflection charms on her pack.

She moved out cautiously, found a group of teens, and eased up behind them so she'd look like one of their number. They had stopped at a table where a woman set down a basket of hot fried breads.

"Are these for everyone?" asked a girl Ari's age. "Where did you get the flour?"

"Take one," the woman said, fists on broad hips. "My man sneaked down to Loving Ducks just now, to fetch up two bags of flour we hid up behind the ancestors. Those snakes and scorpions don't know the back paths." She spat noisily to the side. "If it's true they're on the run, why, me and Roreg from the Three Sailors and my second son's wife, we can between us put together a feast fit to thank the gods for sparing us, and send a few curses after those demons, too."

How to find out what was true? That was what Ari could do — find out truth from rumor.

She was aware of exhaustion dragging at her limbs. She needed sleep. But her mind was far too restless. Muin! After all this time! Muin, now a captain in the army — and the look on his face when she mentioned gallant wanderers . . . She had to talk to him again, to tell him about people like the Ki clan, and Madam Nightingale and her sister, and Lie Tenek and Oriole and the hermit and Reckless, and all the good people she had met on her wanderings!

She glanced toward the command building. There was Muin's window. She saw a shadow cross it. He had company, probably more of the officers, or the physician to change those many bandages.

She grabbed a bread, stuffed half of it into her face, then slipped around corners until she found an empty nook between a stack of crossbows and the wall. She set Sagacious Blade down and signed deflections on herself, then brought up Essence from the fire below the island. Her body ached with the effort, as if she'd sparred too long.

She did Essence breathing as she rose to the rooftop, then whizzed into the cold night air, and arrowed toward the harbor town below. It was mostly dark, except for golden lights along the wharf, and on a row of navy ships — two more spear ships, and a pair of heavy deck ships with four cannon each.

She briefly closed her eyes and reached with her inner sense. She sorted the different blobby lights. From the orderly manner of clusters of light-blobs, the navy was conducting a determined search for any Shadow Panthers trying to hide in the town. Ari was fairly certain that last blast of fire from the harbor wall had kept them away, but a search was always a good idea. She hated the thought of some family of shoemakers or weavers coming back to find an angry Shadow Panther ready to pounce.

She drifted up higher, looking farther. Distant light clusters had to be the Shadow Panthers on the run. Closer by, the watery blobs were likely undersea creatures. A huge crowd of human blob-lights over there, in what looked like a warehouse. Another next to it. That had to be where the navy had stashed the prisoners they rounded up.

A promising gathering trooped aboard the biggest ship. She approached, high overhead, looking down at the swinging lamps. Yes, officers. Coming aboard and going straight to the stern housing, where the captain had his rooms — and there was a messenger loping up the ramp.

She swooped down and around, careful to avoid lookouts, and hovered outside the frame of the oiled-silk windows.

". . . prisoners insist that Firebolt of the Redbark sect is here, and attacked the Shadow Panthers with fire."

"Firebolt? Where have I heard that name — "

"On the Capital List. Raided a brimstone mine. Feuding with these scum — attacked one of their strongholds. Two of the prisoners swear they lived with Firebolt, who they curse as a traitor."

"Get an exact description of Firebolt from them, and we'll send it on to the imperials. Mind, keep them separate, so they don't collude. Compare them. Like as not they'll say anything if they think it'll win them a lighter judgment by turning in one of their own . . ."

Ari shivered, and slowly drifted away. Muin was right about the Capital List! And here she was, wearing the same outfit she'd worn when she escaped Screaming Hawk and burned down the Shadow Panther manor.

She let the wind blow her a distance from the ship, as she was afraid to move and catch someone's eye. When she felt she'd gone far enough, she flew around in a wide circle back to the garrison, and landed in the same secluded spot. There, by starlight, she changed into her girl clothes again, shivering the while. She was not sure what else to do, except to keep her head down. Thanks to Muin, she would be known as Captain Muin's sister. No one would think to point a finger at her and yell about Firebolt, as long as she avoided the warehouses where the navy was herding in those Shadow Panther prisoners. From the sound of it, some of them had been at that horrible training manor that she and Shigan had burned to the ground.

She wandered out between the buildings, unsure where to go next. Not ten steps later a swinging lantern caught her attention, and an older woman's voice scolded, "Here's another one strolling around as if it's Kraken Boat Festival! Get inside, girl! It's still not safe!"

Ari found herself swept into what smelled like a laundry room, where bedding had been laid along the walls. Whispers and giggles made it clear that this had been made into a sort of girls' dormitory.

Some women handed out water and food. Another pointed out the area set aside as a privy, and then the girls were chivvied into the sleeping room and told to settle down and be quiet. Ari was very happy to do that; she fell profoundly asleep to the sounds of whispering and wonder-ing.

She slept hard. Exhausted from her exertions, she went right back to sleep three times, until she woke to more whispering. She turned on her side, suppressing a groan. She'd fought briefly but hard the previous day, after weeks of no chance to spar at all, and only intermittent drill. That was on top of the cumulative effects of that horrible flight. Every muscle in her body was protesting.

Without thinking she began to stretch, until silence abruptly fell. She looked up, seeing four faces more or less her age staring. She blinked, then realized she had pulled one leg to her face. She let go.

"Are you a dancer?" a girl asked. "I don't remember seeing you. Who are you?"

"Ari is my personal name," Ari said. "Ryu Ari," she amended.

"*You're* Captain Ryu's sister? Where did you come from?"

"I was traveling around, and it happened that I ended up here, just as trouble was starting," she said vaguely, hoping to avoid further questions.

But the girls were not interested in her. One said in an eager whisper, "Do you know if Captain Ryu is engaged?"

Ari stared back, completely unable to cope with this kind of conversation. "You ought to ask him," she said uneasily, her face burning. How Shigan would laugh at her if he heard!

"Oh, leave her alone," the first one said. "What boy tells his little sister his love stories? And we all know if he's got eyes for anyone, it's Third Miss."

The others began talking at once. Ari mumbled that she had to get to the privy, and grabbed up her pack before making her escape.

The older women had organized basins of hot water. After a year of living in a mountain cave, Ari had gotten very adept at basin bathing, consequently she was as tidy as she could make herself before she ventured out. Hot, weak tea and more fried bread seemed to be the only available meal. She was midway through getting these inside her when a young conscript appeared, saying, "Captain Ryu wants Miss Ryu."

Ari finished her tea and crammed the rest of the bread in her mouth as she followed the conscript to the command center.

Muin sat up on his bed, at least half his body bandaged. He looked, and felt, terrible, but his eyes were alert. He dismissed the conscript with a flick of his eyes, and waited until the door was shut.

"Sit down, Little Third," he said, nodding at a waiting mat beside the bed, which was on the floor. Papers had been stacked on the floor next to his bedding. The room had no furnishings other than that.

Ari sat, eyeing Muin, who sounded very much like an elder brother. That was even more pronounced when he said, "I don't remember a lot of our conversation yesterday, but a few things stuck. Afan Arikanda, you are *not* going to the imperial city to attempt a rescue on Second Brother."

Ari was ten again, scowling from the rooftop when First and Second Brothers were planning to sail their self-made boat all the way to the harbor. "Somebody has to," she began.

"Somebody is not you. Listen to me, M—Ari. If Yskanda is still alive, and I really hope he is . . ." Muin looked away, his mouth tight and unhappy. "I really hope he is. And if he is, then that means the emperor is in no hurry to kill him." *Which gives me time to earn enough merit to free him. I hope.*

But Muin could not say that out loud—it sounded too arrogant. And what if the emperor grabbed him, too?

He shook that dilemma off for later. "You've been here one night. After a battle. Yet everyone in this garrison is talking about my sister. We look a lot alike, and you know how much I'm said to resemble Father. If you were to go to that imperial city, there is no chance whatsoever that someone won't recognize you as Danno's child. I was there, and I saw the security measures. You won't get past them. *I* wouldn't have gotten past them, and I spent two years learning how to make and break security measures."

"If you were there, why weren't you recognized?"

"Because I smashed my face in to make myself completely unrecognizable. If you come up close and look at my nose, you'll see the dent where I did it. It hurt worse than I feel now. I don't recommend the experience."

"Oh." She sighed. "But Muin, I can use my Essence —"

"If you mean that deflection talisman thing, the palace is full of talismans to prevent people slipping by. They *know* about those things. We heard all about it at Loyalty, my fifth year. As for your flying, the wall sentries are not just staring down at the ground, but they look outward, they look out at sea, they look up Mt. Lir. They'd see someone on a flying sword. Even if you go up into the clouds, they will see you coming down. I'm serious. Don't do it."

"But we can't just leave Second Brother there."

"No. But we can wait. You know Father will be trying to get Yskanda free." Muin wiped a hand over his tense forehead. "Which brings us to you. I was thinking. You ought to stay here. With me. It's an excellent post. If you want something to do, we could make you bodyguard to Second Miss, that is, Falik's wife. I think you'll like her. Even if she's a Yulin." He smiled faintly.

Ari was sorely tempted—except she longed to be Ari of Redbark again, walking free, her staff in hand, and Sagacious Blade loose in its sheath on her back, not hidden away in her pack. Ryu Ari, Muin's sister, would be a role. She didn't mind roles for missions, or to hide from enemies. But living a role would be so confining.

And why should she?

She put her hands on her knees. "Is this offer to keep me from going back to the gallant wanderers?"

"Partly," Muin said. "Partly because I'd like to have you here. One thing I miss is having a family, even a small one."

"I miss that, too. But you've got the wrong idea about

gallant wanderers."

"I think *you* do," Muin said. "The proof is out there, running away from the navy right now. I know you loved those hero tales, but life isn't like that."

"It can be." Ari shook her head. "I mean the justice part. I know it, because I was there. Let me tell you about Master Ki, and Lie Tenek, and Benevolent Winds, and why I raided that mine . . ."

His expression was set, but he listened. Her heart leaped when she heard him mutter, "Nobles," in a sour tone after she got to the description of the wretches with no shoes in contrast to the expensive wedding and the pots of gold.

He listened all the way to the end — but it was clear to her that he was thinking about it like an army officer, not like a potential gallant wanderer. He said, slowly, "I think I understand why so many of us were shifted around, and we ended up without a full complement. No, I'm not blaming you! I think you did the right thing — though maybe you went about it wrong. Because the fact is, you still have a price on your head."

Instead of answering, Ari dropped a pack he hadn't even noticed she was carrying, and in a few swift movements snapped together the most beautiful staff he'd ever seen. She glanced around, moved a few steps to the middle of the nearly empty room, and then set the staff to humming. "Made for me by monks," she said, snapping it apart again. "Monks! I'm sure there are evil monks out there, like anything else, but my point here is that martial arts *monks* are the local justice up north at Dog Leg Passage, because the imperials don't bother patrolling up there."

Muin sighed, his wounds aching badly. "*That's* not true. One of the reasons we're undermanned is a shift of people northwards to cruise the border up there, where the Westerners have been raiding more and more. It's not just for the search at Benevolent Winds. But I don't know any more than that — and it seems, neither do you. If you leave . . . do you even have a place to go?"

"I do," Ari exclaimed. "My Redbark sister inherited an inn. She sent me a letter inviting me."

"Redbark! You stay away from them," Muin said.

"What?"

"There's two ships of pirates down there in the warehouses right now, claiming that the Shadow Panthers were trying to recruit them. They all said they are Redbark, which already has a bad reputation—"

"Redbark," Ari said, "is five people. Ayah, three now. But it was five. Including me."

"But there was a report last summer—ah, it was after the mine raid."

"Muin! *I* made Redbark up," Ari said. "And those people in that warehouse are Shadow Panthers, *not* Redbark. I destroyed their rudder, and they took those traders."

Muin pinched his fingers between his brows. "I hate to expose you to the questioners, especially as we'd better hide that you know anything about Redbark—"

"You don't have to," Ari said. "Shadow Panthers all have neck tattoos. They must be hiding theirs."

Muin lifted his head. "Yuju!"

The door opened, and the conscript stuck his head in. "Captain?"

"Tell Dun to pass along to Captain Ing that those Redbark prisoners are probably Shadow Panthers. Check for neck tattoos."

The door shut. Muin said, "In a way I envy you. . ." He shook his head. "What happened to the other two of your Redbarks? Dead?"

"No. Yaso . . . went wandering." That was the best way to describe Yaso, who hadn't been a martial artist at all. But still was Redbark. She hesitated. How to explain the truth about Shigan? She wasn't sure she ought to, even to her brother. It was Shigan's story to tell—and how much of a burden might it be for Muin to know? If Redbark was too dangerous for her to admit to being a part of, she had better keep silent, at least until they had a better understanding of each other. So much had happened while they'd been separated! "And so did the other," she said.

Muin sighed, leaning back—his mind was already moving on to Lord Oru's funeral. "Arikanda, please don't do anything until the funeral—and as my sister, and a civilian, we'll have to get you a mourning robe."

He looked miserably down at his hands. "Falik is not yet awake, and they say he probably won't be able to stand when he does waken. He took a bad stab in the back, all but severed his spine, along with the rest of his wounds. If I can't convince you to stay here with me by then, I'll get you onto one of the ships going north."

Ari blinked at how her brother's mind leaped from Falik to her, then the thought struck her that in their years together, Falik and the Duns had become like brothers to Muin. Of course they had. Didn't she feel the same way about Redbark?

She suppressed a sigh. She did see the sense of his words about going to the imperial capital, though part of her decision to stay away was fear of discovering that Shigan had stopped being Shigan, and had turned into the evil emperor's son, a white-eyed wolf. "I'll stay. I'll be glad to help the healers." And resume her studies, she thought, remembering her vow made at Imai Harbor.

"Good." Muin looked wearily around his bare room, mentally surveying the wreckage outside, the representatives from the duke, the prefect from the Ministry of Works who had come with the naval detachment, the Registry assistant from town, and even the tax people, all waiting to talk to him on Falik's behalf. "I'd be grateful if you would stay. We could really use another pair of hands."

ELEVEN

WE RETURN TO THE imperial capital, and to First Imperial Princess Manon, whose next goal was small, and practical: she wished to be invited to attend court.

To that end, she chose a court day to arrive a little late — not too late — to make her bow to Imperial Father. She had dressed with care. Robe, ornaments, headdress, and fan were very fine and very flattering, but simple. It would never do to be too obvious, and full court dress would be obvious. As she examined herself in her mirror, she judged her clothes unobtrusive for court, but much finer than the careless robes Jion favored, or the extravagant fashions Vaion chose. (Gaunon, though nearing sixteen, Manon considered too negligible to spare a second thought.)

She and her maid set out for Golden Dragon Pavilion, all calculated very carefully — but after all, unless one actually has access to the imperial graywings, one cannot know everything going on.

Such as a report that was both intriguing and irritating that the emperor received moments before Manon was announced.

She, like everyone in the family, was an expert at assessing the subtle signs of the emperor's mood. He was impatient.

She chose a brisk manner, humble and modest — always modest — *that* had been slapped and drilled into her by her mother — but one of assessment, of self-command. The manner of scholarship was her favorite, as she could draw upon quotations and rank points in order of importance, as in debate.

Seeing Imperial Father's impatience, she abandoned the quotations she had chosen so carefully. It was time for words of gold and jade in the form of admiration for their imperial blood line. "I have been comparing the court records of the first years of each of our Jehan ancestors' rule," she said. "Without going into detail, it is interesting to contemplate how very characteristic these are."

Imperial Father glanced to the side—and there was Melonseed, holding Imperial Father's court robe. Manon knew that the graywing only came when summoned or when duty required his presence, but he had managed to position himself at the edge of her vision. Though the old graywing meant well—he was fond of the imperial children, many of whom he had helped guide their first steps—to Manon he was only a graywing, could never be more than that, and she resented the presumption of a not-so-subtle hint.

She turned her shoulder to block Melonseed from view, and launched into her comparison. But she was not gaining Imperial Father's interest. She could feel it. Once again she mentally readjusted her approach, this time abandoning reasoned and ranked observations, sticking only with the most important facts. Perhaps he would ask for elucidation, and then she could expand into her thoughts on imperial matters of the past.

But when she reached his rule, her face covered in gold and her words honeyed, he said, "I trust you will forgive me, Beloved Daughter, but I well remember my own first year — and each thereafter." He forced himself to stop there.

He had to remind himself that he had not given her any task worthy of her talents since the Journey to the Cloud Empire, so here she was, showing initiative by making one. He knew why she did it, just as he knew why she had come late on a court day, her dress precisely calculated. It was that sense of her jogging his elbow, rather than actually doing something to ease his burdens, that irritated him. But how could she ease his burdens when he kept her — and her mother — well away from the throne and its demands?

He turned to her, and handed her a verbal reward. "I'm sure you realize that you are constrained by what the Grand Historian deemed worthy of putting into those records. It might be enlightening for you to read what the family said in their own private records. Though I warn you, there is a lot of it to get through."

Her indrawn breath made it clear how much she appreciated this gesture. Unlike Jion, who had been offered those records but had only once set foot in that locked and guarded archive sometimes referred to as the "dragon and phoenix" archive. A locked, guarded archive that the emperor himself never knew existed until the year before his grandmother Empress Teyan died.

"Bitternail will give instructions to my guards to permit you access," he said, well pleased at her obvious pleasure – and beneath that, glad that he had given her something to do that would occupy her attention for a goodly while. "Right now, I have a report to finish reading before court."

"This grateful daughter would be glad to read it to Honored Imperial Father while you are being robed."

And there she was, jogging his elbow again. "Thank you for your very kind offer; there is also a necessary meeting I must squeeze in," he said, and though his voice and manner had not altered, she knew she had overstepped.

She could only bow and withdraw. She had not succeeded in gaining an invitation to court, nor had she been invited to learn of, and comment upon, whatever problem he found so urgent, but she had won a significant goal in another direction: access to the dragon and phoenix archive, where emperors' and empress's own writings, and those of their immediate families, were stored – she had learned of it through her mother, who had winnowed it out from the dowager empress.

Triumphant, but always looking toward the next goal, she decided to take a walk in the imperial garden. The weather was cold but sunny; she might as well see who might arrive.

Back in the emperor's outer chamber, Melonseed came forward with the robe, and the emperor reread the report as the body servants, under Melonseed's experienced eye, put the finishing touches on the emperor's hair and outer accoutrements.

Then he spoke. "Send that messenger in. And get the Minister of War as well."

Melonseed went to execute the order, saying for the messenger's ear, "It's best to be succinct."

He nodded, grateful for the hint of impending imperial thunder, and mentally rehearsed his words as he passed to the interview chamber and bowed to the ground.

The sun was nearly up. The Minister of War forgot his dignity enough to hurry in, glad he'd read the copy of the report that had been delivered late the previous night; it had caused him restless sleep, from which he'd considered prudent to rise and dress in case he was summoned.

The emperor wore a frown that alarmed everyone in the interview room.

The messenger who had sailed day and night gave a terse account of the attack on the Green Jade Island. He said from the floor, "Admiral Sun required me to then summarize by observing that by virtue of your imperial majesty's grace the criminals then went into full retreat, with two deck ships in pursuit."

The fact that the emperor had not yet gestured for the messenger to rise was testament to his mood — had anyone suffered much doubt. "You are telling me," the emperor said, "that an untried company of a hundred at the point of starvation, after holding out for two weeks, suddenly routed nearly two thousand criminals? If they are that mighty, why did they not rout them at the outset?"

The navy messenger had hoped there would be no such questions. His voice dropped as he said to the floor, "There are conflicting reports, your imperial majesty. I was told to say that more will become clear once the interrogations are complete."

"Tell me what you do know. And stand up. I can barely hear you."

The messenger, an unexceptionable lieutenant who had served well in his five years so far — which was probably why he was chosen for this particular duty — looked as unhappy as he felt as he stood stiffly.

"Begin with the attackers. These are all from the criminals calling themselves Shadow Panthers?"

"Not all, your imperial majesty."

"But enough of them, attacking directly in the center of the kingdom, nearly two thousand strong, and no one had any idea they were coming?"

"Your imperial majesty, two ships worth of captives claimed they are Redbark sect —"

"Redbark! I've heard that before. Minister of War Cor Gu: how do you explain the fact that two sects of criminals allied and no one knew?"

The Minister of War could only go to the floor. The messenger knelt again, and spoke up bravely. "There was some confusion, your imperial majesty. The day I was to leave, I was kept back by a late report that those claiming to be Redbark might actually be Shadow Panthers. They bore Shadow Panther neck tattoos, we discovered, on investigation."

"Allied or a subset, it matters little," the emperor said. "If he is so competent, why did not Young Falik route this rabble at the beginning instead of waiting two weeks?"

"The tide of battle, various eyewitnesses attest to, was turned by the arrival of a sudden comet, or bomb, or perhaps an Essence artifact. Which then exploded like a bomb, flattening all combatants. Then confusion set in, but there are a number of prisoners who insist it was Firebolt of Redbark who caused the conflagration. The result was, the attackers fled back to their ships."

"Firebolt of Redbark was fighting for which side?"

"That is unclear so far, your imperial majesty. The attackers retreated, but Firebolt was described by three witnesses crouched over both Commander Falik and Captain Ryu, who had been fighting his way to Commander Falik's side. He was then chased off by Quartermaster Dun approaching with a party of defenders. He vanished in the confusion."

"So Falik was killed, or nearly killed, by this Firebolt criminal?"

"Your imperial majesty, Captain Ryu Muin, who was nearly as badly wounded as Commander Falik, insists that Firebolt, or whoever it was, administered an Essence medicine, which saved Commander Falik's life."

"How coherent was Ryu?"

"Captain Dun Duan testified that he was rational, your imperial majesty. Immediately, while his wounds were being addressed, he issued orders in Commander Falik's name that were all very much according to procedure, Captain Ing Iog of the Dolphin Division of the Blue Jade Defense Fleet testifies. And that continued to be the case. Captain Ing also testified to that."

"All right, then we can regard Captain Ryu as reliable testimony for now, despite his wounds. Did he identify this mystery individual as the criminal Firebolt?"

"Your imperial majesty, Captain Ryu said there was too much blood in his eyes for a detailed examination other than youth, armed with a staff. But he witnessed this individual putting a medicinal pill into Commander Falik's mouth, after which there was a glow of Essence, and Commander Falik's breathing became noticeably stronger. When he looked up the individual had vanished."

"Leave that subject for now. What about damages?"

"Other than the numbers of dead and wounded, which I began this report with, your imperial majesty, the reported damage was to the south buildings of the governor's manor, and to some warehouses, otherwise mostly theft. Several storage houses packed with silk bales for spring trade had been loaded onto the criminals' vessels while the rest were besieging the garrison. Captain Ing offered the observation that the invaders were intending to take possession, that this was not a mere raid."

The emperor was going to pounce on the word *mere*, but he held that back: the context was clear, and infuriating. Pirate hit-and-run tactics were infuriating enough. But someone who dared to take, and hold, one of the inner islands? That was a strike at his rule. In that sense, *mere* was exactly the right word. "No word from the pursuit?"

"Nothing was heard as of my leaving to report, your imperial majesty."

The emperor glanced down at the report. "Another question. Isn't there a garrison directly north of Green Jade? Ah, yes, here it is, Milky Springs Harbor Garrison. Commander Wei. 'Did not send reinforcement as he had no orders, and regarded Young Falik's prediction as the wild guesses of a young captain eager for fame.' Did the man actually know either of the Faliks? The former Cavalry General is famous through the empire as one of the bravest, and from all reports son and father exemplify the saying that a tiger does not have a rabbit for a child."

"Your imperial majesty —"

"In fact, I recollect now, wasn't Young Falik posted at Milky Springs Garrison for a time? Never mind, I am merely thinking aloud, but Minister of War Cor Gu, I believe this Commander Wei might do better somewhere at a distant outpost, as a quartermaster, perhaps, where he will not be confused over possible attacks *on the heart of the empire*," the emperor finished with withering sarcasm. "See to that."

"As your imperial majesty wishes."

The emperor frowned, one long finger tapping the arm of his throne. "What it sounds like to me," he said slowly, "is that this Master Night not only knew that Green Jade — which has been peaceful for generations — was undermanned, as apparently a spy informed him, but he seems to have known that our forces were strained to such an extent that no reinforcements were in the offing."

The Minister of War, still on the floor, swallowed in a dry throat. The imperial eye turned his way, black and hard as obsidian. "If there is a leak in your department, you will find and explain it."

"As your imperial majesty wishes," the minister said from the floor, and rose to depart. "I will institute a full investigation at once."

"Overseen by Chief Fai Anbai," the emperor said in that deceptively mild voice that froze the marrow of his listeners. "Where *is* Chief Anbai?"

Fai Anbai and his father had come by different routes to the small set of rooms belonging to Agent Tek Banu, who had unaccountably not reported in for well over a year, a serious departure from the norm.

Even though they had every right to be there, they had chosen to break into her rooms when no one was around in order to keep questions to a minimum. The ferrets were already dispirited due to various discoveries that put them if not at fault, seriously behind — but far worse was the suspicion that there was a traitor among them.

Neither Fai Anbai nor his father believed that Tek Banu, whatever her faults (and there were many) was a traitor. The center of her existence had been the emperor as Heaven's Chosen, and as wielder of order. They needed to know where she'd gone, in order to send someone after her. The emperor had not chosen to tell them — they had their suspicions — and after months of discussion, had decided mutually that if Tek Banu had not reported in by New Year's, they would investigate.

Her door was locked, which was not proof against either of them.

Fai Anbai surveyed the two rooms without touching anything. They were characteristic: except for the dust inevitable in a room untouched for a year, everything was scrupulously tidy, rigidly ordered. The bedding on the narrow kang was stashed in military rolls. There were two trunks, one the regulation trunk for clothes. In the second Fai Anbai discovered neatly racked rows of clean, polished implements used in interrogation. He was certainly no neophyte in the matter of interrogation techniques, but he shut the trunk again, his stomach clenching at the loving care those implements displayed, a care not given to the old, mended clothing in the first trunk.

He left that room and went back into the main room. Table, a single mat. He could not imagine her ever having had a visitor. Corner stove, dishes for one stacked precisely. Against one wall, a neatly organized bookshelf labeled by year, going back to her training days: from the looks of it, her training notes, and then summaries of her missions, written in the ancient characters that the ferrets had adapted as their own code.

He leafed through. The reports evoked her flat, unmodulated voice. He suspected that the same wording, or nearly the same, mirrored the reports she had written and turned in after missions. Except for tiny symbols here and there. Those were definitely not in any written report he had ever seen.

Notes referring to what? Not others' reports — she had been famous (infamous) for insisting on solo missions, as no one else was ever meticulous enough, or ruthless enough to suit her. He stood back, then turned as his father entered from the bedroom.

"You'd better take a look at this," Grandfather Fai said.

Fai Anbai followed his father back into the bedroom. The second trunk lay open — and Grandfather Fai took out the tray of interrogation implements. Beneath that lay wrapped and stacked weapons: knives, a crossbow, quarrels. Digging tools. There was the bottom —

No, that was a false bottom. "I didn't see that," Fai Anbai admitted.

"You were put off by the torture collection. As intended. Though I'm very certain those were not there for show, but they are old, from our training days. She travels with newer ones." Grandfather Fai gestured. "I've known her since she was in training, and so I was looking for something like this. Likely she has another hidey as well. But let's see what we have here."

Together they felt around until they found the subtly worked latch that sprang, loosening the false bottom. Once that was lifted out, they saw neatly stored . . . reports?

Grandfather Fai took these out, and went to the oiled paper

window to hold them to the murky light, which was enough to read by. "Ah. Mission notes — for herself. Ho! Some of these are in another code."

"My wife can deal with the code — "

A tap at the door.

Fai Anbai went to find a young page. "Chief Fai, there's a graywing with a summons from the emperor."

"I will come at once."

"I'll go through these," Grandfather Fai said from the far room. "And I think I'll look around. I'm almost sure there's more."

Fai Anbai sped away, wondering why the emperor wanted him. He knew about the report from Green Jade of course — a pigeon had arrived the previous day with a summary of the unsuccessful attack. He'd assumed it would be a straight-forward report, and that if anyone was to be summoned it would be the Minister of War, as it was a military matter.

Fai Anbai sped through a couple of shortcuts before crossing over to the emperor's residence, where he found, to his surprise, the emperor alone with Prince Jion.

As he prostrated himself, the emperor was still speaking. ". . . apparently the criminal calling himself Firebolt of Redbark was either allied with the Shadow Panthers, or fighting against them."

"It would be the second, Imperial Father," the prince said. "Firebolt would never ally with the Shadow Panthers."

"Never?" the emperor repeated acidly, then turned to Fai Anbai, gesturing for him to rise. "You were investigating this criminal, Chief Fai. Have you any observation to make?"

Investigating Firebolt of Redbark had been judged a low priority by Fai Anbai, until more urgent cases could be solved. He'd finally sent someone during the autumn, who had returned with nothing. "There is so little but rumor, your imperial majesty, and that old, that I find I have nothing to contribute here."

"Old?"

"No trace of Firebolt of Redbark since the mine raid last spring. I was beginning to wonder if he was dead."

"So you did not know that his name cropped up along with the attack on Green Jade Island?"

"That report might be waiting for me, your imperial majesty. I was involved in one of our other investigations."

The emperor turned back to his son. "Since you, out of all the people available to me, have actually met this individual, I believe you may go and clear up the anomalies. No?"

Jion looked up, startled. He had not thought his expression had changed, but his father must have been watching him carefully. Of course Jion did not want to arrest Firebolt—but surely Ryu would have fled, if she was even there. However, he was not about to explain any of his thoughts. What could—ah. "Imperial Father, I was trying to figure out who could take my place here."

"Here?" the emperor repeated.

"As you are probably aware, after New Year's, the scholars who work as assistants to the scribes pending their passing the examination have been coming to my manor on court nights to discuss the classics. No one minds my leading, as they all know imperial princes don't take the Imperial Examination. We've made the discussions as like Scholar Shan's as we can."

The emperor's expression cleared. "I see. Do you have a suggestion for a replacement?" And waited for Jion to defer to Manon, as usual.

But that did not happen. Jion stared thoughtfully at the floor. "Vaion is too young, and he comes intermittently. Also, he doesn't have nearly the memory for classics that Afan Yskanda does, for example. In fact, if he were not the assistant court artist, *he* would be the best, as he's passed the Imperial Examination. And he leads discussions by the younger apprentices while they work."

"Afan Yskanda," the emperor repeated, very interested that Manon's name had not come up. "He has an excellent grasp of the classics. A fine suggestion. I do not want to see that group disband—it was a commendable idea. These boys are our future ministers." His tone lightened at every sentence.

But then his eyes narrowed. "To resume the original subject. I've far less interest in the criminal world's squabbles and alliances than I am in the fact that we believed we had rid ourselves of the Shadow Panthers, between your purported burning of their training manor and the raid we ran shortly after. I want to know," and here the emperor turned that unblinking gaze on Fai Anbai, "why they have what sounds like an army. Which brings their crimes from mere lawbreaking to rebellion."

A beheading crime—not just the perpetrator, but their

entire families.

"Jion, you will both go to Green Jade Island to investigate. I want Young Falik and his captains commended, as you look into their situation, and if Firebolt is there, you will identify him."

One glance at the implacable set of his father's mouth and Jion bowed, hands clasped in his long sleeves. "As you wish, Imperial Father. When are we to leave, so that I may inform my household?"

The emperor glanced at Bitternail, who came forward with a box of ebony carved with dragons. The graywing turned toward the silent graywing behind the throne, who lifted the lid of the box and remained bowed over it.

Bitternail came down the steps and bowed to Jion, offering the opened box.

Inside lay a tiger-eye tally made of gold. The emperor watched Jion narrowly. What he saw was uncomprehending blankness, then came the impact. Jion frowned a little, as though considering, as he carefully took it.

"With that," the emperor stated the obvious with only a thin layer of irony, "you may take any ship in the harbor, and appoint yourself an honor guard. But permit Chief Fai to see to the logistics. You will depart on tomorrow's tide."

He rose and walked out, leaving the two bowing. In silence they departed, Jion stashing the heavy, cold gold in his sleeve. This was definitely another test, and like many, had come out of nowhere.

Neither spoke until they reached the outer door. Fai Anbai bowed and said, "This servant begs leave to inform his imperial highness that tomorrow's earliest tidal turn is expected at second Phoenix."

"I will inform my household," Jion replied, and they parted.

Jion was stunned at the sudden change in his life. He'd veered between belief that his father would never let him out of his sight again, and nightmares of being sent to cut off Firebolt's head—those were the exact words Imperial Father had used last spring, after the attack on the mine. Oh, this was definitely a test.

As he meandered along the path, looking up with distracted eyes at the drifting plum blossoms, he fervently hoped that Ryu of Redbark was far, *far* away from Green Jade. What possibly could have brought her there in the first place?

A movement caught his eye—there was Manon's maid, half-screened behind an artfully shaped juniper. Waiting? Watching for someone?

For him? He took a step toward her, but when he took that step her face blanched and her eyes widened into such stark terror that he slid his gaze away and changed direction, walking past her and into the garden as if that was where he had intended to go all along. That look of terror was a fairly graphic reminder that the Su servants were not permitted to speak to anyone unless to deliver a message.

That brought to mind an earlier discussion. The Su servants were trained at their manor, a fact that had disinterested him when young. Now he wondered if their rules were such that if he approached that maid with a perfectly legitimate question, she might very well have to pay for it. By Manon's decree or Honored Second Mother's?

Why was she even there? Ah. Here was Manon, sitting on one of the benches, as if it were midday in spring, and not a very cold morning. As he approached, she rose, the low winter sun dappling her robe embroidered with tiger-head orchids and gracefully darting golden fish. "Manon, Elder Sister, good morning," Jion said. "You look exceptionally fine. Going to court?"

"Merely making my bows, Younger Brother, after which I stopped to observe the last of the plum blossoms. I trust all is well?"

And that, he suspected, was why she was really there. He was very aware of the heavy weight of that tiger-eye tally in his sleeve, which he kept hidden; he knew that she would misinterpret Imperial Father's test as an encroachment on her intention to be promoted to imperial heir. He suspected that she wouldn't believe it was a test—but then she hadn't seen that speculative narrowing of Imperial Father's eyes, or heard that sardonic note in his voice.

Jion laughed. "I'm out here walking off my temper. It seems I'm being sent off with the chief ferret as guardian."

"Oh?" she asked, pausing, her head a little tipped, so that her long, delicate phoenix earrings winked and gleamed in the sun. It struck him that she always wore phoenix ornaments in or around her head. Phoenix embroidery was common, but no one but an empress was permitted to wear phoenix ornaments on a headdress. "Where to?" she asked. "Anywhere interesting?"

Jion said, "Imperial Father deems it necessary to send me to the Silk Islands again, as either a lesson or a warning. And after I've tried to be so good!"

"But the chief ferret will insure you return safely. Your family will be relieved to know that," Manon said, smiling the same smile she'd used when saying that Afan Yskanda was a mere parrot—with Yskanda right there listening, and unable to speak unless spoken to. She was probing to find out who was in command..

And he discovered that he didn't want to say that he was, because again, he wasn't certain of that at all. He had the appearance of command, but had no doubt that Fai Anbai would have orders about him if he made an error. And such was her hunger for that heir's crown he knew she would argue about it.

Better to explain after it was over. "Speaking of my return. When that happens, may I accompany you to your bookstore?"

Her eyes widened. "Nothing would delight me more. But why this change of heart?"

"Why does one do anything? Interest—curiosity—a desire to see the latest storybooks, for younger sister and brother."

Manon smiled and dipped her head. "I shall be delighted to have your company."

Jion smiled back, bowed, and continued on, thinking over yet again what Lily had said. He had no expectation of seeing any mysterious suitor or lover; he was more interested in repairing the relationship between them, beginning by trying to understand her better. For she had increasingly shaken his former conviction that she would make a sage empress.

Ayah! That was for his return. Now he had to ready himself for this sudden, probably humiliating journey, at the other end of which, he thoroughly hoped, Ryu would safely be islands away.

This reminder of the unlikelihood of ever seeing one another again worsened an already grim mood. The orders were no surprise. *Find this Firebolt. Bring me back his head.* He'd had that threat hanging over his own head since summer, but he'd been able to forget it—or rather, to hope his father would forget it—as the weeks and months had passed. But his father did not forget such things.

He returned to his manor to report the new orders to

Steward Whiteleaf and to change clothes. He left the servants to deal with preparation while he headed for the west court to work off the mood. When he arrived, he walked into an air of anticipation — even excitement.

By now he knew the names of all the guards who rotated through to practice with him, though they kept a proper distance that he never tried to cross. That, he suspected, was exactly how factions formed — and though he had no intention of forming a faction, he was aware that one was judged by what others perceived.

He said easily, "What's going on? A war game planned?"

Some glances of surprise semaphored between guards, then big, fast Yim grinned. "Ha Gar, there, and Tun-Tun and I, we've been assigned to your imperial highness' honor guard."

"Ayah," Jion exclaimed.

As he worked through his warm-up drills, he considered this news. He'd expected to be surrounded by tough, grim-faced veterans who would treat him as an erring puppy for the duration. Had Fai Anbai actually chosen people Jion liked? Of course that could be construed as a different type of threat — that if he decided to run off, these guards he worked with every day would be first on the execution ground — but since he had no intention of running off, he might as well regard their inclusion as an unlooked-for benefit.

"Let's spar," he said, plucking a staff from the rack. "While we've got solid ground under us."

TWELVE

ARI KNEW SHE OUGHT to take the next ship out of the Green Jade Island bay.

She was very aware that staying in the midst of imperials while she was on the Capital List was akin to bedding down next to a sleeping tiger for its warmth. But it was so very good to see Muin again, and to watch his improvement day by day. As for Firebolt, nobody was actually searching for this mystery criminal, who rumor had it was a bulky young man. Ari kept her Ryu clothes in her pack, along with her wrapped sword and staff. She carried her pack everywhere, and refreshed the deflection charms on it before she slept and on waking each day; because no one was looking for it, they just didn't see it.

She liked helping with the nursing in the garrison—and the physician readily made not only his books available to her, but his charts of meridians and acupoints. There were so many wounded that her help was desperately needed. She discover-ed that most of Mother's lessons in making medicine came back to her; on finding that she was acquainted with the fun-damentals of medicine, the army physician put her to work making and delivering medicine—and so she was learning from him, too.

It felt good to be learning again. It also felt good to escape up to the grave mounds, where no one went during winter, to do Redbark drills and to work with her fan form. She was finally getting the fan to whirl back to her hand, after countless false tries when she had to chase it all over.

But the recovering wounded came first. She was there when Falik Tan opened his eyes at last, and though he was too weak to speak, it was clear that he recognized his orderly Pigear, whose tough, bony face shone with silent tears. "I'll go fetch Second Miss," Ari offered.

Pigear nodded, hovering over his commander, ready to leap at the slightest twitch of discomfort.

Ari sped from the infirmary up to the command office, and knocked at the door to the modest two rooms set aside for the commander.

"Enter," called a female voice.

Ari slid the door open, to discover both of the Yulin daughters there, like her wearing the rough, undyed fabric of mourning for their uncle, slaughtered with the duke's guard that he had commanded. Though Falik and Second Miss had a pretty manor near the duke's own manor — where Third Miss had a palatial suite — invariably the sisters were to be found here at the garrison. And not expecting to be waited on, either. They had been sharing nursing duties with Ari; they had also donated a great deal of the manor's fine furnishings to replace the tables and chairs and shelves that had been cut up to make arrows.

Second Miss, Falik's wife, lay back on the bed, her complexion unpleasantly mottled. "Second Miss," Ari said, consciously making the commoner's bow to a duke's daughter. "Good news! Commander Falik opened his eyes!"

Both sisters started up — then Second Miss gave a little cough, the sort of cough that means stomach upset, and clapped her hand over her mouth.

Third Miss turned wide eyes to Ari. "Miss Ryu, can you take her pulse? Do you think it's . . ." She, friends with animals as well as with people, was Ari's favorite, though she liked them both. "If Sister were a mare, or a dog, I'd know."

"I'm not very good at pulse taking," Ari said as she came forward. That was true. Her mother had barely begun teaching her when she left with Muin.

She put her fingers on Second Miss's limp wrist and closed her eyes. She wasn't actually listening to the pulse, but sensing the lights. Second Sister's was a somewhat sickly orange. But within that light was a pinpoint light, a bright blue spark. Ari usually shut these auras out, as they were more distracting then revealing, but for once she was pretty clear about what she was seeing.

She opened her eyes. "I think . . . I think it's there. Two pulses within you," she amended quickly. "Yours, and a new one. It's very strong and steady."

Second Sister's maid, hovering in the background, gasped. Third Sister said with satisfaction, "There. I told you. Bad rice, tchah!"

Second Miss's eyes were closed, tears leaking from beneath her lashes, making an already unprepossessing face look more mottled. Ari remembered the physician warning them that because of a vicious sword strike that had all but severed Falik's spine (actually it had, Ari remembered that much) even if he recovered, he might not walk again. Or be a husband in the fullest sense. That part of human relations was still a mystery to her, but she could see how very important this news was to Second Miss.

"Go see," she whispered to her sister. "If he can talk, I'll come. But I'll have to have a basin."

"I'll make you some ginger tea," Ari offered. "And brink you some aromatic incense—jasmine, or—"

"No jasmine!" both sisters exclaimed, then Second Miss groaned.

Ari stared from one to the other. "But jasmine is very good for—"

"Not for some members of our family," Third Miss said briskly. "It'll make her *really* sick. Honored Father, too. The taste, the smell, even the feel of it—no, no, no." She looked up from rubbing her sister's shoulders. "Doesn't bother the rest of us, but we had to give up having it around. Not so much as a jasmine seed dares come into our garden."

Ari frowned, memory tugging at her. But she didn't have time for whatever it was; she said, "Ginger plain. I can see to that."

"Thank you," both sisters chorused.

By the time she got down to the kitchen, made the tea, and got upstairs again, the entire garrison buzzed with double good news: the commander's waking, and the news that his wife was with child—Second Miss's maid, determined to be first with the news, having lost no time in running ahead and blabbing to anyone in sight.

Muin sent off notice to The Duke at Blue Jade Island, who was their superior, that Falik had woken.

Now the mourning period was past, the duke's augur offered several auspicious times for Lord Oru's funeral. The men had already been buried, each with a fine mound and a grave marker (the dead Shadow Panthers had been dumped into a common grave at a stony site considered inauspicious, with ghost-warding charms at all four corners), but Lord Oru rested in an elaborate marble coffin in the ducal ancestral hall — which was more than he would have gotten if he had died on Gold Jade Island, where he was born. The duke's wife insisted that her brother deserved the finest of funerals, and the duke, still recovering from his syncope, agreed as always. The proper prayers had been offered every five days for five weeks, and now it was time to bury the body, which it was hoped would completely free the soul to await the journey to rebirth.

The duke's wife chose one of the auspicious dates she was offered, and sent a messenger to the garrison, for it had been agreed that the funeral ritual would include all the fallen.

By now Muin was conducting drills again; if the Shadow Panthers reappeared, he planned to be ready. But everyone felt the weight of what was due to the many, many dead. It was he who had insisted that the funeral include the garrison fallen as well as the manor guards.

Muin himself did not know whether the rites conducted on earth truly affected doings in Heaven. But he remembered his father telling him when he was small, "Once you command, never forget that most of your conscripts will be very far from home. How you honor the dead will be a sign to them how they will be treated if they give up their lives."

Muin meant for his sadly diminished company to see that every man, no matter how humble his background, would receive the same incense, the same spirit talismans, and the same prayers as those born higher on the tree of rank.

The rite for the men began early that morning. Falik's wife was too ill to help, and Third Miss had to aid her mother with the funeral for her uncle, so it was Ari, as Muin's sister, who had taken on the job of burning the spirit talismans for each of the dead.

As she trudged up the hill, carrying a heavy basket of spirit papers, below in the garrison it was a sober company who stood for inspection. Muin took the time to examine every man, though he still leaned upon a stick. Falik was wheeled in a cart behind him, his eyes alert and searching.

Then all made their way up onto the hill where fragrant cedars sheltered both the garrison's burial mounds and above them, the ancestral mounds of the Yulin dukes and their families.

First there was Lord Oru's funeral rite. Many of Lord Oru's men had been locals, so there was quite a crowd standing respectfully back of the Yulin family; at first, no one noticed the new additions who had come straight from the harbor as they quietly took up positions at the back.

The duke was still too ill to lead the ceremony. His wife conducted it, aided by her third daughter, after which the military part of the gathering marched down to the garrison mounds.

Then it was the manor guards' and the garrison's turn.

Ari was nearly finished when she heard the arrivals. She did not look around — she knew what to expect — though somehow the atmosphere had changed. She knelt before the brazier, eyes closed against the sting. Was that the sun, strengthening toward spring, or something else, flickering vaguely across her eyelids? She could not believe she could see the spirits of the dead. It had to be the sun, though she could feel its warmth on her left shoulder. A new aura, one that was really, really bright? That brightness intensified against her eyelids until she opened her eyes, and through the drifting fingers of smoke made out a tall male silhouette.

She blinked away the distracting aura — and stared straight into Shigan's eyes.

Shock froze her. It froze them both.

Falik, in his rolling cart, with patient Pigear behind it, joined Muin at the altar. Falik lit incense and made the offerings, helped by Pigear, as Muin spoke the proper sutras, and then slowly, with deliberation, both men poured out the libation. Ari stilled, a few spirit talismans still in her basket; she could burn them after the libation.

Thump! The men knelt, fists to chests, heads bowed.

Falik's head also bent, and tears glimmered below his eyelashes. Muin finished the rite by full and formal bows, forehead to the ground, three times to the altar.

When he rose for the last time, signifying the end of the ritual, he glanced distractedly at the two new arrivals. The garrison began filing out, satisfied that their brethren had been seen off properly. Muin's heart was heavy — he had known every one of the dead at least by name — but garrison life had to go on. He frowned, wondering if one of those newcomers didn't look familiar as he retreated to stand with Falik and Dun. These newcomers had to be important, as those were imperial guards in the background.

By now Ari had recovered from the stunning discovery that Shigan was *here. Now.* She realized there were others with Shigan. When she recognized the planed jaw and subtly sculpted cheekbones of the man behind Shigan, her hand faltered.

The tiger was awake and snarling — that was the head ferret! Heart hammering in her throat, she dropped an entire fistful of spirit talismans. The paper flared to light, sending up smoke, which did not hide her from his sight.

She scolded herself: be calm. You are Miss Ryu. No one had pounced on her. In respect for the dead? Had Shigan turned against her? Why was he *here* — with *him,* that ferret? She forced her attention back to her empty basket, as Jion stared at her, equally stunned. That was Ryu — dressed as a girl in a mourning robe, her hair braided elegantly around her head instead of twisted up into a messy topknot, but he would have known her anywhere. Her small, strong hands, the turn of her shoulder, the shape of her ears. Her eyes, her lips.

His gaze snapped back to the captain, whose eyes were shadowed by his hat — but the lower half of the young man's face was familiar enough for him to recognize First Ryu, the elder brother, now with the shadow-darkened upper lip and chin of a man who had to shave now and then.

Commander Falik — Jion recognized him, too — signaled from his cart, his thin, wan face puzzled: he had no idea who they were, but the sight of imperial guards indicated someone important. Oh, wasn't the one in black one of the legendary ferrets?

Knees watery, Ari stood up, then moved to stand behind her brother, who stood uneasily at the sight of those imperial guard uniforms. Falik made the signal to follow the last of the garrison now leaving. Those who wished to remain behind could, to make their own personal offerings.

The imperial guards watched their prince, who had specifically said on their way up, "The rite takes precedence. I'll announce myself when it ends."

Ari followed her brother, intensely aware of the newcomers' footfalls. She gazed out at the harbor, where a long, narrow naval fast courier rode in the bay. She glanced to one side, and there were the imperial guards in their red cloaks and the armor with the golden tiger eye on the chest. She was poised to run—but there was Shigan.

When they had cleared the cedar boundary, Shigan turned to Falik, holding up the golden tally as he said, "I am Prince Jion, sent by his imperial majesty—"

Falik waved for Pigear to halt his cart, and all the imperials, including Falik and Muin, made a military salute northward to the emperor. Ari caught herself putting her hands together for the gallant wanderer's salute, and hastily made a maiden's bow. Then Falik's captains and their orderlies dropped to one knee, right fists to their chests to salute the prince, as representative of the emperor. Falik tried to bow but all he could do was bob his head, wincing.

"—to finish up the investigation, and to provide what aid we can. Please rise! This is Chief Fai Anbai, also sent by his imperial majesty."

Muin stared in cold shock. Caught—square—with his sister there! But the habit of assessment had been trained into him. The prince was too young to have met Danno face to face, and so was the ferret. Yes. The latter's attention was on Falik. The imperial guards were even younger.

Falik blinked from the prince, resplendent in shades of blue, pale green, and peach, to the man dressed in black. "Your imperial highness. This is an honor—had we known, you would have had precedence." It was clear that it was a strain to speak.

"I did not want to disturb the rite for a mere question of protocol," Jion said easily, trying not to stare at Ryu, who was hiding behind her brother. "I feel confident that the fallen will overlook it."

More bows, then Falik murmured, "This is my second in command, Captain Ryu Muin." Indicating Muin, with the silver panther embroidered on the chest and back of his robe. "And his sister, who has been helping in the infirmary."

"Miss Ryu," Shigan—no, *Prince Jion*—said.

Ari bowed without speaking. In her mind she said *Prince Jion, Prince Jion, Prince Jion* over and over. She was terrified to speak, lest "Shigan" pop out. Was he an enemy or not? She forced her gaze to remain on the ground, her hands clenched inside her sleeves.

"We don't have any visitors' quarters, I have to confess," Falik said, barely above a whisper. "And even if we did, we turned most of our furniture into arrows. Ordinarily the duke would be extending a welcome, but—"

"We know the duke's situation," Jion said. "We arrived at the beginning of the ritual up on the mountain there—and we could see how much there is still to repair on the ducal manor."

Falik bobbed his head again. "My wife and I can move to the infirmary, and—"

Jion held up a hand. "Commander, make yourself easy. We found sufficient lodging in the harbor. I am not here to add to your burden. It is his imperial majesty's wish to aid you where possible, and to, ah, prosecute the investigation into the attack."

Ari's gaze was resolutely on the ground, but she felt his eyes on her—every nerve flared.

Muin spoke up. "Your imperial highness, prisoners are all in the warehouses, according to orders from Blue Jade, pending interrogation."

"We will begin there after we've spoken to you," Jion said, indicating Fai Anbai at his side. All eyes shifted to him, taking in his silent demeanor, his black clothing. No weapons were visible, but his aspect was so quietly ominous that their gazes shifted quickly away. Everyone knew of the ferrets' reputation for interrogation expertise.

Trickle appeared then, and executed a smart bow. A real prince in their midst! Would he be handing out any largesse? But what was the purpose of the sinister one in black? Did princes travel with their own interrogation specialists? "We've brought in more furnishings that the ducal manor kindly sent, and set it up in the commander's office, if you would care to follow me. A hot meal is on its way." He bowed again, in case one bow wasn't enough.

The involved task of getting Falik's cart up the stairs to the office gave Ari and Jion an unexpected reprieve. Both stared at the other furtively, then away again quickly, each very aware of the ferret chief's sharp gaze.

Fai Anbai waited patiently for the prince to get to their questions, so that he could move on to the warehouse to conduct the interrogations. He still had a mountain of papers to get through in the poison investigation. And how was his father doing with Tek Banu's papers?

"We'll have a ramp up these stairs by week's end," Trickle said into an oddly tense silence he could not quite define. It had to be the presence of the imperial prince — and the fact that their already overburdened schedule of repair and recovery was now completely destroyed, as imperial princes popping up took precedence. "Commander Falik insisted we repair damage relating to defense first, and then people's homes. The carpenter is putting together a pulley system to get our commander up and down. He says it will be easy for one orderly to do it . . ."

He went on talking about the pulley system to fill the silence, though no one listened. Falik, in his misery, had been dreading being broken of his command due to his injury. He'd thought that would come later, but it seemed that was to be now.

Muin was also worried about that, and mentally marshaled arguments against it (if he was even asked, which he doubted would happen), and hadn't he seen that imperial prince before? Except he didn't remember seeing any princes during his brief visit to the imperial palace. He had seen the emperor, and this prince looked very like the emperor. Maybe that was it?

The orderlies got the cart upstairs, and Falik out of the cart and onto a mat, propped with rolled blankets and pillows. The others sat when the prince did, and Trickle gestured for the waiting conscripts holding trays of dishes that the cooks had hastily put together as soon as word reached them that the newcomers included an imperial prince.

Falik, Muin, and Ari waited for the prince to pick up his chopsticks; Jion, seeing them waiting, said, "Please, this is not the imperial court. Commander Falik, permit me to offer you a toast to your splendid defense." He picked up the small cup of white wine an orderly had just poured, and bowed across the table.

Falik was not able to bow, but he lifted his cup, and they drank, then Jion addressed Muin. "Captain Ryu?"

Fai Anbai turned to Imperial Prince Jion, expecting him to begin with the emperor's questions, but he was staring at Muin's sister. Was he that desperate for female company after only a few days of sailing away from his harem? "The emperor desired us to investigate the matter of Firebolt of Redbark," Fai Anbai said, in an effort to get the prince to remember why they were there.

Ari stared, terrified. That ferret was right in reach of two of the emperor's targets for that execution square! She simpered. "Shall I go fetch Second Miss? Oh, but she's so ill!"

Falik was immediately distracted by that. He cast a startled glance at Jion, afraid he and his wife were committing some kind of protocol error by her absence. "I beg your imperial highness to excuse my wife. Her belly is sensitive right now."

Jion clasped his hands. "Congratulations! Please ask her to forgive our intrusion when you see her, and I hope to meet her later."

Fai Anbai merely waited, and then said, "What can you tell us about Firebolt of Redbark? First of all, was he even here?"

Falik shook his head slowly. "That I cannot answer, except by repeating hearsay."

Trickle looked expectantly at Muin, who usually spoke for Falik on military matters. Which this was — in a sense. But the senior captain was busy pouring out more wine.

So Trickle spoke up. "We're told that it was Firebolt who saved the commander's life. But that's all hearsay, as Commander Falik just now said. The commander was unconscious — near death — and the captain here nearly as bad, his face covered with blood. We were fighting our way to them. It was only after the enemy ran that we could get there, and whoever it was had already gone, but the captain said he gave the commander some kind of Essence pill. It was glowing."

At this, Muin looked up long enough to nod. "That's right." He looked down again, as rigid as before.

"So there is no description of the criminal that we can use?" Fai Anbai persisted, though he still carried that clear mental image of Yaso, the supposed Healer who abandoned the Redbark youths the night before he and his task force secured the prince and captured Screaming Hawk.

Ari got to her feet, her meal untouched. "Commander Falik, you are looking very pale. I'll fetch more willow concoction," and whisked herself out.

Falik had leaned back on his pillows, but at those words, he straightened with an effort they could all feel. "They say he saved my life. He came out of nowhere. Shot fire at those pirates and sent them running. And *saved my life.*" His gaze was earnest and steady. He spoke with the conviction of two generations of utter loyalty, "If I had the chance, I'd do the same by him."

Muin looked up at that. "Captain Ing of the naval ship *Kraken* reported to us that some of the prisoners claimed to be part of Redbark, and to know Firebolt of Redbark, but they all turned out to have Shadow Panther tattoos. We think they lied to escape judgment."

"That," said Fai Anbai, "I can establish once I interrogate them."

It was clear to Fai Anbai that none of this company had anything to offer with respect to Firebolt of Redbark — and out of deference to their commander, they were not going to pursue it. He was very certain that Firebolt would have decamped faster even than the Shadow Panthers, but he still was going to look into every face at the makeshift prison, in case "Yaso" had been swept up with the rest of the prisoners. He moved on to the next question. "The spy Pa Jan. It was you who had her followed? Was there any result?"

Trickle sighed. "I can answer that."

"And you are?" Fai Anbai inquired, not without humor.

Trickle flushed. "Company Quartermaster Dun. I was my brother's orderly."

Falik nodded for him to continue, and Fai Anbai saw how much even this small interview was wearying the commander.

Trickle went on, "I sent one of my volunteers to follow her, but none of us orderlies are trained in tracking. He came back saying he lost her in Emerald Bay. He thinks she saw him and landed there because it's busy. By the time he landed his sailboat, she had abandoned hers and was gone. He looked around for a couple days, then returned empty-handed."

Fai Anbai said, "If you can send him along so that we can get as many details as we can, we can send someone to investigate further."

By then Jion had recovered from the shock of seeing Ryu here, of all places, and dressed in a mourning robe, with her hair down, like an unmarried girl. Which she was. However she ended up here, he did not want Fai Anbai curious about Captain Ryu's sister! He had better concentrate on his orders.

"My father the emperor also wanted to hear a more detailed report on the attack. We have an excellent summary, but there are questions. Such as, where was the ducal guard?"

Falik's eyes closed.

Muin looked up. "As Commander Falik Tan is related to the matter, in a sense, it might be better if I answer. You know we were undermanned — though I do not offer that as an excuse."

Jion said, "We understand that to have been the case, yes."

Muin started with a short, quick report on the sequence of events. But under Jion's sympathetic questions, he began to expand. Fai Anbai sat back, impressed with the prince's ability to pull a more detailed response from the silent young captain. There was even a revealing sidestep — stated in factual, unemotional terms — how it was that the ducal guard and the diminished company had always been kept separate, according to Lord Oru's will, and even how the ducal guards' training apparently consisted of riding around in patterns, their drills more like games of polo, using swords instead of mallet and ball.

Falik nodded now and then in agreement as Muin described what happened each day, from the sighting of Master Night's ships to the day the enemy leader ran, abandoning those who couldn't get to the bay fast enough. The pivot point was clearly Firebolt's Essence-fire attack, unmistakably and unequivocally against the Shadow Panthers.

Both Fai Anbai and Jion gained the impression of Falik as a straightforward commander dedicated to the welfare of his garrison, which included constant alert and readiness preparation. Fai Anbai had come expecting to be impressed by General Falik's son, but that respect widened to include the two captains — even though Captain Dun was not present, being on duty, his name came up frequently, the others wanting him sharing in any praise.

This recounting went on until the drum tower beat the watch change. Jion rose, knowing that his presence had prevented the two commanders from getting anything done that they had been expected to do. "Thank you. We'll return to the temporary headquarters in the town to speak to Captain Ing, and begin the process of examining the prisoners," he said.

There was no mistaking the relief Captain Muin tried to hide, but Fai Anbai assumed that that was on behalf of Falik, who by then was looking gray from the effort he had expended to sit up that long.

They rejoined their honor guard and departed. Jion looked about covertly: Ari was nowhere in sight.

THIRTEEN

ARI WATCHED FROM ABOVE.

She knelt on Sagacious Blade, her heart thundering in her ears as Jion emerged from the garrison command center, the others behind him. That ferret in black looked around fast—she held her breath—but he did not look up. Nor had the guards stationed around the building and at the gates. Shigan—Prince Jion—also looked around more slowly. Ari peered down at him anxiously, impatiently blinking away the distracting brightness of his aura as she tried to read his mind from his expression. But all she noted was that he looked older in his fine, flattering silks. And even more handsome than he had been in their dusty days on the road.

The warehouses along the wharf had been fenced off by Captain Ing's fleet, and they rotated a heavy guard, both to keep the prisoners inside, but also to keep curious townsfolk from coming to gawk and throw offal at the hated attackers.

She watched as the ferret and Shigan—no, *the prince*—entered the naval building below the harbormaster's house, and stayed there. She could drift for a while, but that got tiring, and she had been up before dawn in order to begin burning spirit tokens for the dead. She was tired, and she was hungry. At least she could get rid of one of those.

She drifted away, and a very short time later, sat on the terrace of a fried seafood place, midway between the braziers, where it was reasonably warm. From here she could see the door to the naval building halfway down the street. Muin had insisted on sharing half his pay with her — which she was glad of now. She ordered a plate of crispy scallops, spiced turnips, and tea, and settled back to make it last as long as she could.

Jion, inside, had been covertly looking around for her. He had no intention of participating in the interrogation of the prisoners if he could avoid it, but he did have to sit through a long, rambling report from the short, square-headed and scarred Captain Ing Iog, who led them point by point through the attack all over again. Only he was far more prolix about the arrogant Lord Oru and his pack of noble hopefuls who thought that clashing swords from horseback once or twice a week while riding around in fancy robes actually constituted readiness.

"I met him when Admiral Shen sent us out here five years ago," he said heavily, his thin gray topknot bobbing emphatically. "I knew he'd be worse than no help. Sure enough, when we got here, Falik was down, Ryu, too, but their handful were fighting like an army of five thousand, whereas Lord Oru's guard was either dead or run . . ."

As Captain Ing went on with his report, stopping every now and then to offer unasked-for opinions on criminal wanderers and every other subject that occurred to him, Jion wished that the good captain had had to sit through Instructors Fumig and Shaz's classes on how to give a proper *and succinct* report.

The sun had long set when he arrived at the end of his tale, and they were at last free to go. As they proceeded up the street toward their inn, Fai Anbai said, "May this servant inquire what your imperial highness makes of the captain's report?"

"Toward the end," Jion said, "I was mainly thinking of my dinner, especially during his long, very long opinion of Master Night. Which I do agree with! My primary impression is that Captain Ing thinks as highly of Commander Falik as do the commander's own captains, but he's more impressed with Captain Ryu. That might only be because he's been dealing primarily with Captain Ryu."

"That is this servant's impression as well, your imperial highness," Fai Anbai said.

"May I, in my turn, ask if you intend to interrogate every one of those pirates in there?" Jion tipped his head back toward the warehouses.

"I don't see a need," Fai Anbai stated. "We've a day or

perhaps two before the army reinforcements arrive, and Captain Ing's fleet will take these prisoners back to Blue Jade for judgment. I need to read the notes on Captain Ing's interrogations tonight. If these are sufficient — if the emperor's questions are adequately addressed — it should only take a day at most. We might even get to Blue Jade ahead of Captain Ing."

Jion understood then that Fai Anbai was in a hurry — and with the poisoning investigation hanging over his head, no surprise there.

Which left one day to try to see Ryu, that is, Miss Ryu Ari . . .

By that time, Ari had finished her second pot of tea. When she saw them leave, she let her hair swing forward to curtain her profile as she crouched over her tea. She sensed the indifferent gazes of the honor guard sweeping over her; the imperial prince's head was turned the other way as the ferret spoke to him.

She waited where she was until they were some thirty paces ahead. When numerous strollers and carters and child-ren chasing and being chased by dogs had filled the road between them and her, she got up to follow. As soon as she saw them enter an inn, she walked away to examine some embroidered scarfs. When she turned back, the honor guard had taken up positions around the inn.

She wandered away, and bought more tea at a different place, to wait until full dark had fallen. She made herself drink it very slowly as she watched the harbor people, who had all moved back home, filling the days with hammering and painting and repairing.

But nighttime belonged to the young people, and as it was a mild night, many were out strolling and enjoying them-selves. When her tea was done she wandered among them until she found a secluded spot. She was still wearing her layers, with the fraying mourning robe over it — which she would not have to wear on the morrow, now that the funeral was over.

She sketched fresh deflection charms over her and her pack, took out Sagacious Blade, and was soon in the air once more. By the time she found the inn again, lights glowed in the oiled silk windows on the upper story overlooking a tiny court. Those had to be the best rooms, deemed suitable for a prince.

She had learned to emulate raptors by staying still, and letting the wind currents do the work of pushing her along. That enabled her to remain in the air for longer times — if the wind was favorable. She was uncertain how to proceed. She suspected that if she returned to the garrison, Muin would pounce on her and bundle her aboard some ship, all for her own protection. That's what responsible elder brothers did, even if a person could protect herself.

And she did need to get away. But not until she found out whether Prince Jion was friend or foe.

She settled lightly on the roof, closed her eyes and reached.

There were the blob-lights of the guards, moving steadily in their patterns. In a large space that had to be the common room, blobs moved around clusters of stationary blobs: waiters serving customers. More light blobs darted hither and yon in what she expected was the kitchen. On the second floor, more guards, and here and there random lights. One was still. She wondered if that was the ferret or Jion. She could not be wrong!

Behind the second-floor windows directly across from her perch there were three blob lights, one still, two moving about. The still one was so bright. No, not bright like a sun — that was wrong. It was the same size as the others, but it was so *intense*.

Could that be Shigan? Ah, Imperial Prince Jion? Much as she hated it, she had to get used to his identity, because that was not going away.

She waited until at last the intense light was alone, the other two withdrawn to another room. When she opened her eyes, she was startled to see how Phoenix moon had jumped across the sky, and Ghost Moon had already risen.

She unslung her pack and left it on the roof, behind an ornamental statue of a guardian chimera. Then she rode the sword gently across the courtyard, focused on that window, and let Sagacious Blade drift down to its level. She remained arm's length away, in case she was wrong and the ferret looked out. Then she leaned over and scratched at the window.

Nothing.

She scratched again, three times.

For a heartbeat or two no response, then from the other side of the silk and lattices she heard a hesitant step. The window unlatched, was pushed out by a hand — and she and Jion stared into one another's faces.

Jion's steeply slanted brows lifted, he looked down, and his eyes widened so much she smothered a giggle. "Ryu," he whispered. "How —" He saw the sword then, and breathed, "When did you learn *that?*"

"Last summer," she whispered, barely loud enough for him to hear, and looked around. No light blobs — and there were no warning red or orange streaks in his. If anything, the blob glowed the brighter, the blue-white of . . . what? Joy? Excitement, certainly.

"Can you fly without the sword?"

"No." She shook her head. "I can leap, but I'm like a leaf, I come down slowly. On the sword, I can aim. I don't know how or why it works — Master Ki didn't tell me — oh, there is so much to tell *you!* If . . ." He might have changed in all kinds of ways since they'd seen one another last, but she did not believe he would glow like that at the prospect of throwing her in prison. "Let me in?"

Instead of answering he lifted the window wide. Unused to making entry this way, she tumbled in, but caught herself and landed softly. Both froze, turning toward the far door. Jion sprinted lightly to the door to the servants' room, and eased the bar across. Then he went to the hall door and did the same.

He turned back as she straightened up, holding the sword by one hand. He held out his arms — but she did not rush into them; having not hugged anyone except her parents when she was small, she missed the cue. Reddening, she took an uncertain step forward, reached with her free hand to almost touch his fingers, then whispered, "You didn't turn into an imperial?" It was always good to make sure.

He shook with silent laughter. "How am I to answer that?" He moved to the bed. "Come, sit beside me so I can hear you, but my servants won't." He pointed at the door.

She trod to the bed, and sat slowly, cautiously, as if it had been strewn with scorpions and snakes, her hand gripping the sword beside her. Jion watched her, his heart swooping through emotions he couldn't name, feelings both painful and tender. She had changed, oh, so much — and in some ways hadn't changed at all.

They both spoke, "What have you —"

They stopped. He smiled. She didn't. "That emperor," she murmured. "He didn't kill you."

That emperor. He recollected a similar reference during their last conversation that night at Madam Swann's, when he had revealed everything — and she hadn't. "They talked about the former commander here, now a general escorting a princess to the Easterners," she went on. "And I thought of the sister you

told me about, your favorite person. I am very sorry you had to
lose her."

Jion recollected his words about Manon—and hard on that
came what Lily had revealed. Thinking about Manon still
confused him, and also hurt. But now was not the time for that.
"I lost *a* sister to a necessary trade treaty," he said. "And I will
miss her. Thank you." Then, "It's your turn to talk."

"My turn?"

"Ryu—*Miss* Ryu—"

"That sounds so strange, coming from you," she muttered,
shoulders up by her ears.

He sighed. She was the most formidable martial artist he'd
ever met, but equally intense were the memories of his little
brother Ryu.

Ah, sister. No, *not* a sister.

He said carefully, "I am so happy to see you. And terrified,
because you ought not to be here. But mostly I'm uncertain
because the last time we were together I told you pretty much
everything. And, ah, you didn't trust me enough to recipro-
cate."

Ari's shoulders hitched even closer to her ears. But she
didn't leap up and run.

She was nearly delirious with joy to be beside him again.
But it was a nervous joy. In all those conversations she had
imagined with him, none had begun like this, with him hurt
because she didn't trust him.

So she took a risk—right then it felt like the greatest risk of
her life. Poised to dive back out that window if it went wrong,
she whispered, "It was not my secret to tell. That was the *only*
reason. And I know I probably don't deserve to ask for a favor,
but may I ask a question? If it wasn't desperately important for
me and my brother, I wouldn't ask. And no, I can't explain why.
At least, not yet. Not without my brother knowing, and
agreeing. It's a matter of, of filial obedience and promises."

Jion held his hands out, his smile crooked. "Ask."

"Do you know of . . . have you heard . . . of someone called
Yskanda?"

During all the many conversations *he* had imagined holding
with *her*, he had never once foreseen that.

He said carefully, "Do you mean Assistant Court Artist
Afan Yskanda? If so, he's safe, and quite well respected."

She was so certain that Yskanda was in prison that she

opened her mouth to say he had the wrong person. But when she heard *Assistant Court Artist*, and that followed with *Afan*, she stilled.

He'd said Yskanda's full name. With the word *artist*.

"He . . . is?"

Her eyes rounded, then she gave a soft laugh — and there it was, the flicker of familiarity that had confused him ever since his first interview with Yskanda. Though she and Yskanda shared little else in appearance, there was a similar expression of the eyes, fleeting but clear as water, innocent of malice or greed. He had seen this aspect of Ryu in Yskanda, and now he recognized that expression of Yskanda's in her. Not exactly the same — they were very different people — but they shared a quality he could scarcely put a name to, especially when they laughed. It was such an open, utterly guileless expression.

"He's your brother?" Jion ventured. "Afan. Not Ryu?"

Her eyes widened with alarm —

"Yskanda . . ." And then it was there, or nearly all of it. "You — and First Ryu, you're all the children of Danno and Alk Hanu," he breathed. "Where does the Afan come from? Oh, that can wait. I will forever hate myself for saying this, as I've wanted, and dreaded, seeing you again, but you had better run, and keep running. You know who Fai Anbai is."

He rose and went to the window to hold it wide, but first scanned worriedly below.

His care had exactly the opposite effect: his light blob glowed around him, an aura of silvery-gold, like candlelight, and for once she understood an aura: he was still true.

Right then, that was all that mattered.

She heaved a slow, silent sigh, let go of the sword, and drew her knees up under her chin, the fraying mourning robe rumpled around her. "Tell me how he is? How did you know? About our parents? Did he tell you?" The questions tumbled out too fast for him to answer.

He left the window and sat beside her again. "He tried most admirably to hide it. But my grandmother recognized your mother in him. She told me the story. Did you know how extraordinary a Talent your brother is? Did you know he sees visions?"

"Visions?" Ari repeated. "I think . . . I think I always knew that. He was always drawing things nobody else saw, as well as flowers and trees and clouds as well as people. When he wasn't staring at the sea. *When* he was supposed to be learning sword skills."

Jion grinned. "Yskanda learned sword? Really? I can't picture him knowing which end of a sword to grasp."

"He was never very interested. More dutiful. If he wasn't trying to sketch raindrops in a spiderweb, or something like that. He told you about seeing visions?"

"He tried most admirably to keep it from me, even after we shared a vision of a kraken."

"A *kraken*?"

"I was as surprised as you," Jion murmured.

"What does it mean?"

"I don't know. He claims it's madness, and he's learning to rid himself of them. Your family is . . . surprising. How did you and your eldest brother end up as Ryu?"

"Muin—born Muinkanda—picked that name himself, when we first went to Loyalty. As a way of protecting our parents." Ari's smile flickered.

"Yet he's in the army," Jion wondered.

She hesitated. The phoenix feather was the last secret, and it felt very much as if she ought to get permission from Muin, or more likely her parents, to share it. But there was another layer of truth. "He has never said, but I think my brother is in the army to earn enough merit to get our parents forgiven. It's . . . it's the sort of thing he would do."

Jion nodded slowly, considering his impression of Captain Ryu, who had deferred to Falik as if it were natural, instead of crowding forward to replace him. He had also made certain to give credit to Dun, and anyone else he believed was due. Jion remembered his grandmother's description of Danno as honest, modest, silent. It seemed his eldest son was the much the same.

"Muinkanda. Yskanda," Jion said. "What is your name?"

"Afan Arikanda," she said—savoring being able to say it out loud. To him.

"Arikanda," he repeated, drawing it out. Hearing her name on his lips made her shiver. "I like that. Very much. 'The peace of Kanda,' in the old language. So appropriate. I'll think of you as Arikanda."

"Prince Jion—"

His hand flashed up. "Jion. Please. No court titles from you. Unless you end up in the palace, but we'd better prevent that," he added quickly, dropping his voice back down to a whisper.

"But . . . Yskanda," she began.

He said quickly, "I will look out for him. I promise. I liked him before I found out his story. Now — knowing that you are related — he will be as my brother."

Her eyes stung with tears. "*Thank* you. I will gladly be your donkey for ten lifetimes. Muin and I have been worried about him, ever since I found out he'd been taken from Imai Island, where we were born. We both wish it had been us instead."

Jion shook his head slowly. "Your brother might surprise you. He has managed to stay in my father's good graces, which is not easy. I love my father," he said quickly, seeing a spasm of fear in her face. "But he has his, ah, burdens. My father still is not completely certain that Yskanda is the son of his old bodyguard, so very different they are in all ways. And yet Yskanda has managed not to be handed over to the ferrets. You probably cannot imagine how extraordinary this is."

Ari studied him; it suggested to her that the emperor liked to play with his prey, the way powerful noble villains did in the story books. But she kept that to herself.

Jion went on, "My father also appreciates talent, and your brother has done some extraordinary work, young as he is. The palace is the best place for someone like that — an endless supply of the best materials, no worries about meals or housing or clothes, something I came to appreciate while a gallant wanderer. He might very well end up a famous name."

"I wanted to go there next, to your palace, to rescue him."

"*Don't*. Do that." Jion's expression changed. "*Please* don't. The guards are on high alert."

She crossed her arms. "You really think I couldn't get in and find my brother?"

He turned to meet her gaze. "I know you could," he said slowly. "But unless you have changed more than I thought, I don't think you're willing to leave a trail of corpses, and that's what it would take."

Her breath whooshed out as if he'd punched her. "No. I wouldn't." As she said that, she got a sudden insight into why Father hadn't already rescued Yskanda. If Yskanda wasn't slated for a terrible death, he'd want to wait, and find a way that wouldn't mean a high cost in lives.

"The imperial guards would fight to the death," Jion said. "Because if someone gets past them, they die anyway. Their lives depend on being vigilant and alert, especially now, due to a couple of assassination attempts on me. *I* thought I could get around the ferrets, as I know the palace well, but I was wrong," he added.

"*Assassination?*"

"Ayah," he breathed. "Who is going to go first? When did *this* happen, and how?" Jion asked, his fingers brushing over the pommel of Sagacious Blade, lying on the bed beside her. His fingers tingled—such a beautiful sword. Someone was not thinking merely of death when that sword was made, but of art.

"Do you remember Grandfather Ki?" Ari said, reclaiming his attention.

"Tell me."

Out it poured, everything that had happened to her since she watched him taken away. When she got to her release of the prisoners at the mine, Jion comprehended why his father had issued that order for him to collect Firebolt's head. Anything that struck at the sources of gunpowder was considered the worst of crimes, bordering on rebellion and treason. Even though she hadn't touched the brimstone, she could have. And if one person could do that much damage . . .

". . . that's when I learned the lightness skill. It could be there are martial artists who can use that skill without a sword. I can't. Maybe I never will. I can't say for certain that Sagacious Blade has a soul. Maybe knowing will come later. Maybe not. But the sword and I together can fly, and I am getting better at it. Somewhat." She made a face, thinking of those wallowing traders that still managed to beat her to Green Jade Island, nearly disastrous for Falik and Muin. "Anyway, I was careful not to be seen flying."

"That's how you ended up on the Capital List," Jion said. "No one in court was talking about the incident, except in whispers. I only heard a little here and there. But I do know the result, because it's my brother Vaion's Great-Uncle Yu who is now the governor at Benevolent Winds, reorganizing the work at the mines. There's talk of sending Vaion to learn from him."

"Are these good people?" she asked, so earnestly and trustingly that he could not possibly take offense. Or laugh.

"What little I know of Great-Uncle Yu makes him sound like a scholar and a careful man. I do know his entire house-hold is devoted to him. And my brother Vaion might be a scamp, but he has a good heart."

"Then there was justice for those people in the mines," she

exclaimed — and blushed.

He said with that steep slant to his brows that meant he was laughing inside, "We're not all evil all the time, you know."

We. She couldn't think about that now. She looked aside, saying quickly, "I was thinking more about Matu's parents. I know I didn't get to all the miners when I asked about them. Not even half of them, I was moving so fast, and it was such a desperate situation. I still don't know if they were alive, and among those escaping. Anyway, when I was leaving the island, I saw that same man, your chief ferret, coming to search — probably for me — and so I decided to go back home to visit my parents."

"Did you see them?"

She shook her head slowly. "I tried. But they'd left Imai, probably after Yskanda was taken. I went to the place they'd always told us to go to if ever disaster struck, but they had just left. And my father was wounded. I was afraid that . . . ayah! That your ferrets came after him."

Jion could not deny it. He sat there for a moment as the pause became a silence, and both of them considered the wall of expectation — even of law — between them. How to resolve it?

"So there it is," she said finally. "I guess things I was afraid of are true, then. The emperor wants to capture and kill us. Especially me. I'd better go."

To his horror her eyes sheened in the guttering candlelight.

"Ryu — Arikanda — " he began helplessly.

She rose and took a step toward the window, then turned. "You said assassination. Someone is trying to kill you, too? Come with me. Come back to the gallant wanderers. You know how you loved it. We could . . . we could be Redbark again."

He shut his eyes, tempted almost beyond bearing. Almost. That sweet freedom again, with her tramping by his side. Sparring every day, finding justice for those who could not get it themselves. But hard on that came the inescapable thoughts: his mother's devastation if he were to vanish again. Vaion, how betrayed he would feel! Imperial Father's half-smile when he promised that northern ice floe if he was caught again — and that would be the lightest he could expect.

Mostly, though, it was this poison threat. Whoever it was still roamed free. And if he ran off, that person won. Who would be next? It depended on why he was attacked — if it was his proximity to the throne, then Manon would surely be the next target. Then Vaion, and innocent, butterfly Gau-Gau . . .

His hand had reached unconsciously for the locket he had worn every day since they parted at Madam Swan's. He said, "Then who would protect Yskanda?"

And saw that strike her, a blow straight to the heart.

He sat back—and felt the locket thump against his ribs. He said, quickly, apologetically, "Do you want this pill back?"

Until he brought up Yskanda, she had been glaring at her hands, waiting for him to agree, but knowing with every breath that he would not run away again. She had to accept that, the way he accepted all she'd told him.

She faced him. "No! You must keep it—what if your assassin tries to poison you again? I can tell you that it really works. I think both the mine guard and Commander Falik were dead, or very near." She stood up, resolute. "I'd better leave."

"Wait." Not just like that—he couldn't see her for these precious few moments, just to lose her again! "Arikanda, no one knows who you are. Let's meet once more—let's figure out a way to communicate. Is there somewhere we *can* safely meet here?"

She sank back down, her fingers restlessly running up and down that beautiful bronze blade, as reluctant to leave as he was to let her go. "Yes. Where I've been doing my Redbark drills, most every day—not this morning, because of the funeral. But other mornings I go right there, to the graveyard. It's quiet, and secluded. I sweep the snow away. I don't think the dead mind." Her voice wavered a little. She sniffed and straightened up. "Early mornings, I change bandages and take medicine around, but by the last drum of Phoenix I—"

The latch clicked.

Both heads turned sharply.

The latch rattled, then came scratching at the door. "Your imperial highness?" Min Ko called. "Are you all right?"

"Sleeping," he called.

"Is there someone in there with you?" The door rattled in the frame. "I heard voices."

Jion and Ari stared at each other, both realizing they had gradually begun to speak instead of whisper.

Ari lunged up, ready to throw herself out the window, but halted when her inner sense warned her of light-blobs converging below. She could put a deflection charm on herself, but that was not proof against searching gazes.

Jion shot a questioning look at her, and she shook her head, holding up four fingers and pointing below. He cursed under his breath, flashed a grin, then whispered in her ear, "Forgive me, but this is the only out."

Before she could speak, he yanked the ribbon binding up the front part of her hair. With the other hand, he reached for the fraying mourning sash at her side. She shot a questioning stare at him as he pulled the sash, and then poked at the tie at her right hip. "Off." He mouthed the word, and she yanked off the mourning overrobe, standing there in her quilted under robe. "Get into the bed."

"What?" she squeaked.

The front door reverberated under a hard rapping. Chief Fai said authoritatively, "Your imperial highness, open the door."

"I have to get dressed," Jion yelled as he dived for a trunk in the corner and flung it open. He rooted down underneath, then yanked out a glorious bed robe, and began ripping off his clothes and flinging them into the trunk.

Ari shut her eyes and turned away — then had to laugh at herself. All those years with Shigan changing right in the room with her, she'd never cared. But now — despite danger rattling the door — she found herself wanting to peek, and intensely embarrassed because of that want.

"Hurry." His whisper was barely a breath.

Now that she couldn't see him, she understood his intent. If there was a girl who seemed to have nothing to search lying in the bed, ayah! There would be no search.

She could not bring herself to strip down all the way. She yanked her quilted robe half off, and pulled one arm out of her undershirt, holding the rest tight under her armpit. Cold air made her shiver. She vaulted into the bed, taking the sword with her. Then pulled the covers up to her bare shoulder, and shook her hair around her face to hide it.

Jion cast a glance at her, and flashed the old smile when she'd got in a good hit while sparring. He was barefoot, dressed only in that fine silken robe with long-tailed swallows embroidered all over it, his hair loose.

He yanked open the door. Ari raised her bare arm to block her face, but peered under it, through the locks of hair, as several sets of wide eyes took her in, flicked to the prince, then determinedly away in an *I didn't see anything* manner. Of course there would be some rule about catching nobles and royals in intimate moments!

She suppressed a nervous impulse to start giggling, but her belly trembled warningly as Jion said in a weary pout, "Give us time to get dressed and I'll throw her out."

He slammed the door in their faces.

Ari jumped out of the bed as if someone had lit her butt on fire, and shoved her arm back into her clothes. Her entire body prickled with embarrassment, and . . . and a secret wish to stay, but she was *not* going to admit to that with him standing *right there*, and an army of enemies right outside the door, their auras blobs of yellows and storm-sky greenish blue.

With her winter robe pulled tight around her again, she bent to pull the sword from the bed, and with nowhere else to put it, turned her back on Jion, pulled her robe open again, and stuck it down inside her linen underdrawers.

"Here," Jion whispered in her ear, handing her another bundle of cloth—a beautiful silk robe with a red silk sash. Probably one of his inner layers, but finer than anything Ari had ever seen in her life. She pulled it on over the quilted robe. It looked like something an entertainment girl would wear. "The mourning robe would give you away."

As she tied the red silk hastily around her waist, Jion reached up to pull her loose hair around her. "You're a town girl," he whispered softly, his breath warm on her forehead. In spite of imminent danger, she shivered again at the warmth, and of the feel of his fingers in her hair.

Then another authoritative knock. "Your imperial highness, we beg forgiveness, but—"

"She's just leaving," Jion called, looking over his shoulder at Ari. He mouthed the words, "Head down."

How was she supposed to speak? This wasn't going to work—

But Jion opened the door wide, and smiled at her, his black eyes bright with fun. She put her head down, aware of a bubble of laughter still under her ribs, in spite of the danger. Maybe because of it.

Jion elaborately pushed something into her hand. Startled, she looked down at a golden tael then up at him, her hair curtaining her face as she blinked hard against the intensity of the auras threatening to give her vertigo.

Jion smiled encouragingly. "Thank you, it was most entertaining, farewell." He patted her shoulder, gave her a little push, and she kept her head down, her shoulders hunched as she sped stiff-legged past the tall figures standing in the hallway, swords drawn.

Jion said, "I was so bored, and there she was. What could I do?"

Ari duck-walked awkwardly down the stairs, trying not to cut herself on the blade. Behind in the hallway a man said plaintively, "I deserve to be flogged, but your imperial highness, our job is to protect you. That means we have to clear *everyone* who comes in. How did she even get in here?"

How would he answer *that*? Their voices sank below the general noise in the common room. She darted awkwardly among tables, head down, feeling stares on every side. She was glad of her long hair curtaining her face as she ran for the door . . . and out.

Fai Anbai, at the top of the stairs, watched her go; why did she walk like that? She had to be drunk. He tried to shut out the press of fatigue—he had been sitting in his room across the hall, working through those interrogation notes, when the rising voices of the servants had disturbed him, upset because the inner door was unaccountably locked with the prince inside talking to someone.

He'd grabbed up his weapons and leaped to the door, but it turned out there was no danger. From the smirks of the guards not on duty, they obviously thought it hilarious that their prince—known for having a harem at the imperial palace—could manage to pluck a lover out of the air his first day at Green Jade Bay.

Jion saw they were all waiting for an answer, and it occurred to him belatedly that the duty guards had to have an answer, that their lives depended on no surprises.

"It seemed to me you knew her," rumbled Min Ko, the poison taster servant who was actually a ferret.

Jion's mind darted desperately—and lit on an amatory story one of the Ran twins had smuggled into class when they were all fifteen, about a fox demon who was fond of sneaking into the bedrooms of handsome scholars by night to steal their hearts as well as their souls.

"I did," he said. "I met her on the way to the privy this morning, while most of you were checking over this inn for assassins and hidden doors. Don't you remember seeing me chatting with a girl?"

There had been a number of harbor people who had tried to speak to him once the word began to spread who he was, but the guards had fended them off. Though they had not followed him into the privy.

He went on, "It wasn't long. I thought. But long enough for her. Tonight she apparently got onto the roof with some friends — all drunk — on a dare, and came down a rope. What could I do but let her in the window?"

Ayah! A collective sigh rose. "Just like Lilu the Nine-Tail Fox Fairy," Yim said, thereby revealing his own taste in reading material.

"Was she pretty?" asked Tun Ro, known as Tun-Tun — and at sour looks from both Fai Anbai and his Imperial Guard Chief Ha Gar, he uttered a strangled noise and braced to attention, his gaze going diffuse.

"She couldn't possibly be an assassin. There were certainly no knives or poisons under that robe," Jion went on. And at another smothered laugh, he added in an apologetic voice, "But I can see that I disturbed you all for no reason. I humbly beg pardon for that."

It was mollifying, as princes did not have to apologize. Ha Gar said, "If his imperial highness the first prince will remember that these incompetent guards must first meet *all* who come and go into his imperial presence, it will make their jobs much easier."

"*Indeed* yes," Jion said. "I wasn't thinking. I'll make sure of that in future."

Fai Anbai sensed his barely-suppressed laughter, and considered the little signs — the glance between the prince and the enterprising young woman before he made his grand gesture with the golden tael, how he'd watched after her as she left. He wished now he'd stopped her and got a look at her face, but it was mild curiosity, without suspicion. If she was an assassin, she certainly wasn't very good at it — and he still had Yaso's face firmly fixed in his mind for the mysterious, power-ful Firebolt, who could singlehandedly bring down an imperial mine.

Ayah, no matter — nothing had happened. And it was the first time the prince had behaved the way the ferret chief had expected to face every day when they first met in that harbor a year and a half ago.

He dismissed Jion's promise as so much air; they would simply tighten the ring of security.

FOURTEEN

ARI SPED INTO THE safety of the shadows, then ducked into a narrow alley between two shops. Here she sketched deflection charms over herself and then pulled Sagacious Blade free of the billowing folds of slithery silk. One more check, then she knelt on the blade and shot upward into relative safety.

She zoomed over the roof, grabbed up her pack, and soared upward and away. Elation swooped through her, though her troubles were far from over. Shigan was a prince, but his heart had not changed! They were still friends!

She reached the garrison, shivering happily. They were still friends. In all other aspects of life the river had become a sea and the hill a mountain, but at least that hadn't changed.

Now she had to face the mountain and the sea. First was Muin, whom she'd left behind at that funeral dinner. He would be very worried by now. Maybe even angry with her.

As she flew over the garrison's inner buildings, she shut her eyes briefly. Blobs in Muin's chamber. Lights in the window, too; she wobbled, then clutched hard on Sagacious as vertigo swept through her, unsettling her stomach. Her empty stomach.

Her descent was swifter than usual—she was so very tired. She landed in her usual spot. She wrapped Jion's silk up in a tight ball and shoved it deep into her pack before pulling out her rose traveling robe. She'd returned her sword to her pack in its wrapping, and the harness as well, when she heard a messenger call beyond the building, "Have you seen Miss Ryu?"

"No," someone called back. "You go report."

"I don't dare."

Ari suppressed a groan and ran out, calling, "Here I am! Here I am! Sorry to have troubled you."

She had to repeat that four times before she reached the command building. Muin slammed his door open, his eyes stark as she ran the last distance. She shot through the door and he slammed it shut again, saying, "Where did you go?" and, lower, "Why didn't you keep going?"

"It's all right," she said. "I apologize, Elder Brother. It was that ferret, listening, then the questions about Firebolt, and I wondered how much the ferret knows, and I got scared and thought I'd better just get out of the command office."

"That ferret is still here!" Muin's whisper was hoarse. "Not *here*, but with the prince."

"But he doesn't know who I am." And, because she knew it would go a long way toward mitigating the anger and frustration he was feeling, she said, "Yskanda is safe. He's safe, and acknowledged as a Talent, and he *did* pass the Imperial Examination, just as Master Bankan said."

"What? How do you know that?"

"Jion is Shigan—you remember, at Loyalty? Left with me? I didn't tell you because I thought—oh, it doesn't matter right now. But I asked him. I saw him at the inn, when he was alone in his room. He's Yskanda's friend—and Muin, he knows The Story. But hasn't told anyone."

Muin had been on his feet far longer than usual. He limped across his room, sank onto a chair, and put his head into his hands. Then looked up, his face distraught. "Arikanda, I don't even know where to start. Having that ferret turn up — with the *son of the emperor* . . . you here . . . Firebolt . . . Falik so worried about Second Miss—and that they are going to replace him . . . I don't know where to turn first, but my biggest worry is *you*."

"I am a bad sister to bring you trouble, Elder Brother."

Muin let out a long breath, his eyes closed. "You are not a bad sister. But this is a bad situation. 'Jion,'" he repeated. To him, nothing good could come of being that comfortable with using a prince's name.

"If it helps," Ari said, "think of him as Shigan. I do, in my heart."

"Except he's not Shigan anymore. If he ever was. He's the son of the emperor, surrounded by people who probably have orders to drag Firebolt away in chains because of that mine you raided. And I . . ." He rubbed his tense forehead. Then he dropped his hands and took Ari completely by surprise as he said, "Do you ever think about the phoenix feather?"

"Not really," she said. "Ayah! I did when we were at Loyalty. When it was hard, that first year especially, I remembered that I was helping you on your road to greatness. It was very cheering." She smiled.

He did not smile back. "I gave up on the idea of my own greatness before I left Loyalty," he said. "I thought that if there was any truth to it, the greatness would be in Falik's achievement, and I would share it if I could be his captain. But now . . ." He stared at the wall. "I know he's afraid that this is the end, for him. There is no general who cannot walk."

Ari's soul chilled. She rubbed her hands up her arms. "I hope . . ." She shook her head. What did she know about imperials, except that they were in some wise her enemy? But that was "imperials" as an idea. The individuals she had met while staying on Green Jade Island she liked just as much as she liked the gallant wanderers she'd met. They seemed the same sort of people, the best ones striving to do their work well, to do what was right by one another.

Given that, she could not pretend to predict what sort of future Falik had. She was not going to try — and returned to the subject. "When I was little, it was simple. Mother and Father were sure you were destined for great things. Second Brother and I thought so, too."

Muin's smile was pained. "If Second Brother is a Talent, maybe it was meant for him."

Ari had never dared to tell Master Ki The Story, but they had talked a lot about symbols and meanings. She said, "Maybe we were all wrong? All we really know is that a phoenix must have flown over Sweetwater when Mother and Father said their wedding vows before the village, and dropped a feather down. Perhaps it was . . . a blessing? Ul Keg never said he believed it was your road to great leadership, I recollect that now. He didn't deny it, either. But now, when I think back, I wonder if he thought it was a blessing, too."

"What do blessings *mean*?" Muin burst out. "Maybe it's

luck? If you hadn't happened to show up that day, I — and Falik — would be lying up in that graveyard now, silent bones. That was luck."

It had not felt like luck to Ari, who had toiled so hard to follow the trader much less get ahead of it, and was almost too late. But she would not argue with Muin, who was so tired, still healing, his heart knotted. "Maybe that's what it means," she said. "I don't know. We could ask a shaman. Or find Ul Keg. I would love to find Ul Keg," she admitted on a sigh. "Sometimes, when my thoughts were as tangled as my hair, he could always comb out my mind."

Muin flexed his hands. "I never asked questions. I thought it was easy, a straight path before me — work hard, be filial, be truthful, be just. But you know what they say about straight paths."

"We banished the demons," Ari said, pointing to the bay.

"They don't stay banished," Muin retorted, limping to the window to look out. "Enough of that. Your prince and that ferret are here to question those prisoners about Master Night, but they are also here to evaluate Falik. I have to make sure the garrison is properly run, until the reinforcements arrive — which might be with a new commander. Whatever lies in the future, I've got to see to it that it doesn't happen right now if I can. It would kill Falik, sure as an executioner's sword."

Ari bit back a protest, and then closed her mouth against uttering reassurance that everything would be fine, words she could not guarantee. "It's very late," she said in a small voice. "I'm so sorry. I'll go away, back to Te Gar. Tomorrow, if you think it best." Though she would meet Jion once more, if she could.

He sighed, the tension and regret coloring his aura a deep, night blue that bled through to Ari until she blinked hard to shut it out before her stinging eyes betrayed her.

"The sooner you get distance from that ferret, the less I'll worry about you," said Muin. "I'll talk to Dun about finding one of our locals to get you away on a boat, and once you are safely away, I'll think of a way to get messages to that Blue . . . Blue . . ."

"Hibiscus. On Prince Ratha's Miracle Victory Way, in Te Gar Harbor."

"Blue Hibiscus. Prince Ratha's Miracle Victory Way. I'll remember that. And I'll find a way to keep in contact that will not compromise everyone, is that agreed?"

"Yes, Elder Brother."

Everyone got scant sleep during what remained of that night.

In the morning, Ari left the little closet off the infirmary where she had her temporary bed. She meant to get an early start on her usual round of duties, so that she would be free to wait for Jion if he could get away from his guardians. Or guards.

As she passed the main room with its row of curtained-off beds, she heard a familiar choking cough: Second Miss was there. Ari poked her head in.

Second Miss turned her wan face toward the door. "Oh, Miss Ryu! Could you get me more of that ginger tea? It truly helped yesterday."

"I would be happy to," Ari said. Remembering how much the sisters loved the fresh scents of gardens, "Are you sure you don't want a pinch of jasmine — oh I beg pardon. I remember. Itches. Is there another aromatic tea that you would like? Ginger doesn't smell like much, and I was thinking yesterday that things that smell good might help."

"Just the ginger," Second Miss murmured, eyed closed. "I don't want any strong smells. Even herbs."

Ari mentally added ginger tea to her list of morning medicines to deliver, and headed to the kitchen, where she found the usual cluster of orderlies waiting for breakfast trays. She darted around them with an ease practiced over the last stretch of days. Keeping busy had been the best way to avoid the idle questions that people asked each other when living in the same place. That was another benefit of having been an orderly, she thought as she waited in line for bowls of congee — she'd gotten accustomed to keeping to herself, in the background.

That allowed her to think about that conversation with Jion as she piled things on her tray. She was so deep in memory while moving by habit that she headed for the door without Second Miss's ginger tea. A whiff of raw ginger being chopped up by a cook caused her to stop and turn back.

The tea was only a matter of moments to make, as there was always hot water to hand. However, she had miscalculated how much she could carry, and stood there, wondering if she ought to take Second Miss her tea right away, or deliver the rest and make the poor woman wait for last.

She looked up and there was Trickle. "Miss Ryu? Did you forget something? Or are we out of something? I can send someone down to the herbalist."

"No, it's a carrying problem. Second Miss has morning sickness. Ginger. *Without* jasmine," Ari added, nodding her head at the pot there on the sideboard. "My mother always used to put a pinch of jasmine or chrysanthemum in ginger tea."

Trickle grinned. "Not for Yulins!"

"Yulins?" Ari repeated—and then remembered Yulin Pel of their Loyalty Fortress days. But Muin's sister wouldn't know that. So she looked a question.

"Jasmine is poison to half of 'em," Trickle explained. "Don't dare have jasmine around if the duke comes visiting. If that's all, I can take it—I'm stopping by Commander Falik's anyway, as Pigear is busy supervising a bath."

Ari thanked him, hefted her heavy tray, and began her rounds. But her mind stayed back in the kitchen. The duke—Yulin Pel and Weed—stomach upset—stomach churning—

She stopped suddenly, and nearly dropped her tray when memory hit her: the recruiting ship, she and Shigan, their heads aching and stomachs churning after drinking that tea with some kind of sleep herb in it. First Brother Banig . . .

She looked down at the various pots and cups, then bolted onward, determined to get all the deliveries done, collect the dirty dishes, and then find Muin before he began the drills.

But she was too late. Everybody had to stop her to chat a little. By the time she was done, he was—as expected—out in the courtyard, overseeing his cavalry conscripts at their warmups. Ari wrenched her eyes away, both disappointed and also longing to be out there with them. Muin had worked fundamentals from Heaven and Earth into the old Loyalty drill. It surprised her how much like her Redbark drills these were—but when she'd showed Muin her Redbark drills, he had exclaimed, "That's excellent, and Father will shed tears of pride. But you cannot do that here. Everyone will be talking about you. And then will come the questions."

So she'd gone up to the graveyard to do Redbark, which reminded her of her orderly days, out behind the kitchen garden. At least the grave mounds plateau only smelled like cedar and the sea.

Muin cast a glance her way, his lips tightening. She kept moving, very aware of new watchers on the balcony outside the commander's office—Jion among them. But she resisted looking, as she knew that ferret was there as well.

She hurried on as if she had something pressing to do, hoping that the ferret would keep his attention on Muin's cavalry.

Jion watched her without moving his head, trying not to draw Fai Anbai's attention; the man was far too observant, and Jion suspected that his ruse in getting Ari safely out the door had not been completely successful. While a couple of the imperial guards had made jokes that morning about the prince's talent at finding willing women appearing out of the air, Chief Fai had remained silent, his brows slightly lifted. Jion had been glad when the subject dropped.

Ari disappeared below, and he turned back to the drill, wishing he could join them. There was a lot of Redbark in that drill. Ryu Muin's doing, most likely—both he and Ari had been trained by the famous Danno. Oh, he understood so much, now.

Fai Anbai stood beside Jion, equally tired and stressed; he had the interrogations waiting, and after that, all those reports still to sift through in the poisoning case. Fai Anbai turned his attention down to the courtyard, where Captain Ryu limped back and forth, leaning on a stick as he watched his conscripts with an eagle's gaze. This drill was as precise as anything the ferrets did, with elements of the old imperial guard drills. That surely was General Falik's influence, as he had done five years with the imperial guard in his young days . . . How definite were the physicians about Commander Falik never walking again? The Duke would surely ask. So would the Minister of War . . .

On Fai Anbai's other side, Falik Tan sat in his cart, straining to get his legs to move even a finger's breadth. He could not bear to imagine what his life would be like if they replaced him . . .

Down in the courtyard Muin signaled for sparring, very aware of those watchers. They were one tide from getting Ari safely away. Dun had summoned their usual supplier of fish to the garrison before sunup, and Muin had paid him double to take his sister to Gold Jade, supposedly to get her away from a persistent lover. As soon as the tide turned at midday, Ari had better be down at the wharf . . .

The practice lasted until the drum ending the first hour of Phoenix Watch. The conscripts were dismissed to their labors, patrolling and repairing, many sending a practiced eye skyward in hopes that the dark line of clouds would hold off the snow until evening.

On the balcony, Commander Falik straightened as much as he could in his cart, and said, "If you'll come inside, Captain Dun is waiting."

Jion said to Fai Anbai, "This is your last interview before the interrogations, which I will be no help with. Imperial Father will want a detailed description of the damage to the duke's manor, and to know that our respects were paid to his grace the governor."

Fai Anbai said, "This servant begs his imperial highness to recollect his imperial majesty's order, and take Yim and his team."

Jion had hoped for more freedom to maneuver, but expected less—and had come prepared. He agreed and left, beckoning to Fennel, who bore the gift that Jion was to take to the duke, and went down to collect his honor guard of five. They soon had horses saddled—Jion did not even have to take his tally out of his sleeve—and rode up the mountain to the ducal manor.

This was enormous, the size of a small town. Though the garden had been shockingly hacked up by the invaders, he could tell that it had matured over generations, and no doubt the damage would vanish within a year or two of careful pruning and planting. The buildings, like the imperial palace, were only visible by the double rooftops, each with its five guardian animals ranged along the Heaven-turned corners.

The consort received them in a secondary hall. He'd seen what the invaders had done to the ancestral hall on his way in; the consort went to her knees, apologizing elaborately for the wretchedness of their home and the terrible welcome.

Jion had expected all that, replied with equally elaborate politeness, and then learned that the governor was still in bed recovering. "His speech is much clearer than it was, but very difficult to make out, and his right side is . . ." She shook her head, her expression real for the first time in their dialogue. "If his imperial highness desires a personal interview, this humble consort will obey at once, but he is so embarrassed at his faulty speech, and the fact that he cannot rise to bow."

"I do not wish to trouble the duke," Jion responded, and gestured Fennel forward, who bowed as he proffered a beautiful carved box. "His imperial majesty sends this medicine made from a century old Longevity Root, decocted by the Imperial Physicians Department. He hopes it will aid the duke's recovery."

After she thanked him, and offered refreshments that he turned down with equal politeness, he and his train climbed back on the borrowed horses and rode through the ruined gates.

When they passed the gate leading to the Yulin burial mounds, he turned to his escort. "I brought wine and offerings so that I can pay my respects to the garrison dead. His imperial majesty will want every honor observed, and there was no chance to do it yesterday, as I had to interview the commander first."

The honor guard received this with impassive faces: orders were orders.

Jion then said, "I might spend some time at it; I would like to recite some sutras. If you would rather wait at the entrance for me, I did order some extra hot wine in case, which should still be warm, and a box of dumplings from that vendor across from the inn."

Here, six faces brightened in characteristic fashion, and Jion began to hope that this would actually work.

Was Arikanda prepared? She was.

Two of the imperial guards insisted on pacing the circle of the garrison grave mounds, sweeping for any possible danger. As Jion had hoped, Ari had expected it, and was nowhere in sight. Unless she hadn't come at all?

The five guards and Fennel settled with the food and wine around a huge, flat boulder just outside the entrance, visible under one of the towering cedars. Jion ventured alone into the graveyard, carrying the incense, the small jug of cold wine, and the plates of nuts and cakes that he'd brought for the purpose. He lit the incense, then set the food offerings on the ground before the statue of the Sun God. He recited three sutras that his grandmother had taught him as a child as he poured the wine out in a libation.

When the jug was nearly empty he toasted the fallen

silently, drank the last drops, and bowed. As he backed up, he heard a step—and there she was, standing behind a fresh mound, which she kept between herself and the guards now sharing the meal at the entrance.

The mourning period was officially over—luckily, as he'd had to thrust her undyed robe into the brazier the night before, rather than explain it to the servants. She wore a rose-colored robe cut for travel, and when their eyes met, her face brightened in that happy grin that had never been tutored into a courtly simper.

He held out his arms, just a little. He was very ready and willing to close them around her, but she faltered a few steps away, her head a little to one side as she eyed him uncertainly. He wondered if his princely robes were another invisible wall between them, and said, "I hoped you wouldn't forget to come."

She glanced at the unheeding guards at the entrance some hundred paces away, then made a sign on her body from shoulders to waist. He blinked as her edges blurred. If he concentrated he could see her, but his eyes wanted to slide to the sky, to the cedars rustling in the wintry breeze, to the broken branch she dragged toward him.

He blinked in puzzlement as she said low-voiced, "I figured you'd have guards, but I hoped you'd make them stay outside there. Take off your cloak and lay it over this branch here. From a distance it will look like you're kneeling before the statue. It won't fool them if they come, but we can go behind the mounds for a bit."

They each checked, but the guards were busy passing the jug and eating dumplings, the well-trained horses peacefully nosing the ground a few paces away. He took off his warm cloak and slung it over the branch where she indicated. There was a broken twig more or less at the shoulder height of a kneeling man. She must have searched around to find a suitable piece of fallen wood.

As he did that, she sketched that sign over her front, and the strange blur vanished. He blinked away the ache in his eyes.

"You really had trouble seeing me?" she asked. "I never knew how well this deflection charm worked."

"I could see you, but it's a little like trying to read underwater. With sun glare," he said. "I kept wanting to look away, but I could see you if I concentrated," he explained as he paced beside her.

She led him around behind the Sun God statue to the older mounds. Some were so old that the ground had smoothed to gentle humps.

"This is where I do my Redbark," she said. "I haven't felt unwelcome."

He had never really come to term with the idea of ghosts — had preferred to think of other things. Like, why did she seem so uncomfortable with him? "I haven't been able to do Redbark except in cramped quarters aboard the courier, and my inn room, for days," he said.

It was exactly the right thing to say. Her uncertainty vanished. She unslung the pack he hadn't even noticed, and pulled out her familiar staff, and the new sword. Then she hesitated, and came to him with the latter. "Would you like to have a sword in hand again? Sagacious Blade is very old."

Light winked in the huge pearl in the pommel. Jion noticed that the bronze blade gleamed a different shade from the bronze he was used to, and admired anew how the blade had been worked with an overlapping scales pattern. It was beautiful craftsmanship. "The color? Is there something besides bronze in the blade?" he asked as she put it into his hand.

"Yes. Master Ki said that a piece of a star from the Heavens was folded and hammered in."

Jion swung the blade experimentally. It fit surprisingly well into his hand, though his hand was so much larger than hers. It was not a small blade. He struck a pose and slashed the sword in Pheasants Rise in the Wind. It felt natural, an extension of his arm, so natural a pulse of regret surprised him. It was going to be difficult to let it go. "This is a very impressive blade," he said as she snapped together her staff.

They took up the familiar stance side by side, with space for the swing of their weapons, breath clouding in the air. Anticipation sang through Jion as Ari smiled his way, and he flashed a quick smile back. They both were aware of happiness, but tempered with the heightened awareness of imminent departure. She was committing the sight of him with Sagacious Blade to memory.

Neither noticed the cold.

Then, under the slowly approaching clouds, as the wide bay below them turned from blue to the gray of stone, once again they worked through Redbark. Oh, it was so sweet, so bittersweet, to perform the familiar movements that both had had to do in solitary silence over the past year and a half! Once again they breathed in synchrony, moving first slowly, then whirling and snapping through her variations on Heaven and Earth, as the rising wind toyed with clothes and hair. Three times they did Redbark, each time moving a step closer as they found their old rhythm, fighting together without fouling the other's weapon. Ari gloried in the familiar rhythm, the sense of him at her side, the golden glisten of his aura, a light like a thousand beeswax candles.

They finished, breathing fast. He handed the sword back, and as she sheathed it and tucked it into her pack, he clasped his hands in the gallant warriors' bow—

Before he could speak the drum signaling the end of Phoenix Watch reverberated from the hills.

"I need to go," she said, startled. "The tide will turn soon."

"Go? Where? I thought we'd have the rest of the day," he said, sharply disappointed—then he saw the stricken expression in her face, and the telltale track of tears on her cheeks.

It had happened during that last Redbark form, which had been so perfect. Heartbreakingly perfect, because they would not be fighting together side by side. They would not even drill together. Maybe never again would she see, and feel, that golden glow beside her. They were friends. He had come to the graveyard, and he had smiled. But between them loured the shadow of the emperor. Who he loved, and she could make no argument against a son loving his father. That would be a sin.

She saw no resolution. But at least she could continue to work for justice.

She knuckled her eyes, and said in a low, urgent voice, "You recall Yulin Pel at Loyalty was allergic to jasmine?"

"I don't think I ever knew that," he said, startled that she would bring him up, of all people. "If I did, I forgot. I tried to forget *him*."

"Shigan—Jion—listen. This is important. I think. Duke Yulin also has trouble with jasmine, as does Second Miss."

"Why are we talking about someone I'd rather forget?"

"Remember when Water Cat and the rest forced us into the Shadow Panthers? That very first day, I overheard First Brother Banig talking to one of the tattoos who had robbed someone of a chest of teas. First Brother Banig made the tattoo toss the entire chest overboard instead of sending it as tribute to Master Night. Just because there was jasmine tea among all the others."

Jion stared. "So you're saying, you think Master Night is one of the Yulins?"

"I don't know. All I saw was his mask, and even if it had been off, I don't know if I would have recognized him if he is Yulin Pel's father, or uncle, or third cousin. And I'm sure there are plenty of other people who have that same trouble, but wasn't there talk of our Yulin's father getting into trouble and vanishing? Isn't it worth investigating?" As she spoke, she stowed away her staff and slung her pack over her shoulder.

"I will pass that on," he said.

"I hope that will be a good enough trade for not killing Firebolt," she said, her smile very lopsided.

He looked back, understanding that she needed reassurance. "There was no Firebolt to be found," he said. "Fai Anbai will corroborate that. Firebolt vanished the day Master Night vanished. I only met the heroic commander, his equally heroic captains — and one captain's sister."

Muffling a sob, she darted close and before he could react she stood on tiptoe and kissed him. It went awry, as first kisses sometimes do; he opened his lips, tasting a hint of salt tears, but before he could close his arms around her at last she whirled away, her dark hair streaming as she threw down her sword. He had the space of a heartbeat to see it glimmer with its own light before she sketched that complicated sign on herself, and then she blurred as she rose into the air. Between one blink and the next she vanished. He squinted against the clouds, and found a blur again, moving fast, but then it diminished, and maybe that was only a sea bird.

Fighting impotent fury and hurt and disappointment, he trod back to the statue. Here he bowed, then pulled his cloak from the branch. He dragged that off to one side, where it would look as if the wind had blown it from one of the trees, and stood before the Sun God, who stared into Heaven with infinite patience.

He fought to regain his equilibrium, one, two, three breaths.

When he turned toward the entrance, Fennel was packing up the remains of the snack. He rejoined them, and said as lightly as he could, "Shall we go?"

FIFTEEN

"THE ROAD IS STREWN with setbacks, but the seeker of paths will find one as long as the sun still rises."

Ul Keg had made Ari write that as an impatient nine-year-old. In an effort to ease the knot in her heart, she whispered it to herself as she tramped around Milky Springs Harbor until she found a trader going north; by then she had been able to trade Jion's golden tael for cash. By now she had a better sense of what things were worth. That tael would easily pay for passage all the way to Te Gar without her having to offer herself up for scut-work to crabby captains.

And she wouldn't have to try flying between islands again. No doubt real Essence masters could do it without a blink, but her attempt to reach Green Jade to warn Falik had been a miserable experience, learning one after another of her limitations. The most important being, at least so far, unless there was an enormous pool of fire below an island, she must continually reach for Essence to keep her in the air, especially when she was in the middle of the ocean in horrible weather.

She still had dreams about her flight at times being as slow as walking, buffeted by icy winds, while she was desperately hungry and thirsty. With no money, she'd had to creep into places to sleep, and steal food — which she had tried hard to take from those who looked as if they could afford it.

And she had almost been too late.

That thought twisted her dreams into nightmares, and humbled her.

Feeling even lower at having to say farewell to Jion — maybe even forever — she remembered that Capital List, and decided she had better travel as a law-abiding subject, if she couldn't find gallant wanderer transport. As she was now in the very heart of the empire, the signs or sights of gallant wanderers were rare indeed — even the storybooks about them were kept in the backs of stores, if sold at all. Twice more she spotted *Firebolt and the Mine of Shame*, and slunk away as if someone like that sinister Fai Anbai might pop up and point an accusing finger from the book to her before sending an army of imperial guards to bury her in chains.

At last she found a trader in secondary silks going north. Two more transfers over the succeeding days swallowed pretty much all her cash, in addition to a few purchases she made, but at least it brought her finally to Te Gar.

The closer she got, the pain of parting with Jion and her brother eased enough to allow her a mild sense of anticipation. She would see Petal and Matu again!

She got off the latest boat at Te Gar, unprepared for the tide of feelings the familiar sight, sounds, and smells brought back. Some things had not changed, such as the garrison towers off to the right, and the curved roof of the Justice Building, with the big drum out front for subjects who came for justice. She tried to image Petal marching up to that building. What bravery that took!

But there were changes. Old Rock was gone, replaced by a vendor selling embroidered house shoes. She hoped wherever he was, his life was better, for both him and Lotus Bud.

As she made her way along the winding thoroughfare, her heart began to beat fast in anticipation. There was the Blue Hibiscus — same sign, but out front were a pair of neatly trimmed hibiscus enjoying the sun of early spring. From the branches hung wish ribbons of several colors — including the white that belonged to gallant wanderers.

She opened the door. Gone were the fussy spirit screens. The space was simple now, with only more hibiscus plants against the back door to the courtyard. An aproned innkeeper appeared. Ari blinked at the broad-shouldered, barrel-chested young man with the thin mustache and the long hair clipped back —

"Matu?"

He had come forward with the proprietor's ready greeting, but at this his step faltered, then his face lit with a genuine smile. Reddening to the ears, he exclaimed, "Brother Ryu — ah, Ryu?" His gaze took in her rose-colored robe and her ribbon-tied hair.

"Ari," she said.

Matu turned his head. "Petal!" he called, voice ringing.

Here came Petal, much stouter than she had been, well dressed as an owner must be. She paused, her mouth rounded, and she let out a short breath.

"It's Ari," Matu said.

"Sister Ari," Petal said softly, beaming. "I knew you would come."

A short time later Ari had an offer of the best room in the house, a hot bath, and a hot meal to be brought to her room at once. When Petal finally realized that Ari was increasingly embarrassed at being treated like a princess, she stopped herself after an inward struggle, and then asked, "What would you like?"

"The old seahorse room will do. Really," Ari said. "I spent what I had in fares, so I'll be looking for work for a time. But that can wait till after I visit our old bath house. Is it still there?"

Matu had been standing by, completely inarticulate. At this he and Petal exchanged glances, then Petal said, "It is indeed. In fact, this spring we've commenced building a nice pathway down there. It goes through your old drill site. Which is now the outer courtyard. We still offer baths, of course, but it's more expensive."

Ari nodded. "I know. Heating and hauling all the water up, then back again. That's why I thought of the bath house. Now I'll get to see the women's side."

Matu hadn't said anything, but it was clear he had something on his mind. His stare was unwinking, his face still red. Ari got more uncomfortable by the moment, wondering if his dismay at her awful blunder so long ago had turned into dislike.

But once Ari returned from her bath, wearing the new travel robe she'd bought in Green Jade (her rose robe had been handed off to the laundry side at the bath house, to be fetched on the morrow), she found Matu waiting for her. "Petal would be here, but she has some bookkeeping for a supplier that won't wait," he said abruptly. "Would you . . . could you come to the kitchen?"

"Certainly," Ari said wonderingly. Uncomfortable they both were, but she was not hearing any resentment in Matu's voice.

She followed him through the main room, which was filled with delicious smells, customers at nearly all the tables. Matu led her through to the kitchen, where a burly man with a gray topknot was overseeing busy kitchen help chopping, stirring, doling out hot food, and over in the corner washing dishes.

Matu led her up to the man, who looked up, his brows rising. "Matu?"

"Meet . . . Ari," Matu said in an odd voice, and then added in a fierce undervoice, "It's Brother Ryu."

The man turned a startled face to Ari, then to her dismay, he began a deep, profound bow.

She darted forward, catching his hands. "No, please don't. You are an elder—I ought to be bowing to you, Uncle . . .?" She turned helplessly to Matu.

The man cast a look around the kitchen, gave a short nod, then said, "Come into the storeroom."

The three of them stepped down into a cold room that smelled of chili paste and plum sauce. Matu pulled the door shut, and said, "This is my father. He goes by Chef Ki."

Ari gasped in delight. "Then . . . you made it?"

Chef Ki said, "I have you to thank."

"I don't understand—I never saw you. I never found you. I thought I had failed," Ari exclaimed.

"I was a cook at the guard camp," Chef Ki said.

Ari was horrified. "But . . . I used the fan on you!"

Chef Ki nodded. "Yes. You did not know that some of us in that camp, actually, all the launderers and cooks, were prisoners. How could you? But you didn't kill anyone. So here I am."

"But . . . how did you get free?"

Chef Ki said, "I could tell you that story perhaps later? I ought to be overseeing the dinner preparation now. These workers are mostly new to the kitchen out there." Chef Ki smiled a little—and it was Matu's smile, on his older face, kind to the heart. "Also . . . I'd like a little time to get my thoughts straight in my head. I always hoped to meet you to thank, but did not believe it would happen soon. Or so suddenly."

"There is nothing to thank," Ari said seriously. "I can see I made a horrible mistake."

He shook his head. "We shall speak later, if you will?" Another bow.

"Of course, of course!" She clasped her hands and bowed back.

The sun had gone down by the time she'd eaten an excellent dinner, and retired to her room, where she gazed out into the courtyard at a row of young trees. Not much could be seen in the darkness.

Petal had given her a large room (no Seahorse) — large enough to do a few rounds of Redbark, which felt good after being cooped up on board a small ship. Then she walked the length of the room and back, her thoughts like summer fireflies, darting here and there, until at last came that tap. She opened the door to find Matu, his father, and Petal there.

Petal said, "The inn is quiet for the night, the kitchen set for morning. My night crew has the desk, so we can talk."

Ari heard the pride in that *my*, and smiled inwardly, rejoicing for Petal. It was so good to see her in a handsome robe of a soft peach, with crimson berry clusters embroidered on it, amid tiny hummingbirds done with iridescent silken thread. And it was good to see Matu so proud, with his father — but she was afraid to ask about the rest of the family. She sat silently as Matu carried in a heavy tray laden with tea and a stack of Earth Wishes Festival pancakes.

"Tell her the story, Dad," Matu said, passing out the cups and plates.

Chef Ki clasped his hands toward Ari, then lifted his tea in a little salute. "I only remember you as a blur. I was making soup along with my wife — who is with my mother, back on Ten Eagles."

"They are alive?" Ari said happily, then turned a puzzled look to Matu. "You didn't tell me your father was a cook. It would have made the search so much easier."

"I didn't know," Matu protested.

Chef Ki patted the air with his hands. "I wasn't what you call a trained cook, as one would put it. Third Uncle and I were caught when I was fourteen, and put to work for the imperials, this was up north, a navy camp during a campaign against the

Westerners, who were raiding something terrible then. I was too scrawny for much so they stuck me in the kitchen, where I was the scut-worker, but I learned plenty before the navy went to battle the Westerners and we ran. I didn't think of it until I was arrested off the streets the very day I reached Benevolent Winds, where I'd gone to find a cousin outside the Ki family. When I saw those mines, in desperation told them I was a cook. It worked — they couldn't get anyone to stay, so they were using prisoners."

"And Mother saw him when she was taken there," Matu said. "She said she was a cook, too, though she didn't know anything about cooking, outside of decoctions."

"I see," Ari said. "But . . . I didn't rescue you. I used the fan tap on you both, and I'm sorry."

"You couldn't know," Chef Ki rumbled.

Ari turned to Matu. "What about your grandparents?"

"My mother is very frail," Chef Ki said. "You passed right by her in the mine. She was one of the sorters, which meant at least she didn't have to move much, though she was coughing blood from the dust — the same dust that killed my father the winter before."

"I am very sorry."

"Thank you — we were glad he escaped the pain of the lung rot at last."

"Tell her what happened," Matu said.

"That I will, as I got ahead of myself, or out of order, you might say. We were making soup when we saw a blur — you — and then nothing, until we woke up lying on the ground, very thirsty, with aching chests and bees in our fingers and toes. That feeling went away as soon as we got up. And none too soon. The guards woke, howling for food, for water, for the captain. They were milling around while my wife and I tried to figure out how our cauldrons had gone completely empty — and that is when one of the garrison captains showed up, very angry."

He smiled reminiscently. "What a panic they were in! From all the cursing, we discovered that someone had put bombs in the mine, and all the prisoners were gone, save us in the camp. My mother had gone right by us on the barge, we found out later, helped by some of the other sorters, without seeing us lying there hidden by the tall grasses along the riverside. Just as well, you might say, though we did not know it yet. Ah, where was I, son?"

"Cursing garrison guards."

"Ayah, yes, the guards. Very frightened they were — they wanted to know how many armed attackers had gone up the path to the mine. Nobody in camp knew anything, it seemed, so they speculated more and more, and ran around, and some hiked up the path to get a look at the damage, then came down to curse some more. We thought it prudent to keep the food and the tea coming, with the result no one much minded about us."

Chef Ki paused to drink off his tea, then he turned the cup around in his big, broad fingers as he said, "My wife was down at the riverside washing a tub of dishes — this was two, three days later, you might say, I forget now — days of no one to cook for save the mine guards, for we discovered all the prisoners had vanished, and secretly glad we were, though I did wonder about my mother."

Matu smiled.

"As I was saying, it was days later when my wife took her turn washing the dishes, which was something we traded off, as it was a little escape that enabled us to get a wash and breathe air that wasn't camp guard, when what sounded like a thunder of dragons appeared on the road, sending dust up into the air. It was none other than imperial guards, at their head an imperial ferret, all dressed in black, just as in the stories, only not carrying instruments of torture."

Ari shivered. She could picture that so easily.

"Three ferrets there were, two men and a woman, who got the guards lined up, and started asking questions while the guards ordered the rest to break camp. Then it was our turn. When they found out we were bonded, and we explained how long it had been, and the fact that we'd been taken right off the street, the both of us, the ferrets did not say much, but once we'd all been put on a barge and taken back down the river, then to the garrison, to our surprise, they turned us out onto the street."

"Without a tin, or even decent clothes," Matu said in a low growl.

"Ayah, we were so happy to find ourselves free that that did not matter to us. And even if it had, who is going to go back and bang on the door and ask imperial ferrets for our travel things returned, mine confiscated ten years ago? Not us!"

Matu was still scowling.

"Though we were not sure what to do or where to go," Chef

Ki admitted. "Worse than the frog at the bottom of the well, we were, until we stumbled toward a temple. If I followed any god, it was the Fox God, and not the Snow Crane, who I always thought was the god of beggars and thieves and the lazy, their shamans full of trickery — ayah, it was my Cousin Anu's Uncle Ban who was taken in by a crooked shaman, the Year of the Great Frost, and remembering that, I thought we ought to give them wide berth, but then we saw some of the miners we knew in their courtyard, eating buns, some of them with what you might call new clothes. That is, old clothes donated, but newer than the rags we'd always seen them in. They called out to us, so we went in, thinking that as we had nothing to rob, we might as well."

He paused to cover his mouth over a great yawn. "I am so sorry! I rise very early to get the baking done, and it's a long day for old bones like mine."

Matu said gently, "The Snow Crane shamans told you where to find Grandmother . . ."

'Yes! It seemed the shamans were not averse to trickery here, but it was the kindly sort. They were parceling out people to houses around the temple when the patrols came by. We found ourselves claimed as uncle and aunt to a family we'd never laid eyes on." He chuckled deep in his chest, a sound very like his son's laugh.

Ari smiled at how much alike the two were.

Chef Ki set the teacup down. "While we were recovering, we found out that Firebolt had been our rescuer, and there was all kinds of trouble going on at the garrison and the south side, specifically the governor's house, and the Justice Department. Justice! Some justice that was."

"Tell her how you . . ."

"I'm getting there, son! We found out that the shamans and the monks at the Phoenix Moon temple between them had been assembling lists of people pulled off barges, who were looking for other people. My mother was ill, taken in by the Phoenix Moon monks and handed off to a band of nuns. They said if we had a skill they could find a way out, and near the top of the list was cooks, so I was able to get a berth on a trader going north, with my wife and mother."

Matu said, "Once my dad got them to Ten Eagles, and Grandmother in the care of the aunts, they told him about me, and came here. He got here just after Harvest Festival."

Chef Ki rose. "I'm falling asleep on my feet, but I want to thank you again, for getting all those people out. So many of them were like me, yanked off the street. It was terrible." His smile dropped and he looked down at his hands, which Ari saw were thick with scars. "I had to watch my father waste away, but at least he died with the three of us there with him." He shook his head. "I send a part of my earnings to the Snow Crane temple each month, now, and tell them to put in a good word for him in Heaven, in hopes when he comes back, it'll be to our clan, and maybe even to my son here, now that he's found himself a wife, and a very fine one at that."

He clapped Matu on the shoulder, not noticing how red his son became at these words. "I have you to thank, and if ever I can do anything for you, say the word, Broth—ah, Miss Ari. With that, I'll say good-night."

One more clasp of his hands and a quick gallant wanderers bow, then he was gone. Leaving the others looking at one another.

Petal said, "You'll stay, I hope. We have some Redbark recruits."

Recruits? Ari thought that odd, but decided not to say so. "For a time," she said instead. "I have something I have to do — I mean to take down that Master Night."

"Can we help?" Petal asked, without even a pause. In her mind, of course Sister Ari would, and could, rid the world of Master Night.

"We would very much like to," Matu said, but he looked worried.

"Certainly," Ari said happily. "But first I need to find out some information, like where he hides. I thought I'd visit you, then get started for the north, for the Sky Island — what?"

Both Petal and Matu were shaking their heads.

"Sister Ari," Matu said soberly, "the imperials put a price on your head. There will be searches for you — there are already searches. My cousin wrote that First Uncle over at Eagle Island heard from one of the Sky Island masters that there was someone asking up north there about getting a ride to the Sky Island Competition. Knew weapons, has the stance, but didn't know that you have to be invited to the competition. Word is, the Sky Islanders think she was an imperial spy."

"A ferret?" Ari said. "I guess the invitations is a good idea, except I remember all those Shadow Panthers."

Matu said, "It isn't foolproof—all it took was one to get himself invited, then he asked a friend, and so on. But First Uncle said Sky Island sect is being much more careful now, and though that woman was well behaved, something she said or did made them suspicious."

Petal said with a worried expression, "They're still looking for a boy, right?"

"Yes. Both my brother and Shigan helped with that, a little."

Matu frowned. "But that doesn't mean the ferrets won't sneak up anyway. It's what they do, I hear. And it isn't as if the island is hidden."

Petal said in a low voice, "And it's not just the ferrets who will be searching for you. I remember on the beach that night, how much screaming about revenge there was from those Shadow Panthers. Don't you think Master Night is sending spies everywhere to find you first?"

Ari sighed. "You're right. I can't go to the competition. But how am I going find what I need to know?"

Matu grinned. "That is a different matter. Remember I told you a cousin nearly got grabbed by them? The one who knew where Screaming Hawk had that training manor."

"Yes," Ari said.

"He's the one to start with. He hates the Shadow Panthers so much he'd be glad to help." Matu leaned in. "I'll send a letter off—I know who's going north not two days from now—but in the meantime, you can trade this room by taking over the training. We need it."

"Some," Petal muttered, "more than others."

Ari thought rapidly. "I'll do it, and gladly. But I have one condition, and I won't change my mind."

"What is it?" the other two asked, almost together.

"I train as Ari. Not as Firebolt. There will be no talk of Firebolt."

Petal looked disappointed—she cherished her dream of Blue Hibiscus becoming known through the gallant wanderer world as Firebolt of Redbark's headquarters—but Matu nod-ed slowly. "Given what we were just talking about, that would be best."

SIXTEEN

THOUGH TE GAR WAS closer to the Silk Islands than the imperial island, Ari and Jion arrived at their respective destinations at about the same time, Ari having had to scrounge for transport while Jion sailed from Blue Jade Island to the imperial island in a fast courier, with only a couple brief stops.

During the journey Fai Anbai was mostly sequestered in his small cabin, working steadily late into the night, judging by the lamp glow under the heavy hempen flap that served as a door.

Jion had been given the largest cabin, in which he was mostly alone save when Min Ko or Fennel came in with food and fresh clothing. He wished he'd had the foresight to bring reading; there was little to do except play Circle against himself, try to do Redbark and dance warmups, or gaze out to sea and wonder where Arikanda was.

When they neared the imperial island, he began rehearsing to himself what he would say to Imperial Father, a preparation he was glad of when they found Bitternail at the quay as the courier floated into the bay: the emperor awaited them. He conducted them along the back ways. Jion reflected on the vast difference between this arrival and his last. Everything else was so different, he had to suppress a weird bubble of humor at the strange twists life could take.

When they reached Golden Dragon Pavilion, Bitternail bowed the prince and the ferret chief into a small anteroom, saying, "Please wait while this servant sees if his imperial majesty is alone."

He slipped through a door. Fai Anbai, who knew this ante-room well, leaned against the wall and used the opportunity to thumb through his report for one more check. Jion, midway between restlessness and boredom, began to pace back and forth.

Behind the wall, the emperor glanced through one of the many palace peepholes — some centuries old. Survival during his young days having taught him to assess at a glance, he'd discovered that these moments before an interview were often quite revealing.

Fai Anbai looked exhausted, absorbed in his never-ending sheaf of papers; Jion looked bored. There was no hint of mutual agreement, much less collusion. He had not expected it, but life with First Brother Hojai had taught him that it was always good to be vigilant. He turned away, sat down, and Bitternail opened the door.

The two entered and went to the floor before the throne. When bade rise, Jion then came forward and offered the golden tally, laid across both palms. The emperor's mood had improved at each step so far; it seemed that his venture in granting his eldest son a limited measure of power had had the proper effect. At last Jion was growing into a sense of responsibility.

The graywings took charge of the tally, then the emperor sat back. "What can you tell me about this rebel leader who calls himself Master Night?"

Jion glanced at Fai Anbai, who spoke. "Our interrogations as well as those of Captain Ing, your imperial majesty, furnished similar information: he never spends much time at any of his manors. Apparently he has several, though no one appeared to know where his primary lair is. His recruits are now trained at temporary camps, then moved around. No one uses real names, or places of origin. He possesses enough ships for at least one fleet of five, possibly more, but takes care to move them with as little witness as possible. He appears to have called out his entire fleet for that exploit at Green Jade. Our navy ships chased the five remaining ships until overtaken by a storm. When that cleared, there was no evidence of any of them, suggesting a strategy of dispersal under cover of a storm."

"That much I've learned from the early report via pigeon,"

the emperor said. "What else can you tell me? Jion, speak first. What about Firebolt of Redbark — what is rumor and what is truth?"

"There was little chance that we would find Firebolt, Imperial Father. According to all witnesses, he vanished off the field once he drove off the Shadow Panthers, using Essence fire."

"There was no alliance between the criminal sects?"

"None. It was all Shadow Panthers, some attempting to disguise themselves, most likely to escape retribution," Jion said. "I did not speak to any of the prisoners — I've had no training at that. My time was spent with the commanders, and I also visited Duke Yulin, who was too ill to see me . . ."

Jion went on to paint a verbal picture of the duke's situation, the damage to his manor, to the garrison, and to the harbor town. Then he said, "Commander Falik impressed me with his loyalty as much as his bravery, and with his leadership. He and his captains. He depends on them, and they are scrupulous in carrying out his orders."

"Did you make a recommendation to Admiral Shen or The Duke at Blue Jade?"

And that had been the most surprising aspect of the entire journey — aside from finding Ari at Blue Jade.

But he did not let himself think of Ari while standing before his father. He kept his mind firmly on his visit to the naval base at Blue Jade, where, surprisingly, the gold tally had truly meant something. Gold tallies had always been something read about in histories, something the elders wielded. There had certainly been no gold tally the first time Jion was sent to the Silk Islands. Even so, he'd regarded it as an empty gesture, like a toy; Fai Anbai would hold the real power.

Except that it wasn't a toy in the eyes of those commanders. Though Jion had little experience compared to those scarred and sun-seamed veterans, he had sensed that he could have issued any kind of orders and they would have been obeyed, however crazy — or dire, like the orders from Bloody Emperor Maoyan, Jion's great-great grandfather, had been, in particular before he died.

Jion paused, their waiting faces vivid in memory. So this is how power begins, he thought. Of course, every action has consequences — he had learned that well while living with Ari and Redbark.

"When Admiral Shen asked for my opinion, Imperial Father, I explained that my military training had only lasted two years, so I could not claim any expertise. He replied that he'd heard I had been inspecting the army training from the inside, which meant I had a fundamental understanding of army structure. I did not deny that or explain it. I only said that in my limited opinion I thought that the two captains and Commander Falik would best be kept together."

It had been a brief exchange, not even a fingernail's worth of an incense stick, after listening in silence for two days, but it had happened — after which they saluted him and said, "As you command."

With those few words, he had affected three lives. No, more. It had been immediately gratifying, and in retrospect, unsettling. He was not at all sure that he liked having power. Mistakes didn't mean losing face, as it had when he was Shigan, but losing lives.

"Excellent," said the emperor. "I will corroborate your recommendation with an edict. That rumor about your covert inspection of our training has propagated nicely," he added, pleased.

Jion had become aware that in permitting the rumor to spread that he had spent time under cover at an army training fortress, his father had not only made a virtue of those two years, he had also done his best to remove the gallant wanderers from the world's awareness of Jion's experience, if he could not remove them from Jion's life.

"Chief Fai?" the emperor prompted.

Fai Anbai was surprised at the prince's succinct and accurate summary. He'd been equally surprised at Prince Jion's frank admission of rudimentary military knowledge when Admiral Shen had put the question back in naval head-quarters at Blue Jade Island. The prince could justifiably have claimed to be the veteran of at least two serious actions, but he had made no mention of any of them.

"I agree with his imperial highness's assessment of Commander Falik and his two captains," Fai Anbai said. "While the state of Commander Falik's physical recovery is uncertain at this point, there is nothing wrong with his grasp of command. I concur with his imperial highness's recommendation to retain him in his post. His company, though small, is superlatively trained, what's more they are quite loyal to their officers. And they fought brilliantly, being vastly out-numbered. Captain Ryu alone seems to have scythed his way through the enemies in his effort to protect the commander, who led the way by riding them down. Here is my report on the sequence of the battle, according to witnesses." He held out one set of papers, which Bitternail took to the emperor.

Who read through a page or so before glancing up. "How much of this is the exaggeration of battlefield rage? This Captain Ryu seems to be almost an army in himself."

"According to many witnesses, the enemy could not stop him. He took terrible wounds, I might add. Fell right after Falik did," Fai Anbai said.

"I'm impressed with the both of them," the emperor said again. "Though I expected something of the sort from Falik's boy. Jion, you may go; your mother and grandmother are waiting for you." And, as soon as the door closed behind Jion, "Chief Fai? What is your general impression of my son's conduct during this expedition?"

Fai Anbai had decided, when writing up his report, to leave out the incident with the drunken girl invading the prince's room, which reflected at least as badly on the imperial guard as it did on the wayward prince—for that matter, on himself, as none of them had deemed it necessary to station crossbowmen on the rooftops in the wintry air, what with Captain Ing's people already on guard.

Prince Jion had kept his promise not to venture into any more such incidents, making the decision easier. The prince's behavior ever since that night had been abstemious and cooperative with his honor guard.

"His highness First Prince Jion conducted himself well, your imperial majesty. Moreover, the people of Green Jade Harbor, who were badly shaken by the attack, seemed to be heartened by the attention of an imperial prince. The first day we spent with the garrison, as we arrived on the same day as the burial ritual, but the second day, once he returned from visiting the duke and paying his respects at the grave mounds, he spent among the people of the harbor, listening, sympathizing, and promising aid—I should mention we had the Registry, Works, and Tax representatives there, whom he consulted on what could be reasonably achieved. When we departed, the entire harbor turned out to see him off, a great honor considering the repair work yet to be done."

The emperor gave a small nod. "So there was no trouble left over from the White Jade incident and the false prince?"

"None, your imperial majesty," Fai Anbai said. "We met only a handful of Green Jade's silk farmers, though they seemed to be aware that the garrison had protected the bridge that gives access to the mulberry orchards. I gained the impression there is little contact between the islands, save at designated trade events. So I can confidently say that no one ever brought up Prince Jion's former visit, whether in his own person or impersonated."

"Good," the emperor. "At least we've had some success there—though we are no closer to flushing out whoever was behind that impersonation. Or the poison matter. Where are you with that?"

"In the process of reviewing all testimony, your imperial majesty. I hope to have an initial report this week, depending upon what my father discovered in his separate inquiry."

The emperor accepted that. "I am pleased that my son handled himself well. I wanted him to see for himself that his so-called gallant wanderers are mere rootless duckweed. Suitable subjects for storytelling, or for boys of a certain age, but useless overall, even worse than useless, as witnessed at Green Jade. If," he went on to add, "Jion shows any interest in your investigation into the poisoning, I desire you to share whatever you have with him." He added dryly, "We shall then see if any of it spreads, and to whom."

Through whom, Fai Anbai thought, but kept that to himself. "It shall be done, your imperial majesty. As for the criminals, you'll find in the report one valuable result, if inadvertent, of his imperial highness's experiences among them. I dispatched both agents from Blue Jade to begin investigation, but the prince gets the credit for recollecting that when the Shadow Panthers tried to recruit him, he overheard gossip that jasmine is poisonous to Master Night. He was reminded when one of the Yulins at the manor chanced to mention that as a family trait."

"Yulin . . ." The emperor had known a couple of the Yulins during his young days. One of his first judgments had concerned a Yulin provincial governor whose populace had nearly revolted after their taxes were tripled—he grimaced inwardly, remembering that.

Other Yulins served in various parts of the army and navy, without any infamy that he was aware of. Master Night might be any of these in secret — but that would at least be easy enough to check, if any among them was absent during the assault on Green Jade. And of course he might not be a Yulin at all. Jasmine being poison was not a trait limited to one family.

Fai Anbai added, "Admiral Shen promised to look into the whereabouts of all Yulins in the army and navy, without making a stir, and I instructed my agents to begin with the feuding Yulins. There is sure to be plenty of information to get them going."

The emperor laughed at that, and released Fai Anbai with a wave.

The ferret chief bowed himself out and rushed home. His wife Yan Yian had had a little over three months to go in her second pregnancy when he left. He wanted to see his family, to reassure himself that all was well, to catch up with reports, and above all to tackle every one of the fronts and work like a demon so that this time — if at all possible — he would be present for the child's birth.

He arrived at their small courtyard to discover his father there, cheering on his small daughter as she practiced balance on a plank raised a palm's breadth off the ground, while his wife filled the air with the aromatic scent of Earth Festival pancakes, one hand supporting the small of her back. The mound of her belly was demonstrably larger than when he'd left. It was such a cheerfully domestic scene it was nearly anticlimactic, for which he was grateful.

"Da is back," Grandfather Fai exclaimed.

Little Treasure squeaked and ran to slam into Fai Anbai's shins, clamoring to be picked up. His wife came out, plate in hand, to say, "I broke Tek Banu's code. Easy, actually. She was a very strange person."

Fai Anbai turned from one to the other. "What did you find?"

"Eat first," Yan Yian said.

"We have a lot to discuss," his father added. "Let's get settled."

This meant not just the meal, but getting Little Treasure down for the night. Once she was asleep, Yan Yian barred both the outer door to the garrison alley and the inner door to their main room before saying, "Easiest first?"

Fai Anbai said, "Neither was easy, is my guess."

Yan Yian shook her head. "Someone that rigid can't bear

randomness, so even if her code had been five levels deep instead of a mere three, once I grasped the main patterns, it was only a matter of toiling through frequencies. The latest entries built a picture of the travel of an unnamed monk."

"We're pretty sure that's related to the Danno and Alk Hanu case," Grandfather Fai said. "The destination seems to be narrowed to a few islands in the extreme southeast—nothing of military import."

Fai Anbai had mentally shelved that case long ago, in the face of far more urgent demands. Unless the emperor placed it as a priority, he wouldn't waste his people on it until the more urgent cases were resolved. They were already spread too thin. "Anything else?"

"Yes. This one is quite odd," Grandfather Fai said. "Not in itself, perhaps, so much as the fact that she made the discovery and hoarded it, along with the tracking of the monk we were just talking about. She seems to have been keeping back discoveries in various cases."

"So that she could leap on them first," Fai Anbai said. "Yes, she often did that, so that she could spring the final resolution on us. I always had to ask her directly for status reports, in which case she would admit whatever she had. But I had to know what to ask for."

Grandfather Fai nodded. "I always knew she resented your promotion. I never understood how badly."

Fai Anbai waved that off. "I'll confront her about it when she turns up."

"If. I still think she's dead," Grandfather said—without any sign of regret. "This silence, without even a hint, is far too uncharacteristic."

His son accepted that, and said, "So what did you find that she had secreted?"

Grandfather Fai said, "She didn't just log the messages to the bookseller the imperial children favor, she copied out the entirety of any message that had to do with the imperial family, mimicking the hand of whoever wrote."

Fai Anbai hid his sharp disappointment. That duty—even the copying of messages—was reserved for beginning agents fresh out of training. It was a matter of routine to intercept the bookstore's mail, unseal, read, summarize it in the log, and reseal it before delivering it. In the same way clearing and sweeping the shop for dangers, then maintaining two rings whenever an imperial prince or princess visited had devolved into duty for imperial guards fresh out of training.

"We've been maintaining that log for over ten years," Fai Anbai said. "It's mostly First Princess Manon who uses that shop, and Princess Lily next most frequently. What could Tek Banu possibly find of interest there?"

"Read it for yourself," Grandfather Fai said, tossing over the translated page from Tek Banu's papers.

Fai Anbai glanced down. The letter was addressed to Imperial First Princess Jehan Manon, written in a fine scribal hand. That was nothing new — she received love letters and proposals from all over, especially when some enterprising soul had managed to sneak a painting of her out, to be recopied and sold for gold. Though admittedly none came to the bookstore. But some moon-smitten scholar might have glimpsed her there. So far, nothing out of the ordinary. Unknown scribe, Azure Tranquility Harbor, after full Phoenix Moon of the third month, Year of the Dolphin —

He looked up, startled. "That's right after our poison month!"

He glanced down, then placed Azure Tranquility in his mental map: he'd been there not that long ago. It was a common naval stop between the imperial island and the Silk Islands . . . "Prince Jion — this is where he vanished!"

"Correct. Read the letter. No, rather, see how it's signed."

Fai Anbai cast his gaze down a letter full of nonsense, mostly references to classical poems and old-fashioned but popular plays. Callow showing off.

Signed: *Shigan*.

Fai Anbai's first reaction was a roll of the eyes. "The prince never mentioned sending this letter. I suppose we can ask him about it, and for that matter ask the princess if she ever received it, since we didn't log letters being handed off to their recipients. But what would that give us?" Then he halted himself, annoyed that his former disgust with the spoiled, willful first prince was affecting his judgment. "Nothing, perhaps," he said in a different voice. "But at the same time as the poisoner was abroad? All right, possibly significant. Which brings us to the messiest case."

Yan Yian was already unrolling a huge sheet of very fine paper — the kind ordinarily reserved for the scribes and the artists, and of course for the imperial children to play around with, for they must always have the best.

The three were sitting on mats on the floor. Grandfather Fai shifted the table to the wall as Yan Yian laid out her paper. "First day of the first poisoning."

Fai Anbai had a much smaller one, which he unrolled and laid it next to the larger one. All three bent over to examine them both.

They depicted maps of the inner palace. Each was covered with the tracks of various individuals who had been reported on duty that day. Those were in one color of ink. In another color, the tracks of witnesses who had seen individuals that day, whether at work, or on route, or just glimpsed, sometimes drawn carefully alongside the tracks of the first set.

They had each made a map for the four days that people had turned up with what had been assumed was a sickness. By going through the records exhaustively, they built up a picture of where everyone was their particular day.

When they first took testimony, it had been for a slightly different purpose: to track the spread of the supposed sickness among the servants, and then, at the emperor's private order, to establish the whereabouts of the Su family, as none of their servants had come down sick in those early days. The overworked ferrets had completed that when five Su servants came down with violent cases, three from Su Manor and two from Second Imperial Consort's Inspiration of Drenched Blossoms Pavilion. After the ferrets established the whereabouts of the elder Su clan, from the wily old Right Chancellor down to the plethora of cousins, suspicion of them had been abandoned, and when no one else came down ill, the records were sealed, upon the emperor's decree.

Grandfather Fai, representing himself as a messenger and general aid (he even swept the office and the court) as something to do during his retirement, had gone to the ferret private archive in the middle of the day when it was busiest to make his request, promising to come back on the morrow to pick them up once they'd been hauled out of whatever vault they were stored in.

Unknown to all, Fai Anbai had gone to a very private vault only known to him and his father and his wife, to retrieve the rough notes from all those original interviews — it was these he had been poring over during these past weeks, at a safe distance from the palace. Nights, he had painstakingly constructed his map of everyone's movements.

Three heads bent over the two maps, and slowly tracked the bewildering interconnection of lines.

And one by one they saw that between the two there was a difference: in Fai Anbai's map, there were three sightings of an unidentified female servant, and more disturbingly, two of a man no one recognized. The unidentified laundry woman's sightings were mostly near Drenched Blossoms. Fai Anbai was mostly interested in the sightings of the man. One was in the imperial garden below Prince Vaion's pavilion, and the other on the north side of Prince Jion's pavilion.

On Yan Yian's map, one sighting of the man near the princes' manor was missing — which meant the testimony was missing from the main archive — and two of the laundry woman's sightings were missing, with a third labeled with the name of one of the servants who had died. "This," Grandfather Fai said, "pointing to the laundry woman's sightings, "could be sheer indifference. Who pays attention to another laundry woman? But this sighting of the man near the princes' manors . . ."

The three looked bleakly at each other. Then Fai Anbai glared down at the maps as if he could use strength of will to force them to match. But they didn't match. Four testimonies, specifically the one about the man, had vanished.

"We've got a mole among us," Grandfather Fai said, and sighed.

SEVENTEEN

"THE FAULT LIES WITH me," Grandfather Fai said heavily. "I oversaw the training of everyone in our department except for two, and both have been largely out in the field, Tek Banu being one of them. Leave rooting out the mole to me. You've enough to do."

Fai Anbai acquiesced gladly. Even so, he spent a restless night, rising very early to get started on three separate lines of inquiry, each which demanded full time: the raids in the northwest; the Shadow Panther assault and its leader; the poisoning. Then there were the subsidiary questions, the least of which concerned the first imperial prince. He forced himself to address that first. He was too disciplined not to; lately it seemed every time he let a tiny rabbit of a question concerning the eldest prince hop away, invariably it turned into a tiger.

At least the weapons court where Prince Jion practiced mornings and the emperor evenings was not very far from where the chief ferret was housed. It was also a place that Fai Anbai knew quite well. He could see everything in earshot, and he trusted the swordmaster to make certain that there were no strays lurking out of sight.

Jion was surprised to see the chief ferret turn up to watch his session. His first reaction was displeasure—nothing more than old habit. The recent journey had proved that the ferret chief was actually almost human.

He was put on his mettle, even so. Likewise his guards, fairly-well known after traveling together for a month. After the session ended, the guards vanished to duty, and Fai Anbai descended from the viewing balcony to meet Jion as he wiped down and racked his wooden weapons.

Jion was remembering the feel of Sagacious Blade in his hand, and started when the chief ferret spoke up beside him. "Your imperial highness," he said with a correct bow, "this servant has a question to put to you."

"Something that didn't come up while we were on the ocean?" Jion asked with a dry smile that unexpectedly called his father to mind. But it was merely sardonic, absent of liminal threat as he set the wooden sword in the rack.

"Yes, your imperial highness."

Jion turned. "Ask."

"Did your imperial highness write a letter to anyone at any time once you had left the ship conveying you to White Jade Island?"

Jion did not hide his surprise. "I did, right before I and the other recruits were shipped off to Loyalty. I wrote—that is, I hired a scribe to write to my sister Manon."

He sensed more than saw the ferret chief's flash of surprise, and felt obliged to go on. "Being an idiot, I had some idea of disguising my handwriting by using a scribe, and I never named myself, but dropped hints like boulders that I was free and about to commence a career in the army at a place called Loyalty—all through play and poetry references, you understand. I even gave the name Shigan, which she knew was my favorite character."

He shrugged. "I asked her first thing when I got back if she ever received it. She said she did not, so I decided not to mention it since it never got to her. I did not want to risk dragging her into whatever trouble I was getting myself into," he finished with disarming frankness. "You remember that ride up toward the Pilgrim's Trail." He waved toward Mt. Lir looming above the north end of the palace. "I still dream about that," he added, half under his breath.

Fai Anbai could have stopped there, but the prince's frankness, his cooperation on the recent journey—and Fai Anbai's own desperation to find any clue, however obscure— prompted him to say, "The letter did reach the bookstore. Whether or not the First Imperial Princess received it, of course

I cannot say. We had not been logging deliveries, assuming that once we released a letter it of course went to its intended recipient. And the usual person who did deliveries at that time joined the tea traders when he came of age."

Jion nodded, understanding that the important matters to the ferrets were who wrote, where it came from, and of course its contents — whether they constituted a threat.

Or, so it had been assumed. "If he even remembers — no, you'd think a letter coming for a princess would stick in mind. Unless she gets a lot of letters there? Why would she?"

"Because it's known that she visits there," Fai Anbai said dryly. "Most of those letters are from would-be consorts to a beautiful princess, who think they are clever in bypassing the inner palace. But we still want to talk to him."

Jion froze, his eyes narrowed. He looked unsettlingly like his father now. "But you have the contents of my letter written down somewhere or you wouldn't be asking now. So it was opened at least once. Maybe more times, is that what you are saying?"

Fai Anbai said neutrally, "Including by someone who might know how to hire mercenaries?"

"Impossible . . . no, it was *very* possible," Jion whispered.

Fai Anbai went on, "If someone read that before it got to your imperial sister — or instead of reaching her — that person would have been the only one to know where you were, and under what name."

Jion said slowly, "Assuming they knew it was I behind all those stupid quotations from poems and stories, and could guess that 'Shigan' was my favorite character from the wanderer tales. If so, then it's believable they would even know what I looked like. I think . . ." He looked upward, his mouth a white line. Then he shook his head. "Maybe you're the one to tell what my sister Lily said before she sailed away: that Manon has more than once spoken to a strange man at the bookstore."

"Now, *that's* impossible," Fai Anbai exclaimed. "The first thing the imperial guards do is remove everyone from the premises. I know they assign that duty to very new guards, it being considered a low threat level, but new guards are not incompetent. Far from it. It would have to be the Su steward, or a guard or graywing."

"Lily's maid Ri-Ri was a truthful person. She knows the difference between guards, graywings, and I am reasonably certain she also knows the stewards from both the Su Manor and at Drenched Blossoms. She saw this man around the time I was sent to the Silk Islands, and again more recently, when we were allowed to go into the city again. Lily saw him, too. She said he had hanging earlobes, like a lot of the Su clan."

Fai Anbai had been ordered by the emperor to share the poison investigation with the prince, but he was not ready to say that the ferrets tracked all the Su clan as a regular thing, on the emperor's instruction. If any of them had been at the bookstore, it would be in the records.

"Thank you, your imperial highness," he said, bowing. "I do wish I'd heard this before."

Jion opened his hands. "Lily told me the day before they sailed, directly after the wedding. I never saw either Lily or her maid again, and I didn't think about it while we were traveling." He looked a question. "Should I ask my sister Manon about it? She could probably help." His first thought was that it might repair the distance between them.

Fai Anbai said carefully, formally, "If your imperial highness would consider waiting before discussing this matter with anyone, it would greatly aid these servants."

"I can do that," Jion said. "Though I don't see how it aids anyone. But then I don't know how you'd go about finding the poisoners, especially after all this time. Since it directly concerns me, am I permitted to ask if there is headway in the poison investigation?"

Fai Anbai said, "His imperial majesty specifically gave me permission to share what I know."

Jion looked around. The two of them stood alone in the middle of the courtyard. A cold wind had begun to kick up, and occasional spatters of rain to fall.

Fai Anbai said slowly, "Before we understood that you never reached White Jade Island, security within the inner palace was relaxed with respect to the imperial clans. The palace staff never checked the identities of the many servants accompanying relations of the Ran, the Yu, and the Su families, for example."

Jion knew that would have been considered an insult, unless there was notice sent in advance, and by imperial edict. He also remembered the large trains of servants behind his various aunts and uncles on the Ran side as well as the Su clan and Vaion and Gaunon's Yu clan as well, when they came to the imperial palace; those had been reduced to the minimum ever since the discovery that he had gone missing.

"Tracking down the movements of an individual all this time after the fact is subsequently difficult. It requires painstaking examination of the records, because there is usually some trace. The gardening staff notes who takes fruit or flowers. The kitchens have records of what was ordered on any given day, and who delivered it. Messengers are sent, they see, they are seen. Then there are laborers, who are logged by the work leader, and who might have seen something. The same with painters and carpenters, as there are almost always some sort of repairs going on. The Household Department has numerous departments under them, and not only are their movements recorded, but sometimes there are hints of what they saw that might have been an anomaly. Usually complaints. All that is written down by someone. Those records must be combed through, and as exact a picture of a given day to be built as is possible."

"But you've surely already done this, right?" Jion asked. "In fact, that's what you were doing on the ship while we were traveling, when you weren't reading prisoner interrogation reports, am I right?"

"Correct on both accounts, your imperial highness," Fai Anbai said, acknowledging the intuitive grasp the prince had. This might not be the waste of time he'd dreaded. So he unpeeled another layer of complexity — with its implied trust. "But in addition to reinvestigating those records, I must also investigate the investigators. And the more people who talk about these matters, the easier it is to alter information. Think of it as footprints. The more people who walk a given path, even to search, the further the existing prints are obscured, or even obliterated. I make no imputation against her imperial highness the First Princess, but if she chooses to speak of such matters before one of her relations, or the many Su servants permitted to go back and forth, we cannot control who those servants speak to outside the palace."

Investigate the investigators . . . *He's afraid they've got a traitor in the ferrets.* Jion suppressed a shiver as he gazed out over the leafing trees. So beautiful a place, poisoned with hidden greed and viciousness. All human traits — the birds and the small animals living in and around the imperial parks went about their daily affairs without ever worrying about crowns.

But then there were also humans like Arikanda, who walked through life looking for ways to make it better for those who could not act, and Yskanda, who lived for beauty. Arikanda and Yskanda — the same family! He never would have guessed it. Never. And yet he sensed qualities they shared, including with their elder brother, who called himself Captain Ryu. A very thin disguise, if Imperial Father once exerted himself to discover them: the man standing with him would figure it out in a heartbeat, if he wasn't burdened with all the rest of these affairs, and had clearly set aside the entire matter as a low priority.

Fai Anbai had been waiting, as a good interrogator does. The prince's thought processes were clear — disbelief followed by examination of the known facts, then reaction, followed by . . . What was he thinking now?

Jion blinked and turned the gaze increasingly like his father's to Fai Anbai. "I see. I will not discuss this conversation with anyone, then." Understood by both: *including the emperor.*

Which was a danger in itself. But it didn't take much thought to comprehend how desperate Fai Anbai was to find the traitor in his own midst before he could delve into the poisoning and whatever else he was ordered to ferret out, which might even be connected.

Jion added, "It might be time for me to do some investigating on my own." He saw the twitch of warning in Fai Anbai's face, and raised his hand. "Not by the methods you use. I have no facility with these — would not know how to tell truth from someone telling me what they think I want to hear. But there are other ways of finding information. First, I have a letter to write — you can read it first; I'll have Whiteleaf send it to you, but it needs to go with the next messenger ship to the Easterners."

Fai Anbai said, "I'll be writing to our people in the East, actually."

"All right. Then how about this? I'll host a gathering or two. Perhaps an opera. It's surprising, how much gossip one hears when everyone is relaxed and laughing, maybe a little drunk. Everyone," he added, "except me."

Gossip, yes — and most of it hearsay, speculation, or exaggeration, in Fai Anbai's experience. But he could see that the prince meant to be helpful, and that would certainly keep him busy.

That same morning, in the courtyard behind the Blue Hibiscus in Te Gar, Ari glanced along the row of Redbark hopefuls — tall, short, young (maybe fifteen or sixteen?), old (possibly fifty? A bit older than Father), four males, two females. One of those was Lie Tenek, Ari was delighted to find. Matu had explained that all of them had been spoken for by at least one trusted source among the gallant wanderers — and all were supposedly seekers of justice.

The justice in the storybooks had always been so clear. But in life, Ari had discovered, it was not always the same thing to everyone.

Her gaze stopped on the last of the newcomers, and now she was fairly certain why Matu and Petal wanted to hand off training. He appeared to be twenty, maybe a bit older. He had a splendid chest, like Matu, but unlike Matu, who had short, stocky legs, he was tall. Not lynx-muscled, like Jion. This fellow was more like a horse — a splendid one, but brawny. However, his main distinguishing marks were his expression, one of challenge, and his hair, which was even more curly than hers, with a definite reddish streak along the top, as if the sun had created a bit of a rooster's crest.

Not surprisingly, Ouyan Jin went by Rooster.

As soon as she walked out to the courtyard, Rooster's gaze scraped from her own unruly topknot to the toes of her boots, and his mouth twisted into disbelief.

She sighed inwardly, then launched into the talk she'd planned out, modeled after Master Ki's lessons. "There are as many definitions of 'cultivation' as there are sects. Maybe even as many as there are martial artists. Who can give me some examples?"

Lie Tenek, delighted to see Ari again, and warned to make no references to Firebolt, said, "The most obvious is to train until a person is better at fighting than anyone else."

The older woman said, "Cultivation to me means challenging myself."

Ari clasped her hands gallant wanderer-style, enjoying being able to do that once again, and began to walk back and forth.

One of the other young fellows said, "Some say a lot of stuff about how cultivation is improvement of the mind, and ascending the Path, but I think a lot of them really want to be powerful, whatever they say." He sidled looks in both directions, and when Rooster snorted juicily, he flushed to the ears.

"I think you're right," Ari said, and was glad to see the flush die down a little.

"There are also Essence masters," Lie Tenek murmured, eyes on the sky.

Ari tromped very near her toes in passing by, but didn't quite step on them.

"There are bullies, like the Shadow Panthers," Petal said, looking serious.

Ari clasped her hands again. "Another truth. One thing I discovered as a child, and there were several bullies in our small villages, is that bullies aren't all the same. Some get that way trying to survive when their lives have had more than their share of bad luck. Some even want to protect weaker family members or friends. And then there are those who just like beating people up. Those are not welcome in Redbark. There are enough sects out there, including Shadow Panthers, who will welcome them."

Rooster had been sighing.

Ari turned to him. "Something to say?"

"I'm trying to be polite, but are we going to have warmups and sparring, or speeches?"

"Wait and see," Ari said. She had already decided that she was not going to start off here by fighting types like Rooster. She knew that whatever she said, that's all they'd remember.

"Redbark's cultivation is to train us, body, mind, spirit, to fight for justice for those who can't get it for themselves. But first we have to learn what justice is. I've made plenty of mistakes about that, and am learning all the time, that there is no single answer that fits every situation. However, there are basic cultivation exercises that will enable us to be stronger in body, mind, and spirit. And those start with breathing."

"Breathing!" That was Rooster. "You're joking, right?"

"No."

"Who are you, anyway? How can you be any sort of master? You're younger than I am."

"One thing Redbarks discover is that we can learn from anybody. Including birds in flight, and insects, and people younger than us. I was going to start right in, but let me make one demonstration—something I learned from Ghost Moon monks."

"Monks!" Rooster gave a crack of laughter.

Ari pulled her staff. Rooster's brows lifted when he saw the two halves—he recognized an excellent weapon, at least. Then they rose further when Ari snapped the pieces together in one fast movement, planted her feet, and without any further words, set the staff to humming.

One hand, then the other.

"All right, that's a good trick, but—"

"See those iron sconces set up at each end of the court?" She pointed at iron candle holders, one at the north wall, one at the west, south, and east.

Without waiting for assent, she slung her staff and sent a blast of Essence wind at the north one. The heavy iron sconce fell over with a loud *clan-n-n-g!*

Voom! Voom! The east and west sconces hit the stones.

Then she whirled and air crackled as a thin stream of fire shot from the end of the staff and hit the south sconce. It glowed red briefly before crashing down.

She grounded the staff with a crack.

"You've got a charm on that staff," Rooster said, but with question in his voice.

Ari tossed it to him. "Go ahead. Try it."

Rooster did—and tried again. He tried to spin it, but the heavy wood clattered to the ground. He came forward, mouth crooked. "No. I cannot do that."

"I'll teach you as much as I can," Ari said. "But we'll begin with cultivation."

She sat cross-legged on the ground, and everyone followed suit. Of course they didn't need Master Ki's aids to Essence breathing and mind-clearing to learn the basic stances of Redbark form, but she figured working on clearing anger from their minds would be a first step.

Before any of them learned Redbark, they were going to think like Redbark.

EIGHTEEN

DURING THOSE FIRST DAYS after that terrifying ferret smashed Danno's kneecaps, Hanu alternated between caring for him and quietly readying for a journey, though the idea of leaving Burning Rock grieved her sorely. She did not want to go, but she shared Danno's conviction that if one ferret could find them, others surely were on the way. In fact, he woke one morning after the initial fever went down, saying, "I thought they traveled in teams of two. Or more."

She didn't care if it was two or twenty. "We cannot endanger these good people."

Danno agreed. "Wolves among rabbits. As soon as I can stand up, we'll go. Give me three days, five at the most."

Five days later he could not stand without going off into a dead faint.

But he forced himself to try. Each day he tried to stand, and then to shuffle forward a step, a process that left him sweat-drenched and gasping from the pain. His first goal was to walk out of there, but the sense of urgency they both felt forced him to settle for getting himself to his cart, which she took apart so that the back end lay flat. The healer had been adamant about not bending his knees in the slightest degree for at least two months. "Three would be better," the physician warned. "You are not as young as you were, however strong you might consider yourself."

The Snow Crane shaman who had been teaching Hanu specialized in spiritual healing, but as she said, spirits in the middle world are inextricably tied to bodies. She listened to the physician, and nodded agreement, saying, "Healing takes its own time."

While he lay helpless, Hanu continued her healer's work, but began talking about aging parents and an uncle who had not long to live. On foggy days, when visibility was poor, she rowed out to the ferret's single-sail boat, and began to prepare it for them.

Her first time aboard, she thought at first it had been abandoned. That she was wrong about Tek Banu having sailed it. The structure at the back was too small and flimsy to be called a cabin. Inside was little beyond a moldering blanket and a trunk.

Hanu picked up the blanket, thinking it ought to be laundered and repaired, but the smell brought instantly back that terrible Tek Banu. Hanu threw it down again, her stomach heaving. She opened the trunk, and found a sack of rice, a cook pot, a chunk of salt on one side, and a tray of cooking implements above a folded robe, trousers, and stockings. Hanu frowned—what would you cook with these things?

She picked up a strangely shaped knife and turned it over, then realized it was a flaying knife, and threw it down again, her breath hissing out. All these implements, designed for tweaking and digging and cutting . . . Were these possibly instruments of torture? Kept with extra food and cooking utensils?

Once again her stomach heaved. Using a tong (what was that for, holding hot coals?) she picked up the rest of the items and dropped them into the middle of the blanket. Then she added the tong, rolled everything up in the nasty blanket and flung the bundle over the side of the craft.

As she watched it sink into the deep, she washed her hands in seawater, wondering what made someone become such a person. Was it upbringing, or did the gods truly create such people for purposes unimaginable to the finite human mind? Not that she considered herself peerless in any sense, especially as a mother. Her own upbringing had been so odd, with a sister leaving normal life for the seclusion of the temple; Danno had been even more hapless about child-raising, as his entire existence had been shaped to exert himself to protect someone else's life.

This had been especially clear after First Son and little Arikanda had vanished—Hanu had seen some of the other parents look askance at how serenely tough Olt had gone about his daily life. It was no false serenity. He was confident that by the time Arikanda had reached age ten he had given her everything she needed to survive, as long as her brother was looking out for her, and surely she'd get even better training than was possible in Imai, while keeping the family secret safe. He, with his singular upbringing, would have sought the same at ten.

Before the three children left that spring, she knew the aunties had sometimes gossiped behind her back, especially about the youngest two. *The first boy is fine enough, a tiger father has a tiger for a son, but that second one has more than a touch of the Ghost Moon about him. Ayah, he's so beautiful no one will ever care. Little Third, she's a rascal, that one, doesn't know if she's boy or girl. If she was mine my hair would already be white the way she runs the rooftops! No daughter of mine would ever be allowed . . .* But however her three children might have turned out in these long years she had not seen them, she had felt the crimson string of love stretching steadily from her heart to them all. She knew that they never would have become the soul-desiccated wretch this Tek Banu had been.

Enough reverie—she had work still ahead of her!

She forced herself to look around, and assess the sailboat for other mute testimony to the dead woman. Hanu had intended to use whatever was left over, but her mind changed; it was all unclean, and over the side it went, even the rice. She would eat no food that had rested within the reach of those implements.

She rowed herself back, the mental list of necessities getting longer and longer.

The next time she came out, it was during a rainstorm, which would give her a natural rinse. She lugged a brush and a jug of soap made of ground honey-locust bean, with fresh herbs to strew about for scent. As warm rain poured down, she scrubbed every length of wood within reach, including as far up the mast as her brush could go, in an effort to remove Tek Banu's unclean touch from the wood.

On a sunny day, she brought Danno's carpentry tools and several bits of precious wood. She had learned about carpentry along with him back when they first arrived in Imai, and in fact had aided him, until the children came along and claimed the time she did not spend as a healer; over the next week she strengthened the shack into more of a small cabin, and then brought out items such as an extra set of clothing for each of them, a thick quilt to sleep on (for she knew that the farther north they sailed, the colder it would get while still winter) and one for a cover.

The prospective journey became inevitable in her mind when she took her hoarded healers' books out, her jars of herbs, and her last bits of Essence paper.

Then she brought to the sailboat a bag of rice, some chilis, pickled vegetables and dried grapes and apricots, which would keep for weeks though she trusted that she and Danno would not remain on the water that long. After that, flint, coals, and cooking oil. Last, four covered buckets on whose sides she had pasted hoarded Essence paper. She had painstakingly inscribed purification talismans on these in case the sailboat was becalmed: she was not adept enough to turn salt water into fresh, but her charms would keep rainwater from turning stale.

Before she brought her last treasure, the phoenix feather, she took it to the Snow Crane shaman with whom she had been studying. To this old woman, she did not lie. "We must go," Hanu said. "Our being here is not safe for the others."

The old shaman closed her eyes. "We do have protections," she said at last. "But these, as in all things between Heaven and the Underworld, have their limits. Perhaps it is your fate to go."

"Before I do, I wish you show you something. I have only showed it to the Phoenix Moon monk who lived with us before." With that, she opened the little cedar box, and disclosed the phoenix feather, which was now translucent, a shimmer of gold through which one could easily see the grain of the wood.

The shaman hissed in a breath, then let it out. "Yes," she said, after a very long pause. She frowned at Hanu. "Safely hoarded, and to what end? Almost all the virtue is gone." Then, to Hanu's dismayed expression, she relented. "It is still here. These things . . . are rare. And difficult for us to entirely understand. But I believe you must use its virtue for redress soon, before it is entirely vanished back to the upper realm." Her gaze narrowed consideringly. "But if you wish to preserve it from inimical eyes while you travel, you would be wise to lay some trinket in the box."

"Won't that destroy the phoenix feather? It looks so very

fragile."

In answer, the shaman poked her finger through the middle of the feather. Hanu gasped, but all that happened was the finger shimmering golden where it penetrated the feather. And when she withdrew her finger, there was the feather, completely undisturbed.

"The villagers saw it when it first fell," Hanu said. "How could it not be seen by some?"

"Your villagers were not binders," the shaman said. "For talismans such as this, inimical eyes are those who use talismanic power to bind and to rend."

"I understand," Hanu said—though she didn't, really, but time was pressing. "My mother's favorite hair clasp, that I was saving for my daughter. It's worth little as an item to be bought, though it is a treasure to my heart."

They bowed to one another, and Hanu went to do just that.

On her next trip to the boat, she took the phoenix feather, now with the hair clasp in its box. As each load went out, she began to erase all traces of her existence from Burning Rock. It took much longer to remove all traces of herself than that of Danno, for he had been raised to live out of a small trunk. The entirety of his belongings only took a single trip of the rowboat, the heaviest item his sword, kept hidden all this time.

At last she was done—and Danno said that very night, "I can get myself to the cart. Rain is coming in. We'll get wet, but we'll be hidden from view, and the buckets will fill with fresh water. Let's leave tonight."

"I'll say our farewells at day's end," she promised.

She took leave of each person she knew, keeping her destination as brief as possible, for she hated lying to those she trusted, and who trusted her. They all had become inexpressibly dear.

In her pack she slid as many fresh foodstuffs as she could fit, and then came the grinding effort and pain of helping Danno to the cart, and taking him to the shore. From cart to rowboat resulted in his gasping for breath, drenched with sweat. As he lay there, breathing against fresh agony, she loaded his cart with rocks and towed it into the water until it sank out of sight. It was a shame to destroy good wood like that, especially when it was so rare on that island. But they must not leave any part of themselves behind for the ferrets to sift for clues: both their little cottages, indistinguishable from most of the others in the valley, were now bare and scrubbed clean.

She rowed them out to the sailboat, where she had erected a rope-pulley from the mast at his direction; with a rope in his armpits, she was able to raise him to the sailboat's side.

That operation taxed the last of his strength. He lay on the deck in the rain, his knees throbbing white fire to the beat of his heart. He whispered, "We'll tow the rowboat with us."

She disassembled the pulley, affixed the rowboat to the rope, and under his direction got the sail set. While she was doing all this work, he dragged himself backward by elbow-crawling until he was under the support of the shelter.

The night airs were mild, but with the sun the next day sailed another band of gray clouds and a brisk wind. The sailboat came alive. Navigation was simple — in the mornings, keep the sun on the right cheek, and after noon, on the left.

So embarked the second great journey of their lives, into the unknown; when they had left Imai for Burning Rock, they had had a destination in mind, and even the name of a shaman at the temple. Now, as they had been at sixteen and twenty, they were venturing into new waters. Before, they had wanted only safe harbor. Now, the goal was for Danno to heal enough so that they could find and gather their three children, and then set out once more for somewhere out of the emperor's reach.

At first Danno insisted that being out in the fresh air was doing him good, and he already felt better, but his color continued to be pale, and he was feverish at night. Hanu dosed him with all the blood-strengthening herbs she had, and while he slept she prayed over him. She even slipped a precious healing talisman under his side of the bedding, though she knew he disregarded such things. "Heaven gave me two good hands, two good eyes, and the brain to use them. It's an insult to beg for more," he had said now and then, when she took the children to attend rituals conducted by the Snow Crane God shaman who visited Sweetwater four times a year.

During the daylight, Hanu knew better than to fuss over Danno, who insisted on sitting at the tiller in order to do his part. He hated leaving the bulk of the labor to Hanu, but he finally had to admit that shifting himself from his cottage to the boat had set him back a little.

"A little" soon proved to be vast understatement. After a week of sailing through intermittent storms, he finally admitted that perhaps it might do him good to remove the bandages, which never seemed to dry out, and let sun and air heal him.

She helped roll up his loose trouser legs to his thighs.

What Hanu saw when she finally got the bandages off appalled her. The unwrapping alone had set him sweating and gritting his teeth, which was a very bad sign. While he sat on deck, his legs stretched out before him, she untied the bamboo supports at either side of each leg and washed them and the ties. Even the air moving over his knees was excruciating. He said nothing, but she could tell he was in pain by his breathing as well as by the fact that he ate very little of the food she made, whereas he was drinking great quantities of water and ginger-willow tea, with tiny pinches of her flower herbs in it to help mask the taste.

As well they had frequent rain to refill their buckets. Hanu insisted he sit inside the shelter while she tended sail.

So it went as they moved steadily northwards toward the flat horizon, without seeing any islands except for an occasional rocky bump on which nothing could land but birds. His legs remaining unbandaged except for the bamboo supports tied at thigh and calf meant she could examine him silently, without disturbing him.

After some ten days, she thought there might be a little improvement. The swelling was not quite so terrible, or surely that was not merely being used to the sight? No, he was eating a little more . . .

She woke one morning to a dark line on the horizon: a storm, from the looks of it much bigger than the cloudbursts that had swept overhead for the past days. She said nothing, but made up some ginger and willow tea for Danno, and made certain that everything was tightly sealed and as tied down as she could get it.

When Danno fell asleep, she sat on the bow, praying over her beads. It was not begging, she had explained once. Prayer was a conversation, a method of gratitude that could be more heartfelt than rituals. But she knew that evening she was pleading as she listened to Danno's hissing breath.

The storm struck in the middle of the night.

Hanu had bound tiller and sail the way Danno had instructed. For a time both held as the waves climbed to wall height, then to roof height, and then ever larger, until the little craft climbed at a steep angle, then slid down into valleys between the waves so deep that they lost the wind, and the boat was ever in danger of broaching. The waves towered higher, the roar of the wind so loud that they never noticed when the rowboat they'd been towing smashed into the stern of the sailboat on one of those downward slides, its splinters washing past them down the deck and out to sea. Danno steadied the tiller, his useless legs braced against the sailboat's sides, his upper body straining to keep them running before the tearing wind.

Hanu clung to the taut rope binding the sail, her mind running in a stream of prayers and memories. Usually she prayed for the children in reverse order, the youngest needing the most, but for some reason this night her thoughts winged to Yskanda, far away in that terrible imperial city, a prisoner.

She imagined him a ghostly figure, something like the grandfather she remembered from childhood, impossibly handsome, distantly kind, his mind so far removed from human concerns. But Yskanda as a small boy had managed to stay tethered to his family by love . . .

She prayed for them all, for Danno, for herself—

CR-R-R-A-A-ACK!

The boat gave a great jolt. The mast split, then, grabbed by the wind, speared into the inky waters and vanished.

The shelter was right behind it, flapping madly like a demented bat. It, too, was gone, with a cruelly deliberate suddenness.

Hanu flung herself down the deck when the sailboat began to rise at that angle again. The wind and the thunder were so loud she could not hear herself cry out. She closed shivering fingers around Danno's, and together they held the tiller still, though it vibrated violently with every new surge.

The children will never know what happened to us. She wept silently, turning her numb, sleet-battered face into her armpit, and grieved at never seeing her children again. But even in anguish she fought to live, trying not to breathe in the gouting rain flying sideways.

She tried to see their sweet faces again in memory, but it was neither First Son—like his father, as solid as earth—nor their fiery sprite Arikanda with whom she felt a steady, insistent tug, every bit as strong as the red string of ancient poems. Perhaps because her quiet, dreaming middle child had been entranced with the sea, her thoughts bent toward Yskanda. She could see him so clearly, the smooth round cheek of childhood, his small hands careful and tender, utterly without the careless cruelty of childhood, when he rescued a cricket from a puddle that must have been an uncrossable ocean to the insect. Her yearning reached for him, a steadfast tug from heart to heart, until memory jumbled into dreams as sheer exhaustion caused her to fall briefly to sleep between waves, then jerk awake again when the ship began the downward slope, water surging down the deck.

Her hands had gone numb as one clung to the base of the tiller, the other curled protectively around the herbal that represented her life's work. Her face turned toward Danno, who had managed to tie himself to the arm of the tiller. Neither of them noticed when the waves gradually began to lessen toward dawn; they dropped into profound slumber, Hanu waking first to a bright blue world of sky and water.

Pain crashed through Hanu's head as she reached first thing for her water buckets. Half of the fresh water had slopped out of each. She quickly replaced the lids, already working out how to ration her own water as she moved to check on Danno. He slept on his side. His legs were still forced into stiffness by the bamboo strips, but they were turned in an awkward position, very worrying.

She tried to straighten him out without waking him. He uttered a soft groan, the first she had ever heard from him. His face was hot with fever.

They had survived the storm, but their ordeal was far from over.

NINETEEN

"I REALLY BELIEVE THIS is even better than the Journey to the Clouds," Court Artist Yoli said — then his eyes rounded and he spat to the side, "Pei! Pei! Pei!" And made hasty signs warding against bad luck.

Yskanda made the same signs. It would never do to tempt the imps of ill luck by bragging before a picture was even finished. And yet in his heart — in both their hearts — they knew that this one would be superlative.

And it was all the better for being the work of many hands, Yskanda believed. His was the design, but Court Artist Yoli had invited certain masters and two very skilled apprentice painters to add their expertise to the portions they had provided sketches for. Both apprentices were about to take the Imperial Examination in a matter of days, which all expected them to do well in. Then they would be folded into service, beginning their own projects.

Yskanda woke each day still aware that he was a prisoner, but never had his captivity been less onerous. There might come a time when he would have to run, and ignore the consequences — such as the fact that the young imperial guards who accompanied him into the city would assuredly lose their lives if he vanished — but that time was not now. Nothing occurred to disturb the quiet waters of his life: He had his work. He had not seen the emperor, except from the uncross-able distance between them in the throne room, since New year's Two Moons.

And he had read all Brother Pine's books on divination and augury, skipping past all the sections on preparation for same, and reading only the portions having to do with closing off one's access to the world of the spirit.

It had taken Yskanda some time to learn to master that inner gate, but determination and discipline had prevailed. Now, every night before he slept, no matter how tired he was, he sat on his bed and concentrated on rebuilding the mental wall around his thoughts, brick by brick. After that he could lie down.

Then there was the fact that Prince Jion had sailed away on his father's orders the month previous, but had left instruct-ions that Yskanda was to take his place leading the nightly discussions of the scholars.

At first he could not understand why he was chosen in-stead of one of the scribes, until it occurred to him that he was in no wise competition. He had already passed the Imperial Examination (and many questions about the experience had been put to him that first night); he had no intention, or desire, to leave his post for one under a court minister. These things he was aware of; what he did not consider was that he was an excellent discussion leader, who remembered everything he had read, but was patient in prompting, and generous in guiding the discussion back on point without using verbal weapons such as sarcasm or confrontation.

After a successful month of meetings, he arrived one night, a few days before the Imperial Examination was to occur, aware of a slight headache building. He discovered the early arrivals again holding a bamboo box of divination sticks, which one of them had just cast. Another had a well-thumbed divination book spread open, his finger on a line.

At Yskanda's appearance, they looked up, a couple of them sheepish, or defensive, and one scowling. "We're trying to divine the likeliest questions," Su Ysek said.

Yskanda clasped his hands in his sleeves as he bowed.

"Do you know how to cast the sticks?" Ran Hamin, son of an exalted prince, asked. He wanted very badly to earn a good post in court, rather than be sent home to sit around as a princeling in boring Ran, where nothing ever happened.

"We did not have any sticks when I was small," Yskanda

said tranquilly — typical of Talents, many of them thought, utterly undisturbed at admitting to low birth and poverty. "And we probably would not have, even if we could have afforded such things. People used shells and small rocks. My father tended to say things like *Depend on your own two hands*, or if the Snow Crane shaman had visited, and people asked her for divinations, *Everything she says is so vague it could be applied to anything, including tomorrow's breakfast*. But our mother was more serious, saying that true readings were another way of seeing the affinities of everything in the world. The problem was learning how to understand them."

The Ran twins gathered their divination sticks as Yskanda spoke — just as Ze Kai appeared. He was easily the best of the scholars, but he had a sarcastic tongue, and had applied it especially bitterly on Yskanda's first night, when one of the other scholars had brought up divining the questions at this year's examination.

"If you put as much effort into reading as you do with those sticks and the rest of it, you might actually pass," Ze Kai had said witheringly. "Leave fate to take care of itself."

Yskanda remembered the hurt in Ze Kai's face the spring before, when Princess Lily's marriage was negotiated, and his pain and helpless anger right after the wedding. As Ze Kai eyed the bamboo box, Yskanda bowed a welcome to him and forestalled a comment by addressing the Ran twins. "I overheard something about placating southeast spirits, which would come under the sun's rule, would it not? Which may or may not give a clue to the examination, but it happens to relate to today's discussion question: You are an official under a governor, who has been called to the imperial city. You've discovered a sect dedicated to the Willow Twig. What do you do?" He added, "This question has appeared on the Imperial Examination four times, the last over ten years ago. So it could appear again."

He saw them make the connection from Willow Twig to Suanek, the early sun goddess, and from there the spirits of the southeast corner of any given space. While his connecting the reading the two had attempted to this question didn't solve or help anything, it might convey a sense of hidden order, never a bad thing with such tensions imminent.

Ze Kai sat down, the long ribbons on his half-bound up hair reaching the floor behind his cushion. The scholars all wore simple ribbons tying their clasps, some longer than others. Ze Kai, as heir to a powerful duke, wore long ones, nearly as long as those of the two princelings, but that was his only affectation. He wore no rings, nor fabulous embroidery on his sober-colored robes.

He said slowly, "I would first inquire whether or not this was a Willow Twig Heresy — which of course must be defined. There were several different ones."

"We'd better know the year and dynasty," Vaion's cousin Kui Zuinan murmured. "As well as the heresy itself."

"I can tell you that," Su Siar said over her fan — she had been showing up, partly to look at Yskanda's beautiful face, and partly to be well-established among the group when Jion did return. She described the dances and the rites of the heresy — and what had happened when it was put down.

Phlegmatic Bi Kandatai chewed his lower lip, then said, "What if the question is about *when* a sect or a popular idea becomes a heresy?"

"That's easy, Cousin." Su Ysek snapped his fan. "Whenever the ritual puts someone — in this case, Suanek — at the center of the rites instead of the emperor." Here everyone bowed toward the throne, hands clasped. "Who is the Chosen of Heaven."

"What steps must our official follow?" Yskanda asked.

He did not know. Further, he did not care, for that was entirely the province of court, but the headache behind his temples had begun panging insistently.

". . . to remember that Heaven and the emperor are connected. If the emperor misbehaves, Heaven retaliates by sending droughts, and by making the fire dragons in the earth move, or water dragons manifest in the sky, igniting terrible storms, which in turn cause destruction and storms," Bi Kandatai stated firmly.

"Exactly," Ze Kai said. "The last Willow Twig heresy maintained that there is nothing Humankind can do to fix the other two powers — Heaven and Earth — except to beg the influence of Suanek, who watches out for Humankind, which is how the rites began placing the sun at the center . . ."

Ze Kai and Bi Kandatai traded off supplying the rules and rites of court, then shifted to a discussion of laws, which was what Yskanda had expected. Between the two of them they had surely given the others plenty of reading to catch up on.

At last the bell rang the middle Dragon hour — time for the discussion to end, and the scholars to depart for home or quarters. He bowed them off, as usual unaware of Su Siar's lingering appreciation; his mind was on tea, which he hoped would warm him. If only he was not so very cold!

The walk, which he usually enjoyed, seemed longer than ever, and though the night was mild, his mind shot back in memory to another night, during the journey after his capture, when a terrible storm overtook the ferret ship he was on. He found himself unconsciously doing the deep breathing Brother Pine had taught him as he recollected the inky waters raising the ship and then plunging it down again, sea and wind and sky in a whirling rage. And though the ship had got a great gash in its side, which ought to have capsized it, it had remained afloat, riding each wave, with Yskanda inside the damaged vessel, watching, watching, as if he could keep it afloat by will.

He felt the same way now. It was strange how memory flooded him. He gave up trying to eat and fell into bed with his tea half drunk, shivering under his quilt as his mind swept up shadowy waves, then down again, serrying through storm memories and circling around his parents . . .

His parents . . .

He dreamed. The dream took him into the heart of a gale so violent he lay gasping for breath, then coughing as if choking on cold brine. Juniper, startled out of sleep in his tiny alcove off Yskanda's room, listened in increasing consternation, then finally rose, lit a candle, and entered Yskanda's chamber. What he saw shocked him into almost dropping the candle.

Yskanda lay tangled in his covers, his hair loose and draggling wet. How could he be sweating so hard on such a cold night? When Yskanda gasped, coughing, Juniper sprang to the bed and tried calling to Yskanda, without any effect.

This was terrible! Juniper hovered. His orders were clear: if anything threatened Assistant Court Artist Yskanda, he was to instantly report to his supervisor. He did so — leaving the door open — then presently fled back, his supervisor, like him in his sleep clothes, on his heels.

After one appalled look, the elder graywing sent Juniper running again, this time headlong down the servants' byways to report to sympathetic Melonseed or austere Bitternail, whoever was on night duty. They would know whether or not to apprise the emperor. The supervisor then roused one of his assistants, and sent him for an imperial physician.

Because the servants' ways are roundabout, Jion, at that moment returning from a dinner and a play the dowager empress his grandmother had hosted to welcome Jion back, spotted Juniper running bareheaded, in his night rail. Jion knew Juniper from his visits to the court artists' workshop, and halted, shocked. Graywings were never seen without their hats.

He put out a hand, and the poor graywing stumbled to a stop and flung himself into a bow. "I must not stay, your imperial highness," Juniper babbled to the ground. "This servant must report to the emperor—"

Jion picked out from the stream of words that Yskanda was sick—out of his mind with some sort of mysterious fever. Knowing that the sight of his father would assuredly make everything worse for Yskanda, Jion acted on impulse. "Let's go back," he said. "I'll take responsibility. We do not want to disturb the emperor if it turns out to be a stomach gripe, eh?"

Juniper's eyes rounded in terror. He bowed wordless agreement and the two raced all the way back.

The imperial physician got there just ahead of them. They entered the room to find him trying to catch Yskanda's wrist as he moved restlessly on the bed, beads of sweat running down his face; the room smelled oddly of brine.

"Hold him down," the physician said to the graywing.

Juniper, a strong young man, went to catch Yskanda's arm—to be blocked and flung off in a martial move that would have been applauded out in the imperial guards' practice court. Poor Juniper tumbled head over heels, night clothes flapping. Yskanda was clearly a lot stronger than he looked.

"Here, let's both try," Jion offered as Juniper picked himself up and rejoined them at the bedside. Juniper bowed acquiescence to Jion, and both reached; Jion saw Juniper hesitate, for which he did not blame the hapless graywing. With the result that Jion touched Yskanda first. "Assistant Court Artist Afan, be calm. We are here to help you," he said as he laid his hands on Yskanda's shoulders and pressed.

Yskanda stiffened, his blind eyes opaque, but then he relaxed into bonelessness.

For a long breath nobody moved.

"I think you can take his pulse now," Jion said.

Juniper backed away a step, waiting for orders as the physician took Yskanda's resistless wrist in hand. Then he looked up, frowning. "It is not a sickness I know. His pulse is galloping, as if he bore a tremendous burden. Perhaps a demon has taken —"

"I cannot believe that," Jion exclaimed, with all the authority of his rank. "Afan Yskanda is the last person I've ever met who would countenance a demon possessing him."

The physician was offended, but because this was an imperial prince, he had to swallow the insult. "Perhaps this ignorant and lowly wretch might fetch a fellow imperial physician, who might be familiar with such a case and teach us all."

Jion blinked at him, and realized he had denied the old fart face. His father would not be pleased. "That is an excellent notion," he said, forcing his voice to cordiality. After all, anytime the imperial family had a hangnail, there were never fewer than five of these imperial physicians muttering and mumbling over their needles and vile embrocations. "Between the two of you, combining your wisdom and experience, you will surely know what to do."

Somewhat mollified, the imperial physician bowed with immense dignity, and walked out at a sedate pace that made Jion furious all over again.

He turned to Juniper. "Run to the . . . yes, I think it's the Ghost Moon temple. Brother Pine, I believe he said. Fetch him."

Strictly speaking, the monks were exempt from secular commands, but when the abbot had been wakened and learned that his sometime student was in crisis, he lifted his hand and Brother Pine followed Juniper back to Yskanda's room.

He sank to his knees beside the bed, where Jion was still holding Yskanda steady — though he had stopped coughing so wetly. The supervisor graywing was also there, which with the newcomer made quite a crowd. Jion moved back to let Brother Pine take his place.

Yskanda gave a great, crackling cough, and doubled up. Droplets of salt water flew off him, startling everyone. Brother Pine sank down, eyes closed. He paled, then glanced up at the prince. "If your imperial highness could resume what you did before?"

"I just held him down so the physician could take his pulse."

Brother Pine said, "This is a matter of Essence. Did not Brother Afan tell you of your affinity? I can see that your

Essence talent is air—he cannot breathe without your connection."

As soon as Jion pressed his hands once more onto Yskanda's shoulders, the latter's shuddering breathing eased. It was still harsh, a struggle, but he was no longer coughing.

The two graywings faded back, ready to leap in any direction if given an order.

For a protracted time they all remained where they were, Yskanda lying there, eyes wide open, but focused far beyond the simple beam ceiling overhead. Brother Pine sat beside the bed, eyes closed, palms cupped. Jion stayed bent over, hands gripping Yskanda's bony shoulders. He realized he was counting those breaths; he was not certain if it was real or fancy that if he took a longer breath, Yskanda did as well. Beyond question, he breathed with Yskanda, whose complexion slowly lost that terrible bluish cast, as if he were suffocating.

The imperial physician reappeared with a colleague, who bore a bitter-smelling brew. They hmmmed over Yskanda's face, each tested the pulse in his wrist, and then the second physician tried to get Yskanda to swallow the stuff in the covered cup.

Perforce Jion had to free him so that the graywings could lift Yskanda, who groaned, and flung himself gasping to one side. He coughed wetly and spat the medicine out, making a mess of himself and the bed. Then he fell back, hands flailing like someone drowning. Jion pressed his shoulders once again. Yskanda drew a long, hissing breath and collapsed into limp unconsciousness.

For a time no one moved, everyone watching the slow rise and fall of Yskanda's chest.

"We've got him quiet," Jion said to the two physicians. "We will call you if he takes a turn for the worse."

Thus dismissed, the two withdrew, their dignity intact; they both were aware that this assistant court artist was under the emperor's special commands, and no one wanted to be responsible for his death from some mysterious illness.

Jion looked at the supervisor graywing. "Could you fetch new bedding?"

The supervisor, treated as a lackey, bowed and withdrew; he was less offended than he could have been as he, too, did not want to be by if something dire happened.

Jion said to Juniper, "If I must be here all night, perhaps

some fresh tea."

"This incompetent one will see to it at once, your imperial highness," Juniper said, and bowed himself out.

Alone with the monk, Jion said, "This is a matter of Essence, is it not?"

Brother Pine opened his eyes, then waved a hand. The candle streamed, then went out. Jion saw Yskanda shimmer-ing in blue-green Essence.

Not just Yskanda. He realized the glow extended up his own body. He was already lightheaded with exhaustion and with surprise; everything seemed unreal. Just when Jion was convinced he was imagining the glow, Brother Pine waved again, and the candle relit. The glow faded in its light.

The supervisor returned with neatly folded bedding. Juniper returned with tea. After a hesitation he poured out a cup, bowed and offered it to Jion, who grabbed it one-handed and drained it, hot as it was.

Turtle Watch passed into Tiger Watch; Jion finished all the tea.

Phoenix Watch began, with morning nigh, when Brother Pine opened his eyes. "He is asleep."

Jion slowly lifted his hands, gazing doubtfully down; he could not tell the difference between unconsciousness and sleep. His back creaked from bending over for so long.

Yskanda was breathing normally, though his cheeks showed the flush of fever.

The two graywings set about moving Yskanda's resistless body to change the sodden bedding, and Jion followed Brother Pine out into the hallway. As soon as the door was shut, he said, "What's this about Essence? I don't have any Essence talent."

Brother Pine shook his head slowly. "You appear to have an affinity for air, which strengthens Brother Afan's water affinity. In turn his Essence affinity, which is very powerful, strengthens yours. He did not tell you?"

"Not about that. He told me he was going to learn how to shut it all out . . ." Jion stopped there, not wanting to get into why Yskanda would want to keep something like a wild Essence talent secret. Though all paths led to the emperor.

Brother Pine let a small sigh escape. "And so, here he is, as I warned him. He ought to have been practicing to master Essence flow."

Jion said, "Air Essence? Could that also have . . . affinity . . .

with a fire Essence, ah, person?"

Brother Pine studied him, then said, "Air is volatile, as is fire, but unlike fire it has affinity with everything."

Not exactly helpful. Ayah, he hadn't expected much. Jion said, "What exactly happened in there? Is he sick, or not?"

Brother Pine's expression altered. "That," he began, "is harder to explain. I am still a seeker, and have never seen anything quite like this matter. But it seems he was sending Essence to someone at a distance, and using himself up entirely, instead of sending the Essence through him harmlessly, as he would have learned if he had practiced the way I taught him. He was also absorbing as much of the danger as he could. At a guess, someone had fallen into a lake, or a river, or maybe even the sea, and there appeared to be . . ." Brother Pine hesitated, unwilling to say that he sensed intent in that storm. He was not certain at all—this was something far outside his experience. That, and proximity to imperial power, made him shake his head. "I know nothing more."

"How can I learn about air Essence?"

Brother Pine said, "He recopied all the books I gave him. I saw them in there."

Jion thanked him. The monk took his leave. Jion was tired after that long night, but when he heard the rise and fall of voices from inside, he laid his hand to the door again.

The two graywings bowed. Yskanda's face turned wearily on the pillow. He began to struggle up, but Jion said, "Stay there." To the graywings, "I'll be going straight to the palace to inform my imperial father what happened here. No need for you to make a special trip to report—I suggest you get your rest first."

Jion saw them take "I suggest" as an order, as he intended, and the two graywings bowed themselves out.

Jion hunkered down beside the bed, so he could gaze straight into Yskanda's face, which he was annoyed to discover was still flushed with fever. "Why," he said remorselessly, "did you neglect to tell me everything about Essence affinities? Same reason you neglected to learn properly, and so nearly killed yourself?"

Yskanda's eyelids closed.

Jion relented. "I know, I know, you don't say anything because there is always the worry my Imperial Father will hear it also, and use it against you. But that doesn't explain why you didn't . . . what did the monk say . . . practice the wards properly, so that you wouldn't be harmed when something like this happens."

"I didn't want it to happen," Yskanda murmured, barely audible. "I am not certain what did happen."

"You were helping someone. Who? Do you even know?"

Yskanda's lips parted, then closed and he stirred restlessly on the bed.

Jion sat back on his heels. "There is that wall again. Yskanda, when are you going to learn that there are things I will never tell my father? I believe that you, and your family, mean no harm to him personally or to the empire. So I have no moral uncertainty about keeping your true identity to myself. Ayah, speaking of knowing—I meant to tell you that I know your sister. And your brother."

Yskanda's eyes opened, stark and staring. He tried to struggle up.

Jion put a hand on his chest and pushed him flat. "Your sister lived with me for two years as fellow cadets in the army. Then we wandered in the northern islands for almost two more. I did not find out she was a girl until the day the ferrets caught me."

Jion saw that he had Yskanda's undivided attention. "I learned a little about Essence then. Your sister is fast becoming an Essence master. Only her affinity is fire. Yours seems to be water. At a guess, your elder brother's is earth—slow to move, but nigh unstoppable when he does. The Alk gift seems to have manifested in all three of you. See? I know it all."

"I don't understand," Yskanda murmured, eyes too bright in his fever-flushed face.

"We should talk this out, but not right now," Jion said. "The imperial physicians were here. Two of them. You ought to get some rest, and I need to get to my father first, so that he will have the right context for the inevitable reports. I'll tell him that when you get fevers, you have visions, but it's all water-related. That means you have no talent as a geomancer, and you don't want what you have. Since he dislikes augurs, and values you for your art, there ought not to be any problem."

Yskanda winced. "I tried to close it all out. But I had this nightmare. About my parents."

Jion understood now—or thought he did.

"They were in a storm, at sea. Small boat. Coming apart. It

was an arrow of a storm. It felt . . . aimed," Yskanda said.

All right, that was a little surprising. But—nightmares. Who could say what was true and what wasn't?

Jion rose to his feet. "You'll tell me everything later, and I'll tell you about seeing your sister and brother at Green Jade Island—which, by the way, nobody but the two of us here, and they, know. We both need to catch some sleep. I was going to take your books, but I think, when you're better, you are going to teach me these Essence matters—after you learn to do it correctly. No more pretending it's not there. Your sister would tell you that. Oh. She goes by Ari now. Arikanda."

TWENTY

AFTER WAKING ON THE ruin of their sailboat and discovering that they both were still alive, Hanu uncurled herself, pulling her precious herbal out from where it had been digging into her hip, and her medicine bag and the cedar box beneath her rump. The herbal was unharmed, its pages intact, but she had not expected mere water to damage it: she had overlaid it with every protection she had learned, and then, as she learned more, she obscured the writings about talismans with illusion mirroring the earlier pages on which she had drawn various herbs and their properties.

Everything was intact, including the precious few sheets of Essence paper she had left, tucked behind the stiffened board of the back cover. The cover was sadly discolored and slightly warped as well as gritty with brine, but the paper was unharmed.

She felt among the detritus on the deck to see what, if any, of their supplies had survived. A jug of soap was intact. Her pickled vegetables were all smashed, only shards remaining. She hoped bitterly that undersea creatures would regard those vegetables as a treat.

The rice bag had been ripped by splinters and was water-logged: a tentative taste revealed it was seawater, already brackish, and not rainwater. She would have tried cooking the rice if it had only been rain; her cooking oil was miraculously intact, cushioned behind the rice bag, though it was half empty. Her food was gone, but Danno's leg was resting atop her bag of chilis, garlic, and leeks.

The medicines had survived despite being sat on, with the phoenix feather beneath them. She had one coal left, and her flint. After a hesitation, she used a small amount of water and made ginger and willow tea. She drank a third to banish the headache, and saved the rest for Danno, in hopes it would help with his fever.

Thus began three days of calm, floating there on the water as, one by one, their buckets of fresh water emptied. She permitted herself only the tiniest sips, barely wetting her mouth. Danno slid in and out of fever; one of his knees had burst the swelling and was bleeding. Her healer training did not compass such a wound as this, but at least her shamanistic training had reached the cleansing of blood. She drew the correct talismans over his chest, forehead, and legs above and below the wounds, as she murmured the rituals. Some of the hectic flush in his face died down, though otherwise he remained unchanged.

She rigged a semblance of a cover with a shirt that had tangled itself around one of Danno's legs, the single extra garment not swept to sea. Using this shirt and Danno's sword, she at least was able to shade Danno's head and upper body.

On the third day, she dragged herself to the prow, knelt, and threw her spirit into the air in wordless prayer. Shameless begging. If the gods had turned their faces away from her, who would know? She had never had any particular pride about such things. She tried to pray herself into resignation for death, grateful that at least she and Danno were together, when a crackling noise disturbed her peace, changing to an unmusical cawing squawk. At first she shut it out, endeavoring to recapture the fragile semblance of submission to fate, when the sound became more distinct. Insistent.

She opened salt-gritty eyes to see a vague shape against the bright sun. A bird—a heron? Yes, a long-necked heron, white of feather, with a great sharp orange beak. The heron flew around the boat, uttering that crackling caw, then squawked, until another heron appeared. The two flew around overhead. Did they wish to perch on the sailboat? She sat still, wondering if these were sea birds or freshwater herons.

Or . . . she glanced over at Danno, still slumbering.

"Mother?" she called softly, looking upward.

The female heron sailed downward, circling Hanu, then launched upward in a beating of wings. The two herons continued to wheel and dive overhead, occasionally cackling and cawing. Hanu watched, wondering what they meant, until the thought occurred that if this was truly her mother, of course her nature would have altered with her form: words were surely as much noise to birds as their sounds were to humans.

Presently the pair flew off, and Danno stirred. She crawled back down the deck. By the time she got some water into him, she heard the birds return amid a great cackling, croaking, and high-pitched screeling. They had brought with them a siege of birds — mostly herons, but among them seagulls and egrets and a dozen other types, flying around and around. Splat! Something dropped on deck. She withdrew her bare feet, thinking it was bird guano, but then she saw it was a crab, good-sized, freshly dead.

She snatched it up and popped it into the cook pot. But she had no coal other than one precious lump! Yes, but there was the remainder of the mast, and a wad of splinters piled in the bow, now quite dry.

She gathered these and lit a small fire, feeding it splinter by splinter.

She would not think about tomorrow. She tossed pinches of herbs and a chili into the cookpot, and made a soup that Danno drank down gratefully. And when she saw sweat burst out on his forehead, she cried with gratitude that the fever had broken, at least for now.

The birds vanished with the sun, but were back the next day. Once again crustaceans were dropped on the deck, along with a miracle — a small coconut that one of the birds must have found floating on the sea after the storm. She broke that open and cooked the milk with the crustacean over the last of her coal. Danno ate that, too, but then sank into sleep, his cheeks hot.

She performed the blood cleansing over him once more, then sat back on her bare heels and looked at him helplessly, wondering if they would get hungry enough to eat raw crustacean (if the birds even returned) when the wheeling spiral of birds flew upwards in a great beating of wings, crying and cawing as, out of the east, a smudge resolved into . . . a ship.

Hanu stood, wondering how to get its attention. The coal

and the splinters were gone, so she could make no fire. She had no flags, nothing to wave except that shirt shading Danno's face. It didn't occur to her until the ship bore down that it had probably seen the birds long before it saw their sailboat.

Beautiful, red-lacquered sails brailed expertly up part way, sailors calling to one another, as the fine luxury vessel, built for speed, slowed. A fine-featured man with long, curling graying hair came to the rail. He wore a silk robe embroidered with bamboo shoots and nightingales. An exquisite jade ornament hung at his belt, with a long golden tassel—he had to be a nobleman.

"Ho there," he called down genially. "We had a bet going—whether this might be a ghost ship or a treasure ship. The birds seemed to think it was both!" As he spoke his ship was gliding past.

Sailors laughed at his humor, and Hanu smiled tremulously. Was he truly going to leave them there? "If the esteemed nobleman could see his way to helping us to a little water," she called, trying to recollect the manners of nobles she'd learned so long ago. She put her hands together, though her sleeves were mere tatters, crusted with salt, and she gave him a court bow.

But his attention was not on her. As the ship slowly slid by, she saw his attention sweep over the boat to Danno, and stop at the sword, revealed and concealed in the cool sea breeze.

"I can do better than that," the man called suddenly. "You are about two days from the nearest island — or, two days if you had a sail. But it seems yon gentleman is indisposed? I have never seen an excellent sword like that used to make a tent before. Very innovative, ha ha." He gestured to his sailors. "Help them aboard. And—careful. He is wounded, if I am not mistaken?"

"The storm was very bad," Hanu said. "As you see, we lost our mast." If their rescuer wanted to assume Danno's knees were ruined as a result of the storm, all the better.

Calls on the deck resulted in sails being pulled up and the anchor splashing down. The big ship rolled quietly, casting shade over the ruined sailboat below. Under the benevolent eye of the gray-haired nobleman, his sailors fashioned a kind of sling from a hammock with a plank laid in it to stiffen it, and affixed booms to either end. They lowered this, one of the sailors coming with it. He helped Hanu to get Danno onto the plank. As they carefully lifted him to the ship, Hanu had packed everything of value into the shirt—the phoenix feather at the bottom—and tied it over one shoulder.

The plank was lowered once again. Hanu seated herself on it decorously, despite her tattered, filthy clothing.

"Don't forget the sword," the nobleman called down. "From here it looks like a very fine weapon. Valuable, too."

Hanu picked it up, and with it lying across her lap, she sat down again and was swung up on board.

There, she bowed to their host. "These wretches are so very grateful to our esteemed benefactor."

"It's what anyone should do, ha ha. And we are not at court—no need for extreme politeness."

She bowed again, thinking that he was dressed for court in at least three layers of silk, the over robe's sleeves detailed with dragonflies and cassia blossoms among the bamboo shoots, his fingers graced by expensive rings. She said quietly, "As you see, we have nothing to offer as payment. However, I have my skills as a healer, and I would be glad to serve if you have need of such, your honored grace."

"You do me too much honor." The man chuckled. "I am a simple merchant, dealing sometimes in salt, sometimes in silk, whenever I can arrange a good cargo. My undistinguished name is Ye Daq. If, once your man recovers, he wishes work, I believe that will be very easy to arrange. I always am on the lookout for skilled individuals, but all that can wait. The first order of business is to rest and recover. What adventures you must have had! Whom have I the pleasure of rescuing?"

"I, one Afan Iley, am a healer's assistant," she said. "My husband is Olt, a wood-carver—"

As soon as the words were out of her mouth, she belatedly remembered that commoners were forbidden to carry swords. Danno, as Olt, had kept that sword hidden all the years they were on Imai, and it had also been hidden at Burning Rock, as weapons were forbidden. She stuttered to a stop.

But Ye Daq didn't seem to notice anything amiss. "I have an excellent physician," he said. "We'll have him take a look at . . . Olt, you say? He is in luck—we have one bed free."

Hanu bowed with grace and dignity despite her torn and ruined clothes and her bare feet and her hair draggling down her back. Ye Daq then asked how it was they got stranded in the storm, she told her story about rushing to the bedside of an ailing uncle, and then they talked about the severity of the storm until a steward approached, bowed deeply, and announced that dinner was ready.

"Will you honor me by sharing a simple repast?" Ye Daq asked.

From the delicious aromas wafting on the air Hanu was thinking that the food was anything but simple. Hungry as she was, though, her thought arrowed straight to Danno. "I would be honored," she said. "If you'll permit me to wash my hands, and to make up some ginger-willow tea for my husband . . ."

"The physician has him already bandaged and settled for the night. You must be exhausted. Let's get something into you, and you can rest."

Hanu had been her own boss for so long, or had existed among healers who agreed on everything by consensus, that she was unused to being swept into someone else's ideas of what to do. But she suppressed objection. This man had generously rescued them—and she was so very, very tired. She permitted herself to be swept, until she stretched out on a hammock in what felt like a closet . . .

She slept so hard that when she woke, at first she did not know where she was. She was so grateful for utter comfort that for a time she lay there in the hammock she had been pointed to, enjoying the rocking of the ship and the smell of congee with osmanthus syrup added.

Gradually memory returned, and with it, movement—and the sore muscles of extreme effort. Sensory awareness floated back, bringing with it the urgencies of yesterday: Danno's fever; the lack of food on the sailboat; the fact that they were lost.

Then the details: they had been rescued, by a noble. And she had been given this hammock off the galley storage, with a cloth hung up for modesty, as she had not seen any other women on board.

Ayah, here came the questions, which meant it was time to rise.

She found clean clothes laid out for her, plain, soft under robe and pants, and a sturdy over robe that probably belonged to servants, not that Hanu cared. Lukewarm clean water awaited her, set on a barrel of almond flour, and a covered ceramic cup of equally lukewarm tea to rinse her mouth with.

She rose, winced against the pangs of a headache, then readied herself as best she could in a very cramped space. When she was done, she unhooked the hammock, which was now covered with the dried brine that she had not been able to clean off for days, picked up the basin of used water, slung her pack over her shoulder, and ventured out.

Almost at once a servitor wearing the mauve and green she wore saw her, and kindly directed her to leave the used bedding and basin for the servants, and told her that the master awaited her pleasure in the dining cabin. Master, not lord. A very successful, well-born merchant, then.

She went where she had been pointed, to discover Ye Daq seated at a fine table, with servitors around him. He murmured low-voiced, then flicked his fingers in dismissal. All three bowed and withdrew.

Hanu reverted to the manners she had been taught so long ago, as she traveled to the imperial city for that disastrous consort-selection.

"Good morning, Healer's Assistant Afan," he said. "I trust you slept well?"

"I did, thank you, Master Ye," she said, bowing. "I wonder if I might look in on my husband first?"

"Did not my steward show you to the infirmary?" Ye Daq's brow rose. "And—I understand that my stupid servants stuffed you in a closet, and gave you servants' clothing. I will have them all beaten."

She bowed in negation. "Please, sir, the hammock was quite comfortable, and they gave me clean clothes, which is all that matters. You cannot imagine how good that feels, after days of drifting without being able to wash. As for the infirmary, perhaps they would have shown me had I asked, but I did not think it good manners to keep you waiting. Please forgive them."

"Ah, very well, very well. It shall be as you say! Please! If you wish to see, ah, Mr. Olt, I believe you will find him asleep."

Her expression did not change, but a warning jolted through her at that knowing *Ah* before the words "Mr. Olt."

"I am told by my physician that the fever broke midway through the night, though it is back again. However, I am also told that is to be expected, and he should be soon on the mend, a strong man like that."

Hanu bowed again, expressing relief, though inwardly she meant to see him for herself as soon as she could. The only thing that had stopped her was the distinct memory the evening before of hearing that there was one bed — which suggested a space filled with sick or injured men. She was not going to venture there until she had a better sense of this ship and its master; she also recollected a careless wave of one beringed hand toward the galley storage the evening before. It had not been the servants who put her in that closet.

Servants then came in bearing exquisite porcelain trays, and set out far too many dishes for only two people. "I trust a simple repast might not be amiss?" Ye Daq asked. "It might be rougher than our esteemed guest is used to, but at least it is hot."

Hanu demurred, thanking him again. This genial man seemed to have a taste for reassurance; perhaps he regretted bestowing her in the closet? He had saved their lives, so she could certainly accommodate a bit of oddness.

She forced herself to eat slowly. It helped that she had to stop frequently in order to answer a stream of questions: she was a healer's assistant, having left the Snow Crane God temple, and they were on their way to visit an ailing uncle, but she feared they had been swept far out of their path.

"Ah, which island is that?" Ye Daq asked.

"Peach Orchard," she replied — knowing there had to be at least a dozen islands with the same or similar name, if not more, as the Peaches of Immortality were part of Suanek's worship..

"I'm afraid I don't know it," Ye Daq said easily, "so I will not be able to set sail for there. But I can offer you hospitality, and perhaps more, when we come to Kanda Sutra."

Hanu bowed again. Without consulting Danno, she was reluctant to agree to anything — not that there was much she could do now anyway.

Ye Daq then took over the conversation, talking about the storm, and recent storms, and about trade, and silk. He sounded inordinately proud of his cargo, which — he was delighted to report — had come through the terrible weather intact, and there was nothing like watertight compartments, was there? Really, he seemed to be gloating. He must have made a very good bargain.

It was a pleasant meal, each exerting themselves to please and be pleased. And when it was done, Ye Daq excused himself in the politest way, which indicated to her that he had been raised by nobles, whatever his claims to roughness. He invited her to reassure herself by visiting her husband. He even pointed the way to the infirmary.

Every bed was not only full, there were two pallets on the deck. She was surprised—the ship had not exhibited commensurate damage. The others there fell silent, all eyes staring her way. She said, "Good morning. I guess the storm was even worse than I thought!"

A quick smile from the man in the next bed, who looked barely old enough to shave, as an older man across from Danno said, "We were drinking, and didn't notice the storm until it threw us nearly on the beam ends."

"That's right," exclaimed the others, a little too loudly, too jovially—as if they all shared a hidden joke.

She spoke polite words of commiseration, noticing as she did that their wounds were not fresh, but judging by the color of bruising on visible skin, more like ten days or so old. They had to be referring to an earlier storm. One or two lay unbandaged, their wounds straight slices, not the tears she'd expect from wooden splinters.

She turned to Danno, whose color really was better. His knees had been expertly bandaged, so there was really nothing for her to do, and she sensed that her presence put a check on the sort of conversation men liked to have with one another without women present.

The physician appeared, and said anxiously, "There was infection, but the rainwater rinsed most of it away. We left his wounds open to the air through the night, but rebandaged them this morning."

"Thank you," she said. "We had been leaving them open as well."

"Very glad to help, very glad," he replied, bowing as if she were a princess, in spite of her chambermaid clothing. Once again she sensed that there was an undercurrent here she could not see. The physician went on obsequiously, "I observed from the state of his wounds that he received the best of care before the storm stranded you."

"We had help from the senior healers at the temple," she said. "I am only an assistant, but if there is anything I can do to help you, I would be honored."

He thanked her, and went on to the next patient.

She turned back to Danno, who held out one hand. When she laid hers in his, he gave a little tug. She dropped to her knees beside the bed. To her surprise he tugged again, until she laid her head on his breast, hiding her surprise, as he had never been demonstrative before others' eyes.

But his arms came round her, hugging her up against him; when her head bumped against his chin, he turned his head to nuzzle her ear. She blushed, murmuring, "This is not the place."

His lips pressed against her ear and he whispered, the veriest breath, "He recognized me."

Then Danno let her go.

Now fully on alert, she straightened up, patted his cheek fondly, and said, "Do everything the physician tells you, *Husband Olt.*"

"I will be good," he returned.

She rose, bowed to the company, and withdrew — hearing good-natured chaffing behind her, and a couple of envious comments such as, "I wish I had *me* a pretty wife." It felt almost as if she had come among some sort of military group.

Hanu moved away, the personal comments sloughing off as irrelevant. What did that mean, he recognized Danno? That might lie behind her going to sleep in a closet as an unwanted but tolerated burden, and waking to treatment like a well-born woman. Which, strictly speaking, she was — but she had given up that life along with her true name.

The rest of the day stretched out before her with nothing to do. The ship was beautifully made and decorated, but it appeared to lack books; she occupied herself as best she might in wandering the deck in the fresh air.

She dined again with Ye Daq, who asked about temple life. This she was able to furnish, probably more than he wanted to hear, but it gave her a safe channel of conversation that carried her through the meal. They parted with mutual compliments and she visited Danno once more before retiring — not to the closet, but this time to a tiny but well-appointed cabin with a silken coverlet on the bed built into the bulkhead.

The next morning started much like the first until she got to the infirmary, which she found open to the air so that sunshine flooded in. She glanced more carefully this time, alert to every detail, and noticed that many of the healing wounds were now exposed. There were no rashes, and no one appeared to be sick. She was not at all an expert in identifying the wounds that resulted from war, but she knew what healed sword and knife and arrow wounds looked like from Danno's own body. She was very certain that these were all the slashes and smashes of the damage that humans do to one another.

On the surface everything was friendly, comfortable, generous. But she remained vigilant, even uneasy, after that encounter with Danno, short as it was. His words about the wounds—his wanting to speak in private—made her all the more uneasy because of the benignity of their host and his servants.

During the day they passed several small islands, and in the distance one larger one. Hanu knew too little about navigation to understand that their ship was taking a very roundabout route. But evening brought them in sight of a distinctive island with three sharp peaks; judging by the shouts and laughter of the crew, the home port was in sight.

By Dragon Watch they flowed in with the tide, and soon were under a rain canopy held by waiting servants. Hanu was escorted to a covered cart with cushions inside, which she shared with her host. The last she saw of Danno, he was taken on a stretcher with the other wounded into a longer, plainer cart.

Hanu was uneasy, though Ye Daq was as friendly as ever, talking about how beautiful Kanda Sutra Island was, and how perfect the seasons. "Welcome to Three Guardians, of my many homes the pearl in my palm. Pearl in my palm, eh, you know the classic poem? We shall soon have your husband on his feet," he promised. "My physician assures me that he is healing well, and once he's in a regular bed for a day or two, out of the stuffy air of a ship, the fever will subside. In the meantime, I can offer you accommodation at my humble manor, or perhaps you might wish to stay with the women?"

She said, "Wherever is most convenient. Perhaps other women will have clothes I can borrow until I can earn the wherewithal to buy more?" As she spoke, she realized she had been maneuvered in that direction—separate from Danno.

It was very late when they reached the manor. In the rain and darkness she gained only an impression of thick walls and a well-guarded gate, then they were inside. Courtyards, gardens, then the master went off to the north, and she was taken to the east, where she found several maids dressed, like her, in mauve and gray. But they bowed and one conducted her to a resplendent guest chamber.

"I'm to say that your husband was taken to our doctor, whose advice is for him to lie flat, and sleep. You will see him first thing in the morning, if he has a good night."

Hanu was about to protest that she was a healer, but she was so very tired. There was no danger. Danno was clearly in good hands. She would see him come morning. Meantime, a good rest in a stationary bed would be the best aid in clear thinking.

She slept hard, her dreams uneasy, and woke once again to a strange environment. Yskanda lingered in her mind, her gentle, dreamy second son whose gaze so often strayed to the sea. Like her mother's had.

Her throat tightened when she thought about the heron pair, and the birds who brought food. Was that truly Mother watching over her, or was that flock of birds sent by the gods? Both were easier to believe than mere random happenstance.

If that was Mother, she was alive, and she seemed to have found company, unlike her life as a human; Hanu found it difficult to believe her mother could survive as a bird, she who had been first and foremost a scholar, devoted to the study of words. Birds did not deal in words. Hanu blinked back the sting of tears. She would not weep. Mother or not, the red string of love still bound their hearts together, and she hoped Mother was happy wherever she was.

Hanu rose, determined to set about her day. First to check on Danno. Clean clothes and hot water had been set out for her—but these were not servant garments, not this smooth, slippery cloud-patterned silk. What woman had worn this beautiful over robe with the delicate peonies embroidered over it? And these golden hairpins?

She washed up and dressed. Then she did up her hair, using the most modest of the hairpins. It had been years since she'd done her hair up—braids had been sufficient for decades. But her instinct was to look her best for whatever was to come. Not that she arranged an elaborate hair style. Her fingers were too untutored for that. She coiled it on top of her head, pinned, it, and looked in the polished brass mirror.

The scars had faded, looking more like a superficial skin rash that never went away—very different from the livid furrows she had endured for years. She studied her face, having not seen a mirror for well over twenty years. Thirty, her inner voice corrected remorselessly. What looked back was a woman with her mother's gaze beneath the arch of brow. Fine lines around her eyes, and the skin beneath her chin had softened, signs of age she had earned.

A quick glance at the rest of her: a thin woman of middle age, her hands work-worn. There was also a tray of rings set out, some of jade, others with fine gems. Thoughtful gesture? Kindly invitation? She would lay no claim to a style of life she had turned her back on years ago. She regarded her rough, ringless hands with pride—evidence of her skills as a healer. She would never hide the marks of hard work, knowing that she had striven to do good in the world.

Thus bolstered, she also ignored the pretty fan laid out—the weather was early spring, no need of a fan—and walked out into the courtyard.

She was pointed through an archway to another court, where she caught a medicinal smell that suggested she had found the manor's infirmary. Here, she encountered tattooed Phoenix Moon monks sweeping the flagstones and cleaning railings. Phoenix Moon nuns were hanging out bedding on lines.

Monks! Nuns! She had not realized that she had become tense until the sight of them made her shoulders ease.

She began to pass by, on her way to the infirmary, ready— as she thought—to face anything.

Until a familiar rounded shoulder, a long gray braid, caught her eyes as a monk bent over to trim a shrub. She turned her head, and suppressed a gasp. The monk was a little grayer, a little more lined, but it was definitely Ul Keg, who had lived with her little family more than ten years.

Their eyes met, then he hefted his basket of clippings and walked right past her without so much as a glance.

TWENTY-ONE

SHOCK KEPT HANU GOING without a pause. Her mind, already alert and uneasy, raced to catch up with this new change in the winds of their lives. Was it possible Ul Keg did not recognize her with the scars nearly healed on her face, and her hair worn high instead of in its village braid?

No, not possible. That was a glance of recognition: she felt it. He did not want to acknowledge her . . . Or was it that he did not want her acknowledging him?

In another place, and time, she would have turned right around and chased after him, wanting to know what it was she had done to be ignored. But caution kept her silent — that and the urgent wish to get to Danno, and see to his welfare. Now that she was awake and aware, it seemed odd to her that the two of them had been gently but insistently separated.

She arrived to discover their rescuer sitting at Danno's bedside in a room off the infirmary. Danno had a room to himself, across from a much larger chamber with a row of beds in which she glimpsed most of the men from the ship, and a couple of unfamiliar faces.

Danno and her host looked up at her entrance. Ye Daq gave her a broad smile. "And *here* is the princess," he said. Then, to Danno, "See, I remembered!"

Shock rang through Hanu again, more painful than her sudden encounter with Ul Keg. "Our rescuer must forgive this confused assistant healer, who was never at any time a princess."

"But you married Second Prince Enjai before he took the throne," Ye Daq said. "It *was* you, was it not? First in the old selection custom for prince and princess consorts. And very pretty you are, if a man may be permitted to say so before her husband."

He was slightly disconcerted when she only bowed, attributed it to modesty, and went on. "It was the sword I recognized first—the sword only given to the imperial guard. And he looked so familiar, then it came to me midway through the night: the famous guard to the second imperial prince." Ye Daq chuckled. "Whenever we scholars heard you were to be in one of the competitions, we nearly had duels over who would get a place to watch." He chuckled again, hands on his knees, eyes crinkled in mirth.

Thoroughly unsettled, Hanu reminded herself that this man had rescued them. She bowed slightly, then said to Danno, "I came to see if I could make you anything. I managed to preserve most of my herbs. I could brew up an aromatic tea with willow bark, if you are in pain."

Danno's cracked lips twitched in a grateful semblance of a smile. "I'm full of tea. Thanks to the generosity of our rescuer." He made a nod toward Ye Daq, who chuckled again.

Hanu had known Danno's dear face in every possible expression over the years; it was a very long time since she had seen him as a stranger might. In the very early days she had thought him inscrutable, even a little sinister. Outwardly he had not changed much, except for the silver glinting in his hair, and the slightly softened line of his jaw. There was also the flush of fever in his lean cheeks, but he was once again wearing that inscrutable expression of the alert guard.

Ye Daq seemed to take Danno's few words as encouragement, for he said, "I always thought you'd end up with Prince Hojai. I know he wanted you—he always wanted the best. But fate . . ." He shrugged, and seeing no response to the named prince in either Danno or Hanu, went on. "Though I believe we can make an effort to change fates we don't like."

Here, Danno gave his short guardsman's nod.

Ye Daq's smile widened. "I need a hero," he said. "And here you are. A man you might meet, a man I admire, insists that we can indeed make our own fate, and in making our own, remake the fate of the world. Perhaps that is true! When someone doesn't stand against you. I believe a man has a right to regain what his ancestors intended he ought to have. And create his own clan, a new dynasty! After all, someone was first in the past. Why not me for the future?"

Danno stilled, and Hanu's stomach tightened.

"Oh, I do not covet the dragon throne," Ye Daq said, laughing. "That can be left to one who can hold it. I am wise enough to know when I must bend the knee. We will not interfere with *his* plans."

Hanu's neck prickled when she realized that Ye Daq was not talking about the emperor.

"My sights are set on regaining what my father and his father ought to have had—and instituting a new name. The old one is tarnished. Ye is an excellent name, don't you think?"

He smiled, his gaze searching the faces before him. He was an expert at assessing hidden desires. He saw none of that here. Yet. It was merely a matter of finding them. So unexpected a prize falling into his hands was worth the time taken.

"What I need is a hero," he repeated. "I can deal with most of the obstructions. But there are others ranging the borders of the empire, claiming to act for justice. An easy claim to make, and seldom means anything more than greed, covetousness, and the claws and teeth of the tiger." He laughed. "I know human nature! There are two such threats at present. How much do you know about current affairs?"

"Nothing," Danno said. "We have made good lives for ourselves by staying out of politics, local and imperial."

"Are you truly happy?" Ye Daq leaned forward. "Hiding your talents for years? Doing what, catching fish? That's right, carving wood. Anyone can carve wood. Few can defeat every threat the way you once did."

"I don't know if I'll ever walk again," Danno said abruptly.

Hanu was sick—this was the first time he had ever admitted to this fear. Which she shared.

Ye Daq pulled a fan from his long sleeve, and snapped it open to wave back and forth. "No, no, my friend, have no fear on that score. My physician is one of the very best. He stakes his life that you will be walking again. Quite literally stakes his life, ha ha—that is a compliment, testament to how important you are to me!"

He paused, and when the two before him did not seem to

be impressed by the value he placed on Danno, he went on. "Though he says it must come perhaps a little slower than you would like. He said that whoever attended to you immediately after the attack—it was an attack, not a fall, let us both be clear about that—did everything correctly, in aligning the pieces of your kneecaps together so that they will reknit properly. It is the reknitting that takes its own time."

Hanu bit her lip. This was good news. But she was afraid, hearing it come from this man whose words were so unsettling.

". . . that is what you must be patient about. Bones do not reknit overnight. Then you must strengthen again—but that will not take long. To resume. My plans are progressing, in spite of a recent setback. But two outstanding problems remain—that is the disadvantage of the wandering world. One of them ought to be dealt with soon—I wish I could send you. It would have been so much easier."

"Me?" Danno repeated.

"These self-righteous martial artists pop up every now and then, with a fingernail of talent and a dragon's worth of presumption. But I have ships on the way to Sky Island and Ten Leopards at this moment. I believe I will soon be there to personally witness the death of Firebolt." He paused, and seeing no comprehension in either of them, smiled with inward satisfaction. Danno the Swordsman, ignorant these thirty years! Unbelievable luck.

"There is a worse problem. My old enemy, Waoji Lion's Mane." Ye Daq's tone hardened with residual anger. "Rid the world of him, and any other such, and you shall have anything you want."

Danno's eyes closed briefly. "What if I just want to be left to a quiet life?"

"Then you shall have it! After a little exertion. Tell me you do not miss the excitement, the challenge, the best against the best."

Hanu saw the answer in Danno's face—and so did Ye Daq, who laughed and slapped his hands to his knees. "I thought so. I thought so. Ayah! A tiger does not turn into a rabbit even if a few years slip by. Why, you are three or four years younger than I, and I am in my prime yet." He laughed again. "There is much to be done, and you must be about your healing. I will assign one of the monks to be your personal servant. They are even silent—the best possible servant. No luxury is too much, my friend. We are going to accomplish great things when you recover."

Ye Daq rose and nodded politely to Hanu, saying, "Let us find something for you to do, shall we?"

She was not going to get to talk to Danno alone, then. Thoroughly unsettled, she rose and followed her host out. He took her to the physician and introduced them, saying, "She's a descendant of the great Alks, that much I remember. Surely she is knowledgeable enough even for you. And you, dear princess, will not be bored as your husband goes about his recovery."

Ye Daq left her there. The physician, Chu Cho, then put to her a series of questions rather like shooting arrows. She gained a sense of a man whose entire life was wrapped up in affinities, herbals, the details of what made up the world. She did not get a sense that he understood the souls of that world, but (she scolded herself) that was a judgment too quick to make.

At the end, she made her first try, mostly to gauge the emerging unspoken rules. "I would like to prepare for my husband his favorite tea. I was able to preserve a good part of my stores," she added. "Enough so that I can combine ginger, treated willow bark, a pinch of longevity root, and jasmine for scent and taste."

Physician Chu's eyes widened. "Jasmine," he repeated in a voice of doom. "No, no. You must not open that here." His hands waved. "Get rid of it!" And, at Hanu's astonishment, "It is poison to the Master. You will not find any jasmine anywhere on this island."

"I'm glad you told me," she responded. "I will get rid of it at once."

To her absolute surprise, he nodded vigorously several times. "Do that. Right now. That is, do not burn it, or throw it in the stream. Bring it to me. I'll send it out with the fishers to be tossed into the sea. Then on your return, I will have readied a schedule. You can take over examining the recoveries of a morning, and some of the medicine preparation. With the population here growing, and always more wounded appearing, I am always behind."

Hanu walked out, retracing her steps. She found the room she had been assigned, and reached for her little bag of belongings—aware that they were not quite as she had left them. She paused, studying carefully. Someone had gone through everything, and had put it back nearly exactly as they had found it, except the knots binding the silk strings around her herbal were right-handed, not left. Most people would not even notice such things, the world being mostly right-handed.

Someone had leafed through it, but nothing was missing — the untutored fingers had missed the precious Essence papers inserted into the warped back binding — or they did not know what they were. She uncapped her surviving herbs and spices one by one, sniffing carefully. Nothing added. The jasmine was even there, seemingly untouched.

She capped it again, set the little pots right out in a row, an unspoken challenge: if someone needed to go through her things again, she'd make it easier for them.

She retraced her steps and handed off the jasmine to Physician Chu, who by then had written up a list of all current patients who did not need his immediate care. "You'll accompany me on a round so I can introduce you, then they are yours, unless something requires my attention," he said.

Hanu had to suppress all her questions, but patience had been one of her earliest lessons.

The introductions went well in the sense that no one questioned who she was or where she had come from. In the course of checking bandages, she corroborated the age of the wounds. None were new — they could not possibly be from the recent storm. What's more, though the men came in various sizes and a range of ages, she noticed the edge of a tattoo on all their necks. Sect marks?

All she knew about tattoos was what Ul Keg had explained about his own: Phoenix Moon monks traveled through the world on their Ul-journeys, teaching. Because they were so often away from their temples they had talismanic protections as tattoos, including a way to find the bodies of brethren who might die far from the temple, so that their bodies could be located and brought home.

She did not know if sect tattoos had talismanic protections, and she was too unnerved, too wary to ask anything but what strictly related to medicine.

She had by her second day convinced herself she had imagined Ul Keg when she caught sight of him planting bulbs in the freshly turned earth outside one of the infirmary outbuildings.

She hesitated till she saw his work-worn hand furtively make a quick, waving motion: go away. He did not lift his head.

She walked by, glanced down again, then saw him flash two fingers upright before he picked up a bulb to plant. Two? Two what?

She walked on, hoping to find time in her routine to speak to Danno alone, but each time she wrested free moments from the routine of grinding roots and gathering dew and all the other arduous and exacting tasks of medicine making, she found Ye Daq with Danno. By the way their host interrupted himself, and asked how she was, and if she was happy, she got the sense that she was an intrusion. When Danno did not speak up to ask her to stay, she left again.

Two days later, she woke to a change in atmosphere. She felt it, but could not define it, except that it was somehow easier to breathe, as if a sultry, airless summer day had given way to a fresh, cool breeze straight off the sea.

She'd risen, washed, and dressed when a quick tap at her door brought her to her feet. The only person she wanted to speak to was Danno, who could not walk. Dreading a visit from her host—though so far he had been nothing but hospitable—she went to her door, and to her surprise found Ul Keg.

"Come in," she said on an interrogative note.

He entered. "Forgive me, dear Iley," he murmured. "It was necessary. Our only defense is our silence. But Ye Daq departed, and so I dared approach you."

"Defense?"

"Yes. Ye Daq's pirates took our ship when we were on our way to take over an orphanage at one of the western islands that was devastated in a raid. He was going to slaughter us all when he remembered that monks and nuns cannot take money, and chose to make us slaves. We invented a vow of silence, the only protection we had against having our tongues cut out."

"Ayah, that is abominable! He is worse than I feared. Where are we? Is there a chance of rescue?" She realized as she spoke that she no longer regarded Ye Daq's rescue as such. Not when she got the increasing sense that they were prisoners.

"I can only tell you that we are within the sea boundary of Ran, south of the main island," Ul Keg said. And, seeing her incomprehension, he added, "Where treaty forbids the imperial navy from patrolling."

Hanu knew nothing of the ins and outs of sea patrols, and

cared less. "He recognized Danno," she said. "He wants him to attack some man."

"I know. They've all been talking about it. Strange," he added reflectively. "How people assume if you cannot speak, you cannot hear. Of course we help by pretending not to hear. But perhaps that is a discussion for later. This is what I can tell you. Ye Daq is the master of a sect called the Shadow Panthers. They are pirates. Thieves. The government might term them rebels in that when he encountered you and Olt, Ye Daq was returning from an attempt to take the Silk Islands, their faces full of the dust of defeat."

"So I was right, those *were* wounds from fighting, and not from the storm," she said. "Even worse! We might as well revert to our true names. It seems they are known. Our true personal names," she added, remembering how much pride her phlegmatic husband had taken in Afan, a name bestowed at their wedding. Afan Iley was gone, a memory both dear and fraught. She was now Afan Hanu, descended from the Alks. She liked the sound of that.

Ul Keg's steady gaze remained patient until she recollected herself. Then he said, "Ye Daq did not leave until your husband received a Shadow Panther tattoo. Do you think Danno wishes to become Ye Daq's man?"

"I don't know. I can't get to him alone," she admitted.

Ul Keg then surprised her. "As I said, Ye Daq set sail this morning, to oversee some nefarious plan in the north. He rarely stays long in any one place, though he visits here most frequently. Now that he is gone, there will be a little more freedom. For example, if you express concern at Danno's complexion and pulse, offer to take him for an airing. Then what is more natural than to summon the closest monk to push the cart?"

"Yes," she breathed. "The closest monk," she repeated. "Is this why you ignored me when we first came? So that we would not be seen to know one another?"

"That is exactly it. Ye Daq seeks conspiracy everywhere. He would put me to death in a heartbeat if he suspected we knew one another. He didn't even want the two of you together until he had his tattoo on Danno."

Sick at heart, she wondered what that meant. She made her rounds, careful to behave as she had previously, then stopped by Danno's, after which she took her concern to the physician.

"Even if he were not my husband I would be worried," she said. "I do not think he is thriving. Perhaps some sun and fresh air? The spring weather today is quite mild."

Ul Keg was lurking around with his broom outside the infirmary when Physician Chu poked his head out the door. "Here, you. This man wants an airing," the physician stated. *He* didn't worry about who talked to whom about what.

Hanu's heart beat fast as she said, "I'm going along. I want to coax more food into him. He's much too thin."

The physician agreed — he was terrified of losing so important a patient. He was paid very well, and given freedom to experiment on prisoners — but he also knew his life would be forfeit if the master was displeased. He'd seen it happen.

The three of them were soon tooling along the bluff overlooking the sea, as a brisk, cool spring breeze fingered hair and clothes. Once they were thoroughly out of hearing, Danno said, "It's good to get outside. Hand me that soup. I'll drink it now, so you do not have to carry it."

When he was done, Hanu got right to the point. "Ul Keg, tell Danno what you told me."

Ul Keg repeated his story, at the end of which Hanu added, "I was half out of my mind the day his ship found us, but after a night of sleep I remember quite distinctly how I watched as they sailed by, afraid he was about to leave us there in that ruined sailboat. Until he saw Danno's sword."

Danno spoke. "He was proud of recognizing that sword." He frowned out to sea. "I knew from the beginning that he was hiding something. I might have been so sick I was hallucinating, but I know a war ship when I see one, and that ship of his is a war ship. It's no trader, though the hold might be stuffed with silk. There was at least one more following us, that I gathered from overhearing the wounded talking. That's absolutely forbidden."

"I recognized wounds from weapons," Hanu said. "Did you once know him?"

Danno said, "Soon as he started talking I was fairly certain I recognized him as Yulin Enk, a provincial governor's son. Not one of the military Yulins. This was the one who formed part of Prince Hojai's court until he was sent home for cheating on the Imperial Examination, that same spring when you came to the manor. Anyway, he seems to think I want revenge on Prince Enjai — on the emperor — for what happened back then."

"Do you?" Ul Keg asked gently.

Danno said unemotionally, "The truth is, I betrayed Enjai. He knows it. I know it."

Hanu had been holding his hand. As her fingers gripped convulsively, he smiled up at her. "I'd do it again. Because it was your life against obedience to a bad command."

She let go, and slid her hands up her arms, looking back down the years. "I guess if anyone is at fault it was I. I never ought to have come to the imperial island, but I was curious — I thought I would be able to get lost in the empire's greatest library, and . . . Oh, those days are gone, more than thirty years gone, and though I might have done many things differently, the outcome perhaps would have been the same. He was so *angry.*"

"Had reason," Danno said.

Hanu smiled tenderly down at him. "I know. I remember. I only met Prince Hojai twice, but I saw immediately that he was so very much worse. However, in my refusing Prince Enjai — and in our leaving as we did — we humiliated him. Many things can be forgiven, over time, but the poison of humiliation lingers the longest." She shook her head, her smile fading. "I understand that now."

Silence fell between them, broken by the hiss and wash of the sea below, the wind soughing through the grasses, and the distant mew of a gull.

"You accepted the Shadow Panther tattoo," Hanu said. "Does that mean you will do what Ye Daq asks of you?"

Danno gently fingered his neck, which was red and puckered. "Had to," he said. "Can you give me an assessment of the situation here? He made it clear that Hanu's life was in the balance."

"Mine," Hanu exclaimed.

Danno turned his gaze up to her. "Yes. I'd still retained some gratitude for his saving us. Even though it's clear he did it only because of the sword — because he's hungry for fighting men. But the gratitude ended when he made his little speech about loyalty or death." He dropped his hand, then turned to Ul Keg. "What is the situation here?"

Ul Keg shut his eyes to think out what to say. When first those pirates had clambered aboard their ship on its mission of mercy and murdered the two eldest and most fragile as a warning of the price of disobedience, he had begun to wonder what terrible sins he had committed in a past life, to deserve such a blow. The pirates had then flung their bodies carelessly out to sea so there would be no chance of recovery.

As the ship made its journey to this island, the Phoenix Moon brothers and sisters had done what they could to placate any wandering ghosts, but they themselves began to wonder, especially as life became a grind of slavery for a brutal master, if they ought to commit the double sin of suicide, offending both the gods and their parents who had united to give them life.

Kanda had written that the world of Heaven and Earth is good, and that goodness is born into human hearts. The Way taught that Purpose is the stuff of which Essence derives. He had lost sight of goodness and purpose in recent days, with so much careless evil around him. But then he turned around with his basket of pirate underclothes he had finished scrubbing, and there was Afan Iley. Surely this was Purpose.

It was going to take work to aid it.

He said, "I would not know how to give you a military assessment, of course. But we monks are sent on errands all over the island, which he has taken for his own. At the east and the west ends are training camps. Those people come and go. The permanent structure is the north side bay, where a shipwright Ye Daq took from another island oversees the repair and the building of three more warships. That is a slow process — every tree but those in his gardens has been cut down, so they depend upon raids for wood."

"How many guards does he have overseeing all this? He must have an army," Danno asked.

"Not as many as you would expect. Instead he has two Cobra Sages, from the Westerners. Third level. He took the old master with him. The young one is at the north end of the island."

"Cobra Sages? But . . ." *They are outlawed*, Danno was going to say. "Right." Now he had an identity of sorts for the cold-eyed bald man who had put the tattoo on him.

"Third level?" Hanu repeated, horrified. There was only one level above the third, the ghost and demon level. She'd been told those who mastered the bindings that affected the spirit world were powerful indeed.

She said, "Third is what they call the blood level — that is, they master the talismans binding not only wind and water, fire and metal, but beast and blood." Her eyes narrowed. "I believe I know now why I get that sense of impending lightning storm whenever I am in proximity of those tattoos. There is a blood talisman worked into them."

"Yes," said Ul Keg, who could feel the evil Essence from a hundred paces. He could feel Danno's. "The recruits are told that if they try to run, or betray Master Night in any way, their blood can be poisoned through the tattoos and they won't last a week. As for Cobra Sages, we've heard whispers that there is a fourth level sage coming, but in company with the man they refer to as the White Dragon."

Hanu felt sick, as if she had placed her foot on sure ground to find herself tumbling end over end in the air.

"Sage," she said. "Making a mockery of the term."

Ul Keg gazed out to sea. "I'm told they give up a great deal for their power. Such as names and identity."

Danno grunted. "They don't have names? If you meet a pack of them, how do they tell one another apart?"

"They have internal signs that no one can see, or if seen, do not understand. The younger one here has a diamond etched onto her forehead. The old one has a star. I expect those tattoos also have Essence bindings worked in."

Danno looked up at Hanu. "Can you do something about these tattoos? You understand this Essence talk, am I right? You can fix the poison threat?"

"I understand what lies behind it," she said slowly. "Much of my work these last two years at Burning Rock has been with the shaman who teaches the cleansing of poisons from the blood. The principles are the same, she said: ours to heal, the Cobras to harm."

Danno took in their anxious faces, then gazed out at the clean, eternal sea, and spoke words he never thought he'd say aloud—that had remained knotted in his heart all these years. "It's not just my life I'm thinking of here. But all these men. I've listened to them, these past days. Some of them are bloodthirsty killers, but not all of them. I'm a killer myself—I was trained to be one. I know the difference."

Ul Keg clasped his hands in agreement. "There are many who I suspect would leave if they could. Especially at the north end. But your life is important, too."

Danno said, "My life was already forfeit. It was only a matter of time before First Prince Hojai made another try on

Prince Enjai, probably sooner than later, and I would have had to kill him. They would all have been relieved, maybe even secretly grateful. I hoped they'd be so grateful that someone might slip me a cup of some deadening elixir before I had to die of the thousand cuts in Lotus Blossom Square. Because a commoner must never be able to kill one of the imperial family and live."

He glanced up at Hanu. "By betraying Prince Enjai I gained thirty years, with you. Thirty good years. The best. And three beloved children. None of which I was ever supposed to have. So if I must give this oath-broken life back to Prince Enjai, it'll be by taking Ye Daq's organization apart from the inside. I owe Prince Enjai that much." He closed his eyes, frowned, then said, "Ran. I remember where that is on the map. The imperial island is straight east, more or less. But I have no idea where these other islands you named lie, or how far it is to sail there and back."

Ul Keg, who had traveled all his life, said, "I believe Ten Leopards is part of the northern clusters. Call it a month or so of sailing there, and a month or so back."

Danno held out her hand to Hanu. "We have two months at the earliest to arrange a surprise for our host's return. What do you say?"

She gripped his fingers. "I will start by finding a way to break the binding in those tattoos, and we can change the panther into . . . oh, a chimera. There is a symbol for good luck! I will begin with you."

TWENTY-TWO

ARI KNEW BY THE end of her third day of training that she had made a far worse error that first morning than she would have had she challenged Rooster to a fight.

She met with Matu, Chef Ki, and Petal in her room that night. "I was stupid the other day. And I'm afraid I'm going to get us into trouble."

"They all promised not to talk," Petal said. "When we agreed to start Redbark again."

"I think . . ." Ari tried to get her thoughts in order. She reached back to Instructor Shaz's lessons on intelligence gathering. Then she recollected Master Ki talking about human nature while they sat in their cozy cave, watching the snow fall in the little valley.

"I don't believe any of the new recruits are spies," she said slowly. "At least, not spies for the imperial ferrets, whose foundations have to be as good as the Sky Islanders, or for the Shadow Panthers. *Their* foundations are narrow, always a forward push. Never evade or retreat. Shigan and I called theirs the Stomp and Smash Style."

She paused, as always any mention of Shigan hurting. "It's hard to hide foundations, especially from somebody with training, which I have, and from a trained person watching closely, which I've been doing these past few days. Take Taoh Ahlin," Ari added, referring to the middle-aged recruit. "It's so clear that she's studied nothing but Eel Style. Years and years of Eel Style. Her foundations are all balance—which I was taught was the most important of the Four Pillars. I'm not saying balance isn't important, oh no."

Petal nodded enthusiastically here. "Especially for women."

"Exactly. I was trained in some Eel forms when I was small, but now I realize the ones my . . ." *my father* ". . . master picked were for male bodies. I asked her if she will train me in forms designed for women, with our balance point in our hips. Oh. I forgot where I was going."

"Mistake," Matu said, a little anxiously. He had come to love the inn so much he was afraid to lose it.

"I tried to go back to basics, but they're waiting me out. They all remember what I did. They keep bringing it up. What worries me is that word is going to spread about that stupid fire I made as demonstration. As showing off. We can ask them not to talk about it, but people are people—telling them not to talk about what excites them most is like trying to draw water in a basket. Someone will say some little thing, and that kind of little thing is exactly what the ferrets listen for. And who wouldn't want to collect the huge reward for turning me in, dead or alive?"

"I'll talk to them," Matu muttered.

His father looked stern. "If anyone blabs, they're out."

"But don't you see, the word would already be out," Ari said, hands wide. "I'm trying to make them think it was a . . . fluke, that I was trying too hard. Which is why we're all doing basic foot work."

Matu had already overheard Rooster claiming that Firebolt couldn't be any better than Ari, his voice so full of admiration Matu hadn't known what to say. Until that day, Rooster had been enthusiastic, but difficult. Now he was all eagerness to learn—and Matu knew Rooster was just biding his time until they could get to the good stuff.

"What if you two Kis do some teaching for a few days? I'm going to tell them that I have to recover, that what I did was no more than a trick, and it made me so weak I have to rest. I hate lying, but I want them to forget the fire, to concentrate on martial arts, both for their own sakes and to avoid chatter about Redbark being a sect that uses fire as a weapon. And they'll forget about Firebolt altogether."

Matu said fervently, "We can ask them to swear, no talking about Firebolt, or Redbark, at all."

"Except someone has, or they wouldn't be here. I don't mean Lie Tenek. She said she never mentioned Redbark after she left me, and she was careful to break her trail several times over, after I left her last summer. Before she even got here."

Petal looked down unhappily. No one was leveling accusations, but she knew she was to blame for bragging about Redbark. But she had been so very careful, only talking to people she found trustworthy. Taoh Ahlin had been teaching girls in the town where her sister lived. Hat Pin-Pin was sixteen, the son of Matu's cousin-connection at the herb shop down the street. And Rooster had been sent by another Ki cousin, after they'd ended up fighting against Shadow Panthers together.

Ayah, Rooster was a bit prickly, but Ari had always been firm about everyone getting equal chances, not just People You Like. So Petal had let him stay. Her secret, happiest vision was of an inn full of Redbark justice warriors.

Ari went on, "We'll also make sure they know that Redbark means a lot of hard work. Years. And not everyone has an Essence talent. But they can still be a good martial artist, with dedication."

"Like Shigan," Petal said.

"Exactly! If a talent shows up, that's fine, but it needs training and control. Also, sometimes, a different way of learning."

"Grandfather Ki taught us that," Chef Ki said approvingly.

"That's who I learned it from," Ari said, smiling. "We've begun with basic foot forms, no matter how experienced they are with some other style. Ki Style is just as good as Redbark for foot work, and better with knife forms — I need to work on that. Until they have excellent foundation not just in body, but in mind." Here, she was echoing Waoji Lion's Mane. "Redbark is for justice, not for throwing fire around at annoying people."

Petal said, "Can we still take in new recruits, then? If we are really, really careful?"

Ari wanted to say no, but this was Petal's inn. "All right," she said. "I'm agreeing because I love Redbark. It hurt when I thought we were ended. But I also have to remember that I'm on the Capital List. At least your names aren't on it. If they come, it will be just for me."

Matu said urgently, "If they do come, please get away, as

fast as you can. Don't worry about us. We'll be all right."

"Yes," said Petal. "I am a respectable inn owner. And we were right here when you were crashing that mine — any number of witnesses will testify to that. They cannot prove anything."

Ari nodded. "That's the only reason I'm staying here, because they can't stick my crimes, what they call my crimes, on you." She rubbed her eyes. "I'm trying to learn to think ahead, not just about the situation, but about me in it, the way Shigan and I learned at Loyalty. I always saw myself as invisible, and I, oh, I talked about the mulberry while planting the peach. Planning *around* me, you might say. I've got to think a new way now."

Petal looked confused, then her brow cleared. "You mean, stop using fire?"

Ari shook her head. "Not that. Though it's a part. Shigan said the ferrets aren't just good at fighting and sneaking around, they're good at finding clues and stringing them into a net. I think the only reason they haven't caught up with me yet is because . . ." She remembered what Jion had told her about the poison mystery, and realized that she was stumbling into very dangerous territory.

Again.

". . . because they are busy with more important imperial affairs. But one of them, maybe that one who tried to get into the Sky Island competition, might pick out of the gossip about Firebolt that he dresses as a girl, is a girl, is sometimes a girl and sometimes a boy. And then they are going to come hunting me. They might be right now," she added, remembering the eagle-eyed Fai Anbai, so sinister in those black clothes with all the hidden weapons. His foundations were good, all right, she'd seen that much just in the way he walked.

She looked around, as if those sinister, omniscient eyes were on her right then, in her room at the west side of the Blue Hibiscus Inn. "So no more Firebolt tricks, and if I see anyone suspicious, I'm going to fly." And I mean fly, she said to herself.

At that same time, in their private training court at the extreme northwest corner of the imperial palace's military partition, Fai Anbai was feeling the very opposite of omniscient.

He fought two on one against a pair of ferrets-in-training. They kept at it until they were all dripping. "Again," he said, when one of them bent, his hands on his knees, his breath rasping in his throat.

Wearily the candidate straightened up, mute misery in his face. Fai Anbai was very near his own limit, but he refused to acknowledge it, and squared up — then caught sight of his father standing behind the stuffed target.

Grandfather Fai didn't move, but the sight of him was enough to give Fai Anbai a needed pause. He waved off the grateful candidates, who made themselves scarce.

When they reached the safety of their private lair, Fai Anbai faced his father. "I can't get past the awareness that the Traitor has to be one of mine," he admitted. "Someone I oversaw, who I shared field experience with. Who I taught, I trusted."

The chiefs did not do all the training, of course — they would never get anything else done. Instructors were brought in, most of whom never knew what they were training their students for. Other training was obtained in the field, again under various guises. That was after extensive early work, and interviews. And finally, potential candidates did field work together with the chief or with one or two very trusted senior agents (now all in the field, alas). There was no better way to truly know a person than living beside them, striving against danger and hardship to achieve a solution that would go unacknowledged by the world.

Ferrets were very carefully selected, with many washouts early on. Most of the earliest candidates did not even know they were candidates, being chosen from imperial guard recruits, sometimes underlings in the scribes, infrequently from other branches, including the graywings.

Errors at the higher level came to quiet ends, which was one of the pitfalls of the ferrets' proximity to power. "Errors" being those who disclosed a hereto hidden taste for power, for influence. For riches. Those who were otherwise blameless but who discovered they could not bring themselves to the lethal part of ferret practice worked in other regards — Fai Anbai's wife was one of these.

We cannot send an error out in the world, trained as we are trained, his father had said. *The only thing we can do is make it quick and painless. They never see it coming.*

Fai Anbai had not had to administer a surprise death

personally, but he knew his father had. And still mourned those, regarding them as personal failures. Fai Anbai had known one — his own age — in training. He'd trusted that candidate, laughed with him, drank with him, sparred with him . . . until he vanished, and his father told him why. For a year or two after, Fai Anbai had not trusted himself or anyone around him. It had made him far more cautious.

Their traitor had to know what was coming.

His father checked the windows and doors methodically as he said, "Min Ko just reported to me that Menace was called to Afan Yskanda's room last night. This after Di Lifan's report that Afan Yskanda's window was glowing with Essence all night."

Di Lifan was one of their prowlers. Sensitive to Essence, she and her team roamed the inner palace ceaselessly, using whatever sense it was that warned of Essence being used.

"I did not hear that," Fai Anbai said. "Afan Yskanda. Is this something we must look into? It will have to be reported to the emperor."

"Menace did that himself," Grandfather Fai said. "Menace" was the old code name for the first imperial prince. It ought to be changed, Fai Anbai supposed — though he suspected Prince Jion would enjoy it if he knew. "The assistant court artist appears to have a fever-induced talent for augury, and an affinity for water. He turned to the Ghost Monks to train him to control it — to shut it out."

Fai Anbai was relieved that this was not a new problem leaping up to attack them. "The emperor hates augurs. He will approve of that."

"So it is. When you see the prince again, you might ask about it. My advice is to not trouble the young artist, who at this moment is back with old Yoli, finishing up the wedding painting." Then, seeing that his son did not take the comfort from this relatively easy resolution to a minor problem, Grandfather Fai added, "*It* has to be living in fear, waking and sleeping."

"It" was the traitor, to which they did not put a gender pronoun, lest it lend unconscious bias.

"I think It's gloating day and night," Fai Anbai said bitterly. "I hoped It would be Tek Banu. Would make things so easy. But she was in the field all that spring. Or she probably would have figured out who the poisoner was in a day."

His father uttered a humorless laugh, and shook his head.

"I can't sleep—can't eat," Fai Anbai admitted. "I hate fishing in muddy waters. What did I not see?"

"You cannot continue wearing out the candidates," Grandfather Fai admonished. "They are going to begin believing you don't trust them. Worse, they will begin questioning what is on your mind. Which is what they are being trained to do. I need everything to be as usual, to not wake the sleeping snake."

Fai Anbai grimaced. "I'll remember that."

Grandfather Fai nodded; his son had a little metal Essence in him—not enough to be trained, that the shamans had said when he was small—enough to make him stronger for longer, so that he seemed to be made of metal rather than flesh. Until he dropped. "I believe It's one of mine," he said.

Fai Anbai's head whipped around. "What makes you say that?"

"It's . . . more instinct, at present. And the fact that there is no overt reason. I've combed through the accounts. Nothing amiss there. There is no trail of peculation, or even of interference in military matters or court. Minister of War Gu is certain of his leak, who had nothing to do with us."

Fai Anbai already knew that, of course—he'd presided at the interrogation before the man's summary end. His contacts led straight to the Shadow Panthers—and there dead-ended.

"I've also matched up dates of missions. I'm down to five."

"Who?"

"Not going to say. Yet. If circumstances require you to report to the emperor, I want you to be able to say truthfully that you don't know."

"We're on borrowed time," Fai Anbai murmured on an outgoing breath.

His father looked grim. "The emperor is too busy looking northwest—and we are well represented there."

Mother, Fai Anbai thought. He'd largely grown up without a mother, as she had gone into deep cover years ago. Extricating her, his father had carefully explained, would be a risk to her life. The emperor knew it, too. He counted on those reports smuggled out with great difficulty, now more than ever before.

"That should buy us the necessary time I need," Grandfather Fai said.

Fai Anbai translated that out to the time it would take to get a courier to the Easterners and back again. That question kept gnawing at Fai Anbai: *Including by someone who might know how to hire mercenaries?* "You are counting on Ri-Ri's testimony. Getting a ship there and back . . . that will be months."

"We need the time," Grandfather Fai repeated. "That letter Tek Banu hid is troubling enough. She had to have a reason to keep it. My guess is, the case was fresh enough that she took the journal with her. Until she returns, we won't know the connection that she saw. I'll say no more, except to wish that we had thought to put a shadow on the princess long ago."

The only one of the imperial children with a ferret shadow had been Prince Jion, merely because he was so troublesome. It had been for safety reasons. If he'd managed to get himself into a dangerous situation through his erratic behavior, the ferrets and the imperial guard would pay for it. Princess Manon never got into trouble. She was so very good, so very obedient. Her mother had been shadowed ever since she killed her first maid, even before the emperor asked for the ministers from the Su clan to be watched.

However — Fai Anbai realized now — that daughter had grown up in proximity to the second imperial consort. What did such a poisonous atmosphere do to a child?

More to the point, who could she possibly have been meeting in secret? They needed to know — to rule out some hapless admirer or the like — before they dared to go to the emperor. Then they had to find out, if they could, what part, if any, the princess played in whatever this person had as intent. She could — probably was — an unwitting victim, but one thing for certain: any kind of accusation would have ineradicable political consequences, which quite literally could not come at a worse time.

And yet, if they put a shadow on the princess now, it could be that they would unwittingly be assigning the traitor to her — thus revealing what, so far, no one but they, and Prince Jion, knew.

Fai Anbai sighed. "I have to go over to guard headquarters, and check over the security for the Imperial Examination."

They parted, each in silence.

TWENTY-THREE

JION WAS NOT ABLE to pin Afan Yskanda to a chair and pry lessons in Essence out of him any more than Yskanda was able to find out the details of the prince's encounter with his brother and sister. They both were kept busy over the days following that strange incident with the water vision, Yskanda with his art and Jion resuming leadership of the scholars. In those few days leading up to the Imperial Examination, the scholars met earlier and earlier, trading off frantic talk and even more frantic reading and rereading. (Also secret divinations, but we need not list those.)

Jion invariably ended the discussions with the best quality hot rice wine brought round, as the scholars between them were at least tangentially connected to the most powerful families in court, perhaps in the empire. And a connection, however tenuous, meant proximity to the sort of gossip that might lead to the poisoner.

Even abstemious Ze Kai unbent enough for a tiny cup, it was so delicious. Su Siar also accepted cups, which put a glow in her complexion; under its influence she went so far as to admit that she was not taking the Imperial Examination, as a high score would merely land her in some dusty ministry office, wearing an ugly robe, which "will do neither of us any good."

Tongues definitely loosened—a cascade of words. In that sense he'd been right. He knew that Su Siar would never be so blatant otherwise. She was on a Su family campaign, for which there could be no blame. She'd been raised to it from birth. He could even see the political sense of it, as Su Siar, through her mother, would inherit the largest tea trade fleet in the empire — they held the precious seal bringing the Easterners' superlative red tea to the Thousand Islands.

He had always liked Su Siar—and still did; it was out of kindness that he didn't tell her this campaign was a sea chase in boats of straw. One person lived in his heart, though she he could not marry.

Ayah, his father had refused to crown an empress, and the empire had not turned to dust. He could do the same.

Especially as he had no intention of ruling, he reminded himself. None! No chance.

He was appalled at the direction his thoughts had drifted, for the idea of fighting over the throne sickened him to the marrow. The more he talked to Manon now that they were both considered adults, the more he sensed that she — his childhood companion—would fight, and fight hard, against any of the siblings she saw as rivals. Including him. He could only use the last of that lingering bond to try to influence her toward being a better empress.

The morning after his first attempt at high-level intelligence gathering, when big Min Ko, the ferret, came in to taste Jion's breakfast, Jion looked at the man, wondering if he could be the traitor. No—surely a poisoner would avoid being appointed as a poison taster.

Bolstered by this profound insight, Jion said to him, "I told Fai Anbai I'd be listening for gossip that might reveal some-thing—but I don't know what's useful. Can I sum everything up for you, and you can pass on what you think Fai Anbai needs to hear?"

Min Ko bowed, impassive as always, but he did what he was asked.

Fai Anbai listened to the end, commenting, "Nothing of use here—nothing new. But this is actually a good idea. Keep him at it if you can."

The day of the Imperial Examination dawned under a clear sky. By the time the scholars left, the sky had darkened with a spring deluge. Some regarded that as an augury of ill luck, others of good; when the scores were posted after the customary agonizing wait, Ze Kai's name was first.

Prince Ran Hamin passed, and his brother didn't, which surprised no one, as the second prince had only tested to keep his brother company. They had reached the age to accept that from now on they would not share everything, but nothing would ever shake their reliance on one another.

Somewhat to the surprise of Second Prince Vaion and his cronies, Lu Fan did quite well—just behind pedantic Bi Kandatai—and even more surprising, Vaion's cousin and best friend Kui Zuinan actually scraped by, second to last.

No one was surprised who knew her when Su Inek came in fourth. Among the Su cousins, only Su Siar was fond of her, but then she was fond of everybody; Manon had tolerated Inek when they were all small, as Inek, daughter of a subsidiary family, had been taught to be humble, and she was at least as passionate as Manon about reading. But Manon had dropped her hard when, at age eleven, Inek not only knew all the quotations Manon brought out to impress the elders, she could cap them with better ones.

Another surprise to the Su clan was Su Ysek's very respectable number in the low twenties. But he, like Inek, was regarded by the old duke as a child of a subsidiary branch — that is, descended from Su daughters. How the old duke felt when he heard that this flighty great-grandson had also passed, while his favored and spoilt great-grandson Banek (descended through sons and first consorts, and who had disdained the prince's gathering of scholars) had failed, was not shared outside Su Manor, but no one in the family was (overtly) claiming green smoke emanated from the Su ancestors' graves in pride.

Of course Ze Kai received many expensive presents. Manon sent over a beautiful white jade waist ornament with a carved three-toed water dragon, sign of wisdom, suspended from a silken holder double-knotted in the Shared Luck style, with a very long tassel appended. She sent a note saying only that she had worked the silk knots herself, believing that of course he would come in first.

Instead of a present, Jion sent messengers around to all the scholars, inviting them to a celebration in Ze Kai's honor. He invited those who passed as well as those who hadn't, with a personal note for each saying it was also a commiseration party. It was to be on the night following Ze Kai's speech before court. Directly after that speech, everyone knew, there would be a feast in Ze Kai's honor: very formal, very strict, and with so many courses that Jion promised his party would be nothing but drinkables, with entertainment guaranteed not to be the least bit political.

It was a brilliant, rain-washed spring day when Ze Kai rode down the main street of the capital to present himself to court. He wore a huge red rose made of silk ribbon, much like bridegrooms wear, and a new, tasseled loaf. A high court position was guaranteed — it remained only for the elders to negotiate between them as to who would get him.

He was preceded by drummers and buglers. People along the street cheered and clapped — and proud, wily Left Chancellor Ze made sure there were servants in Ze Kai's train to throw out shiny brass coins to the crowd, which was guaranteed to keep the Ze name spoken with smiles, and gestures to bring luck.

Right Chancellor Su had to maintain an impassive demeanor as his hated rival's grandson came forward to bow to the emperor, then, as was customary, to read one of his examination answers to the court. It was beautifully written, full of praise for gods, empire, emperor, and laws — but in the choice of quotations, Ze Kai struck straight at the Su clan's cherished plan to put forward a law once again controlling all empire trade — with, of course, the Su clan overseeing the collection of customs.

The ministers, in their compliments, added their own shafts hidden in flowery compliments and quotations — everyone with one eye cocked toward the emperor on his throne. Who smiled benignly, favoring neither side.

Afterward the Su elders united in impotent fury, which spilled over into Drenched Blossoms. Manon — who still had her sights set on Ze Kai as the worthiest consort for a future empress — prudently decided to be elsewhere, and, remembering a promise she'd made Jion, sent over a note asking if he would like to visit the bookstore on the morrow. His party was to be held that night, but of course he did not have to do anything for its organization. He pounced on the invitation, though he knew very well that Manon would not be meeting any mystery men while he was in her company. But he looked forward to the outing as a chance to try to regain their old friendship.

When he climbed into Manon's carriage the following day, he found her as expected, wearing silver and deep purple with hints of gold glinting in the darting swallows embroidered on her robe, and in the golden tassels hanging from her waist tally. She wore a huge hat with a sheer veil, which permitted the interested to make out her lovely profile, while modestly obscuring her features. He had taken that veil for granted for years, but as he settled across from her, he wondered if she had tried varieties of diaphanous fabric to get that effect.

She put the veil back and greeted him.

"I expect the mood is one of bitter herbs over at Drenched Blossoms?" he said with sympathy.

"Honored Mother is furious on Great-Grandfather's behalf," Manon said. "He has worked so hard to regularize trade, and our imperial father has seemed inclined to favor the plans. We all hope this will not augur a setback."

"I don't attend court," Jion said, "but I've heard from some of the scholars that he has been less inclined to agree to reinstituting the trade law ever since that fiasco at Benevolent Winds."

"That was not the fault of the family," Manon stated. "*One* uncle, who has ever had a reputation for rampant avarice. So much damage done to the clan's good name — so undeserved. The Sus build ships for trade, and operate medicinal shops for the good of all."

Her calm tone of conviction was overlaid by another voice in Jion's memory, a shrill voice, thick with the accent of the local dialect, at Madam Nightingale's establishment. ". . . and those Su shops are the worst thieves of all! Did you know they are owned by a noble clan? And it's not just one family, it's all of them, the same thievery protected by the law!"

"Of course they're owned by a noble clan," another dancer had put in scornfully. "Who else would dare to hire bully-boys to beat anyone harvesting medicinal herbs on the back mountains, and force the pickers to bring back twice a normal load? Then charge swingeing prices . . ."

Jion looked into Manon's unblinking, steady gaze, wondering if she knew. "So much better than the disagreeable rumors I once heard about shops that charged prices so high the people could not afford medicine."

"I do not interfere in the family business," she replied. "My concerns are far wider. Such as the awareness that our beloved empire is safer with all gunpowder controlled by the government, which not only keeps it out of the hands of criminals, but guarantees it is pure, and properly handled. The same philosophy guides the family businesses — and that success leads to assurance that the same might be applied to governing trade and custom fees."

Jion bit back a retort that that sounded lofty and empress-like, except how well did it truly translate out in human terms? He was aware that he himself was new to this sort of thinking, and further, this was not the time to start an argument that would affect nothing, and ruin the day. It wasn't as if he didn't know what she would say, in loyalty to her mother's clan. There was nothing new here.

He was aware of restlessness as he gazed out at the imperial garden. It was such a beautiful spring day — cool, with a hint of rain in the air. He would have enjoyed a walk, but Manon did not walk. Jion had never considered how, from her earliest years, Manon regarded a curtained carriage as a necessity for entering the city. Not just to preserve her clothes from dust, but Jion now saw something he had never before noticed: from the slight lift to her chin to the posing of her hands, his sister was glorying in the panoply. Gone were the days of his taking for granted that it would require the labor of upwards of thirty people and six animals to get two people (for her maids were expected to walk behind the carriage) into the city.

He wondered if she would rather ride in a palanquin.

They rolled through the south gate, and the outriders began clearing people from the street. Vendors and shoppers and delivery people alike hastened to either side, then turned to stare openly.

"Tell me, Honored Sister — I ask only to be educated — would you ride in a palanquin if it were permitted?" Jion asked.

Manon turned her obsidian gaze to his. She regarded him in silence for a breath or two, then she said, "That is a strange question. But as it happens, I would, and proudly, too. The

Heavens have chosen us to be born with imperial blood, and that is one of the outward trappings to remind these good common people to whom their luck is due. Do you see how the common folk are well clothed? No one is thin with hunger? The street is swept, the houses well kept. The vendors sound cheerful, not desperate. They *should* be bowing right to the ground in gratitude."

"'If we cannot meet on top of Mt. Lir,'" Jion murmured, "'then we shall surely encounter one another on the jade terrace among the stars.'"

Manon's brows lifted. "I'd expect that poem from someone older. We both have long lives ahead of us. This puzzled sister certainly wishes a long and prosperous life for her first and best of brothers."

"As does he for his best of sisters," Jion returned, bowing slightly — hiding his regret over the fact that he was no longer sure that "best" was true.

Manon flushed delicately; to her, it was clear, there was no ambiguity.

"Here we are," she said, as the carriage rolled to a halt.

Jion leaped down, waiting as Manon was helped by her maids, her train shaken out behind her, and her veil protecting her face from the gazes of the vulgar. As Jion had expected, the imperial guard and the two rows of servants had gone ahead. The ordinary folk not only had been cleared from the shop, the servants had swept any floor the princess might walk, and dusted or wiped any surface she might touch, while the guards kept the crowd at a distance of some twenty paces. There was no chance any mystery man was going to be slipping past the guards with their wickedly sharp spears held sideways, keeping the crowd well back.

Brother and sister walked into the store, where the owner and his clerks bowed low. If they regretted the custom they lost through these doings, there was no sign of it. Perhaps, Jion thought as he stared sightlessly at a new stack of *Reports from the Imperial Court, Illustrated,* as soon as he and Manon were gone, those waiting outside for a glimpse would rush in asking what the imperial pair had bought, or looked at, or said, and business would be brisk.

Manon went straight to the shelf of historical and philosophical works. Jion browsed the poetry, then wandered to the rear of the store where older books were kept. The back door was open, as he'd expected in this balmy weather.

There was the alley leading toward the temple—he could see its heaven-turned eaves in the distance. And, nearer, there was the fence covered with vines, beginning to bloom, where Ri-Ri and Lily had stood. Definitely close enough to recognize a person, if not to see details like the shade of eyes or the number of moles.

Jion looked about him. It was a small space, almost a little room in itself, stacked with copies of very old books that were probably put out on the street for a pittance to lure custom. He had a clear view to the walls, thus it was a good place to not be overheard, but few would browse here. All the newer books were in front.

"Jion?"

He turned, to find Manon framed by the inner door. "Anything here is worthless. The few of value, we have copies of."

"I was looking for old storybooks. For Gau-Gau," he said.

"Oh? Which books?"

"*The Flower Fairy Histories.*"

It was not quite a sparring match; he saw her take in his empty hands, the stacks of dusty books (which he was now studiously examining) and her smile widened with a hint of pity. "Does she still read such things? I remember Imperial Grandmother gave me those when I was eight or nine."

"Gau-Gau still likes them," he stated. "*I* know she's getting older, but does *she* know that?"

"She ought to begin realizing it," Manon said mildly. "But I suspect she will always be a baby to our honored imperial parents."

He shrugged, his hands behind his back. "This fond elder brother believes Honored Sister is entirely right. In any case, no flower fairies, or any fairies, seen here. But copies can be made—her birthday isn't far off."

He followed Manon to the front again, and this time she went to the poetry and he to the history section. When he brought two books to the proprietor, she was there at his side, looking down. "I did not know you had an interest in Cor Keyin's interpretation of Kanda's historical writings.

He didn't—he bought them entirely to introduce Ze Kai's name. "Ze Kai suggested them. He's right when he points out that what Kanda actually wrote on government is very little,"

Jion said.

Her lips tightened at the sound of Ze Kai's name. That suggested some kind of feeling—so the mystery man was less likely to be a lover? Or was she, like he, diffusing the adults' speculation by her own method, as he did with his supposed harem?

Jion gave no sign that he'd witnessed this tiny revelation; he was hunting a tiger, armed with shadows and smoke. "Or, at least, what we have of Kanda's words. He might have written great tracts—he was, after all, a court official to two different kings—but we'll never know, unless something turns up in some obscure mountaintop temple in a far island somewhere. Everything else is an interpretation."

"Except the absolute law," Manon pointed out as they settled into the carriage again. "That the ruler has the mandate of Heaven. Everything begins from there."

"And we come back to our starting place. Ayah, the scholars will do that enough later tonight. No, I amend that—tonight is sheer celebration. I expect the scholarly discussions are over, at least for another three years. But you are welcome to join us."

"Thank you. All things considered, it is perhaps inopportune; I know Honored Mother expects me at her side. Will you continue meeting once it is over?" Manon asked, as the carriage began to move.

Jion waved his fan idly. "Do you really think any of them will want to?"

"They will come," she said, "if you summon them."

"Summon! I don't summon anybody," he said. "Summonses are for heirs."

"And yet, Imperial Father sent you to the Silk Islands," she observed—yes, here she was, hunting her own tiger. "You even had a military tally. Which you neglected to mention when we met in the garden."

"I didn't believe it was real. That is, I knew I had it, but I assumed that all the decisions would be made by the ferrets—who chose the courier ship and the honor guard, and the schedule. Did whoever you heard that from also tell you that the graywings made it vanish again as soon as I returned? And that my sole use of it, if it could even be considered a use, was to make a recommendation the military leaders had already decided on?"

Manon could not figure out Jion's mood. Did he want to use

the coveted tally? Which she had never been offered, but then she had never left the palace, except in company with the entire imperial family. Once again she subdued regret, bending her thoughts away. "Tallies," she mused, and probed in another direction. "I expect these things are kept in a vault somewhere in Imperial Father's pavilion. I've never actually seen where they, and the imperial seal, are kept."

"Certainly not under Bitternail's bed," Jion said, laughing.

She ignored his flippancy and asked more directly. "Has Imperial Father showed you where such things are kept?"

"He has not. All I know about them is what I did while I had one — which was to keep it in my sleeve pocket during the day, and Min Ko had it at night. I was terrified of losing it."

"The fact that it was yours for that time," she said, "could be seen as a test for an heir."

"Then there must be many, many heir candidates running around out there. Including the ferret chief, who I know had that same tally when he caught up with me the Rat year." Jion twirled his fan.

"It could be viewed as a test of a possible heir," Manon repeated, wanting to see his reaction. Wanting him, very badly, to deny it, to deny the heirship. To go back . . . but she knew there was no going back. And there was the inward spike of distrust.

"It could be viewed as the act of a prince following his father's orders," Jion countered, brows slanted with wicked humor. "I had enough of being confined to my manor. I am the most obedient of princes. Besides, I enjoyed the journey. Very much, and for reasons that had nothing to do with the tally."

Was she going to ask what he enjoyed about the trip?

No, he saw with regret. She had no real interest in what he thought of ship travel, or his view of the mighty cascades either side of the bridge at Blue Jade. Or in the heroic commanders, about whom books lay right back there in the bookstore, *One Hundred Heroes against the Shadow Panther Army*. Her discerning eyes were so firmly bent on her imagined trail that she missed Mt. Lir above her, and the sky full of stars beyond that.

Pity prompted him to say, "I hope I can spend a lifetime traveling about the far reaches of the empire, inspecting — nothing too arduous — like Prince Ratha of old. Who was heard to say that he pitied his imperial brother, stuck in the palace, never to leave, except to examine the orchids once a year. Much as I enjoyed the Journey to the Clouds, thanks to you, I can imagine that fifty years of it might get old."

Manon smiled, making a small nod of acknowledgment at the compliment. And then she went right on hunting her tiger. "Speaking of princes. And brothers. Have you ever gone into the dragon and phoenix archive, where our ancestors' own writings are kept?"

"Once," he said. "Not long before I was sent off to the Silk Islands the first time. Speaking of which." He turned, his voice casual, his posture relaxed. "Did you ever get the letter I sent, the first time I was sent? I sent it here, through a scribe — I thought I was so very clever, not using my own handwriting."

"You asked me that before," she reminded him, her gaze steady, but the pulse in her neck ticked. Then she raised fingers to her face, her brow furrowing. "Oh, don't remind me of that terrible time. How I wished I had — it would have saved us so much worry."

Contrite at upsetting her with the memory, he said apologetically, "Did I ask before? Forgive me for bringing it up! Anyway, you asked about the emperors' archive. I went there once, with some grand idea of looking up the records of our ancestors' battles. I had this idea of glory in martial might, and wanted to see it from a prince's viewpoint. I made the mistake of looking at one of Great-Great Grandfather Maoyan's later . . . edicts. Then I walked right out, and never went back."

She had been about to point out that she was deeply involved in studying Maoyan. Taken aback at Jion's reaction, she considered whether admitting to her own interest would be too revealing — or had she just received the assurance she wanted? "There are those who find him a perfect example of both a warrior king and Lao Sha's sage king."

His face lengthened in an appalled expression. "You're joking, right?"

She frowned. "Why would I joke about our ancestors? So unfilial!"

"Manon, it might be unfilial, but I can't forget that he killed off a good part of the family over imagined conspiracies! The cousins, one by one. Half his grandchildren. All his brothers, at the end. And that doesn't touch the deaths of ordinary subjects that he ordered."

"Who is to say they were not conspiring against him?" she asked.

"A ten-year-old child conspiring against the throne?"

"A ten-year-old can carry poison, and know she is doing it," Manon stated. "If some evil person tells her it is right. What does a ten-year-old know?"

Jion was going to point out that ten-year-olds can be shipped off somewhere safe to be educated, but that would merely start an argument about hypotheticals. "What makes you find him a sage king?"

Manon hesitated, reluctant to admit that she was fascinated by Emperor Maoyan's writings, especially as a young prince. If Jion knew, surely he would read them, too. Maoyan illustrated more clearly than any others of the family exactly how to gain, and build, power. Fear, he said repeatedly, was a dragon's greatest weapon — and so it was true for a dragon emperor. He could be the best swordsman in the empire, but that only assured one defeat at a time. Fear forced squabbling siblings into polite silence. Fear tamed an unruly populace.

Jion leaned forward, elbows on his knees as the carriage swayed and jiggled gently. "Honored Sister Manon, you might not have reached this part yet, but he had *an entire island* put to the sword, just to chase one rebellious duke. Who he wasn't even sure was there. That's what I found that day, and I've never been back."

"I know," she said, surprising him with her calm. "I read that. It was a very small island."

"It wasn't small to those who lived there, I'm sure."

She ignored this speculation on his part. "His reasoning makes sense, if you accept the philosophy of the emperor — who cannot be everywhere at once — using his power to cut out the rot for the greater good. He said one clean strike and he averts civil war."

Jion lurched back in recoil. "There is nothing *clean* about slaughter. I've seen it. Twice. And I saw the effects of it in the fresh mounds on Green Jade Island. I repeat, Emperor Maoyan was not even sure that duke was there."

"But the empire was quiet thereafter. That makes him right, whether or not the man was actually dead. Duke Viar might have crawled into some hole or other until he died," Manon said quickly. "That is effective use of force, rather than the horror of half the empire embroiled in civil war."

They stared at one another. He said, "Except the entire empire was about to erupt into civil war before he died."

"He had plans for that, too. I've just begun reading that part. But he became ill and died before he could bring his plans to fruition," Manon stated. "I'm still reading — there are so many testaments to get through — and yes, some of his rulings seem drastic, but these were drastic times, with famine in the north, and devastating floods in the south, and dragons spewing fire rocks right there above where we sailed last spring, not counting the war with the Westerners."

"Proving that Heaven was not happy with their chosen," Jion said, reaching for humor, to hide how shocked he was.

Manon dismissed his words with a flick of her fan. "We don't actually know if the natural devastation caused the unrest or Heaven was dissatisfied with him and caused the devastation. The list of auguries alone is laughable — the geomancers saying one thing one day, and another thing the next. Trying to preserve their lives."

"I'm not about to defend the augurs and geomancers," Jion said, and pushed aside the curtain with his own fan. "Ayah, here we are. Good luck with Bloody Maoyan. I'll be interested in how you assess his later years. I haven't the stomach to read those records myself."

With a flick of his fan and a half-smile, he whirled out of the door and joined Min Ko, who had been walking beside the carriage, carrying the books Jion had purchased.

Manon remained in the carriage, which, at her orders, passed by the Pavilion of Sun's Grace, now empty, where the imperial heir would live. For years she refused to go near it until it should be hers, but of late she liked passing its long walls, observing the beautiful fruit trees above those walls, the upturned corners to the buildings, and wondering what the private garden was like that this pavilion alone shared with the emperor's own residence.

When Emperor Maoyan was a prince, he, too, had walked by that same building. Then he had come to live in it . . .

Prince Ratha. Manon sat back, shutting her eyes as the carriage rounded past the ancestral shrine, and the long train of guards and servants quietly dispersed, leaving only the driver and the six maids. If Jion could just be satisfied as a Prince Ratha, everything would be so very much better, so very much.

Jion watched her carriage vanish under the leafing trees toward the Pavilion of Sun's Grace. Interesting that she went that way now. She always used to avoid the empty heir's pavilion as if the place were haunted. Though they'd been told no one had lived there since the death of their aunt the night Great-Grandmother Empress died.

Manon admired Emperor Maoyan? He would have thought she would model herself after Great-Grandmother Empress, who had managed to settle the empire into peace after Emperor Maoyan's bad years. Who had been about the only family member left standing when Emperor Maoyan died, being a sister more interested in books than the sword.

He knew he ought not to feel responsible for changing Manon's mind. She would resent it if she thought he was attempting it. And there were elders to educate her. But if she wanted to be the heir, then she ought to be the *best*. Another Emperor Maoyan would be the opposite of the best.

Except that she clearly did not think so.

He walked back into his manor, aware of Min Ko putting the new books in his study. Jion stood uncertainly, torn between diving into that reading, and his pursuit of that strange business about affinities and Essence. He did not feel he had any Essence talent, that was for certain. He knew what an Essence Talent looked like — Ari. He certainly was not able to summon Essence while fighting. He'd tried.

"Air." Hah. What an irony! If he truly had a talent, it figured the gods would stick him with something completely useless, like air, instead of Ari's amazing fire and metal. Ayah! He couldn't go to the west court to work out his mood with staff and sword, for his designated period was early mornings.

For the first time a thought slipped in: if *he* were to move into Pavilion of Sun's Grace as imperial heir, he would have his own court.

No, no, no. No bloody battles for that accursed throne.

He shed his silks, and danced away the bad mood.

TWENTY-FOUR

"NO, YOU ARE NOT going off to your temple again," Court Artist Yoli said. "The emperor is pleased with The Wedding Procession, and I'm told it will hang in the formal interview hall. The first imperial prince is honoring us by hosting a celebration in the evening. Of course we must be there. And I, for one, plan to get so drunk I cannot find my feet. We've got a rare few days to do absolutely nothing. Enjoy it! You won't get many. You can hunker over musty old tomes any time."

Any time he was free, Yskanda thought to himself, but utterly without rancor. He liked painting through all the daylight watches, whereas he still felt that studying affinities was a duty. And so far, not a particularly successful one.

"We don't even have to stuff ourselves into those hideous hempen boxes this year," Yoli added with satisfaction—having in old age had a surfeit of same, though he was aware that his young self would have been appalled by this attitude; the Journey to the Clouds this year would not be graced by the imperial family, the emperor had decided. Being the emperor, he did not have to give a reason.

Court Artist Yoli cocked an eye toward his assistant. "You're not grieved over missing the Journey, are you? I could try to get you sent—we can always use fresher sketches. We used all the best of the old ones in last spring's painting."

Yskanda did not want to point out that the emperor would

never let him go. Nor did he want his name put before the emperor. He had been miraculously overlooked for weeks, which he hoped would continue. "This assistant thanks his honored master for the thought, but there is plenty of work right here."

Yskanda looked around as if to get started on it. He was reaching for a roll of paper when Fennel appeared with a spoken request that Assistant Court Artist Afan was to come directly from the Hall of Glorious Harmony to play Circle with the prince before the gathering.

As soon as the page was gone, Court Artist Yoli said, "Cultivate that connection! It could be that he will be the one giving you orders when this old corpse of mine finally decides it's had enough. But you didn't hear that from me."

Anything Yskanda could say to that was such a bridge of knives he merely bowed and went out to exchange his work robe for his court one.

One of Jion's harem had a sister who was part of a dance troupe. When, earlier that morning, his grandmother mention-ed when he paid his daily respects that the emperor was going to receive the new painting at court later that day, and he'd designated it for one of the formal halls, Jion recognized a new excuse for a celebration. He stopped at his manor long enough send off a messenger to hire the dance troupe, and told White-leaf to invite the entire imperial family as well as the artists.

Then he went on to make his bow to his father, who received him amid a welter of reports. Imperial Father seemed tense, and his greeting was brief before he released Jion to his day. Jion withdrew, sensing imperial thunder in the air. Why? Try as he might, he could find no fault in his own behavior. Nor in his siblings'.

He carried on with his usual schedule — practice court, and then back to sessions with Master Zao — trudging through the Grand Historian's court records, but he finally gave up, knowing he was marking time. Before he changed to court clothing for the presentation of the new art, he sent off the messenger to Yskanda, as we have seen.

The Wedding Procession hung on the north wall in the formal interview room to the east of the throne room, where sunlight would never fall directly on it and fade its brilliant colors. Mornings, when interviews were likeliest to happen, the room filled with diffuse light, which enhanced the vibrant and lifelike shades.

Those inclined toward art — and those who for whatever reason wished to be perceived as appreciative of art — crowded before the painting. This, as did the previous year's painting of the Journey to the Clouds, told a story as one moved along. Or rather it told two stories. The surface story was, of course, the grand procession for the wedding of Princess Lily to the Easterners' Grand Prince.

But for those whose eyes were captured by the exquisitely rendered houses, animals, and people along the streets, it was a story of the imperial capital in all its busy life. Many hands had contributed to this work, but there was no piecemeal appearance, testifying to the genius that oversaw all.

It was human nature to look for one's face first of all. The ministers were all there, each carrying his jade tally of office, his robes of office perfectly rendered in all detail. Being satisfied with their own profiles (Yoli, wise and experienced, had admonished his artists to slash ten years of aging off those portraits, but otherwise keep them recognizable) the ministers and courtiers were at leisure to look at everyone else's, and then wander outward westward and eastward, in one direction to where the great river curved around to empty into the sea, and the other framing the city with jagged mountains rising toward the great snow-topped pinnacle of Mt. Lir.

Vendors, carters, strolling scholars, scurrying messengers, flirting young couples (and some not so young), shopkeepers, customers, children, chickens, dogs, cats, horses, donkeys, and myriad birds all were captured on silk, caught forever in a moment to be seen centuries after they had long left these lives.

The emperor summoned the court artist to receive his reward, which he was to share with his assistants as he deemed fit, and they were all dismissed. As always, though the emperor had been nothing but complimentary, it was not until Yskanda saw his train receding through the great double doors solely used by him that he could relax and smile more naturally when bowing to receive praise.

Then all dispersed, Court Artist Yoli, who had been coughing irritably, to get in a short nap before the celebration, and Yskanda perforce accompanying Jion back to his manor. As they were followed by Jion's servants, the conversation was solely about the art.

When they entered Jion's study at last, the prince did not bother with politeness — He shut slid the door shut and stood with his back to it. "You wanted to know about —"

Yskanda spoke at the same time, desperation crumbling his usual wall of reticence. "Your imperial highness once mentioned this unworthy's brother and sister —"

They both stopped, and Yskanda flushed at his own temerity.

Jion said in a quick, low voice, "Once we both get a chance to walk in the garden, I'll give you all the details. They're both well, your brother in the army, and your sister a gallant wanderer. And a martial artist of some renown."

"She was excellent," Yskanda said, with pride. "Far better than I, though I am older."

With his back to the door, Jion felt the subtle reverberations of someone approaching down the hall. He moved away from the door, saying, "Let's not sit and do all that breathing. I did enough of it in martial arts exercises and in dance training, and I still don't see any effect. Ah, did I tell you I used to do a lot of dance?"

Min Ko entered, bearing a tray.

Yskanda made a business of setting his books down, red about the ears. "I don't think so . . ."

Jion waved that off. "It's frowned on, though I regard that as inexplicable, since it's easy enough to point to records of past imperial family members who entertained one another, and court, and anyone else they could get, by dance, by singing, by music. There was one emperor who as crown prince had a play written for him to dance the lead role in that went on for a day and a half. I hope for the sake of his court he was a good dancer. Anyway, you will surely find plenty to draw tonight — I'm told the girls are all pretty, which is all my brother and his friends ask — except maybe Cousin Ysek, who'd much prefer pretty boys."

Min Ko was bringing out the Circle board. They sat down across from each other, and Jion cocked an eye at Yskanda in question. "Nothing to say on the subject of pretty girls — or boys? Vaion's crowd usually has plenty to say, the prospect of passion being one of the first requirements for a successful entertainment."

The second prince and his noble-born companions had the luxury of saying what they wished, but they were not prisoners, or hostages. Yskanda did not wish to point out that he had cut that kind of passion out of his life, lest it be used against him.

However, Jion had become unsettlingly adept at reading him. "Ah, monkish living is a defense? Of course it is." Then he mercifully passed on. "Essence study. You've been at it for weeks. Is it useful or not to pick the theoretical from the practical?"

Yskanda considered the question as a servant placed fine carved and gilt boxes of Circle markers at their right hands.

"If you look at what is sold in bookstores, most of the works on divination are about determining ways to avoid disaster," Yskanda said as they began to set up their markers — they had fallen into the habit of trading off, one match Yskanda with white and Jion with black, then the reverse for the next match. "But it is an error to think of the Path as something purely mechanical."

Jion knew the answer to that one. Master Zao had been very tiresome on the subject. "Yes — it also states that righteousness is the substance of the world seen and unseen." He repeated the precept as one who had had to write and rewrite it a thousand times as soon his hand could grip a brush, as his opening moves attempted Golden Eagle Strikes Hare.

Tick! Tick! Tick!

Afan Yskanda might be diffident in manner, but he was merciless on the Circle Board. "That is indeed so," he said kindly as he struck back with Crab Wrapped in Lotus Leaves. Tick! "It appears that what we regard as divination is three ways of thought woven together."

Jion was startled by that. "Three? But the Westerners follow different ideas, and the Easterners are still Suanek's children. Or so I was told." Tick!

Tick, tick, tick! "Many assume that the Path mostly concerns geomancy."

Tick! "Where to build, balance in arranging rooms, doors on the south," Jion said, and pounced, capturing one of Yskanda's scouts. "I'm not arguing."

Tick, tick! Tick, tick!

"They also associate the Path with the stone talismans that help ease the turning of dragons under the earth, because when the ground shakes and the stone plinths glow with Essence light so strong everyone can see it, they become a visual manifestation of the charms, rituals, and talismans that affect the physical world." Tick, tick! "It's easy to forget—and some never learn—that the Path also includes the stars and the moons and their influence, all with their affinities."

Tick! With a thoughtful air, Yskanda captured a square of Jion's cavalry. "True."

"It's also easy to forget Kanda's notion that the endless interaction of Heaven's Essence and Earth's is what brings about everything that exists in the material world." Tick, tick! "We mostly turn to Kanda for wisdom in how to live this life well."

"Brother Pine tells me to contemplate the visible manifestation of Essence as consolidated in matter," Yskanda said, thumb resting on a piece as he turned his profile toward the window, beyond which starlings braided upward in flight. "And how all matter dissolves and becomes invisible again," he said slowly. "I hear each word, but I can't find my way in them, when it comes to practice. Suanek's way, putting Essence in the world of the spirit, seems both easier to understand, and more dangerous—like the world of dreams." Snap! His attention returned to the board.

"I'll agree with that," Jion said, distracted by an image of tentacles looming up five stories overhead—and they began a duel for the northwest corner of the board as he waited, knowing a point was coming. Ze Kai had said recently at one of Jion's gatherings, *Afan Yskanda speaks his mind seldom, but when he does speak, I've always found his point worth listening to.*

Yskanda picked up a piece and turned it in his fingers as he said, "Separating out three different ways of thought helps me to understand why it is I have such trouble with what Brother Pine thinks so simple," he said. Now he was staring out the other window at the golden cassia, brilliant flowers bright as metal, the brighter as the leaves had yet to bud.

Then he blinked and turned back to the game. Snap, tick! "I have worked on the breathing—correctly now—until I can feel myself sitting on a world of water, with more in the sky above. But it is there, and I am here. I can no more use it than I can assuage thirst by looking out a window at a rainstorm."

"Ari struggled with that, I know," Jion said, wondering what Yskanda was building toward in the south and west of the board. He couldn't be . . .

As always, when Jion mentioned Ari, Yskanda's smile brightened. "Oh, if only we could see one another again!" he breathed, one of the rare times emotion broke through his control. Sure as the autumnal flight of the swallows the smile vanished, and Jion knew Yskanda was thinking *Not here*.

But he had too generous a heart to say it aloud. He knew Jion would free him if he could. Yskanda went on quickly, "Yet the way she found to use Essence probably would be no more useful for me than Brother Pine's. It wasn't until this past few days I've begun to wonder if I have been using Essence all along, through wood. Through my brushes."

"You mean when you paint?" Jion asked. "Of course."

"That makes me wonder if I have any actual ability at all, or it is merely Essence acting through me."

Jion snorted. "You can talk to your abbot about that, but I suspect he'd say that the Essence is a part of you, not some separate entity."

Yskanda said slowly, "I can live with that. I think. If that is how Essence and I co-exist. But at the same time, if it is true, I will not be able to do what you ask — I could invite you to our classes and teach you about employing the brush in art, yet I don't believe that will aid your own learning."

Jion snapped his fan open and used it to push the idea away. "No, no. The memory of Master Zao and his endless lessons in painting bamboo leaves when I was eleven . . . No painting lessons!" Then he scowled down at the board. "You are! You're trying the Dragon's Tail of Ten Galloping Horses!"

Tick, tick, tick.

"And succeeding." Yskanda's smile was briefly mirthful, then rueful. "Unlike my attempts with Brother Pine." He scooped up the captured markers. "You were not paying attention," he added with gentle reproof.

"I'll get my revenge. And you could not be less successful than —"

Whiteleaf entered, bowing low. "His imperial highness, Second Im —"

Vaion banged through the door and pushed past the hapless graywing, finishing cheerfully, "My imperial highness is here early, but you won't mind." Behind him appeared several young men in their finest silks, tasseled sleeves swinging, ribbons fluttering from half-pulled up hair, the rest braided down their backs with gems glinting in the ties.

"We had to escape," Su Ysek said, eyeing the game. "Are you losing, Cousin? You're losing! I didn't think you *could* lose."

"Yskanda pays no heed whatsoever to my imperial esteem," Jion mourned. "Escape what? If you're bringing the guards down on you, I'll thank you to walk right out again. The servants just got this place cleaned up and the candles lit."

"Su Manor," Su Ysek said in a voice of doom. "The uncles have been arguing ever since Cousin Banek failed the Imperial Examination. I think he really believed that his august birth would waft him to first place."

"Oh?" Jion asked. "What could the uncles be arguing about? They don't change the scores once they're posted."

"It's not that." Su Ysek looked around. "Where's the rice wine?"

"The kitchens are still preparing things for the party that is supposed to start *in an hour*," Jion said.

"Tell him," Kui Zuinan said, snickering. His reddened face made it clear he'd already begun his own party.

"Our excellent Prince Jion already knows my honored great-grandfather is, or was, randier than ten goats," Ysek stated airily, and Yskanda—who had at that moment been drinking from the tea at his elbow—choked.

Vaion pounded him on the back. "You certainly wouldn't think it to look at him," Vaion said. "That is, you wouldn't think that any woman would want him. Even a hundred years ago when he was our age. That nose! And I say so with the greatest respect."

"It's the bastards again," Su Ysek said in a slightly lower voice—that could be heard clearly all through the room. "Great-Grandfather was yelling down a thunder of dragons on Uncle Jifar for wasting so much on the extra tutors for Banek, until Grand-Uncle Ja Ne came back at him about how much *he's* wasted on the illegitimates, then Great-Aunt Li agreed, saying that *her* children certainly never got . . . Oh, you know the rest."

"Illegitimates? I know he has a lot of consorts," Jion said. "I don't think I've met them all."

Su Ysek sat on the edge of the table. "Two died, and a few left him. But we're talking about the ones he never married. At least three—grandmother says—tricked him by having children for instant riches. But there are some he never acknowledged, and there's been trouble over it, though we're told it's not filial to ask."

"How many children does he have?" Vaion asked. "Is it strange to have cousins pop up that you never knew?"

"Very," Su Ysek said. "Especially when I hear about them but never get to meet them. It's like being haunted by ghosts. *I* say, why not have them in? Su Manor already has half a city's worth of residents, what's a few more? Grandmother says to send them right out again, or more will turn up like stray dogs. But we like stray dogs! Don't we?" He turned to his younger brother.

"We do," Tarek spoke up. "A stray dog is a bath and a meal from being a pet. And they always love you. Which is more than I can say for cats."

"Or cousins," Su Ysek said, thinking of bad-tempered Banek. "Anyway, when the elders get going at the main hall, that's time for us run to the west hall — except Banek is throwing tantrums all over there, so we decided to come here. We knew you'd not mind us early."

"As long as you don't drink everything before any of the guests get a chance to show up — ah, just in time," he added, hearing women's voices. "The dancers are here."

"Dancers?"

"Dancers?"

Vaion said, with feeling. "Jion, you are the *best* brother!"

The game was summarily ended. Soft-footed servants appeared to sweep it away as the young men adjourned to Jion's larger hall, where he had thoughtfully provided a side desk with paper and inks in case Yskanda was inspired, but (he hastened to explain) he was not expected to paint unless he saw something worth painting.

The tone was set early by Vaion and Su Ysek and their friends and relations. By the time the rest of the imperial family arrived, the warm, candlelit air was redolent with the fragrance of wine, and conviviality ringing in all voices. The second imperial consort remained long enough to realize that the emperor was not going to attend, therefore she would not get credit for her generous condescension in putting up with the noise of His Imperial Majesty's various relations she liked least. She left, missed by no one.

Manon arrived, with one intent: to see if Ze Kai wore the double-luck knotted water dragon jade she had given him.

He did not.

She tried listening to the music, but its excellence was

destroyed by the noisy merrymakers. She endured the crowd and the chaos until she, too, was certain that Imperial Father was unlikely to put in an appearance (a wise choice). She despised the noisy boys, cared nothing for the sleeve dancers, and wondered why Ze Kai was playing this game of detachment with her; she would have been astonished to learn that the moment he saw her gift he cut the silk off with his father's sword, tossed it tassel and all into the fire, and gave the jade to his personal servant.

Manon, like her mother, departed early — missed by no one, which never occurred to Manon. She had from the age of twelve been the most interesting person in the room, and believed that increased with age. But she was very aware that no one pursued her. At one time Jion would have chased after her, begging her to stay, but he had coarsened, and become more arrogant. Was it age, or the increasing attentions from the emperor?

Both, she decided, as she climbed into her cart. Ayah, she had far more interesting pursuits, and returned to her poring over the papers of Emperor Maoyan, glorying in the fact that his blood ran in her veins.

On the departure of mother and daughter the rest of the company all seemed to brighten with an unconscious sense of release. The dowager empress smiled benignly, genuinely enjoying the dancers, who (seeing her august presence) had hastily reorganized their program, favoring traditional dances. She and Jion's mother looked on smiling, even when the leader of the dancers — after Vaion got up and tried to dance with them — dared to draw Jion in.

She might have had mixed intentions — who would blame her for trying her hand at attracting a handsome, rich young imperial prince? — but her words were sincere when she said, "I've heard about your dancing. Are you really able to do the Leap? Would you dance for us? No, dance *with* us!"

Jion tried to demur, protesting that it was unseemly. He cast a laughing glance toward his mother and grandmother, but when the dowager empress — on her third cup of excellent wine — said, "Why not? I remember seeing my grandfather dance the Leap when I was a child," he bowed.

"As you command, Honored Grandmother."

He shed a couple of layers right there. And then, for the first time as himself, danced in public. The music was superlative, and after a couple of surreptitious awkward steps and hasty readjustments, the dancers faded back from their usual formation, ringing him as he danced with exalting grace.

The empress dowager wept to see the Kui brilliance emerge once again, unweighted by Jehan metal. Opera was her favorite diversion, but watching her grandson was even better; no one in all her memory leaped so high, and with such effortless grace.

After Jehan danced, of course the boys had to get up and try it as well, he made it look so easy. Their abject failure ignited gusts of wine-inspired mirth. The party ended soon after that, everyone giddy with good feeling; the leader of the troupe complimented the prince, who accepted with smiling absence, his gaze polite but not inviting.

"Told you so," her sister murmured as they packed up their scarves and things to depart.

"Can't blame a girl for trying," was the tart reply — a lot less tart for the promising weight of the clinking bag the prince's steward had given them.

Jion never noticed Yskanda vanishing, several sheets of drawing paper with him; he staggered off to bed once he'd booted his brother and friends out the door. "Min Ko," he said, heavy-eyed. "Tell Yarrow not to wake me come morning. Listen, here's what I need you to pass on to the ferrets. I'm sure none of it is worth the air it takes to speak, but a promise is a promise . . ."

And, as *he* had promised, Min Ko made his report the next day to the Fais.

Fai Anbai listened all the way through, slowly shaking his head. He would not admit out loud that he was relieved there was no new thing requiring him to drop all his current lines of inquiry, each more urgent than the next. But then he saw his father thumb his small beard, a bad sign.

"What?" he barked as soon as Min Ko left. "What in that morass of gossip could possibly catch your notice? Not Su's miscellany?" He named the most absurd of the many bits of gossip.

To his surprise, his father said, "It might be."

"Ayah! Surely you've had people run all those down years ago. In fact, I know you did. I had to follow one of them myself, until Guai Li returned from aiding Mother in the north. And I distinctly recollect that Peony had made us a chart of all Old Su's consorts, married and unmarried, offspring, and whereabouts."

"Which I will have to fetch out, as Peony is still tracking down those mercenaries," Grandfather Fai said. "What caught my ear is that business about new ones."

"Third hand. No, fourth," Fai Anbai muttered tiredly, though he knew he should not discard any scrap of anything without its being duly checked. But right now he was buried in investigations — and the Sus were so *very* well spied-on.

"Let me do that," Fai Anbai's wife spoke up unexpectedly.

Both men turned doubtfully to her as she stood there with one hand pressed to her lower back, her very pregnant belly like the prow of a ship.

Yan Yian grinned. "Every midwife in the imperial city knows the others. What easier subject for me to investigate, looking the way I do? I'm a naval consort, my husband recently relocated to the capital, so I must seek a midwife. A few swipes to my brows, my nose, my neck, and my face is completely different — and forgettable. They'll all be looking at my belly anyway. I can say I don't know anyone, but I trust whoever serves noble families — very auspicious for my child — and find out who is connected to the Sus that way. Any woman trying to attach to the Su name, and fortune, won't be shy about that. I think I can find what you want in the month or so I have left, and no one the wiser — including the traitor, as I will not go through any of our usual methods or people."

Fai Anbai and his father knew Yan Yian was one of the best researchers the ferrets had. With a strong sense of relief, he waved the entire subject over to her. "It's yours. Now, where were we with . . ."

TWENTY-FIVE

WHEN THE SPRING WINDS came up off Te Gar's bay and Ari was out in the courtyard, she could sometimes hear the reverberations from the big drum outside the Justice Building. She reassured herself that this was proof that justice for ordinary subjects of the empire was possible, because any subject of the empire could pick up the red cloth-tied mallet and strike that drum. If the judges had been terrible, surely she would have heard whispers from the umbrella-maker two doors down, or the herb-seller, or any number of other gossips up and down Prince Ratha's Miracle Victory Way.

The imperials weren't all bad, she told herself. If they had been, Shigan — Jion, that is — would have escaped again, she told herself.

And yet . . . and yet she kept thinking of all those out in the world who did not dare come drumming for justice. Some nights, as she stared out her open window at Phoenix Moon sinking slowly toward the horizon, she tried to pretend she lay on lumpy ground somewhere on the open road up north, where there were no justice buildings. Redbark would surround her, Shigan at her side, and the next day they would travel to a new place, meet new people, and try to make life better for those who could not find justice . . .

The cure for restlessness and heartache was work. There was plenty of that.

She started by learning Eel. This martial arts style had been devised specifically for nuns, back in the days of writing on sticks. It had been adapted by female guards around the First Empress. All the basic stances, and shifts in balance, were familiar. All she was really learning were new combinations. Much as she enjoyed these, a month was enough to master the best of them — the rest were refinements that she had already superseded with her staff training.

She turned to Chef Ki for more training with the Ki fan form, putting that together with the training in acupoints that she had received from the physician at Green Jade garrison. She went up on the roof very early in the mornings to do Redbark with full Essence, and the rest of the day she supervised Matu's training of the new recruits.

He was turning out to be a very good teacher. He was patient, and thorough, and he never lost his temper. He also never got bored going over the basics, even when two new recruits showed up — another Hat brother, and one of Tao Ahlin's best Eel Style students, a girl Ari's own age named Shao Cassia.

At the end of these hard-working days she read until her candle guttered out. She reread everything she'd read so reluctantly as a child. Much of it was new now, with more understanding of the world; when she read the herbal she'd borrowed from Auntie Hat down at the medicine store, she heard her mother's voice reading the words.

The days slipped by, marred only by the occasional restless dream, until the summery day two Ki cousins suddenly turned up, a familiar tall, shaggy-haired figure behind them.

Matu and Ari were out in the courtyard with the Redbark recruits, working on blocks and throws when Petal came out, leading three people.

Matu gave Waoji Lion's Mane a puzzled glance, then moved to his companions, and his face beamed. "Cousin Hitu!" he exclaimed happily. "Welcome, welcome! I did not expect . . ." His voice trailed off when the two cousins did not smile back, but instead exchanged uncomfortable glances. "What happened?" he asked more quietly. "My mother?"

Chef Ki materialized at his side, as anxious as his son.

Waoji Lion's Mane caught Ari's eye and beckoned. The recruits stood around awkwardly as the Ki family closed in, murmuring softly.

Waoji Lion's Mane made no attempt to introduce himself.

Remembering that he'd preferred being known simply as "the hermit" during her time in Master Ki's valley, Ari said to the staring recruits, "Take a break, everybody." And when the martial arts hero gave her an approving glance, she joined him. "Is something happening?"

"Let's go somewhere else," Waoji said.

He led the way to the front door, then into the street.

They didn't speak until they reached a tea shop that had an awning shading low tables from the early summer sun. Both headed for the seat with their back to the tea house wall, and a full view of the street and the side alley. Ari grinned, saw no answering smile, and let him take the best defensive position, sitting opposite him.

"Ari," he said, believing that bad news was best delivered quickly. "Master Ki died at the end of winter. I was with him."

Ari gasped, her eyes filling with tears.

Waoji put up two fingers to the aproned young man, who sped off to fetch tea and snacks, then he bent toward Ari. "He spoke of you at the end. He had messages for you all—his family, of course, and for you, his student. His message to you was full of praise for your hard work, and he said that the valley is yours if you want it."

"I should go light incense at the temple," Ari said, her voice wobbling. "And s-say the sutras for his soul."

"You could do that, but I think it would be more for you than for him. I never saw a more peaceful death, and I have seen many. Too many. But he was content—I would stake my life he went straight to the Ghost Moon god, first in line."

Ari wiped her burning eyes. She could believe that.

"Also. There's more."

She was trying not to cry, though her eyes burned and a boulder had lodged in her throat. She did not want people staring at them. "More . . . what?"

His mouth pressed in a white line, then he said, "There is no easy way to tell you, so I'll make it fast. But first: you are not to imagine blame to yourself. All the Ki elders insisted."

Ari had actually been glad to see him. She hunched up, a ball of pain and shock and heartache roiling inside her as he told her low-voiced that Ten Leopards had sustained an attack from the Shadow Panthers.

Who were looking for *her*.

Waoji Lion's Mane had come down from the mountains

after burying Master Ki properly, and tidying the cottage. He'd reached the Ki family the day before the attack — they were at their ancestral shrine, having pulled the patrollers in so that the entire family would be there for the memorial ritual.

"A mistake, which none of us knew," Waoji said. "Ten Leopards having been peaceful for more than a generation. They were able to sneak up and hit us. But they paid heavily for that surprise," he added with a wintry almost-smile. That hint of bleak humor vanished when he added, "The surprise is probably the only reason they were able to get away with the two smallest Kis. They left a message for us —"

"I can guess." Ari's stomach roiled. "They'll kill the little cousins if I don't go. Where?"

"Blissful Solitude Temple on Little Otters Island." And, in a neutral tone, "What do you want to do?"

She started up — but he put out a hand. "Fishing in muddy waters will net you nothing but duckweed. You know that."

She halted, but did not sit down. "All I know is that of course it has to be a trap —"

"Yes," he said. "Sit."

"I have to go. You say it's not my fault, but they were looking for *me*. This is *my* problem. I *have* to go after those small Kis. First, I have to find a ship — someone who knows where that island is —"

"I thought you might say that. Sit down. Rushing off without planning is hurling yourself into a river of knives."

"But —" she began in a heated voice, then lowered it to a whisper as glances turned their way from other tables. "But I don't know how long I have to get there — two weeks from when?"

"It's two weeks from now — they said forty days. I've kept a count," Waoji said. "They gave you little time purposefully."

Another thought struck her then. Appalled, she whispered, "Did they follow you here? Do they know about the inn?"

"They do not. No one but the Kis know that Matu and his father live here now. They also hit Sky Island. That was a mistake," he added. "My son dealt with them. I understand you met Reckless."

"I did," Ari said. She looked down at her tea and snacks, too upset to touch them.

"Drink your tea," Waoji said. "Eat something. First of all, I know Little Otters well. My wife was born there. She died there, defending our two when they were small. Yulin Enk, who calls himself Master Night, has used that same strategy for years: capture someone defenseless, or an entire manor or town, and stake their lives against whatever it is he wants. In this case, you."

Ari's mind was recovering from shock and began to stream with questions. "You came with the Ki cousins. Does that mean they want to go to Master Night's trap with me? Or in my place?"

"That's why you and I are here alone," Waoji said. "The Kis kept the Shadow Panthers from taking Ten Leopards, but not without cost. Those two are about the only Kis who didn't take wounds. I brought them because they were coming anyway, to tell Matu and his father about Grandfather Ki. I plan to be gone before they return from lighting incense at the local Ghost Moon temple."

Ari's throat was too tight for speech. She made herself drink the tea without tasting a drop. It helped enough to enable her to say, "I have sparred with both. They're pretty good, but not good enough to face the Shadow Panthers. They want to go anyway, don't they." It wasn't even a question.

"Trying to talk them out of it was like teaching a tiger to read. Ayah, I've told you, and now I'll be off."

"Not without me."

He rose. "Are you certain? You know Master Night intends no good end."

"Just because he intends it doesn't mean I have to cooperate. I have to go, either with you or by myself."

"To tell you the truth I expected as much. But I wanted to give you the chance to say no. We can be gone before they return from the temple," Waoji said.

"I'll get my pack, and slip out the side door. They won't even see me," Ari said.

Waoji gave her another wintry smile, and a short nod of approval. "Let's move."

Ari drank off the last of her tea and grabbed up the snacks, since they had paid for them, and she wasn't sure when she would eat next. As she slipped in the side door of the inn and light-footed up to retrieve her pack, she sent up a mental prayer for Master Ki's soul—and an apology for not going to the temple to do it properly. I will when I return, she promised.

She hesitated at her door, the urge to tell Petal very strong.

But if she did, she'd be asking Petal to keep a secret from Matu. Secrets had already caused trouble in Redbark. She slipped down the back way, and as she hoped, spotted Lie Tenek in the courtyard. Then she hesitated. Lie Tenek would want to come — and Ari would love to have her along, but how to extricate her without the others finding out?

Better to make a clean break.

Ari sketched her sight-warding talisman over herself, reflecting that she hadn't had to use it for nearly half a year. Good or bad? She hadn't brought justice to anyone, either. Bad, she told herself firmly, and ran down to join Waoji, who waited a little ways down the street. He didn't react until she was right next to him. He stilled, hand tightening on his staff, then he gave a curt nod. So he hadn't seen her! "Good thinking."

"The umbrella-maker over there is a very good, loyal friend, but the words 'five aunts and ten grandmothers' were invented for her. She won't see me. She doesn't know you. Should we split up to find a ship?" she asked.

He murmured, "That has been taken care of."

Ari suppressed her questions firmly. If passers-by saw this shaggy-haired tall man with the walking staff talking to himself, or heard her voice seem to come out of the air, they'd start looking for her. And they'd remember.

She stayed quiet until they reached the bay. Waoji Lion's Mane peered up and down the shoreline, and then uttered a low, "Ayah. There."

He led the way to the public pier, where rowboats could be hired to take people out to the ships anchored in the bay. He went straight to a rowboat where a tall young man wearing a conical bamboo sunhat sat in a rowboat.

"Wait," Ari said, low-voiced. "Do you think Master Night will be there, at Little Otters?"

Waoji looked down at her expressionlessly. "Probably — he'll be curious about you, and he likes to play with his victims before dispatching them. Though if he thinks there is any danger, he'll run and leave his followers to fight. Why? Second thoughts?"

"No! It's just that I promised to tell . . ." She reddened. "There's someone — in the empire — in the imperial capital. He would tell the imperials. If we can rescue those children first, wouldn't it be a good idea to have the navy deal with the rest of them? I know they want to."

Waoji smiled. "The navy already knows. Or is about to—my daughter is a navigator aboard a naval spear ship. She'll see to it they find out."

That wasn't telling Shigan, but Ari reflected that it was the best she could do without going to that garrison and telling them—then of course having to deal with all their questions about who she was and how she knew.

"All right," she said. "Good."

They made their way down the barnacle-studded ladder into the boat, at which time the young man looked up.

Ari gasped. "Waoji Reckless?"

"You remembered me, Firebolt of Redbark," he murmured, laughing as he lifted the oars.

Ari was about to protest, then she realized that she had become Firebolt again. It was Firebolt Master Night wanted to kill—and if she wanted to keep her real life to herself, she must become Firebolt once again for this mission, and if she survived, she could vanish as Ari again.

"Did you pay off the trader?" Waoji asked his son.

"If you squint, you might make them out hull-down on the horizon," Reckless said, grinning. "Long Knife and Minnow are out there right now spreading the word that the Shadow Panthers are all over the Otters Islands. Nobody will take the Kis anywhere near Little Otters."

"Good. Take us out to the *Gull*. If the Kis spot Long Knife or Minnow, they can surely make up some reason to be in Te Gar, but they should not see us."

Reckless pushed away from the pier and began rowing.

Ari said, "Didn't you come with the Kis?"

"Yes—the usual trader that stops at Ten Leopards took them on, and I came with them, but Reckless and the others followed along behind, without them knowing."

Reckless put his back into skimming them over the choppy green waters, and said over his shoulder to Ari, "I was coming to bring Father the latest letter from Sky Island when we spotted the unfamiliar ship. We hid out further up the coast, and when we saw smoke rising from the plateau, we went up a back trail to help. By then it was all over." He looked angry. "While we were going over the back route, the demon-cursed Shadow Panthers were muscling those two children down the main road, or we could have taken them on. I'm still angry over that."

"We will have our chance," Waoji said. "He won't have killed them—he needs to brandish them alive to lure Firebolt."

Ari's insides squeezed. It was the anticipation. Seeing danger and running to help, that was easy. Not easy, maybe, but it didn't feel as horrible as this sense of sailing, one salty wave at a time, toward a deliberate trap.

But she was not facing Master Night and his sect alone, she reminded herself, and looked around. Their craft was a small ship built for speed. Ari and Waoji climbed up the side, to be greeted by the captain, an older woman with a white braid wrapped around her head in the style Lie Tenek had taught Ari. "Welcome, welcome," she said. "If Long Knife and Minnow remember the tide and get here before flood, we can set sail by last Horse."

Which was exactly what happened.

The *Gull* lifted red-lacquered wings and began chasing the sun westward as Waoji's small company gathered on the weather deck.

"We've got two weeks to get ourselves ready," Waoji said. "First, let's introduce everyone. Reckless, you have met . . . how do you want to be addressed?" he asked Ari.

"I'm Firebolt now," she said firmly. She was going to explain, then she realized she was talking to people with martial arts names, who might very well be protecting families, friends, or homes as well.

"Firebolt it is," Minnow whispered as she perched on the rail, her sharply-boned, triangular head cocked to one side. Her smooth black hair had a decidedly reddish cast, and her smile, with an edge of white teeth, was cheerfully predatory.

Reckless said, "It was an auspicious day—very—that brought Minnow to Sky Island before the attack. Long Knife here is an expert with all weapons, especially the long ones. He also has a water affinity—he can make fog."

Long Knife was about Reckless's age, some years older than Ari; Minnow's age was hard to guess, especially as her light blob was distractingly different from the others. Not only was it intense in a different way completely from the intensity of Shigan's, it kept . . . shimmering, or undulating.

Reckless went on, "You'll remember First Uncle Ki."

"Yes—the best of the Ki knife fighters," Ari said.

"He's asleep below. Wounded in the fight, but he insists he'll be well by the time we reach Little Otters." Reckless lowered his voice. "You know of course it's his boy and girl who they grabbed."

Ari's throat tightened. "I know."

"He was coming home with me," Reckless went on. "He still blames himself for showing us the other path—but we really thought . . ." His gaze dropped to the deck.

Minnow's head cocked the other way, listening. Sniffing.

She's a fox, Ari realized. Her light blob was blurry because it was animal and human together. Not just a fox, but—she blinked, struggling to bring the aura into focus. Yes, those undulations were tails. She was a nine-tail fox—the avatar of a god?

Minnow's smile widened—showing more teeth—yet this was not a threatening smile. There was too much humor as well as awareness in her black eyes. "This human who calls himself Master Night is very cruel to my kind," she whispered, just for Ari's ears.

Long Knife certainly had not heard. He cast an uneasy glance in Ari's direction, then addressed the father and son. "What's our plan?"

He did not know Firebolt, except by reputation. She was awfully small and young for all those stories, and he wondered how much was exaggeration—in other words, would she be any help or a hindrance?

Waoji peered around at sky and sea, then nodded to Reckless to take over.

Reckless said, "Since it's just us, we don't need anything elaborate. We martial artists train to take on problems as we face them. My sister learned about strategy at the naval training fortress. What all that study and practice seems to come down to, at least in my mind, is outflanking the enemy as well as outthinking them."

Ari said in a tight throat, "I thought the condition was that I go alone."

"Oh, they will see you come alone," Waoji said. "The *Gull* will look like a rundown trader by the time we reach Little Otters, and we'll let down a rowboat for you to row in."

"But before that, we're going to leave, one by one," Reckless said. "You'll have to hold them off long enough for us to get into place." He clapped his hands. "Flank, gallant wanderer style—we'll hit them from all sides."

"Just us?"

"Just us."

Minnow bared her teeth and uttered a growly laugh that was not friendly at all.

Waoji said, "This means that starting in the morning, whatever the weather, we will be working very hard to hone our skills."

Reckless clapped his hands and rubbed them. "Very hard."

TWENTY-SIX

FAI ANBAI SAT CROSS-LEGGED on a cushion, his newborn son cradled in his lap.

It was very late; a sliver of Phoenix Moon shone through the window, sinking slowly in the early summer sky, and in the window on the opposite side of the room, Ghost Moon rose. He had set a single small oil lamp far behind him, as the midwife had said that flickering lights would bother the infant's eyes.

Whether that was true or not, the new Little Treasure had not cried once he'd been dressed warmly. Before going to bed, his small daughter had been elated to discover that with this brother's birth, she had been promoted to Big Treasure; of course both children were given proper names, but those would wait until they ventured out for schooling. In the family, they were Treasures.

Fai Anbai, who had not seen his daughter's birth, was utterly enchanted by the small face, the tiny lips working. Miniature hands bobbed in the air, fingers spread, perfect in all details yet entrancingly minute. His chest ached with a mixture of love and wonder and a little worry, too.

"I promise I will exert myself to give you a safe and peaceful world," he said, low-voiced.

The infant's hands flailed. He made a noise like a kitten. It struck Fai Anbai straight to the heart.

"You can be a scholar if you like," he said to the small face, whose tiny tongue poked out. "You and your sister both—I would be happy if you become scholars. Or poets. Or makers of porcelain. We work so hard to give you as peaceful a world as we can..." A lifetime of caution stopped him here, even though he knew he was alone, just himself and his little son not two watches old.

Even so, he was straying into dangerous territory. And besides, the baby's brow began to pucker. "Ah. I expect you're looking for something that I cannot give." He laughed a little, rising with the little bundle safe in his arms.

Sure enough, by the time he reached the bedroom where his wife was dozing, the babe let out a wail like the mew of a gull.

Yan Yian's eyes opened, and she held out her arms.

Fai Anbai stole away, to find his father in the outer room. "We made it," he said, as a yawn took him. This past week had been increasingly tense—every day expecting some assassin, or brigand, or traitor somewhere, requiring him to mount horse or ship in pursuit, which would cheat him again of a child's birth. "My only disappointment is not anyone's fault, certainly not my wife's."

He meant her search for the hitherto uncounted (and therefore unwatched) last of Right Chancellor Su's progeny. Yan Yian had found him, all right—his name was Ris Jun. According to the embittered mother, part of her payoff from Duke Su was that Ris Jun could not presume to the Su name. As he had run away to sea when he turned sixteen, she had not seen him since.

Grandfather Fai remained silent.

Fai Anbai began to say that he was off to bed—and then it struck him that his father was still here, though it was very late, and the birth had happened a watch and a half ago. And he had not said anything.

It took all his effort not to curse. You got to see this child's birth, he reminded himself. Do not take the gods' gift lightly, or you will surely pay for it. "What is it," he said in what he hoped was not as surly a tone as he felt.

Grandfather Fai said, "A messenger came. Just as her labor began."

They were not the only ones awake that soft summer night. The imperial guards patrolled ceaselessly along the palace walls and the pathways of the inner palace. Soft-footed graywings glided along halls within the pavilions.

The quiet was broken by the gasping, braying laugher of boys on the verge of manhood — Jion had hosted Vaion's going away celebration. Tomorrow he was off to Benevolent Winds to serve under his Great-Uncle Yu. He and his two favorite cousins, plus Lu Fan, staggered out of Jion's manor down to Vaion's, which was right next to it — a relatively short distance except perhaps to a collection of boys who thought they were much better at handling their wine than they really were.

Vaion had insisted Jion come with him to see the new painting he'd bought — at least that was how the journey began, but halfway there, Vaion forgot what it was he wanted to show his brother, and then he forgot why his brother was with them.

He also seemed to forget where he was going, and twice turned abruptly, to be gently but firmly turned back by Jion, until his steward appeared to take Vaion and his guests in hand.

"No — we were going somewhere, weren't we?" Vaion protested, turning around in a circle.

"This way, your imperial highness," came the patient, quiet voice.

Lu Fan began singing. Vaion stopped dead, then whirled around. The long tassels on his waist ornament and hanging from the embroidery at each shoulder whipped around, almost slapping Zuinan in the face, as he had been leaning on Vaion. "Opera! J-Jion invited us . . ."

"You just came from the opera, sot," Jion said. "Go to sleep!"

Vaion turned again — then nearly fell over his own feet.

By then the steward had given some kind of signal, or maybe Vaion's household knew what to expect, and graywings appeared like shadows, each to an unsteady boy, as they began bawling a bawdy song from the opera.

Jion smiled as he watched them vanish into the pavilion, mentally totting up the gossip of the evening. Nothing that hadn't been discussed over and over. This plan of his that had sounded so impressive and helpful a couple of months ago had turned out to be about as useful as a straw boat. There was no use in reporting to Min Ko, he decided as he turned away. Then halted, his gaze catching on the glint of gold framed in the circular moon door leading into the imperial garden not fifty paces away.

A man stood on one of the many little arched bridges, silhouetted against the pale stone of the pagoda, his head bent. He seemed to be staring into the lake. Jion was going to continue on toward his manor, but stilled when something familiar in the lineaments of that figure registered.

Imperial Father? It couldn't be. This late? Jion mentally calculated — wasn't this a court day? Dawn was scarcely two hours off.

The figure turned, gold glinting in his hair clasp and among the long braids — yes, that was definitely Imperial Father.

Jion started toward the moon door, halting when two imperial guards materialized from the gloom on either side of the door, spears crossed.

"It is I," Jion said. "First Imperial Prince Jion—"

He felt their gazes rake down his body, and, seeing no weapons, one turned to the other, giving a short nod. The second one vanished up a shadowy side path as the guard bowed then said, "His imperial majesty gave orders for him not to be disturbed, your imperial highness—"

But it seemed the emperor heard voices on the still summer air, and his own voice was heard, "Let my son pass."

The spear lifted, and Jion hurried along the three zigzags until he bounded up onto the bridge and bowed. "Honored Imperial Father is still awake?"

The emperor's face was in shadow, but Jion could hear the smile in his voice as he said, "I was about to ask the same of you. Get up."

Jion sensed that his father was not in the mood for extreme formality, so he reverted to the less formal title. "Father Emperor, I just walked Vaion and my Kui cousins to his pavilion."

"Ah, yes, the opera. *The Demon King and the Goddess of Spring* was it not? To celebrate Vaion's going away?" The emperor recollected his Kui grandfather once said it was old when he was young, but then an erotic romp very thinly disguised as a cautionary tale involving the gods was sure to be a generational favorite, as long as there were young men to watch it.

"There's a new dance troupe, Father Emperor." Jion explained. "They team up with the Magnolia House singers."

The emperor started down the bridge. Jion took that as invitation and walked beside him. They paced together for a short time, Jion ready at any moment to be dismissed. Then the emperor briefly turned his flattened palm outward, and the inner circle of imperial guards dropped back obediently.

Aware of how sound carried in the light summer airs, the emperor did not speak until they reached the little waterfall. Under cover of its hiss and splash, he said, "Are you aware of your sister's project?"

"Sister." Neither of them thought of Gau-Gau, who at sixteen was still a butterfly, pretty and kind, but seldom looked past tomorrow.

"This unenlightened son believes First Sister is writing a history of the Jehan rulers," Jion said. "We've talked about it."

"She appears to be living in the dragon and phoenix archive," the emperor commented. "Every time I have occasion to venture into that part of my house, I nearly trip over her."

No doubt she arranged that, Jion thought—and then was disturbed at the meanness of the thought. But he knew it was very likely true. And further, from his tone, their father was aware of it.

The emperor said, "I gave you a chance to read anything you liked in there once, did I not?"

"Honored Imperial Father granted this foolish son that privilege once," Jion said. "It wasn't long before I left for the Silk Islands."

"You never had an interest in returning?"

Jion sighed. "The truth is, Father Emperor, I scared myself. My idea at fourteen or fifteen was to look at Great-Great Grandfather Maoyan's military record, and find something sufficiently glorious to use to convince Father Emperor to let me train in martial arts. What I read . . ." He looked away. "An entire island, put to the sword. On what amounted to a rumor. I ran out of there and never wanted to return."

"I see," the emperor said in a musing voice. "You never told me that. I assumed you had no interest."

"This callow and ignorant son was more disturbed than disinterested, Father Emperor; and at fourteen, no one wants to seem weak," Jion said with a laugh.

"I remember that one. It disturbed me as well. My grandmother required me to read it . . . But that was long ago. Your sister perhaps has not ventured that far into Emperor Maoyan's records. He's much more bearable in his early years. But I think she could learn a great deal more from my grandmother."

"That's what I thought, Father Emperor," Jion began — then stopped himself. It felt like tattling behind Manon's back. Even though he disagreed with her — sharply, in recent months — she had always been loyal to him. For the sake of their old companionship and bond, he said, "I forgot what I was going to say. Too much wine with my brother and too little sleep." He faked a huge yawn.

The emperor let that go, because it was not Manon's reading that banished sleep and drove him to walk through nights. And — so far — Jion's answers were far less frivolous than they had been — and far less calculating than Manon's.

"Your sister's thoroughness is commendable. Yesterday she asked my permission to delve into the graywings' records, to corroborate certain details of our ancestors' actions."

"This ignorant son believes that Honored Sister Manon is a true scholar, Father Emperor," Jion said sincerely.

One more test.

"I remember," the emperor commented as they passed under the soft glow of moon-shaped hanging lanterns, "when I brought up the prospect of a treaty with the Easterners. You asked if there was trouble in the west. Do you remember that?"

Jion had to think back. It had to be before the treaty marriage that took Lily away — before the betrothal, even. "Ayah, I recollect, Father Emperor. Before the Journey to the Clouds."

"Why did you go from the Easterners to a question about the west?"

Surprised, Jion said, "Isn't it obvious? We first year cadets at Loyalty got drilled in Lao Sha's and Liad II's basic strategies, one of which is that the wise ruler avoids fighting in two directions at once. I thought, if you were really considering a treaty with the Easterners — which has been a subject I've heard about since I was small, and I knew it was old then — I figured something had to be brewing in the west. As I recall you didn't say anything about that, though, Father Emperor."

"That is because . . . I was not ready to," the emperor said slowly. "It is . . ." He interrupted himself, the falter so rare that Jion forgot his pose of tiredness and glanced at his father in concern.

The emperor looked into Jion's face, illuminated by the glow from a lamp shaped like a plump, happy luck fish. His expression revealed his concern. The emperor said, "What do you know about the Westerners?"

Bewildered, Jion began counting up the few facts he remembered. "This ignorant son knows little, Father Emperor. We call them 'Westerners' because we have to sail west to get there, but their islands lie in a mighty cluster in the north, where the water freezes in winters, except where they have fire mountains. They call their empire some long, impossible name in their language. They elect their rulers, but only certain ranks can vote, and it's almost always one of the royal family who gets elected. They look more or less like us, except most of them have what many call 'ghost eyes' though Grandmother Empress doesn't like us using that term — she says 'sea eyes' is less rude, and more like the truth as the colors can be gray or green or blue, according to Uncle Pandan, who has sketched them. Though I've seen her make the ward against inauspicious omens whenever Uncle Pandan brought out drawings of Westerners with eyes colored blue. Demons are said to have blue eyes as well as red."

The emperor smothered a dry laugh. "Go on."

"I don't know much more, Father Emperor." He stopped there, and when his father stayed silent, he went on. "Let's see. They follow the dragon god, but their shamans practice a kind of Essence that is forbidden here. Master Zao said it had to do with snakes and blood. The work is mostly done by slaves, especially on their galleys, which are fast and maneuverable."

He stopped again, and again the emperor maintained silence, so Jion said, more randomly, "I know that I had an uncle whose mother was a Westerner, Uncle Hojai. And I remember hearing about random raids, when I was traveling around in the north."

"*Random* raids," the emperor repeated. "Is there such a thing?"

"It sounded like it from what I heard," Jion said slowly. "But then, gallant wanderers would think that, Father Emperor. They don't think in military terms. They don't form armies — except the Shadow Panthers, apparently. The rest fight one to one, or at most sect against sect, or sect against pirates or a gang of brigands. But . . ." Master Fumig's dry voice spoke in memory. "Raids are never random, are they? It takes planning, and logistics, and if you want to be successful, you drill as much as you can in similar terrain." He turned to his father. "Might this ignorant son beg Father Emperor why he asks?"

"What do you know about Jehan Hojai?"

Startled, Jion said—diplomatically—"That he was Father Emperor's brother, that he died about the time Great-Grandmother Empress did."

"That's all?"

"I don't know much more, but what I do know makes him sound like . . ."

"A white-eyed wolf? If that's what you were about to say, you would be right." The emperor's voice sharpened. "He was not my brother. Though we had to call one another 'brother' because our grandmother willed it so, as we did share blood through her two sons. He was the son of the first prince, and so he was the First Imperial Prince, though we were never really sure if he was born before I was. The Westerners did not always tell the truth, except when it suited them. For example, they never mentioned that *he* had a brother, one of shared blood."

Jion stopped on the pathway, turning a startled glance at his father. "He did? When did you find out? Where is he? What's he like?"

"To answer your first question, yes. As for how I found out, Fai Anbai's mother did not actually run off with a silk merchant—I don't know if you heard that story. Her family was told that, as they believe the Fais to be mid-level scribes in the tax department. She lives in the guise of a hairdresser in the Westerners' imperial palace."

"That's got to be dangerous!"

"Yes. To resume, his faction calls him the White Dragon; I do not know his given name. They are even more protective of their names — we, out of filial respect, they because they appear to believe names can be bound with Essence talismans. Perhaps they can, through the Cobra Sages, their shamans, who practice forms of Essence manipulation that are forbidden here."

"This ignorant son did not know that, Father Emperor."

"Traditionally a forbidden subject—I myself only found out that the White Dragon is related to me relatively recently. The expected favorite was the eldest granddaughter, who is two years my elder. She and the White Dragon between them were dueling covertly, then not so covertly—until the election, at which she was unanimously chosen, whereupon she took a ruling name, as we do. And then began the purges of those who lost. White Dragon fought them to a bloody standstill, then turned his eyes eastward. To us. And so," the emperor's voice was sere, "he has been testing the grounds up north."

"He's bringing his war here?"

"Apparently—"

The emperor stopped. Jion was so amazed by what he was hearing that he paid no attention to his surroundings, but the emperor was alert and aware at all times. "Bitternail," he said. "What is it?"

Jion turned; there was the chief graywing, standing some fifty steps off, hands in his sleeves, gaze lowered as he waited patiently.

"Your imperial majesty, a pigeon message from a naval courier," Bitternail said.

The emperor held out his hand, took the little paper and unrolled it. His brows slanted steeply, and he handed the paper to Jion—who was aware that he was seeing his first imperial message.

Master Night hunt criminal Firebolt at Little
Otters Island mid-month.

Jion stilled, jaw locked against a shout of anger—of desperation. He looked up, to find his father watching him with that inscrutable, unblinking gaze that always shot through the nerves to roil in the pit of one's stomach.

"This unworthy son believes he can prove himself by catching Master Night," Jion said, falling to his knees. "Imperial Father, I beg you, please send me."

The emperor had clasped his hands behind his back as he watched his son's intense reaction—far more intense than any reaction previously seen, even when he was first offered a golden tally. "Catch him, First Son," he said, gesturing for Jion to rise. "I would prefer alive, so that he can end his worthless life in Lotus Blossom Square, a lesson to all traitors—but if you have to kill him to put an end to his depredations, don't hesitate. Mid-month . . . I'd have to look at the map, which lists customary sailing times, but I suspect there is no time to lose."

"No," Jion whispered, handing back the note that he'd crushed in his hand. "May this eager son withdraw, Imperial Father?"

"Go."

And when he'd vanished through the moon door in the direction of his manor, the emperor said, "Summon Fai Anbai."

The ferret chief had spent the time between Grandfather Fai's news and this expected summons arranging his affairs as best as he could.

He was waved through to the emperor, who said, "I presume you have also received word of Master Night's latest move."

"Yes, your imperial majesty."

"My son the First Prince wishes to capture the traitor. I'm sending you to facilitate that."

"Yes, your imperial majesty."

"Also." There was the slight smile. "We both know that Jion's true impulse is to rescue his criminal friend. I'm very sure that in his headlong rush, he will lead you right to Firebolt. Capture Firebolt, Chief Fai. Don't kill him unless you cannot avoid it. I'm curious. Also, with that much notoriety, I think it best sends a message if he, too, dies in Lotus Blossom Square, witnessed by would-be heroes, rather than in some obscure spot."

"Yes, your imperial majesty."

TWENTY-SEVEN

DANNO HAD NO IDEA who Waoji Lion's Mane was, but the Shadow Panthers on Kanda Sutra Island were very willing to fill him in: famous gallant wanderer, never lost a fight, nearly sent Master Night to the King of Hell years ago (whispered, in case the master was somehow listening).

None of that mattered to Danno. What did matter was his plan to hollow Ye Daq's sect from the inside. He had been a leader by the time he was sixteen, and all those skills were still there.

He began very simply. Once he could haul himself to his feet and stand without falling in a faint, he walked until he could manage with one crutch. He made his way to the practice yard, very aware of the stares and the sudden silence, though he did not react until several of the more aggressive Shadow Panthers strolled up to him.

Before they could start with the challenges and the goading that were pretty much inevitable from certain types of men, he clasped his hands as best he could, gave a short bow, and said, "I'm new. Please teach me how things go here."

It was what the boys had had to do in the intensely hierarchical imperial guard, where everyone was aggressive or you didn't advance.

The Shadow Panthers exchanged looks, shifted stances, one licked his lips; by little signs that Danno read from long experience, he saw that one man was acknowledged as leader. This was the man he had to win over.

"We heard you're the best. Former imperial guard. Then you ran?"

"I was the best. I did run, thirty years ago. I'll need to get in some practice." His tone was quiet, neither aggressive nor deferential.

The big man looked him over as he stood there with the crutch under his left armpit. Danno winced, then switched it to his right, shifting his weight and wiggling his left leg, which had been taking his weight.

"Who did for your knees?" another spoke up.

"Imperial ferret."

Low comments, then the big man reclaimed his position as leader by saying, "I saw the master took your sword off to Ten Leopards."

Danno lifted a shoulder. "He's welcome to it."

"Practice rack over there—we don't bother with wood. Metal is good enough for us. Though the swords there on the lower rack aren't sharp."

Danno hitched his way to the rack, and looked the blades over. Several were what he thought of as pirate blades—too heavy in the blade for the handle, or too much ornamental addition that would put his balance off that small amount that made a difference in speed.

He chose one that seemed better made than the rest, and swung the blade, warming up his arm. It had been weeks—he could feel it. But warmth and tone returned fast enough.

Danno had discovered back at Sweetwater that drilling barefoot felt good. He never questioned it. He liked the sensation of the solid ground beneath his feet, the sense of the world's strength coming up through his heels the way tree roots draw up nourishment from the earth. He spent two or three days working with one hand, then the other, in the air, then hitting the stuffed target at the far end of the practice field. He watched the others, noting how aware they were of being watched.

The inevitable challenge came on the fourth morning. "You can spar a little, right? I'll go easy on you," the big man said.

Danno gave a short nod, and resettled the crutch under his right armpit.

"You want to go with the other hand first?"

"Thank you, either is fine."

Danno had seen the style favored by the Shadow Panthers. It was a blinkered style, its single focus forward force. Stamping, slashing, yet without any awareness of side defense much less rear, and no semblance of working in line. They all competed to be faster, to be first. It had to be frightening and effective to a batch of civilians who had never even seen weapons, but against trained warriors, they'd be bamboo shoots instead of a wall.

He moved his feet into correct stance, mentally seeing the circle around them — and when the big Shadow Panther tried a testing blow or two, Danno finished gauging his speed and his strength. The man made his move. A heartbeat later he blinked, looking uncomprehendingly from his empty hand to the sword lying in the dirt a few paces away. "I slipped," he said. "Here, we'll try that again."

"Sure."

This time, in spite of the crutch, the man grunted with effort as he brought the sword down. Danno turned shoulder, hip, the blade whooshed a hand's breadth from his arm, and he brought up his point at the exact moment that the strike lost its force, twisted and tapped.

Thud! The sword hit the dirt.

Danno knew what was coming next — an escalated attack, then two, then three — and he dealt with all of them, no change of expression. After disarming the three, he winced, switched the crutch over, and wrung his right arm.

"Hurt your sword arm?" someone asked.

"Armpit," Danno replied.

There were one or two left-handers there, but no one able to switch. They eyed the sword in his right, wondering if he'd be even tougher — then one of the men mumbled, "Show me that disarm?"

"Sure."

After demonstrating slowly a couple of times, then faster, before walking them through it, the atmosphere changed around the time he'd hoped it would.

At the end of the session his hands throbbed after so long without practice, but he knew that would clear up in a week. He watched them move off in clumps, muttering, with a few glances back.

Good start, he thought. It was going to take work, but good start.

He made his way back to his room—he and Hanu had continued to sleep apart, until his knees could bear the bed jarring when she turned over.

Hanu found him sitting on the floor, which had become his habit so he wouldn't have to bend his knees. Seeing him staring sightlessly at the wall, she set beside him the tray she had been carrying, and dropped down on the other side of it. "You seem disturbed."

He looked up. "Puzzled, not disturbed. I wonder why Ye Daq would take my sword. He has to have a hundred of them here. Most of them aren't very well made, but he has enough gold to get good ones."

Hanu said, "From what I've been hearing, he probably thinks it might bring him luck. Or that it has Essence worked into it. Or, that you have an affinity for it."

"That sword?" Danno slewed around. "It's just a sword. I kept it all these years because I knew I wouldn't be able to lay my hands on another. It was there for protection of my family—and the village, should any pirates or the like have turned up."

"I know that, but he seems to think differently."

Danno shrugged it off, and began to eat the shrimp in chili sauce that she'd brought, with rice to soak up the sauce. "I think I've got a start."

"How long do you need?" she asked.

"Give me a few more days."

A few days later he was conducting drills just like the old days, except he still could not do Heaven and Earth. But his eye was as exacting as ever, and if the Shadow Panthers forgot that, he scrapped occasionally, easily beating all comers one-handed, the other gripping his crutch. Right hand, left hand, didn't matter.

While he taught, he listened to the others' chatter, including covertly expressed complaints, mentally separating out those he suspected would leave if they could. A younger brother was pulled along with his elder who thought the Shadow Panthers were the best gallant wanderer sect; an angry young man whose family had been partly killed off, the rest scattered by the vicious son of a count; a very good fighter who believed Ye Daq's glowing promises of loot and women and land, and who discovered that once he got the tattoo, he could not get free again.

Working in the garden barefoot, he found he healed more rapidly than lying in the bed. Meanwhile, word spread rapidly that the old (to twenty and thirty, fifty being "old") ex-imperial guard was unbeatable, even bare-toed and using a crutch. To men who gauged the world in terms of fighting skill, that made him interesting—and worth listening to.

"It's time," he told Hanu one night. "I'm not teaching any-one Heaven and Earth, my knees being my excuse. But I can use that only so long. Let's begin with the tattoos."

"I'm ready," Hanu said. "But I must warn you, I am going to have to use the phoenix feather for that Cobra Sage. It fell that day for us both. So I believe you have a right to know."

Danno smiled up at her. "Essence was always your skill. Not mine. Do what you must. I've got the memory of that thing fluttering down, and landing on your palm. That memory is all I need."

The tattoo was the easiest matter; she did not even have to use her precious Essence paper to break the binding in the tattoo. After years of acupuncture, she found that inked needles were no mystery. She worked on Danno herself, first undoing the lethal binding, and then turning the panther into a chimera.

Danno went out as usual, saying nothing. But within a day or two, men had come up to him separately. "How did you do that?" "Master Night said that if we alter the tattoos we die. And he can always find us." "I like the chimera—very auspicious."

Danno explained, soothed, and meanwhile Hanu taught the tattooist, who himself had been forced to join. Chimeras began appearing, a new one or two every watch.

Time for the next stage.

She had prepared with her usual thoroughness. Physician Chu, who always preferred being left alone, had been given long doses of her following him around asking questions. She could see how he forced himself to answer—how he tried to rein in his impatience.

She chose a day that promised clouds. When she came to him the next morning and said, "Everyone I've been seeing to is recovered, or nearly so. Why don't I take a trip to the north end, to see if there is anything I can do there?" her reward was relief in his face, which he tried to hide.

"A very fine idea," he said. "I ought to have thought of it. They usually cart their bad cases over the hill to us, but why not save them a trip, eh?"

"Indeed, thank you, Physician Chu. I do so need the practice. Ah, shall I take a monk to drive my cart, in case I have to bring a patient back?"

"Take any of the monks. That's what they are there for," the physician said, already done with the subject, his eyes straying toward his never-ending experiment to find an eternal youth elixir, as Ye Daq had ordered.

Hanu was soon on her way north, driven by Ul Keg. They waited until the narrow path wound its way alongside a stream trickling through a thick stand of bamboo. The air was cooler, the light a soft green. Despite the pressure of expectation and need, Hanu found herself relaxing a little.

"This is as good a place as any," she said presently.

Ul Keg obediently pulled over onto a grassy area above the stream. The horse immediately bent its head to slurp water from the stream as Hanu withdrew the little cedar box from her sleeve. She had left her mother's ornament in there—the box must look the same when they returned, though none of Ye Daq's people had been able to see the phoenix feather, just as the shaman had promised.

She half-expected her hand to pass through the feather, but when she carefully reached to pick it up, it lifted away from the box. She laid it on her palm. It was translucent, light as air. She scarcely felt it except as a slight coolness that might be her imagination.

She set aside the box, closed her palms together around the feather, shut her eyes, and recited the healing sutras that she had been taught.

Then she pulled her hands a finger's breadth apart and peeked.

The feather was gone.

She turned her palms up, and stared down at the shimmer around both. Or was that the reflected green light from the bamboo forest?

She replaced the box in her sleeve, then handed Ul Keg a narrow strip cut from her precious Essence paper. On the strip she had carefully inscribed a talisman. "All you need do is wait for a substantial cloud to cover the sun, and touch the talisman to wood. The side of a house, a cartwheel, a tool, a table. Anything will do. Very quietly." After the monk took the talisman, she said, "We can go."

They reached the top of the rise soon after, then started down the northern slope. The northern inlet appeared when they cleared the trees, giving them plenty of time to look it over. At one end, ship-building was going on, two ships in various states of construction. At the other end, a small village built round the usual square. Out in the quiet waters, two small ships rode at anchor. They looked like fishing boats to Hanu. The sea beyond was calm and green, with two islands in view, one fairly close, from the looks of it barren and uninhabitable, and one farther away, a silhouette in the haze.

As they neared, Hanu watched workers moving slowly in the summer heat, heads bowed.

They were going the last distance when Ul Keg warned, after a short inward struggle, "Please do not assume the Cobra Sage is as friendly as she sounds."

Hanu thanked him gravely, remembering that Ul Keg tried not to disparage other living creatures. But they were surrounded by danger, and Cobra Sages did not use binding Essence for any kindly-meant purpose here. There was no healing in the blood-binding these ones practiced. Only controlling.

When the cart rolled into the village, a sprite of a woman with wispy curls artfully escaping her elaborate hair style glided to the door of the biggest building. She was dressed in silk woven in the expensive swans rising mode. Golden ornaments dangled around her face from a graceful circlet around her hair. In the middle of her forehead a diamond tattoo glowed with an oily sheen. Hanu looked away, remembering who she was supposed to be: a slow, painstaking, unimaginative assist-ant physician. She should not reveal curiosity about that glowing tattoo.

A host coming to the door was a signal honor—but in the next breath it became clear that this person only appeared because she was bored. "Oh, it's only one of the monks—ayah, and someone new!" She giggled, then added in a breathless gurgle, "Oh! You must be the assistant physician."

Hanu bowed from her seat on the cart. She was then swept into a round of introductions. The Cobra Sage spoke in a stream of words, her lisp girlish amid constant mouse-squeak titters, her tone falsely confiding in way that made Hanu grit her teeth. Despite her companion's dimpled smiles she could feel lizard-quick glances darted her way. The "sage" was older than Hanu had first surmised, nearer to Hanu's own age, which meant plenty of experience. But she was also jaded, and Hanu rejoiced in signs of overconfidence and even careless-ness.

Hanu spoke slowly, painstakingly, and very soon saw the welcome signs of boredom in the Cobra Sage. Whenever clouds covered the sun, she drew the Cobra Sage's attention away from the monk and toward herself with questions: How long have you lived here? What is the purpose of that house there? Where is the dispensary? Her purpose was to create an impression of painstaking dullness, which would suggest its own reasons for someone well into middle age still being an assistant physician.

Hanu was taken around to various sites, where an aide banged on a gong and announced that by the grace and generosity of Master Night, a physician was here to tend any with complaints. The captive workers all bowed low when the Cobra Sage walked among them.

The Cobra Sage stuck right next to Hanu as the patients came in with bruised joints, upset stomachs, and the like.

At first Hanu could scarcely hide her elation when she discovered that the phoenix feather aided her in healing, without her having to search for and draw the correct talismans. How powerful was it? Visions of healing Danno with a touch enchanted her, then faded as she began to discover the limitations: the phoenix feather Essence, though powerful, mainly negated Essence bindings. It also aided her in the healing process, but only through proper methods.

The shipwright appeared in the long line, his face lined with quiet misery as he spoke of headaches. Hanu longed to comfort him—to promise the end would be soon—but she did not dare do more than ask him to sit at the side while she dealt with some faster cases, and she would apply her needles presently. She had glimpsed Ul Keg surreptitiously swiping the talisman against wooden pillars, walls, tables, carts, and the like as they passed—but it seemed this cloud overhead was *never* going to end.

Until, quite suddenly, the sun burst through. Ul Keg sat stolidly on the cart, and Hanu was binding a badly treated broken wrist when shouts and exclamations rose. The talisman brought out wood's latent wish to root. It was utterly harmless, and the sprouts would wither away soon, but Hanu suspected that to a Cobra Sage, whose entire study was bent on controlling, binding, and limiting, the prospect of all the wood in the village reverting to trees would be alarming.

"Look, all, the wall is sprouting!"

"What's wrong with this table?"

"Ayeeeeee! The cart is haunted!"

The Cobra Sage shot a suspicious glance Hanu's way, but she was staring wide-eyed, her mouth open. The Cobra Sage sped away, for once not giggling.

As soon as she was gone, Hanu finished the wrappings on a bandage, sent the woman off with a word, and turned to the shipwright. "Come, sit," she urged. No need to take his pulse — she could see by the vein beating in the man's temple the stresses he was under. "I will ease the immediate pain, but I want you to know that I will come again, and keep coming, until the bindings on *all* your tattoos are undone. You must spread the word among those who do not wish to be here. I'll fix yours now — bring anyone you can before I leave."

The man turned bloodshot eyes to her. "My family? She's holding them hostage at Master Night's orders . . ." He pressed his lips tight and shook his head. "If they are even still alive."

"My guess is that they are," she soothed. "Master Night does not have to tend them. And if they live, he can brandish them. I'll find out what I can."

The shipwright was beyond question; he let out a slow sigh and closed his eyes as she placed needles in the acupoints where such tensions were held, then concentrated on sending phoenix feather Essence down each needle.

When she saw some of the pain in his face ease, she laid her palm against the tattoo on his neck. The ugly binding writhed like a worm of molten fire, but when she whispered the simple peace sutra, and envisioned snow, it abruptly died out. The tattoo now was just ink — as she had hoped, she did not have to ink in the talisman to break the binding. If any Essence lingered, the Cobra Sage would not see it, any more than she could see the shimmer about Hanu's hands.

And best of all, though she had quietly removed some dozen tattoo bindings, the Essence in her hands had not diminished.

Hanu removed the needles. Already the man's tired eyes were clearer. "Thank you," he murmured. When he went away, he walked without that invisible yoke around his neck.

Before the sage returned, Hanu took binding out of eight more tattoos. When the Sage stalked up, a frown between her brows, Hanu slowly packed up her needles and herbs, promised dully to return, and climbed onto the cart, her hands tightly gripped in her lap.

The summer sun began its westward slide by the time they reached the relative safety of the bamboo forest. Hanu forced her hands open, afraid to discover that she had used up the phoenix feather's essence. But when she gazed down, the shimmer, even in the cool greenish light, was strong. Quite strong. She rubbed her fingers cautiously over each palm. In fact, it seemed stronger than it had been. That ran counter to the logic of things, but the shaman who had been teaching her had talked metaphorically about rivers and flows.

When she returned to Three Guardians, she found Danno waiting. She told him everything she had learned, including about the phoenix feather. He said nothing, but the hope in his eyes made her hold her breath as she tried laying her glowing hands on his knees.

"That feels . . . warm," he said finally. "Thank you."

She knew from his quiet tone that she had guessed correctly — this was no miracle cure. But the Essence enhanced her own knowledge. "I'll keep trying," she promised. "As I learn. I must also figure out a way to negate the power of that Cobra Sage."

"That has to come first," Danno said soberly — as she had expected. "I'm healing fine on my own."

TWENTY-EIGHT

ARI HAD NEVER WORKED as hard as she did on the small deck of that ship. She was the only one not expected to take a turn at the tiller or as a lookout—the entirety of each day was spent in staff, knife, and fan sparring. She did five rounds of Redbark on rising, and again before she slept. Sometimes Waoji Lion's Mane joined her, and finally Reckless as well. The limited space forced her to be precise in her footing, especially when, during scrapping, both Waojis and Minnow came at her at once. Which they did. Repeatedly. Everyone knew she was going to be facing whatever lethal traps Master Night had planned; she had to hold them long enough for her allies to get into position.

Over meals they studied the map Waoji made of the small island, once a summer retreat for the local branch of the Yulin family. Once they'd evolved the plan about as far as they could, round and round with all contingencies, the conversation sometimes branched out.

One night, when Waoji Lion's Mane was eating supper with the others below and Reckless was taking his turn at the tiller, Ari learned a little of what had happened when Reckless and Feckless were very small, and their mother died protect-ing them.

"We found out that Yulin Enk was the eldest son of the old count. He was thrown out of the imperial city after cheating on the Imperial Examination. His father disinherited him. Wrote him out of the family register, and put the second brother in his place. After the father's death, Yulin Enk prevailed on his brother to let him be tax collector."

"Was the brother another villain?"

"Mother said he was just lazy. The only thing he took an interest in was gambling. As long as he had money to spend, he didn't look too closely at how Yulin Enk got it. Mother grew up here," Reckless said, gazing in the direction of Little Otters Island. "She was good at whatever she did. Especially martial arts, which is why she was invited to train in the Eagle Sect, as her lightness skills were excellent. But when her own family was beggared by taxes, she found some way to investigate — we don't know how — and discovered that Master Night had doubled taxes, and even made up new ones. But he was also cheating the imperials, which could get the *entire island* punished if discovered. She copied out his ledgers and the real ones, and gave them to some imperial — that was the start of the trouble."

He looked toward the ladder to the deck. "I don't know all that happened, except that he captured us to get revenge. Yulin Enk poisoned his blade. She won the duel in the sense that she saved us and finally disarmed him, cutting him badly, but he'd also got a cut in. He ran off and she collapsed, dying. Father got there too late to do anything about Yulin Enk, or to save Mother. With her last breath she made Father promise not to take revenge. I remember that as if it was yesterday," he added, looking away. "My sister as well, and she could barely talk, she was so small."

A surge of hatred burned through Ari. "I *wish* Waoji Lion's Mane had killed that man."

"Ayah, he couldn't that night — she was dead, and we were weak from no food and being tied up all the time. Also, Mother had used a weapon, forbidden to commoners, and she was from a sect that was outlawed for flying. Father had to get us away. As I said, Yulin Enk had already run, leaving the residual mess to his brother."

"From the sound of it, not much happened to the brother," Ari commented. "He's still got his title and everything, right?"

Reckless solemnly nodded. "He does. It was early in the emperor's reign. It is said that he believed the count, who swore an oath before his ancestors that he had no idea what his elder brother was doing — he gave him the position out of filial loyalty. The emperor granted mercy. Though I'm told there's a special tax collector who examines the accounts, which stopped the rivers of gold. Anyway, Yulin Enk vanished, leaving behind his wife and baby son. The imperials thought he was dead."

"But he wasn't dead, was he?"

"Rumors among gallant wanderers said he was gone to the Westerners, dead, alive, but the most persistent rumor was that he turned up in the Shadow Panthers, and eventually took them over, calling himself Master Night and making them into what they are now."

Ari said, "The son. He wouldn't be named Pel, would he?"

Reckless shrugged.

"Put in the army is all I know," First Uncle said, coming up behind them. "But there are a lot of Yulins in the army — most very distant relations of Master Night, if at all. It's an enormous family, its head down in the Silk Islands."

Ari remembered the kindly duke at Green Jade, and crossed her arms. "I think it would be justice, not revenge."

"What is the difference?"

That was Waoji Lion's Mane, coming up as well. The watch had changed, and one of the other crew was now at the tiller, freeing Reckless.

"Is that a real question?" Ari asked, still angry on Whirlwind Bi's behalf — when she was a small girl reading about gallant wanderers, she had cried over the version of the story sold in bookshops, and she hadn't even believed Whirlwind Bi was a real person. "Kanda says to repay evil according to the laws. That's justice."

"That *sounds* so clean and simple." Waoji spread his hands. "We know the first rule of filial respect, but what about a child who kills a father who was a tyrant, beating the children, murdering their mother, assassinating neighbors, and so on?"

Ari said more slowly, "Kanda's rule is that anyone who kills a father can never be just. Anyone who kills a brother might have a reason, but must be exiled, and so on. He says repay evil with the law, and kindness with kindness, and don't mix them. I never quite understood that part."

"Nor has anyone else," Waoji commented. "Or at least, there are rooms and rooms of writings on the subject. Kanda is the strangest when he insists that if you repay evil with kindness, then how can you handle those who treat you with kindness? His insistence that one repays evil strictly according to the laws seems to imply a belief that laws are inherently good."

"Which everyone knows they are not," Reckless said.

"Another reason why I stay away from imperials, who will argue your nose off your face," First Uncle commented. "Grandfather Ki used to say . . ."

". . . those who want revenge ought first to begin by digging two graves," Ari finished. "But what we're doing is justice, isn't it? Master Night has killed so many people. He has your children and threatened to kill them," she said to First Uncle. "He killed your mother, Elder Brother Reckless. He wants to kill me. I just want to stop him, but it seems to me the only way to stop him is by death."

"Are you willing to slit his throat?" Waoji asked. "We probably ought to discuss that now."

"If I have to," Ari said grittily. "I've killed one person. He was a Shadow Panther, and he used to talk about how wonderful Master Night was. I felt terrible after. Sometimes I still do. But I think, if I went back, I would probably do it again. Let them start with a new life."

"And so you are a god, dispensing justice over lives?" Waoji Lion's Mane asked, smiling painfully.

Ari flushed, and he raised a hand. "This is a question my wife raised with me. That was even after Emperor Maoyan, who was a terrible emperor, ordered the Eagle Sect massacred simply because they taught the lightness skills."

"She really did fly?" Ari asked, drawing a breath of delight. "I read that in the stories . . . I apologize. I interrupted." She clasped her hands and bowed.

"I've made my point. Or, rather, I made no point. I think the question must be answered by each of us. However long it takes to find the answer."

Ari wondered if she had just stumbled on the reason he had become a hermit. Or maybe it was one reason. She said, "I don't like deciding things by fighting, but I can. I want to defend people who can't, against people like Master Night, who decide everything by killing and fear."

"Then that is the thought you take with you in two days, three at the outside," First Uncle said.

Ari took his words seriously, as she took all martial arts teaching.

She was serious enough to ink the word *justice* onto the front of her headband before they reached the waters near the cluster of islands Little Otters was a part of. They had made it with three days to spare, so they waited in the lee of one of the uninhabited rocks poking up in the cluster until the storm on the horizon struck.

As the first fat droplets of rain spattered the deck and sails, Ari got out Sagacious Blade and used it to keep her steady in the air as she traced her warding talisman on sails and on the hull. When the storm rendered the sky, the air, and the sea a uniform gray, the *Gull* emerged from behind the rocky precipice, and under Waoji's direction, cruised the coast of Little Otters — keeping a careful watch for Shadow Panther boats posted in inlets as lookouts.

Ari closed her eyes, reaching for light blobs. Oh, yes. There they were. She recognized the tight clusters that meant hu-mans aboard ships, and — still with her eyes shut — pointed them out. She left navigating as well as visual scouting to the others.

They sailed by the main bay, well-watched from a distance, the next day — but though Ari sensed a great many light-blobs in ship-clusters, far more than the previous day, none of them ventured near. Ari's stomach boiled with nerves — she hated the anticipation part, especially knowing that Master Night would cheat in any and every way possible. But Ari had found the blob-lights belonging to the two children, sickly green with terror.

There was no going back.

The *Gull* had been fixed up to look like a trader. The crew, under the captain's direction, let down a battered little rowboat. The gray-haired captain stood at the rail, her eyes concerned, as Ari clambered down, and a scrap of remembered conversation flitted through Ari's mind — *Why are there so many older captains women? Are there young ones?*

Didn't you know that women make the best navigators — definitely considered good luck. Many male captains marry their navigators, and if they're a lot older when they marry, or suffer ill luck, leave widows who take over as captains. I know you are luck-blessed and strong, Firebolt, but I have grandchildren your age. Be careful, promise!

They sailed on, having already let Minnow, First Uncle, and the Waojis father and son off at the end of the rainstorm the night before.

As Ari rowed herself toward the empty shoreline, her senses were alert to a painful degree. Sights, smells, sounds —

and that inner sense that revealed figures hidden in the tangle of shrubs that began where the sand ended. She noted them, and forced her attention ahead.

The terrified children were there, next to a hard, red-veined blob that had to be Master Night. Only, what was the blob glowing a dark red like embers off to the right? Could *that* be Master Night instead of the orange and red-veined one with the two frightened little blobs? Oh no, now there were five, three big ones and the two small. That glowing ember one a ways away from the five made the back of her neck itch — something dangerous there.

She had her sword and her staff loose in her shoulder harness, and her fighting fan stuck through her sash. She no longer needed the fan for hitting acupoints with Essence, as long as she was close enough to aim with a finger, but it was useful in so many other ways.

Ari waited until she had trod up the beach, then stopped well out of range of those shrubs. She faced a wide clearing that once had been a garden approach to what appeared to be a ruined temple. She cast her gaze to either side. The clearing was quite wide. Though there were blobs hidden among the forest to either side, any arrow shot would be all but spent by the time it reached her.

She yelled, "Let the children go."

A pause, then a man shouted, "You'll have to come here and talk like gentlemen."

She wanted to yell that gentlemen don't threaten children, but kept her teeth gritted.

"Now," he said, harder.

Two tall, brawny figures stepped out of the shadow of a plane tree, each forcing a small figure in front of him. Another man, equally brawny, dressed in shimmering silk, strolled between them. He wore a black mask decorated in silver. He was the orange blob, more red-veined by the moment.

"You've caused me trouble," he said in a booming voice. "But I like initiative. And I'm curious. These urchins here have outlived their usefulness in getting you here. But if you please me, they can go. Makes no difference to me, alive or dead."

While he spoke, Ari swept her gaze over the scene, noting how many she stood against, where they were, what weapons. And she counted the hidden light blobs.

"Talk," she called, and began her approach.

Fai Anbai had seen First Imperial Prince sulky and sullen, moody and fractious, then cooperative and suave, patient and sympathetic. He'd seen him drunk and sober, serious and silly, but until this journey he had never seen this sword-sharp intensity.

The prince spent the first two days and nights of the journey at the prow of the fastest messenger ship in the harbor, standing there as if he could get to Little Otters that much faster by sheer will. He scarcely slept, and—much like their first journey together—ate almost nothing.

Fai Anbai understood now that this was not sulkiness. He debated warning the prince of his orders concerning Firebolt of Redbark, but somehow he could never quite bring himself to it—especially as the last couple of pigeons had carried troubling news from Grandfather Fai, without any good news to balance it.

"Your imperial highness," Fai Anbai said on the third day, once they were out of range of pigeons. "We will get there no faster with you here, and no slower if you get your rest."

Jion arrowed a bloodshot glare his way, then blinked. "Yes. Thank you for the reminder, Chief Fai."

He turned right back to scanning the western horizon. But sometime later, he at last consented to go below to eat. And later Min Ko came to the weather deck to report that the prince was asleep.

"Does he know about your orders?" Min Ko asked, low.

"No."

Mink Ko looked westward. "There's going to be trouble." It was not a question.

"Let's consider our plan of approach," the ferret chief answered.

He did, with the chief of the naval Imperial Third Fleet, which rode in station a ways behind them, coming on as fast as they could.

These plans they laid before the prince once they were firmed up. He listened to all contingencies without speaking, then said, "I will lead when we make landfall. That's my one order."

"As your imperial highness commands . . ."

Ari closed the distance at a slow walk, not daring to shut her eyes and risk vertigo trying to track the familiar light blobs belonging to the Waojis for First Uncle. She had to trust them to get into position as fast as they could.

She stopped ten paces or so from Master Night—close enough to see the children's desperate eyes. The Shadow Panther chief stood with his back to a solid wall of very old magnolias still in flower, the ruined temple directly behind it.

"I'm here. I'm listening," Ari said.

"You're really Firebolt? If this is a foolish ruse," Master Night snarled. "Where is the famous fire?"

In answer, Ari aimed a small spurt of fire into the air. Alarm pulsed through Ari: for the first time, she felt resistance to her effort. No, not resistance, it was more like something reaching past the fire to pull Essence out of her.

Master Night grinned behind the mask. "Ayah, that seems convincing enough. I confess I'm a little surprised that you're so short, or maybe you're still growing? How old are you, fourteen?"

"Nineteen." *Next year.*

Nineteen seemed old to her at not-quite-eighteen, but Master Night laughed. "All the more impressive." He leaned on a sword in an attitude of ease that did not convince her for a heartbeat. "Now, hear me out. I can forgive some things, especially as you and I have never met. We've no reason to be feuding. The gallant wanderer world is wide enough for all ambitions, and as they say, it's only the foolish rabbit that eats right next to its own warren. I reward my people well. Very well. Why not be generous, when we all get what we want?"

"Let the children go," she said. "And I'll talk further."

The grin below the mask didn't lessen, but Ari noted the tightening of Master Night's muscles: he didn't like hearing that. No, was it a signal, too quick to catch—wait, that sword. She *knew* that sword—

The guards at either side of the children pulled knives, and held them at the children's throats. Ari's attention snapped to them, but before she could move, something whacked behind her knees, knocking her off balance.

She hit the dirt. But she was only there for less than a breath.

All that practice with Shigan's dance moves prompted her to land in a backward roll and flip up into the air, to land in a perfect horse stance.

One. Two! She sent spears of flame at each of the guards holding the children. But midway there the flames vanished as if swallowed by something that hummed on a deep harsh note more felt than heard. Not just swallowed—it sucked the Essence from her.

She brought both hands up and sent more flame. This time it vanished almost from her hands, as a cold, metallic smell smote the air around her, and yet more Essence flowed out of her

Danger, danger, danger. She yanked her two staff pieces and launched at the guards, who staggered back, the knives still at the children's throats, but as yet they had not cut: Master Night's policy was that prisoners can be made dead at any time, but no one can bring them back to life once gone. And he would need a shield to get to safety if things somehow turned against him.

He stepped behind the two guards, so that the children stood between him and Ari, who skidded to a stop. She was close enough now to see that sword. It was familiar. Very much like Father's sword. In fact, she knew that sword, having practiced with it—he wasn't here, was he?

The thoughts streamed as fast as an arrow: No, he would never be here. If Master Night knew who he was, he'd be throwing threats around, the way he does with families. *He stole Father's sword.*

"Drop your weapons, boy," Master Night said. "Girl? Which is it?"

"All right," Ari said, ignoring the question. The staff dropped at her feet, and she stepped past. Eight paces. Seven.

"Sword."

She drew Sagacious Blade, and laid it down, aware of light footfalls behind her. This was looking tough, but she had to get to those children, whose eyes pleaded desperately. Another step, five paces—

Behind, a man shrieked.

Everyone started violently. She glanced back, astonished to see a Shadow Panther bent over to pick up Sagacious Blade. As he closed his hand around the sword's hilt, virulent greenish light flickered over the blade and up the man's arm. He howled and dropped the sword, then crashed senseless to the ground next to it.

And Ari leaped, both hands out, first two fingers pointed. Thud, thunk—air struck the acupoints in the guards' chests, and they froze, eyes wide.

"Behind me," Ari said to the children, who stumbled toward her as fast as they could with their hands tied behind them. She whirled and snatched up Sagacious Blade, which none of the Shadow Panthers closing in would touch. The one who'd tried to grab it lay moaning on the ground, curled around his hand.

Ari slashed it in a circle, adding fire—but once again that vanished, and again she felt that cold, metallic yank of Essence from her core. *Something* terrible was not only eating her Essence, the thing was trying to worm inside her to get it all.

She could fight without Essence.

She used Sagacious to force the Shadow Panthers back, then whirled the blade securely back into her harness, scooped up her staff and snapped it together, and set the staff humming, forcing the Shadow Panthers to stumble farther back. She tried to move slowly, aware of the trembling children pressed to either side, off-balance with their hands tied.

"You rabbits!" a voice boomed at the back. "Charge, all at once—"

The command cut off with a squawk of pain. Crack! Thok!

Another staff hummed, and then—to Ari's utter astonishment—here was Shigan, knocking Shadow Panthers left and right.

He slanted a question toward the children, and tipped his head; Ari sidestepped, and just like the Redbark days, she and Shigan understood each other without a word. Each took a defensive stance on either side of the children as they plied those staffs with whirling speed.

Jion fought with fierce joy, aware that Ari was better than she'd ever been. He couldn't even see her staff except as a wood-colored blur as she cracked shins and shoulders, dropping Shadow Panthers—but scarcely had he wished they could do this forever then he saw her staff slow, and she faltered a step. Had she been hit? No, she still fought them off, but slowly, as if she were underwater, her face crimson with effort, her breathing harsh.

And from behind the ruined temple, sheltered by dove

trees, the elder Cobra Sage gloated to himself as he set another invisible hook in that girl, and yanked on her Essence core. As promised, he covered Master Night's retreat. When Master Night had vanished up the narrow trail, the Cobra Sage rubbed his hands. He wanted those children for his garden. All he'd had to hollow out of late were Master Night's prisoners or victims — unaesthetic every one. He also had plenty of animals, which were only worth practicing on in idle moments when he was bored. A pair of gracefully posed children would look well on either side of the sundial.

But first he had to get rid of that accursed Firebolt.

She was fighting unexpectedly hard against his hooks. He settled back, prepared to enjoy himself, for he had what the high-level Cobra Sages called her Essence register now. She was barely trained, and astonishingly ignorant, but oh, so much power! It would be all the sweeter to pull it out of her a little at a time, so she'd really feel it before he reduced her to a stone husk.

Which he could pose alongside the chil —

A crack of a twig behind him.

He whirled, to find a tilt-eyed, sharp-faced woman emerging from behind a dove tree, her ruddy brush of hair reminding him strongly of a fox's . . . He hurled one of his poison-tipped needles.

A blur very like a cloud of tails knocked it away. "You," she said in a husky snarl, "have been killing my kind."

"Begone," he said, inscribing a talisman of protection between them. "You dare not interfere between humans."

The crash of a shrub caused him to whirl again, to face a wolf springing. With a contemptuous flick of his fingers in a talismanic sigil, he hardened the wolf's life Essence to fine milk-white jade, and uttered a laugh when the new statue thudded to the ground. A fox and a badger attacked next, then another wolf.

"Is this all you have, fox-god?" he drawled, glancing over his shoulder, to discover that the fox avatar had slunk away in defeat.

Or so he thought.

Four more animals hardened to jade before the fox, who had transformed to the shape of a hairy spider, reached the Cobra Sage's shoulder, two claws in front bearing the needle he'd thrown at her. Which she then stabbed straight into the cobra etched along his spine, between knobs two and three below the neck.

The Cobra Sage did not have time to scream before he turned to stone, though alive on the inside. The poison was something special the Cobra Sage had devised to be particularly cruel.

The animals were dead—but not for long. Leaving the Cobra Sage there to scream inside his beautiful golden jade outer form, the fox-avatar touched each of her creatures, who glimmered then vanished in a flourish of tiny lights, straight to the lap of the Ghost Moon God to await rebirth. The fox avatar looked around, touched a few vine tendrils, which promptly started growing up around the golden statue, then she, too vanished.

TWENTY-NINE

FAI ANBAI STOOD AT THE prow of the messenger ship long enough to observe the naval spears surround the Shadow Panther ships, then had himself rowed ashore. Perforce he'd had to let the prince ashore with the party sent to capture the small cluster of criminals gathered in the clearing before the ruined temple. But he assumed the prince would remain at the back, permitting the imperial guards to round up the criminals.

Before Fai Anbai's astonished eyes, attackers streamed out from the manicured garden at either side of the path, and converged on . . . *was that Jion at the center?*

A soldier pounded up. "He got away from us," the young man panted. "One moment we had him in a protection circle, and next he was outside of it, running. He's *fast*."

On the word fast, Fai Anbai was also running, the soldier pounding determinedly behind him. The battle changed rapidly, almost at each step; at first it had been two, sheltering two small figures, fighting five or six criminals. But as Fai Anbai sped toward them, more criminals joined the circle, the number increasing faster than the two could knock them down, until a swordsman slammed into the circle from one side, and a man with two knives from the other, breaking the circle into a melee.

Shadow Panthers dropped, but there were far too many still around the prince and a short figure with a topknot fighting alongside him. Fai Anbai kept his gaze on the prince as he slashed his way through a pack of howling Shadow Panthers.

On the other side of the melee, Waoji Lion's Mane took in the emperor's force converging. "Ki," he said.

First Uncle Ki dove under a blade and rolled to the feet of his children, who broke down at last, sobbing at the sight of their father splattered with blood. He cut their bonds with two fast strokes, saying urgently to Ari, "Imperials. Run!"

He took his children by the hands and vanished into the ornamental bamboos, right behind Waoji Lion's Mane, both convinced that of course Ari would be right on their heels.

But Ari was in the center of the fight, beside Shigan once again (his identity as Prince Jion forgotten) as she stumbled and struggled to breathe.

Crack! Jion's borrowed staff splintered in his hands as he blocked an axe stroke.

Black shadows roiled at the edge of Ari's vision. By instinct she reached for the hilt of Sagacious Blade in order to toss it to him. The sword began to slip through her grip, but then it lightened the way it usually did when she flew, and it arrowed across the gap and smacked into Jion's hand. He blinked for a single heartbeat in surprise, then waded in, taking on the axe fighter trying to brain Ari. Belatedly she recollected what had happened to the Shadow Panther who'd tried to grab the sword, but Shigan . . . Jion . . . seemed fine . . .

A rustling sound and a something settled over her head and arms. A net? A net with that same horrible cold sensation that had been trying to gut her. The net buzzed with Essence bindings.

Instinct was strong: she threw fire at it—

And icy cold smashed her into unconsciousness.

The shouts and screams faded behind Ye Daq as he raced beside his newest bodyguard—chosen not only for his size and strength, but also because he was stupid, which meant he would never presume to make unwanted suggestions, much less to argue. Unlike his predecessor, now frozen into a jade statue somewhere on the island.

"Rockhead! Keep a sharp eye," he snapped.

"Yes sir," Rockhead replied, breathing hard.

Ye Daq was also breathing hard, but he did not slacken his

pace as he pounded through a very old maze, toward the garden gate door that would lead down mossy stone steps to the hidden inlet where his brother's elegant boat lay. Where was that stupid Cobra Sage? Playing with his statues, of course. As long as he was covering Ye Daq's retreat while he played . . .

Confronted by a tangle of vines that had begun to obscure the trellis before the gate, Ye Daq said, "Cut those down, Rockhead." They were probably full of nasty insects, and would certainly mar his new shimmer-silk, which shone in two colors.

Rockhead obediently hacked the vines down, then Ye Daq waved him back. "I'm fine from here. Go make sure that lazy Cobra Sage isn't hiding in the house, and tell him if he is not down at the boat by the count of fifty, then he can find his way back to Kanda Sutra. I'm waiting for no one. That includes you, so be quick."

Rockhead grunted an affirmative — forgetting to bow, but Ye Daq only sighed. There was plenty of time to beat proper protocol into the idiot once he was back at Kanda Sutra. He shook out his robe, and, breath slowing down, stepped through the archway toward the gate.

Then he jolted when a slim figure materialized from the gloom beside the gate. "I thought you might scuttle this way," Waoji Reckless said.

"Who are *you*?" Ye Daq demanded.

"Someone who spent his childhood here, tending this very garden," replied Reckless. "Before you murdered my mother."

"I did no such — "

Reckless had sometimes thought about what he might say when he caught up with his mother's murderer. He and Feckless had talked about it endlessly as children, though Father had done his best to dissuade them from revenge.

Reckless didn't feel this confrontation was revenge. It was merely the two of them — Waoji had even let the bodyguard go, to live or die as fate decreed for him. He had thought about what to say, but now he discovered he had no interest in whatever lies this man would spin. Of course they would be lies. "Master Night" even lied to himself.

"Now we can negotiate," Ye Daq began. "I like initiative — "

Moving so fast Ye Daq had no time to be surprised, Reckless struck, slitting his throat. Eyes distended in shock, as if this could not possibly be happening to him, Ye Daq — Master Night — Yulin Enk fell dead.

Reckless began to step over him, then looked down at the sword that dropped from the dead man's fingers. Though the handle was worn, and showed a few nicks and dents, the blade itself was very fine, a lot like the one naval officers had, judging by what he'd seen of his sister's shipmates.

He picked up the sword and ran up the path — and when he saw imperials in search parties, faded back again, and ghosted along paths only known to denizens, until he reached the secluded grotto he'd shown the others. First Uncle Ki sat on a rock, one arm around each of his children, who leaned against his side, still shivering. Waoji stood guard over them.

Waoji's face eased in relief. "You're here," he said. "I don't think Minnow is going to join us. She said she had completed her mission. Did you find him?"

"Dead," Reckless said. "He said before he died that something, or someone, called a Cobra Sage was to meet him at Kanda Sutra."

Waoji frowned. "No idea where that is. But we can find out, as soon as these imperials clear off. They're searching fairly thoroughly"

"I'll show you where to hide," Reckless said. "But where is Firebolt?"

Waoji Lion's Mane and First Uncle looked sick, but didn't speak before the children.

"No," Reckless whispered.

Waoji Lion's Mane scowled upwards, then at the forest, then at his son. "There are too many of them for us to snatch her back. We'll have to leave her to that prince she was fighting beside."

Reckless looked bleakly at his father. "You have an idea?"

"Yes. Let's finish her job. She'll want that. We'll find our way to Kanda Sutra, and clean up the rest of this trash."

"Chief Fai. You've got the wrong person," Jion began.

Fai Anbai motioned a pair of soldiers forward, hands gripping the arms of a Shadow Panther.

"Who is this," Chief Fai asked, pointing.

The Shadow Panther stared down at Ari, who lay stunned beneath the net. "That runt is the traitor Firebolt. That one standing there in the fancy robes is Shigan. I'd know them anywhere." He sneered, "I'll die happy seeing the both of them decapitated right beside me."

One of the imperials cuffed the Shadow Panther. "You presume to address his imperial highness with your filthy words?"

"What? Imperial what?"

Another smack, and the man was muscled away, still protesting.

Jion had already forgotten him. He pointed at Ari. "Let h — uh, him go," Jion said, turning the stumble over pronouns into a cough. After that sweet kiss among the grave mounds, he was never able to think of Ari as a boy again. "You saw. Firebolt was no friend to Master Night."

Fai Anbai looked down at that young face. That young familiar face. Ari's face was smudged with dirt, but he was sure he'd seen those eyebrows before — and recently, too.

"I have orders," he said, and raising his clasped hands to the east, "from his imperial majesty himself."

Jion remembered the last orders he'd received about Firebolt. It struck him hard, merciless as a deliberate arrow between the eyes, that he — Jion — had in coming to the rescue led the ferrets, and the navy, straight to her. "You can't," he wanted to say, but he knew that Fai Anbai could. Not only could, but must. Fai Anbai had to obey or die — and if Jion tried to countermand an imperial order, he would die, too, as many princes — oh, so *many* princes — had died in the past.

A ferret turned to his chief, holding ropes, his eyes questioning.

"Don't touch her," Jion said fiercely — and then paled at the slip.

And Fai Anbai had it. Shock silenced him. Loosen the top-knot, clean the face, swap the gallant wanderer headband and clothes for pink silk robes, and he was facing Miss Ryu of Green Jade Island.

How was that even possible?

"Get . . ." Fai Anbai hesitated; what had begun as a straightforward mission had gone horribly awry. Beginning with — he realized — causing the prince to lose face, inauspicious at the very least. He bowed to Jion, saying, "All thanks to your imperial highness, without whose presence we could not have achieved the emperor's orders."

Jion was furious, but not so enraged that he missed the

needle beneath the flowers. They had to obey — too many had seen her. Knew who she was.

But they were not at the capital yet.

"Get the prisoner on board," Fai Anbai said heavily.

Two ferrets picked up Ari's limp form, which was wrap-ped in the net imbued with some kind of Essence binding meant to hold Essence masters. Fai Anbai had no idea how it worked. He didn't need to.

Still holding tight to Sagacious Blade, Jion followed, furious at them all, but especially at himself. He knew his father. He knew Fai Anbai. He should have expected it would not be easy to separate her off and spirit her away before the imperials could catch up.

He glanced back, toward the orderly groups of imperial soldiers carrying out the search for hiding Shadow Panthers, others herding off the captives. All according to the plans, but not on his orders. In spite of the tally, the truth was he had absolutely no power here. If he ever had — most likely all those plans had been set before, might even had been carried out anyway, even if he'd disagreed, he thought bitterly.

He had to find a way to save Ari.

They had just reached the shoreline when a shout came from behind, "Chief!"

Fai Anbai stopped as an army runner pelted up, sand flying behind his heels.

The runner sketched a salute and waved back in the direct-ion he'd come. "They found what they think is Master Night."

The entire party waited until a group came up with a man lying on a stretcher, one arm hanging. The party came to a halt and dropped their burden unceremoniously. The black and silver mask obscured a face none of them recognized. His throat had been slashed by an expert.

The abundant gray hair above the mask, the rich robes, Fai Anbai had seen from the shore, but in the time that man had vanished from the scene and reappeared dead anything could have happened; he could as easily be some local, killed and dressed to resemble Master Night to cover his escape.

"We found this on him," the leader of the patrol said, hold-ing up a gold-handled key. "No weapons, no other identifying objects."

"There's an abandoned house on the other side of the garden," a ferret spoke up. "The key might fit that lock."

Fai Anbai had learned that the Yulin count who ruled this small island cluster, loaded down with gambling debts, had left this island to itself, as he couldn't afford the staff to tend to it. But even if the key fit the lock to a house, it still told them nothing concrete. "Sketch his face, then bury him," he said, and jerked his chin at the rest of the party to continue to the ship. "We'll include the sketch when we question the prisoners."

The imperials shuffled and eyes shifted at that—every-body knew what ferret interrogations meant. They picked up their burden and moved off, and Fai Anbai's gaze snagged on Prince Jion's white-lipped fury. This was the prince's mission, but he'd taken it over entirely. He sighed inwardly: caught between father and son, of course he had to obey the father. Even if he liked these orders less and less.

He glanced down at Firebolt's face, now fairly certain of Firebolt's identity. Firebolt of Redbark was a girl, most likely Ryu Muin's missing "brother" who had left Loyalty after the mercenary attack. "He" and Prince Jion had left together. Firebolt had turned up again at the Green Jade Island attack, in support of her brother—and had assumed girl robes, hiding in plain sight. He wondered if the superlative, straightforward Captain Ryu knew about his sister—and then memory arrowed back to the girl who had turned up in the prince's room. He would wager anything that had been Firebolt swinging down from the roof, and not a random drunk.

It all made sense now, including Jion's barefaced lies to protect her identity. Deliberate deception of the emperor was an automatic death sentence. His head began to pang; what had seemed so simple a mission had turned complicated. A quick glance at the prince—enormously complicated.

They piled into the waiting boats, Fai Anbai and Jion sitting in silence. Presently they boarded the courier vessel, whose hold—unknown to the prince, who had never ventured down there—had been prepared for the Firebolt of report.

Jion followed them down into the hold. When he saw the cage that one of the emperor's shamans had hung with talismans designed to counteract any Essence attack, he exclaimed, "You can't put her in that!"

Fai Anbai cast him a coldly ironic glance. "Your imperial highness, this cage was prepared for the Firebolt you yourself described: huge, brawny, hairy, I believe the precise description went."

Jion flinched inwardly, but rallied. "I lied," he stated. "I lied through my teeth to keep you away from her because she's never done anything wrong, ever."

"Establishing what is right and wrong, your imperial highness," Fai Anbai stated, "is a matter between you and his imperial majesty. That includes deliberate deception of the emperor."

Jion turned abruptly and regained the weather deck in two vaulted steps, Sagacious Blade still gripped in his hand.

He stopped with a jolt, and looked down at Ari's sword. Which could fly. He noted then the two pieces of Ari's staff, laid on a bench with the other stuff being catalogued by a pair of ferrets.

Ayah! There still might be hope yet.

THIRTY

A FEW IMPERIALS CAME aboard to report. The island had been
swept; there was nothing but some peculiar statuary scattered
here and there in the vast gardens, all very realistic stone statues
of people, but every one of them in awkward poses no one with
taste would want to look at.

One end of the house had been recently occupied, a second
silver mask found, along with a trunk of gold, and in another
room some books written in what someone insisted was the
Westerners' tongue, a couple of them with a cobra incised on
the cover in what looked like dried blood. No one wanted to
touch the books, so they'd used their swords to push them into
a sack.

"Prisoners in the holds," the last one reported to Fai Anbai's
assistant on this mission. "All five ships. Captain says to report
that our orders are complete, and if you want to question them,
he's ready."

"I hope I'm not assigned to them. I want to witness the
interrogation of Firebolt," the youngest of the two ferret
trainees said cheerily to her companions.

"We'll get to watch the chief in action at last," he replied.

"Too bad the other cage is empty and Master Night is in the
ground," the first commented. "Would have been interesting to
compare his methods with each."

One of the listening sailors winced, and a couple of listening imperial soldiers side-eyed each other, each thinking horrific thoughts; they found these ferrets in their crow black inauspicious at best, without considering that the context was the art of information-gathering, and assessing it for truth, rather than the infamous torture that was ritual in treason cases.

The ferrets continued to speculate on the approach the chief would take, looking forward very much to what surely would be an interesting session. But to their surprise, when, that night, word came the prisoner had stirred, Fai Anbai said to them, "I'll handle the initial interview alone. No one to be permitted in."

They already knew he'd had orders from the emperor about this Firebolt, so there was nothing more to be said. They went about their duties, Fan Anbai first scanning for the prince. In his cabin. Good. Fai Anbai went down to the hold, where Ari struggled sluggishly through what felt like smothering shrouds to get to air. Her mouth was dry, her limbs heavy and aching.

Through it all a soft voice reached, ". . . Arikanda. Miss Ryu Arikanda, can you hear me?"

"Trickle?" she mumbled. "Where's Muin . . How did I get here? . . . So thirsty. And . . . I can't breathe." She got one hand free of whatever it was wrapped around her.

"Here's water."

A hand held a cup through the cage bars, the cold ceramic touching the top of her hand. She fumbled to get it, and tried to sit up, but shadows bloomed around the edges of her vision and she felt back, the cup spilling as she gasped for air.

"Here's more. Try again."

She groaned and tried to sit up, but her head swam. Her fumbling fingers found the refilled cup, and this time, expending all her effort, she got it to her lips through the holes in the net and drank gratefully. Then dropped back, head panging, the water sloshing unpleasantly inside her. If only she could get enough air!

"Who brought you here?' came the quiet voice.

"Muin?" she asked. But no, she couldn't be at Green Jade Island. Could she? Bits of memory returned: Otter, something Otters, Master Night. The children!

"*Gull*," she murmured, and finally — clumsily — got the net off. Vague alarm at the question spiked through the miasma. She remembered the horrible Essence attack in the middle of the fight, like clawing fingers of ice scraping her from the inside. Then Jion appeared. That was wonderful, until this cold net tangled her limbs, and she tried —

She was a prisoner! She was not only a prisoner, but she'd answered to Ryu Arikanda. "Alone. Came alone," she stated, still in the mutter that indicated speaking took great effort.

Fai Anbai knew she had become conscious — there was the first lie. He tried a different approach. "This cage is bound against Essence attack," he said.

"I can't breathe . . ." She sighed, her head dropping back. "Can't get. A whole breath —"

The hatch banged open then, and Jion leaped down. By now he hadn't slept much for two days, and hadn't eaten for one. He flung the golden tally at Fai Anbai's feet, saying, "If that actually means anything, then you'll listen when I *command* you not to touch her."

Fai Anbai — sitting on a stool outside the cage — lifted both of his empty hands, palms out. "As you wish, your imperial highness."

Jion scowled down at Fai Anbai. "I suppose you're under orders from Imperial Father to shoot me dead if I let her go?"

Fai Anbai looked askance; because they were (almost) alone, he said, "Not quite, your imperial highness. But close enough."

Jion snorted a bitter laugh, the words wrung out of him. "Do you know the carrot dangling in front of my nose? It's to be raised to crown prince. And yet he trusts you more than he trusts me."

Fai Anbai could hear the genuine upset in the prince's voice. "I swore an oath when I first began my duties, and have carried out that oath since before you were born," he replied, in a voice that sounded dispassionate to Jion and to Ari. Neither had any idea, as yet, how very careful was his wording. Then, because they were alone, he deployed a deflection. "How long have you been carrying out your duties, whatever those might be?"

Jion was far too disturbed to take the bait. He peered into the cage, which was square, barely the length of a man, and half a man's height. Ari lay against the far wall, her ribs shuddering as she gulped in breath. It really sounded like she was drowning. "What did you do to her?"

"Nothing, your imperial highness," Fai Anbai said — it was his turn to sound genuinely surprised. "She ought to be fine, once she recovers from the recoil of her Essence attack." But as he said these words, he wondered why she still seemed to be struggling just to breathe. Unless it was an act, meant to get him to open the cage door.

Jion grabbed the bars, then snatched his hands back. Then, tentatively, he touched them again. "Chief Fai, why are these bars so icy?"

Fai Anbai was also underslept after a couple days of almost ceaseless labor. He'd sunk down onto a stool near the cage because he was too tired to stand. At Jion's reaction, he got up and laid his hand on the bars. "I don't feel cold, much less ice. Please honor the unenlightened by explaining, your imperial highness?"

Jion wrung his hand. "Is there some kind of Essence talisman worked into this thing?"

"Of course," Fai Anbai said. "There's a binding on the joints — see those tags hanging? The larger the space, the more difficult it is to counter Essence attacks, that I've been told. Thus the size of the cage. You'll note that means we don't have to use manacles — until we make landfall."

Jion leaned close without touching the bars. "Did you hear that, Ari? What does that mean to you?"

"Can't draw air," she whispered. "Like there's . . . a cabbage in my chest. Or a coconut."

Jion turned to Fai Anbai. "Open it. Let her out. I'll take full responsibility."

Fai Anbai sighed. "Your esteemed imperial highness, his imperial majesty is aware that you would be troubled by conflicted loyalties. The orders I was given were in part a protection for you."

Jion turned his head. "Do you promise not to escape while we're at sea, Ari?"

"Anything," she muttered huskily. "Anything."

Fai Bai did not like the situation any more than Jion — the emperor had been specific about wanting Firebolt alive. He ranged up where he could see Ari's face. Her forehead sheened with sweat, her face pale. Her lips were bluish. That would be difficult to fake.

If she set fire to the ship, now that they had left the islands behind them, she would perish along with them. But there was always personal attack. Though Fai Anbai was fully armed, including with a miniature crossbow with a poisoned bolt, he had a healthy respect for her rumored skills. He said precisely, "Will you promise to avoid attacking me or those under my command if I let you free?"

"I promise." Ari's eyes opened blearily. "I don't want to hurt anybody."

"One wrong move, and I have orders to kill you," he warned — mostly for the prince's sake, as Firebolt looked as if simply crawling might be beyond her.

He unlocked the cage.

Jion barely waited for the door to open then dove inside. He recoiled, shook himself violently, then reached in again, holding out his hand.

She clasped his hand, but her fingers slid through his as if she could not hold on. Jion gritted his teeth, ducked inside again, clasped his hands under her armpits, and hauled her out.

At once she gasped in a full breath, then another. "Oh," she exclaimed. She slipped through his fingers to slump on the deck, just breathing.

Fai Anbai ducked his head inside the cage. He felt nothing. Then looked down at Jion as he sat back on his stool. "Has this reaction something to do with Essence affinities? Didn't Afan Yskanda say something about your having an affinity?"

At the name *Afan Yskanda* Ari jerked. She turned it into a coughing fit, but Fai Anbai saw that, and the fast look exchanged between Jion and Ari. New questions bloomed in his mind, along with the possible consequences of both question and answer.

Jion said quickly, "I do have an affinity. Air. Which is as useless as it sounds. I am not certain why they even call it an affinity, as air is, well, air." He was babbling.

"My Essence cultivation is just that," Ari put in breathlessly when he abruptly stopped. "I learned a little about talismans once. . . But I didn't get very far. . . Before I ended up at Loyalty being orderly. . . To my brother, *Ryu Muin*."

"Essence binding should be fairly obvious, then," Fai Anbai said, giving Ari a dubious look. "That is what the shamans among the geomancers do to the ground to keep the quakes from killing everyone when the sleeping dragons turn. You ought to know that — it's general knowledge — the Essence bindings keep buildings solid, bridges, dams on the islands big enough to need such, and even roads, in some places, though many insist that a well-constructed road does not need talismans. The important point right now is that Essence bindings in our empire are confined to objects."

Ari shook her head. "You can't bind living things with Essence."

"That is not true," Fai Anbai said. "I wish it was."

Jion said, "Master Zao made us read a long scroll listing all the ways the Westerners are barbarians, one being that they do study the Essence binding of living things. Animals. Fish. Birds. People. Some to help, like binding diseases, others to harm."

"Or to control," Fai Anbai said. "Their shamans are called Cobra Sages."

"Cobra?" Ari said, still drawing deep lungfuls of air.

"At least according to Master Zao's text, they began with using snake venom back in ancient days. The cobra is sacred to them."

"Oh." Ari sat up, pressed her knuckles into her temples, then turned a questioning glance up at Fai Anbai. "I guess you had to arrest me to get revenge for the mine."

Fai Anbai said dryly, "You brought down an entire brimstone mine single-handed. That is a crime under any law."

"Not to Suanek's laws!" To his astonishment, her eyes gleamed with tears. "If you had seen those people, many of them barefoot, covered with festering sores, coughing up blood. And few of them had actually been guilty of any crime. They were snatched off the streets because the miners were dying off too fast. I *had* to shut it down." She crouched on her heels, arms wrapped around her legs, her chin on her knees. "Or they'd be dying there still. No one was doing anything about the vast injustice."

"I will not deny the injustice," Fai Anbai said. "I witnessed it. But first, there are a number of ways within the law to redress those ills, and second, why did you choose that mine, out of many possible sites of injustice? There is currently a pressing need for brimstone in the north, and it could be assumed that your actions were in support of the enemy massing there."

Ari ground her chin into her knees. He was right in a sense — her initial intent had been to rescue the Ki family. But she had changed that goal when she saw the suffering of the miners.

But "supporting the enemy"? She looked up, stung. "I don't support *any* enemy of the empire. Especially pirates."

"You were not aware of the increasing number of raids by Westerners up there?"

Ari's bewildered look was a plain enough answer. Jion said,

"We heard about raids now and then when we traveled with Redbark, but most villages don't pay much attention to anything beyond their own shore, or valley, or island. I certainly did not know that the Westerners were massing until my father enlightened me."

Ari gazed from one to the other, appalled. "You mean, a war is coming?"

"I believe his imperial majesty would prefer to avoid it if possible," Fai Anbai retorted, then relented slightly. He was very aware that the two before him had exerted themselves mightily to distract him from that reaction to Afan Yskanda's name. He needed to think.

He rose, and scolded the rabbit to warn the tiger by addressing Ari, crouched miserably on the deck, "Remain here. If you so much as poke your nose above the hatch, you will be shot."

He bent to pick up the golden tally still lying at his feet, laid it on the stool, then left, closing the hatch behind him.

The two were alone. "That," Jion observed, "was entirely for me."

"Don't want to go on deck if a bunch of ferrets are there." Ari stood up, wincing against the crash of pain in her head.

Ever since she left Green Jade she'd dreamed about hugging Shigan—Jion—the next time she saw him. She'd thought during warm spring nights about getting their next kiss right. But now that he was actually here, looking forbiddingly tall and princelike in all that silk, she felt hot and itchy all over, much too aware of how grimy she was. Ayah, where was Lie Tenek, to tell her what to do next? Except that Lie Tenek's advice always sounded so easy—like saying to the new Redbark recruit, "You just use Wind Through the Forest followed by Snake Strikes Wolf," without first telling the recruit what weapon to use, or how to stand, or which foot to begin with.

Jion, with plenty of experience, eyed her uncertainly, gauging her emotions by how high her shoulders hitched to her ears. He took a careful step toward her, hand half-reaching. "I'm so sorry, Arikanda. I led them straight to you. All I could think of was you facing off that villain Master Night, and my plan was to keep them busy rounding up the Shadow Panthers while I got you away."

Ari backed toward the cage, aware of her grimy fingers, and how disgusting it would be to let her grubby clothes touch that silk embroidered with flying cranes. "I heard what he said. That emp—uh, your father, sneaked in orders behind you. It's not your fault." She edged near the cage, and put out a tentative finger. Then snatched it back. Still icy. "I better learn about this matter of Essence binding."

Jion gave her the space she seemed to need. He slipped the golden tally into his sleeve and dropped onto Fai Anbai's stool. "They took some books out of a house nearby. I am guessing these books belonged to a Cobra Sage. You say you felt bad before you were put in the net?"

"Oh, much worse than the net. Much worse. I mean, the net was terrible, especially when I tried to burn it. I know not to do *that* again. But this was much worse, as if the darkness of hell had reached fingers from the underworld to pull me apart from the inside. It still hurts."

Jion nodded. "Let me see if I can get you those books. Someone said something about the Westerners' language, but maybe one is in our characters. I can try, at least. This tally ought to be good for something."

She sank down onto the deck again. "Yes!" Then cast an assessing gaze around, and lowered her voice to barely a whisper, bringing him to crouch right beside her, their heads together. " Before you go, how is Yskanda? What's happened to you? And where is Sagacious? Also, Jion, I'm very, very certain I saw Master Night holding my father's sword . . ."

Up on deck, Fai Anbai, listening at the scuttle, heard the voices drop to inaudible whispers, and turned away. One of his ferrets—all were watching—gave him a questioning look and made a motion toward the hatch, but he held up his hand. For reasons he could not define to himself at the moment, it was better to let them think he'd permitted the prince to question their prisoner.

He needed to consider what he had discovered. Thought he had discovered. There was only one way that that girl could possibly know Afan Yskanda, who was from an ink dot of an obscure island. It all fit together too perfectly, answering questions that he had not had the leisure to pose as yet, the entire Danno matter having been superseded by much more urgent affairs. Oldest child a boy, youngest a girl. Boy in the army. Girl at a temple. Everything fit but the last—however, the matter of Firebolt's identity as male and female, the missing army training cadet Prince Jion had left Loyalty with, the

Essence talent—everything else added up.

Everything except the older boy's motivation for entering the army, given his father's history. It was always possible that he was a mole, or a plant for some long-reaching revenge plan, except how could Danno concoct such a plan while living on a tiny island for thirty years, among fishers and mat weavers? Also Ryu Muin—or Afan Muin—did not behave like a mole or plant. No mole in Fai Anbai's experience would fight to the point of surrendering his own life to protect his commander, or care for the recruits the way Ryu Muin had. Moles had a way of vanishing when trouble loomed, then turning up with plausible stories.

The ferret chief leaned against the scuttle, making a radical alteration of the plans. He had about two weeks before this courier ship would be in contact with anyone, even by pigeon. He'd intended to keep the big, brawny Firebolt locked up tight, on very short rations, interrogating him at leisure, until they reached the capital. But if he turned the actual Firebolt loose, making sure that someone was in listening distance of her or the prince at all times, he might learn more.

He beckoned to his team, and issued new orders, beginning with the secondary naval courier going out with the news of Master Night's death, the rounding up of the Shadow Panthers . . . and the capture of the criminal Firebolt.

THIRTY-ONE

WORD FLEW AHEAD: FIREBOLT captured!

"Good job," said imperial military and merchants to one another, as the fast navy courier stopped for fresh supplies and news, then sailed on the next tide. Though a few of them said it to be heard, without much conviction — especially those aware of the rumors about the spectacular corruption out at Benevolent Winds. The occasional tip or gift between profess-ionals preserved face all around — no one would argue with that — but snatching people's grandmothers right off the streets and selling them to the miners made everybody lose face.

When the news reached Te Gar, Petal sank into a chair, pale as death, but when she roused, she summoned the Red-bark candidates, and in a low voice told them the bad news. And then, quite firmly, she said, "Here's two boaters. Go, all of you, and buy all the red and white silk ribbon you can find."

"What will we do with them?" asked the youngest recruit.

"Hang them from every tree. Not just the temples. Hang them from shrubs, from eaves, from banner poles, if you can without being caught. Bring them here first, so I can write Firebolt on the red ribbons and Justice on the white ones. Because Firebolt *never* did anything evil, *ever*."

Overnight Te Gar burst out in red and white streamers, the word "Firebolt" on everyone's lips.

From there the idea spread. In imperial cities, it was mostly taken up by young people who had eagerly read about Fire-bolt. There were those among their elders who were ambivalent about Firebolt's criminality, and thus, in certain firmly imperial cities, when red and white ribbons began appearing tied to trees, shrubs, and even banner poles, many respectable merchants and even patrols never seemed to see them.

When the news reached Benevolent Winds, within a day the entire north side of the harbor city buzzed with it. The next day, a handful of scarred victims turned up before the Justice Building, kneeling, heads bowed. They did not hit the drum. They intoned "Justice for Firebolt," over and over.

A clerk was sent out to shoo them away. They ignored him. A higher-ranking secretary came out, in her hat and robes. She used all the authority of her calling to order them to disperse.

They ignored her, and kept chanting.

Annoyed, she looked up, then smiled when she saw the thunderheads piling over the barren mountains. She'd let the weather clear the streets.

The storm struck at sundown. Nobody moved.

The next day, when the Justice Building staff reported to work, there were fifty people kneeling and chanting. The Chief Justice ordered the guards to use their staffs to clear the way, but while the guards were perfectly ready to whack brawny young men, they were reluctant to begin beating old women and children and people with missing limbs—all survivors of the mines, or relatives of those who had died.

The following day there must have been two hundred, and the despairing Chief Justice sent pigeons off to beg for an edict—rain or shine, the crowd just got bigger by the day.

In gallant wanderer circles, the appalling news spread fast-er than wildfire. Red and white ribbons festooned trees, ships, and shops—anywhere the imperials looked, a blatant but silent protest.

It was not only the military who used birds, of course, so word of Firebolt's capture winged literally as well as figurative-ly, until it reached the Silk Islands, where General Falik had lately arrived to await the birth of his grandchild.

When he, his son, and the Dun brothers saw tough Captain Ryu sink down onto his cushion as if gutted, they nodded wisely, attributing his reaction to Firebolt having saved both their commanders. Captain Ryu was as quick as Commander Falik to give credit where it was due.

Unaware of these repercussions, the naval courier carrying Firebolt, Prince Jion, and Chief Fai Anbai sailed sedately east. The return trip was twice as long as the journey to Little Otter, due partly to the winds being now directly against them, punctuated by a series of storms that blew them back, and also by the naval ships' holds being heavily laden with all the prisoners taken from both the island and the retaken Shadow Panther vessels.

Ari never forgot she was a prisoner, but she was certain that as long as Jion had Sagacious Blade, she'd be able to grab it and run in spite of there being no fewer than three or four of the seven ferrets aboard at any time, in addition to their chief — the rest rotated between the ships to question the Shadow Panthers — and the imperial guards. The younger of the female ferrets was not much taller than Ari, and quietly offered to share her civilian robe, which she'd brought in case she had to go covert. Ari accepted gratefully.

Jion — aware of his father's orders and the consequences of not obeying them — made no attempt to counter imperial orders. He kept his goal small: to obtain one of those Cobra Sage books long enough so that Ari could read it. He hoped that somewhere in that book would be some Essence sutra or ritual that would enable Ari to escape without needing Sagacious Blade. Because he knew that he was constantly watched, and he had no hope whatever of sneaking a sword to a prisoner marked by the emperor's personal orders. Especially a sword that . . . *moved*. Why hadn't Ari told him about that? Twice now he'd shoved it into a trunk to hide it, to wake up with it lying by his hand. Once, he could believe he'd absently retrieved it. Not twice.

Jion tested the boundaries of his relationship with the ferrets by casually asking the youngest one — no older than he was — over breakfast one morning if he could take a look at the confiscated books, to be reminded that Firebolt was a very dangerous prisoner, and that putting possible arcane know-ledge into her hands might get them all killed.

Very well. Wolves on the walls and rats in the temples — for all the easy-going atmosphere, the boundaries were as tight as an impending battle.

Ari kept experimenting with the cage, in hopes of learning how to counter its binding. After a couple days of recovery, she could even go inside it, though she kept a hand pressed to her middle. "I breathe Essence all the time," she told Jion one morning. "I think that's why it feels like a boulder sitting on my chest when I'm in those bindings. But it's not as terrible as that first day, after whatever it was that attacked me while we were fighting the Shadow Panthers." Her brow furrowed. "Cobra Sages. I really need to learn about them."

"They sound evil," Jion observed, with a gesture of repudiation. "But if you can use their evil Essence to break that ice binding on the cage . . ."

"Essence is Essence," she reminded him. "Binding spells holding bridges together aren't evil. I remember my mother's herbal saying something about cobra venom, if properly decocted, being able to help when people are in terrible pain, like after being burned by fire. Those who intend evil can use Essence just as they use anything else." She sighed. "How to define evil? I'm sure these imperials think I did evil when I collapsed that mine, even though I was so very careful not to let anybody get squashed, guards as well as miners."

Fai Anbai, listening above, detected the ring of sincerity in her voice. He and his other senior ferret traded off listening, but though the two chattered about their Redbark days, and about martial arts styles, and many other subjects, there was no mention of her identity: they could not know that during that very first conversation, whispered as Ari recovered from the Cobra Sage's attack, they agreed to never make reference to her origin, or to Yskanda. Or to Sagacious Blade and flying. If the ferrets wanted to think that Jion had picked up that sword from a fallen Shadow Panther, let them.

That meant they couldn't talk about the sword's odd habits.

But they had other matters to occupy them. Five days into the journey, Fai Anbai permitted Ari come to the weather deck in the sun and air, for which she thanked him with a grateful bow. And since they already knew about Redbark, what was the harm in getting in some drill? She found Jion moving through the warmups the following gray morning, sea and sky shrouded in mist. She ventured to the forward deck, and when the sailors and the ferrets on watch did nothing to stop her, she fell in with his own breathing pattern, shut her eyes, and began to move through Heaven and Earth.

Jion had already arrested the eye with his skill and grace. But when he started over in tandem with Ari, it was as if he had sloughed off a suit of clumsy armor. Each was superb in distinct ways, Ari smooth, no movement wasted, the embodiment of power strictly leashed—a fire roaring safely between impermeable walls. Jion's control was a different quality, the summer sun spangling water as a brilliant, even seductive reminder of its power.

Everybody was watching as they built up to speed. At the end, Ari sighed, kicked her bare toes into the deck, and mumbled, "I guess I can't have my staff? Ayah, we can spar without."

They did. It wasn't just their skill, or the easy laughter that made that skill seem effortless as air. They entranced the younger ferrets, and made the elders thoughtful. Fai Anbai came up from his work, watching soberly. He recognized that he was witnessing something both rare and troubling in the sense that if things turned dire he was confident he could take down Jion with some effort, and probably Firebolt if she did not use Essence, but not both.

It was disconcerting because he caught no hint of threat in either of them. Growing anxiety, yes.

Jion was sublimely aware of their matching, movement to movement, breath to breath: the promise of transcendent passion when she was ready buoyed him against the stresses, whereas that sun was still hovering just below the horizon for Ari. Though it glimmered now and then in secret little aware-nesses: the glint of dawn's light on the stubble along the fine cut of his chin; the thump of Yaso's pill locket inside his shirt; the curve of muscle along his thigh, hidden and revealed as the long lengths of his robe panels whirled and snapped. The brief touch of his hands in blocks and feints.

The days flowed by, broken by ferrets and messengers moving back and forth between the command vessel and the naval ships, on which Fai Anbai's agents conducted interroga-tions. He himself had to stay aboard the ship containing the emperor's prisoner, so his agents made a list of those to be interrogated again by him.

What they learned was disturbing enough. According to several, there was indeed someone behind Master Night: no less a mysterious figure than the White Dragon. As soon as he heard that, Fai Anbai took out the books the searchers had found in the summer house, and though he had not studied the Westerners' language for ten years, he sat down every night, as soon as Firebolt was reported to be asleep, and forced his way through as best he could. The arcane rituals and jargon-laden Essence talk he skimmed. He was looking for any scrap that might point toward the White Dragon's plans.

Meanwhile, Ari, finding the ferrets less bloodthirsty and grim than she'd dreaded, talked readily about martial arts, and even sparred with them, for she was always thirsty to learn new styles. Once the ferrets saw that she was holding back her Essence, and knew precisely when to pull a kick, punch, or jab to acupoints, put down the weapons they had hidden all over the deck, and enjoyed watching until it was their turn.

This was the pattern until a rainy afternoon that kept everyone penned in the main cabin outside the galley: it was the first cold storm of the season, a hint of autumn not all that far off, on the other side of Ghost Month.

Jion was trying to shape an approach that, if he could not get Fai Anbai to look the other way while Ari escaped, might mitigate his father's ire. Why not try his ideas on the ferrets? At first two or three of the younger ferrets got involved in the discussion of natural rights, and moral questions that transcend boundaries.

But Jion forgot the potential political weight of his title. As soon he got onto the subject of the sage ruler, the younger ferrets all found they had duties elsewhere. No one was going to risk discussing even hypothetical kings with an imperial prince.

Fai Anbai had no such reticence. And duty kept him right there. He had twofold purpose in testing the prince's opinions, the first and most obvious to discover, if he could, whether Jion was going to make a move against him on Afan Arikanda's behalf. He said provocatively, "One of the measures of the sage ruler that I've seen written, your imperial highness, is in the reasonable departments of government, as well as its judgments. And who can judge them, and apply judicious force to avert evils, but the sage ruler?"

Judicious force, Ari thought, scowling. But she didn't want to start arguing about force, because then they'd surely bring up collapsing mines as an example of injudicious force.

Fai Anbai's gaze went from her silently mutinous expression to Jion's watchful gaze, and he went on, "If this uneducated person may, for the sake of discussion, dare to remind your imperial highness that Kanda's time was one of greater unrest than that of Lao Sha seven centuries ago. I'm no scholar, but experience has taught me that the world we live in shapes our thinking." He paused.

"You will get no argument from me," Jion said. "All that seems self-evident—at least, Master Zao insists on the first, which I can't prove or disprove. But what I've read corroborates your point, Chief Fai. And so?"

Fai Anbai said, "You'll also agree that Kanda and Lao Sha did not live in the same environment as well as in the same dynasty or era. Lao Sha had the benefit of free travel and well-established law under one emperor. Kanda was driven from island to island by either war breaking out or threatening, each by different kings who all made their own whims into law."

Jion snapped his fan open. "Again, all the writings insist that Kanda's time was one of terrible unrest, the kingdom divided into as many factions as islands, as the saying goes. We're all agreed on the obvious so far . . ."

"Given that, your imperial highness," Fai Anbai said, "it seems to this remedial scholar that perhaps one can under-stand Kanda's preoccupation with kings — in particular the sage king, who, in acting on behalf of his people, is justified in making laws for the good of all."

Ari sat upright, cast the chief ferret a doubtful look, then sat back.

"Go ahead, Arikanda," Jion urged.

"I stopped lessons in history at ten, except for what we got at Loyalty," she said uncertainly, the color coming and going in her face. "You know that. But it seems to me that there is a difference between the kings who make laws and follow them, and the ones who throw laws around but don't follow them."

"Ah," Jion said. "The emperor who is above the law. My sister is preoccupied with . . ." He paused, and shook his head. "Forget I spoke. I believe that when one disagrees, one ought to let that person speak for themselves."

Ayah! And there was Fai Anbai's second purpose, to find out if Prince Jion knew whatever it was that First Imperial Princess Manon was studying with the emperor's permission — and which inspired her to go delving into archives that usually went ignored.

Jion went on, "Clear laws can be understood by all, from

high degree to low, and that includes foreigners – unlike customary laws, which arise out of circumstances of a time. And once that time passes, the laws become opaque. At best. In particular to foreigners, who have no such laws. Like the avoidance of hot food on Tomb Sweeping Day."

"Or," Ari said, greatly daring, "the law that forbade common people to wear blue on certain days, as an excuse to grab them and force them into mines."

"That law has been rescinded," Fai Anbai murmured, considering how to bring the discussion back to Princess Manon's project.

Jion said, "Master Zao lectured us endlessly, insisting that most subjects cannot understand the rites and rituals of government. Yet no one argues that they are not still subjects. And, they can be got to understand, and to abide by, laws that are clear and unambiguous."

Ari's rare smile flickered. "Remember Instructor Shaz quoting Kanda? He said that if a person, he said man, but I think it would go for women, too, if anyone looks into a mirror and sees a charging tiger coming up behind, they will naturally run and hide. But – going back to bad, or obscure, laws – if the tiger is obscured by palm leaves and the mirror has been painted over with the latest popular color, how is it possible to see the tiger?"

"Good question," Jion said, consciously avoiding a glance at Fai Anbai. Instead, he smiled at Ari, reminded of their old debates while they lay side by side under the stars. "A very good question. That can go for bad orders as well as laws."

Ari leaned forward, encouraged by his smile. "If old tarnish – old laws – smear the mirror, and aren't wiped away simply because the mirror is old and venerable, handed down countless generations, even though there's no reflection left, and some young cousin comes along and says, 'Why don't you take a cloth to it?' and the elders shout, 'But it's our tradition to leave it untouched,' then what good is it? A mirror that acts like a mirror is useful. A mirror that collects dust, ayah, it seems to me that it will cause arguments about how things look and whether to wipe it or not, which is the opposite of harmony."

"I recognize the gallant wanderer path of thought," Fai Anbai said. "For the purpose of discussion, what laws do we save, or are we to throw away all laws?"

Ari, too, was reminded of the past. But for her it was Ul

Keg's gentle voice reading and talking to her and her brothers during long rainy days. She closed her eyes, pulling his voice from memory. "As Mana Ta says, we must always come back to natural law. It is the only true law of general purpose, eternal and unchanging; it outlines the duty of the civilized being, and its prohibitions are solely there to curb wrong-doing. Therefore to alter, or abolish, natural law is a sin against Heaven itself."

Fai Anbai rose. "As soon as we begin assuming we can speak for Heaven, I know I am finished. I can only speak for myself. Besides, I have been smelling pepper fish for a while now, and my stomach is reminding me with increasing fervor that midday is nigh."

That broke things up. In the course of getting the meal and finding a place to sit, he cut Jion out, and said, "You were about to describe First Princess Manon's current study, your imperial highness? She is an impressive scholar. I'd be curious what draws such a mind."

Jion looked down at his dish, then up. "I happen to disagree very strongly with the direction her studies are going in. So I am reluctant to speak, lest I misstate her ideas."

Fai Anbai said, "I salute your forbearance, your imperial highness. And I have found myself in similar situations. May I offer a suggestion?"

"Please. I would be grateful if you would."

"You might ask yourself if anything you might say will endanger his imperial majesty, or the Empire of the Thousand Islands."

"Neither."

"Further, you are aware that his imperial majesty has given her highness full approval. So anything you say will fit within a safe context, I venture to suggest."

Jion nodded slowly. "It's Great-Great-Grandfather Maoyan," he said. "She seems taken by him. Not even dissuaded by the bloody events — in fact, she seems to be fascinated by his later rule. I'd thought she would learn more about becoming a sage ruler by studying the words of Great-Grandmother Teyan. But . . ." He turned away. "Of course it is up to Imperial Father to determine who will make a sage ruler."

Fai Anbai barely heard these words. Shock ran through him, and he struggled to hide it; this was the very worst possible time to be constrained to the slow pace of prisoner-laden navy ships. But he was tied to them until the interrogations were finished.

As soon as he could, he disengaged from conversation, forced himself on his regular rounds, and then withdrew to his tiny cabin to pen a deeply coded note. And over the next day and a half, he stationed himself so that he was nearly always in sight of the pigeons in their cages — and at the very first flutter that indicated they sensed land nearing, he chose his father's two pigeons, and cast them into the midnight air.

THIRTY-TWO

THE NEXT MORNING, THEY were considerably startled to discover Ari looking . . . odd. Jion realized with a hastily smothered gasp of shock that she had methodically plucked out most of her eyebrows. The skin was still reddish, though it had probably been worse the evening before; she had reduced her characteristic straight brow to two thumb-sized "moth wings" more or less in the style that Madam Swan's women favored, only of course without the precision, so they were somewhat lopsided.

He stared at her almost unfamiliar face.

"Why did you do that?" he asked—then realized as her shoulders hitched up that he sounded too blunt.

She was about to speak when a shadow flickered in the open hatch, reminding her that they were listened to. "Everybody always says my eyebrows are ugly. I thought, if I got rid of them, the emperor might not want to kill me as fast. If I looked nicer."

Jion had no idea what to say to that. He was so used to Ari, who had never once, in all his memory, taken the least interest in her appearance outside of neatness or the disguise of a ruse. Her reasoning about the emperor sounded completely insane. Then the obvious struck him: she was terrified that his father would somehow recognize Ari's father in her face. She certainly resembled her brother.

The absence of that line of heavy brows definitely changed her face, which he'd thought he knew so well. Her features were unremarkable as features — it was her expression that made it distinctive. Her brows had dominated that face, but now her eyes did. It wasn't that they were suddenly larger or smaller. And their color was the brown most often seen in faces all around. It was their expression, that clear, guileless gaze that she shared with Yskanda.

Jion realized she — without any mirror — was waiting for judgment. "I think what you say will be more important than your appearance."

"Do I look terrible?" she asked anxiously.

"No. It's just that you don't look at all like you," he said, and sure enough, a grin of relief flashed, as quickly hidden. "Let's get breakfast. Ayah, I can smell land on the wind! We can't be more than a day out." When he saw worry crumple her brow, he made a gesture as if holding a sword to remind her. Her brow smoothed. Trust. She trusted him to get Sagacious Blade to her.

He was not at all certain how he was going to manage that. Was its peculiar reappearances to his hand an attempt by the sword to get back to her? The idea of a sword having even limited volition was mildly disturbing; it might have been more so except that this sword was not craving blood, the way that one Ari had smashed had been.

Whatever it wanted, or didn't want, he *had* to get it back to her. She was relying on him.

They tumbled up to the deck and joined the ferrets not on duty for breakfast. Ari was self-conscious at first, but no one seemed to notice her eyebrows. Or if they did, no one commented; they probably had heard her below, sounding like a fool. Better than the truth.

While they ate and enjoyed the warm sunlight after the previous night's storm, Fai Anbai sat alone, a slip of paper crushed in his hand. His father's terse line, *Owl alone in graywing archive* — Owl being First Imperial Princess Manon — could mean anything. At any time during the past rule, the past dynasty, the past centuries. "Alone" signified the fact that she used her authority to forbid any servants attending her, so no one was able to see where she went or what she looked at.

But what Prince Jion had said about her current interests — that was a very bad omen.

Up on deck, Ari and Jion finished breakfast.

"Shall we do Redbark?" Jion asked.

"As soon as I wash out this borrowed robe," Ari said. "I want it to have all day to dry since it's cloudy out."

Jion nodded, and crossed the deck to begin his dance stretches, which he could do without having to think about them. The courier ship was so close to land. What if he got down into the hold and tried laying the sword just inside the bottom framework of the cage? Or he could . . .

While he made and discarded ever more unlikely ideas, Ari conscientiously filled a bucket with wash water from the rain barrel, and lugged the awkward, sloshing thing below-deck to fetch the robe. She was midway in setting it down when a quiet step right behind her caused her to set it down with a thump and a splash.

But she was already too late. She stilled as a knife blade pressed against the side of her neck, and an arm like a steel band clamped around her. "It's time," Fai Anbai said, and maneuvered her efficiently to the cage. A quick shove, she stumbled to her knees, and the door slammed. The lock clicked.

She clung to the bars. "I wasn't going to . . ." she began, choking on the words.

"Maybe not," Fai Anbai said, with a hint of compassion. "But his imperial highness was very much going to, probably with that sword you loaned him. Yes, I saw that from the beach. This way, there are no painful choices — and his imperial majesty's orders are obeyed. You probably don't know how many lives were in jeopardy," he finished.

Ari's insides twisted with sick regret and anger. She swallowed past the knot in her throat and said, "Can you put that robe in the bucket to soak?"

"I'll return it. She'll take the gesture as meant."

And he was gone. A short time later male voices rose from somewhere above, muffled by the deck. She recognized Jion's furious tones.

She did not see him again — the ferrets had gone into guard mode. She sat in the cage, which was bearable — just — and reflected that they had allowed Jion and her that one last breakfast together. Kindness or taunt? Her mother, and Ul Keg, would want her to believe it was kindness.

When two ships sailed into the harbor below Three Guardians Manor on Kanda Sutra, the island Ye Daq had taken after slaughtering the entire family of a cousin, Danno and Hanu had been putting together their plan to take the north end of the island, the one most heavily guarded. Those guards were still largely devoted to Ye Daq—or, more correctly, devoted to his promise that once the ships being built launched, each of them would shortly thereafter become lord of his own island.

Danno controlled the rest of the island now. When his lookout over the bay pelted up to announce the two ships, he nodded at the gathering and said with his usual mild tone, "We drilled this. Everyone to your places. I'll go to the bay to welcome the newcomers."

Nods and affirmative grunts, a few surreptitiously stroking weapons—for some don't change all that much.

Hanu remained behind, silent but worried as Danno made his way down the ancient steps cut into the gentle slope. His knees still twinged, but he could run if he had to. And he could fight.

Ul Keg went with him, his heart racing like a deer in his chest. He could see little past the haze, but he relied on Danno's excellent distance vision.

"Ayah," Danno said presently. "I don't see Master Night among them. Isn't he usually at the prow?"

"He always has been," Ul Keg murmured. "In our experience. Admittedly not all that long."

A cook named Lentil Lu piped up from behind Danno, "I don't recognize a one. I thought every recruit at one or another time has sat before a table of my dishes."

Danno appreciated the expert way the newcomers approached in a loose arrowhead formation, no one fouling anyone's reach, swords still sheathed but carried in left hands. Then he frowned, his attention going to the handle of the lead man's sword. "That's mine," he said involuntarily.

The man, tall, scarred, with a mane of gray-streaked dark hair loosely tied in a tail behind him, lifted his chin as the sound carried. "You once a guardsman?"

"I was," Danno said. "You?"

The tall man hesitated, but the younger one at his left, with a mane of dark hair, shouted, "He's come to announce that Ye Daq is dead. I took that sword off Ye Daq's corpse after I cut his throat."

Lentil Lu turned to Danno, grinning. Danno said, "Ayah! It seems someone has cooked the rice while we were fetching the water."

From behind came a shout of surprise, and cheering. The newcomers, seeing this, relaxed their stances as the questions and answers flew back and forth.

When the emperor left the palace it was usually with musicians and drummers and banners going before him, then marching imperials with spears raised, after which his fifty-man palanquin came, followed by more guards, graywings, and serving maids.

When he desired to eschew notice, he had several modes. One of these was to ride in a closed cart, with graywing attendants and perhaps a guard at the horses' heads. Of course more guards would be stationed on rooftops and at all points in the surroundings, some wearing imperial guard armor, others dressed like civilians, on the watch for sneak attacks. Anyone who saw this cart knew it was from the palace, and to stay well out of its path.

Then there was the rarely used invisibility mode, in which he put on the scholar's robe, and walked alone, or perhaps with a guard also dressed as a scholar. The circle of guards would of course still be there, but also dressed as civilians—except for those bearing crossbows, roosting on rooftops.

The emperor, whose mood of late had been grimmer with every new dispatch, had originally intended to make a display of the prisoner Firebolt, who had dared to slap the imperial face by attacking a mine in the heart of the empire. No "gallant wanderers dispensing justice one villain at a time on the edges of the empire," that. It was not just a mine at the heart of the empire, but a brimstone mine, crucial to the making of gunpowder.

But over the last week, a flurry of increasingly unwelcome pigeon messages had arrived—only one of them about the traitor who had called himself Master Night, who apparently had a lair in an island tucked within the treaty-protected Ran principality.

All the rest concerned Firebolt.

The peace and order of the empire had not only been seriously disturbed by the increasingly dire news from the north, but by proliferation of the Firebolt ribbons — and reports of subjects kneeling before Justice buildings first in one or two cities, then ever more with each new dispatch. The emperor was assured that governors were busy quashing such disobedi-ence — underage commoners caught hanging the ribbons were given ten strokes and their families fined; adults refusing to disperse were hauled off and sentenced to six months' labor at Imperial Works for disrupting public harmony. Some governors were harsher, they righteously (and obsequiously) assured the emperor, but to his imperial majesty, that meant only that Firebolt had succeeded in fracturing the peace at the very time he needed it most.

Then, at last, came a message by pigeon from Fai Anbai, to inform the emperor that the infamous Firebolt was not, after all, a brawny brawler whose mastery in martial arts was legendary, but a small teenage girl, whose brother was in the army. A brother famous for his heroism.

She was also very close to Prince Jion.

Jion was going to be explaining this discrepancy, most like-ly after a lengthy time for reflection on his knees before the shrine of his ancestors, but before that, the emperor intended to get an early glimpse of this infamous beguiler before she was locked up in prison.

The sun had barely cleared the eastern arm of the peninsula when the tide brought in the courier ship. The imperial guard did not have to do much to clear the wharf of the curious, for the morning was cold, enormous sky-reflecting puddles everywhere after a series of storms.

The emperor in his civilian garb stood obscured by a redbark tree at one end of the quay as a cage was boomed from ship to wharf. There in the cage sat a small, woeful figure with an utterly undistinguished profile. With no fanfare whatso-ever, imperial guards closed in on either side, and the cage was trundled off to the west gate.

Once it was gone, Fai Anbai appeared with Jion in tow, both taut with tension. Every line of Jion's body radiated wrath as he stalked down the ramp to the wharf.

The emperor issued orders, and then withdrew.

Ari didn't notice any of this. She had told herself that she would not be ashamed of being stuck in a cage, but when it actually happened, she had to remind herself that the binding on the cage prevented her from using her sight-warding talisman — and thereby drawing the attention of the guards whose alertness she could feel. She knew without being told that all their lives were at stake. She was an imperial target. If they were anxiously peering into the cage to make sure she was there, they would be reminded of her Essence talents, and then they might be moved to put more of those horrible bindings on her.

All I need is my sword, she kept repeating to herself. She had absolute faith in Jion. She knew he had to be trying; the question was, how could he get it to her when he, too, was being guarded, and kept separate?

Her cage bumped along a stone canyon with high walls topped by sentries, and then inside a massive gate. There to the right was a huge drum, and in a court a sundial, reminding her of Loyalty Fortress. She was rolled directly to the door of a building whose only windows were located under the roof: this had to be the infamous prison of so many stories, legends, and ballads: the House of Eternal Peace.

She was right.

She was surrounded by a double patrol of armed guards, and taken down a long dank-smelling stone corridor. Voices echoed off the stone, mostly in the local accent that she always thought of as northern. But she was not to be put near any of these prisoners, it seemed. Down steps below the surface of the ground, to another corridor, this one torchlit, past empty cells, all the way to the end. She was locked in a cell that contained a rough, low table, a narrow plank bed with a folded blanket, and a covered pot in the corner.

Jion, following at a distance, saw Bitternail coming. The old graywing said, low-voiced, "His imperial majesty desires you to repair to the ancestral shrine to reflect."

Jion gripped Sagacious Blade as he stood poised, the more discerning around him holding their collective breath. He shut his eyes, one heartbeat from throwing it all away and going after Ari, scything down all who got in his way. But that was the likeliest way to get them both killed — and what would she say to him if she saw him appear, covered with blood, leaving a trail of bodies behind?

"This son hears and obeys," Jion said tiredly, and turned to

Fai Anbai, holding out the golden tally. "You might as well hand this back to his imperial majesty. This was your mission, not mine."

He turned away without seeing the shared sighed of relief, and crossed the garrison. He found Yarrow waiting, and handed off his things, including Sagacious Blade, which at least had not been taken away.

Off he went to kneel on very familiar stones, as Fai Anbai bowed before the emperor. As always, he handed off his report and the tally to Melonseed, who carried both up to the emperor.

The emperor looked down at the tally, then took the report. He glanced through, then his brows shot up when he reached the sketch of the dead man. "This is Yulin Enk! I thought he was dead, years ago."

Fai Anbai remained silent, a tacit reminder that the ferrets had been shut out of that investigation early in the emperor's reign when he thought he had to appease the powerful clans at court. The emperor leafed on, then exclaimed, "*Two* Cobra Sages? Two? Then he has — had — connections among the Westerners?"

"We'll be conducting more interrogations, your imperial majesty, but it appears that he has been receiving funds as well as these Cobra Sages, in return for supplying information on our harbors and defenses to the White Dragon."

The emperor read silently — without asking about Prince Jion. Then looked up. "Is this girl who calls herself Firebolt really related to one of my most promising captains?"

"She appears to be the missing cadet after the attack on Loyalty, your imperial majesty."

"She was with my son all along."

"It seems so, your imperial majesty."

"How does this fit into the Redbark Sect and the rest of it?"

"It appears that Redbark was her invention — there was no sect. Or rather she started it, with a couple of other youths. Before that she followed her brother into the army as an orderly, dressed as a boy. She discovered her Essence talent during training, and after the mercenary attack left the army to seek a master in Essence cultivation."

Silence; Fai Anbai waited for the question he would have to answer about why no one had investigated Second Ryu past Te Gar, but it did not come. For the emperor, the matter of Second Ryu's background was so low in priority that he dismissed it with an internal shrug: he had no interest in the obscure corner these Ryus had come from. His interest was fixed on what she had become. And how she had convinced Jion to throw off his imperial identity to go traipsing all over the north, looking for duels in the name of justice.

That was the crux of the matter. All four of his children appeared to have loyal hearts. In the latter two it was unthinking; in the elder two, the loyalty *appeared* to be unswerving. But while Manon's every word expressed dedication to the empire, Jion's erratic actions centered around this demon-cursed girl.

The emperor waved at Melonseed to take the tally away, wishing the entire disaster could go with it. But then that left the other matter that kept him up through nights: the White Dragon, who, denied one throne, wanted another. One could say he was a barbarian Westerner, but to the emperor his behavior was *exactly* like Hojai.

He glanced up, and remembered he had not dismissed Chief Anbai. He observed caustically, "Now that you are back, I trust we will see some resolution in *any* of the other matters. Request your esteemed father not to trouble himself if his years are pressing."

Fai Anbai bowed, accepting the rebuke to both his father and himself, and the emperor moodily waved him away.

The Cobra Sage of Kanda Sutra's north bay found duty tedious in the extreme, but she had been promised that once Ye Daq successfully accomplished his plans, she would be able to join the White Dragon's elites, who would be executing the first wave of attack on the Mud-Eyes' empire.

And the days were tedious — until the day they weren't.

She woke to the sounds of sword fighting. She threw on her wrap and ran out, to discover the guards fighting against a swarm of newcomers. She ran back to fetch her Book. Time to ignite the blood poison in the hostages as promised.

The rash-faced assistant physician appeared out of nowhere.

"Get out of my way, stupid," the Cobra Sage shouted. "I need to . . . what are you doing?"

The assistant physician was rubbing her hands, which glowed with Essence. Power, raw and wild, and the idiot had never sacrificed a drop of her own blood!

"Where did you learn that?" the Cobra Sage demanded.

The woman did not answer, but opened her hands — and a cloud of wild Essence enveloped the Cobra Sage, tickling like a thousand insect wings brushing her skin. Her domination tattoos chilled before that onslaught, draining her power. The Cobra Sage clawed at her own flesh to waken her blood but the assistant physician sketched talismans in the air, which glowed golden — and the domination marks deadened one by one.

The Cobra Sage screamed as all her hoarded power fled into the void, leaving her as defenseless as a street sweeper. "No, no, no! I'll kill you!" She snapped open her Book, Written in her own blood, but the words turned to mush in her mouth.

The assistant physician's gaze shifted, and that was all the warning the Cobra Sage had before a sack enveloped her head, and a rope bound her limbs to her sides. Someone yanked her stumbling into a space that reeked of rotting garbage, unwashed bodies, and chamber pots left untended.

The tugging halted. A door slammed and locked. She knew the sound of that lock.

When she finally freed herself from the rope-bound sack, she discovered she was locked in the same room in which she'd kept the shipwright's family, with their filthy blankets and the garbage she had refused to rid the room of. The doors and windows were locked.

She began to howl, banging on the door, while elsewhere in the dreary little village, the shipwright and the now-freed workers prepared to finish the most forward of the ships and sail away to freedom.

Others roamed around helping themselves to the former guards' considerable stores, and celebrated.

The Waojis and Danno led the way back through the bamboo forest, exhilarated after as neat a skirmish as could be — no one killed, the former guards locked in their own prison, the hostages and prisoners free, their tattoos having been defanged by Hanu.

"I haven't gone through Ye Daq's things yet — I was considering whether to leave them for his return and pretend a little longer so I could get his plans out of him," Danno explained.

"He can explain his plans to the King of Hell," Reckless said. "Let's see what he's got."

As former Shadow Panthers whooped, hollered, paraded

around in Ye Daq's silks, and got steadily more drunk, the three divided up Ye Daq's suite of rooms and systematically went through them.

The gold and wealth was set aside to be divided, as Danno had promised. Some would use their share to begin a new life, others would no doubt drink it in a week, but that was their fate. He had his sword back — Reckless having surrendered it at once when Danno explained — and as for the rest, as long as he could get to the capital to rescue Yskanda, he was content.

"The imperials ought to be along in two, three weeks," Waoji Lion's Mane observed. "You'd be welcome to join us at Ten Leopards, or Sky Island. Everyone insists there's trouble coming — more and more Westerners' galleys sighted, and fast raids more frequent."

"Once I find my children, then I might join you," Danno said.

"You'd be welcome," Waoji Lion's Mane said, bothered by the sense of familiarity about this man. Too bad they had worked from different sides of the north harbor, so he hadn't seen him fight.

"I thank you —"

"Ho, look at this," Reckless exclaimed. He had been digging through a trunk and found a false bottom. Trays of rings and fine hair clasps and belts were set aside, disclosing sheaves of papers.

He began sorting and setting aside, then paused to examine a drawing of a boy's face, with writing down the right side. "That, I'd swear, is the prince we saw on the beach at Little Otters," he said.

"Prince?" Danno repeated.

"Let's see," Waoji Lion's Mane said. "A little young here, but unmistakably the same boy. Now a young man."

Danno stared down at the drawing, stunned. This drawing could have been Second Prince Enjai when they were boys — except that Enjai had never had a grin like this. But the eyes, and especially the dramatic tilt to his brows, were the same.

"This is a target description," Waoji said, reading over Danno's shoulder. "Loyalty Fortress?"

"It's an army training fortress," Danno said. "Or was, back in my day." He didn't explain that reading was not one of his skills. He said, "May I take it? I might find a use for it in the capital, trading for information about my son."

"It's yours," the two Waojis said, and began reading through the papers.

Danno left them to it.

Hanu turned up a short time later. "I put jugs and buckets of water in reach of all the cells, and bread and root vegetables. If they are careful, that ought to last until the imperials arrive and unlock them." She sighed. "Ul Keg says the monks and nuns are ready to go. We can leave them at any temple we see, and they will continue on from there. The rest, some are preparing to leave, but many are too drunk to hear me when I warned them that the imperials are probably on their way."

"Then there is nothing more to be done after we divide the loot," Waoji Lion's Mane said, with a questioning look cast Danno's way.

Danno agreed with a nod, and left that to the Waojis. He found his muscles sore after the earlier exertions. For him, there was only one solution.

He picked up one of the blades and went out to the practice area to do Heaven and Earth, slowly at first, stretching and smoothing the cramps and kinks. Then he shut his eyes and whirled through the pattern he had known all his life, the sword hissing and vooming in the air.

He stopped with his feet in the precise prints he'd made when he began, let out a long breath, enjoying the singing of blood in his veins.

He opened his eyes, to find a row of staring eyes — both the Waojis, and the gallant wanderers they had brought along.

"Where did you learn that?" Waoji Lion's Mane asked.

"Imperial guard," Danno said, surprised. "You knew I was once an imperial."

"But that's Redbark," Reckless exclaimed. "Or very near."

"Redbark?" Danno repeated. "What's that?"

The two Waojis exchanged astonished glances, then Reckless said, "Firebolt's martial arts drill. She calls that Redbark. It's not the same," he added. "There are differences. But . . ."

"It's the style I've used all my life. Taught my children."

"How many children?" Waoji Lion's Mane asked, his gaze focused on Danno's puzzled face, the straight line of his brows. "Is there a girl among them?"

"Three. My daughter Arikanda."

"Ari," Reckless breathed. "Firebolt's name is Ari."

"This," said Waoji Lion's Mane, "changes everything."

THIRTY-THREE

"THAT FOOL JION," SAID the second imperial consort, "is in the shrine court again."

"I know." Manon had gone herself to see, and to reassure herself he wasn't there lighting incense and reciting sutras in order to impress Grandmother Empress, or some other sneak attack to threaten her ascendance. But kneeling in the court meant one thing: Imperial Father was angry with Jion.

"If my steward is to be believed, he was stupid enough to argue with his imperial majesty about that common-born wench over in the prison that everybody calls Firebolt. *What* a fool Jion is! Just like his mother. I sent Hao over to get a look at her. Said she's as plain as a turnip, if you are curious."

"I'm not." Manon set her teacup down. "The prison stinks, and I trust we'll be summoned before nightfall to watch her head cut off. We'll see enough of her then. What matters is what Jion will do. I half expect him to leap into Lotus Blossom Square waving a sword around, or maybe even worse."

It was gratifying, and maybe a relief, that Jion's own nature would work against him, so that she need not. It was his Ran half at fault. Though the Rans were a far older family, they had never risen to dynastic greatness. Mediocre Ran blood had polluted his Jehan blood. Manon promised herself she would make him happy in the future—he could be sent on diplomatic visits, where he could eat, drink, dance, and flirt with stupid women. Because she really was fond of him—within reason. And that was the essence of command, everything within reason, no weaknesses for conspirators to worm their way in.

Manon glanced disparagingly at the silk hangings in her private room, everything embroidered with symbols denoting the phoenix. Hangings, screens, cushions, were exquisite, but this was not the Hall of Glorious Harmony, which she had been in often enough of late that she had begun to think of changes she would make once it was hers. She smiled. "I think I will have this hall redone. I want to experiment with a style that might suit the heir's palace."

The second imperial consort eyed that smile. "Daughter, do not get overconfident. His imperial majesty is furious. Any little mistake and you will be out there kneeling with that silly boy."

"Everything is going exactly as I planned," Manon replied coolly.

It was true. Diligence had paid off in a thunderstrike—clearly Heaven intended for her to rule, and she had to prove it by not wasting her opportunity now that she had her proof. She had been waiting patiently for almost three weeks for Imperial Father to be at his angriest. How very fitting that it was Jion who gave her the perfect opportunity!

In fact, that must be her beginning, especially if Jion was kept out there through a night again. Commence with filial piety. Imperial Father liked displays of filial piety. Then go straight to her horrifying discovery, and a humble plea for advice . . . she must not even hint that she was passing judgment herself . . . A private plea, wearing thick robes beneath her white swan robe for sorrow, so that if she knelt in supplication her knees would be well cushioned . . .

She slid contentedly into sleep.

In spite of her hope that Jion would still be in the ancestral courtyard the next morning, the emperor merely let Horse and Dragon watches go by before he summoned Jion. He was very tired, and irritable from far too many matters too complicated to resolve with a simple edict.

Melonseed had come for Jion, on his own bringing a cool, dampened cloth for the prince to wipe his face and hands, and water for him to drink before they proceeded to the imperial garden. After two long watches of self-castigation alternated with increasingly stupid plans for wresting Ari to safety, Jion had to concentrate on walking while enduring the painful return of circulation to his legs.

Melonseed evaporated before they reached the aromatic magnolia.

The weather had stilled, all those puddles making the air sultry. The emperor sat under the gilt-eaved roof of a tea house built on one of the platforms where the stream feeds into the lake, stirring the air a little — and incidentally muting sound. Glowing lanterns in the shape of fish and moons lit the scene as Bitternail oversaw silent graywings bringing out chilled fruit, and first flush red leaf tea, sent by Lily and served in porcelain decorated with water dragons gracefully undulating around each cup as well as the pot.

Jion winced as he knelt and went to the fine tile floor.

The emperor knew he would not sleep at all until he saw Jion; though his list of aggravations began with threats to the empire, and court brangling over the trade issue, when father and son were alone, he was impelled to burst out with the strongest emotional injury: "Get up, get up, get up. I want to see your eyes. Jion, you stood before me and lied right to my face about that Firebolt."

Rivers branch in incalculable ways; this conversation might have gone very differently if Jion had tried to deny, or looked away and pretended not to remember, or had even gone to the floor in a groveling plea for mercy. But he gazed straight back at his father, grubby as he was, and said, "I did lie, Father Emperor." He used the more intimate term, rather than Honored Imperial Father, the public honorific, which Manon preferred, because one day she would be Her Imperial Majesty the Honored Empress, and everyone would *always* use every single word.

Jion stood straight, hands flexing once, then said, "I lied because I wanted to protect Firebolt. Because I do not believe she is any threat to the empire, to you, to anyone except the likes of Master Night. When we got there, she was fighting alone, trying to rescue a couple of children Master Night was using as bait. It seems to have been his favorite ruse."

"I know what she was doing," the emperor snapped. "I read Chief Fai's report. What I want to hear is how you imagine that destroying one of my gunpowder mines, at a time I need them the most, is not a threat to me or my empire? She might very well be an agent of White Dragon. As apparently Yulin Enk turned out to be."

"Impossible, Father Emperor. She could never be."

"How can you be so sure?"

"Because this unworthy son of yours, when believing that assassins from our own people were after him, lived beside her, worked beside her, sometimes shared food out of the same bowl. Trained beside her, fought beside her, each saving the other's life several times. Living that way, you learn to know someone, almost better than you know yourself."

"And yet," the emperor replied, his deceptively mild voice at its most sardonic, "you did not know she was a girl?"

Jion spread his hands. "She didn't tell anyone — and boy or girl, it didn't matter, especially then, when we were so young, Honored Imperial Father. This unworthy son might be ignorant about much in the world, but I know *her*. Neither she nor this ignorant son had ever heard of White Dragon until Imperial Father enlightened me, directly before I left. If you wish to punish someone for those lies, punish me. I won't complain — I deserve it. But not her. When everything she does is for the good of others." Jion's voice rang with passionate sincerity. "If this unworthy son may be permitted to save you the effort of asking the next question, I did intend to rescue her, but I also intended to destroy Master Night and his army as I promised to do when you gave me that tally. She was fighting alone, as I said, just as she came to rescue our people at Green Jade Island when he attacked there."

"Yes, I know that, too. Apparently Yulin Enk had some idea of setting himself up as duke there. Family vengeance." The emperor waved away the subject of Yulin Enk, dead and unmourned. "Does Captain Ryu know his sister became Firebolt?"

"He does — according to her, Honored Imperial Father. I did not discuss it with him. She told me he tried to convince her to stay in Green Jade but she felt she could not accomplish anything there that the duke and the army wasn't already doing. She left before I did — I only saw her one day. She wanted to go back north to the islands where our law does not reach, and someone like Firebolt is needed. That was before Master Night staked those children's lives against hers."

"Somewhere up north," the emperor repeated. Where the Westerners were massing. He wanted Jion to be speaking the truth, to not be a rebel, as too many princes had become. The emperor had believed that he would avoid the ultimate pain of son against father if he gave his children everything they desired, and kept steel out of their hands.

Scowling, he waved dismissal. "Go to bed. Tomorrow as soon as you waken, go reassure your grandmother and your mother that you are still alive and breathing."

Jion bowed and began to withdraw.

"Jion."

The prince turned. "Father Emperor."

"You will remain in your manor for a week in self-reflection. After which I am not limiting your movements, except in one regard. You carried out my orders in all other respects—Fai Anbai praised your part in strategy planning, and how well you fought. But do not go anywhere near the prison. It's their lives at stake if you get past them, as I'm certain you probably can."

Heartsick, Jion bowed and left, thinking tiredly that that just destroyed most of his possible plans for getting Sagacious Blade to Ari. Why wouldn't that sword do its weird moving thing to *her* hand?

He returned to his manor, agonizing over what to tell Yskanda, a problem he still had not resolved when at last he fell into troubled sleep around dawn.

He was deep in unpleasant dreams when Manon rose, dressed with her usual care, then performed her morning greetings to her mother at the other end of the manor, to her grandmother at a time when the other consorts were usually there so she would not have to visit them respectively—oh for the day when they had to come to her and bow down!—and then to the emperor's residence. Only this time it was not to study. She went directly to Bitternail and requested an interview.

It was immediately granted, which was auspicious; she had made certain that Jion was not in the ancestral court anymore before she went to her grandmother's manor, so she had time to rearrange her approach.

She cast an eye over the emperor. Good, judging by the marks under his eyes, his mood was terrible—and surely Jion had to be the cause.

Falling to her knees, she said in her lowest, sweetest voice, "Honored Imperial Father, this wretched daughter confesses that there is one comfort afforded her, that she did not see First Imperial Brother reflecting at the ancestral shrine, and trusts that he has been forgiven his trespasses." She paused as if for breath after this reminder of Jion's transgressions, hoping to hear that Jion had really thrown away all his merit over some criminal in the prison.

Imperial Father said nothing, so she moved to her triumph, every word practiced. Going face to the ground, she begged in a tremulous voice for enlightenment and advice, for she dared scarcely to speak . . .

The emperor heard this mellifluous flow, admiring how very practiced it was. Galled to the heart as he was, it struck him that such a quality, much as he disliked it personally, would do very well before a fractious court. But he had little time, so he cut in, not unkindly, "I note, however, my daughter, that you *are* speaking. And I am waited on by many. What exactly is the problem? Look up, don't talk to the floor — I cannot hear you well."

She looked up. "Imperial assassination," she whispered.

"What?" He expected almost anything but that. He sat back down, his heavy brocade dragon robe forgotten. "What? Who? When?" Why wasn't he told?

"It was Great-Great Grandfather Jehan Lanek, Emperor Maoyan. He was poisoned to death by Graywing Melonseed." And with not-so-covert spite — knowing that the graywing could not speak unless addressed — Manon said, "I found the evidence in the graywings' own records, thanks to your gracious permission, Honored Imperial Father."

The two chief graywings' duty hours always overlapped mornings, when the emperor was readying for court, or interviews, and evenings, when there might be events to attend, so they were both there. Decades of habit built on hard training kept them soundless, without moving, but Bitternail could not prevent a shocked glance, quick as a lizard, at Melonseed, whom he had known pretty much all his life.

Melonseed stood as still as a statue, his eyes closed.

The emperor took them both in, and frowned down at his daughter. "What evidence? Did he write a confession that has been tucked away unseen all these years?"

She was astonished at the sharpness of his tone — almost as if *she* had sinned against the very Heavens, which assassin-nation of an emperor amounted to.

"No, Honored Imperial Father. The evidence is in the fact that he was the last servant to see our honored ancestor before he died. He brought medicine. No one else was there — this humble daughter also checked the records of the imperial guard, and who was on duty. The emperor's death is recorded very precisely, his end progressing exactly in the manner of one poisoned." She felt a sharp look, and added inadvertently, "Which I know about from a few years ago. My maid. And others. When we thought they were sick."

The emperor's head turned sharply. "Melonseed," he said. "What is the truth here?"

Imperial guards materialized as Melonseed prostrated himself. "It is true that I administered the medicinal draught from which he did not recover," the graywing said. "I believed it to be medicine to relieve pain. He was in so very much pain."

"He's lying," Manon said—and regretted the words as soon as they were out. She dropped gracefully to the floor in a cloud of gauze, and apologized humbly and abjectly, then said sweetly, "This daughter begs for punishment, though in her heart there is only a desire for the lawful protection of the imperial greatness that sheds its benevolent light upon us all. It is her poor and weak understanding that there can be no mercy for any who dare to raise a hand against Heaven's Chosen— and in justice to the law, this ignorant daughter pleads for permission to witness the interrogation that she might learn."

The emperor nodded to the guard captain, who saw to it that Melonseed was taken away. "Send for Chief Fai," the emperor said to Bitternail, who stood rooted in shock. This command furnished the impetus to move, as Manon lifted her head in hopes of taking her place at Imperial Father's right hand for what was about to unfold.

"You may withdraw, daughter, and assemble your proofs."

She was going to reply that she had already done so—in fact she had written no fewer than six drafts—but her father's soft tone caused her neck to tighten, and she thought it better to withdraw for now.

The emperor was left alone with Manon's thunderstrike, which had had all the effect she had desired—if not the end. But only in those absurd operas that Imperial Grandmother and the rest favored did the masked emperor in gold ever turn abruptly from shocking news and proclaim the righteous as heir then and there.

She made her way back to Drenched Blossoms, satisfied with imperial father's reaction—but not so satisfied that she forbore ripping off the ruinously expensive gauze outer robe that had taken the embroiderers months of work to make, and stuff it in a brazier to burn away the residual feeling of having to prostrate herself on the floor.

THIRTY-FOUR

THE IMPERIAL MESSENGER FOUND Chief Fai at the ferrets' headquarters. Knowing that his father would join him once he reached a certain corridor, he walked out and very soon there he was, falling in step beside him.

Word had already reached Grandfather Fai, who looked as sick as his son: what they had feared most had come to pass.

"He's so old," Fai Anbai said.

"He makes *me* feel young."

"After all these years . . ."

"Never," said Grandfather Fai, "underestimate the reach of ambition."

Fai Anbai clasped his hands to his father, neither pausing their brisk pace. It did not do the keep the emperor waiting at the best of times.

"You know what to do," Grandfather Fai said.

"You are the one who taught me."

"If we can, we shall press for time. At least we ought to have the Easterner courier ship arriving soon."

They reached the end of the corridor and parted unobserved

The day dragged by.

Two became three, and then a week, each of our principals troubled for different reasons; Melonseed sat patiently in prison, knowing what was to come; the staff tried in silent ways to ease his incarceration by sending a thicker blanket, putting good tea instead of the army regulation dull brick tea in the pot, and filling it with freshly boiled water instead of the water that often arrived lukewarm; making sure his food was delivered hot. Melonseed recognized all these little efforts, which reached his heart, though he found it difficult to eat, and to sleep.

Manon had expected to be hailed for her loyalty and perspicacity, for it really had taken sustained effort and painstaking work to track down an anomaly that she confidently assumed had bypassed everyone else among the older generation, to sit gathering dust in the archive. But the emperor did not summon her to lead the investigation, nor did he issue an edict (preferably before the assembled court) promoting her the imperial heir as a result of her vigilance and selfless effort in the name of the imperial dynasty.

Jion slept little, and ate less; he felt terrible for Melonseed, but judgment was reserved solely for himself in not keeping that implied promise to Ari—who explored her cell, noting ancient talismans much like those on the cage. Most of her fear was for Jion; she was sure that if only she could get through that door, she could rescue herself. But how to wrest him away from these imperials? She did Redbark feverishly, so that she would be ready when the opportunity came.

Grandfather Fai had calculated correctly in predicting that the advent of the next courier ship from the Easterners was nigh. The first pigeons arrived, one of his own as well as those to the imperial guards. He trusted that this arrival would distract the emperor. Anticipation also heightened in the dowager empress's and the first imperial consort's households, mitigated by the deeply upsetting news about Melonseed, who was well known to, and well respected by, them both. But they could not interfere; Manon had made it a matter of state.

Before the week was up, Grandfather Fai reached the ferret office, where everyone was elbow-deep in work. "The latest pigeon has the Eastern courier coming in on the morning tide," he announced. "Whoever is disrupting our function will no doubt be expecting it as well, so I'll need someone to serve as backup for our agent."

Two or three eager younger ferrets stepped forward, as

expected, plus one older, steady agent. "I just returned empty-handed," Peony said, referring to her long mirage of an investigation into the mercenary attack on Loyalty Island the Year of the Rooster. "I'd welcome a good, hearty dust-up, should the unnamed enemy be so obliging as to offer one."

Some laughter met this, and Grandfather Fai turned to her. "Then go, Peony. Be there before dawn. Do you want backup?"

"I shouldn't need it. Especially as the graywings will no doubt have people there in anticipation of whatever the princess has sent, along with the usual red cloaks."

Grandfather Fai accepted this, and turned back to the pile of grim reports from the north.

Peony, a short, solid ferret a year or so older than Fai Anbai—trained in the same cohort—paced the entire wharf well before dawn, not only noting the regular naval guard, but the deployment of imperials in readiness for the courier ship. She also noted secluded nooks where people could hide, still shadowy with the sun rising later each day.

The courier floated in on flood tide and expertly tied to the wharf, which caused a flurry of activity, naval people going back and forth around the imperial family graywings who of course had precedence. Maneuvering through this tangle was the ferret agent, a tall, gaunt, serious woman who invariably went undercover as a maidservant. Her arms were full of imperial mail.

She saw and recognized Peony, then glanced around for the backup, for she well knew the importance of the messages she carried. "No backup?" she said abruptly, though she had not seen Peony for years—but to her, Peony had been a mere recruit. Once a recruit, always a recruit.

"There's news," Peony said. "It's worse than you think. Chief Fai is waiting to brief you especially—the office has been compromised."

"Ah," said the senior agent, proving that deserved flattery rarely fails in convincing people to overlook protocol, which is so often their undoing.

So it was now. The world was still blue with the sun a finger's breadth below the horizon; Peony led the senior agent to one of those shadow-obscured places among the rocks on the peninsula, while flood tide surged and ran between them, and then jostled her senior, whose arms were laden. As the latter teetered on the rocks, Peony knifed her between the ribs, caught the package, and set it aside while she weighted the senior down with rocks and sent her splashing into the water to sink.

Then Peony sat down on the rocks and used all her skill to break the seals on the messages. She read them one by one, pausing when she came to one addressed to Grandfather Fai's scribe desk. Inside was an expert sketch of a familiar and beloved face. Peony tore that paper into tiny shreds, then dropped those into the breakers, watching till no scrap remained before she breathed her fire starter to life to affix each seal she had broken. She waited until these had cooled and hardened, packed them all up, and returned to the office to report that the senior agent had gone straight to her well-deserved liberty, entrusting the messages to her.

Grandfather Fai took them with a distracted air, leafed through, then sighed in sharp disappointment. "Lay them on my desk, will you, Peony? Then take over the observations class — the emperor has summoned me."

He finished up what he was doing, straightened his robe, as one does before attending the throne, and then left, stopping only to speak orders to two waiting people, who ran off.

Grandfather Fai found his son inside the garrison gate closest to the imperial pavilion. He was holding a paper, which he had just fetched from their agent among the first imperial consort's maids; this woman had sorted the messages from the East, and while the consort and the dowager empress exclaimed over the gifts and letters they had been sent, quietly extracted the hidden message from Ri-Ri, Lily's maid, and awaited Fai Anbai's arrival.

Grandfather Fai shook his head, his face grim.

"Peony?" Fai Anbai exclaimed. "It can't be! I've known her since we were first learning to read!"

Grandfather Fai was more upset that the senior agent had not come — for he did not believe for a heartbeat that she would go straight to her liberty without reporting in. "I really thought she would be on the watch — that if Peony tried an attack it would have gone the other way. With all her experience . . ."

Fai Anbai was very sorry to lose an older agent, though he had scarcely known her, and time was not just pressing, but a tiger's hot breath on their necks. "Do you know this man?" He held up the second drawing that Ri-Ri had sketched and sent in the hidden message, as requested.

"No. He does look like a Su, though, doesn't he?"

Fai Anbai was reflecting that fifty, more like a hundred other people also looked like Sus, which availed the ferrets nothing; Grandfather Fai was reflecting sadly that once again they had missed a hint, a cue, vital as it was.

Ri-Ri had been an early ferret recruit, until it became clear that her temperament was not aligned with ferret duties. Otherwise utterly trustworthy, she had become their agent in place with Imperial Princess Lily—who gained her devotion. Grandfather Fai stared down at the drawing, saying, "It never occurred to her that the presence of this man in secret at the bookstore might constitute a danger."

Fai Anbai agreed. "And she didn't speak until her princess asked her to." They could not call that misplaced loyalties.

"Now we have to figure out who he is, and where," Grandfather Fai said heavily.

"At least we have our mole," Fai Anbai said grimly. "Did you put someone to tail her?"

"Two," and his father named them—both experts. Then Grandfather Fai's thoughts winged out to implications and consequences. "How long has Peony been lying to us, and about what? At the very least we've the mercenary search to begin all over again." He held out the paper. "Get that copied. Until we have Peony tied down, don't use our people for that."

"Who? Court artist?"

They had had recourse to the court artist over the years, he being as discreet as he was disinterested. "He's sick," Grandfather Fai said. "Once the interrogation is over, take it to the assistant."

Fai Anbai tucked the rolled paper into his sleeve, and they parted.

Ari remained vigilant. To no avail.

Food was brought twice a day, and the covered pot in the corner swapped for a clean one, accompanied always by too many well-trained imperial guards for her to fight. They wore thick chest armor, which would prevent her from using the acu-point freeze, and she refused to neutralize the flimsy Essence-preventing talismans on the cell and burn the guards. No. No, no, no.

She had to find another way to get out.

She knew she was not completely alone in that torchlit corridor. The second day, they'd brought in a new prisoner. At first she was not certain what was happening, but the rumble of voices, and an apologetic, "You'll be here, Graywing Melonseed. Would you like another blanket?" followed by the raspy tones of an older man, "Please," made it clear enough.

She peered through the bars toward the stairway, but could not see anything from her angle.

After that, the string of days during which there were the sounds of the other prisoner getting his food, which meant her turn would be next.

Then one day (unknown to the prisoners, this was the day the Eastern ship arrived) a lot of noise broke through Ari's fifth round of Redbark drills: scrapings, as if something heavy was being dragged, clankings, and even the singeing drift of hot iron as from a brazier, and the soft murmur of voices in the courtly accent whose specific words she could not quite make out. Was that a woman's voice? Instinct curled warning along her nerves — and then came the gasp of pain that made it clear what was happening.

After that, the slightest sound, and there were many, lacerated her nerves, especially when the man gasped and groaned. And then she heard the chief ferret's voice — kindly, patient, which she found so much more chilling than threats.

"Did you act alone?"

"Yes . . . yes!"

"Who gave you the poison?"

"No one! I prepared it myself. It was . . . ah-h-h-h! It was a matter of . . . mixing a theriac with a decoction . . . I'd been told . . . it was effective."

"Who told you?"

"The old shaman, Rui Naneg."

"Who acted with you?"

"No one!"

It went on like that, round and round, until a silence, followed by, "He's unconscious. Do you have all that down?"

"Yes, chief."

Then more of the sounds of things clinking and thumping and the shuffle of withdrawal. Followed by blessed silence; Ari could not see anything — including the emperor and Manon, who were witnesses.

Manon had made it clear that she wanted to attend, to prove

that she was a dedicated heir determined on justice, but her expectations faltered when Imperial Father sat outside the cell on a cushioned stool placed for him. Under cover of the noise of the ferrets setting up the implements of interrogation inside — for prisoners this important were not hauled upstairs to the regular interrogation rooms — he'd said low-voiced to Manon, "I detest these things."

Exasperating as Jion was, from him he knew he was likely to get a similar admission — but from Manon he received a lifted chin, and a melodious, "When it comes to protecting the imperial name, I will do my duty."

The emperor suppressed the impulse to retort that duty was understood — why else would they be in this dank, dark stone corridor?

Manon was not certain her words had had the proper effect. The next interval was even more unsettling — and thoroughly unpleasant. She made herself look into the cell, to show her firmness of purpose. The sights, the sounds, the smells, made her stomach roil. She told herself that after all that man in there was a mere servant, who had dared to raise his hand against Heaven's Chosen, and bringing him to justice proved that she was a worthy guardian of the precious imperial name.

It went on until the emperor, still with his eyes closed, raised a hand, and a moment later the noises ceased, except for Fai Anbai addressing the scribe writing down all that was said.

The emperor rose and walked out, Manon perforce following, leaving the ferrets to pack up and withdraw.

Melonseed had been a child and youth during the reign of Emperor Maoyan, whose era names had all been words of peace, but whose actions had progressively become more sanguine. In those days, the entire palace was forced to watch the frequent executions, and sometimes public interrogations. There were levels to these things, he'd learned by the time he was fifteen: for the most part, the first level was the stripping away of dignity as the body craves surcease from pain. But beyond that there were levels of horror, the last being the mutilation that guaranteed one would not be buried with a whole corpse. Which meant, everyone knew, wandering as a ghost, too shamed to return to the ancestors who had given one life in that body.

Pain there had been just now, but endurable. He knew quite well that Fai Anbai was capable of far worse — the chief ferret had been trained by his father, the expert. There was a semblance of communication beneath the questions and the use of force here, a tacit agreement going both ways. Melonseed remained firm in repeating that he had acted on his own in making the poison and administering it.

Ever since that long-ago day, Melonseed had lived believing himself on borrowed time. The Heavens would surely hold him accountable eventually, though he had been granted decades of peaceful existence. Until now. But everyone eventually comes to a day of reckoning before the King of Hell.

Outside the prison, the emperor did not speak until they left the neatly swept stone world of the garrison and crossed into the peaceful grace of the imperial garden. "Daughter, what did you learn by witnessing that?"

Manon was startled by the question. She thought rapidly. What *had* she learned? That human flesh was fragile; that she never wanted to witness such again; that she wanted it *over*, and her merit firmly established. That, after all, was the entire purpose—and of course to protect the imperial name.

Her mind worked fast, concocting an answer that would make her sound like a future empress, and was this how Heaven chose for the throne? So far there had been no shafts of illumination, no sense of the gods leaning down to crown her, neither in omens or dreams, and certainly not in any real sense.

"Honored Imperial Father, this ignorant daughter learned," she said precisely, "that he acted alone. Which establishes Heaven's desire for justice."

"How do you figure that, Daughter?"

Manon did not at all understand the glance cast her way. Though she knew every shade of sarcasm, thanks to her mother's tutelage, she only perceived irony when it reflected elsewhere, never toward herself. She said, "Heaven displays its approbation of Honored Imperial Father's benevolent and wise reign by putting this humble daughter in the way of discovering the truth."

Did she really believe that, the emperor wondered. Her self-satisfaction would certainly indicate so. These were all the right words, this the right attitude, so why did he feel an emptiness within her words and actions, like one of the musicians' beautifully painted hollow gourds on which they rapped and knocked in time to their harmonies?

Manon was everything an heir should be—oh, she certainly

needed tempering, but what young person didn't? He ought to elevate her now. He was ready to get the matter resolved, at least *one* matter resolved.

No, there was no need to act in haste just because there were so many other unresolved questions. He pulled his mind back to the threatening chaos, which ordinarily he loathed contemplating. But that was better than this inward sense of betrayal of Melonseed, whose kindness and benevolence he had taken for granted his entire life.

"Do you," he began, his voice a shade harder, "feel we ought to make a spectacle of his end?"

Her ear caught that shade, though she could not interpret it at all. He could not possibly regret the justice of her discovery and its right true end? She was thinking fast. Imperial Father had held a few public executions during her lifetime — they had expected to hold one for that criminal calling himself Master Night — but always for the perpetrator of a series of heinous crimes. Really, the only heinous aspect of Melonseed's action was in daring to presume to medicate one of imperial blood without going through the usual protocols. Emperor Maoyan had been quite ill then — she had seen the imperial physicians' recommendations for rituals, incense, decoctions. Melonseed had said repeatedly he had taken it upon himself to mix two medicines to kill the emperor's pain. It was more presumptuous than heinous; even if it was Tiger Watch, surely even a seventeen-year-old would have the wit to call his seniors and not act on his own?

Mainly, she wanted the matter done, Melonseed out of the way and attention firmly on her virtue. Was it not time for praise for her diligence? It seemed she was still being tested. Ayah, the way to the throne was never meant to be easy, or everyone would be kings.

And Honored Imperial Father did not like his elbow jogged. Yes, that was the safest approach: when in doubt use modesty as a weapon. "This humble daughter, in her ignorance, begs Honored Imperial Father to enlighten her . . ."

When the emperor perceived Bitternail waiting patiently in the doorway to his pavilion, he waited until Manon was done with her claims to humble supplication and sent her off.

Bitternail had been rigidly correct all week. He was so now. "Your imperial highness, a naval courier has arrived with urgent messages."

THIRTY-FIVE

JION'S WEEK OF REFLECTION being over, he randomly picked a couple of hangings he cared little about, and made himself cross the palace to the eastern end, where Court Artist Yoli's workshop was located. Jion knew it was cowardly to hope that Yskanda was otherwise occupied, but no, he was there alone, filling the air with the reeks of mixing paints.

Yskanda had isolated himself as much as he could after word spread about Melonseed in the prison, and the following day, toward the end of a class in brush techniques that he was teaching, he overheard a first-year scribe student whispering a little too eagerly that, "You know they torture people in state cases. I hope we don't have to see it."

"Since you have the time to chatter," Yskanda said, "you two may clean all the brushes over the morning break."

He was not the only one who made disapprobation clear—his punishment was by far the mildest. Graywings, like every-one else, varied. He had learned early to avoid the roaming protocol graywings, such as those he'd encountered his first day in the palace. Their purpose was to make certain that the staff behaved with proper decorum at all times, and never trespassed where they were not permitted; the graywings given this duty had the temperament to enforce it, as Yskanda had discovered.

Melonseed, far above even these, had so different a temperament. He and Bitternail had ruled their part of the palace world with justice and kindness, and Yskanda, grieved and unable to do anything about Melonseed's fall, buried himself in the world of color.

Until the day Jion came to his workroom, a pair of rolled hangings under his arm.

At the sight of Jion, Yskanda smoothly suppressed the leap of his heart, and made the mental shift from the glorious world of art and color to the mundane one of courtly protocol and bowed. "Your imperial highness. I heard that you had returned."

Jion told himself, get it out at once. "Yskanda, I am sorry, but Firebolt—Arikanda—is here. In the prison. I couldn't prevent it."

Yskanda's face blanched. He whipped around, launching toward the door much faster than Jion thought he was capable of moving. Jion caught him by the arm and held him back. "Yskanda, don't."

"I can't just let—"

"Do you really want to make things worse?"

Yskanda stopped straining against Jion's grip, and Jion let go. "How is begging for her life worse than doing *nothing*?" He bit off the last word with soft violence.

"Because my father has done nothing, which means he's in no hurry. The worst danger was that first night or so." Jion paused, but he was not going to describe his own wakefulness after he had been dismissed from the tea house, and how he had resolved that if they were summoned to Lotus Blossom Square, he would have taken Sagacious Blade, and . . .

He still didn't know what would have come after *and*. Except that he would do anything to save Ari's life. Including relinquish his.

He cleared his throat. "So far, a miracle has happened—the ferrets have not figured out she's Danno's daughter. Maybe because they're too pushed by other matters, most of which you don't know about, and maybe because they discovered she is the sister of Captain Ryu and that's satisfied them as to her identity. But if you go running to my father, he *will* figure it out, probably within the space of three breaths."

Yskanda sank down. "You're right." His sightless gaze wandered from object to object on his desk as if he had never set eyes on brushes or paints.

Jion pursued his point. "My father has left the matter of your identity all this time. He has other concerns. But if you come to his notice, you will bring all those questions back, and he is not in a mood for mercy right now. There is too much going on that has nothing to do with your family, but a reminder of that matter is sure to make everything worse."

Yskanda sat there at his desk, his expressive hands for once still, purposeless. He looked as shattered as he felt: that which he had tried so hard to prevent had happened—the emperor held another of his family, even if he didn't know who she was. He had been living with awareness of how very flimsy that ignorance was. He turned to Jion, his expression distraught. "Has she changed that much? She always had a look of our father."

Jion felt, if possible, even more wretched than he had since his return to the imperial palace. "She still does. Through here." He pointed to his brows. "She knows that. Before we left the ship she pulled most of her eyebrows out. Or nearly. It's a court style of some ten years ago, now mainly used by courtesans and rich merchants' girls. Not that Ari would care even if she knew." Even so mild a joke did not elicit any semblance of a smile. "It changes her face. It was clever thinking . . ." Jion's words dried up at the mute misery in Yskanda's expression, the sheen of tears in his eyes.

He realized then that his company was no comfort, and held out the hangings. "I brought these as my excuse to be here. If you could put these back in the archive, and find a couple of new ones?"

Yskanda's expression eased slightly—here at least was something he could do. He rose to take them, and laid them carefully in one of the waiting shelves for works to go back to the vaults. "I'll be glad to fetch new ones. What subject would your imperial highness prefer?"

"I don't know."

"I could bring something for the new year."

"A Rabbit year. Isn't the element water?"

"It is. We have some very fine paintings along the river that were done by two new masters, your imperial highness."

"Do that." Jion turned toward the door, to find himself nearly smashed back into the room by Fai Anbai.

They had not seen one another since that bitter parting on the wharf. Jion's first instinct was to move protectively toward

Yskanda, which was not missed by Fai Anbai, who knew, of course, that the two met frequently, and he had long suspected that Jion had figured out Yskanda's real identity. That conviction was underscored by the discovery of who Firebolt really was.

He hesitated on the verge of politely booting the prince out, then remembered that the emperor had given orders to include him in the poison investigation. Which might go a ways toward mitigating what Fai Anbai suspected was the bitterest resentment for the arrest of Firebolt.

He bowed low, removed the drawing from his sleeve and gave it to Yskanda. "By imperial order, the need for five copies of this supersedes all else. Nothing to be said about the matter."

Yskanda nodded absently—he never talked about work matters anyway, except with Yoli—and he looked down as he fingered open the tightly rolled paper, fighting to get his mind to focus. If the ferrets did not know his sister's true identity, then they would not know he was related. He must get control of himself!

He sat down at his desk with his back to the ferret chief, surreptitiously thumbed his eyes, and smoothed the paper, which wanted to curl again.

Then made a discovery. "This man is familiar . . ."

"Where have you seen him?" Fai Anbai demanded sharply.

Yskanda blinked up in surprise and a little shock. Fai Anbai saw the reddened rims of his eyes and recollected who Yskanda really was. The prince must have just disclosed the news about the prisoner in the House of Eternal Peace; if Fai Anbai had needed proof that his conjecture was correct, here it was. But a pulse of sympathy, scrupulously hidden, was all he could afford.

Yskanda's gaze dropped to the drawing. "I . . . can't say for certain. I know I have seen him. But not recently."

"Perhaps you'll remember while you copy the sketch. I will wait here while you do so. This is quite urgent." He turned to Jion, still in the background. "Your imperial highness, the Easterner courier ship arrived. I believe there are letters for you."

Jion could not bring himself to speak to the ferret chief. He slipped out and crossed back to his manor, to find his household still in the cold state of silence it had been in all week.

Which brought right back the shocking news about Melonseed. Why couldn't Manon keep her mouth shut? Throwing an old graywing in prison over something he did two reigns ago was utterly useless. No. Not useless. She would never exert herself this much if she did not believe it would lead her to the throne.

In that moment, Jion despised her. Realizing it shocked him—it was so unfilial to feel that way about his own family. Hatred in the same house never led anywhere good.

He looked down at Lily's handwriting on a sealed letter without seeing it. His mind rattled around, but he felt trapped, powerless—where could he go that wouldn't drag this futility, this rage, with him?

The emperor had no time to feel pleased that Lily seemed to like her new surroundings, and apparently was much cherished by the Easterners. He was still trying to assimilate the news he had just received from the north when another messenger announced the arrival of General Falik, summoned out of semi-retirement a month ago, when the news of raids in the north began accelerating. The emperor had known that General Falik was at Green Jade awaiting the birth of his first grandchild, but he'd assumed the man would take his companies and go straight north.

"Esteemed General Falik," the emperor addressed the elder man. "I ought to say, Esteemed Golden Gentian General Falik, for you are in the process of taking command of the northern defense, are you not? Please rise. I did not expect to see you."

The general bowed his balding head, then spoke painstakingly. "Your imperial majesty, it will be this old and unworthy soldier's great honor to carry out your imperial majesty's orders—and the requisitioned companies I have the honor to command are on their way north—but first I must beg to be heard on a matter involving my son."

"Please speak. I am very pleased with your son's bravery and skill. I am also sorry that he was so grievously injured."

"He would have died," the general said bluntly, betrayed only by a slight hoarseness. "That's what the physicians say. As it is, when I went south to Green Jade, which your imperial majesty's benevolence and mercy permitted me to do, I brought my own physician, in truth a very learned shaman in Essence matters, who said that something, or someone, far more powerful than he intervened. He said that the Essence binding my son to life is located in a place on his spine that is vital. Usually no one survives such a stab wound. This old and unworthy father desires to assure your imperial majesty that my boy has begun to recover feeling in his toes. I saw them wiggle."

The emotion in this stiff, dignified man robbed the words of any possible humor.

"It pleases me to hear that," the emperor said, knowing a preface when presented with it. "And so, has Commander Falik a request?"

"Not a request as such, your imperial majesty. This unenlightened father begs to assure his imperial majesty that gratitude for the merit that shines from your throne is enough for any man to hope for, and yet my son, who cannot come to speak for himself, requested me to speak for him. For the news reached Green Jade the day I was to leave, that Firebolt had been captured while facing down that white-eyed wolf who called himself Master Night. My boy requested me to beg his imperial majesty to spare the life of Firebolt, who spared *his* life—not only in the medicine he gave provided, but in fighting off the criminals who tried to kill him."

"He." The emperor did not miss that. "Did you know," he said, "or hear, that Firebolt is actually a teenage girl?"

General Falik's eyes widened, and his jaw dropped. "A girl?"

There was no mistaking his genuine bewilderment. No conspiracy of silence then, except on the part of a brother. The emperor was aware that his own weakness was a respect, even a longing, for the fraternal loyalty that he himself had never experienced. Muddied waters indeed.

"Assure your son when next you communicate that nothing will be done in haste. Now, as to the north. I've placed Dragon Claw Army . . ."

Once the general had been sent on his way again, the emperor sat alone, frowning into the distance. Instead of Melonseed, there was a new graywing. Equally well trained, silent, deft, quiet, but he was not Melonseed, who had watched over him as a small boy. Melonseed's hands were the only kind ones the emperor had known, outside of his mother's and his nanny's. Melonseed had risked his life to save the imperial seal on the Night of Blood; less spectacularly, but profoundly important, he existed in a blur of daily memories, never failing to see to the emperor's comfort, to soothe, to comprehend when to speak, and when to remain blessedly silent.

The emperor forced memory away, and said to that new face, "Summon the First Imperial Prince."

Jion had been expecting something of the sort. At least he'd managed to get to Yskanda, though he was still not certain what he'd accomplished there, except causing, and feeling, fresh pain.

When the emperor's summons came, Jion changed into court robes, and even had Yarrow brush out the part of his hair that hung loose, and check that the braids were tidy. "Gold clasps," he said, touching a braid. "This is in almost all respects a court visit."

Yarrow didn't speak, but exchanged glances with Min Ko over Jion's head.

A short time later, father and son faced one another for the first time since their conversation in the tea house in the imperial garden. The emperor had given Jion a week to either do something stupid, or to remember what was important. To contemplate his loyalties. He was dressed immaculately, but his eyes were circled with the bruised skin of sleeplessness, his mouth a thin line.

"Melonseed's interrogation proved that he acted alone," the emperor said.

Ayah! Then Jion's theory, concocted in the middle of a sleepless night, was a straw boat, as so many night theories were — he had convinced himself that Melonseed was part of a hidden conspiracy — one of the many Emperor Maoyan was always looking for — and had been given instructions in secret to prevent one of those tragedies that inspires centuries of sanguinary plays and melancholy poems.

"Since Manon is credited with the discovery, I asked her what ought to be the result, but she declined passing judgment."

Jion, alert to every shade of his father's voice, heard the irony, but did not understand it. He understood nothing, except this: on his walk over, he had promised himself that he would do whatever he could to prevent Manon from inheriting the throne. That meant, to begin with, he must not give in to the impulse to lose his temper, to let loose wild talk, to act rashly.

Ari was still alive, not even put to the question, according to Min Ko. He might still be able to effect a rescue. He said, "This ignorant son begs to be enlightened about what exactly was learned from this interrogation?"

The emperor's brows rose. "Besides the fact that he acted alone, he thought he was alleviating pain by mixing two medicines."

Jion suppressed a snort of disbelief. How could any graywing, no matter how young, be permitted anywhere near the imperial dispensary much less be allowed to take whatever concoction he brewed up into an emperor's chamber? Jion's private conviction rushed right back, but he was not going to speak his mind, as he had no proof, and there was already too much threat in the air. Instead, he said, with an irony to match his father's, "This ignorant son was not present, and so knows too little to voice any opinion."

"You have no opinion, Jion? Very unlike you."

He was being goaded—he knew it—but after such a long stretch of sleeplessness his command of himself slipped just enough for him to retort, "Since Honored Imperial Father desires a response, this ignorant son must obey, observing first, why ought anything to be done at all? Melonseed has been present all my life, never endangering anyone. The very opposite. He has proved his loyalty every day of all those years. One would think a measure of mercy due to years of exemplary service." He halted—he would be condemning Manon next— and said more calmly, "The fact remains that he did kill our imperial ancestor, however inadvertently, so perhaps there is a necessary consequence. But if it was left to me, I would permit him to take poison—if you cannot give him the one they call the Imperial Sleep, then as merciful a poison as such a thing is possible."

"The Imperial Sleep," said the emperor, "is granted at imperial command. Your summary matches my own preference." Then the blow, "Do you wish to be there for Firebolt's interrogation?"

Jion shut his eyes, exerting every nerve to remain in command of himself. Then he said, "I don't see the necessity at all. She talks readily, and I can corroborate the truth of what she says."

"And yet," the emperor said, quite mildly, "you looked me in the face and stated that 'he' was tall, brawny, and hairy. Jion,

I am exerting myself to avoid involving you in this matter."

And Jion lost his grip. "I wish you wouldn't! Put me to the question instead!"

"But you were here when this criminal brought down the brimstone mine. So my question remains, do you wish to attend her interrogation?"

So many pitfalls here. He could not bear the thought of anyone causing Ari pain. Instinct prompted him to hide, unable to see or hear. But he'd *know*.

He had to be there. Proximity might give him room to act if worst came to worst . . .

Jion forced himself to bow, though his body vibrated with fury. "Whatever Honored Imperial Father wishes, this son must obey."

THIRTY-SIX

FOR ARI, THAT BLESSED silence slowly eroded into threat: she knew it was her turn next. She had been exercising over the week, but now she threw herself into repeating Redbark, as if building strength could possibly aid her in withstanding being burned or torn apart or whatever was to happen.

She struggled every day not to break the weak talismans keeping her from using Essence and throw fire at the group who came to her cell door—always a group, one or two with the items, and big guards with wicked-looking blades affixed to long poles to keep her well back of the door, plus more guards in the corridor.

They came back again, this time without food or a fresh pot for the corner.

She scanned them, ready to spring, except there were so many, and she fought her own instincts to destroy them all as a wooden frame was dragged in.

They were going to bind her to that! They'd drag The Story out of her! Terror caused her to leap, somersaulting over the head of the lead guard. She blocked a lunge from another, and leaped again, to kick aside one of the guards with the poles. She landed whirling, blocked another, and almost made it to the door.

But there were too many of them, and she still couldn't kill, not those anxious, determined eyes in people she recognized, people she had thanked for bringing food and water. She could see in those gazes they had to stop her, not kill her. She backed up a step, and as she calculated a plan of attack, chains snaked in. She jumped, batted, deflected—but all it took was one to wrap around her ankle and she crashed to the ground. At once the men with the poles pinned her limbs. More swarmed and grabbed her, two to each arm and leg. She struggled mightily, but they got her to that frame and then clamped her into it so that she couldn't move.

Next a brazier was put near her bare feet, burning rods of various types set into it. Brands. They placed a small table on the other side, with a rack of shiny instruments laid on top. The sight of those made her belly tremble.

In came Chief Fai, his aura an intense gray-blue that she could not comprehend. Other light blobs bobbed around, until she shut them all out as a distraction she did not need.

Fai Anbai carried in a stool, which he sat on. Behind him stood a ferret with a whip that had a tiny, glittering thing on its end. "Now, Firebolt," Chief Fai said. "It's time for the truth."

"I told you the truth," she protested.

"Who raided the mine at Benevolent Winds with you?"

"No one!" She heard an echo of the unknown Graywing Melonseed, wondering desolately if he had been telling the truth or a lie. Maybe every interrogation started this way, and when would they get to the questions about her identity?

"You're trying to tell me you acted alone in incapacitating an entire company of guards and bringing down two mines?"

"I told you that. On the ship. I *did* act alone. I used fire on the mine. I froze the guards with—ah!"

The one with the whip flicked it with a horrible snapping sound. Pain burned the top of one shoulder—whatever that glittery thing was cut right through the fabric of her robe to her skin. A warning of what was to come?

She gritted her teeth, as Chief Fai repeated the questions. Each time she repeated her answer the whip flicked her again. Bicep. The side of one leg. Her other shoulder. Always the lightest flick—but the metal bit on the end, sharper than the sharpest sword, cut through the fabric of her clothes to the top layer of her skin, no wider or deeper than the sliver of a fingernail, just enough to bleed. She was determined not to make any sound other than answering the questions she could answer. As for the ones she could not . . . She began to shiver uncontrollably, terrified not of pain, but of betraying her parents because of pain. How much could she endure?

Three times, the same questions, and then Chief Fai rose, and picked up one of the brands. He waved it in front of her face. "Let's go over that again," he said, and brought the glowing tip close enough to her face for her skin to feel the warmth. She could not prevent a gasp.

And he smiled. A quick smile, so fast and so slight she was not even sure she'd seen it, and she could not interpret it at all, for it was not the grin of enjoyment or triumph or even cruelty. In any other circumstance it was the quick smile of the teacher who sees the student get a move right at last.

The brand jerked toward her face, sharper, and closer. She let out a yelp — and there was the smile again. Did he *want* her to yell? If yelling would keep those terrible questions from coming, she would yell.

She let loose the howl she had been valiantly suppressing, and there was the grim smile.

"Now," he said, "let us talk. Where is White Dragon?"

"Who?"

Snap! Flick! The whip blade bit the top of her ankle — she had gotten into the habit of going barefoot in the cell as her socks were so grimy — and there had been no time to get her boots on when they came in with that frame thing.

She wailed.

That sequence repeated, along with the same round of questions, round and round, always about who the White Dragon was, where he was, how he communicated. She yelled louder and louder, "I don't know!"

Another flick, this time to the top of her cheekbone. It was just deep enough to bleed profusely, but so near her eyes that she startled herself as well as the ferret chief with the sob that burst up from deep inside, and once she started, she couldn't seem to stop.

Chief Fai stood up and pressed a finger against the side of her neck. She knew that acupoint — had used her fan form on it to knock out Shadow Panthers in that fight. Blackness boiled up around her vision, and she began to fade until a voice came dimly, "She's passed out. Wake her up."

Splash! Cold water hit her in the face. She gasped — and it all began again.

Through it the calm, repeated, remorseless questions about

someone she had never heard of, which made everything so much worse. Chief Fai had dropped the brand, and the whip was coiled and held—it was only her, crying in great, shuddering gulps, and the endless questions. Until a last press to her neck, and she felt herself sag in the frame.

"She's unconscious, your imperial majesty."

"I've heard enough."

The emperor withdrew from the corridor beyond the cell, Jion—blazingly angry—with him, followed by the two guards who had stood immediately behind them, hands on their swords, an entire patrol directly behind them, and another at the entrance to the dungeon. Some of those guards Jion knew from the west court—he could take most of them one on one, but not two or more.

Rigidly controlled, Jion bowed to his father and when dismissed ran back to his manor as fast and as hard as he could—but he could not outrun the sound of Ari's sobbing. She had *never* cried like that. Being forced to stand there in silence listening to those sounds was like a tiger clawing out his heart.

His father had kept him outside Ari's cell for her interrogation, partly to spare him the sight, but he had said before they descended into the dankness below ground that he didn't want her seeing him. "I want her attention solely on Fai Anbai, not on you. I must know if she is part of White Dragon's conspiracy. He seems to be using Essence masters as part of his campaign."

"Honored Imperial Father, this son—"

"This son told me many things, half of which were lies," the emperor cut through, sharp as a knife, and that was the last either said until the emperor sent Jion to his manor when it was over.

He slowed near Vaion's manor, which was dark and silent, and had been ever since Vaion was sent to Benevolent Winds. Beyond was his own manor. Every nerve jolted—he had completely forgotten that the study group was coming to him that night. He had invited them a few days before for the night his period of reflection was to end, thinking it would help him get through the horrible wait. Except that his manor was quiet. None of the lamps lit in the side wing or the garden.

When he entered, Fennel was waiting. "Your imperial highness, I'm to tell you that her imperial highness the first princess invited the gathering to her manor, as you were with the emperor."

Jion leaned against the wall, his eyes shut. With every nerve he longed to remain right where he was. But that would bring all the questions he wanted to avoid, howling like a pack of wolves. He knew he was watched. He had to act normally, until somehow he would think of a way . . .

He forced himself to move.

A short time later the steward at Drenched Blossoms conducted him to the formal hall, which had been redecorated yet again, this time with the colors of autumn, gilt with real gold. Manon presided in her mother's south facing chair, which looked more like a throne than ever. Manon was dressed in gold and white, with crimson accents in the shape of beautifully stylized parasol trees — the symbols of love, loyal and true. The earrings at her ears danced and caught the light: phoenixes again.

Jion looked at the beautiful sister who had been his most faithful companion all his early years, and he hated her.

He knew that she had nothing to do with Ari's imprisonment or interrogation, but her confidence, bordering on complacency as she smiled a welcome, was a forcible reminder that she was quite capable of ordering such things without any appearance of remorse. Exactly as she had sacrificed Melonseed; she said, and she might even believe, that her actions defended the prestige of the imperial name, but was any name worth trading for innocent lives?

". . . that pirates are the outward proof that if the government is not failing, its trade laws are," one of Jion's Ran cousins was saying.

"It's not merely laws and pirates, the very heavens make their disapprobation known," someone else said, as Jion made his bow to Manon, and tried to force his mind to whatever it was they debated.

"I'll agree with that," Su Siar spoke up. "One of my mother's tea fleets was nearly swamped, after a storm in which five water dragons were seen off the prow, hanging in the air upside down, their whiskers trailing in the billows breaking over the ships' rails. Five!"

"I've never seen one," Ran Hamin exclaimed. "And I cross back and forth to Ran all the time."

"We have lost the original topic," came Ze Kai's dry voice. "The last point having been made that control of all trade sounds well but is impractical, even disastrous."

Trade law — again, but it was a pressing topic now that the

Easterners no longer paid tribute. Jion tried to wrench his mind to the subject, but the words had no more meaning than the chatter of birds. He heard only Ari's sobs.

He forced back that memory, and saw Ze Kai standing at the far end of the room among those of the lowest rank, his expression absorbed, while Manon studied Jion from under her lashes. His eyes looked as if he had not slept for a hundred years. Ayah, he simply had to learn to be firmly subordinate to her! He would never be able to rule, he was far too weak, too lenient. She promised herself once she was on the throne she would favor him, surround him with music and comforts, to make up for . . . necessary steps a ruler must take.

She waited for a natural break in the flow of arguments they had all heard each other make repeatedly over the past year, then came forward gracefully. "My honored brother has returned from our esteemed Imperial Father, here to join us." She paused in case he might choose to say why this summons so late at night. When he did not, she said smoothly, "The musicians are ready, and I long to hear Honored Imperial Brother's opinion of the new pieces I commissioned." She stepped toward him to take his arm, and guide him to a comfortable place.

No "First Imperial Brother." Another of her little reminders that she considered Vaion and Gau-Gau almost as negligible as Lily.

Jion could have let her take his arm, and put him in a place of honor, but he was done being manipulated by her, even in a setting such as this. All he could think of was Melonseed, probably at this moment drinking poison. And, again, the sound of Ari's sobs.

He stepped adroitly out of her reach, saying, "Here briefly to make my bows and apologies. You all know how fond I am of music. It's a measure of how badly my head aches that I must plea for a postponement."

"Of course," Manon said in her sweetest voice. "I live to serve."

Za Kai turned at that, and crossed the room to Jion's side, his strides so long that the tassels on his robes swung and danced. "I am shameless enough to beg his imperial highness to give me a moment of time, concerning a possible change of debate topic for your next gathering. If this importunate one may accompany his imperial highness?"

Su Siar fell in step between the two. She bowed a polite farewell to Manon, who, being one generation lower, could not say anything unless Su Siar did. The three left.

The walk toward Jion's manor was mostly made in silence — Ze Kai had no question, nor did Jion want to hear one. Su Siar, gliding between the two tall young men, watched her embroidered slippers wink in and out from beneath the fragile gauze of her robes. On the one side, cold rage; Ze Kai still had not forgiven Manon for maneuvering Lily into the Easterner marriage. On the other side, hot rage emanated from Jion, she was not certain why. But she could hear it in his breathing.

Presently she stopped and snapped her fan open, obliging them to halt as well. "I once advised my esteemed niece the first imperial princess to refresh her reading of Suanek's wisdom, beginning with the observation that harboring anger within one's breast is like drinking poison and waiting for one's enemy to drop."

"But you're not telling *her* now," Jion said, a faint spurt of amusement flashing through him, gone in a heartbeat.

She had also seen his eyes, and unlike Manon, she suspected he grieved for Melonseed — for the Su clan was better informed about inner palace matters than most, though not completely: about Firebolt she knew only that the infamous gallant wanderer was in prison.

"My very dear imperial cousin," she said, tapping his delightfully muscled forearm with her fan. "You enchant us all by dancing one night, then you dash off to fight singlehanded alongside the famous Firebolt to defeat the evil traitor, and you." She turned her gaze up to Ze Kai. "Your wit is as sharp as his sword at the brilliant parties Prince Jion holds, and everyone looks to you as the future Left Chancellor. You are the leading two of the empire's Five Handsome Bachelors, and I am the leader of the Five Beauteous Wits. Did you even *know* that?"

Jion cared so little she might have been speaking some tongue from the far side of the world.

Za Kai gritted his teeth, a muscle jumping in his jaw.

She smiled. She, too, had a campaign to conduct. "Even popular Princess Gau-Gau knows, and in another year, I expect she will be Number Two, just because she is so well liked. And yet my dear niece First Imperial Princess Jehan Manon has slipped to number five, in spite of all her wit, beauty, and grace — and I strongly suspect she recently discovered that.

These things do matter. I hope you will remember that." After another valedictory tap, she bowed, and minced away to the cart awaiting her at the other side of the garden wall.

Ze Kai turned his shadowed eyes to Jion. "If Manon takes the throne her reign will make Emperor Milo Giha into a sage king by comparison. Which I will proclaim from Lotus Blossom Square," he added bitterly.

Jion raised a hand. "Peace. Peace. I think you know by now I'm not in the habit of running off to tattle." And then he addressed the true matter, "She is not the imperial heir yet."

He knew as he spoke that however careless the words seemed, they were not; now that he had spoken them for another to hear, he had taken the first step on a road from which there was no retreat. But first he must save Ari.

Kai said nothing; he stilled, his chin nicking upward in hope.

Jion said tiredly, "The Easterner courier ship came. You probably know that. I had a letter from Lily. Would you like to read it?"

Ze Kai looked upward, then down. There was no changing fate. The sooner he schooled himself the better, all the elders told him that. "Just tell me, is she truly well?"

"I think so. She praises everything, probably to be expected. Not just things — music, food, and the rest — people. She especially spoke of the empress. They've become friends."

Ze Kai accepted that, bowed, and walked off. Jion returned to his manor, where he sat for a time with Sagacious Blade lying across his knees.

Presently he moved to his desk, ground some ink, and in his dashing calligraphy wrote out the proper honorifics, then the message: *This son dares to make a request of Honored Imperial Father.*

The emperor, preparing to leave his manor, sent the servant back with an invitation to speak, and considered what to say when Jion made the inevitable request for clemency toward that wretched girl.

But Jion surprised him. The note that came back said, under the same list of formal honorifics: *This ignorant son requests the honor of admittance to the ancestral archive.*

The emperor wondered if this at last was Jion's challenge for the heirship.

Granted.

THIRTY-SEVEN

IN THE CELL, ARI gulped in air, regaining consciousness as Chief Fai got up off his stool, and in reverse order they withdrew: brazier, brands, instruments that had never been used, and last she was unbuckled. Two ferrets gripped her upper arms and carried her limp, trembling body to the plank bed and left her there.

The cell door was locked. She hunched up tightly, then looked down at herself. Except for the stinging cuts here and there, they had done no gouging or breaking or peeling or beating. It could have been so much worse, so very much worse.

Or was that to come? Though there had been hundreds of questions, most of them the same ones, not once did the chief ferret ask about her place of birth or her parents. She got up and walked around her cell. Nothing wrong but the sting of the tiny cuts, which, combined with the water they'd thrown on her, made huge, bloodstained blotches on her grimy clothes. Looking down at herself, she reflected that she looked a whole lot worse off than she really was.

She wrapped herself in her blanket and lay down. After a time the stings lessened, leaving an ache around her ribs where she had sobbed so hard. Very brave, Firebolt, she told herself. Those ferrets were surely throwing open the doors of their mouths, telling the world that the famous Firebolt was a blubbering rabbit.

Ayah, who cared what they thought?

Except where was Yskanda, and Jion, and what rumors would they hear? She worried at that, unable to sleep. Then she sat up, and though she had promised Master Ki not to try the soul wander thing, she did her breathing and attempted to force herself, but all she succeeded in doing was giving herself a headache.

In the distance, the watch drum boomed the change to Turtle. She became aware of noise. Someone was coming. Already? She was so tired, so very tired, nearly dizzy with exhaustion. She knew she had very little fight in her—and she could not use fire, no, no, no . . .

She sat up and tugged the blanket tightly around herself, as if that would protect her, and pulled her knees up to her chin, ignoring the pull of forming scabs here and there, and the coolness of air on her cheek—that little cut was bleeding again, thanks to the water thrown in her face.

She tried with all her strength to will the guards away, but a whole troop of them appeared, along with the regular prison staff in gray. Her covered pot was swapped out early. That was strange—before her interrogation, they had not done that. She hunched up as the guards stood stiffly to either side, and a tall man entered, dressed in fine robes. Gold glinted on his head, a beautifully worked clasp for his hair in its topknot.

Her gaze traveled more slowly from his embroidered hem to his face, sharp-etched in the ruddy torchlight, and her mouth dropped open—it was Jion. Except older, harder. No, that was not Jion.

She knew with a painful jolt exactly who it was.

She was facing the evil emperor.

Inadvertently she let the blob-lights distract her. His was an intense, dark blue veined with crimson. As usual, impossible to comprehend, so she shut it out again.

A soldier gave her a cuff that knocked her sprawling, and she remembered her cadet days and the exhortations about how to bow and to whom. She rolled up and fell into the soldier's bow—right knee on the floor, right fist over heart, left hand hanging down. Belatedly she realized it was probably the wrong bow, but too late now.

The emperor found that interesting as his gaze took her in from the bleeding cut on her face to the reddish stains all over her clothes.

Two prison guards brought in a chair, on which the emperor sat. "The problem with people like you," he said as if they were continuing a conversation, "is that in some ways you are more trouble than the likes of Master Night, who at least is somewhat predictable. Your random offences aren't."

Ari glanced up — remembered her eyebrows — and hoped none had grown back in the week since she'd yanked them out one painful hair at a time.

The emperor waited, but the girl said nothing, only sent frightened glances his way.

He considered her. Surely rumor had exaggerated her skills — she was small, a round, unmemorable face, her expression bewildered and frightened — about as threatening as a chipmunk. "Can you really command fire?" he asked, more amused than not.

At that her expression changed. She gave him a look of hurt dignity and then she rose and crossed to the bars, her knees still watery; he did not miss that stiff walk, mis-interpreting it as pain so bad she could scarcely stand. The guards shifted, closing around her until the emperor lifted a finger and they dropped back so that he could see unimpeded. She ran her hand lightly along the bars, then slowly sketched something in the air over the door frame.

The emperor saw so brief a greenish flash he could not be certain what it was, or if he'd imagined it. Then with another of those stares, she stuck her arm through the bars. "Move away," she said to the guards assembled outside the cell, her voice high and thin.

Eyes turned the emperor's way. He opened his hand, and they moved to one side. Ari shook her head, which still ached from her useless, stupid attempt to reach Yskanda, and she pulled up Essence from beneath the palace. Oh, so much Essence! She could feel it now that she'd neutralized the binding on the bars.

She breathed it in and raised her palm. A spear of flame shot out to splash against the far wall. It was precisely aimed, to avoid the guards, now a row of frozen stalks with wide eyes.

Hot air rolled back into the cell, smelling of burnt rock. The guards inside the cell recoiled, then began to advance on her, but after the briefest hesitation, the emperor once again lifted a finger and they dropped back, leaving clear space between Ari and himself.

For a moment no one moved, many contemplating the fact that that girl could turn that power onto the emperor — maybe onto them all. And if she was as good a martial artist as they insisted —

The emperor leaned an elbow on the arm of the chair and his chin in his hand. "What do you know about Cobra Sages?"

Ari blinked, having completely forgotten the name brought up on board the courier. "What? Cobra, did you say? Is it a martial art?"

"So you are not an Essence master?"

"I don't think of myself as one," Ari said, bewildered by this conversation. So far, no sign of any more torturers. "It's true I learned a lot of things from an Essence master, but I only studied a year. There is a lot more I don't know. I certainly don't know anything about Cobra . . . what you called them."

"Sages. Cobra Sages use a type of Essence skill employed mostly in the West. I'm told they bind Essence, they don't release it. I am not certain what that means to you."

"Ayah!" Some of the talk aboard the courier ship returned — including her intent to learn more about them. But then the cage happened. She shook that off. "There was a very old binding on the bars. I had to break it to make my fire," she said.

"Why did you not do this previously?" the emperor asked curiously, as if they sat in the garden over tea and almond cakes.

"I can't kill people," she said. "I mean, I can, but I don't want to. I did once, Shigan can tell — that is," she caught herself, appalled at the slip, and blushed, blotting her cheek with her sleeve, which smeared the little trickle of blood. She was afraid that mentioning Jion would cause him to get dragged in here — a terrible betrayal. "The people bringing in food and water, I can't trade their lives for mine," she mutter-ed.

"Could you kill someone like Master Night, only far worse?"

Her arms crossed. "If someone is far worse than Master Night, I could. In a fight. I don't think I could in a sneak attack. I don't *think*. Life is . . . a matter for the gods, except when the evil ones go about murdering and destroying." A glance at the sardonic slant of his brows, and she added, "And, uh, a matter for the laws."

The emperor suppressed a comment about her awareness of laws, about which it was very obvious she was ignorant. He had a purpose here. "There is a threat to this empire who calls himself the White Dragon, who has already done vast murder and destruction in his own empire, and now he is bringing it here because he wants my throne. I intend to keep him from getting it. To that end, he's been raiding increasingly frequently in the north."

Her lips parted.

"Ah, you have heard something of those raids?"

"Yes," she said. "I thought . . ." She looked away.

"You thought what?"

She said to her feet, "That you didn't care. Because it's not the empire. It's gallant wanderers."

"You appear to be completely ignorant of the tangle of treaties up there, between the Westerners and us, and between some of the northern peoples and ours, but that is immaterial at present. White Dragon and his army are ignoring all those in favor of building his attack."

The emperor dropped his hand and leaned a little forward. "I'm told you spent some time at Loyalty Fortress with your elder brother, so you'll understand at least in part that I have the navy as first line of defense, and Dragon Claw Army on its way. Reserves as well. But I don't know how much an army can do against Cobra Sages. I've learned recently he is drawing numbers of them to our empire. Their intent cannot be beneficial for us."

There was no mistaking Ari's genuine horror.

The emperor said, "At present, according to the rumors, you are the strongest of any with an affinity for fire who also knows something of the martial arts. I am sending geomancers with earth, fire, and water affinities north, but I need a martial artist to find a way to defend against White Dragon himself."

She dipped her head in a tentative nod, utterly ignorant of proper protocol around emperors.

"What I propose is this. You and your master, and who-ever else you can trust to employ, go north and destroy White Dragon. The army and navy will be at your back. If you are willing to do that, the charges against you will be negated — the very least of the rewards awaiting you. What do you say?"

Ari opened her mouth to point out that her master was with the Ghost Moon God now, then it struck her that he was offering her freedom. In exchange for something she would have done anyway, if this White Dragon was truly as terrible as he said.

"I'll do my best."

"Excellent," the emperor said. "The tide will turn midway through this watch. A ship will be prepared."

He walked out. The others as well, then the door slammed shut as the emperor gestured to Fai Anbai, who had been ordered to wait outside and listen. When they got to the upper floor, the emperor said, "I want you to send someone to see that she gets there. I also want word spread far and wide that the mighty, hirsute Firebolt, he who collapses mines at a gesture, who routed a five-ship fleet singlehandedly, is heading north with my blessing to challenge White Dragon. That ought to put an end to the demon-inspired ribbons and the crowds interfering with my Justice Departments."

"He?" Fai Anbai repeated.

"Absolutely," the emperor said. "I want her to make it all the way there, to keep White Dragon well occupied looking for that hairy, brawny martial artist. Once he discovers that Firebolt is a singularly ignorant girl of what, sixteen, he will, I am very sure, solve the problem for us both. Until then, Firebolt is the bait, and Golden Gentian General Falik's army the trap." He turned to the silent prison staff waiting at a respectful distance, heads bowed. "You. Make sure she goes straight from here to the ship."

He went off to get the first decent rest he'd had all week, while Ari sat alone in her cell, wondering if that was real — if she truly would be able to leave.

She was startled when the staff returned, but this time with new items. For the first time in the week of her imprisonment she was brought a basin of steaming water, and folded cloth that turned out to be the long gray tunic and loose trousers that prison staff wore, with a cloth sash.

They left those and vanished again. Ari moved to the basin, eager to wash up.

She shook her head, her gaze on the steam rising from the water. Odd, how it seemed to glow with color, almost. She bent over the water, wondering if it would reflect her own face in the dim light from the corridor torches — then she stilled, startled.

She knew that face! "*Yskanda?*

THIRTY-EIGHT

ARI'S HAND PLUNGED INTO the water before she could stop herself. The image splintered and she bit back a wail, thrusting her face down in fierce hope that Yskanda would reappear.

There he was, still visible in the rippling water. She let out a glad cry as he said, "I hear you in my head. I don't think you have to speak aloud."

At that moment she realized she was hearing him inside *her* head, not a voice inside the cell. The image in the water had not changed. She could see him, and yet through him to the bottom of the basin. His mouth did not move. This had to be the soul wander Master Ki had spoken of, or a version of it.

"How do you do it?" She mouthed the words without speaking aloud.

"I've been trying to reach you all day, but you never heard me. What do you see?"

"You. In a basin of hot water. You have not changed at all!" Maybe she could think the words, but it was easier to shape them with her lips.

"Ayah, I ought to have expected that! It turns out I've an affinity for water. And wood. Mostly water. Perhaps what you are seeing is your last memory of me. Little Third—Arikanda— I cannot see you, at—are you truly well? There was a rumor the ferrets were to put you to the question."

"They did. But . . . ayah, it was nothing, Second Brother.

Well, not nothing. But it could have been so much worse." She remembered the look of those coldly glinting instruments on that table, none of which the chief ferret had touched, and added, "Truly."

Yskanda could feel her conviction, and she sensed his relief.

"I have this hot water because I'm to go on a ship. Very soon, I think. I'm supposed to be washing up. The emperor was here, and I am going to the north to face someone called the White Dragon. I think he's an Essence master. A real one. Not like me. But he's something called a Cobra Sage. I was so scared that I'm afraid a lot of my wits fell out of my head, along with what I was told. But I expect someone will tell me again."

"Mother was dealing with a Cobra Sage."

"Mother is here?"

"No. I can . . . in a way . . . hear her. Speak to her, but only in her dreams, or when she is praying. I don't know if the gods aid her, or us both, or if she is only able to hear when praying. It's so much more difficult in her dreams because if I am too direct she wakens and looks for me."

"I don't understand that."

"I don't either. I know it's true because what I learned from her, Prince Jion learned from other sources. I mean about the end of Master Night, and much related."

Ari heard footsteps in the distance. "I might have to hurry."

"Use the water, Little Third. I am not truly reflected there."

Her throat ached and her eyes stung at hearing herself call-ed Little Third again. Maybe it was the warmth in Yskanda's voice, and maybe it was just reaction from the earlier terror, the *helplessness*. "I don't dare. If I didn't hear you before and you called to me, then I'm still stupidly unable to do this soul wander unless I can see you in the basin. Ayah! Mother is where?"

"That's what I began to tell you, then distracted myself. It is difficult to speak like this. My thoughts want to race in ten directions. I have to shape the words with my lips."

"So do I!"

"Ayah, a pair, are we not? Arikanda, Mother and Father are on the way here. If I am right, they are only a week from reaching the capital."

"No, they can't! Father will be caught!"

"He is with some gallant wanderers who seem to have friends here. What I want to tell you is, Mother had to deal with one of those Cobra Sages. She wrote it all in her herbal. She dreamed about it, which is how I know—and I tried to share some of what I learned from Brother Pine, oh, that can come later. Ten directions, all so important."

Ari's breath hissed in. "I'm supposed to get my 'master' to help, on the emperor's orders. I think—I suspect—I won't be going alone, but with guards to make sure I do what I was told. Or to kill me if I don't. This is just the sort of mission I would do on my own. But I don't think they believe it. Anyway I need to learn more about Cobra Sages."

Yskanda said, "Little Third, listen. One thing I've learned while here is that court wording saves face, which is very important in dealing with ministers, nobles, and imperials. But also, if you word things so that they can agree, many times they will agree."

"You mean . . ."

"If you call Mother your Essence Master, will the emperor's guards let you meet with her?"

"I don't know—ayah, there's noise. I'd better change. But first, Yskanda, if you talk to Jion, tell him I'm all right. I'm sorry I have to go without him. And also tell him that I think . . ." She remembered the way Sagacious Blade had flown out of her hand. "Tell him I think the sword ought to stay with him. It might even want to stay with him. Master Ki's affinity was air, and so is Jion's. If they give me my staff, I'll be fine."

"I will."

"Ayah, people are in the hallway."

Yskanda's inner voice was gone. Ari cast a frightened look at the torchlit corridor outside the bars of her cell, but the noise stopped outside the cell of the other prisoner.

She hastily divested herself of her grimy, damp, blood-stained clothes and scrubbed with the cleanest corner she could find. She rubbed and scrubbed, careful around the small cuts, which really were remarkably shallow, then relaxed only when she had shrugged herself into the sturdy, thick new clothes, and securely tied the sash. A pair of socks had fallen out. She pulled those on, and her boots. When she finished, she realized things were quiet in the far cell, and so far, no one had come near her.

She felt her hair for the first time in days. Ugh! She dunked her entire head in what was left of the water, hoping to get rid of some of the prison smell. Then she tried to comb her tangled, sodden locks with her fingers, and braided it tightly.

Footsteps again. This time they did not stop at the other cell, but approached hers. She neatened the blanket, grubby as it was, and sat on the plank bed. Then, to her surprise, one of the ferret women from the journey back from Little Otters entered with a prison worker in gray. "Come, Firebolt," she said. "I have your staff. Our ship is ready."

Ari got up and followed her out, scarcely aware that she was the only one left in the corridor reserved for the most important prisoners. She was too tired, too bewildered, and too full of regret at not being able to see Yskanda or Jion.

But an entire company of imperial guards awaited her, as well as black-clad ferrets, some familiar, some not. They surrounded her in silence, and did not break formation until she boarded another of the small, swift courier ships, which immediately set sail.

Jion endured the most wretched night of his life.

All night he paced his room, furious and grief-stricken by turns. Every remembered sob of Ari's was a reminder of how her trust in him to save her had been betrayed. How could he save her? He had no power except what he could achieve with his own hands. And yet he knew that if he fought his way into the prison, and she saw the trail of bodies, would she even go with him?

Twist, twist. Plans and regrets mercilessly ripped his heart in different directions until a bleak dawn. He wanted to sit in his room, but what would that gain him? He could go kneel before his father's manor, but that would make the matter into a contest of will, and he did not have righteous virtue on his side: that reminder about his lies, which he had so enjoyed speaking, had been purposeful.

Then there was Manon, sacrificing Melonseed for the heirship, without any apparent regret. Which made him wonder how far she would go to get what she wanted.

He finally dressed, and went to make his bows without speaking more than the politenesses he uttered each day. His father, seeing his ravaged face, secretly rejoiced to see him there. Jion's self-command was improving by the day.

Jion saw the satisfaction in his father's manner, and came very close to hating him for it. He had to remind himself that he had lied — which was a capital offense — and now he was paying the price for those lies.

In that mood he retreated to the west court. One look at those black, glittering eyes, that set mouth, and the imperial guards knew the rumors had to be true: their prince had collected yet another lover, this one the infamous Firebolt. And from the looks of things, she was first in his heart.

They braced for rage, and rage is what they got. Jion broke two wooden swords that day. Afterward, he felt no better. But he had to keep going; he wanted to be in as strong a position as possible when his father called for him again. That meant going to the dragon and phoenix archive, to which he'd gained access once again.

Manon was not there; she was at her wing in Drenched Blossoms, supposedly writing up her history of the Jehan rulers, but her eyes kept straying to the floor plan of the heir's manor.

Jion spent a little time looking about to see who might be curious enough to spy on him, and chose records at apparent random. When he had come as a reluctant, ignorant fourteen-year-old he'd remembered it as musty and dim. Now he was surprised to discover that when the imperial rulers wrote only for themselves, there were no elegant illustrations, no elaborate dragon-binding of the books. Records were as simply bound as student books, though made with the very best paper and written with the finest ink.

Not surprising, there was very little private writing in his father's section. Either that was kept nearer to his father's suite as records of a sitting emperor, or more characteristic, his father did not put his thoughts down where any but he might see them.

Jion wasted a little time looking in his great-grandmother Empress Teyan's records, specifically the year that Emperor Father had his brief, disastrous marriage with Yskanda's mother. Information was scant. Jion had wondered if Manon had read any of it, and suspected she had never made it that far. You had to know what to look for, and the references were cryptic: the edict declaring there would be no more selections for consorts; the edict confining Second Prince Enjai to his manor, followed by a private family edict requiring all additions to the capital list to be submitted to the imperial eye. Nothing, he thought sardonically, about gaining and using power, so Manon would pay little heed.

By the time Jion had glanced through these ink-faded papers, he figured anyone who might have been watching him was not going to interfere. He went back and grimly set himself to read everything Emperor Maoyan had written, so that he could check the consequences in the court records. Henceforth he was not going to remain silent when Manon offered Emperor Maoyan as an example of a sage king. He would counter every utterance with truth, proving that Emperor Maoyan's brutal, intolerant style was the very opposite of the sage king.

The early years were innocuous enough—he even saw himself, a little, in Emperor Maoyan's eagerness to master martial arts when he was a prince. Jion would have to ponder that later; but just because the dragon might be in his blood did not mean he had to let it slip to ream the world.

Jion read until hunger gnawed at him. He hadn't thought he could eat—any time he paused his mind shot straight to Ari—but life is stubborn. He mentally marked his place, restored everything the way it had been, and returned to his manor, to be surprised by another first: Afan Yskanda had written a note to him.

Jion winced as he sat down to read it. Of course Yskanda wanted to find out what had happened to his sister, but he would not be able to ask directly. Any number of eyes would have read the note first. Unsurprisingly, Yskanda said politely that the artists were planning ahead for the turn of the year, and if his imperial highness still wished any part of his manor renewed, he had set aside some hanging scrolls that Jion had requested (untrue) and begged to be informed of any further instructions.

Jion longed to ignore it. But he owed it to Ari, and to Yskanda, to face the unpleasantness in person. He forced down a quick meal, told Whiteleaf that he was going to the court artists' workroom to issue some instructions it would take too long to write, and ventured out to endure the gate of swords.

He found Yskanda at the workroom, talking to a pair of students whose paint-rimmed fingernails marked them as artists. Again, Court Artist Yoli was not present. As soon as the page announced Jion, the students both turned, shocked to find a prince in their territory, and at a nod from Yskanda they bowed and fled.

Jion expected to see a miserable face, but Yskanda was

composed as always. He picked up a couple of rolled silk hangings that he had set aside to replace the ones Jion had brought previously, and they walked out into the garden where they usually spoke when they wanted to be private. Here, Yskanda laid out one of the scrolls on a flat rock as Jion said, "Court is not in session today. Where's Old Yoli?"

"Still in bed, your imperial highness."

"Still? I did not know he was ill."

"It's been two weeks, this time. He insists he is fine, but that cough lingers, and wears him out." Yskanda looked worried. "The physicians want him to build his strength against the coming winter, and as there are presently no imperial orders, he must remain in bed. Though he insists he's too ornery for the King of Hell to get him yet."

"I hope he's right," Jion said. "Old Yoli has been a fixture all my life. I don't want to see him gone."

Yskanda bowed his thanks, and Jion drew a breath to confess his failure, but then Yskanda surprised him. "If your imperial highness will permit, I spoke to my sister last night."

"What?" Jion managed to keep himself from yelling — just. "How did you ever get into the prison?"

"I didn't." Yskanda laid out the other hanging so that they could stand side by side looking at them, as an imperial patrol passed some sixty paces away. "Your imperial highness, Brother Pine taught me to rely on my affinities. I'm still trying to understand how, and when, I am successful. I think I told you that it began with my mother."

"They were in a storm."

"Yes. I . . ." Yskanda looked skyward, still reluctant to attempt to capture his experiences — which he did not wholly understand — in words, so dangerous and misleading. He could not really know if he had actually kept that disinter-grating boat afloat, or only wished to.

In any case, that was not the subject. Here was Jion, his eyes ringed with exhaustion. "I read in one of the older books that water could be a conduit for water Essence affinities. And so I used water all day, every chance I could get, to call to her. Last night they gave her a basin of water. She saw my re-flection. It enabled her to hear me." He tapped the side of his head quickly, and then, for the benefit of any watchers, pointed at the paintings as if describing something.

"Last night? When last night?" Jion's voice was sharp. "Did

you *see* her?"

"No. We could not actually see one another. But we heard one another's inner voices."

"They put her to the question," Jion said tightly. "I had to endure it."

"This ignorant one is aware, your imperial highness. She insisted that she's all right," Yskanda said quickly. "I could hear her emotions under the words. She was still very unsettled —"

"She was sobbing," Jion whispered, and leaned one hand on the rock, staring down sightlessly at one of the paintings — though later he would never be able to tell what either of them was about. "Sobbing her heart out. I know Fai Anbai was doing what he was ordered but I wanted to kill him. I still do."

"She was not hurt but superficially," Yskanda said.

"You cannot possibly know that," Jion retorted, all the more heated because he wanted so badly to be convinced otherwise.

"I was not there," Yskanda said carefully. "As you are aware, your imperial highness. But I truly heard her thoughts last night. She has small cuts, no worse than happens in martial arts sparring. One on her face. Another on an arm. Those came through clearly because she was thinking of them — she touched the one on her arm. I . . . I felt it, or an echo of the sting. It is difficult to explain. I don't understand it myself." And seeing Jion unconvinced, Yskanda sighed, and looked away. "Court Artist Yoli told me that when he was small, the entire palace used to have to attend such things, both interrogations and executions."

"Under Emperor Maoyan."

"Yes. He was talking about, oh, anatomical matters, in reference to drawings, and it came up. This was after he fell, and sometimes the medicine would make him ramble. I never thought I would say any of this — and I will only summarize — but he said they learned that young or old, male or female, there were categories of pain, you might say. So I will ask: did my sister ever scream in agony?"

"Yes of course . . ." Jion tipped his head. "Actually, no. Not *agony*. I've heard agony. A couple times." He grimaced, thrown back to the Shadow Panther training camp. "She never screamed like that. At first she didn't even cry out, then suddenly she began, and then it gave way to sobbing, before she fainted."

Yskanda accepted that, brushed his fingers over the river in the painting, then said, "Secondly, if I may ask your imperial highness, were there any questions about our identity?"

"No, never. I dreaded that. It was all about the mines, over and over, and then some about the Shadow Panthers, and then endless questions about the latest threat up north."

"The White Dragon. She told me that," Yskanda murmured, and Jion was now convinced that whatever had happened between brother and sister was true, because the emperor had not released that name as yet. "At any rate, she said she was ready to go."

"Go?"

Yskanda's profile had sobered as he began rolling the paintings. "The emperor has sent her to challenge White Dragon, your imperial highness. They sailed last night."

Jion leaned against the rock, sick with fury. Yskanda waited beside him until he looked up, then said, "If this unworthy inferior may be permitted to observe, his imperial highness knows that Arikanda would have gone on her own without being sent."

"I know." Jion's eyes were shut, his face distraught. "But I could be with her. At least I could have said goodbye. Given her that sword."

Yskanda said, "You'll be able to say goodbye, or anything else you wish to say, through me, if you so wish, your imperial highness. I cannot promise when she will have the chance, or remember to try gazing into water—we might try to fix a time." Yskanda tucked the paintings under his arm, making a mental note to send them along to Prince Jion's manor with a page, which ought to satisfy any curious ferrets about his visit. "As for the sword, she thinks it ought to be with you. Ayah, do you know what that means? I did not quite understand how a sword 'ought' to be with someone, unless it's a matter of ownership."

Snow fell on Jion's lacerated nerves. Ari and he were not cut off from one another after all, despite his father's wishes. He let out a shaky breath. "As an excuse to meet, I can always start Circle competitions again."

Yskanda bowed his acquiescence and Jion walked away, thinking wryly all right, perhaps he would not find a way to kill Fai Anbai.

Which Fai Anbai would have been relieved to hear, had he been present.

His life was already too much like a gallop downhill on a

maddened horse. The sun was setting when he finished a task and found a trusted messenger waiting. "I was to tell you from Senior Fai that last month's accounts don't match."

News! "Carry back my assurance that I will fix them tomorrow," Fai Anbai said.

That was their private code for an urgent meeting. As Fai Anbai vaulted a fence and sped along an old alley full of broken roof tiles and bits of wooden cartwheels, he wondered if his father had taken care to alter the accounting book. Of course he had.

He used his lightness skill to leap to a high fence, then spring to a complicated rooftop from which most of the lower palace could be seen, without anyone seeing them. His father waited there, a shrouded lamp beside him. "There you are," he said. "Firebolt gone?"

"Sailed out of the harbor at midnight. What news?"

"The identity of our mystery man." Grandfather Fai laid down a copy of the drawing that Yskanda had made. "We have his name now — Ris Jun. I took care of this one myself, figuring his mother might eventually come to trust someone closer to her age. I was right."

"Ris?" Fai Anbai frowned, then had it. "The woman who tricked Old Su by having a child?"

"One of several women," Grandfather Fai stated. "Like the others, the duke bought her off, refused his name, the son ran away and joined the navy. Or so she says — she was very bitter. She thinks he's amassing a fortune and will come back to surprise her."

"Not navy at all. No one expects to get rich in the navy. Piracy?"

"Or smuggling. Except that he's not on the water. She recognized him at a glance, beard and thinning hair. That means she's seen him since he ran away, at least once, and relatively recently, but she's keeping that dark."

Fai Anbai sat back on the tiles, gazing skyward as he let the implications build. "If this is Owl's man . . ."

". . . what is he doing, meeting her secretly?"

"At a guess, playing the victim, using blood-relationship to gain money."

"Except when has Owl ever been known to dispense largesse?"

"She gives very expensive presents."

"To family, or those she wishes to impress."

Fai Anbai gave up. Not enough facts. "We can't question her."

"No. Especially as it seems she is being seriously considered for the heir's palace. Before we go to the emperor, we need to know why they are meeting. Whether it's merely another internal Su matter. Or even a flirtation, unlikely as that sounds. He's around forty, and she's nearing twenty-five."

Fai Anbai said, frustrated, "Even if we had the extra agents, we can't put anyone with her — she only permits Su-trained maids around her, and the rest of the servants stay out of her sight. There's the far perimeter watchdog already in place . . ."

". . . who is useless, as Owl has access to all kinds of imperial nooks we haven't a way into. And the bookstore meetings seem to have ended." Grandfather Fai waved the drawing back and forth. "Meanwhile, Peony is still behaving like the most exemplary of agents. I still cannot be sure whom she might have corrupted."

Fai cursed her, and her ancestors, back ten generations. Then he said, "We're going to have to wake up the plant around Viper? At least Owl is used to seeing our plant with her mother's maids."

"Yes," Grandfather Fai said. "Let's give her the signal."

THIRTY-NINE

ARI MOSTLY SLEPT FOR a couple of days, waking frequently to nightmares.

Every time she woke she requested water. Cold water, hot water, basins morning and night. At first they complied — aware that she'd been locked in prison for a week — but by the second day she got the side glances that probably meant they thought she was mad.

The following morning right at dawn, she gazed down into her wash water — and there was Yskanda again.

She barely restrained herself from shouting aloud. She had been given a tiny cabin of her own, but she knew that sounds carried easily aboard such a small craft — and the imperials were surely required to listen to everything she said. They certainly had listened to what she and Jion had talked about, she'd discovered after that last journey.

"You're here," she mouthed the words. "Yskanda, you're here!"

"I am. Are you generally awake at dawn? Most days, this would be relatively easy for us to meet like this."

"I can be. Oh, I'm so happy you're back! I was beginning to wonder if I dreamed it when we met before."

His laughter was like a stream of silver, no, like summer sunlight winking on the waters of a river. "Let's try, then. I'll tell Prince Jion. I feel certain that if he can be here, he will."

Yskanda had never been so formal in his speech before they left Imai. She wondered if that was a result of living in the palace, then he went on. "Arikanda, this is important. Mother and Father have landed at Flowering Plum Island—I think, I'm fairly certain, that they are coming here to try to free me. You must send them away."

"How? What is Flowering Plum Island?"

"I believe it has to do with the navy. Mother did not quite understand, so I don't understand—remember, I cannot ask directly. However, I believe if you can find her, you can convince her to take Father away somewhere else."

"Where do I find her on that island?"

"That was the part that isn't clear. There seems to be a connection, something reckless, or feckless, which does not sound promising."

Ari drew a breath of sheer pleasure—then looked around guiltily. "Do you mean Waoji Feckless? She is a navigator in the navy, though she comes from gallant wanderers."

Yskanda's tone lightened. "I believe you have it. Try to find out if there is a guest house, or an inn, or a court, with the word 'fruitful' in it. Mother was remembering a bit of conversation, though memories are so quick, like catching butterflies, and sometimes they distort—ayah, never mind. There goes the bell already, and I have a class to conduct on decorating wood trim."

"I'll try to have water and be right here at dawn tomorrow."

Ari blinked. She could still see the reflection of Yskanda's twelve-year-old face, but she could feel that inner door shut, his voice gone. Ayah, was this how it worked for her, then? Master Ki had said it was different from person to person.

She finished getting ready, considering how to approach the imperials. She remembered what Yskanda had said about wording, and later on, over a meal, she asked, "Are we going to Flowering Plum Island?"

Several turned her way. "We are," said the ferret Bo Ya, known as Ya-Ya. "Though we almost never use the island name, but only the harbor, which is home base to the Capital Fleet. Why?"

"The emperor told me I ought to bring my Essence master. Who is here. I mean, there. At Flowering Plum Island. Somewhere called Fruitful . . ."

"Fruitful Blessing? That's an entertainment house. An inn, too."

Curious looks her way turned wary.

She said, "My Essence master is there. I think. The emperor did say to get my Essence master — she's also a very good physician." Ari knew she was babbling, but she had to convince them to let her go!

Exchanged looks, then the imperial guard captain said, "Ferret Bo and I will accompany you. Along with a suitable escort."

Ari agreed, grimly aware of how little they trusted her.

A day later their tiger-eye banner got them flagged past all the other ships in the harbor — most of them navy. They'd decided since they were stopping anyway to take advantage of the chance to get fresh food aboard, and some other supplies missed in their hasty departure.

Ferret Ya-Ya led them toward the inn. The imperial guard captain marched along, his armor and red cloak clearing the way for them as he watched in every direction. Ari composed herself as best she could. They reached Fruitful Blessing Inn and the two imperials accompanying them did a thorough search.

At last she was permitted to enter. What if Mother wasn't there? What if she was, but she was angry about what Ari had done with her life? What if she exclaimed Ari's name, Afan Arikanda?

Worry and anticipation gibbered in her mind until she saw her mother sitting at a side table, her eyes closed, her fingers on the pulse of what appeared to be a dancer, judging by her practice clothes and her lithe form. Ari took in the white strands in Mother's hair, but otherwise Mother looked healthy, and she had always been beautiful to Ari's eyes, despite the terrible scars. Even the scars seemed to have faded.

Mother whispered to the dancer, who looked on as Mother felt over her ankle. No, not just felt. Ari watched, amazed, as Essence glowed a deep green around where Mother's fingertips pressed. The dancer gasped, then her face cleared into a smile. "Ayah, you have the name of a healer, and the shadow of Suanek! It's *good* again! Better!" Then she scowled. "But I was right, I was cursed. And I know who cursed my ankle to turn each time I leaped. Can you place a curse on her?"

"I do not make curses," Mother cautioned. Oh, her well-remembered voice! Ari watched, her heart overflowing as her mother leaned forward to whisper to the dancer. The girl's scowl altered to uncertainty, then she rose, bowed, and flitted away, leaving mother and daughter face to face.

Hanu froze, her complexion draining of color, then flooding.

Ari approached cautiously, her lips shaping the word *mother*, but then she remembered that this was supposed to be her Essence master. The moment her mother's eyes turned her way, she bowed, then said in the quick dialect of Imai Island, "Essence Master Iley, here is your student . . ."

Hanu had been warned by the Waoji father and son that Ari, in her guise as the gallant wanderer Firebolt, had been taken by the imperials. And there at her shoulder stood a curious red cloak. She squashed the impulse to hug her daughter, to let out all the years of worry and wonder, saying only, "Arikanda?"

Ari dropped to her knees and made a full bow. "Master Iley," she said loudly. "I am ready for more Essence studies — I have received orders from the emperor himself."

Hanu rose slowly, her hands under Ari's to raise her as well, her mind racing along two separate paths. Both con-verged at the fact that her strange dreams centering around Yskanda appeared to be true visions. "Arikanda," she said again.

Ari's eyes blurred with tears, but through them she could see that her mother had shrunk! Ari was on eye level with her, but sturdier of build — Mother was like a bird, with small hands and tiny wrists in her plain sleeves. "I need to talk to you about —"

Ferret Ya-Ya stepped up. "Better to discuss your orders in a less public place," she murmured for Ari's ear.

"Come aboard our vessel, *Master Iley?*" Ari asked.

"Yes," Mother gave a short nod; though she had been bewildered by the dreams that seemed so real, and she had feared coming to this island full of imperials, she and Danno were desperate enough to find their children that they were willing to listen to, and try, anything, Including following vague symbols and directions in Hanu's dreams.

They had discussed contingencies endlessly. She was ready for this one. "I can go at any time. I have only to fetch my things. It will take one moment."

The ferret and the guard relaxed minutely now that their not-quite-a-prisoner had found her master, without any gall-ant wanderers leaping out waving bloody swords. Time to meet up with the staff getting the supplies from the garrison quartermaster, and resume their journey.

The garrison lay at the other end of the street, a vast pile centuries old. The west gate opened onto an enormous court where an entire army could gather. Ari and Hanu saw imperial army soldiers everywhere, dotted with the blue robes and kingfisher-feathered hats of captains, one of which watched stern-eyed as a gaggle of slump-shouldered recruits desultorily swept. Ari, seeing them, was thrown right back to her cadet days as an orderly.

Imperial Captain Ha Gar stook out in his bronze tiger eye chest armor and red cloak, gathering curious glances. But Ari didn't notice that because she spotted a familiar face not twenty-five paces away.

It was Father!

He looked exactly like always, except that he was dressed like the wharf laborers. He stood beside Waoji Lion's Mane next to a cart full of fresh hay.

Father saw her at the same moment. His eyes widened in surprise, then he smiled and started toward her just as the north gate opened to a swarm of chattering conscripts, practice weapons in hand. A huge young cock of the walk strutted in the lead.

This conscript, no older than Ari, glanced around, bawling, "What's this? You say the famous Firebolt is *here*? Where is this godling, more famous than Erku the Hero?"

And he spotted Father, mid-stride—to anyone with even a little training, Father's walk was that of a martial artist.

Father stilled. Ari looked in horror from the red cloak to the other officers in sight. None seemed to be old enough to remember Danno, but what if there was one drawn to the noise?

The brawny thick-skull advanced on Danno. "Let's see if you're as good as they're claiming, eh?"

Nooooo! Before anyone could move, Ari leaped over Ferret Ya Bo, somersaulted in the air, and landed in front of one of the broom squad. She grabbed a broom from a surprised recruit, kicked the end, sending the bound straw flying, and then whirled over to land in front of Thick Skull, broom-staff at the ready.

"What is this, one of Firebolt's mice?" Thick Skull asked, tipping his head as he looked down on her.

Ari whirled the broomstick over her head, set it humming,

tossed it to the other hand, and then brought it down to the swept stones with a *c-r-a-c-k!* Not as apocalyptic a sound as her own staff, still locked up on the courier, but satisfying enough to cause laughter and admiring whistles—and joking comments at Thick Skull, "Looks like the mouse bit your nose, ha ha ha!"

The brawny recruit grinned, always ready for a brawl, and slashed his wooden sword down toward Ari, who evaded with a turn of her shoulder. As the blade whistled by, she whipped the broom handle around, and yanked. The wooden blade went flying.

At that moment, a captain rushed up, bellowing, "What's going on here? What are you doing?"

His voice clashed with the red cloak, who had waited to see what Firebolt would do. He recollected his orders, assumed his sternest face, and raised the tally the emperor had given him. Not everyone could see the tiger shape, but the glint of gold was unmistakable. No one under the level of a general ever had a golden tally.

The captain in charge of the recruits gasped, "It's the emperor's tiger tally!"

All the imperials went to one knee, belatedly mimicked by the bewildered recruits. Ari flung herself down next to her father, both heads bowed.

"Do you need help?" Father asked, low-voiced.

"No," Ari said. "I could get away if I had to. I'm doing something I would have anyway. But Father, Yskanda wants you to stay away from the imperial island."

"After I see his situation for myself." Father's voice was calm, soft, perhaps a little huskier than she remembered, but rock solid with conviction. "If you see him, do not tell him I'm coming."

"But—"

Twenty paces away, the red cloak said loudly, "Rise. Do not impede us. We carry the emperor's orders."

The imperials got to their feet, Ari and her father as well. "You've done well, daughter. I'll find you when I know Yskanda is safe." Father squeezed her shoulder, and glanced across the yard at Hanu. Both nodded, understanding the other.

Then Danno hefted the yoke of the cart, Waoji Lion's Mane pushing from the back, head bowed, and they trundled away, ignored by every soldier there.

The recruit captain promptly began scolding the recruits as Father and Waoji Lion's Mane vanished beyond the gate.

"That," Ferret Ya-Ya said to the red cloak, "was ill-handled."

Captain Ha Gar looked a little shamefaced. "No harm done. I guess I didn't really believe she's Firebolt."

Ferret Ya-Ya had had private orders from Fai Anbai, warning her of what the emperor wanted. She reflected that by the time rumor of that silly encounter spread wide enough, Firebolt would be as big as that rock-skulled recruit who was probably even now sweeping the entire parade ground all by himself.

Ari was thinking along a similar path. She said to Ya-Ya, "I thought our mission was secret. They seemed to know Firebolt is coming, just not who I am."

Ferret Ya-Ya's expression was difficult to interpret. "Let's try to outrun the gossip," was all she said.

Ari had to be satisfied with that; besides, she was far more curious to find out where Mother had been, and what had happened.

They met up with those who'd made the supply run, regained the ship, and set sail. Mother was allowed to stay in Ari's tiny cabin. They retired early, where at last they dropped the pose of master and student, and hugged tightly, mother and daughter again.

Then they sat on the deck with their heads together, voices a whisper as Ari said, "I'll tell you everything, but first, how can we get Father to stay away? He *can't* sneak onto the imperial island. Somebody is sure to recognize him!"

Hanu briefly told Ari about the drawing he and the Waojis had found. "Waoji Reckless's sister has a friend in the quartermaster's. He said he would get the map to the right person, and in trade — he was certain there would be a reward — he was to give them information on getting into the capital undiscovered."

Ari wanted to argue. But she knew her parents would do what they thought was right. And her mother was waiting to hear her story. Good and bad, it was time to confess.

When she was done, the night was mostly spent. Ari fell asleep immediately, but then tossed and turned in a nightmare, muttering, "The door . . . the door . . ."

Hanu slipped out of the narrow bed, and knelt beside Ari,

who was rolled up in her sheet and blanket on the deck in front of the bed. Hanu tenderly cupped her hand to her daughter's face, her breath hissing when she felt the tear tracks.

"Ari," she murmured. "Arikanda. Waken. You're having a nightmare."

Ari snorted, then sat bolt upright. "Oh! Mother," she whispered. "What? Why are you awake?"

"You were having bad dreams. About a door?"

"The cell door," Ari muttered in the darkness. "It's always that fight that I lost, when I was trying to get to the door."

Hanu sat back, sighing. "I am so proud of you. And I heard your own pride in all you accomplished. As is just. Yet I feel very guilty, too, that the secret we imposed on you children — meant to keep you safe from our past cursing you with ill luck — has instead become a terrible burden."

"But it's not, Mother," Ari said earnestly. "Ayah, it's true I was afraid that ferret would ask, but he didn't. And their torture wasn't much of a torture. It was far, far worse in the Shadow Panther training camp. It was even tougher at Loyalty. I don't know why I keep dreaming about that fight, and not any of my other fights. Maybe because I wanted to use fire? But I *didn't* use fire on them, people I knew, people doing their job. I didn't do it, so why am I dreaming about it?"

Hanu was fairly certain she knew where she was now. "Tell me the dream, child. Unpleasant as it is. Perhaps we can banish the ominous aspects if you do."

Ari obediently described the nightmare, huddled in her bedding much like she had as a small child. At the end, she looked trustingly into her mother's face.

Hanu stroked her cheek. "I think I understand why you dream of the fight, and not the interrogation."

"Why?"

"I believe it's because that is the first fight you lost."

Ari shook her head. "I've lost plenty of fights."

"Not important ones, from what you told me earlier. It's true you did not use your powers, and that might be a part of it, but Arikanda, in this life you have chosen, and for the best of reasons, you must confront the fact that one day, you will face someone stronger. This is something your father said. Surely you must remember. Every martial artist has to face the fact that there is one day going to be someone stronger. Always."

Ari shook her head, hunched her shoulders, and sighed. "I

don't . . . ayah. But . . . how can I get justice for those who aren't as strong as I am?"

"There are many ways. In the meantime, you are formidable. And you keep getting better. And," Hanu added, "there isn't one answer. Now, curl up, darling daughter. Try to get some proper rest. I am going to sit right beside you, the way I did when you were small. Be small again—not everyone gets that chance. Be our little mouse again, and rest."

FORTY

DURING THOSE FIRST FEW days, Jion studied in the dragon and phoenix archive with ferocious concentration, mostly late at night, after the musical entertainments that Manon had begun hosting; while her invitations to Jion were effusive and fond, he suspected she was deliberately pre-empting his debate gatherings.

That was all right—for now.

When he didn't keep himself busy, questions bit at him like buzzing insects, such as: if Fai Anbai had deliberately avoided Ari's origins, was it possible he might have done something similar with Melonseed's interrogation? In other words, was it possible Jion's original supposition that Melonseed could not have acted alone be true?

He did not expect his father or Manon to think along that path—he would not have, either, before he became a gallant wanderer, and saw how much work went on that nobles were unaware of.

If there was a conspiracy, did it still exist? Second, and potentially a more disturbing question: were the ferrets aware? Jion had lost most of what little trust he'd begun to repose in Fai Anbai. He knew that the ferret chief had to carry out the emperor's orders. But the fact remained he had dared to give Ari pain. Jion's resentment kept him from communicating with the ferrets, even through Min Ko. Let them spy on him if they wanted to know what he was doing. Of course they were already doing that.

Then there was the frustration of not being able to go to Yskanda each day without drawing attention; he knew he was under especial scrutiny, surely on his father's orders. Though he'd suggested the Circle competitions, it turned out that Yskanda was frequently busy until very late, covering both his and the court artist's duties while the latter was recovering. To demand Yskanda's presence for game playing when there was an entire palace full of people who could play Circle would draw exactly the sort of attention he wanted to avoid.

Jion no longer felt any desire to talk to Manon. During his free time, he roamed the imperial garden, consciously trying the Essence breathing that Ari had tried to teach him long ago. The idea of sitting and breathing without doing martial arts or something useful had made him impatient at seventeen, but he was no longer seventeen.

He turned onto the Path of Enlightened Virtue and paced alongside the water, doing Essence breathing as he imagined shedding the anger. Even the "righteous" anger, which was poison, Kanda said. Poison—he had completely forgotten that matter, though he knew the ferrets hadn't. His attempt to aid them had obviously failed, but they seemed to have reached dead ends in their own investigations, or he would have heard.

He reached his manor—and there were his servants, waiting with his clothes for west court practice, question in their eyes if not on their tongues.

It was then that an idea occurred to him: if Manon could redecorate her wing, making it look more and more like an heir's palace, why not do some redecorating of his own? New Year's was the time for that sort of thing. And that would justify summoning Afan Yskanda, in hopes he'd heard from Ari.

Jion had not summoned his "harem" since his return from Little Otters. He did not want anyone around, especially when he found out that his favorite among the women had reached twenty-five and had left palace service with her promised bag of boaters. He knew she had a family debt to pay off, and a life of her own to begin.

He exempted only Yskanda from his isolation. Yskanda

came each evening as ordered, and over a stack of drawings, murmured Ari's daily doings: study, sparring, and catching up with her parents' history since her departure with First Brother at age ten. Jion listened as closely as he would to any vital empire news, longing for reassurance that Ari had recovered from the interrogation from which he'd been powerless to save her. But easy as the news seemed to be, he knew Ari. He was afraid that she hid the hurt in order to spare his feelings. That made him feel worse.

He continued to turn down Manon's invitations to her gatherings. On the night of the third, Ze Kai turned up at Jion's manor, luckily after Yskanda's report. He claimed to have a question, but what he really wanted was to measure his own Circle skills against Yskanda's. The artistic consultations turned into games; Yskanda's time was his own at night, but he knew that he would never turn Jion down.

The fourth night, Yskanda only had time to say, "Arikanda says our mother believes the reason Arikanda's staff is fire resistant is that the monks must have worked all five affinities into it—"

Before Jion could ask what he meant by that, Whiteleaf was at the door to announce Ze Kai, two Su cousins, and Jion's Ran cousins. The isolation had officially turned into a gathering.

Ari and the staff lingered in Jion's mind. When he was alone, he often took Sagacious Blade down from the rack, as handling it brought Ari closer. His father had to know he had it, but no edict had been passed down. The sword was still there each time he returned to his room. He was not going to test matters by taking the sword outside his manor.

He didn't even want to. He liked taking it to his own quiet courtyard and working through Redbark, while imagining Ari's hand where his gripped. The sword was so light, no, that suggested flimsy and it was not that. It was so very well balanced—so natural—so much a part of him; it wasn't until that evening that the idea occurred to him that if this sword had taught Ari to fly, was it possible he could as well?

He scoffed immediately. He knew he had no powers, whatever "air affinity" meant. Except, ayah, what did one fly through?

He was very tired, and a little drunk, or he probably would have scorned himself out of making the attempt. And he almost gave up when he placed the sword on the ground of his quiet courtyard, stepped on the blade . . . and nothing happened. He frowned, remembering that night in Green Jade's harbor, when Ari sat next to him, telling him in a fast whisper what she'd learned on the rooftop in Benevolent Winds' main harbor before she crashed the mine. What had she said? She felt light.

He always felt light when he danced — that was one of the pleasures of dance. What else? She'd looked somewhere, and saw herself there. That didn't sound likely. Nevertheless, he fixed his gaze on the guardian lion at his rooftop, bounced lightly on the sword, and tried to see himself rising . . . rising . . . was it actually happening?

He looked down.

The sword clattered to the stones, and he tumbled, long habit turning the fall into a bruising roll instead of breaking bones.

He'd done it.

And so, what now? It wasn't as if he could actually fly anywhere in the palace without immediately being seen by the wall sentries, as he did not know those talismans for warding sight. He also remembered Ari's grim description of toiling through the air before the attack at Green Jade, sometimes moving as slowly as a walk, while expending tremendous effort. All right, he knew that at least rising into the air was possible — but in the way he knew it was possible to eat ten sesame cakes in one sitting. That did not mean he was going to do it.

He went inside, put the sword on the rack, and retired to sleep.

Most of the rest of the inner palace also retired, as it was quite late, both moons in the sky, Phoenix Moon dropping toward morning. But there were those who did not sleep, beginning with the night patrol in their ceaseless rounds.

Over on the west side, Grandfather Fai and Fai Anbai stared speechless down at the just-delivered, crinkled, grubby drawing of a young First Imperial Prince Jion, with a precise description of his clothes, and his habits. An imperial courier had brought it, with a verbal message from the garrison commander at Flowering Plum Island, the imperial island fleet's home port: *Isn't this your investigation? We're in the midst of maneuvers — you will know best how to use it.*

Yskanda was also awake; though Court Artist Yoli had insisted on getting out of bed to attend court, Yskanda had in his turn insisted on doing all the tasks that required running around to consult the imperials' wishes. He hoped to get that done in the mornings, if they would consent to see him, so that he could get back in time to get at his regular day's work.

By now he was used to organizing the army of Painters (who executed wall and trim repainting) and Artists (who designed as well as painted) to begin the refurbishing of upper palace pavilions for New Year's Two Moons. Yskanda had to chalk up a chart of who was to go where when, so that they could still get the Sky Wishes Day lanterns constructed and painted well ahead of time.

Then, at opposite ends of the palace, two people paced in almost identical fashion, though their emotions were very different: First Princess Manon had received with very mixed feelings the news that her honorary Uncle Ris Jun was back from wherever he'd gone; when she was young, it had been so exciting to meet with him in secret, but she was so close to having everything she wanted, and what had been exciting at age fifteen was more of a risky burden now.

So she paced, working out a graceful, but firm, speech that would wish him well while parting, and of course she would never tell anyone, ever, about their having met.

At the other end of the palace, the ferret mole Peony paced impatiently, excited to see her lover again. While Manon was unaware of Peony, the ferret was very aware that the princess would probably get his attention first. It had always been that way.

Until midway through Tiger Watch, he surprised her.

As the sun rose, he took his time assuming his disguise, thinking that this would be the last time. Though there was a certain amount of pleasure to be had in passing right under the noses of imperial guards and courtiers alike, none of whom gave a second glance to a hunch-shouldered old nanny carrying a basket of smelly cloths, who bowed humbly out of the way of anyone who passed.

He entered through the back of Drenched Blossoms, where the Su servants, who had seen this nanny off and on over the years, assumed "she" was one of the Su Manor servants who the Second Consort or her daughter sometimes called for. Asking questions was considered presumption, and presumption carried a heavy penalty among the primary Su families.

Ris Jun made his way into Manon's wing, which she had in

various ways caused to become further separated from her mother's wing. He found her in her study, books all about her, and saw immediately in the smooth way that she turned and laid down her writing brush that she had arranged one of her little scenes. They had been amusing when she was young, but had over the years become more assured—and more arrogant.

"Dear Uncle," she said, rising.

"Dear Niece," he responded. "I see you are flourishing."

"Quite well, though very busy finishing a task I was given by his imperial majesty. As it happens, I have come under much scrutiny of late, and—"

"Daughter," came the Second Consort's irritated voice from the hall. "Are you in there? I do not like these permanent screens that force me to go out of my way." The door was thrust open.

The Second Consort saw her daughter with a servant, mentally dismissed the servant, and transferred her gaze to her daughter's face. "You," she stated, "are the one insisting on changing the formal hall yet again. Your expertise is sought," she finished acidly, and waved her fingers at Yskanda, who entered with an armful of sketch designs.

He bowed to Manon, who had found that if she did not look directly at him, she scarcely felt the unwanted reaction. Soon, she believed, it would wither like a weed plucked from the garden.

His gaze flicked to the servant, whose features were familiar—almost familiar?

The servant stared back as Yskanda bowed again, backing to the door. "Forgive me, your imperial highness. This person of no talent would be happy to leave the designs for her imperial highness to approve at her convenience."

"Leave them and go," Manon said with a flick of her fingers, her shoulder turned.

He was already gone.

Manon stared down at the pile of sketches, determined to rid herself of any vestige of reaction to that low-born paintbrush wielder. Why was Honored Mother in a mood again—

"Niece Manon," Ris Jun said sharply.

No one spoke sharply to her. She tolerated his lack of protocol and the familiar address because it had pleased her to have a secret relationship with someone who could accomplish things for her that no one else could. It had been delicious to hoard that secret, that sense of power — but all that was so very childish. She was close to gaining real power now, which meant no missteps. And certainly no unfortunate connections. "Honored Uncle," she began in a sweet, chiding voice.

He made a dismissive gesture. "Who was that just now?"

"No one of any import," she stated emphatically, wondering if she had betrayed herself somehow. Impossible. She had not even looked at him.

"That 'no one' recognized me."

Manon glanced up, confused. "Impossible," she said aloud. "He was brought into the palace after you left last time. And he was nowhere near this end of the palace when you visited last spring."

"Send a servant to fetch him," Ris Jun told her. "I think he recognized me."

Manon did not want to send for Afan Yskanda, and she very much disliked being given an order by anyone. "He could not possibly have recognized you."

"You," Ris Jun said even softer, "were not even looking at him."

It was exactly the same soft voice Imperial Father used when he was most displeased. This was Manon's house, and she certainly had rank, but his steady, unwinking gaze, his tone, thrilled warning through her. She knew some of the things he'd done — including for her.

Maintaining her dignity, she lifted her voice slightly to call for her maid outside the door. "Tell the steward to summon the assistant court artist back here. I have questions." When the door shut, she said coolly, "I suppose it will be as well to be assured."

"The only assurance," Ris Jun said, "is silence."

What did that mean? She did not quite like to ask. And what did it matter, she told herself — and began telling him about her project, to remind him that she was part of the hallowed provinces of power, the future Heaven's Chosen. She intended to work around to her carefully prepared speech suggesting they part as friends until he interrupted and told her what he had just done that morning to preserve silence.

In the meantime, Yskanda hurried through byways to Jion's manor, carrying the rest of his sketches. He found Jion just returned from the west court, still in his practice clothes.

"Yskanda," Jion said when the servant had let him in. "Was

I expecting you this morning?"

No, but of late their nightly meetings had somehow become parties. He might as well shift the excuse of redecorating to mornings, since he had to be in the north end anyway. "This person of no importance hoped to take a few moments of his imperial highness's time . . ."

Jion waved off Whiteleaf, who waited for orders, as he said, "Those the sketches for the hall?"

"Yes, your imperial highness."

As soon as the door shut, Jion eyed him. "Is there bad news from Ari? Why do you look like you lost something?"

Yskanda shook his head, trying to banish the distractions. "I had to stop first at Drenched Blossoms. It's the nanny her imperial highness was speaking with. I'm certain I saw her — no, I know what it was," he said suddenly. "She must be related, that's it."

"Related to my sister Manon?" Jion asked in disbelief.

"This foolish lackwit apologizes for confusing his imperial highness." Yskanda resorted to formality. "It was that drawing I made for Chief Fai." He reddened. "I beg forgiveness, the news from my sister was the same as yesterday — sailing, Redbark drill, and studies. Apparently the ferrets handed over a copy of a Cobra Sage's herbal, or text, and she and Mother have begun studying from that."

Jion thanked him, spread the papers, and was about to start sorting them when Whiteleaf announced from the hall that the steward from Drenched Blossoms was there to fetch the assistant court artist back. "I am to repeat that her imperial highness is quite insistent," Whiteleaf said.

Yskanda looked bewildered. "Her imperial highness did not seem to have time to . . ." He turned to Jion, clearly uncertain what he was to do, for he did not know whose rank was higher.

Jion laughed. "Go, go. Manon's redecorating is far more elaborate than mine. See what she needs. I can wait."

Yskanda bowed and withdrew, to find a big, grim-faced steward waiting for him. In silence they returned to Drenched Blossoms, Yskanda mentally making the shift to the princess's designs as conveyed through a servant. How he wished Yoli would oversee this one — he really felt winter's ice in the princess's presence, however beautiful she was.

No servants were in sight as they entered through the back of the princess's wing. But instead of being taken to the princess's rooms, he was waved into a cold room behind the kitchens, where the nanny and the princess awaited him, but it was the nanny who dominated the room.

"You," said the nanny in a man's voice, "drink this." He pulled a vial from his sleeve, and uncorked it.

A sickly, acrid smell drifted from the bottle.

The princess's eyes widened. "Not that—not here!"

"You'll have to get rid of the body, but you've managed that before. Silence is the only way out for you, my girl."

The princess's eyes were stark and round. "Uncle—I thought you'd question him—bribes for silence work perfectly well . . ."

"Nothing works as well as silence, Su Manon. I've told you that repeatedly." The man in woman's clothing laughed. "Oh, my humble pardon! *Jehan* Manon. Both families equally doomed, and I get the pleasure of watching it happen."

"*What?*" For once she forgot to modulate her voice.

"Now is not the time to pretend innocence, girl. I'll see to that."

Yskanda backed toward the door—to be pushed forward by the steward, who had long been in Ris Jun's pay. "I don't understand," Yskanda said, eyeing the vial. "I don't know you—"

"You don't have to understand," the man said. "You just need to die."

He pounced.

Yskanda raised his arm in a block. He remembered enough from childhood to fend Ris Jun off for three or four moves, but he had never sparred with an adult. A knee behind his own knee, a brutal strike across the face, and he fell heavily. Then the man was on him, smothering nose and mouth as the steward stepped on his arms, pinning them to the floor. Yskanda struggled to breathe, fighting futilely. When the man pulled away his hand, Yskanda gasped—and in went the poison. Then the man shoved his hand over Yskanda's mouth again. He choked, swallowed, then choked hoarsely as corrosive fire seared its way down into his stomach.

Manon said, "You don't have to do this—I could have . . ." Whatever she was saying began to fade as Yskanda's body fought the fiery poison, and lost.

Jion was left thinking, drawing? Then he recollected Ri-Ri's drawing of the man Manon had been meeting. Did this man have a sister or mother over at Drenched Blossoms? That would solve the mystery after all—except why would Manon meet any relation of a nanny? It was unlike her to have any relationship with a servant at all, except to hand out orders.

For that matter, he thought, staring down at Yskanda's drawings, why would she have a nanny at all? Unlike his grandmother, who provided homes for all the aging nannies of both the Kui and the Jehan families, neither Second Mother nor Manon was the least sentimental about old servants.

Then he remembered Madam Swan's, and himself dressed as a girl to escape Screaming Hawk—

"Whiteleaf, could you send for Chief Fai? It has to do with a drawing he had the assistant court artist make. I think that person—or a related person is at Drenched Blossoms right now?"

Min Ko, the ferret, appeared behind Whiteleaf. "This is bad," he said, startling both prince and steward. The ferret then bolted away.

No servant had ever behaved that way in Jion's manor—or anyone's. What news had passed to Min Ko without Jion knowing—"Yskanda," Jion breathed. If there was something strange or even threatening going on, Yskanda would be defenseless, and Jion had promised Ari—

His first thought was of fetching a sword. Then he recoiled as Sagacious Blade smacked into his hand. His thoughts reached instinctively for Yskanda. He jolted again, even harder, and tumbled to the ground, the sword clattering beside him. He was in a cold room he'd never seen before. Manon and a man stood side by side, staring. Then Manon gasped in horror. "Jion?"

Jion paid no attention, for there on the ground an arm's length away lay Yskanda, with green foam mixed with dark blood coming out of his mouth, his nose, his ears. Manon whispered, "How will I get rid of him?"

Ignoring her, Jion threw himself down beside Yskanda, vaguely aware of the rustle of fabric behind him—it was the man, leaving; Ris Jun had no more poison, and Prince Jion, whose prowess was a common topic in barracks-room gossip, had a sword. Time to make his exit.

Jion never noticed him leaving. What do to — what to do — as he bent over Yskanda, the locket in his shirt banged his ribs, as it had ever since the day he and Ari first parted. Jion smacked his hand to his chest, then yanked open his clothes and ripped the locket free. His fingers trembled as he pulled a round pill from the locket. He forced open Yskanda's mouth, horrible as it was, and shoved the pill in.

"Come on, come on, brother," Jion said. How did you get someone who looked very dead to swallow? But then Yskanda drew a shuddering breath, choked, and moaned, sweat springing out on his forehead. The gray in his complexion slowly receded.

Jion ripped off part of his robe and wiped Yskanda's face as a greenish glow spread over his body. One shallow breath. Two. Jion counted them, breathing with him, willing him to breathe deeper; Manon stared down, excuses running through her head. Could she possibly shift the blame for poisoning onto Jion . . .

Yskanda sighed, and his eyes opened, staring upward.

Uttering an inarticulate cry, Manon ran past toward the door — but then she backed up again as Min Ko entered, armed with sword and knife. "Don't move," he said to Manon.

"How dare you address me that way! I'll have you beaten to death . . ."

She began uttering threats, ignored by Min Ko and unheard by Jion, who breathed with Yskanda, watching anxiously for any more blood.

Then footsteps approached, and suddenly the room was filled with imperial guards and ferrets. Fai Anbai looked around, knives in either hand, but when he saw Jion kneeling by Yskanda, and Manon standing with her back to the wall, her fingers spread, and Min Ko on guard, he lowered his weapons. A reflective glance at Sagacious Blade, then he bowed to Jion. "Thank you, your imperial highness."

Jion said numbly, "For what? I really don't understand." Then he turned to glance up behind him at Manon. "Was it you who poisoned Yskanda? Why?"

Her lips moved. "It was not I," she managed. She flung her head up. "What was that you put into his mouth? I saw you put something into his mouth!" It would be his word against hers —

"Is this your handwriting, your imperial highness?" Fai

Anbai asked, holding out a paper.

Jion craned his neck, and caught a glimpse of — "That's me! Ayah, I know that sketch. I remember when you made that." He turned, gazing up at Manon, who stared back, utterly confounded. "We were sitting in the tea house by the pagoda, and I was complaining about Master Zao making us draw bamboo shoots . . ." He stopped, his countenance radiating the questions he could not give voice to.

Fai Anbai looked down at him inscrutably. "This was found at Master Night's principal hideout. There is evidence that the mercenaries who attacked Loyalty Fortress were Shadow Panther recruits. They used this sketch as a guide."

Jion thought he had endured enough shocks, but this one detonated inside his heart like gunpowder. He turned to Manon. "It was *you* who sent them? *You* who tried to poison me?"

"No." Her voice cracked. "He — Ris Jun — it was all *his* doing."

Jion turned on his knee, still holding the bloody cloth. "Manon, you said you never got my letter. You lied to me. You were the only person who could have known where I was — and don't start telling me he got the letter and you didn't, because who but you could give him that sketch you made? Why?"

Manon's breath came fast. She spoke to Jion, but her gaze darted between the ferrets and the imperial guards. "He's my uncle. In a sense. A Su ought to be able to . . ." She could see that the pride of being part of the Su clan was not an argument that would sway them.

She marshaled her wits, and pitched her voice to sorrow. Her voice quavered — let it. "I never wanted you hurt, ever. He said he'd make you go away — Imperial Father was always petting you, not me, and he, my uncle, kept reminding me that it was *you* who was going to get the throne you didn't deserve, just because he likes you better — "

Jion got to his feet. "I told you, over and over, I didn't want the throne. I thought you should have it."

She retorted in a passionate, shaking voice, her mother's careful — painful — lessons forgotten, "Who believes that? Of *course* you want the throne. *Everybody* wants the throne."

Jion cut in, gazing directly into her face. "Not I. I never lied to you, or to Imperial Father, about that. What I wanted — still want — is the sun and the wind and the satisfaction of justice one person at a time, won with my own hands. But I'll say yes to Imperial Father right now if it means keeping *you* from the throne; if you can so badly misunderstand me, the person who trusted you most, loved you the best, believed in your scholarship and your wit, how can you understand your subjects?"

They stared at one another, she furious and desperate, he still trying to cope with how utterly she had betrayed him.

She was about to try to accuse him of the poison again when a quiet voice rose from the floor: "Graywing Melon-seed?".

Everyone stared at Yskanda, who said conversationally, "Forgive me, Graywing Melonseed, I seem to be lying on the ground. I don't . . . quite know why. But it is very good to see you again." He sat up slowly, apparently unaware of the blood smeared horribly over his face, his neck, his hair, and down his gray robe. "Oh, my head feels . . . strange. And I am so very thirsty," he murmured as he gently picked up his loaf and set it crookedly on his head again.

"Yskanda." Jion knelt at his side again. "Melonseed is not in this room."

"He's right here." Yskanda pointed between Fai Anbai and the closest imperial guard.

Jion put a hand under his elbow. "Come, Yskanda. I think we'd better get you some water." One last look toward Manon, one of total betrayal, then he turned his back on her, and helped Yskanda from the room.

Fai Anbai nodded at Min Ko to cover them, and the guards closed in on First Imperial Princess Manon, ignoring her commands not to touch her, and then her wild threats rising to a shriek of disbelief.

FORTY-ONE

A SEARCH OF BOTH wings of Drenched Blossoms Pavilion," Fai Anbai said before the throne in the private interview chamber an incense stick's worth of time later, "disclosed poison vials secreted among the jewel cases of both the Second Imperial Consort and First imperial Princess Manon. They each deny knowing those items were there, as do the maids who actually clean those rooms and tend the objects therein."

"Su-trained," the emperor commented, white-lipped with fury. "And we've just heard proof that all of them are liars."

Jion, who had been summoned, turned to Fai Anbai, who said neutrally, "This incompetent of no talent desires to address that, if your imperial majesty pleases." And at the expected hand wave, "Pursuant to the enlightened orders with which your imperial majesty chose to grace these your servants, we had placed a maid at Drenched Blossoms, introduced through the household of Su Afar and brought in after the previous . . . incident spring of the Rooster year. Under my orders five days ago this agent began active duty, listening and searching rooms. She testifies that the poison vials appeared today, during the time she was tasked by Second Imperial Consort Su Shafar to inventory the winter clothing. She was thus not at hand to identify Ris Jun or to aid in the pursuit, but she had made a sweep of the Second Imperial Consort's rooms before she left."

"What you are saying is that it's possible Ris Jun planted the poison on his way out," the emperor said. "Why would he do that, if he was plotting with Manon?"

"Imperial Father," Jion said, "before Ris Jun forced the poison on Afan Yskanda, the assistant court artist heard the conversation between him and my sister. Ris Jun was heard to say that he intended to destroy both families, ours and the Sus."

Fai Anbai bowed. "We have now placed Ris Jun among those unidentified persons during the Dolphin Year poisonings. The unidentified, or incorrect, sightings of a laundry maid were most often around Drenched Blossoms Pavilion. We suspect now that Ris Jun was the individual in question, dressed as a nanny. However, the patterns of the poisoning vary."

"I remember," said the emperor. "The Imperial Physicians initially believed the cause a disease that was more virulent among the young, but now they think that two different poisons were used."

"That is correct, your imperial majesty. One poison administered outside Drenched Blossoms, and one from within, on two young maids, and a seamstress from the Fabrics Department under Imperial Household. The Imperial Physicians say they need more time for proof, but they are fairly certain that the poison we found in our search corresponds to the poison that killed these three."

"Servants in every household died," the emperor said. "It's beginning to sound more like a rehearsal for imperial assassination. Beginning with my son. Have you placed mother and daughter separately in House of Eternal Peace?"

Fai Anbai and the commander of the imperial guard both bowed, the latter standing in the background, silent until now; neither was going to inform the emperor that that was standard procedure. "We have, your imperial majesty, though so far there is no evidence that the Second Imperial Consort was colluding with her daughter and Ris Jun. The relationship so far appears to be entirely between him and First Imperial Princess Manon. And that he was the source of the poisons, though it is . . . unclear . . . who is responsible for administering them."

The emperor's eyes narrowed as he recollected Manon admitting to recognizing the effects of poison, and her hasty verbal recovery, the morning she accused Melonseed of causing Maoyan's death. That hasty recovery had been odd in one who normally calculated every word. "You're implying my daughter poisoned the maids and the weaver?" His voice sharpened.

Fai Anbai bowed, saying, "It is possible, and becoming more probable, though the only proof so far is in the conversation Assistant Court Artist Afan overheard before he was poisoned."

Jion looked away, sickened: he was remembering that Manon had complained about one of those maids being impertinent, and the other of looking at young noblemen in the imperial garden. But he had been told that one had been sent away to get married, and the other dismissed. Then he recollected the terror in the current maid's face when he almost approached her during the summer, before he went to Green Jade—

The emperor turned to the commander. "No sign of the traitor Ris Jun?"

The commander had to admit that the searches had only disclosed the two corpses—both ferrets, apparently killed early that morning.

"One was the mole named Peony, the other was detailed to watch Peony," Fai Anbai said, with difficulty hiding his own fury. "We'd been watching her in hopes she would betray any other conspirators. But we are fairly convinced now that she was the one who killed the false prince and the graywing in the prison, on Ris Jun's orders." The night before she was sent to investigate the mercenaries—which meant she was left out of the intense questioning of staff, as it happened, but Fai Anbai was not going to admit that unless asked. "She was kept in information-isolation by Ris Jun; he might have others in his pay, but she was not cognizant of them."

The main of Fai Anbai's rage was due to the knowledge that Ris Jun had always been one step ahead. And still was.

"I want to hear exactly what was said between him and Manon. Where is Afan Yskanda now?"

"At my manor, Imperial Father," Jion said. "We left him there, with extra guards, to get cleaned up."

"He was somewhat delusional, your imperial majesty," Fai Anbai said. "Whatever it was that his imperial highness gave him definitely saved his life, but might have affected his brain to an extent. The imperial physician who examined him said that was the residue of the poison, which burns through anything it touches. He suggested that the delusions might fade once Afan Yskanda has rested."

He paused there, in case the emperor wished to know more

about the delusions—very unsettling delusions, specifically speaking to the dead—but his imperial majesty had no interest in what, by definition, was not real. "Have you sent searchers to the Su Manor?"

"Yes, your imperial majesty," said the commander. "They have been mobilized and should be on their way."

"Report immediately on any findings," the emperor said. "Bitternail! Better make it an edict: the Su clan is confined to their manor pending investigation. Put a couple of rings of guards around Su Manor, for their safety as well as ours. Everything done with utmost respect. The court will be in an uproar over this, and at the worst time."

"Understood, your imperial majesty."

"Jion, go back and keep an eye on Afan Yskanda. If he wakens sane, I'll want to hear what he has to say, though he seems to be a completely unwitting victim in this despicable and treasonous affair."

Treason. The word was not as easily defined as some believed—mostly, treason was what a ruler pointed at. But everyone knew the penalties, and as Jion bowed himself out, he felt a pulse of pity for Manon, and for Honored Second Mother, who apparently was ignorant of what was going on at the other end of her manor. While it was true that Manon had betrayed him—not in a moment of anger, but with careful planning—he knew why she had done it, and he'd seen the terror in her face when Fai Anbai and the others burst in.

Manon and her ambition were very much on his mind when he reentered his manor. He was still wearing his court clothing, and wanted a bath, though nothing was going to clean his mind from the evidence of the grime of poisonous ambition. He also needed some time to figure out what exactly had happened with Sagacious Blade, now resting innocently on its rack in his bedroom. (Good. It had stayed put!) But when he asked Yarrow, "Is the assistant court artist awake yet?" the answer was, "He never slept, your imperial highness."

Jion sighed and went to the guest room, calling, "Yskanda?"

The door opened. "Your imperial highness," Yskanda said, dressed in a fine gray robe that Fennel had given him. "This unworthy servant wishes to express his utmost gratitude for, ayah, everything, from saving my life, to the gift of having a bath to rid myself of the stench of the poison. I don't think I will ever get that smell, or its attendant pain, out of my memory."

"From all the blood, I would hazard a guess it was akin to a tiger clawing you from the inside."

"A tiger competing with a fire dragon." Yskanda brushed his fingers over his ribs; the beating he'd received on his first day, which had until then been the worst pain he had ever endured, was a mere tickle compared to the savagery of that poison. "But what you gave me, it was snow on parched, burnt land. What was that — where was it from?"

"Didn't I tell you about Yaso and the restoration pills? Ay-ah, I don't remember what I told you. The important thing is, I had only the one. And Ari and I are pretty sure Yaso was a god, or sent by a god." He briefly described the crane that app-eared at the dance when Screaming Hawk was chasing them, what seemed a thousand centuries ago. "I should warn you," he finished, "my father is likely to send for you at any time. Right now he thinks you are sleeping off your delusions."

"What delusions?" Yskanda asked.

Jion looked away. "You recovered and, ah, started talking to Melonseed. Who is dead."

"I know," Yskanda said peaceably. "I think he knows he's dead. I think he lingers to get justice, or perhaps to reassure the other graywings. He was very much respected by them, you know. Still is."

"Yskanda," Jion said carefully. "Do you think you see ghosts?"

"He's right there." Yskanda waved a hand to Jion's right. "You don't see him?"

"No. I see my Five Cranes in the Peach Garden screen," Jion said, trying to be precise. "You think he is haunting my best guest room?"

Yskanda gazed in that direction, then slowly turned in a circle, his focus disturbingly distant. "I don't think anything," he said presently. "I *see* him. Them."

"There's more?"

"Two much brighter ones. A woman somewhere around the chief ferret's age, I would hazard a guess. She wears ferret clothing. And a man, also in ferret clothing, a bit older than that. Balding, with a mole on his ear. They are very bright, very. I think they might be new. They look a little lost. And very angry."

The ferrets Ris Jun had killed early that morning? Yskanda can't have known that. Could he? "Where *is* Melonseed, if he's not in the guest room, yet you see him right there?"

"I suspect that distance is not a material thing," Yskanda said slowly, his eyes narrowing. "Melonseed stands adjacent to a great dragon painting. Oh, I do wish I could examine that! It's magnificent. Over there is a very elaborate sword rack. A great bed canopied with brocade that way."

He was describing Imperial Father's bedroom, which Jion had only seen once in his life. No, more correctly, that was the imperial bedchamber, for his father did not have a brocade canopy over his bed. Jion hadn't really looked at it—his interest had been in the sword rack, and a little in the dragon painting—but he remembered an impression of light, gauzy fabric, and while his father could have had it changed, he very seldom altered anything in his pavilion, which was always maintained in perfect condition.

Could it be *Emperor Maoyan*'s bedchamber, years ago? Or a mere delusion?

Jion was aware of a sense of dread. He hoped that Yskanda had not been miraculously restored from the poison just to become insane. "I heard you speaking to Melonseed right after you woke. Did he, ah, talk back?"

"No," Yskanda said. "But he seemed so lonely. So I spoke, in case he did hear me."

Jion hid a sigh of relief. That made a little sense, at least. He said, "I'm sorry I sent you back to Drenched Blossoms before I figured out something was wrong. I wish I'd been faster."

"You could not know. *I* did not understand at first that they were talking about me. I'd done nothing to cause so violent an intention—did not even know the man dressed as a nanny. I figured it out too late. Ayah, perhaps I was condemn-ed the moment I entered that cold room, as that steward made sure I stayed right there in the room."

"He did? The servants all maintain they knew nothing. He says that he was sent to get you, then dismissed."

"No," Yskanda said. "He made certain I couldn't leave. He stepped on my arms while that man forced the poison down my throat. I can feel the bruises." He flexed his arms and winced.

"I'll be right back." Jion went to find Min Ko, and told him what Yskanda had said.

The big man listened grimly. "That's the worst of it, your imperial highness, if I may speak. This Ris Jun may have paid informers all over the palace."

"This is one you know of. If you can find him," Jion said.

"Oh, we know where all the servants are. At least there's that." Min Ko gave a short nod. "In fact, with your permission, your imperial highness, I'll see to that right now."

Jion left him to it, and returned to Yskanda, who was closely examining the painting on a porcelain vase. "This is a Rabbit vase, for a moon year, with willow twigs," he said happily. "A rabbit vase for next year, if you don't mind that the symbols aren't for water."

Jion uttered a laugh. "I'll have to move it out front, and find more paintings to match it. If I don't get sent over Sun's Grace." He tested the idea. It felt like a yoke settling around his neck.

"The heir's palace," Yskanda commented. "Her imperial highness sent a servant to ask its dimensions, one of the geomancer assistants told me a couple of weeks ago, as a warning that we might be painting it soon, once they established which corners are the most auspicious." His eyes widened. "You? Oh, this stupid and thoughtless person ought to be congratulating—"

"Don't, Yskanda. The truth is, the idea makes me feel sick. Manon was willing to kill for that throne. She is only one of a long line going back in imperial history. I see it as a burden. If *you* make a mistake, you lose face, a little, then order new silk and paints and do it over. If an emperor makes a mistake, lives are lost. But if he's not to die of remorse, he has to become hardened to it. I *hate* that. How does anyone with any moral sense reconcile to it? I'd better read my great-grandmother's thoughts on it. Unlike Emperor Maoyan, she was sane."

"If your imperial highness will forgive an impertinent question from this ignorant one, is that not why you have court?" Yskanda asked sympathetically.

"In a perfect world," Jion said with all his father's irony. "That means dealing with the problems they bring, along with their advice. How much of Heaven's will is there, really, in choosing an emperor—for to any answer there is Emperor Maoyan. Bringing me back to my theory that Melonseed was not acting alone . . . Ayah, I'm jabbering. I got started on this thinking of ambitious princes and fights over inheritance."

Yskanda looked up from the vase. "If that is a real question, your imperial highness, should you inherit, it will be expected—the emperor's son, well-educated, benign, well-liked."

Jion waved away the compliments—"Please, no gold-faced

talk. Not from you. I expect I'll get enough of that if it does happen."

"But this clumsy servant is not intending flattery, your imperial highness. I come from a small and distant island, so in no way speak for all, but I can corroborate from my reading that most commoners want the emperor and imperial problems to stay far away. Civil wars as well as wars with foreigners are only interesting to hear about as long as they happen to someone else. I believe most want an easy change from old to new, an expected change, such as your accession. Easy — eldest son, well-educated, well-liked. They want a government that is benign as well as distant, that will keep the granaries full, and the roads fixed, so that if Heaven punishes us with drought or flood, or demons cause them because they feed on misery, the emperor can be trusted to come to their aid. Did you not find attitudes much like that when you traveled with my sister?"

"Yes, and no," said Jion. "In the far north, no one expected help from the empire. Only interference." He smiled. "Be sure to tell Ari about the last pill. I wonder if she thought I'd lost it after all this time?"

But Yskanda surprised him by looking away. "This unworthy fool seeks forgiveness, but I do not think I will reach for Arikanda through water for a time."

Jion stared. "Why not?"

Yskanda was silent for a while, then said, "If you put a drop of ink in water, what happens?"

"It spreads."

"Just so. Neither of us are able to contain our emotions. For the most part, it does not matter. But I do not want Arikanda feeling what I felt when I was poisoned. I know what it will do to her spirit, and now is the time when she needs to face north, heart and mind. It will not help her if her mind faces north, but her heart is with us — you, almost poisoned, and I, who did get poisoned. And that man still at large."

"Ayah," Jion exclaimed, thinking that whatever the truth was about the ghosts, Yskanda's words now didn't sound insane. "I never thought of that. Then I leave it to you to do what you can, and tell me anything I must know. And ready yourself," his voice changed to warning. "My father is waiting to question you about what you heard in that room between Ris Jun and my sister."

FORTY-TWO

"LET US BEGIN WITH what you truly know," Hanu said.

The weather was balmy, so they were on deck, Hanu sitting on a mat, and Ari balanced on the rail, her arms extended to either side. She had saved all the seeds from her breakfast so that she could play Tree with the birds wheeling about a small island as they passed. Mother had said it was good practice to call their little lights to her.

Ari glanced upward, balancing on one leg, the other extended straight forward. "I know that the study of Essence, of nature, and of destiny is a single act."

"A good place to begin. Continue." Hanu watched her daughter's quick grin as a pair of water birds landed on either shoulder, pecking up the seeds there.

"You taught me that true knowledge of Essence leads to knowing right from wrong." Ari slowly swung her leg to the side, as she sent calming thoughts to the birds. Safe, safe. "But I've seen that there are people who know Essence, who don't seem to know right from wrong. Or, their definition of right is what I call wrong. How do I know I'm not wrong, and they are right?" And there was the essential Ari, always full of questions.

Hanu said, "We will come back to defining those things. For now, let us remain with Essence."

Ari ducked her head in a nod, checked in a quick glance that all the seeds weren't gone, and extended the other leg. "Knowledge forms the basis of cultivation. And of conduct— ayah, I'm going toward the moral life again." She swung the leg out to the side, easily riding out a bumpy cross-current. "Essence governs the five elements, in both the sun phase— action—and in the moons phase, resting. Light and dark. Without Essence, no object can exist. Essence has no shape or shadow, but everything is made of it, everything, from the butterfly on a flower to the stars overhead, and so, its funda- mental nature is often called Purpose."

"Good, go on."

"Living things as well as non-living things, at the moment of their making, receive Essence, so that they may have a form and a nature of their own. And so we come to right, which is to live in harmony with nature, the seen and the unseen world, and with one another. Wrong is to destroy that harmony."

"Now define the world, within the context of our studies. Specifically the raising and binding of Essence."

Ari closed her eyes, reaching toward the little lights drifting and circling. She had remembered her lessons as tedious, but that was before she began to travel, to see how wonderful the world really was. "I understand the realms seen and unseen as connected by circles within circles, ever greater, eternally wheeling with the stars overhead. Years, months, moon cycles, elemental cycles; it all is connected, from that blade of grass with its bead of Essence, to the immense fire dragons breathing Essence beneath the greatest islands."

She opened her eyes, surrounded by birds as Bo Ya the ferret listened from the opposite rail, and Imperial Captain Ha Gar from aft. "Master Iley, I *sensed* those dragons, asleep below certain islands! There is a great one below the imperial island, and—no, I should go on. The fire dragons sleep for thousands of years, and when they turn over, the talismans placed along ago, and tended ever since, kept the quakes to a gentle shake. And when the dragons waken and fly upwards, their mountains spew burning rock in glowing rivers. There are signs ahead of time, each understandable to its living form: humans have to read the stars, because we don't hear or see as well as the animals that read their signs in nature. And the undersea world knows in yet another way, so that all go away before the dragon rises."

"All right, I'll accept that. To talismans, now."

Ari hated studying talismans, though she had ended up using some of the simplest ones. It was the way they wiggled, not physically, but in your mind, giving her an unsettling touch of vertigo. "The talismans that bind the earth are called natural, as they destroy nothing. They fit within the vast harmony of the circles. Master Iley, I get their importance now, but I really don't see how I can learn a fingernail's worth of what the geomancers learn so carefully in order to wield Essence within that harmony. I told you about that horrible storm I unleashed — and . . ." Her voice dropped to a whisper as she shifted to her island dialect. Beneath all the noisy cawing and cheeping and squawking, she murmured in their home dialect, "Ayah, Yskanda doesn't know it, but I saw that storm in his memory. He was on his way to the capital when it happened, and they nearly died! And I never would have known I'd killed them!"

"But they didn't die. From what I know now, Yskanda's own Essence talent kept them afloat." Hanu glanced out to sea, where in the early morning light, could be seen a stream of refugee boats of every imaginable size and description flowing southward. She now suspected that that terrible storm that had taken apart the boat she and Danno rode in had been sent by the gods for Yskanda. Oh, he was stubborn!

However, that was Yskanda's path, which (if she was right, and she was never sure about that) he must walk. She resumed in pure imperial, "You and I are sitting here now to discuss that balance because you are right, you cannot master a life-time of study in a few weeks. However, you can learn how to sense this destructive force, and to dismantle the talismans that aid it."

Ari put her hands together and bowed.

"Let us talk about demons," Hanu said relentlessly.

In occasional whispered conversations, Ari had discovered that her mother had had to learn about Cobra Sages and the demons they attracted while she and Father were on Kandra Sutra, Master Night's Island. Ari did not want to know anything about demons, but if she was going to be facing Cobra Sages, she had to remember what she'd been told.

"They are not human. Like Essence, and anything else, they can be bad or good. The good ones leave us alone. The bad ones might draw on an illusory human shape to lure a human, but you will always be able to see past that. More dangerous by far is when they lure a human to permit them to possess their body, usually by promising something badly wanted."

"What can anyone possibly want that would let them invite a demon inside them?"

"Usually power. Revenge. A desire for war, all things demons favor, because that creates the chaos and suffering they feed on, and in that sense they keep their promises. But they never leave the human victim to enjoy the fruits of victory. Never. When they have finished using the human they leave the husk behind and go on, ever hungrier for souls to feed their own lust for power."

"Very good," Hanu said, in her pose as Essence master. "Now we shall work again in talismans."

The birds flew off, and Ari leaped, turned two somersaults in the air, and landed barefoot on the deck. Then grinned as she watched the flock of birds return to the island.

From the rail and aft, her escort listened; each day that went by they were beginning to see themselves not protecting the empire from her, but her protecting the empire.

Until the imperial guard caught Ris Jun, the ferrets and the imperial guards were on high alert.

Nobody believed he'd run off. Tension gripped everyone, intensified by the second imperial consort and her daughter very present in their absence.

The latest change was the emperor summoning Jion to attend court. On the days there was no court, Jion fought the onslaught of wild emotions by keeping himself moving from the time he opened his eyes until he retired, each night later. The worst of the feelings centered around Manon, once his closest sibling, the person he admired most. Who had colluded in the poisoning of a number of people, and who had personally poisoned three.

Who had tried to have him killed.

How that hurt. Yskanda, whose memory was so formidable, had made that clear when he knelt before the throne in the private interview room and repeated the conversation that had taken place between Manon and Ris Jun before the poison was forced down his throat. By the time Imperial Father summoned Yskanda, the ferrets had wrenched a confession out of the Drenched Blossoms steward, who had corroborated everything Yskanda said, and a lot more.

Jion didn't want to hear it. Even if he could do anything about it, what would he do? Condemn her to death? Thinking about it made him feel physically sick — even anxiety over Ari wasn't as bad, because he had Yskanda to warn him if something happened. (Again, though he was powerless to do anything.) He often reminded himself that she would have gone after White Dragon even if she'd made it safely to Te Gar, or to Ten Leopards, but that made him wish even more strongly that he could be with her.

He filled his days to keep from going insane, fighting through the toughest of the imperial guards in the mornings, and in the afternoons he spent his time in the archives, where his ferret watchers couldn't go. He hunted through his ancestors' writings, his goal now to seek any scrap about Essence-bound swords. He found absolutely nothing, beyond the edict forbidding subjects from making, selling, or owning them.

He discovered more at the large archive, but as the elderly graywing in charge said when he took Jion to that section, "Much of what is written here is legend, I believe. You know that none of these things still exist. But here is what we have. The older scrolls have been recopied, you'll see . . ." And he went on about the history of each.

Jion found nothing about Sagacious Blade — which continued to remain on its rack, behaving itself. Herself.

He tried to think of the sword as "she" but without success. The sword remained a sword, not a person, until such time as he heard a voice. At first he took it down to hold, thinking hard at it to go to Ari the way it had come to him. Nothing happened.

After a day or two of only giving himself a headache over that fruitless exercise, he flew on it around his room, mostly to reassure himself that the sword really did fly. His balance was so good from years of dance that he could arc in any direction — even briefly upside down — but his continual state of worry kept him from enjoying it. He found he could also call it to him if he stood across the room and held out his hand as if to pick it up.

But he could not reproduce that eerie jolt when he found himself right next to Yskanda. That meant the sword had passed through walls. It had to, and yet there were no smashed walls, so splinters — moreover, *he* was in one piece. Surely being hurled by a magic sword through a wall would have smashed him up.

Yet it had happened. Yskanda would be dead if he had not gotten there that fast, and put the pill in his mouth—that poison was so terrible that nothing would have been left of him had Jion been forced to run the distance between his manor and Drenched Blossoms.

Contemplating that increased his longing to see Ari again, to talk about the sword, and about everything else. One night, after he could neither send the sword to Ari nor get it to jolt through walls, in frustration he turned and slung it toward the rack. It spun in the air, and circled right back to smack into his hand. Just like certain swords in the oldest stories, wielded by martial arts masters . . .

He fetched paper and set up targets around his room, and experimented with the sword, which was once again light in his hand, as if eager to fly, or eager to be used. "I wish you would talk to me," he said to it.

No answer—but when he snapped his wrist just so, using controlled power, he could get the sword to slice through some of the papers before it returned to his hand. Which led to experiments with spin, and force, and distance, until at last, at last, he was tired enough to fall into sleep.

Days passed.

The dowager empress declared, when the emperor asked about Sky Wishes Day, that no ill-mannered liar and traitor was going to ruin one of her favorite festivals. The weather being balmy for what was probably the last time of the year, the considerably diminished imperial family gathered in the imperial garden, sky lamps readied by Afan Yskanda and his seniors—though Old Yoli was much improved, the Imperial Physicians insisted he stay inside at night, which he was glad to do.

That left Imperial Princess Gaunon (no one was using the "Second" before her title anymore) to be the center of attention. At almost seventeen, and without any Second Imperial Consort or her daughter to squash her with cold looks and annihilating sarcasm, Gau-Gau was very ready to blossom.

Though no one in the imperial garden that night said anything about the absent—long tradition had made prudence into protocol—each of those women in that small gathering was aware of how comfortable it was without Second Imperial Consort Su Shafar's derisive coldness, or her daughter's icy deference. The former second consort had been exiled for life to the cold palace north of the ancestral shrine, where she would spend the rest of her life earning her daily meals by mending garments for the poor. The rotation of female imperial guards, none of whom had ever had a kind word from her, would see to it.

As for Manon, no one quite dared to ask. Nor did anyone ever think even once of wanting to visit her. Even among the palace's student and apprentice population, her former glamour had vanished when word was whispered that she not only tried to kill Prince Jion, but she'd forced Afan Yskanda to take poison. (As Court Assistant Yoli that morning observed caustically to his chosen cronies among the scribe instructors, "Only Yskanda could manage to become a hero while not noticing."

The Head Painter laughed. "The fact that your assistant appears to be utterly oblivious to the wind of sighs that follow him everywhere merely adds to his allure."

Yoli had chuckled in agreement, keeping to himself the discovery he'd made when he chanced to see Yskanda's gaze rest on Prince Jion. He said, "What I find astonishing is the fact that since the poisoning he sometimes talks to himself while walking along seems to add rather than detract from this allure.")

The conversation among the consorts, the dowager empress, and the female relations began with Duke Su's death. All turned to Gau-Gau, who though not actually related to either the Su clan or the Rans, had always regarded them as cousins. Though she was frightened of old Duke Su, and disliked arrogant Banek, who had grown up counting on being the heir, she had acceded to invitations to visit Su Manor more often than she preferred out of sympathy for the secondary branch cousins. And so she had been there when the old duke died.

She looked wide-eyed at the consorts, her Kui and Ran aunties, and her grandmother. "I wasn't in the room when Duke Su collapsed," she said breathlessly. "And I'm *so* glad! Ayah, I was very frightened by him — very — and I *knew* that he only invited me because he wanted to marry scowly Cousin Banek to me, but I never had to stay on the west side — they let me stay with my friends, the east side cousins."

"Start at the beginning, will you, my dear?" the dowager empress asked, amused.

Gau-Gau paused in the act of painting JOY on a lamp, and held the brush in the air. "We were playing pitch pot for jujubes while we waited for the opera—the duke only let the east side cousins have an opera when I was staying, I told you that, didn't I?

"You did, my dear. But what happened?"

"All of a sudden people started yelling, and there was a great rushing of feet, and suddenly imperial guards were *everywhere*."

"Did they arrest you?" the third imperial consort asked her daughter, appalled. "You never told me that."

Gau-Gau threw down her brush (quietly picked up and replaced by one of Yskanda's senior students) and swooped on her mother, hugging her. "Do not be frightened, it was only a little scary, but mostly exciting. We had to gather in the Hall of Manifest Virtue for the imperial edict. At first everyone was asking everyone else what was going on, until the shouting started, and Ysek had been winning, for he and Tarek had a bet going that—"

"Who was shouting, dearest?" The first imperial consort, familiar with Gau-Gau's style of storytelling, hoped to curtail a long sidetrack into the game.

"It was the duke! After the graywings went away once they delivered the edict. Bellowing about traitors being written out of the family book, and then horrid Great-Aunt Li yelling back that it was his fault, and the next thing anyone knew, they were shouting that the duke was choking and had fallen down."

"Ayah," the third consort exclaimed with comfortable pity. "He didn't die at once?"

"No. He couldn't speak too well, past gasping for breath. The servants carried him to his bed, where the family all had to kneel again, in order, or maybe they wanted to, thinking he was dying? I had to go along, because where else would I go? While he lay there, in a whisper he disinherited everyone in the west wing—the great-uncles, their sons, and the daughters-in-law, and of course Honored Second Mother—do we still call her that?"

"Just go on, we all know whom you mean," the dowager murmured, as graywings brought around more hot tea and fresh almond cakes.

"She, and Honored First Imperial Sister—do I have to keep calling Manon that, as it turned out she did those horrid things?

Anyway she was disinherited and cast out of the Su family, and then, he could scarcely speak, but he ordered the servants to change the wings right then and there. He made the servants start taking all the west wing things to the east wing, and the east wing things to the west wing, while nobody knew which room they would end up in, and in the middle of it the servants found jars of something smelly that hadn't been there before, and Aunt Zi was telling them to throw it in the privy while I was kneeling next to Cousin Lanek, who said he was afraid he would go to bed and find he had changed to Cousin Inek, and *she* said he should be so lucky, but if she woke up and she was he, she'd hang herself, and they were poking each other until two uncles turned around and scowled."

Gau-Gau shivered, then looked around as if surprised to have been able to say that much without Manon scorning her into silence. She resettled herself, still holding the Joy lamp, and said, "The duke declared that Aunt Zi was now head of the family. He made them write it out, and he put his seal to it, with the great-uncles bellowing like thunder gods and Great-Aunt Li caterwauling like a demon-thing that they ought to put the Ris woman to death, and *that* was when the searchers came in and started to comb through the things the servants had *just* been putting right. Then he collapsed again, the duke, I mean, and he was dead by morning, and they sent me home before anyone had passed out the mourning cloth. I never did find out who went where."

"Su Zi," the first imperial consort repeated. "She passed the Imperial Examination, I remember hearing that, though of course it was before my time."

Everyone's head turned as they looked across the grass at the emperor; no one wanted to guess whether or not Su Zi would take the old duke's place in court once mourning was over. Then one of the Ran cousins approached with a pack of teenage Kuis. They bowed to the dowager empress and the two consorts, then ran off with Gau-Gau to set their lamps flying.

The empress dowager and the consorts then returned to easy chatter with the Ran and Kui elders, everyone angled so that if the emperor spoke, or rose, they would be ready to go silent or to bow as needed. So far he sat away from everyone else, with only Jion at his side.

The dowager empress, expert at the courtly side-eye, had observed worriedly that neither had spoken to the other, though they sat together; she knew that Jion was somehow connected to the mysterious prisoner called Firebolt who had come and gone from the prison, but she did not know his heart, as he spoke readily to her about all other subjects but that. And now, Jion's profile was a match for his father's: handsome, inscrutable.

Presently the emperor said in too low a voice for anyone else but Jion to hear, "You have not spoken in court."

Jion's grandmother had said to him the morning after Ari vanished aboard the naval courier, *You will probably be summoned to court soon. Speak as little as you can; if you have opinions, don't air them before the ministers. Even if he asks. It will never be wrong to say you are still learning. Later, when he goes over the memorials with you, just the two of you, then you can talk things over.*

Jion murmured, "This ignorant son has too much to learn, Honored Imperial Father."

He had not used the more intimate "Father Emperor" since Firebolt's incarceration. The emperor found that he missed that. But he had learned early that his well-meaning imperial grandmother, in requiring the younger generation to use terms of intimacy, had not made them intimates, and he refused to insist on it much as his heart yearned to hear it again.

Jion was thinking about his own grandmother. She had also said, *You are likely to be proclaimed heir, and I can see from your expression that you understand the weight of it. Good. You might believe you have little freedom now, but it will be worse, because my son will want to know, always, what is in your mind. He won't be able to stop wondering if what you say is true, and if you are looking past him to the throne, because he grew up hearing so many lies from those with secret ambitions. And Manon just made that worse.*

The emperor studied his son's closed-in expression without being able to divine the direction of his thoughts. He finally said, "What shall we do about your sister?"

Jion glanced up, startled. Then his expression shuttered once again, his tone flat and a little husky. "Honored Imperial Father must make that decision; this son dares have no thoughts on the matter."

Manon would have spoken the same words had their fates been reversed, the emperor suspected, but her tone would have been so sweet, so empty of her real thoughts, and she would not have quite been able to hide the satisfaction in her eyes. At least Jion was no longer defending Manon, much less arguing that she ought to inherit the throne.

You will have to make decisions like this one day, the emperor was thinking, and tried again with an easier question. "The two of you were once so close. When did that change?"

Jion considered the question. He could learn to be prudent, even reticent, but he sensed that this was not the time for silence. "After my return from Redbark, Imperial Father. I tried to recover what I had cherished, but . . ." Jion looked out over the dark lake, and the reflections of the sky lanterns rippling on the water. "I began to realize it after the wedding." He stopped there, not wanting to risk possibly implicating Ze Kai.

"That was a generous gesture on your part," the emperor said. And at Jion's quick look, "Of course I knew, or the ferrets would all be silent bones right now. You will discover that permitting people to sneak around the precincts of court is nearly always a bad idea. Your benevolent and entirely innocent gesture the rare exception."

Jion could only bow.

The emperor watched closely, then said, "Manon consistently calculated everything I wanted to see, to hear. Though I approved in the sense that if a ruler is to survive, that kind of calculation is a necessity, I found myself never quite trusting her. I . . . attributed that sense to other things." A short breath.

Jion, hearing it, glanced over, and for the first time really observed the tension in his father's hands, in his forehead. It was so much a part of him that he couldn't remember seeing him without it.

The emperor continued, "In this position, the power you wield is directly proportionate to the thickness of everyone's mask. No one, including you, tells me the truth of their thoughts."

"May this unworthy son venture to observe, Imperial Father, that no one wishes to die for a thought that might be as ephemeral as a leaf on the wind?"

"Tell me a truth," the emperor said. "Nothing will happen."

Perhaps not now, but you'll remember it, Jion was thinking—at the same time, he, too, longed for the honesty of his Redbark days. "I miss Ari, Imperial Father," he said. "Firebolt. Though she never called herself that. It happened up north, when she fended off pirates. The name stuck."

"I'm aware," the emperor said dryly. "Ryu Ari. 'Peace.'"

Jion's heart banged against his ribs; it seemed a miracle that Fai Anbai had not guessed who Ari's father was. Or that she and Yskanda were related. "I miss her like I'd miss my right arm if it was cut off."

"I spoke with her," the emperor said, as Gau-Gau gave a cry like a gull, clapping at the row of lanterns loosed into the air. Each had been decorated in Afan Yskanda's arresting style.

The emperor turned his gaze to Jion, who stared straight back, unblinking. "I found her credulous, profoundly ignorant, and lacking even a rudimentary sense of protocol. But the impression that lingers is that I believed every word she spoke was what she thought, ill-informed as it might be. In that, she could not be more different from Manon. Let us see how your Ryu Ari does there in the north."

Manon's first day in prison was spent sitting upright, décorously, on the edge of the wooden bed.

When the prison staff brought in a bowl of rice with fish stewed with cabbage—the meal all inhabitants of the prison got, prisoners as well as staff—and set it on the floor inside the door, Manon ordered them to serve it properly. She used her sharpest voice of command, ending with, "I am still *First* Imperial Princess Jehan Manon, and I shall tell the emperor that I was *not* treated with the respect due an emperor's daughter."

But the bowl sat where it was. No one spoke, or even looked at her.

She refused to touch any meal that had sat on the ground, where feet walked and animals fed. When her back began to ache from sitting upright, she lifted the single blanket with forefinger and thumb, then dropped it on the floor in disgust as the scent of some other person rose off it. It wasn't even clean! That would net someone a flogging. She would see to it personally.

She pulled her silken robes around her and lay down on the ill-fashioned, straw-stuffed bed, counting up the com-plaints she would make once Imperial Father came to interview her. But she had better have her defense ready as well. Ris Jun's lying promises—his actions, all *his*. He brought the poisons. As for using them, no one could *prove* anything. She had been very careful about that.

As for Jion, he was scarcely a victim. Honored Mother had once said, *You tattle on him to the emperor, and you will never again hear what he really thinks. Save up his ill-bred remarks and his stupid trespasses, and use them when they will be most effective, for you are likely to only have one chance.*

Manon had not wanted to have to use them. She was *fond* of Jion, in spite of him being the pearl in the emperor's heart, which he did not deserve. But she was fighting for her position, perhaps her very life . . .

We need not follow her path of thoughts farther; she sat decorously, rehearsing her defense, as day followed day. The staff never spoke to her. They never changed the blanket, which she was forced to use when it got steadily colder, and the meals continued to be set on the floor, whether she ate them or not. She ate.

Imperial Father never came.

She firmly believed that he would restore her to her position after a little suitable groveling and tears, and each day she was ready to grovel and to weep, until one night when the door was unlocked to a new arrival — Bitternail.

To summon her? But then she saw the silver salver he carried, on it a single cup. She gasped, cold with shock. She had relished descriptions of the ritual executions for traitorous imperial family members. She knew what was in that pure white porcelain cup.

"So Jion won after all," she said, all pretense of fondness shed like the skin of a snake. "What did he say against me? I suppose you were there to hear it." Her voice shook, and she stopped, though her knees trembled. Jion had outsmarted her, had acted the victim, oh that didn't matter. Nothing mattered except the fact that if she could not rule, and it was clear now that Imperial Father would not restore her to her proper position, or he would have come himself — she might as well be dead.

"At least," she stated bitterly, "an imperial princess should be granted the Imperial Sleep."

Bitternail gave a short nod, not even a proper bow. "His imperial majesty did indeed grant it." She did not hear the implied *but.* She had never paid the least attention to any sort of emotion lying behind servants' words.

Her attention was thoroughly on herself. She smoothed her long hair and twitched her grimy over robe into place. She was determined to die with dignity, and smite Imperial Father with her grace and orderly disposition once she lay in her marble coffin.

Bitternail merely waited until she snatched the cup off the salver — though she didn't spill it, knowing that if she didn't drink it, they would force it down her throat. But when she raised the cup to her face, the smell made her recoil. "What is this?" she demanded.

Bitternail's eyes were coldly implacable — as were those of the imperial guards at the door. It was only then that she understood that though Imperial Father might have issued a decree, these underlings had conspired not to obey it. And all-powerful Imperial Father would never know.

"It's *your* poison," Bitternail said.

FORTY-THREE

"EXCELLENT, MY ASSISTANT, EXCELLENT — " Court Artist Yoli began, then his words broke into coughing.

Yskanda patted his back, glanced past the court artist struggling for breath, and scowled. "Sir, you did not drink your medicine."

"Pah," the court artist grumbled. "It tastes like the unwashed loincloth of a demon."

"Court Artist Yoli," Yskanda said inexorably, "the Imperial Physician made me promise to see that you drink your medicine."

"A demon with a scrofulous rotting disease!"

"If you drink it," Yskanda coaxed, "I promise you will have hot Osmanthus cakes. I smelled them baking when I returned from the four virtues lecture."

Court Artist Yoli cocked a wild eyebrow at his assistant. "Did they try to wheedle you into letting them skip to orchid?"

Yskanda was not to be distracted. "They are all beginning with bamboo," he said tranquilly. "As always. And I promised them that diligence will move them the quicker to plum. The medicine, this unworthy person of no talent dares to remind his venerable master exalted beyond human perception — "

"Ayah! You're worse than my old nanny, and *she* ate tigers for breakfast."

" — that it will taste no better cold."

"Teeth and tails!" Court Artist Yoli grumpily slurped down the medicine, gagged loudly, muttering about useless physicians, then smacked the cup on the tray, scowling. "There. See that you don't forget those hot cakes. And bring tea to rid me of that vile taste!"

Yskanda cast a glance at the page, who was hovering wide-eyed—he'd already ducked a thrown cup of medicine once that day. As he'd wiped it up, his eyes had watered from the smell, and he hadn't the heart to be angry with the irascible elder. With a strong sense of gratitude toward Assistant Court Artist Yskanda for thus effecting his escape, he scurried off to fetch the tea and cakes.

The court artist, grumbling mightily, resettled himself as Yskanda glided through the workroom, fetching his senior's favorite brushes and getting him set up. "Lakes and streams, lakes and streams," the court artist muttered. "Rabbit year with water element. At least we don't have to drop all for a grand funeral." He looked up sharply. "You do know that the former First Imperial Princess Manon was forced to take poison last night? Is the subject troubling you? Rumor was fairly consistent that she tried to kill you. I can give you light duties if your heart is sore."

Yskanda had woken to Manon's ghost hovering there in his room, pale of face and clothing, except for her black eyes and her river of pure black hair flowing down to her knees, like shadows against moonlight. "My heart is not sore beyond grieving for any life so ended," he said, avoiding the question about killing entirely.

Yoli studied him from under wild, furrowed brows, then grunted. "Very well, then, it's as well. They say she was carrying on with a low-born criminal, though I don't believe it. Too sharp an eye, that one. A rebellious duke or a prince, now, that I'd believe. It was that way when she was five years old," the court artist muttered as he sifted impatiently through a stack of sketches. "Moon burial," he added—meaning a quiet night-time burial, no parade, and not so much as a paper brass-piece burned to send along with her. But then, as far as he knew, no one had ever come back to complain about their funerary accommodations. "No mourning allowed. Not even her mother there. Very sad."

"Very sad indeed," Yskanda said, retrieving the sketches from an altogether different stack and laying them before the court artist before neatening the first stack and lifting them to their shelf.

He had spent some time reading sutras to the princess's ghost, without knowing if she heard him, or even why he saw ghosts. He would ask Brother Pine at his next visit to the Ghost Moon God's temple, but before then, he would not ignore them in case they did some day talk. They had to need some-thing, or they would not be there, he reasoned; and like anyone else, they could probably use some kindness.

The visit to Brother Pine turned into an interview with the abbot, who questioned him closely about everything that had happened since their last interview. At the end, the old monk fixed Yskanda with a brow-lowered gaze, and then, in the manner of someone scolding an erring puppy, "I strongly suspect that your storm was the result of your stubbornness."

Yskanda stared, appalled. "But my parents — other people —"

"Other people's fates are not your concern. As for your parents, they did not drown, did they? You finally began to do, clumsily, and at great danger to yourself I might add, what you ought to have managed with a little exertion and no further trouble. If you slap the faces of the gods —"

"O venerable one, this ignorant one did not —"

"If you slap the faces of the gods," the abbot intoned on a lower note, and Yskanda shut up, "you will discover what they think of ingratitude. As you did."

Yskanda bowed, thoroughly chastened.

"I admonish you to renew your studies with Brother Pine, and this time, pay attention to what he wishes to teach you, not merely to what you want to learn for your own convenience."

"I shall, O venerable one."

"Good." The abbot's tone lightened slightly. "As for the ghosts, that, too, is a divine matter. There is little we really know about ghosts. They may speak, in the sense that you say you spoke with your sister through the waters, or they may vanish altogether. Your instinct to help them find peace is good. We generally believe that souls still bound to the earthly realm without their bodies have some need, or perhaps a fate, to accomplish. They might even have a task. We cannot know unless they tell us, and even then, who is to say that ghosts are more truthful than the living?"

Yskanda had no answer to that.

"Now. Brother Pine will give you . . ."

Yskanda left with a daunting list of cultivation exercises. He was as self-disciplined as he was stubborn, so over the following day or two, he began working these exercises into his daily routine while doing weaponless Heaven and Earth.

He continued to see ghosts now and then, Manon most often, usually hanging in the air above him. Melonseed only appeared when Yskanda ventured into the upper palace. The two ferrets had vanished, or perhaps he did not see them; others occasionally appeared, probably freshly dead. He found it interesting that many looked young — including Melonseed. Was this how they remembered themselves? Certainly not how he remembered them, the way Ari saw him in the water. He had not been alive when Melonseed was young.

The exercises he practiced soon proved to have an unexpected benefit: he could control his emotions when listening to his mother's dreams. That meant he could resume the water contact with Ari.

Which was good, because just past the turn of the last month of the year Jion summoned him, and said abruptly, "We can drop the pretense of changing hangings in here. My father is promoting me to the heirship on New Year's Two Moons, and I'll need you to take charge of the paintings for the outer chambers." He did not look elated, nor did he frown. "I . . . should we tell Ari? Are you back to contacting her?"

"I will tomorrow morning," Yskanda said, bowing compliance.

Ari always began her mornings by looking into her wash basin. Days had gone by, but she never missed a morning, for which she was rewarded on the second day of the last month. As always she looked into the water, but so many days had passed without her seeing anything but the bottom of the basin, or her own reflection (depending on where their lamp was) that she jumped when Yskanda's face appeared, gazing past her right shoulder.

"Ys—" she yelped, and finished voicelessly, "—skanda. There you are! Are you all right? Is Shig, ah, Jion all right?"

"We are both well," Yskanda replied. "He can't be here, but I'll tell him anything you wish to pass on."

"There's nothing to say. Mother and I work on learning the Cobra Sage ways of Essence, and we are now very far north. They want to stop once more, then the next harbor after that should be where we find the army—and First Brother! At the last stop, there was a lot of news about General Falik, and they mentioned Muin, whose company is doing all the scouting for the general."

"Thank you for telling me. I always pray for him, as well as you, and our parents, but I will add more incense," Yskanda said. "In turn I have news for you. Prince Jion is to be elevated to imperial crown prince on New Year's Two Moons."

Ari felt as if someone had kicked her right in the heart. With an ice-covered boot. But surely Jion would be happy? And everyone would be proud of him? It was certainly better than him being in trouble, so much better. "That is great news," she said, forcing a smile.

Yskanda's voice softened. "Ari, I can hear your emotions."

"Don't tell him!" she responded quickly. "It's just, I feel him being taken away. Which I know is silly. It's not like I 'had' him. I knew . . . ever since those ferrets surrounded him outside Madam Swan's, that . . ." She clamped down hard on her emotions.

"Ari, I can promise his first question when I see him next will be about you. I think also he would be quick to say that nothing has changed between the two of you."

"Maybe," she responded, "but that won't last. If—oh, I need to stop what-iffing. It's so stupid. Father always said not to."

Yskanda's thought was still gentle. "Father told us to stop when we didn't have enough facts. Thinking up possible paths is what strategists do, and you're a strategist. You wouldn't beat me constantly at Circle if you weren't. What-ifs come with strategy. But when you go straight to the possible road with the most lions and knives without any signposts, then you're just hurting yourself."

Ari's throat ached. She tried to stuff that awful feeling back down.

Yskanda went on, "He will be asking for details about you and your quest."

She forced herself to smile, hoping her inward voice sounded more normal. "We're passing more ships going south each day. Packed to the rails. Rich people as well as ones as shabby as I look. There's something we can't figure out—so many of them are wearing red headbands, or white ones. Both, maybe? Armbands, headbands."

"That's interesting," Yskanda said. "And your preparations?"

"As I said, we cultivate Essence, and the imperial guards let me spar with them."

"Ah, the watch bell is already ringing."

Yskanda's voice vanished, and Ari found her mother waiting. "Yskanda's back. He's well, getting ready for the new year." Ari stopped there. She was so uneasy about Jion's pending elevation to crown prince that she couldn't get the words out.

That became the new pattern. Yskanda was not there every day, especially as the month wore on — there was a great deal of preparation for the New Year, and for Jion's coronation as crown prince. Yskanda shared the artistic end of that preparation, describing with pleasure the themes and decorations that the entire artistic population of the palace staff participated in bringing into being. He reported that Jion's spirits seemed to improve day by day, especially since his brother, Second Imperial Prince Vaion, had returned from Benevolent Winds, and Ari was to know that the mines were now strictly inspected, the workers supplied with silk masks to filter the terrible dust, and sturdy boots and gloves. That went for all the imperial mines.

Ari was cheered to hear that. She and Hanu had not been permitted to leave the ship, after that first encounter at Flowering Plum Island. They stayed aboard while others fetched supplies and news. Ferret Bo Ya and Imperial Guard Captain Ha Gar stopped the courier at what they intended to be the last supply a couple of weeks later.

On this stop they asked about the headbands. As they returned to the wharf, leading a couple of flunkeys with a wheelbarrow of supplies, the captain said to the ferret, "Ought we to tell Firebolt about the headbands or not?"

"No," Ferret Ya-Ya said decisively.

"Do you think it will make her arrogant?" the captain asked.

"The opposite," Ya-Ya said. "She already believes she has to defend the defenseless of the world. To discover how many are counting on her Firebolt mask I think will distract her. We want her mind entirely on how to defeat White Dragon."

Captain Ha Gar accepted that as wise.

When they reached the ship, Ari confronted them, but not because of the headbands. "Did you get any army news?" she asked—she did not bring up her brother's name, though she was pretty sure they knew about her relationship with Captain Ryu Muin. But it was always safer to mention no names.

"Troubling," Ha Gar said in his rumbling voice. "Celestial Waters Admiral Lin and Golden Gentian Commander Falik are dealing with the raids, but there are rumors that the Cobra Sages are increasing in number, and preparing to destroy the islands in the north altogether. The initial reports speak of the talisman plinths being destroyed on one island or another, loosing the quakes."

"Destroy them?" Ari asked. "Why?"

But that information had not been passed along. It was clear to Ari that though the imperial forces were well able to deal with the military side of this attack, they had little defense against the Essence attack.

She said, "I can't sense enough while in this ship, or on the water. You know something about affinities, right? Mine is fire. I really, really need to set foot on an island that has hot springs." She looked earnest. "Please. I need to discover what I can, and the only way for me to do that is through fire Essence. Anyplace with a hot springs will do. You can tie me up if you don't trust me. You can come with me. I only need a little time."

The two exchanged a look, and finding no answer in the other, Captain Ha Gar said, "We've an army installation at Ruby Bay a day or so to the north. I've been there, before I transferred to the imperial guard. It's honeycombed with hot springs. I was going to bypass it, as we got supplies here. But we can stop there for a short time." He added roughly, not hiding how uncomfortable he was, "We'll be with you for protection. In case one of those Cobra Sages is lurking around. Not because we think you'll run off."

Ari flushed, looking very much younger than eighteen. "*Thank* you!"

Their auras had been pure green for days. She still did not trust those auras, but certain colors seemed consistent: spring green seemed to be benign. They really wanted her to save the empire from White Dragon. *She* wanted to save the empire!

She did not, as yet, understand that green could also signify regret: the captain and the ferret knew that she was the emperor's bait

FORTY-FOUR

TWO DAYS LATER, ARI woke to the heady sensation of tremendous fire Essence potential, a vast lake of it. She bounded to the deck, doing her breathing as they entered a bay framed by jagged rock glittering in the morning sun. The island was full of wild beauty, but what claimed her attention was her sense of a mighty fire dragon curled up below the ground. While it was not nearly as old or as powerful as the fire dragon sleeping below Mt. Lir on the imperial island, she could already feel the Essence it slumbered in burning through her.

Hanu watched her daughter glow with Essence as they drifted into the bay. All her instincts clamored. She had seen Ari low, and she had seen her working with the single-minded focus on martial arts that characterized Danno. She had yet to see her daughter drawing on potential power. This must be the Alk gift, she thought, elated and also a little fearful, aware that her daughter was growing past Hanu's own knowledge and experience.

For days, as the number of refugee boats increased, she had been struggling within herself. She saw the lingering glances that the imperials sent after Ari, and knew pity and regret when she saw it. Was it right or not to tell Ari and perhaps destroy her confidence, which was tentative enough? All her life, Ari had asked *what-if?* One of the reasons Danno had insisted on including her in the martial arts lessons he gave the boys was so that she would gain the confidence to face a world full of questions that did not always have answers, or right and true resolutions.

"I have to go. Stay here, in case something happens," Ari added under her breath. She shrugged uncomfortably at the resignation, even sorrow in her mother's face. If Mother made a fuss, would they even let her land? She *really* needed to land. "Please don't worry. I'll be very careful climbing. You know I've always been good at climbing. I'll even take my staff to help me up that cliff I can see over there, with the steam rising. And my fan, in case I get overheated."

Hanu made herself nod, and step back, and resume her pose as Essence master. Right now Ari did not need a mother, she needed the reassurance that a teacher could give. "I wish we had more time to dig farther into the Cobra Sage book, but I am confident you have the fundamentals, and of course you have our studies. Go. Do your best."

Her reward was the easing of the tension in Ari's face, and a semblance of her old eager smile.

Captain Ha Gar brought all four imperial guards as they rowed ashore. There were a lot of soldiers and sailors around, but the festival atmosphere that the captain remembered was gone. The pools were famous among the military; from the looks of things, those using them were recovering from wounds.

"How bad is it in the north?" one of the guards asked a sailor waiting for a boat, as the others climbed onto a floating dock.

"It's a hotpot up there," the man said. "Flame mountains without a bridge. Quakes. Raids. Random, completely random."

"Quakes?"

"Bad ones. Geomancers are howling like wolves. Centuries of work, gone. Those blood-snakes are doing something to the old plinths, loosing the quakes."

"What's the use of conquering an island full of rubble?'

"Maybe the demon-eyes eat rubble," the soldier answered, and spat into the water before jumping down into his boat.

Ari's company was grim and silent for a time. Then Captain Ha Gar said, "I might as well go among the wounded here, all fresh from the north, and gather as much first-hand news as I can."

Ari clasped her hands. "A great idea. Please ask if anyone knows where White Dragon can be found."

So far, the reports were consistent that the White Dragon remained at the head of his army, which had taken a foothold on one of the outer islands at the western border, above the important Grand Dragon Passage. There was no reason to suspect that the news would be any different, but in an impending war, no one took any scrap of information for granted. The captain trod off toward the main building, which doubled as an infirmary as well as a waystation.

The four imperial guards followed Ari, who headed up a very steep trail. She relished the sense of the vast lake underneath, but she needed to be able to *see*. The trail very soon narrowed to treacherous twists.

She used her staff to test the dirt for stability as she toiled upward. So out of practice, she thought, disgusted at how quickly she'd begun panting. Until she glanced back, seeing the four strung out along the trail below, their faces crimson. The air was not that hot, so late in the year, but the sun on their armor had to be broiling them alive.

Ari kept climbing, one foot in front of the other, as she let her inner eye scan the light blobs. Clusters, clusters, clusters . . . ah. *There*. All her instincts sharpened to alertness on a glowing coal light, similar to the one that had tried to gut her Essence from within during the fight on Little Otters. This light blob appeared to be higher up, though distance was as always difficult to determine.

Ari stepped near one of the steam vents, then paused, eyes closed, sensing ramified cracks in the living rock, reaching down and down. Essence hummed in these cracks, a dam about to burst . . .

She opened her eyes, breathing fast. The sunlight had turned to glare, and below in the garrison flags fluttered from no palpable wind. A deep rumble of grinding stones froze everyone in atavistic alarm. *Quake coming.*

Ari closed her eyes again. Now the ember sped away, down the other side of the mountain, where it was met by two ordinary light blobs. Ari turned, gazing up at the mountain peak where the ember had been. Then she glanced back at her companions as they toiled the last few paces up the path, looking around warily.

Ari had begun to suspect that her staff, which her mother

said had been worked with Essence from all elements, would respond to her Essence: if it was true the skill for flying was in the person, and not in the thing that helped them balance, then she didn't need Sagacious Blade anymore. Right or wrong?

She let the top of the staff fall to the ground, and put her dusty boot on it. Drawing up Essence into herself, she lifted from within—and her wonderful monk-made staff rose with her a hand's breadth off the ground.

She was right.

She turned to the four. "Sorry," she said contritely. "I really will go after White Dragon, but first I have to stop the quake. I think it'll be a bad one. Then chase that Cobra Sage." As she spoke she rose above them. The staff whipped around and raced skyward so fast she had to narrow her eyes as she sketched the sight-ward talisman over herself.

To the stunned four, she flew up into the sky and winked out. They looked in all directions, but all they saw was a brief blur in the air.

They exchanged glances. "Better go report," one said heavily.

"No one will believe us," another mourned.

Down they headed; Ari had already forgotten them. Everybody knew about the plinths that kept islands stable. Ari hadn't seen any because she had never gone mountain climbing. But she knew where they were likely to be—her inner sense showed her the cracks all through the ground as thin lights, and the plinth where they met, at the highest point. The geomancers always put the plinths in or near these cracks.

There it was, tall as a man, carved from rock that would last centuries, and inscribed with talismans. They had gone dead. She dropped down as fast as a hawk stooping. She sensed the ground about to let go several hundred years of stabilizing, which would surely kill everyone on the island. She could feel the horses in the garrison panicking . . .

She shook free of the light blobs, and studied the plinth. "Thank you Mother," she whispered as her eyes ran over the talisman, the key fire and earth lines obliterated.

Using her fan, she aimed hot fire at the rock, and fought a sneeze as the lines that the Cobra Sage had destroyed recurved into the plinth. Was it right? Was it enough? Had she got it in time? She sensed the dragon down below, and instinctively shared the calming thoughts that she had learned to give the

animals in Master Ki's Valley, and all the birds when she did
Tree. The dragon's own thought stirred, strange and
incomprehensible, sensation rather than words: it was not time,
rest, rest.

The dragon resumed its slumber, and the shaking settled,
except for tiny rocks bouncing down here and there.

Ari opened her eyes. The talisman in the plinth glowed
reassuringly. One breath, two, to make sure she was steady.
Then she looked around for that Cobra Sage — ahhhh!

On the far side of the mountain a trail led downwards. She
caught sight of three figures hurrying toward a tiny inlet where
a sharp-prowed single-masted boat rocked. It had a slack sail
that looked like it was made of hemp, with no lacquer to protect
it from the elements. Ari swooped down, examining the three
Westerners as they jumped into a rowboat and plied the
paddles the short distance to the boat.

On board, two sailors. Five altogether, all with soot-black
hair, much like people of home. Ari shut her eyes to make sure,
but that middle one was definitely the ember-glowing blob
light. So far, no one had looked upward. She circled once more,
considering her strategy. No weapons in sight, but that didn't
mean they didn't have swords and knives and bows hidden
around the deck. Five against one, but she had the element of
surprise.

Make it count, she said to herself, and swooped down, her
fan at the ready.

The Cobra Sage, a tall, thin woman around Lie Tenek's age,
was turning toward one of the sailors when she blinked,
gasped, and brought her hands up. Before she could deploy one
of those horrible Essence-eating talismans Ari landed almost on
the woman's toes and snapped the fan into the Cobra Sage's
heart acupoint.

The Cobra Sage froze, her eyes wide with shock.

Ari kicked the end of the staff up to her hand and swung it
with a deep voom, shooting a burst of fire to drive back the two
husky youths who accompanied the Cobra Sage. One had
pulled a blade with a wicked curve. He came at Ari with a lunge
and swing. Three fast moves and the sword went flying over
the rail, to land with a splash. A hard poke in the solar plexus
to the other youth trying to come up from behind, and he
thumped to the deck, gasping for breath.

The swordless one put up his hands. Behind him, the sailors

stood, one frozen, the other reaching for —

Ari didn't give her a chance to grab anything. She sent a thin bolt of fire, driving the sailor back against the rail. Then she used her staff and her fan to knock them down and freeze them long enough for her to find some rope and truss them all up, except the Cobra Sage.

Ari studied the diamond tattoo on her forehead, then — mindful of what her mother had taught her — raised her hands. They glowed green as she sketched the talisman in the air. Sweat broke out on the Cobra Sage's forehead as she struggled in futility against her immobile body. Then the reddish Essence glow in the tattoo died out. The Cobra Sage's power was broken. The woman blinked, her blue eyes tearing.

Ari looked away from the forlorn expression in those weird blue eyes, and leaned against the rail. The struggle against the worming, wiggling talisman had been more tiring than the short fight. "I don't suppose any of you speak my tongue," she said with a sigh. Now what to do?

She jumped when the boy who'd picked up the curved sword said in perfect common tongue, "That depends." His accent was even southern, like Ari's own!

"On?"

She walked over to where he sat on the deck and crouched down to face him. She'd tied his wrists behind him. His fists bunched as he pulled at the knots, then he looked up. He had a tattoo on his forehead, but it looked like a character.

"Are you a Cobra Sage?" Ari asked.

"No."

"But you have one of their tattoos."

"Slave mark." He bit the words out.

Ari grimaced. She remembered what Mother had told her about the workers forced to labor for Master Night at Kanda Sutra, and said, "Are there blood bindings in that?"

His lips compressed, then he said, "Yes." And, "I must obey."

Were his words constrained as well as his actions? Rather than asking, Ari extended her palm. Oh, yes. She felt/saw the same ugly blood red worm wriggling over, or in, the tattoo, and made the sign that Mother had taught her. The worm fought, Ari's hand glowed — and the worm faded to mere ink marks in the boy's skin.

"It's gone," she said.

The boy gave her a look of disbelief, yanked once against the ropes, which held — she still remembered lessons from her Loyalty days. Then the boy stiffened, and said, "No."

He waited, tense all over as if bracing for a blow. But nothing happened, other than the boat rocking gently on the water. He hissed out a breath, then said, "I won't obey." And, louder, "I will run away!"

When nothing happened, he turned wondering eyes to Ari. "What you did, it's true?"

"I told you," Ari said. "I guess I haven't given you any reason to believe me. But I did break it. Her power is also gone. She still has all her knowledge, but at least she can't kill you with a word."

The boy sagged, his gaze moving along the rail as if he'd never seen the ship before. Ari suspected she was seeing the recovery from shock. Or maybe it was what happened when everything in the world suddenly changed.

His gaze rested on the blood mage. "She's not as bad as some. She's been picking islands without people, or when they have people, military ones. But she has to unleash the bindings on one island a day, or *He* will poison her blood. And ours."

"He being—"

"Don't speak the name." The boy looked around fearfully at the clear sky and the blue water.

"I don't think he can get at you now. But I can't prove that," Ari said. "The Cobra Sages have to ruin the stability plinths of an island every day?"

"That is the orders," he said.

Ari frowned. "Why? It seems a really stupid way to invade an empire, reducing it to rubble."

The boy shook his head. "All I know is what we are told to do. We protect our Sage, and go where she tells us to go."

"Where is . . . that person?"

The boy slowly shook his head. "The likes of us are never told."

Ari frowned. She had a lot more questions, but it didn't seem he was the one to ask. "You speak our language," she said. "And your eyes are brown."

"My family was taken in a raid when I was small. They separated us, put the slave marks on us, and put us to work. I have not seen my family since." He looked away, then back. "I was put on this team because I speak the language."

Saying she was sorry seemed inadequate. Ari got to her feet. "She will unfreeze by the time the sun comes up. Between now and then, run or stay, whatever you need to do." She spotted the knife the sailor had been going for, dropped it next to his knee, then hefted her staff.

"Wait! Who are you?"

She hesitated, remembered that she was supposed to be drawing attention, and said, "Firebolt. I wish you luck and a better life." She moved aft, traced her sight warding talisman on her and took to the air.

She flew up and over the peninsula, peering down into the main harbor where people ran around cleaning up after the quake. She spotted the courier ship with its tiger banner, and her mother on deck. She was severely tempted to fly down there and at least wave—oh, and once again, here she was without her pack! But instead she circled around, deciding reluctantly to go. Once Yskanda looked for her in water again, she would tell him to get word to Mother in dreams.

Right now, she needed to get better information. Why not start with Ten Leopards, which shouldn't be all that far away?

FORTY-FIVE

ARI HAD SEEN ON the map that Ten Leopards was close, but she still didn't trust her ability to translate map drawings into travel time; uppermost in mind was that long, toiling flight nearly a year ago, when she tried to get to Green Jade to warn Falik and was nearly too late.

Exhilarating, how fast the wind currents carried her as two island clusters slid below, wooded mountainsides snow-fleeced, and distant islands' blue-white folds gleaming under a wreath of vapor in the clear winter sky. So far, no islands reduced to rubble, though she knew they were there. The boats and ships escaping southward had been silent, frightened testimony to that.

Before the day ended, she thought she recognized Ten Leopards. Blinked. Ayah, it really was!

The sun was setting beyond the jagged western ridge when she circled down toward the Ki clan manor. She spotted two armed patrols, alert and ready for anything—except looking up. Before she landed, she recollected that the Shadow Panthers had attacked this island in looking for her, so it was a wistful, deeply sorry figure who presented herself at the front gate, with her most formal bow.

Thoroughly expecting to be booted right back out again, she began as formal an apology as she could make, to find herself grabbed and drawn into a tight hug by First Aunt, after which she was passed from arms to arms like a bolster, until she fetched up, facing First Uncle.

Who then bowed low, saying, "You saved my children. I owe you a life debt."

Whereupon the two children appeared and dropped to their knees before Ari, foreheads to the ground.

"No, no," Ari exclaimed, her cheeks burning as she pulled them to their feet. "I don't — you don't — they attacked, looking for me — it's all my fault —"

"It's my fault," First Uncle said earnestly. "We were too few to rescue you, and they had you aboard a ship before we could —"

"It's the fault of those vermin," First Aunt said crisply. "And though they hurt us, there's a sizable number of them buried in the shingle off Demon Mountain, their souls bowing down to the King of Hell right now. Come, tell us your news, and see who is here!"

They drew her inside the warm general room she remembered so well. She breathed in the delicious smells of black sesame sauce and braised pepper-fish, then jolted to a stop when Lie Tenek rose from a cushion, followed by . . . "Rooster?"

Rooster grinned, looking like a little boy who'd just discovered fireworks, in spite of his huge size. "Innkeeper Bing sent us north to find you! And here you are!"

No wonder the room was so crowded. Not only were most of the Ki clan there, but Redbark as well. And who were these vaguely familiar faces?

Another huge young man blushed as he said, "We met. On the boat. We left you off here. My friends and I, we've tried to do what you said. Fighting for justice. But then these quakes started, and everyone was fleeing the Westerners, and we thought, me and my friends here, we thought we'd look for Redbark, and I remembered you getting off the ship here . . ." He ran out of breath.

"I remember," Ari said. Though it seemed a hundred years ago — she did remember the three rowdies aboard the ship before she went up into the mountains with Master Ki.

"Ah, are Petal and Matu well?"

"Yes," Lie Tenek spoke up. "As Rooster said, Petal sent us. Matu and his father have organized the waiters, other volunteers along our end of the street, and the colony of weavers beyond the alley, in case the garrison is holding the harbor, or chasing Westerners in the mountains."

"Oh, that's good." Ari looked around at the expectant faces, and saw that they were waiting. For?

"You were taken by the imperials," First Uncle said. "Then we heard that they'd sent you north against the White Dragon. What can you tell us?"

"Not a lot. Yet," she said. "But I've got a plan. It has to do with those Cobra Sages causing the quakes. If you are with me, we'll take care of them first—"

The rest of what she was going to say got lost in a resounding cheer.

When they quieted, as she had expected, the entire family volunteered. She explained what she had discovered about the Cobra Sages and the binding talismans on the plinths. "I expect the more dangerous Cobra Sages are with the army, and of course the worst one will be with White Dragon. These Cobra Sages destroying the stability plinths seem to be apprentices and low rank. They are forced to attack an island a day. They each have two protectors, most likely slaves, so all three will need the binding tattoos broken. I am going to go up to Master Ki's Valley and make up the means—I figured it out while coming here," she said. "While I'm gone, divide up into teams of at least three."

"That's who you're taking on? White Dragon?" Rooster asked. "Alone?"

"I'll be heading to the army headquarters," Ari said. "If they have some geomancers or Essence experts of some kind who can help, great! If not, ayah, my mother and I practiced for this. Don't worry about me, just find those Cobra Sages and defang their attack on our island plinths. The sooner the better." She was proud of that "defang." Wasn't that poetic wit? As no one seemed to notice, she guessed not, and sighed inwardly; even if a miracle happened, she would never fit among Jion's court people with their silk-embroidery manners and debates in poetic fashion. Did she even want to fit in? What if . . .

Stop what-iffing, she scolded herself. There's plenty of work to be done first.

They shared a meal, over which the Kis insisted Ari tell the story of Master Night's defeat and what had happened to her in the imperial city. She described the fight at Little Otters, pausing to enumerate as many moves as she could recollect, to deep appreciation by all the martial artists there.

After that, she summed up her imprisonment in two sentences. By then she'd finished her dinner, and — pretending not to see the questions still in faces around her — asked the eldest if she could beg for incense, as she meant to fly to Master Ki's valley before it got too dark.

That ended the subject, and the dinner.

She borrowed a thick quilt and gratefully accepted some food to take with her, then she flew up and away. Darkness was falling fast when she reached Master Ki's valley.

Everything was exactly as Waoji Lion's Mane had said. Master Ki had been buried on the cliff where both sunrise and sunset could be seen. She knelt in the fresh snow, used her Essence to light the incense, placed half of her food out as an offering, and bowed deeply three times.

She said the soul sutras that she had been taught as a child, because it seemed right, but she could feel in the deep peace that all was as it should be.

She sat back on her heels, looking up past the wood monument Waoji Lion's Mane had carved. "Master, I learned so much from you, and I am so grateful. But I wish we could have had more time. Why did you send me away? There is so, so much more for me to learn."

Was that complaining?

She backtracked hastily, hands clasped in a bow. "Though you taught me great things! Like flying! That is, you told me about it, and I understand it now. I think you could say that Sagacious Blade taught me. But when the sword went to Jion like that, ayah, I sent it, it's true, but whether the sword thought that it was a gift the way you gave it to me, or not, I think it wants to be with him. Air to air. It taught me much, too, but I actually fly better on my staff. Is that real, or just my being practiced? But oh, Master Ki, I wish, I do wish I had not been so slow or stupid. I really, really could use the window you spoke of."

Door.

"You said window, then you said it is different for everyone, and sometimes a metaphor and sometimes real, and—" She stopped. Had she heard that?

Door . . . The word was spoke softly next to her ear, but no one was there. No lips to speak, lungs to breathe the air for speaking; she was alone there in the valley, except for the whisper of wings. She turned her head, but all she caught was a brief glimpse of tail feathers beyond the snow-laden tree.

"Door?" she said the word aloud. "Yaso, was that you?"

From the other side of the tree a great white crane drifted down and down. Before it landed it blurred and lengthened, and Yaso stood before her, barefoot in the snow, dressed in a simple white robe. "You have done well," Yaso said, large golden eyes catching the wintry light. "Master Ki gave you the foundations, as much as he could before his time ended."

"Why did it have to end?" Ari sighed.

"I can aid, and I can mend, but I cannot change things," said Yaso. "That you must do."

She understood—or thought she understood, though her mind was, as usual, full of questions that begat questions. She shut those away, and said, "Door? That was you, was it not?"

"I know that blade of old," Yaso said. "Air with any of the other affinities except metal can reach between specific locations when you inscribe a door. But be cautious, for the space between is—"

Yaso stopped, looking sharply northward. "Ayah!" The word turned into a long cry as Yaso's shape blurred. Whap, whap, two beats of the great wings and the white crane rose rapidly, vanishing over the hilltop.

Silence. Quiet.

Ari shut her eyes, reaching—and found herself high above a dark plane, watching clusters of tiny winking light blobs. Some were the color of embers, moving steadily, but dominating all, a great orange glow, like a moon, straight north. When she turned that way the moon abruptly grew, glowing blood red.

Then came the disturbing thought that maybe it could see her?

Her eyes snapped open. Physical senses returned: the soft chuff of a clump of snow falling from a tree to the ground; the smell of wet cloth; cold. She became aware that her knees were icy-wet, and straightened up. A last bow, then she leaped lightly down to the clearing beside the waterfall where she and the hermit had practiced martial arts nearly every day.

She picked up staff and carryall and entered the partial cave, partial cottage that had been home for a year. It was colder than ice, but she warmed herself up by sweeping out the detritus of a year, and then used her Essence to light a fire in the fireplace. She toasted the buns the aunties had wrapped for her, ate them, and then slipped out to look out at the peaceful stars, the silhouette of the sacred tree etched against the sky.

"I do not want to break your branches," she said. "Come morning I'll hunt around for dropped twigs."

She turned back inside, spread the quilt out on the floor next to the fire pit, and curled up.

She had left the door open so she could look out at the night sky, so clear and bright with the two moons moving ever closer. But look, luminous and soft, the clouds sailed in, rank on rank. Was a storm coming?

She ought to rise, but it was so cold out, and she was cozy and warm. Also, the wind seemed to be from the opposite direction—no gusts blasted in to stir and scatter her fire.

The wind rose, singing among the peaks. Birds winged and darted among the receding infinity of clouds as a magnificent and unmeasured melody unfurled in the air. The wind toyed with sparse grasses and the last withered leaves before rising, and rising again, rattling twigs and branches, rustling dry leaves, and thrumming the rocky spires until everything resounded in a wild and pervading splendor.

All night the winds spun out their song, and Ari, waking from time to time, heard the storm as nature's own sutra until the last stars fled, the clouds running after, leaving the soft light of dawn to suffuse the little valley in a hushed radiance that she remembered well.

How could she have diminished this sight to everyday expectation? Is taking beauty for granted a sin, she wanted to ask Master Ki, but he was not here, his mat still sitting on the other side of the fire, cold and dusty. She spoke aloud to dispel the sense of grief she could feel closing cold fingers around her heart: "Is it a sin or a privilege?"

She knew the answer—she could hear his voice as if he spoke, "It is a blessing, my young student."

She looked out the door, tears stinging her eyes: Master Ki felt so close, and yet far beyond her reach.

Up on the cliff above, a herd of deer lifted their antlers simultaneously, then peacefully returned to nosing the ground. When Ari ventured outside, she found snow softening the contours, and piled up against rocks and crannies. But strewn all across the pure whiteness, the sacred tree had shed twigs.

Her heart brimming with gratitude, Ari gathered these, and

sat cross-legged inside the little hut to infuse each twig with Essence.

It took most of the day. The sun had finished its arc and rested a finger's breadth above the white-crowned western peaks when she finished, carefully bundled her twigs in her borrowed carryall, and looked around more slowly, lingering long enough to impress the peaceful valley on her memory.

Someday, she vowed, I will return.

She fetched her staff, by now so practiced she had merely to drop it, hop on, and she sailed up and out over the cliffs and chasms, to plunge in an exhilarating drop toward the lake below. The descent that took days on foot was a matter of an hour, and she spotted the welcome glow of lights along the opposite lake shore when both moons had begun their night's rise toward one another.

New Year's was nigh, when the two moons would bridge.

When she landed, she discovered the Ki clan and Redbark waiting with a splendid meal, all day in preparation. From the silence, she understood that a ritual was nigh. They shared that meal, and then the younger generation brought out little lotus leaf boats that they had made, as the elders fixed a tiny candle in each.

Then, each person carried the little light, which glowed through the upturned lotus leaves, to the quiet waters of the lake, and set it down, whispering a prayer, or a wish, or a sutra — whatever lay topmost in their heart.

When at last the little lights floated out onto the water, a river of golden stars, the people withdrew to get their twigs along with Ari's instructions. She had kept it simple; though many had never seen the plinths, everybody knew of them. She demonstrated, first how to restore the bindings on the plinths, and then how to break the blood bindings on the tattoos. Everyone practiced once or twice, then carefully stowed the twigs in their packs.

Meanwhile, the two Ki elders had set up a brazier in the central hall. One by one they stepped over it to ward evil, then picked up their travel things, and headed down the well-known slope, to disperse under cover of night.

FORTY-SIX

DANNO REACHED THE CAPITAL by working as a hired hand aboard the supply ship that regularly plied between the naval island and the capital. Before it reached the bay they were each issued a wooden token to identify themselves as laborers. The moment they stepped on the wharf imperial guards came forward to check each token, then they were pointed toward the boxes and barrels piled on the dock to be carried out to the fleet. He worked alongside Waoji Lion's Mane; during all the back-and-forth he slipped away unnoticed.

Not much had changed, he soon discovered. He spent two days reacquainting himself with the capital and the outer reaches of the palace where he had spent his childhood. Before making a decision about his next step, he wanted to see for himself how Yskanda was doing.

Before he came up with a plan for getting into the palace, Yskanda appeared himself, going to and from the Ghost Moon temple. Danno resisted the temptation to slip in and greet Yskanda. Much as he wanted to, he had to wait. Security was far too tight. There was a pair of shadows tracking Yskanda, but these did not harass or bully him. Yskanda might even be unaware of them. He himself looked well, he was dressed well, and carried himself the way a young man does who is satisfied with his place in life.

All these signs enabled Danno to leave Yskanda undisturbed for now. When Yskanda departed from the temple, Danno fell in behind the ferret on outer perimeter. Twenty . . . thirty . . . fifty steps, and the shadow slipped between buildings: he'd been detected.

Not bad at all. Danno drifted up, and when he reached the alley opening, he stopped a step away from entering and said softly, "I want to meet Chief Fai."

A few heartbeats of silence, and the expected ambush slipped out — a young man in black, no older than Yskanda. "Who wants him?"

"Chief Fai knows me. Tell him to meet me at the lower wharf, sunrise." Good sight, people around, no violence expected.

A short nod, the ferret vanished into the murk with a rustle of clothes, and the next morning, Danno sat on the wharf used by local fisher folk, some of whom came and went with fishing gear and nets of catch. He had two lines of retreat, including into the water — the cold water of winter, if he had to.

'Chief Fai' was actually Grandfather Fai, chief in Danno's day. After hearing the description of the man who had approached the ferret, and where, the two Fais had discussed the situation. Timing could not be worse, with Ris Jun loose. It was possible that Danno was tied up with Ris Jun, but it was also possible he was really there to see his boy, and maybe even the girl, if he thought she was still in the prison.

After discussion, it was Grandfather Fai who walked along the wharf, dodging carts of catch, a fishing pole resting on his shoulder. Fai Anbai, as well as a team of the best, had taken up stations high and low, from where they could see and not be seen.

"It is you, Guardsman Danno," Grandfather Fai exclaimed.

Danno sat on a barrel, hands propped on his knees, sword resting at his feet, wrapped like a fishing pole. "Chief Fai."

"Actually my son is now chief. But I'll answer to that for now. I assume you are here to see Assistant Court Artist Afan Yskanda? Why did you want to talk to me?"

"Because you're on high alert. I realize the war is in the north, but it seems you're expecting trouble. If there is any way to help protect my boy, who doesn't know one end of a sword from the other, I'm willing."

Grandfather Fai wanted to see his son's face, but he resisted the temptation to give away the position of his defensive backup. After all, Danno might have his own backup, though they had spotted no suspicious persons.

"You could let me guard him," Danno said. "I will try anyway, if I see trouble coming."

Grandfather Fai stared down at the warped boards as gulls mewed and fishers chattered, their breath clouding. He finally lifted his head and came at the next set of questions sideways. "Ever met anyone called Tek Banu?"

"I remember that name . . ." Danno's chin lifted. "Dead. You sent her after me?"

"Someone else did." The briefest hand clasp toward the palace.

"Ah. Thought so."

"I take it you killed her?"

"Wife did. She'd kneecapped me. Still can't run worth a demon's fart."

"Your wife — Alk Hanu?"

"Yes. Tek Banu was going on about how the trip home would be filled with torture, and Hanu had had enough. Would have left her alone except for that."

"And followed her back here, yes," Grandfather Fai said, eyeing the tattoo on Danno's neck, clear in the morning light. Ah, but that was no panther. It was a chimera.

"Ayah, we were coming anyway, to see our boy. Got sidetracked by a man calling himself Master Night."

Now the chimera made sense. "So that *was* you cleaning up his island! The description sounded like."

"Yes. Then headed here."

Grandfather Fai wavered for about a heartbeat; though many things could have changed in more than thirty years, his instinct was that Danno was the same in essence. He said, "There's an inn over that way, which serves excellent tea. Let's talk."

Captain Ryu Muin was a silver panther captain, with six ranks above him and only two below, but by the end of the eleventh month, he and his company had won such respect that even the newly arrived Dragon Claw Army, notorious for looking down on everyone else in the military world, got out of the way when he'd return from a mission, covered in dirt to those thundercloud eyebrows, often with bandages tied around a limb here and there, to report—and to find out the news.

No one knew why he was so adamant about the news, though Trickle, his company's quartermaster, said he wanted to hear about Firebolt. But Golden Gentian General Falik had issued orders to the effect that when Captain Ryu returned from missions and asked, he was to have.

After which he'd march out of the command tent as grim as before, get cleaned up, and rejoin his company. The next day, if he was not out scouting again, he'd be in the clearing conducting his own particular morning drills—which were the toughest of any service. Though the Dragon Claw Army preferred heavy weapons, the more far-seeing among them appreciated speed as well as strength, and Captain Ryu was superlatively skilled at both.

He was also quiet-spoken, willing to teach anything he was asked, and preferred to take his meals with his company, sitting among them and eating out of wooden bowls, rather than retreating to the officers' tents to eat off the porcelain that the orderlies carried from place to place.

Though the best scouts from all three branches of the military had been sent north, it was Captain Ryu who had located the Westerners' principal base. That was the last bit of information needed. Now the empire's combined forced intended to drive the Westerners from the strait that they had been advancing down with combined military and Essence attacks.

The commanders went into the command tent to gather around the great table map made of dirt, clay, and moss, with silver sand between the mounts of islands, shaped to represent the Grand Dragon Passage.

Muin went to get a covered cup of strong, hot tea, and found himself joined by a familiar face. "Yulin Pel?" The words escaped him as he tightened all over.

Yulin had been promoted to a company captain, too. His features were the same, but different in a way Muin couldn't characterize, other than older. "Do I know you?"

Muin did not know how to respond to that. "Loyalty Fortress?"

Yulin waved one gauntleted hand. "I don't remember a lot there—it's all pretty much a blur. Before I left, an ice storm threw me off a horse onto my head. All I remember is waking up to a pair of frog eyes in a moon face." Yulin looked closer. "You're that Ryu? I remember a Ryu. Brother, too." But he said it without any emotion.

A short laugh escaped Muin. "The moon face sounds like Yaso."

"Yaso?"

"My, ah, brother's orderly."

Yulin lifted a shoulder. "Bandaged my head. I was transferred soon after."

Muin stared in amazement, then cautiously nodded; he remembered Yulin had been different after the accident in which the fourth years were overtaken by a sudden snowstorm while out in the field. Muin never did see what happened, only that Yulin came back with a bandaged head. "Weed?" he asked, naming Yulin's orderly, who had been even more vindictive than Yulin—and sneakier.

"Cashiered long ago," Yulin said, again without any emotion. "Runs a gambling establishment off Ocean's Peace Island, last I heard." His countenance, so well-remembered, conveyed an air of question, as in why Muin would even ask, but before this awkward conversation could go further, another of the Dragon Claw captains ranged up alongside them.

As he bent to pour tea for himself, he said over his shoulder, "Tell Ryu here what you reported in the tent."

Another slight shrug, then Yulin turned to Ryu. "We threw off a sneak attack down south at Dog Leg. In the process of questioning, we found out that the Westerners are getting desperate. Moved their attack on the Grand Dragon Passage to three days from now."

"Right on New Year's," Muin commented. "And?"

"This is rumor only, no sightings," Yulin said. "But Firebolt, the martial artist everyone's been talking about, has—somehow—been deploying Redbark Sect to take out the Cobra Sages. The quake attacks have nearly stopped."

"Which is why we are no longer hunting Cobra Sages," said the other Dragon Claw captain, a burly young man with one ear bandaged, and an old sword cut along his jaw. "Not that we had much luck. The powerful ones have ways of getting around—it's said they ride demons."

At that moment Golden Gentian General Falik came to the door of the command tent to address the captains gathered around the fire. "We have conferred, and we are all in agreement, it is time to clear the strait. Attack before they're ready. Ryu!"

Muin dropped to one knee, saluting. "Sir?"

"We'll use your favorite plan, The Host Becomes the Guest." Falik's wintry smile flickered. "But this plan is for the navy, mostly, with Eagle Commander Shan's companies reinforcing. You will be taking out the White Dragon himself. And his headquarters. Yulin there will join forces with you."

All this news assimilated in Muin's mind, topmost the immense relief that if all that was true about Firebolt, it meant his sister had survived her imprisonment. She was still alive — and apparently free. The rumor from down south must be true, then, the emperor had released her to send her against the enemy.

Muin now had to get there first, for he was not leaving White Dragon to his little sister. As his orders registered, he could not prevent a broad smile, and those looking on were astonished to see his delight at the prospect of taking on the mysterious and deadly White Dragon directly.

Falik waved toward the tent doors. "Soon as this snow stops, you can depart."

"Sir, with respect, the weather is great." At that, Muin noticed the snowflakes falling a little faster. As the gathered captains laughed, he added, reddening, "Ah, snow hides prints. Yulin, if you're in agreement, we'll depart as soon as we get our weapons together."

"Ready when you are." He was, and he wasn't, the old Yulin. The shrug was familiar, the bravado, but the suspicious, glowering wrath was completely missing.

A short time later, both companies stood in orderly lines. Their respective commanders gave them the signal to depart.

Muin led the way to the narrow three-man rowboats they would use to thread a treacherous passage between a pair of islands; they couldn't use regular ships. Muin and his company had spotted all the Westerner lookout posts. They'd see any ship coming up the wider passage on the south side.

The north side was even colder, the shoreline on both sides heavily rimed with ice. They were all bundled up to the nose, though the hard work of paddling warmed them somewhat. Once they beached the craft and took the time to cut and hide them with brush, they faced a long climb over rocky hillsides made treacherous with icy patches. Muin's company had learned to follow Muin, who was the most surefooted among them. He could always sense ice — he could smell it, though he was hard put to explain the scent.

"It's just different," he said — having no idea that he, like his father, had a small but well-developed earth affinity.

He found a narrow goat path through treacherous rocky upthrusts that the Westerners had totally overlooked in their initial survey of the island once they'd conquered it. The locals who had managed to escape the general slaughter had left no signs of their escape routes, one of which was this path that cut straight through to overlook the plateau on which an old fortress that had also served as a trading post, was built.

It took most of a day to thread their way upward until they emerged on a rocky palisade above the half-wooden, half-stone fortress that the Westerners had taken.

Yulin duck-walked up to Muin, who scanned the scene through the cover of a scrubby plant that grew in the cracks between rocks. For a short time, they assessed the half-timber, half-stone fortress with its huge timber tower above the gate, then counted the sentries walking the wall back and forth.

Presently Yulin said, "How do you know White Dragon is here?"

"All their couriers, land and sea, have been reporting here. The triple ring of guards." And a sulphureous not-quite-reek, quite strong. "Saw him, the last day. Could only be him. Everyone dropped to a knee, even their two commanders."

"What did he look like?" Yulin asked as he mentally assessed the structure.

"Don't know. Wore a cloak and hood. Gray made him hard to see from this distance, against the stone and the snow. But he looked around once, and I swear to you on my ancestors' graves that I saw two red glowing eyes in that hood. Just like coals. That's when we backed up and returned to report."

Yulin's mouth twisted in uncomfortable disbelief, but he didn't argue. "I guess we'll find out if that's some sort of Essence trick to put fear in his people."

Muin grunted, and they crawled back to the ravine they had made into a temporary camp. Here they could get a meal and wait for nightfall. Muin saw that their companies, while cooperating as commanded, had separated by instinct or habit into two separate groups. He knew they needed to mix better so that there was a better chance of covering one another in the heat of battle.

He had to begin. He hunkered down next to Yulin, set his dish on his knee, and said, "What was it like, being recruited into the Dragon Claw Army? I hear it's much tougher than what we got at Loyalty."

Yulin grunted, and up came the shoulder. "We were taken on a ship to an island. All during the journey, they kept making us repeat slogans. You know the kind of thing, meant to make you tougher, never fall back a step, stay in line, obey orders instantly. Then they taught us marching songs. Same thing. But when we got to the harbor, we were told carts would be coming to take us up to the plateau where the training camp is. We could see the palisades. No sign of any camp. Hours passed. We'd been left with a barrel of water. Nothing else."

"Some wanted to forage for food," put in one of the Dragon Claw men. Muin noticed that Yulin didn't land on him for speaking out of turn.

"Right. Others argued that we had been ordered to stay put. This was probably a test, and breaking orders would get us punished. We heard a lot about punishment, coming over."

"Then there was the attack," another put in.

"At first we thought it was brigands. We had no weapons, of course. They surrounded us. Some of us fought. Got smashed down pretty efficiently. Tied up, left in a barn. We could hear shouting and battle in the distance," Yulin said. "We decided to make a break for it. Did."

"We didn't get far," the second man said, and there was subdued laughter.

Yulin shrugged again. "Turned out it was an exercise. And test. Those who fought got put in the training right away. Those who stayed put got put in supply and barns. It got tougher from there."

Then, to Muin's surprise, he said, "Sunset is still an hour off. How about giving us the tale of what happened at Green Jade?"

Muin groaned. Trickle cheerily said, "Why, I'd be happy to."

When that was done, here came the questions about Firebolt, which kept Muin silent. Trickle fended those off with the ease of the ignorant, for Muin had not told anyone about his sister's identity — and General Falik had said nothing to their people, but he had passed that order about sharing any news concerning Firebolt.

Muin said, "Dark is falling. Shall we go over the plan one last time?"

They were outnumbered roughly two to one. Now that Yulin had seen the fortress, he offered his ideas, and both companies put together the means while they waited for darkness.

Snowflakes still drifted down from a flat dark sky that hid both rising moons as the companies moved into position. Then Muin's company stood by as the Dragon Claws assembled and set candles inside the sky lamps each had brought in his pack. The sides of the lamps had been painted a flat black to hide the candlelight within, though some glow escaped directly overhead. The glow would not be seen by those directly underneath—the most vulnerable time was when they were released, before they climbed into the sky. Each lamp then got a bag of oil suspended.

The lamp teams moved along the rocks until they found the most favorable spot windwise and released a set. The lamps floated skyward, up over the rocks and drifted over the gully toward the fortress. From the rocks nearest the gate tower, Muin and Yulin watched, squinting to track those faint glows.

They waited as the lamps bobbed gently, rising toward the low clouds. Two, three lamps floated off too far from the gate tower, the rest even farther. The release team clambered over treacherous rocks and released another group. More lamps floated over the gulley between the palisade and the fortress's hill, then the signaler from the release team held up a round fan, white side toward them: it was right over the tower.

"There," Muin breathed. "Perfect. You'll take the shot?"

Yulin hesitated only a heartbeat, then said, "Where's Bi Eagle-Eye?"

"Right here, Captain."

Eagle-Eye perched on a flat rock, and another man lit the thin strip of oiled string around the arrowhead. When the flame took, Eagle-Eye lined up his shot, the bow creaked, and spang!

The arrow hissed across the intervening space—and smacked into the oil bag, which burst into liquid flame that fell straight down onto the wooden tower.

"Heh," Muin exclaimed. "Happy New Year!"

"My favorite kind of fireworks," Yulin agreed, and, "Shoot!"

Spang! Spang! Now all the best shots loosed arrows, most

bursting the oil bags. The alarm went up, but the enemy was now divided between readying for attack and fighting the oil fires that broke out all over the upper structure of the fortress.

Yulin nodded to his signaler, who raised his fan, turned it in a circle then brought it sharply down. The Dragon Claws ran down howling, as Muin led his men around to the other side of the fortress, slapping together sectioned ladders.

The Dragon Claws, with their eerie ululations, kept the Westerners so busy that Muin and his hand-picked team of five could get over the wall and make their way inside the main building. They slipped inside as Dragon Claws poured over the wall, dodging enemies in the billowing smoke.

Muin ran from room to room, trying to locate the source of that weird stench, until he fetched up in the doorway to a chamber hung all over with long strips of paper scribbled over with talismans. He knew Essence paper from childhood, his mother having using these precious papers once or twice. But the stink of blood had never risen from hers.

He stood poised on the threshold, staring into the empty room.

"Need backup—what's that?" Yulin appeared, spattered with blood. He stared at the talismans festooned around the room and began to step forward.

"Don't," Muin said, shifting from foot to foot. That dead feeling beneath his heels might only be the result of sitting in the cold for a day or two, but . . . "I think we're looking at a trap."

"You mean he isn't here? Was he ever here?"

"Ayah, I think he's the only one who could have done this."

Yulin grunted, unslung his bow, lined up an arrow. The bow creaked. He shot.

Before the arrow reached the talisman he'd aimed at, it burst into greenish flame, then the entire room erupted in a ferocious firestorm, knocking the two back. "Whoever did that has a lot of Essence power," Yulin said as he picked himself up.

That, Muin was sure, was meant for Firebolt. "Let's get out of there," Muin said.

They fought their way out, leaving behind a smoking ruin, the Tiger Claws as well as Trickle having raided the enemy supplies for the return trip. It took another day and a half to backtrack to their headquarters. Muin and Yulin went to report their failure to take the fortress or to find White Dragon. Muin finished, "He must have sailed with the fleet to command the taking of the strait."

General Falik turned to Celestial Waters Admiral Lin, who sat near the brazier, a bandage wrapped around his head and one arm. "Any sign of White Dragon in that fleet?"

Muin had not seen him at first, so anxious was he to report and to share his idea about White Dragon's whereabouts.

"We drove them off," the admiral said tiredly. "Barely. We cannot call it a victory — how many more might there be beyond the ice floes? But White Dragon was not among them."

"Then he must be on his way back to the fortress . . ."

". . . setting up another headquarters . . ."

". . . could be anywhere, even on this island, setting off another quake . . ."

While they spoke, Muin became aware of a small figure at the very back of the tent, busy bandaging another of the commanders. Did her hands glow green? He blinked, but her hands still glowed greenish. And there was something familiar about her profile. *Mother?*

She looked up at the same moment, then rose slowly, her eyes wide and shining in the lamplight. Her lips moved voicelessly, "Muinkanda?"

FORTY-SEVEN

WHEN HANU SAW THE six imperials return without Ari, the alarm she had been feeling ever since the quake jumped in intensity. She held herself in strict control, remembering that she was supposed to be Ari's Essence master. So far, the imperials had no reason to look for more than that. She could not give them reason to look by acting like a worried mother.

She also reminded herself she knew all along that eventually Ari would go off chasing the White Dragon. Hanu would be no help in that. She might even end up a liability, as from everything Ari had said, it seemed that using family as hostage was one of White Dragon's favorite tactics. Master Night had certainly favored that tactic. He had to have gotten it from somewhere.

The four guards who had gone with Ari looking shame-faced and worried.

Captain Ha Gar said, "Firebolt is gone. There is nothing we can do but proceed to army headquarters, report and ask for punishment." He sighed. "We're lucky that General Falik is in command. He's reasonable; he will at least listen when you explain what Firebolt said, and the fact that Firebolt has *flying light skills*."

He then turned on Hanu. "Did you know that?"

Hanu said, "I am not a martial artist. My lessons with Ari have been entirely in the classics, the study of Essence, and its history. But she has had many masters, most not known to me."

The captain's spurt of temper faded when he recollected what he had read of Redbark. There was no mention of Master Iley in that report. He said in a less fiery tone, "You'll come along with us. I'm certain Golden Gentian General Falik will have questions for you."

Hanu bowed. From that moment her intent was to make herself as invisible as possible, while occasionally scanning the sky in hopes that Ari would return.

She was so quiet, and reticent, that the others tended to forget she was there. Hitherto their attention had been on Ari, who was a presence even in her absence. For a day or two, as they sailed through a couple of snowstorms, they went around and around, discussing the fact that the quake at the hot springs had probably ended because of her interference, which was probably a good sign, wasn't it, and what could she be doing? They seemed to want to be reassured that Ari hadn't merely run off. That she was truly going after the White Dragon. Under their talk Hanu sensed fear: when they had to report, part of the ritual when confessing a lack of success was to ask for punishment. All of them plainly feared that this might not be empty words.

"If," Captain Ha Gar said, "Firebolt is going after the White Dragon, we ought to catch up with her again when we reach the Grand Dragon Passage. The last three reports all insisted the Westerner navy was massing at the west end, preparing to attack."

"And the White Dragon is with them?" Ferret Bo Ya asked.

"He was when they first appeared there. Surely he will lead the Essence attack."

Essence attack — a few glances flickered Hanu's way.

"I'll do what I can," she said. "But I know so little about warfare. I'm a healer by training. Essence came later in my studies."

Captain Ha Gar sighed, but Bo Ya said kindly, "I'm certain whatever skills you have might be welcome."

Hanu assumed that was mere politeness, but a few days later, when the courier cleared a snowstorm, and the lookout yelled, "Smoke on the horizon!" the imperial guard captain turned to her.

"If a battle is in progress, we might be needed to run messages. And we can offer your skills to bolster the medics, if you are willing."

Hanu bowed.

The captain then turned to the four who had accompanied Ari. "You lot can make up for your failure by accompanying Master Iley here."

The four saluted, hiding their glum moods—a fact that, later, they neglected to mention when the story was told and retold.

By the time the courier had worked up against the wind, the battle had become knots of fighting ships, many of them on fire despite the white-gray sky of an oncoming snowstorm that reduced the ships in the distance to stippled silhouettes.

They had their tiger banner flying; from somewhere a cannon ball voomed overhead, to splash in the icy greenish water behind them. Hanu tightened her fingers to fists inside her sleeves, praying to the Crane God for peace, for safety. There was not a second shot, as an empire ship slid between them and the Westerner with their white banner and blasted two cannon shot directly into the side of the enemy, to devastating effect.

The closer they drifted, the clearer the voices of anguish among the terrible noises of war.

Hanu now knew her duty. She turned to her four. "Take me to the nearest ship, please," she said, and while they lowered the rowboat, she went for her bag—on second thought, she carried Ari's as well, suspecting that she would not see this courier again. There was going to be very much to do.

And there was.

Not only lacerated, burned, torn, punctured flesh, and broken bones, but also a strange, horrible paralysis caused by Essence attack. The signs besides paralysis being grayish skin, distended eyes, and lips in a bluish rictus. Every time Hanu touched these victims, her hands flashed green, and the person slumped bonelessly, drawing shuddering breaths.

Then she chanced to look through a hole blasted in the side of a listing Westerner galley, at the slaves chained to their benches and left to live or die.

"Row me over there," she said to her protectors. And when they tried to protest that the ship looked like it was going to sink, she said, "If you don't, I'll swim. A life is a life. And if I take away their slave mark, there is a chance they will want a different life. Should they not get a chance to choose?"

She had become quite practiced in breaking the blood bind-ing of the slaves back on Kanda Sutra. She worked through floating wrecks full of wounded enemies either abandoned or left for someone else—and those galley slaves able to move banded together to escape in boats, or in some cases, they took over their ships and sailed off into the white wall of snow, long oars rising and dipping swiftly. Some returned because that was the life they knew, but because they had no slave marks controlling them, the Western hierarchy found itself disrupted, and thus, Hanu did as much damage to the Western war effort as all the ship-to-ship action had done.

No one touched the woman who glowed with shimmering light. Word spread ahead through the Westerners that there was a divine being trailing Essence power who healed every-thing she touched, and at no cost. Not a drop of blood demanded.

The Essence flowed through her hands; the more she need-ed it, the more she found, as hour slid after hour, and her four guardians held lamps over her as she patiently healed and bandaged and stitched.

The victims seemed endless, until at last she stood, uncertain what to do or where to go, too weary to think. A woman she did not know came up to her and peered into her face. "Come. Healer Iley is it?" she said. "We'll get you to head-quarters. You can rest there."

Hanu was beyond question. She followed the navigator, whose arm she did not remember binding, and found herself on board a larger ship. She sat down where someone pointed, leaned her head against a barrel, her arms wrapped around hers and Ari's packs—hers was nearly flat, the bandages and medicines used up. All that was left was her second robe, and her extra underthings, a very small bundle.

She fell into a deep sleep with her head propped against the rough wood, and woke when someone touched her, discover-ing that her mouth was hanging open. She blushed, and wiped her chin against her sleeve, but no one looked askance. Instead, they were very, very polite as they helped her down the ramp, and into a bewildering city of white hempen tents.

She was taken to one larger than the rest, where a graying man in armor bowed to her. He seemed to be some sort of military man, judging by the fineness of his armor. "Master Iley? I can only extend my profound thanks for what you did among the fleets this day. I dare not ask for more, and yet two of our commanders neglected their own wounds in their determination to get badly damaged ships to harbor."

"I will be happy to help," she forced herself to say. "But I have completely run out of medical supplies."

"That you shall have," said this man.

She looked into the eyes of the man sitting on a stool, seeing that he was holding himself together by will. His arm had been fractured. She rubbed her hands, laid them on the flesh, and shut her eyes. Ah, splinters there . . . and there . . . and there. She did not ask how the phoenix feather enabled her to see what she usually had to find by touch. She guided the splinters back into place, and when all was right with the bone, like fitting together a puzzle, she used one of the Cobra Sage bindings she had learned to keep the bone in place.

"This will not heal the bone at once," she cautioned the man before her. "You must keep it immobile for a time, to let the bone reknit in its natural course. But at least it should heal cleanly."

"Already it feels better," he said hoarsely, and rose from the stool, to be replaced by another man.

She dealt with that one, wondering where she would find the strength for any more, when she chanced to look up at the sound of footsteps — straight into the eyes of her son.

"Muinkanda?" The word escaped her.

"Mother?"

The one in the armor looked from one to the other. "This confused old soldier understood the healer to be Essence Master Iley?"

Hanu had to think again, and fast. To protect a child, she would always find a bit more strength. "That is my healer's name," she said with as much dignity as she could muster. To her surprise, that was accepted with a deep bow — as yet she was too tired to understand what an effect her actions had had.

General Falik was thinking, Iley or Ryu, it was clear that this was a descendant of one of the great Essence families of the past — who were exiled or even covertly decimated under the pretense of friendship by the last emperor of the previous dynasty, in a desperate bid to hang onto the throne. But it never did to discuss the matters of emperors out loud.

Instead, "Captain Ryu, please conduct this esteemed Essence Master who has aided us so spectacularly to one of the infirmary tents so that she may rest. Master Iley, I don't know if you are aware that tomorrow is New Year's Two Moons; things being as they are, our celebration will mostly be a promise for the future, but our soldiers and sailors will be granted a day of liberty, as I trust the Westerners are too scattered now to mount a return attack."

Hanu scarcely heard these words. She bowed, clutching her two bags, until they reached a tent that to her looked exactly like all the others. As soon as they got inside, she threw her arms around her tall, solid son, trembling with emotion and exhaustion.

"Mother," Muin said, patting her back. How had Mother gotten so small? He remembered her being as calm and strong as the ocean on a clear day, but now she was like one of the birds she had loved so much. However, it was clear that she had done some impressive work out there, judging by the reactions among the commanders and the soldiers whose gazes had followed them. "Here's bedding—I'm going to lay it out for you. I think I overheard one of the women say she was fetching hot water."

"Hot water," Hanu repeated, as if the words were new.

"We will have a chance to speak in the morning." Muin bent and kissed his mother's forehead, and went out, as one of the naval navigators came in with food, hot water, a basin, and a set of clothes.

Hanu badly wanted to ignore it and crawl into that inviting bed, but she forced herself to do a quick cleanup job, and change, then swallow down a few bites of a stuffed dumpling and some tea. Then, oh, then came her reward: to slide under a thick quilt, and drop straight into sleep, not waking until that same woman brought in fresh tea, along with a blast of cold, snowy air. It was still quite dark outside.

"Ayah, I see you are awake," she said cheerfully. "It's snowing—again. As well we haven't any fireworks planned. A few of the gunpowder engineers had said they might be able to put something together, but who'd see it? And we might need the powder if they find White Dragon lurking about," she added soberly.

"Is Captain Muin still here?" The delicious sense of warmth and laziness was fading away as the candle flames flickered and streamed in the cold draft from the tent door.

"He's with the admiral and the generals. It seems the latest plan is to divide everyone and search for where White Dragon has set up his new headquarters, so I guess we'll be setting sail today after all. You're invited to the command tent when you're ready."

"What watch is it?"

"We're an incense stick from Phoenix first hour."

Hanu wondered if the invitation was actually an order. At any rate, she would need to be on hand to check bandages, so she climbed out of bed and got ready, dressing in the thick, warm army robe and trousers. She rolled up her grimy robe, wondering where and when she would be able to wash it, stuffed Ari's pack inside her own, then went out to find her way back to the command tent.

Which direction? She set out toward an empty space glimpsed between a row of tents, then paused when she spotted a short, familiar figure walking along, staff in hand. *"Ari?'*

Ari turned, her bewildered expression clearing. "Mo — ah, Master Iley," she cried. "How did you get here? Of course. I ought to have expected it. I'm trying to find out who's in charge, so I can report in," she added as they fell in step. "And maybe get something to eat. I stole food off the last ship of Cobra Sages I stopped, but I haven't seen any more since yesterday morning, and I'm ravenous."

At that moment they spied the big command tent, at the same time the general came to the door, sending off a couple of runners with pigeons. He turned their way, his brows lifting in surprise. "Master Iley? Who is this?"

"Firebolt," Ari said. "I'm supposed to come here — I promised the emperor I would." She paused when everyone in earshot clasped their hands southward. She belatedly copied them, then added, "Though I guess you don't need me now. How did you get rid of White Dragon?"

"We did?" the general asked, as the name *Firebolt* whispered from lips to ears as fast as the lightning she apparently wielded. Was that really Firebolt, walking into the camp like a messenger, instead of arriving with fire and thunder?

Everyone in earshot listened as the Admiral slowly approached her, wincing at the slightest jar to his arm. "Who told you that? We have no evidence that we took him out."

The general regarded her for a moment or two, his expression impossible to interpret, then said, "Please come inside. I will brief you with the latest myself. Everyone else, you have duties."

Actually they didn't—it being just before dawn on New Year's Two Moons, they'd been granted liberty, but these were veterans, knowing that if someone in command wanted to see you busy, you got busy, or they were likely to dump the worst camp chores on you.

A moment later Muin showed up, his expression easing when he saw Ari. He saluted his superiors, then said to Ari, "You defeated White Dragon?"

"No, I was asking what *you'd* done to defeat him," she replied, and then, seeing everyone's attention on her, said, "I've been watching through Essence eye, is a way to explain it. Every soul is like a little light, except the Cobra Sages are more like embers. White Dragon was a large ember until a few days ago, then changed to a huge, round red moon, kind of." She curved her arms over her head briefly. "Very large, and the color of old blood. Then, it was the night before last, that moon quite suddenly winked out. Almost as if it became aware of my inner eye. I had only peeked now and then because I was afraid he could see me. But I haven't seen that red moon since. I saw the smoke and heard the echoes of cannon yesterday, when I was hunting my last Cobra Sage ship, and I thought you'd gotten rid of him."

"We've not seen a body," the general said, and went on to report the Grand Dragon Passage battle. Muin then summarized his findings at the fortress.

Ari listened closely, eyes narrowing when he got to the room with the talismans, and how it burst into flame. "That must have been what I saw, then. He knew I could sense his presence. It was a fake. To lure me. And I fell for it," she ended with disgust. "I failed."

"Not so." The admiral spoke last. "The geomancers the emperor sent have all been dispatched with patrols to find and repair the plinths the Western Cobra Sages have ruined, but they're finding them already repaired. That was you, was it not? Some patrols have encountered small teams who claimed to have been sent by you."

"At least that worked." Ari sighed. She'd hoped they were done with this war, but instead there was an even larger hole on the Circle board, with no resolution in sight. She scowled. "I really do not understand this strategy. Why would anyone want to destroy the land he's taking, and that so far north, which has the poorest land, and the smallest villages? Who wants to reign over rocks and rubble, and people who have nothing to eat but the Northwest wind?" She rubbed her cheek absently, though the little scar had long since healed over. "I get that it's easier to protect a long supply line up here, but . . . Unless . . . oh, yes. Oh, yes," she said bitterly.

"May I ask —"

"He's not here at all," Ari said.

"We knew that," Muin said carefully.

"I mean he's not here in the *north*."

Muin said, "You think he's dead?"

Ari shut her eyes, then shook her head. "I still don't see that red moon, but that could mean anything or nothing." Another silence. She said, a little desperately, "Don't you see? No — you're not at all used to having to deal with Essence. You can't predict what you don't know. Take out the Essence. That's what I had to learn to do. He doesn't have unlimited ships, right? Didn't he get cut off by the new empress in the West?"

As if they all shared one impulse, those used to military planning gathered around the table map.

General Falik said, "If this were an ordinary war . . ."

"Think of it that way," Ari urged. "I *think* I'm right. But I need to see how it looks to you."

The admiral and the general readily complied, talking numbers, lines of supply, logistics. So far, absent the Essence, they had been dealing with a classic strategy — invade from the west, protecting their attenuated supply lines, burn and destroy as they established footholds, and sow fear and disruption ahead as they main body advanced. Or what they had assumed was the main body.

The news that White Dragon could fake his presence caused them to wonder what else he could fake, for instance, could he create illusory ships in the distance, seen after a battle or advance? If so, a different strategy emerged — far grimmer for the Empire of a Thousand Islands.

Everyone gathered around that table stared down at the contours of the map, trying to find another possibility, one that didn't have them having fallen for a possible feint, as the bulk of the navy, and the army, except for a thin protection around the imperial island, was kept busy up north.

While the White Dragon headed for his primary target —

Slam!

Ari danced back as a slim young man hurtled out of no-where in a flash of light and a blast of air that smelled of aromatic cedar.

Then she stared down in surprise at the figure lying at her feet, dressed in a fabulous purple robe with a huge silver dragon embroidered on the front, Sagacious Blade in one hand. He was bleeding from the nose.

"Jion?"

FORTY-EIGHT

To Jion, the last month of the year passed in the measure of a pair of incense sticks, then suddenly after a sleepless night, the month—and the year—was over. He stood in his room at his pavilion for the last time, and dressed in the purple and silver of an imperial heir.

It seemed unreal—everything seemed unreal. He departed by lamplight, surrounded by a double ring of imperial guards, and ferrets drifting from rooftop to wall to rooftop, shadows against shadows, for everyone was aware that Ris Jun was still at large, and the imperial family was the most obvious target.

In ordinary years, he and the imperial family would await the emperor at the Golden Dragon Pavilion before proceeding to the ancestral shrine. Because of his promotion, his place was inside the Hall of Glorious Justice, waiting before the great open doors for his father to finish his night's vigil among the emperors' tombs and the subsequent parade through the city to this, the public seat of government. Once the gathered court, which represented the people, had witnessed the emperor issuing the edict to hand over the heir's seal, the court would bow three times, acknowledging that all was in accordance with the Mandate of Heaven. And then the two of them would join the imperial family at the ancestral shrine for the customary ritual.

Phoenix Watch was still some time off, but he did not want

to risk being late. Since he hadn't been able to sleep anyway, why not pace the hall that he had only begun to learn of late?

The problem was, Sagacious Blade would not cooperate.

Heirs were not supposed to carry weapons. No one carried weapons in the presence of the emperor except imperial guards. Yet three times the blade smacked into his hand as he tried to leave. Twice he walked back and put it on the rack. The last time, he threw it toward the rack, saying, "Stay!" and when it spun back to his hand, he walked it back once more, and this time tied the sword to the rack with a thick, embroidered sash, the closest thing he had to a rope

"More like a dog than a sword," he muttered as he left his room for the last time — and smack! The blade struck his hand so hard it stung.

All right, then, he'd carry the accursed thing, and let the ferrets or the guards take it away and admonish him about the rules he had grown up knowing. It was a miracle he had been permitted to have it this long.

As he passed Vaion's manor, he saw lights glowing in the windows, and smiled. Even though he knew that Vaion was not actually inside — as a precaution, the two remaining consorts, the imperial dowager, and Vaion and Gau-Gau had been spirited away in servants' clothing the day before, to be hidden somewhere undisclosed. Ferrets had been seen out and about wearing copies of their clothes, surrounded by the prince's and princess's graywings and servants, each of whom had been thoroughly vetted by now. The servants and the two graywings in Ris Jun's pay had been rooted out and executed, three of them after Ris Jun's sanguinary plans for today had been extricated from them.

Jion crossed the bridge over the frozen lake and headed toward the Hall of Glorious Justice, as a distance away, the emperor sat alone in the Shrine to the Emperors at the top of Memorial Way.

Unlike his son, the past month had seemed to drag around his neck like heavy chains. He had actually looked forward to this time of silence, away from all interruptions, especially courtly memorials and couriers. He'd thought to relax, but the same uneasy stomach he'd suffered these past few days stayed with him. He could not seem to find a comfortable position, and yet he was reluctant to move about to find one. While he was here alone, it was so much easier to just slump here, chin on his chest, watching the elaborate golden dragon beneath his white robe jumping in time to his heartbeat. Tick-tick-tick, as though the dragon lived.

He lifted his gaze to the statue of the Sun God, the scent of incense thick in his nostrils. He needed fresh, pure air, that was it, yet he could not stir until Phoenix Hour — and the Shrine was visible from the Gates of Memory below, where the servants and palanquin bearers as well as their accompanying imperial guards all awaited his reappearance.

He had been listening to the drip of the water clock, which almost but did not quite match the rushing in his ears. Maybe it was time to rise and look at it in case he might have dozed without realizing it and it was later than he thought. Not quite yet, though — his limbs did not want to stir. Had to be the cold —

At the sound of footsteps, at first, he assumed it was Bitternail. Or perhaps Old Fai. Who else would dare to disturb him here? If there was some emergency —

He found himself face to face with a man some ten years younger, by his looks. Completely unknown. A courier? The guards had to have passed him —

"Guiyan," this man said familiarly. "Or, Enjai?"

The emperor half rose, face to face with Ris Jun.

Who had decided halfway through the night to change the plans. It was all very well to have his men among the imperial guard surround him during the parade so that he could carry out his spectacle, except that he'd got to thinking. The more people, the fewer would see the royal family die — and there would be more chance of accident. Further, with all the noise that would no doubt occur, he wouldn't get time to toy with them before they died. And there was always the chance that White Dragon might plant an assassin among those in the crowd to do away with him — he was very aware that his entire campaign today was merely camouflage.

He was not even forty yet, born the year of the Tiger. He could take an emperor of fifty, who only touched a sword once or twice a week, against men who knew they would be flogged to death if they seriously hurt a hair on his precious body.

It was only a small change. Wouldn't touch the greater plans. White Dragon would never know. The throne would still be his, and that was what mattered.

"Who are you?" the emperor asked, his tongue curiously heavy in his mouth. Was he getting sick, was that it? He was so seldom sick that he was not quite certain what it was he was feeling other than lethargic is a strange way, except his fingers trembled.

"By rights," Ris Jun said familiarly, "I ought to be Su Jun. But you know what that old reprobate was like. I was very sorry he managed to keel over before I could send him to the King of Hell. I'll make do with you instead, as soon as my men get here with your brats."

The emperor had by his side his ornamental sword, handed down through the Jehans. But the rushing in his ears had increased and he couldn't seem to draw it. His tongue had turned to a sodden sock, his jaw like rock as his right hand pawed, trembling, at the handle.

Ris Jun laughed contemptuously. "I never figured you'd be a coward. I ought to have."

"Gowah." The emperor could not get his mouth to work. "Gow . . .w-w-wugh." He fell back, his hands shaking, as Ris Jun smirked.

"Is this an act? Ayah, let's start with those tendons to make sure, so that neither of us will be interrupted. I'm going to cut them to pieces before I cut you apart, to prove you're just flesh and blood like anyone el—ay!"

A sharp bark as a sword seemed to come out of nowhere, the tip scoring his arm before he could bring down his blade.

"Who are *you*?" Ris Jun barely got the words out before he found himself fighting for his life.

The man who had appeared out of nowhere, breathing hard, was older than he was, Ris Jun saw with affront, then he couldn't think at all. Block, block, block, he was driven back, away from the emperor, who kept trying to rise, to get his hands to work, but the right one had gone dead in a horrible way, hanging lifeless at his shoulder as a thousand bees stung him down one side. The left trembled so badly he could not get a grip on his sword.

Clash, ring-g-g!

Ris Jun found himself backed against a wall, facing eyes narrowed for the death blow, when they both were knocked staggering by a third body hurtling at them out of thin air, and falling heavily.

Ris Jun recognized the prince and snatched up his blade — but his adversary was faster, and as Ris Jun lunged, that well-made imperial sword from the previous generation sank into his body below the heart acupoint.

Ris Jun's blade dropped. His hands clawed at the blade. Impossible, impossible! It was supposed to be so easy . . .

He fell dead on that thought, as his adversary slung the blood off his blade.

Jion had rolled to knees and feet, his first thought to get between his father lying there and those two blades, Sagacious at the ready. He only moved back as the standing man laid down his sword and crouched over Imperial Father.

"Waw-wah," the emperor said, trying to shape a word, his left fingers pawing the man's arm.

Jion watched, puzzled, still a little dizzy, as the man gently picked up the emperor. "Don't speak, just breathe," he said softly. In the light of the golden lamps, Jion gazed in astonishment at a familiar profile. Not familiar—grayish hair at the temples, but a formidable brow he knew well, only heavier. "Danno?" he said.

"I'm sorry I was late," Danno spoke to the emperor. "This is the one place in the palace I've never been. I forgot you'd be here. It was always your grandmother over here, in our day."

Jion sheathed Sagacious and knelt. "What—Father Emperor, what happened? Are you hurt?"

Danno said, "I think he's had an apoplexy. Seen it before. Wife's a healer. Listen, can you use that sword?"

"Want a duel?" Jion asked.

Danno raised a hand, sniffing the air. "This would be around the time that that man's paid traitors should be coming at us." Then he startled Jion by pursing his lips and uttering a sharp whistle.

"You have backup?" Jion asked, heart pounding.

"No—it should be yours. That is, it was the old second ring signal to close in—ah, someone's coming." He gently laid the emperor back down and stood up, sword gripped in hand, feet in perfect Redbark stance, Jion noticed dazedly, as he moved protectively in front of the emperor, whose free hand grasped Jion's robe

Jion took his father's hand with his left, his right holding Sagacious, still sheathed.

Not five breaths later running footsteps approached, Grandfather Fai and his son at the head of a patrol of imperial guards, who spread in a circle, bare steel at the ready.

Jion stared in astonishment at Grandfather Fai bearing a

wicked blade, and Fai Anbai with two bloodied knives. Both took in the scene at a glance—Danno at the ready, Prince Jion crouched protectively before the emperor, holding his hand, his own blade sheathed. The imperial guards encircled all three.

Danno lowered his blade and tipped his chin toward Ris Jun's corpse. "His hirelings in the guard ought to be attacking any—"

"Dead." Fai Anbai raised a hand and the imperial guards dropped back. He glanced at Danno as he finished cleaning his bloody knives on Ris Jun's clothes. "We've been watching all but two of them—caught the last of them just now."

Jion turned to his father, whose eyes tracked Danno, though he still held tightly to Jion's hand. "Chief Fai—Retired Chief Fai—I think something's wrong with Father Emperor. We need to get him to the imperial physicians right now!"

Danno raised a hand before the ferrets could issue an order to the waiting guards. "Suggestion only. I think the safest place now is his palanquin."

"You mean, resume the parade?" Jion asked, twisting around. "But he needs help now! And there might be more assassins waiting!"

"The empress used to say that the first line of defense was ritual. I'm pretty sure what he, or whoever sent him, wanted"— here Danno toed Ris Jun's corpse— "was chaos following this attack."

Jion turned sharply. "Then there *is* a secondary attack coming?" He turned to the ferrets. "I realize you are not required to take my orders, only Imperial Father's. May I suggest we get my father back to the inner palace as quickly as possible?"

Fai Anbai had just finished bowing to the emperor, who was still gazing up at Danno. The ferret chief bowed to Jion. "Your imperial highness, the traitors have been cut out of the imperial guard. They will disturb no one other than the King of Hell this day." He turned his head. "Guardsman Danno? Your notion is a good one. We'll surround him—the main street is cleared, and every other street is packed. Your imperial highness—"

"I can walk at the front as if it was planned all along. As it happens, I'm even in the right clothes."

"If this unenlightened servant may ask your imperial highness, how did you get here so quickly," Grandfather Fai began. "Where is your honor guard?"

"The sword brought me," Jion said with a worried glance at

his father. "The guards did not abandon their duty. I know how that sounds. Let's get Father Emperor to the Imperial Physicians. I'll explain later."

Fai Anbai made his knives vanish and loped away. He reappeared, holding out bunched cloth, which he presented to Danno. "I suggest you put this on. This is the least bloody one," he added.

Danno shrugged into the armor, speaking low-voiced to Grandfather Fai, who shook out the cloak. ". . . went to the wrong building. Got here as he was about to stab Enj—ayah, the emperor. Who was like that when we arrived. Then the prince arrived in a blast of Essence. Took up guarding his father while I finished the fight," he added as Jion and Fai Anbai gently, carefully lifted the emperor.

Jion understood then that the ferrets had known Danno was around. But he suppressed questions as guards and graywings arrived at a run. Jion picked up the Jehan sword as the emperor was carried to the palanquin. The white robe was eased off before they settled him with pillows propping him up.

He was still awake, Jion saw with relief—he did not know what apoplexy meant, except that it was terrible, even life threatening. He hovered anxiously, gritting his teeth against exhorting everyone to hurry—he could see that they were moving as quickly as they could.

The drums began to pound, the horns to toot, and the other instruments to join in. The banner bearers came next, leading through the Gates of Memory to where crowds waited, many wearing white mourning over their bright New Year's clothes.

As the progression reached the main street, white hangings were whisked away, revealing fresh new paint and decorations, new sayings in doorways suitable for a rabbit year. For the first time Jion saw the pageantry at either side, the world of color returning. *Ritual, the first line of defense,* he said to himself, and then his mind began to run ahead, every so often stumbling as he fought the impulse to turn to check on his father. He must not give away what had happened, though that would come soon enough.

He tucked the two swords under his arm and lifted his free hand to either side, as the gold bearers threw boaters to the bowing crowd.

"Your highness!"
"Crown prince!"

"Prince Erku the Hero!"

He forced smiles to those who cheered him—nothing wrong, everything fine—but Danno's words about another attack weighed on him almost as heavily as his desire to turn, to make sure Father Emperor was all right.

When the parade reached the South Gate, they were able to shed most of the followers, and at the palace's Gate of Supreme Harmony, the graywings and guards rushed the palanquin around to the back of the throne hall where there were private rooms for the ruler.

And that was when Jion vanished.

He had been thinking back to what had happened before he found himself hurled through four buildings and three thick walls to the Shrine to the Emperors. He had been holding Sagacious Blade as he thought about his father, then suddenly he was there. Exactly the way he had been hurled to Yskanda after he'd been poisoned.

He fixed his mind on Ari, mentally threw himself—and landed hard in the middle of General Falik's tent, gasping for breath, every bone and muscle aching as if he'd dropped off a mountain. His nose began bleeding as he tried to sit up, then there was Ari! She knelt at his side and pressed a bandage to his nose. "Jion," she said. "How did you do that?"

He wanted nothing more than to lay his head in her lap and close his eyes. But he forced himself upright. "Trouble," he muttered into the wadded bandage that Ari had snatched from her mother.

Ari said, "I knew it. White Dragon is in the imperial city!"

"What?" Jion yelped.

"What?" General Falik barked.

"If he's not dead, then he's in the imperial city. Now the Circle board makes sense," she said bleakly. "We have to go back."

Jion sank back onto the tent floor, mopping at his nose. "I can't do that again." He shook his head.

Ari looked at that bright blood, and said, "No . . ." Then she remembered Yaso in Master Ki's Valley.

She bent and picked up Sagacious Blade. It came readily to her, humming with Essence. She turned to Jion. "I think I know what to do. Explain later. Give me your hand. On mine. Let's combine our affinities. You see in your head exactly where to go."

Jion hurt so much that standing took all his strength. But when his hand met hers, the pain faded rapidly. He leaned against her, his left hand over her right, as she guided the sword up, over, and down, then thrust with Essence. Light flashed. Between the lines the sword had inscribed in the air glimmered a doorway, through which they glimpsed a wintry garden.

"Quick, through," Ari said. "I don't know if I can hold it. And don't touch the sides of this Essence door! I'm not sure what will happen."

Hand in hand she and Jion stepped through — Hanu right on their heels. She was not leaving her daughter to whatever fate lay ahead. "Come, Muinkanda," she murmured, her hand held out to her son.

This was in no way proper military decorum, but then nothing within the past few breaths was like anything any of the commanders had ever experienced. Muin sent a questioning look at General Falik, who would grant anything to the Essence Master who had single-handedly healed a good part of the fleet, at the same time causing complete chaos among the Westerners, as reports through the night had made clear. He nodded permission.

Muin laid his big, sword-roughened hand in his mother's thin, work-roughened fingers and stepped into something that felt like the largest beehive in the world. As he did, one flap of his winter robe swayed toward that weird door — and a bit of fabric sheared off as cleanly as if cut by the sharpest knife in the world, falling to the tent floor as the door disintegrated behind him, leaving the commanders staring at air, and that piece of fallen fabric, evidence that what they had seen was real.

On the other side of that door, Muin stared around at an unfamiliar building on one side, and high walls on the other.

Jion said, "We're at the side garden of the Hall of Supreme Justice. I want to check on my father, then we can plan. Court is gathering in the hall, so we'll go through the scribe door."

He began to explain what had happened so far. They had only progressed about ten steps, and Jion got to Ris Jun and the duel, when a tall, graceful young man in soft gray and a tasseled hat dashed around a corner, nearly running into them.

"Yskanda?" Jion exclaimed.

After all these years of being alone, and fearing any contact lest it endanger his family, they were here. Almost all. Yskanda stared, and stared more, his heart too full for speech as Hanu,

Muin, and Ari stared back. Even with his eyes goggling and his mouth a round O, Ari realized that absentminded Second Brother had somehow grown up into the most beautiful person she had ever seen in her life.

"Mother?" Yskanda exclaimed. Then he was crushed in a hug. "First Brother?" he said over his mother's head as he hugged her back, then extended his arms to his brother, who sandwiched Hanu between them. "Where's Father?"

"Yskanda," Muin exclaimed huskily, and then he yanked Ari in as they all began talking at once.

Jion watched this reunion with a tumble of feelings that spiked when Ari peered under Muin's arm his way, and disentangled one hand to reach for him.

But urgency overrode all. "I have to go," Jion said, stepping past them. "My father—"

Hanu the healer remembered what Jion had just told them. She stepped back and thumbed her eyes. "Take me there," she said. "Let me see what I can do."

The palanquin had brought the emperor to the back rooms of the Hall, where there were private rooms. The emperor had been settled on a couch, the two ferret leaders and Danno with him as he stirred restlessly, trying to speak. The fleetest young graywings had been dispatched to the Imperial Physicians' building.

Jion entered, the Afans behind him.

The two ferrets both started protectively forward, then hesitated when the emperor reached his left hand for Jion, who knelt to close his hand reassuringly around those trembling fingers again as he said to the ferrets, "Let Healer Hanu through."

The ferrets dropped back, and as Hanu dropped down beside the emperor, Jion realized he'd given orders—and the ferrets had obeyed. Was that only because he held his father's hand? Did authority truly pass when he received his jade seal— or did authority rest not in Jion, or his father, but in the decision each ferret made to obey him? Would that not imply that the will to *follow* was the fundament of authority?

Danno said, "She's a healer. Essence power."

Fai Anbai exchanged a glance with his father, then went out. Grandfather Fai remaining.

Hanu paid no attention to any of them as she laid one hand on the emperor's brow, and the other on his heart. He slowly stopped fretting restlessly. No one moved as she knelt there, eyes closed, sinking her awareness deep into the rushing river tumbling through the emperor's head. He sank into sleep, his breathing easing.

When his hand went limp, Jion stood up, Hanu with him. She gestured the watchers to one side. "Prince Jion told us a little of what happened. Though that encounter did the emperor no good, this apoplexy was a long time in coming. The incident broke the dam. It didn't create it."

Bitternail entered, leading two Imperial Physicians.

"Apoplexy," one murmured, instantly recognizing the sag on one side of the emperor's face — and speaking in a way he never would have dared ordinarily. "I warned his imperial majesty . . ."

As the learned medical gentleman began their ministrations, Yskanda drew Jion aside. "I came to tell you that Melonseed keeps appearing everywhere I go."

"Who is Melonseed?" Ari asked, looking from one to the other.

"He's dead," Jion said.

"What?"

"Let's go out here." Jion gestured toward the door. "I should be getting ready for court . . ." He frowned, his head still throbbing from being thrown from one side of the palace to the other, and then from one end of the empire to the other.

They stepped into the hall, where Jion said to the three Afans, "Your father — the ferrets — all think there's some secondary plan."

Ari jerked her head down in a firm nod. "And I think White Dragon is here." She closed her eyes. "But I don't see the red moon."

Yskanda murmured, "Red moon? No. We'll go into that later." He turned to Jion, hands clasped. "This ignorant beginner informed your imperial highness that ghosts are still a mystery, but I have seen Melonseed so consistently ever since I woke that I feel I must bring—"

"Your imperial highness." Fai Anbai appeared at the other end of the hall, a ferret at his shoulder, the man's face blanched. "The lookouts report a Western fleet on the horizon."

"And *there's* the rest of the attack," Ari said.

FORTY-NINE

THEY WERE ALL LOOKING at Jion. All, even Fai Anbai. So it begins, he thought. I'm not ready!

"Whatever defense we have must put to sea, to protect the capital," he said to the imperial guard captain at Fai Anbai's shoulder — and from the unsurprised bow, knew he was merely giving voice to the obvious. But that would be reassuring, would it not?

He turned to Yskanda. "Melonseed. Where, and what do you make of it?"

"He's at the upper palace," Yskanda said, frowning in his effort to focus. He was still singing inside with exhilaration at having all his family together again — all of them! His shoulder still felt the warmth from his father's clap and squeeze, and he tried to blink away the image of Father's proud smile.

But there were ghosts all around them, a reminder that this was not the time for him to go round hugging each one, and demanding their story as he sketched eyes, smiles, hands. Finding Jion's black eyes turned his way in a face taut with strictly controlled emotion, Yskanda forced his attention to Melonseed there in the distance, his profile upraised. "Wherever I go, he's northward of me, facing Mt. Lir. If I were to say anything about a ghost's intent, I would guess he's doing his best to warn me. Of something possibly in that direction."

Ari spoke up. "I can feel a great dragon below, probably the greatest. I felt it the night I left, when I removed the — oh, that doesn't matter. There is a vast, vast, *vast* pool of fiery rock under this island, bright with Essence, that the dragon nests in. If the White Dragon wants to make any kind of Essence trouble here, he'd have to break the bindings. Which are probably up on the mountain, like everywhere else."

Muin stirred. "I can scout a mountain, but from the ground. There isn't anything I can do about the invading fleet."

Yskanda's lip curled in a wistful smile. His eyes had been closed all this time as he permitted himself a last revel in his family's proximity, then he let go. "*I can try.*"

"To stop a fleet?" Jion said slowly.

Yskanda turned his way. "I can try," he said again, a little too firmly. "I've learned some things this past month . . ."

Ari eyed him. Was he offering to sacrifice himself in some mad act?

"Wait."

All three Afans turned at the sound of Hanu's voice.

Hanu had been thinking rapidly. And she settled on a compromise whose only cost was to herself. She was sincerely thankful for all that life had given her, but the greatest moments of her days were those in which she used the phoenix feather Essence to help and to heal.

There was now greater need.

"Yskanda, hold out your hands."

Her second son obeyed instantly, and she laid her palms over his. He drew in a breath, his eyes widening, then gazed down in wonderment at his shimmering fingers. "I . . . don't understand."

"You now have the phoenix feather Essence," Hanu said, looking down at her own hands, which no longer glowed. "The phoenix feather, in my experience, will not act for you. It will only enhance what you know already. Can you use that?"

"Yes," he whispered, and now everyone there understood that he had been willing to spend himself doing whatever it was he envisioned. "Thank you, Mother, yes."

She stepped back.

Muin backtracked quickly, going up to his father, who had fallen back into guard position. "May I borrow your sword?"

"For?"

"Defense."

Danno relinquished it, and Muin hefted the sword that had taught him the fundamentals. It fit his hand as if made for it; it never occurred to either of them that Danno had over the years infused it with a certain amount of earth Essence, to which Muin responded.

Muin returned to the others. "I'm off to look around that mountain."

Ari fitted her staff together. "I'm with you. In case White Dragon is there." But her gaze lingered on Jion.

He turned her way, then said reluctantly, "I can't do anything about Essence in mountains, and dragons. But if there's an invading fleet, someone's going to need to command what defense we've got." He had given the order to defend the capital, but he knew there were only patrol craft in harbor. And once the inevitable happened and the enemy landed, he had only the imperial guard. He had to be there to lead them in the defense.

That meant he had to see them coming. "Yskanda, let's go."

A last shared look between Ari and Jion, a look that expressed all the anguish in both hearts — whatever faced them, they wanted to fight it together. But each needed to go in a different direction.

Muin and Ari ran off, facing a long climb. She wished she could fly, but instinct urged her to remain as invisible to whatever awaited her on that mountain as it was to her. That meant not using Essence. Step by step it is, she said to herself. But it was still good to have her staff in hand.

Yskanda and Jion headed out in the other direction, Yskanda in his soft court shoes and only two layers, Jion glad of his heavy, thick, warm brocade. It was clumsy to run in, with its floor length sleeves and the train, so he bunched that up as he ran and tucked it into the side of his jade belt. They avoided the passage to the throne and dodged around to the scribe corridors — spotted by Court Artist Yoli, whose wild brows had been bristling ever since Yskanda had fled without a word, leaving his paints and paper lying on his desk.

Yskanda was at all times a mystery, veering between fog-brained abstraction to extraordinarily, even unsettlingly acute focus. But he had never been irresponsible. And it was very irresponsible to flit off like that on this day, before the most important ritual of the year — and an elevation, yet. The court artist considered sending a page to fetch him, except for the memory — recurring every year since Yskanda's arrival — of that eerie, prophetic drawing he'd done of the three dragons in the clouds on his first New Year's Two Moons.

Yoli was not one given to fancy, but that drawing was very much on his mind now. When he glimpsed Yskanda speeding down a corridor behind the scribe station, sleeves swinging, and none other than the First Imperial Prince on his heels — the one who was supposed to receiving the bows of the entire court in a very short time — the court artist turned to the two seniors being trained, and said, "Get your materials and follow those two."

They instantly obeyed.

Fai Anbai nodded to a waiting ferret at another juncture, who spoke briefly to a waiting red cloak, and a patrol began shadowing the pair, with the two young artists toiling behind them, clutching their ink, brushes, and rolled paper as they glanced worriedly at the sky. It looked, and smelled, like sleet — but if history was about to be made, they needed to be there, making their careers along with it.

Yskanda never looked back. He had worked very hard ever since his scolding by the abbot. One of the things he had learned was, the more water that surrounded him, the stronger was his Essence . . . reach.

He didn't even have the vocabulary for much of what he sensed. He only knew that he could now, under the right circumstances, access at will that heady, exalted sense in which his greatest art came. Of course, that sense sometimes came with the occasional kraken, but such was a surprise, and above all, *interesting*.

Now, his primary drive was to get as close to the ocean as he could, somewhere he could see without obstruction. He sped toward the south gate, thinking at first of the palace's south tower. No, not high enough. He passed out of the palace — the guards, seeing Jion in imperial regalia, did not impede them but joined in behind the patrol that Fai Anbai had summoned.

The city tower? Yskanda glanced up — no, not right. High enough to see the ocean, but he also saw fire up there in braziers, to keep the sentries from freezing. Too dry, too dry . . .

Through the city streets he raced, utterly unaware of people turning to stare at the beautiful young man who shimmered with internal light, and who glided along in silken slippers that shredded beneath his feet — at his heels none other than handsome Prince Jion in his purple and silver dragon, a sword at his side.

Of course they gathered a crowd, trailing behind the two artists.

Yskanda darted down alleys, between houses, and finally emerged at the very southeast corner of the imperial city, at the long rocky promontory that formed one arm of the great bay. He was barefoot by then. Sleet began falling, which he was also oblivious to.

An icy wind began to rise. He climbed, leaping lithely from rock to rock. He spared a thought for himself, glad he'd kept up with the boring repetition of Heaven and Earth, then he reached the topmost rock, from which he could gaze out unhindered, as the wind and the sleet whipped his clothes out behind him and streamed through his ink-black hair—his simple wooden hair clasp had come loose and dropped unnoticed at his first jump.

Jion heaved himself up behind Yskanda, batting his long sleeves behind him. "What do you see?" he asked.

Yskanda did not hear him. His mind was out there, then below the waters, and then he was himself again as he looked up. "Manon," he said mildly.

Jion jumped. *Manon?* Where?

Yskanda went on, addressing the air right above them, "Manon, if you hear me, can you help us?"

Jion recollected the last vision he'd shared with Yskanda, and clasped one hand on Yskanda's shoulder.

And there, black hair blowing in an aethereal wind, Manon hovered above them, dressed in a simple white robe that she never would have worn while alive. Her eyes dark shadows, yet Jion was very sure she did not see him—her attention was solely on Yskanda.

Yskanda really did see ghosts.

"You love the Empire of a Thousand Suns," Yskanda coaxed gently, persuasively. "Help us now, Manon, and be at peace. Chase them away." He pointed toward the ships now hull up all across the horizon, at least five hundred of them.

Manon stared down, and then, between one heartbeat and the next, she vanished.

Yskanda closed his eyes, his awareness expanding. Jion's expanded with it, though he had no control over what he saw, any more than he'd had when the kraken's tentacle looped up into the sky above his sampan two springs ago. He blinked away the surging gray seas and the clouds racing overhead, the sleet slanting down, and turned his head.

All ten of the navy ships in the harbor had set out by now, but they were fighting against the wind, bucketing hard enough that he could see the shock as the prows came down between billows. The wind screamed from the north, driving the Westerners before it; they slanted inexorably toward the shore. Twice puffs of smoke rose.

"They're shooting at her," Yskanda said, the wind whipping his words away. "I wonder what ghosts are to the Westerners? Ayah . . ."

His mind plunged down into the water, to where plants undulated with the current, and schools of fish glided through the water with sinuous grace as bubbles rose from dark shapes in the deep. Jion felt himself sway dangerously on his feet. Vertigo seized him, and he lifted his hand away from Yskanda. His focus snapped back inside his own head.

For an endless time, the formidable line of Western ships sailed closer. Jion, peering under his hand, could make out the rails crowded with figures, especially around the cannon.

Then Yskanda lifted his voice and spoke. "I call upon the Heavens that overlook this land, the waters, the wind and the sun that protect us, and I say, *you shall not breach this shore.*"

How was it possible for his voice to carry like the exhortation of some godling? Carry it did — the words reverberated through Jion's skull as Yskanda began to glow even brighter.

The enemy heard, too, impossibly: for answer, they fired cannon, which fell splashing into the sea between ships and shore, the last shot perhaps a hundred paces away. Jion held tightly to Sagacious Blade as he tried to gauge where the lead ship would land. He would be there to meet it, come what might.

Yskanda turned his head downward. Again, nothing seemed to happen, until the waters below darkened as if an island of ink had poured into the sea. And then, rising slowly, a great tentacle loop, as thick around as one of the great palace pavilions. Only this time, the kraken was no dream image — water surged off the massive suckers, sending huge waves ringing out.

From the crowds gathering along the shoreline, screams joined the howl of the wind. The people began scrambling back as waves surged up to smash on the rocks. Up and up the loop rose, until the tentacle pierced the clouds overhead, then with inexorable strength it came down onto the water with a cataclysmic *WHAM!*

The tentacle vanished below as two great waves rose and rose, veined with kelp, The one racing toward the Westerner ships towered over their masts before it struck, carrying the ships far out to sea again, some with masts that cracked, vanishing into the water like arrows shot from a bow. The fleet scattered far in the distance, but the danger was not over yet — the second wave raced toward shore, just as high.

"Yskanda, it'll swamp the city," Jion shouted into the wind.

Yskanda did not hear, or could not hear; he raised his arms, and before Jion's eyes the wave disintegrated into a million drops of water, which froze, and then fell harmlessly in a flurry of snow onto the water, the rocks, the shore, and the faces of awe-struck people.

Out at sea, another tentacle rose, and once again sent the Western ships scudding, this time beyond the horizon. Yskanda then spoke in his everyday voice, as if they sat together over a Circle game, "The kraken is having fun."

"I don't even know what to say to that," Jion returned, his voice husky. "How did —"

His words were swallowed by a deep groan of twisting rock that came from the island's deepest reaches, followed by cracks louder than any cannon ever fired.

Most of the city was out in the streets now. They looked at each other, exclaiming and wondering, then turned their faces to the two on the promontory.

Below the island the dragon stirred.

In an eerie mimicry of the ringing waves of water from the kraken's slap, the ground rolled, shaking buildings. Tiles clattered down from rooftops, signs crashing. Then, above their terrified heads, green light speared from eave to eave, the centuries-old guardian statues glowing.

Yskanda and Jion both turned their gazes to the cloud-hidden mountain top. "I'd better go," Jion said tightly — the yearning to fight at Ari's side sharpening to urgency.

Yskanda's smile faded. "I think . . . I think I'd better give you this." He held out his hands.

Jion laid his palms on Yskanda's, and for that moment the emotions shared between them revealed more than the exhilaration of raising a kraken and worry about what was happening on the mountain. Then Jion's entire body surged with Essence, and the icy wind and the sodden state of his clothes were forgotten. Understanding passed between them, all the more intense for being unspoken: affection and gratitude on one side, with no heat, and rueful acknowledgement on the other—not without the sustaining buoyancy of humor. For Yskanda was aware that his anomalous status had changed with Jion's ascendance. The emperor's invisible shackles had dissolved. He was now free to live and to love, without fear of any attachment being held against him.

Jion's mind had already winged toward the mountaintop. He tossed Sagacious down and leaped onto the blade, purple brocade flagging in the wind. Unaware of just how reassuringly heroic a figure he made, he sped away, leaving behind gaping faces and awed whispers, *Is that the crown prince, flying?* as Yskanda sat on the rock, shivering with sudden cold, his bare feet raw on the barnacle-sharp stones.

Jion arced high over the palace—one by one the sentries looked upward, and he thought, that is the last time anyone can surprise them from the skies. Then he forgot about them, and the scattered Western ships, as he flashed toward the mountain on which Muin and Ari had climbed as fast as they could, unaware of everything going on at sea.

They had nearly reached the wayside shrine they'd spotted now and then as they looped up the trail when Muin halted, hand up. He hefted his sword, and Ari gripped her staff, spacing herself so she would not foul Muin's reach.

Then enemy soldiers attacked from up-trail, two each. Muin dropped his a heartbeat before Ari knocked her second one down and stiff-fingered him into immobility. Muin squinted, looking around, then at Ari.

"They're guarding someone," Ari said.

"Yes. I get that stench up that way. Ayah!" He gazed toward the sea, his eyes wide.

Ari turned in time to see the looping tentacle rise, then smack the sea. Muin turned back, saying grimly, "I'll guard this path—there is no other way up, and I'm useless with Essence."

Ari jerked her head in a nod and pointed at the slumped figures on the ground. "Keep these Westerners off my back, First Brother."

This is it, she was thinking. White Dragon is up there. Doing what? Nothing good. Her heart slammed against her ribs.

Muin clapped her on the shoulder, and she started up the trail at an easy lope. She kept hearing Mother's voice, *There is always someone stronger*. That is going to have to be me.

Fifty paces up, the first quake hit. She paused at the top of a loop, looking down as the destructive undulations ground the stones of buildings and walls and streets together. But . . . ayah! She shut her eyes and reached for the greenish glows dotting in regular patterns below, each in fives and tens, one for each direction. The roof guardians! Where were the geomancers? Ah yes, most were sent north, and those left would be performing the release talismans one at a time. But she was not confined to one at a time. Ari shook her head, drew the release talisman in the air, and used her staff to shoot it down toward the palace rooftops. She waited only long enough to see the ancient protection spells release, holding the buildings together, then she began to run flat out.

She was expecting to have to run all the way; when she reached the first drifts of the fog that meant she was nearing the cloud banks, she slowed to a trot to pace herself, and consequently was completely unprepared to round a landslide of tumbled rocks and find herself in a clearing. She skidded to a stop, sending pebbles over the edge of the cliff to her left, to vanish soundlessly in a very long drop.

She scarcely had time to see steam rising from a great vent glowing with reflected red light, partially obscuring a great, mossy plinth, when two figures resolved out of the steam and the swirling fog: one shrouded in a long hooded cloak, the other huge and brawny, a sword clenched in a fist the size of her thigh. In his other hand, a spike-studded iron ball on a short chain. His face was covered by an iron mask, but beneath that Ari sensed a slave tattoo. Ari knew the binding in that tattoo would force this man to the will of —

"Kill. It," said the other, speaking with a slightly unnatural precision that suggested someone unused to the language. Or unused to speaking a human tongue. He, or she, only glanced Ari's way, but that was long enough for Ari to glimpse the glowing red eyes in that hood. Then the figure turned away and bent over the plinth once more, as the bodyguard stamped toward Ari, swinging that iron ball on its chain.

She evaded the first blow, dodged the swing of the heavy sword, and brought up her spear to strike with Essence, for this was in no way a fair fight.

But the demon in human form turned her way and made a casual gesture. A cloud of pure Essence floated Ari's way, seeking Essence to devour—and through it, the host. She somersaulted over the bodyguard's head, letting that cloud of evil blow over the cliff edge. She could not use Essence.

The bodyguard came on again, swing, swing, smash, slow and strong as an avalanche. Without Essence she could not meet any of those blows—he would smash her staff to splinters. He drove her back step by step as she swung and feinted, desperate to find an opening. He wasn't fast, but a weapon in either hand left nothing unguarded.

Another flip—and a yelp as the iron spikes whooshed below her close enough to brush the back of her robe. She was being driven toward the cliff edge . . .

A flash of violet and silver—Jion swooped in on Sagacious Blade, leaped off with heart-lifting grace, opened his hands and sent Sagacious spinning in a glittering whirl, to slice across the armored back of the huge bodyguard. The man let out a grunt and pivoted to advance on this new threat, as Sagacious smacked back into Jion's hand.

Jion flicked a glance toward the demon at the same instant that Ari thought, one to one. Elated at Jion being here—and knowing exactly how to back her up—she shook herself and advanced on the cloaked figure, just as the plinth's talisman flashed bright crimson, then went totally dead.

A quake struck, throwing all three off their feet except for the cloaked figure, who floated off the ground, fabric billowing. Rocks tumbled down, smashing around them. The cloak rippled, swinging wide in the icy wind, and Ari got a glimpse of the man inside before the figure bent toward the vent, raising a hand that glowed red. This had to be White Dragon—or what was left of White Dragon. Chill gripped her when she realized what she was looking at: a demon had possessed him.

In an instant Ari understood what had dismayed Yaso that night in Master Ki's valley: this demon had pounced on White Dragon's chief Cobra Sage and devoured his soul. And then, using the power and the form of that Cobra Sage, had either convinced White Dragon to let him in, or had pounced again. The outcome was the same: possessed of two powerful humans, the demon had swelled to the size of a huge red moon as perceived by Essence. It must have been aware of her, then, too, and so had set up that talisman room to lure her.

Now that the bindings protecting the island had been destroyed, the demon could go after what it really wanted — to lure, and devour, the great dragon, which would give it world-devouring power.

Ari dropped to the ground, sitting cross-legged, hands on knees, trusting the bodyguard to Jion, and in desperation, hurled her mind down into the glory of fire Essence. Oh, yes. Here was the great duel, by minds far bigger, vaster, and stranger than any human mind. But she had learned in the Valley how to reach for the non-human minds around her — how to be peaceful, still, protective. Sharing the little lights' delight in the seeds they pecked from her head and her shoulders and arms had taught her wordless communication.

As the torpid dragon stirred, sending shockwave quakes through the island as it resisted the demon's attack, she sent reassurance, peace, protection. The dragon at first did not respond. It was rousing, the beginnings of anger flickering lightning bolts through the crimson of fire.

The demon became aware of her, and broke off the duel to crush her, a hammer to a gnat. Ari's thought, bird-small, darted under, over, and through that corrosive blast, sending the dragon a picture of what the demon really wanted: the dragon flying to its control, the island nest destroyed — and a harness of demon power to force the dragon to its will.

The dragon's measureless focus swung back to the demon and struck, just as the demon swung its killing intent at her.

Ari shook free a heartbeat before that poisonous whiplash could crush her mind, but she could not evade a withering backwash of demonic rot. She wrenched her soul back into her body, falling back flat on the ground. Her nose bled — for a couple of struggling breaths she couldn't move. She looked up, to find Jion kneeling over her. "Take this," he said, grabbing both her hands.

Warmth surged through her, cool and healing as the phoenix feather's Essence flooded her being, flushing away the demon's poison. She heaved herself over to hands and knees as Jion leaped to meet the seemingly tireless attack of the bodyguard, who was twice Jion's size.

Drawing on all her strength, Ari forced herself to her feet, stiffened her first three fingers, and as the wind blew White Dragon's cloak wide, she drove her fingers straight into the man's heart acupoint as she sent an arrow of pure fiery Essence with the command, *Begone*. Right behind her struck the dragon's blast. The two combined, human and dragon, to lethal effect.

Uttering a strangled wail through its victim's throat, the demon fled powerless back to the underworld, and White Dragon slumped to the ground, the hood falling back to reveal the harrowed face of a man who looked eerily like the emperor, only his hair had gone completely white.

The ground still shook. Though Ari sensed the dragon settling back down, the short, sharp slips in the ground were building, building . . . She flung herself at the plinth, and though every muscle trembled with the effort, she raised her staff and etched the restoration talisman in the air, well-known after using it so much over the past days.

Snap! She sensed it settling into place. But the deep cracks remained, poised . . .

The stamp of footsteps right behind Ari brought her around: the bodyguard swung, still constrained to obey that last command. Ari tottered toward the cliff edge, making a motion with her hand as she slumped against a huge boulder.

Jion vaulted sideways, swinging his sword at the bodyguard's arm. The bodyguard turned his back on Ari, dismissing her as unthreatening — and she leaped on his back, driving her fingers between his mask and his shoulder pieces, sending Essence into the First Branch acupoint where shoulder met neck. He stiffened, then fell with a crash.

"Is he dead?" Jion asked hoarsely, leaning on Sagacious as he gasped for breath.

"No. Froze. For a little. No strength. Help me . . ." Her clumsy fingers scrabbled at the straps to the bodyguard's mask.

Jion crouched beside her, and together they got the mask off, lifting it away to reveal the sweaty, distorted face of a man who had been living for years with the world's worst headache, the slave tattoo glowing in the middle of his forehead. Ari snapped and shook her fingers, then drew the talisman to break that slave mark.

The man slumped limply, his breathing slowing. He was deeply unconscious, heedless of the shower of little stones tumbling from the mountaintop as the fretful little quakes continued; the plinth now held off the great slippage, but the deep cracks were still there.

"Come on," Ari said. "Ugh."

They helped each other to their feet — she became aware of bleeding cuts on Jion's right arm, his side, and a nick over one eye. "Muin," she coughed.

Jion cast her another look in question, but did not ask it as they stumbled down the path. It had not seemed long to Ari on her way up, but now, as she ached in every joint, it felt like the distance of the entire island, until at last they spotted Muin leaning on his sword, surrounded by five bodies.

Ari looked away, not sure if they were dead or alive as she staggered up to her brother. "Hold out your hands."

He laid his father's sword across a boulder and obeyed. She put her palms to his and he sucked in a breath, whistling. "What is that?"

"The phoenix feather. I fixed the plinth, but I think all the cracks are still there. Poised to shift too hard for the bindings to hold."

Sure enough, he said, "I know right where they are. I . . ." Whatever denial of Essence he was about to say was not spoken as his gaze diffused. "Ah. Uhn. There."

Muin sent the last of the phoenix feather Essence to fill and cushion all those cracks. Settle they might, but it would happen over time. Immediately the quakes tapered to very mild shakes, leaving Ari unsure if the ground was still heaving, or if that was her, still dizzy. No more rocks fell — the world had stilled, except that the intermittent sleet had turned to snow, which fell softly.

Muin staggered over to the boulder and plumped down next to the sword, as Ari and Jion turned to one another, each reading amazement, delight — and question. A heartbeat later Ari hurled herself into his arms and covered his face with kisses, until he grabbed the back of her head, and lips met lips.

Muin turned his back; unrelated men and women were supposed to keep a proper distance, and that was his little sister. But that little sister was Firebolt, and she had picked her man. As far as he was concerned, she ought to have him.

He was distracted by the snap of wings overhead. Ari and Jion were too involved in the other to notice the great crane that glided through the air above, white against the white clouds, as snow eddied around them. A host of other birds great and small circled the three, then suddenly shot skyward and away.

FIFTY

"HIS IMPERIAL HIGHNESS THE crown prince has been located," a ferret said to Fai Anbai and his father. "He is on his way to the north gate. He gave orders to extend an invitation to Guardsman Danno and Healer Hanu to stay at his former manor."

The ferret was dismissed.

"Then he did fly through the air on a sword," Fai Anbai said to his father. "We're going to have to figure out how to deal with that."

"For now, leave it to the imperial guard," Grandfather Fai said. "Pending orders, I suggest a serious reevaluation of our own training and practices."

"Ris Jun's legacy," Fai Anbai remarked. "I realized that when I looked down on his corpse."

"You will also have to repair Menace's regrettably shaken trust in us."

"In me." Fai Anbai then surprised his father by saying, "I expect most of that will be done by Firebolt. I'm reasonably sure by now she's figured out what I was doing during that interrogation and why. It will help that her father came to us first."

Grandfather Fai smiled at his son. "I'll see to Danno and his wife."

They separated. Grandfather went to Danno and Hanu, who had stayed with the guards around the sleeping emperor.

"The danger has ended," he said. "His imperial highness invites you to the guest chambers at his old pavilion. No one is there other than the staff."

Danno sent a considering look his way. "Is this an invitation that cannot be refused?"

Grandfather Fai bowed. "Not at all. I expect he's thinking of your comfort, and that your children should be able to find you."

Danno considered the unspoken. He and Hanu had lingered hoping to see their children before they slipped away, because while Danno had understood the surprise, and the gratitude, and even the regret in the emperor's face after Danno fought off Ris Jun, there was no guarantee the emperor would not waken to his old grudge and order their arrest. Hanu had said that there was a good chance he would be partially paralyzed — and the fastidious, proud Enjai of old would utterly hate that, just as much as he was likely to hate discovering Yskanda's true name.

But the way the former ferret chief conveyed the invitation made it clear that the old imperial dragon was sinking and the new on the rise. That meant that even if Enjai issued a command to throw them in prison, it would probably go through his son first. The same son who was very tight with two of Danno's three children.

"I'll thank you, then," he said.

Grandfather Fai smiled. "Before we leave the building, I'd like to show you something. I think the two of you will enjoy this." He led them around a corner, and there was Yskanda's great painting of the princess's wedding the previous year. "Assistant Court Artist Afan Yskanda did not paint it all, of course, but his was the design."

"I think I know which parts are his," Hanu murmured, her eyes caught by the heart-stopping artistry of a redbark tree here, the lifelike detail of a bunch of small children playing with a dog in front of a square of hemp weavers at the far end of humble Gong Street. Their son had grown up, but he hadn't changed in essentials: not for him solely painting the rich and powerful.

Danno shook his head. To him, a painting was a painting. He left it to others to say if they were good or bad. "I never did understand that boy."

Grandfather Fai laughed, then took them to the Grove of Serene Wisdom, while on the promontory, Yskanda himself had begun picking his way down, wincing at each step until a crowd surged forward to surround him, and took him quite literally in hand. They would not let him down. He was carried on shoulders until a palanquin for hire turned up, offering to convey him for free — and for the fame afterward.

By then everyone was talking about him. (In the imperial city they still are talking, as anyone who has visited the Four Roses entertainment house knows. There, for all to see, is a copy of the magnificent painting of Yskanda on the parapet, hair and robe tangling in the wind as he raises his hand and transforms the killer wave to crystalline snow, the defeated fleet scattered in the background. The two seniors had agreed to make one for the palace, and one they could sell, this being within the rules as long as no royal faces turned up in it.)

Up on the mountain, the birds vanished at the thunder of footsteps. Muin, Jion, and Ari were surrounded by a protective contingent of imperial guards, who dropped to one knee at the sight of Jion.

"Rise," he said, and issued quick orders.

At first those detailed to form a protective guard around him moved to cut off Ari, whose unprepossessing appearance was not aided by a battle-dirtied gray outfit that looked suspiciously like what the prison servants wore.

"This," Jion said, holding tightly to her hand, "is Afan Arikanda — known as Firebolt."

The imperial guards halted, muttering doubt and questions amid an impressive display of side-eye.

Jion flashed a grin at Ari. "Show them?"

Even tired, she sensed that immense pool of Essence below. She spun her staff just long enough to make it clear she was a martial artist, then brought it down to the mushy ground. It should have merely thudded, but it cracked like cannon-shot, and lightning blasted skyward to light up the clouds.

Silence, except the distant cawing of birds, sounding rather like laughter.

Then Jion, who meant well, said, "You will obey her as you will me."

And Ari stilled.

Jion did not notice at first, because the reports and questions began to come in a trickle that too quickly widened to a stream, each one needing an answer, an explanation, order. This is what Yskanda was talking about that day, he realized. Especially in an emergency, people turn to the one who has answers — who has to take responsibility.

But after all, he knew what to do. His lessons at Loyalty, the aftermath of the two battles he fought as a gallant wanderer, his chat with imperial guards during everyday drill, all brought to mind familiar rules, familiar patterns. He sent search parties out to comb the forest, mountain, palace, and city for any lingering Westerners. Others were sent to bury the dead enemies. There was also a party of the toughest sent up the mountain to secure White Dragon and the bodyguard — to find only the latter's corpse.

Surrounded by the ghosts of the many sacrificed to his ambitions, the man raised as a displaced prince without ever truly belonging to either empire had hauled himself to the cliff edge, fell, and his soul joined the spirits streaming up toward the sky to await the spirit bridge when Phoenix Moon meets Ghost Moon this one night a year.

The bodyguard, once the most famous swordsman in the West, could not bear the shame of that tattoo that had been forced on him, and all he had done under its compulsion. He took his own life there on the hillside, while looking westward into the sun sinking over his homeland. He too joined the company of souls, longing only for the waters of forgetfulness.

Back in the land of the living, one of Jion's explanations was how Muin had guarded the access to the upper path — evidenced by the fallen. Muin was spirited off by some imperial guards, who wanted to hear every detail about the battles in the north, as Jion led Ari into the upper palace. She was awed and intimidated by the beauty of the buildings and the extensive park, even in quake-caused disarray, as the army of servants went about restoring order as fast as possible.

The pair and their ring of guards entered a huge building with a complication of carved and painted ceiling beams. The rooms they passed through were filled with gold-mounted lamps and candle holders, rich with hangings and beautiful furniture, until they came to a halt in the largest and finest. The imperial guards melted away, replaced by another army of servants who bowed low. Jion said to one of them, "Steward Whiteleaf, how is his imperial majesty?"

"This unworthy servant dares to claim the honor of informing his imperial highness that his imperial majesty is now resting comfortably at Dragon Hall, in the care of the

Honored First Imperial Consort."

"That's good news," Jion said on an exhaled breath. He extended a hand, inviting Ari to sit on a pile of soft cushions as he exclaimed, "Tea, water, and plenty of it!"

That set off an intimidating parade of servants dressed like nobles to Ari's untutored eye. These came forward or deferred in a kind of stately dance, each knowing when and where to move. Everything centered around Jion. Was *she* supposed to be bowing to him? And what did he mean when he told those imperial guards to obey her? That was a terrible idea. She had no idea what the rules were here!

A young man dashed in and performed a deep bow, his tasseled sleeves touching the floor as he exclaimed, "First Imperial Brother, I'm so glad you're safe! They wouldn't tell us anything!" Then, before waiting for an answer, Vaion went on to describe being stuffed in a chamber on the west side for a day and a night, and then everyone's reactions as the quakes struck, and . . .

Midway through this very long description, Yskanda drifted into the room, wearing bed socks pulled over his bandaged feet. He winced slightly at each step, then his face brightened when he saw Ari. "You found and defeated White Dragon? Of course you did." He laughed for sheer joy as he sank down beside her, wincing a little.

"With Jion's help—and the phoenix feather. And you? Did you really call a kraken up? And turn rain into snow with a wave of your hand?"

"It was the phoenix feather," Yskanda murmured. "I won't be doing anything like that again. Though I still might talk to the kraken? If that can be called talking. Do you still have the phoenix feather?"

"I passed it to Muin. He says it's gone. He sent all the Essence that remained to repair the cracks in the island," Ari began, then halted when two young women entered.

One was more of a teenager, Ari saw at second glance. She was dressed in floating gauze embroidered with butterflies, and gemstones glittered on her fingers and in her elaborate hairstyle. But the young woman next to her, though dressed in rough-spun, undyed mourning, was really beautiful. The severity of the mourning garment seemed to enhance her spectacular looks as she sank into a graceful bow. "Who is that?" she breathed.

"The young one is Imperial Princess Gaunon."

"Is she the sister Jion loves?"

"No. That sorry story you will have to have from him. The other person is Su Siar, who was considered by all the court to be matched with Jion, until the Su family suffered a disgrace. Though I'm told that Su Siar's branch is emerging relatively unscathed, thanks to the old duke's change of heart before he died."

"Jion is supposed to marry her?" Ari asked, observing the gorgeous Su Siar.

"The Su family raised her to be an empress, but that does not mean that Jion will comply."

"Doesn't he have to do what he's told?"

Yskanda turned to study her. "Ari, what's in your mind?"

Ari was still studying Su Siar, who stood in a circle with the three imperial children, clearly on excellent, even close terms with them. The elegant rise and fall of their courtly accent was so very different from the accent Ari had grown up with in the south, and had never lost. She turned to Yskanda. "I don't belong here. I see myself as a burden. And though this place is beautiful, I could never—"

"Be empress? It's just a role, Little Third."

"Empress! I don't even see myself as a consort. Whereas I can see at a glance that Su Siar would be perfect in all the ways I'm not." Ari shook her head. "Roles for ruses, that I can do. Roles in life—especially ordering others around—no."

Yskanda sighed. "You know the difference between whim and what contributes to harmony. You've been teaching at Redbark—oh, how much Jion admires you for that. Don't tell me you can't give orders." But as he said it, he looked into her face, and remembered that she was two years younger than he was. Though many empresses had been crowned at sixteen, they had also been raised to certain expectations, whereas Ari was a very young eighteen in the sense that she had lived as a boy for many years, and had not had the benefit of their mother's wisdom after she left home at ten. There were aspects to pairing with an emperor that carried so much more weight than pairing off with a weaver, or a shoemaker, or another gallant wanderer.

Yskanda took her hands. "Little Third, talk to him before you do anything."

"Of course I will." Her brow contracted. "But Yskanda,

when I said that I see myself as a burden, I meant that that emperor thinks I am a criminal. Not because I'm Danno's daughter. I don't think he even knows that. I earned it all on my own, being a gallant wanderer. He's not going to want me here at all, and I don't want to come between Jion and his father."

Yskanda gazed soberly down at his hands as he considered the knife edge he had walked over the past few years in just about every encounter with the emperor. "You're probably right. Ayah, I think I ought to tell you something that I wasn't planning to. I didn't want to make it easy for you to run off."

"Which is?"

"Jion's air affinity, I've learned, lends itself to all the other affinities. What works for him and I with water ought to work for you and Jion with fire."

"Speaking affinities, is it true you see ghosts?"

Yskanda's smile became pensive as he searched the air above the heads of the chattering groups of people. "I do. I did. I am glad to see that Melonseed is gone. I suspect he completed his task. And Manon is gone as well."

Before Ari could ask who Manon was, Yskanda leaned down to kiss the top of her grimy head. "I want to find First Brother, and Mother and Father. I still cannot believe they are here!" He winced his way out of the room again.

Jion finally got rid of all his visitors, dealt with the most immediate of the problems, and turned to Ari. She took his hands, and told him everything she was thinking. He listened all the way through, as he always had, and then argued cogently, then passionately, until both were upset.

But within a few days, he discovered that Ari was right.

Though the emperor could barely be understood, the First Imperial Consort, patient and loving, was getting better at interpreting his speech, and she faithfully repeated his words, whether she agreed or not. The emperor no longer insisted that Ari be imprisoned. He kept his word in that—and even extended the imperial forgiveness to her family. Danno and Hanu were free to go, Muin could take his name back if he wished, along with his promotion up two grades to leopard commander, but the emperor wanted Ari gone. Out of the imperial city, and out of Jion's life. It was more important than ever that he make a traditional marriage with someone who could bolster ministerial approval.

Jion listened to all, and carried out the emperor's commands in everything but this one.

But Ari insisted that she had to go, until the emperor changed his mind. And Jion, yoked by the inescapable bond of filial loyalty and duty, had to stay.

The two experimented with fire, one in one room and the other in another. It worked. At least they had that, they reassured one another bleakly — he, aware he had all the power in the world now, except in matters of the heart, and she afraid that the crown and the throne would slowly but surely take him away. There was no Master Night to fight, or White Dragon to separate them — just the inexorable responsibilities of duty, and filial love.

All the Afans but Yskanda departed one dreary, bitterly cold morning, before anyone was stirring.

The Afans, reunited at last, had been meeting each day — Danno learning Redbark, and in turn making suggestions to refine it, which Ari gratefully accepted. Their time together as a family was all the sweeter for the pressing knowledge that it would not last past a few days. The palace was no longer a place of danger, but it was home only to Yskanda.

At Plum Blossom, Muin departed for Green Jade to aid Falik, who was still learning to walk — though he would never fight again. Danno and Hanu went with him to spend the rest of the winter, and then in spring they would head north.

Ari took another ship for Te Gar, where she rejoined Redbark at the Blue Hibiscus. Petal, heavily pregnant with what she hoped would be a future Redbark hero, had kept her room waiting in hopes of her return.

She took up training the increasing number of candidates who showed up wanting to study with Firebolt. She made sure they accepted the Redbark dedication to justice, and only the most senior got to see her practice with Essence. But those who had Essence, and the hearts to use it for the good of the world, she trained. Before she left again, three of those could fly.

She stayed for half a year, then departed to the north for the Sky Island competition — held once again — and this time won second place. From there to Sky Island to learn horseback riding and archery, and then she began roaming, but every night, no matter where she was, she always went off alone, and sat with a candle until Jion's face appeared, smiling at her through the flames.

Occasionally, very late at night, a door would open in the air of her room, and there he would be with Sagacious Blade in hand; he still needed help making the door, but Yskanda was always willing, and in the early morning, Ari and Jion would put their hands together, and inscribe the door that would take him back to Sun's Grace and the duties of a crown prince regent.

The emperor never sat on the throne again, but ruled from within his pavilion.

Jion, like his father, had been betrayed by someone close. While his father's experience had made him distrustful of anyone, Jion merely became careful.

The emperor had from the beginning kept his consorts strictly out of government, but now that he had to depend on the First Imperial Consort for translation, he gradually came to rely on her compassionate heart and her good sense, and in turn, his mother was able to be less roundabout when she had advice to give.

Though he never appeared before court or subjects again, the emperor had the comfort of three filial children, beginning with Jion who came to him each morning to talk over the day's events, and Vaion, who after his sobering months at Benevolent Winds, took an interest in matters of trade, and began to make himself useful in that regard, proving to be a surprisingly persuasive negotiator. Gau-Gau was a delight because she loved everybody if they let her, and never asked for anything but affection, and when the second Ran prince was proposed as a husband, she acceded with her usual sunny smile, and went off to reign over Ran, where she could play with her children, and plant gardens, and nothing bad ever happened during her long life.

The emperor had almost five years of peace before another apoplexy took him away in the middle of the night, and he appeared in the underworld, freed at last from the golden yoke that had bound him. We are not granted knowledge of how or when souls are reincarnated, but I like to think of him reborn as a poet and a designer of plays, where he could make up for all the laughter and companionship that he had missed in his previous life.

That night, Jion appeared to Ari in the flame, wearing the undyed cloth of mourning, and said, "Arikanda, it is time to keep your promise."

She was far in the north. After having won first place at the Sky Island competition, she was now sought by everyone up there who for whatever reason was shy or suspicious of imperial government. She and both Waojis had put together a martial arts group of Redbarks and Sky Islanders and Kis to clear the islands of the last of renegade Westerners left over from the battles.

Jion wished for her company at once, but he had the grace to wait, which meant she would arrive after the mourning period had ended. It was not in her to pretend mourning for someone she had seen as a threat her entire life.

She stopped first at Ten Leopards, where her parents had been adopted by the elder Kis. Danno's Heaven and Earth greatly enhanced the Ki knife and fan forms, and Hanu, though she no longer had the phoenix feather, was by now a fully acknowledged healer, renowned through the islands in that cluster.

In the capital, the actual transfer was proceeding as easily as Grandfather Fai could have wished — as well, as his wife had returned from her long sojourn in the West at last, and now the most arduous part of their day was getting together with the very small number of retired ferrets, sitting in the sun with their tea, playing Circle and complaining about their grandchildren in a way that was actually bragging — and everyone knew it, as they were doing it, too.

Though Jion had spoken with his father every day, it was Yskanda he had depended on at first to help him navigate the shoals of court. Ze Kai as well, as he was honest and intelligent, but he was also ambitious, whereas Yskanda, acute in observation, had no desire whatsoever to be involved in high politics. With the result that, by degrees, he ended up the new emperor's chief advisor in all but name.

One of Jion's first orders was a reshaping of the army; the perennial problem of Imperial Works could be partly supplied, so he reasoned, by putting a great deal of his enormous armed forces to useful work instead of their eternal war games.

Garrison Commander Falik Tan was promoted to duke on the death of his father-in-law, and Dun was promoted to Green Jade garrison commander, which was the height of his ambition; while Muin had been in the north, Third Miss had gotten tired of waiting, and as she had liked Dun nearly as much as she liked Muin, and he had liked her all along, they married. Muin hid his disappointment when he saw their happiness. It didn't last long, for he was off again. Jion promoted him and sent him to tour the empire's garrisons to evaluate training, and to investigate for any signs of the sort of corruption that had made Benevolent Winds a slap on the face of all the empire's military.

Danno and Hanu sighed over this missed opportunity, for she wanted grandchildren, but as Danno said, "When Muin decides he wants to be married, he'll be married. Nothing short of an avalanche will get in his way. As for the others, the gods only know."

That spring of the Year of the Dolphin, Ari quietly entered the capital city, a young woman of twenty-three, carrying her signature staff. By now the entire empire knew that Firebolt was a woman (Rosefinch had made her fortune writing her adventures, as she had found Redbark through Lie Tenek and thus got the tales before anyone else did) and many was the would-be troublemaker who changed their mind about making mischief on hearing that Firebolt had been seen in the sky.

Sometimes her famous monk staff remained in her pack, decently covered, as weapons were still forbidden in cities except by the local guards. Ari never dressed flashy, but even those who knew nothing about self-defense recognized the martial competence in her walk, and gave her respectful space; gradually the whisper went out, was that Firebolt? But no one dared approach her.

She was stopped at the palace's south gate, but as soon as she said "Afan Arikanda," the imperial guards pulled aside their crossed spears, both pairs of eyes widening. In five years of conversations through the flames, Jion had talked so much about the palace that though this section was new to her, she had a good idea where to go: she crossed a canal, glimpsing walls masked by trumpet flowers and aromatic trees off to the right, beyond which were the warrens where the staff worked and lived.

More staff beyond the Gate of Supreme Harmony, then she saw the Garden of Serene Contemplation, and off to the left the grand triple-eaved government buildings, with a full set of guardians atop.

She sensed plenty of Essence there, and smiled to see that the guardians were still vigilant. That building ahead had to be the Hall of Glorious Virtue, and somewhere to the right, Yskanda was either painting or teaching now, or maybe he was off with one of his many lovers — Ari had discovered through Jion that Yskanda, freed of the fear of anyone he got close to being held hostage against him, had been unable to say no ever since.

What Jion didn't say — and Ari wasn't certain if he knew — was what she had gleaned from the spaces between Yskanda's own conversation and Jion's, that her second brother's favorites all knew that if Jion called, Yskanda would always drop whatever he was doing and go. There were so many kinds of love, Ari had discovered. It was like the sea, always there, but today's sea might be completely different from tomorrow's sea. All were good and beautiful.

Ayah! There was the imperial garden — now she was getting to territory she remembered. She turned up one of the paths, stopped by no one, though a pair of guards walked over on the west side, and a couple of graywings in gray glided ahead, the stiff extensions on their hats lending them dignity.

"Is that Afan Arikanda?" A voice like a waterfall caused Ari to look off to the left. She'd seen the pagoda, of course. She knew that the pretty building next to it was the emperor's tea house, but peach trees had hidden it from view. She stepped toward the canal dividing her from it, and saw young people dressed in silk sitting before low desks. Oh yes, the study group for the next Imperial Examination!

Ari put up a hand to ward the sun, and saw a graceful figure floating over an arched bridge toward her, sky blue tassels swinging from her long, gauzy sleeves. "Su Siar?" Ari asked, recognizing the young woman, who was far more beautiful than she remembered.

"I heard you were coming from his imperial majesty soon to be crowned—" Here Su Siar bowed toward the Hall of Glorious Justice, which housed the throne. "Do join us!"

Ari looked down at herself, then at Su Siar, and though Jion had been teaching her the basics of court usage, she was sure she was breaking some sort of rule. She hefted her pack up over her shoulder and said, "Thank you for the invitation, but I should probably dig out my good robe first. I know this isn't suitable palace clothing." She was gauging Su Siar's light blob as she spoke. It was an interesting shade of peach with a golden shimmer. Ari had learned that colors could vary from person to person but she sensed good will.

Su Siar smiled. "I believe the esteem you have earned is so high that you could wear what you like, and it might even create a fashion."

Ari looked down uncomfortably. "All the more reason to change into a good robe. I don't want Jion losing face over my ignorance."

"Ayah, I don't think you understand how beloved the both of you have become. But you must do what is most comfortable, especially if you are to come among us to live."

Ari tipped her head, her eyes considering. This was the person the elder generation had settled on for Jion's perfect match. How did Su Siar feel about it all? "I will," she said, "but not all the time."

"Ayah, you will continue to roam for justice?"

"Yes—now and then. Until I can hand off Redbark to someone else." And, "Jion does say I can do what I like, but you'll tell me the truth: is that bad in an empress?"

Su Siar was thinking about how easily Afan Arikanda said "Jion." The teenage bond the two had formed had only strengthened over time, she had discovered, unlike most childhood or early teen crushes. When Jion spoke about Firebolt, his tone of voice was a caress.

She could have given Afan Arikanda a court answer, but there was that in Arikanda's straightforward gaze that deserved the truth. "This unworthy believes that though our elders think that following tradition is the only possible choice, I believe, as the person most concerned in their plans, there are advantages to a new type of empress. Especially one with powerful Essence abilities. Sometimes traditions need to be broken in order to form better ones."

"But nothing changes the fact that I'm a commoner from a tiny island at the end of the empire. Surely that still matters."

"It is known that you are a descendant of the great Alk clan—which gives you enough noble blood, should someone demand such. As for the rest of being empress, surely you can learn to walk through the rituals on the necessary days?"

Ari nodded. "Jion's been coaching me. But I wanted to know what you think."

"I think you'll make a welcome addition to court," Su Siar said firmly. "As for your very indirect question, there was a faction in court who wanted me to be empress, and I was raised to be a candidate, but in recent years my ambitions — which are very high — have been to make a place for myself at court. My goal now is to be Right Chancellor against Ze Kai's Left Chancellor. We'll battle wits at court, but at home we shall be in true harmony."

"You want to marry Ze Kai?"

"We both believe it is time for the feuding between our clans to end. I'll be better than the Old Duke was, ayah, but first I must pass the Imperial Examination. I failed the last," she said candidly. "It was a much-deserved face slap. I thought myself so smart, so very learned, but I'd only studied what I wanted to. You see the study group over there? We are deadly serious now, talking today about cloth, specifically silk, as commodity, and going over trade and tribute laws." At Ari's honest amazement, she laughed softly. "You must honor us with your august presence." She bowed.

Ari bowed back, thanked her, and forged on, feeling very much better about the prospect of being here. It would be good to get back to reading again, and repair her ignorance!

Jion was still living in the heir's manor, surrounded by scribes. But when he saw her, he threw down his brush, and ran to pick her up and swing her around.

Which set the tone of the following days. The geomancers had given Jion several possible auspicious dates for his coronation, which he insisted would be shared by his empress-to-be.

Time blurred until the two found themselves in Golden Dragon Pavilion, which once again had matching emperor's wing on the west and empress's wing on the right. It was the morning of their combination wedding and coronation. He had dismissed his chamber servants and the two were alone, helping each other with the elaborate imperial dragon and phoenix robes, so that they could share a private conversation.

"Year of the Dolphin, earth element," Jion said, knees bent, hands propped on them as Ari fixed the jeweled clasp in his upbound hair. "Era of Peaceful Justice. The geomancers united in saying that that signifies parallel roads and opposites complementing and suchlike, which will be translated into building terms for new structures, but we needn't worry about that at this moment."

"You're telling me now because?"

His wicked smile flashed. "Because I'm going to try to ease the tension between the gallant wanderers and the subjects of the empire by making martial arts sects legal. That is, if they register, they then enjoy the rights and protections of all subjects, wherever they roam, as long as they obey local laws."

Ari considered that. "Are you trying to prevent more Shadow Panthers in the future?"

"Yes. Yulin Enk was very aware of the laws, most specifically the gaps between the laws. And of course he lied and threatened and bribed a lot. Enough of him. I hope you will encourage the sects you encounter to register."

"Redbark shall be the first," she promised. "I think that will make Petal very happy, though I expect Matu will be wary. And possibly his father."

"I know. I mean to make it up to them, and all those like them, if I can. Ayah, that reminds me. I had three reasons why I wanted to talk to you alone."

"Not the name again," Ari said. "I know you have to have an emperor name, and I'm already used to Shiyan, because it's so close to 'Shigan' only with the tone dropping on the 'shi.' But I already have two names, Firebolt and Arikanda. Can't I be Empress Arikanda? The next empress can have an empress name."

"Very well—I'll make it an edict. Then the elder ministers can grumble among themselves, but they cannot argue."

"What's your second thing?"

"Over the past five years, I've had plenty of time to delve into the records, where I've found some interesting things."

"Such as?" Ari asked. "Here, can you help me get this headdress over my braid? Whoever designed these things has to have hated women."

Jion smiled to himself at the fact that Arikanda, so famous and powerful, was still too shy to have personal servants dressing her. "Yskanda tells me we have to look larger than life."

"He'll paint us that way anyway. Here, let me shake out your train. Ayah! The embroiderers who did this dragon ought to get a reward." She had to laugh at how absurd she felt, dressing up like an empress.

"You can bestow that reward, you know. And it will be

gratefully received. Sit down, this is serious. You need to hear it before you have to sit on that throne next to me."

Ari's bubble of laughter cooled. She turned a concerned face to him. "What did you find? Please don't say you discovered a traitor or an assassin among the people you care for."

"I hope that Manon was enough for one lifetime. This news is centuries old, and yet renewed each time the ferrets change over. Graywings to a certain extent, too, though they are constrained due to even older misdeeds."

"Oh, this is about throne rot." She sighed.

"Yes — ours."

"Ours?"

"I'm quite certain that I was right — I'll tell you later what led me to consider it. The important thing is, I believe that Melonseed did not act on his own. He was part of a conspiracy, the evidence of which exists as, oh, call it holes in certain records. This conspiracy acted to keep Maoyan from committing his worst atrocities yet. It seems to have been formed after Milo Giha's misrule: the ferrets not only act as extensions of the emperor's will, but they also act as watchdogs over the emperors. From what I pieced together, mostly in reports of the sudden deaths of our six worst emperors, and some other scant details, that should any ruler go the way of Milo Giha — or Maoyan — they will take him out. They sacrifice themselves doing it, to protect the secret. I think Melonseed was exempt because the palace then was in such a terrible state they needed him, young as he was."

Ari's eyes widened. "Have you asked Fai Anbai about it?"

"No! Don't you see, we are not supposed to know. I find that curiously comforting. Don't you?"

Ari considered. "If the ferrets are honest, yes. But who is to watch over them, if both they and the monarch are — ayah, I'm spinning what-ifs, useless ones. There are no guarantees, I tell the Redbark candidates that. If we become an evil sect, I tell them, I *want* others to deal with us the way we dealt with the Shadow Panthers. But Jion, that's such a sobering thought, that though we talk about peace and name our buildings and eras after peace, we never seem to keep it."

"That doesn't mean we don't keep trying." He kissed her. "And raise our children to do the same." He laughed to see her blush and look around the room, which was empty besides themselves, to see if anyone was listening. "Bringing me to the last matter: how many would you like to have?" he asked — to make her blush again.

But she saw at once what he was doing. "Oh, three is always a good number. And I think that if one of them shows an aptitude for Essence, and wants to cultivate, that one ought to get a chance to use the Alk name."

He was serious again. "Done. I promised you your freedom, and I will keep that promise — if Firebolt needs to wander for a month, a year, then we'll manage. And if a future child takes to the road, he or she might inherit Sagacious Blade. But what I really want is one of them to be so great a scholar and so wise that I can take this thing off again." He tapped the crown, setting the beads swinging. "Emperor Shiyan becomes gallant wanderer Shigan again. My hope," his voice husked, "is that we will one day be able to wander together."

She understood then that the knot in his heart was still there. Though he could make the door to anywhere, and he could fly on Sagacious Blade, he was a bird with clipped wings. He would never truly escape the burden of the throne until he could hand it off to the right person.

She took his hands. "Then we'll have to raise them well. Your mother will help, and mine, too. And my father. And Yskanda and Vaion will be the best uncles in the world, you know that. But meanwhile," she smiled, "the emperor can dance."

He smiled back. "The emperor can dance."

Whiteleaf — now chief graywing, Bitternail having gone to honorable retirement — tapped at the door. "Your imperial majesties, the auspicious hour is nigh."

"Your imperial majesties," Ari murmured, admiring the embroidered feathers on the sleeves of her outer robe. Feathers — phoenix feather — life had taken such a strange turn! "I don't think I'll ever get used to that."

"Says she who was a he, an army cadet, a gallant wanderer, a hirsute and brawny brawler, and a lightning-shooting hero, under how many different names? At least 'empress' comes with all the best tea."

She laughed, as they walked together through the door into one of the greatest golden ages of the Empire of a Thousand Islands.

ABOUT THE AUTHOR

Sherwood Smith studied in Europe before earning a Masters degree in history. She worked as a governess, a bartender, an electrical supply verifier, and wore various hats in the film industry before turning to teaching for twenty years. To date she's published over forty books, one of which was an Anne Lindbergh Honor Book; she's twice been a finalist for the Mythopoeic Fantasy Award and once a Nebula finalist. Her YA fantasy novel *Crown Duel* has been in print for over twenty years.

She reviews books at Goodreads and blogs intermittently at Dreamwidth.

Visit her website at https://www.sherwoodsmith.net and sign up for her newsletter to learn about new books!

About Book View Cafe

Book View Café is an author-owned cooperative of professional writers, publishing in a variety of genres including fantasy, science fiction, romance, mystery, and more.

Its authors include New York Times and USA Today bestsellers as well as winners and nominees of many prestigious awards such as the Agatha Award, Hugo Award, Lambda Literary Award, Locus Award, Nebula Award, RITA Award, Philip K. Dick Award, World Fantasy Award, and many others.

Since its debut in 2008, Book View Café has gained a reputation for producing high quality books in both print and electronic form. BVC's e-books are DRM-free and distributed around the world.

Book View Café's monthly newsletter includes new releases, specials, author news and events. To sign up, please visit https://www.bookviewcafe.com/bookstore/newsletter/

www.ingramcontent.com/pod-product-compliance
Lightning Source LLC
Chambersburg PA
CBHW050609110726
47899CB00001B/33